THE DISGRACED MARTYR TRILOGY

OMNIBUS EDITION

M. F. SULLIVAN

The Disgraced Martyr Trilogy Omnibus Edition

ISBN: 978-1-7326691-5-4

Text: M. F. Sullivan
Editing: Michelle Hope
Cover Design: Nuno Moreira
Typesetting: Jennifer Cant

www.paintedblindpublishing.com
publicity@paintedblindpublishing.com

FIRST EDITION

THE HIEROPHANT'S DAUGHTER

Ah, not Cassandra! Wake not her
Whom God hath maddened, lest the foe
Mock at her dreaming. Leave me clear
From that one edge of woe.
O Troy, my Troy, thou diest here
Most lonely; and most lonely we
The living wander forth from thee,
And the dead leave thee wailing!

—Euripides, *The Trojan Women*

I

The Flight of the Governess

The Disgraced Governess of the United Front was blind in her right eye. Was that blood in the left, or was it damaged, too? The crash ringing in her ears kept her from thinking straight. Of course her left eye still worked: it worked well enough to prevent her from careening into the trees through which she plunged. Yet, for the tinted flecks of reality sometimes twinkling between crimson streaks, she could only imagine her total blindness with existential horror. Would the protein heal the damage? How severely was her left eye wounded? What about the one she knew to be blind—was it salvageable? Ichigawa could check, if she ever made it to the shore.

She couldn't afford to think that way. It was a matter of "when," not of "if." She would never succumb. Neither could car accident, nor baying hounds, nor the Hierophant himself keep her from her goal. She had fourteen miles to the ship that would whisk her across the Pacific and deliver her to the relative safety of the Risen Sun. Then the Lazarene ceremony would be less than a week away. Cassandra's diamond beat against her heart to pump it into double time, and with each double beat, she thought of her wife (smiling, laughing, weeping when she thought herself alone) and ran faster. A lucky thing the Governess wasn't human! Though, had she remained human, she'd have died three centuries ago in some ghetto if she'd lived past twenty without becoming supper. Might have been the easier fate, or so she lamented each time her mind replayed the crash of the passenger-laden *tanque* at fifth gear against the side of their small car. How much she might have avoided!

Of course—then she never would have known Cassandra. That made all this a reasonable trade. Cold rain softened the black earth to the greedy consistency of clay, but her body served where her eyes failed. The darkness was normally no trouble, but now she squinted while she ran and, under sway of a dangerous adrenaline high, was side-swiped by more than one twisting branch. The old road that was her immediate goal, Highway 128, would lead her to the coast of her favorite Jurisdiction, but she now had to rediscover that golden path after the crash's diversion. In an effort to evade her pursuers, she had torn into a pear orchard without thought of their canine companions. Not that the soldiers of the Americas kept companions like Europa's nobles. These dogs were tools. Well-honed, organic death machines with a cultivated taste for living flesh, whether martyr or human. The dogs understood something that most had forgotten: the difference between the two was untenable. Martyrs could tell themselves they were superior for an eternity, but it wouldn't change the fact that the so-called master race and the humans they consumed were the same species.

That was not why Cassandra had died, but it hadn't contributed to their marital bliss. And now, knowing what she did of the Hierophant's intentions—thinking, always, what Cassandra would have said—the Governess pretended she was driven by that ghost, and not by her own hopelessness. Without the self-delusion, she was a victim to a great many ugly thoughts, foremost among them being: Was the fear of life after her wife's death worth such disgrace? A death sentence? Few appreciated what little difference there was between human and martyr, and fewer cared, because caring was fatal. But she was a part of the Holy Family. Shouldn't that have been all that mattered? Stunning how, after three centuries, she deserved to be treated no better than a human. Then again, there was nothing quite like resignation from one's post to fall in her Father's estimate. Partly, he was upset by her poor timing—she did stand him up at some stupid press event, but only because she hoped it would keep everybody occupied while she got away. In that moment, she couldn't even remember what it was. Dedicating a bridge? Probably. Her poor head, what did the nature of the event matter when she was close to death?

That lapse in social graces was not the reason for this hunt. He understood that more lay behind her resignation than a keening for country life. Even before he called her while she and the others took the *tanque* to the coast, he must have known. Just like he must have known the crash was seconds from happening while he chatted away, and that the humans in her company, already nervous to be within a foot of the fleeing Governess, were doomed.

Of the many people remaining on Earth, those lumped into the group of "human" were at constant risk of death, mutilation, or—far worse—unwilling martyrdom. This meant those humans lucky enough to avoid city-living segregation went to great lengths to keep their private properties secure. Not only houses but stables. The Disgraced Governess found this to be true of the stables into which she might have stumbled and electrocuted herself were it not for the bug zaps of rain against the threshold's surface.

Her mind made an instinctive turn toward prayer for the friendliness of the humans in the nearby farmhouse—an operation she was quick to abort. In those seconds (minutes?) since the crash, she'd succeeded in reconstructing the tinted windows of the *tanque* and a glimpse of silver ram's horns: the Lamb lurked close enough to hear her like she spoke into his ear. It was too much to ask that he be on her side tonight.

Granted, the dogs of the Lamb were far closer, and far more decisive about where their loyalties stood. One hound sank its teeth into her ankle, and she, crying out, kicked the beast into its closest partner with a crunch. Slower dogs snarled outrage in the distance while the Disgraced Governess ran to the farmhouse caught in her left periphery. The prudent owners, to her frustration, shuttered their windows at night. Nevertheless, she smashed her fist against the one part of the house that protruded: the doorbell required by the Hierophant's "fair play" dictatum allowing the use of electronic barriers. As the humans inside stumbled out of bed in response to her buzzing, the Disgraced Governess unholstered her antique revolver and unloaded two rounds into the recovered canines before they were upon her. The discharge wasn't a tip-off she wanted to give to the Lamb and her other pursuers, but it hastened the response of the sleeping farmers as the intercom crackled to life.

"Who is it?" A woman's voice, quivering with an edge of panic.

"My name is Dominia di Mephitoli: I'm the former Governess of the United Front, and I need to borrow a horse. Please. Don't let me in. Just drop the threshold on your stables."

"The Governess? I'm sorry, I don't understand. *The* Dominia di Mephitoli, really? The martyr?"

"Yes, yes, please. I need a horse now." Another dog careened around the corner and leapt over the bodies of his comrades with such grace that she wasted her third round in the corpses. Two more put it down as she shouted into the receiver. "I can't transfer you any credits because they've frozen my Halcyon account, but I'll leave you twenty pieces of silver if you drop the threshold and loan me a horse. You can reclaim it at the docks off Bay Street, in the township of Sienna. Please! He'll kill me."

"And he'll be sure to kill us for helping you."

"Tell him I threatened you. Tell him I tricked you! Anything. Just help me get away!"

"He'll never believe what we say. He'll kill me, my husband, our children. We can't."

"Oh, please. An act of mercy for a dying woman. Please, help me leave. I can give you the name of a man in San Valentino who can shelter you and give you passage abroad."

"There's no time to go so far south. Not as long as it takes to get across the city."

It had been ten seconds since she'd heard the last dog. That worried her. With her revolver at the ready, she scanned the area for something more than the quivering roulette blotches swelling in her right eye. Nothing but the dead animals. "He'll kill you either way. For talking to me, and not keeping me occupied until his arrival. For knowing that there's disarray in his perfect land. He'll find a reason, even if it only makes sense to him."

The steady beat of rain pattered out a passive answer. On the verge of giving up, Dominia stepped back to ready herself for a fight—and the house's threshold dropped with an electric pop. The absent mauve shimmer left the façade bare. How rare to see a country place without its barrier! A strange thing. Stranger for the front door to open; she'd only expected them to do away with the threshold on the stables.

But, rather than the housewife she'd anticipated, there stood the Hierophant. Several bleak notions clicked into place.

One immaculate gray brow arched. "Now, Dominia, that's hardly fair. Knowledge of your disgrace isn't why I'll kill them. The whole world will know of it tomorrow morning. You embarrassed me by sending your resignation, rather than making the appearance I asked of you, so it is only fair I embarrass you by rejecting your resignation and firing you publicly. No, my dear. I will kill these fine people to upset you. In fact, Mr. McLintock is already dead in the attic. A mite too brave. Of course"—he winked, and whispered in conspiracy—"don't tell them that."

"How did you know I'd come here?"

"Such an odd spurt of rain tonight. Of all your Jurisdictions, this one is usually so dry this time of year! Won't you come in for tea? Mrs. McLintock brews a fine pot. But put that gun away. You're humiliating yourself. And me."

Dominia, with some delay for her trembling, slid the gun into its holster, then entered a building that gleamed with history. Such a nice ranch house, with generations of pictures on walls that had themselves been carefully preserved, or identically restored. People were meticulous with homes like these. They lived. This one had been around a long time. Two millennia, based on the style. Centuries of love and care, about to be disrupted by a terrible bath of blood.

A friendlier dog than the ones outside greeted her at the door, and the Hierophant bent to ruffle its floppy black ears. "A new friend for the Lamb, perhaps, after you've cruelly killed three."

"As poor a guard dog as he's proved tonight, I don't think he's the hunting sort."

"Of course not. But we can always use more pets, can't we?"

Wasn't that the use of courtiers? She kept the joke to herself. In an intimate, doily-filled drawing room, the Hierophant drew an antique oak chair from the matching table and patted its scroll-carved back. Dominia lowered into the place set in anticipation of her coming, wherefrom she, scowling, studied him with she had already begun to consider her "good eye." The Hierophant, that eerie smile never leaving his pale lips, poured the tea as he spoke.

"I remember when you were first martyred. You'd pout at every supper, refuse to eat your food. I ought to have seen this night arriving."

"You did. You only pretended not to."

"True! I always like to think I've some small say in destiny. That if I ignore inevitability hard enough, it shall not rear its head. But that never seems to be the case. These tedious things all end the same."

"This is drugged, I suppose."

"It's as if you don't know me. How passé! No, my dear, I only wish to speak to you and—Carol?"

Now the berobed, befuddled woman Dominia had expected made her belated appearance. The Hierophant flashed her a smile stupid men cherished and wiser men feared. "I don't suppose you've a few spare pastries?"

"Some donuts for the children," she mumbled automatically, paling to have reminded herself, and the Hierophant, of their existence.

"Well, far be it from me to take food from the mouths of babes. Why not bring them to share with us! Rouse the tykes from bed. I love to see sweet, sleepy faces."

"Please," said the woman.

"No," said Dominia.

The Hierophant's black eyes danced between them. "I suppose it is rather late for sugar, but you ladies are taking this much too seriously. Carol, dear: go get the children. Or would you rather I fetch them?"

That suggestion chased her right up the stairs. The Holy Father smiled as he plucked with huge hands a delicate teacup adorned with painted roses; the gesture resembled that of a better father, playing tea with his daughter's tiny plastic saucers. "What a hostess. Up at two in the morning with such moxie!"

"Why are you doing this?"

"Don't you wish for a bit of civility amid all the violence and terror? You looked like you could use a sit-down. Please, drink the tea."

With a sniff that detected nothing but jasmine, she did, and broke up the heretofore uninterrupted taste of blood to which she had adjusted. Meanwhile, the flow of blood had stopped above her left eye, and a little shard of glass was pushed out by the work of the sacred protein. That good protein, her one friend. While she blinked the shard away in relief to know she was not fully blind, she finished her tea and tried to calculate a way out of the house before he got his hands on her.

No chance of that. A bonny pair of children soon tumbled down the stairs, wired from their mother's angst and promises of midnight donuts. The Hierophant laughed in delight and clapped his hands, and the girl gasped in wonder.

"Isn't that the Holo Man?"

"It's the Hierophant, Betty." Exclaiming this, the boy froze at the entrance of the room. Their mother whisked past, her anxious stare trained on the Hierophant to whom the girl, brash with innocence, giddily darted. Wiser with his eight years of dread, the boy licked his lips. "Has our family done something wrong?"

"No, no. There will be donuts." Pleased, the Hierophant turned his attention to the girl, whose golden locks fell in disarray while he whisked her up to bounce upon his knee. "I do love children," sang the martyr, far taller in the presence of the doll-like girl. Dominia gripped the table to remind herself of her own size. "They take joy in such simple things. Their courageous connection to the moment, that *joie de vivre*, has yet to be deadened by social laws."

The Governess couldn't hold her tongue. "By your laws."

"God's laws. There are men, and there are martyrs. That is a fact about which nothing can be done—no more than anything can be done about the martyr's inherent superiority. Thank you, Carol." He turned his smile to the tense woman who deposited plates of donuts before her unwelcome guests. On eye contact, her pupils shrank to pinpoints. With a lingering stare for her daughter, she hustled her son to the corner of the sofa and sat with him, one iron hand clamped to the base of his neck.

"You always had a problem accepting that," resumed the Hierophant, breaking up the powdered pastry and offering half to the bright-eyed girl. "Our superiority, I mean. Oh, you tucked your ideals away with enough years' worth of tutors, and enough time spent in the proper culture, but I admit that I saw your regression the instant you took up governance of the Front. Even after your sordid military career, your heart is too soft for these more difficult matters. Will you continue to let Cassandra's unraveling destroy your future?"

"She didn't 'unravel.' You drove her insane. She died because of you. She—"

"Is this a topic for young ears? Please, dear. I must apologize, Carol: despite my best efforts, my duckling never grew into a swan as did her younger sister. There are always kinks worked out with older models. Your name was 'Betty,' wasn't it, princess?" At the oblivious girl's happy nod from behind her powder-coated fingers, the Hierophant offered her the other half of his donut. "Well, Betty, you remind me an awful lot of my Lavinia. Do you know who Lavinia is?"

At the name, the girl's eyes widened, and she preened as any small child would when compared to royalty so high. "She's the real princess! The best princess in the whole world, and the prettiest!"

"She certainly is. What do you think of Lavinia, darling girl?"

"That she's pretty," emphasized the child again. How old was she? Three, going on four? How old had Dominia been when the Hierophant martyred her? Seven, or eight. He preferred that humans did the bulk of early raising; bed-wetting increased the transition's already unbearable difficulty. She had to lean on her notion of his preference and hope that he had only bluffed about his killing mood. There was no moving faster than him. No wasting a bullet on him. At the slightest provocation, or none, he would snap the girl's neck and be on the mother and her son two seconds later. Dominia already saw it happening and willed the images away as the child continued rattling off that Lavinia, "Gets to live in a castle with a lot of horses and doggies and all her friends. And she sings pretty, too."

"Ah, doesn't she." The Hierophant smiled with fondness, then pointed across the table at Dominia. "Do you know who that is?" he asked in a half whisper. The girl, who had been glad to have the donuts but reluctant to look at the bloodied Governess, now followed his finger and shook her head.

"What's wrong with her eye?"

"I know who she is," called the boy, to his mother's visible anguish. "She's the Governess of the whole United Front, all North America."

"'Was' the Governess, lad. Come here." The Hierophant waved a regal hand, and over came the boy, in danger far graver than his sister by virtue of age. As Dominia's breath stilled, the Holy Father reached across the table to pluck up her donut in offering to the boy. "What's your name?"

"Murph McLintock." Donut acquired, the breathless child edged toward the Governess as much as manners allowed.

"Do you see the Disgraced Governess's eye, Murphy?" asked the Hierophant. The boy turned to regard the (slightly) less notoriously evil martyr.

"It's all full of blood."

"Let's play a game. What do you reckon the odds that the Disgraced Governess's eye will stay intact 'til morning?"

The grim boy regarded the jelly extruding from the edge of the donut. "What happened to her?"

"Dominia? Would you tell Murphy what happened?"

With a resentful glance at her Father, Dominia turned her good eye toward the boy. "I was in a car accident. On the way to the shore."

Her Father pressed. "To do what?"

"To…leave."

"To run away," corrected the Hierophant, his solemn expression still aimed at Murph. "To abandon her post and deliver information to the enemy. This woman is a criminal."

Face writ with anxiety, the boy stepped back from the table. The Hierophant's smile never wavered.

"Have you ever met a martyr before, lad?"

The boy shook his head.

"What do you think? Is a martyr different from a human?"

"Dad says—"

"I don't care what 'Dad' says. I want to know what Murphy says."

Between the Hierophant and the Governess, the boy swallowed like his saliva had been replaced by sand.

"Yes. Martyrs are different from humans."

"And how are we different?"

"Well, humans are born, and then we die. But martyrs are born human, and then they die, and then they're born again as martyrs."

"And what happens when they're born again? What makes a martyr superior to a human?"

The boy's face tightened, and Dominia thought, that's right, we're not superior, there's nothing that makes a martyr superior, nothing that merits his treatment of humans, and you don't have to say it; but, of course, she didn't vocalize this thought. Instead, she sat frozen as she'd been in the instant of Cassandra's death. She was back in that dark and bloody room until Murph said, "Well, they're fast, and strong. Some are geniuses—magical, almost, like you. They don't have to worry about anything, even if they get into an accident and need a wheelchair like my aunt Hilda. 'Cause they get better so fast. My aunt doesn't live here," added the child, chin raised in a defensive posture. The Hierophant chuckled to himself.

"And what does a martyr need, my boy, to sustain that second life?"

"Human flesh." The boy spared a reluctant glance for his sister in the Hierophant's lap. "Or blood."

"That's right: although, flesh is better. And how is a martyr made?"

"By eating," whispered Murphy.

"Yes, dear boy. By eating the flesh or drinking the blood of a martyr. And other means, of course, not suited for young ears." The Hierophant winked at pale Carol, who rested her elbow upon the back of the couch and cradled her forehead in that worried hand. "What other things are passed that way, lad? Outside of martyrdom?"

"Well, sicknesses. But it's a sickness, isn't it? Martyrdom? It's a kind of sickness, and that's why all the rich people left in—when was it, Mom? I saw on the history program one day, but I don't remember. After Mars was good enough for people to start living there."

"1744 Anno Lucis," his mother answered from behind closed eyes. "My ancestor wasn't quite seventeen, too young to go with her fiancé, so they forged her documents and pretended she was eighteen. They had to leave their baby behind, and that's why we're still here."

"To think, Carol, you begged before to know why I was here—coming as you do from a family of criminals! Martyrdom is not a sickness, my boy. It is the cure to sickness—all sickness. But it is more than mere earthly cure. It is a mission. A privilege. It is an honor in which one becomes part of something grander than oneself. Grander than one might ever comprehend. One becomes a gift to the world. To reject that, and see that as anything but a privilege...do you suppose that is right, Murphy? Do you think it is *fair* that a martyr should reject the role chosen for them? Should they deny the importance of their task, and the importance of the tasks being done by their brethren?"

Caught in a trap by the sensibilities of his age, the reluctant boy shook his head. The Hierophant's hands spread in Dominia's direction. "There you are, my girl! I have no choice."

He snatched her right eye from her skull in a motion so quick Dominia could only scream in tandem with the children before propelling from the table to writhe upon the floor. Blood oozed through her fingers while her legs kicked to fend off the pain; meanwhile, the girl's panicked feet carried her cries to her mother. With his most feline expression of amusement, the Hierophant dipped the much-abused sac into his tea.

"We never did place a proper bet, lad, so I'll count that as a 'win' on my part, if you don't mind. Do you like your life the way it is?"

"No!" Dominia arched her back against the pain and gnashed her teeth, unable to lift her hand away to view the unfolding scene. "Don't do it! Don't do it, you bastard!"

"I will deal with you at an opportune juncture," said the Hierophant. "Come here, Murphy. Answer the Holy Father."

Again, obligated by well-instilled values, the boy neared with but a flicker of attention for the crying mother who cradled her second child and prayed for her first. Amid all her screaming pain, Dominia thought to herself how praying would only make the situation worse, but she had no strength to say it as her free hand fumbled around her belt.

"I love my parents."

"And your sister?"

With more reluctance: "Yes."

As the boy answered, the Hierophant lifted the lid of the sugar bowl and scooped a few generous teaspoons into the cup. "What if I told you that you could keep your family safe from me forever? All you'd need do is trade your life for them."

"No," cried Dominia again, a word useless to him.

The wise child asked, "You don't mean really die, do you?"

The Hierophant smiled in that mockery of patriarchal tenderness which was his trademark. "No, I don't. It has been a long time since I've been a new grandparent."

"Murphy, don't." His mother made one futile plea, but the boy looked in her eyes and saw her fear, saw her neck wet with the tears of his sister. Strangled with grief, Murph turned back to the Hierophant.

"I'd do it for them."

"You'll come with me and grow into a man who will never age beyond his apex. Never sicken. Never die. You'll have wealth beyond measure, more friends than you could count; I'll make you a duke, or an earl. Not so bad a trade for your old human life? For your family's lives?"

Mute, the boy shook his head. The smiling Hierophant offered the cup of tea and blood. That nauseating admixture stood poised millimeters from the boy's lips when Dominia managed to lift the gun and, half blind, pull the trigger.

She would wish for the rest of her life that she had gotten the shot off sooner, and that Murphy's last memory of life before the bullet ended his suffering wasn't the tea of ocular matter nearing his lips for the sake of his cowering family. She would wish and wish and it would never change, that second of realization that she had killed a child to save him from martyrdom. Nothing about it would change, neither that cry from his mother, which pierced the air for miles around, nor that cold, dead-faced look from the Hierophant, who regarded the corpse, then his daughter, with disappointment.

"That was a stupid thing to do."

"Well, you know me." Dominia took a haggard breath while the Hierophant, in a petty rage, stormed across the room to snap the necks of both mother and daughter. It was the most painless death possible for either of them after the night's direction. "I've never been your favorite."

"You could have been, had you ever tried to adapt. Nothing you could have done for me, for the Family, ever could have made you my favorite child until you accepted my love into your heart! Yet you have always refused it, that love. All the things I gave you—all the sacrifice, the attention and education. The land. Your governance! Oh, Dominia, what an awful shame!"

Feeling pathetic, Dominia endeavored to turn her last bullet on herself, but recalled as she pulled the trigger that her last had been spent on Murph. The Hierophant swept the gun out of her hand, as angry as if she'd been successful. "No, no, no. You ridiculous woman. Shall I take both your eyes? Eager as you are to destroy your world, I would do you a favor by blinding you to it."

"Fuck you," she said, and was whipped across the face with the handle of the gun.

"I have never been as humiliated by your mouth as I was tonight. What a pitiful waste."

He drew back his leg and kicked Dominia once, hard, in the stomach. As her hand shifted protection from her eye socket to her winded gut, the Holy Father clutched her by the throat to fling her against the table. Precious more than a rag doll, she lay upon the broken shards of a porcelain vase and its half-dead posies. The Hierophant regarded her with a heavy sigh.

"Oh, Dominia, my dear. How sad I am to leave you thus. Should I tear out your tongue to let you drown in your blood? That would be easiest, perhaps. Instead, I'll take these." He bent and, with one great hand, forced open her jaw. With the other, he reached into her mouth. After a sickening snap-crunch-pop, first came one silver fang, then came the next. Dominia kicked and screamed, and the family's border collie crawled into the room to bark in an effort it knew was fruitless. The Hierophant was careful his fingers were free of her teeth before allowing her to shut her mouth again. Then he slipped the cuspids into the pocket of his waistcoat, wiped his hands clean of blood on Dominia's leather breeches, and smiled at the dog.

"Hello, hello! How are you? Aren't you a lovely boy."

As the towering man approached it, hand outstretched, the dog's ears pinned back. It edged away with a growl.

"So upset. Wouldn't you like a new friend?"

Once, twice, the dog barked, and Dominia, when she turned her head, caught a glimpse of white tooth. Please, go hide! But the Hierophant chuckled over his shoulder at the Disgraced Governess.

"Perhaps I'll leave him to keep you company while you die." With a lamp from an end table, the Hierophant shattered the most modern object in the room—the holo-center and its attached phone, all tucked in the corner by the couch. Too woozy to protest as he shattered the projector and tore wires from the installation within the wall, Dominia let her head roll back against the floor. "Call some friends on your watch if you'd like us to trace their numbers, assuming you haven't excised yourself of friends as you've tried to excise yourself of family. It's a few hours until dawn. When it comes, why not crawl to meet it? A few minutes after, you'll have nothing to worry about. Oh, but—leave the door open behind you. Wouldn't want the dog to starve once his family is down to bones."

As her Father's back receded along with her gun, her teeth, and her sense of reality, existence faded into the whine of the dog. How funny: after all this time, all this luck, all one thousand battles, Dominia felt certain she'd die in her sleep.

Fate, of course, would never be so kind.

II

Adrift

René Ichigawa seemed a resourceful man, so Dominia wasn't surprised when she jolted half upright to find herself enclosed in a casket that was, in its turn, enwombed within the sound of waves. No, the surprise came when she tried to lift that casket's lid and discovered her enclosure had no lid at all. As her nostrils were assailed by the smell of wet dog, she turned to make visible the McLintock border collie, once hidden in her new blind spot. The delighted dog barked, and while Dominia struggled to regain her bearings, footsteps hurried across the deck. A shaft of light belched into the lazaretto where she'd been stowed alongside other odds and ends with no place topside.

"It's still hours before dark, Dominia. You'll need your rest; go to sleep." René's face appeared, the Franco Japanese professor's foxy features softened by what looked to be gunpowder (or mud) that contoured his face and ears. "The fishing boat is still on schedule to pick us up, and the wind is with us, so we may make it to them by tonight's scheduled rendezvous."

"And if we don't?"

"Then we'll sail all the way to Japan!"

Dry-mouthed, Dominia regarded him, then the dog. "All the way to Japan, with me and some mutt sharing a storage locker?"

"Purebred, I thought. He's not yours? He insisted on following us and wouldn't get off the boat."

"The Hierophant killed his family." Her mouth felt wronger with each word, and as she remembered her missing incisors, she rubbed her upper lip and grimaced at the bare gum. As her hand moved up and encountered fabric around her forehead, René reached into the lazaretto to slap at her fingers.

"Leave that alone! Martyr or not, infections are real. Count yourself lucky he left you alive, and with that." He pointed at the diamond resting on her heart; her hand lowered to Cassandra's smooth facets. Oh, Cassandra!

Dominia pushed the image of her wife's lost body away with a tight swallow while René carried on. "I made a bandage out of my tie—you're welcome—but when we get to Japan, we'll have to get you a new one."

"A new bandage?"

"A new eye." He glanced between Dominia and the dog, certain he'd get his answer from one of them. "What happened?"

"There was a mole. There must have been. Someone who knew we left tonight. The escorts you arranged had me almost to the coast when Elijah and his cronies crashed into us. Without Cicero, no less, which means they're serious. I don't think I've seen them apart since 1994."

"The Lamb! What a nut. The fang trend, I suppose I get, but ram-horn implants?"

"Don't laugh. He needs them to filter all the pleas if he's going to focus on one prayer at a time."

The human did laugh, of course. "Like a tinfoil helmet! So he's just a schizophrenic?"

She didn't feel like arguing. That the Lamb's miracles had physical effects were a given. Not believing in him was like not believing in gravity; but so was believing in him, because nobody could fully explain gravity, either. "I don't understand how any of it works—hardly anybody does but my Father—but it does. Without those implants, he hears all prayers, all the time. Of course he'd seem insane without them. When you can make anything that's possible happen with surety, you're going to be the focus of a lot of attention."

"Like he'd waste his time helping a non-martyr...or even a martyr, most of the time."

She wasn't yet inclined enough against her Family to trash the Lamb along with the rest of them, and said, "He saves martyrs every week, every time they get dragged in to Mass to taste his blood—that's one whole week of not having to eat human flesh. Not if the martyr doesn't want it."

"And how is this different from the Lazarenes?"

No reason to get annoyed; she hadn't believed the tenants of the Holy Martyr Church in years, shouldn't be getting sensitive about it. Better to keep it about her Family. "I wasn't sure I'd made the right choice in leaving. Not until I saw the Lamb in the *tanque* that hit us. Now, I realize this is my only option."

Irritation marred René's face. "I thought you were committed to this."

"I am now, aren't I?" When his features didn't relax, she scoffed. "It's ridiculous, isn't it? Throwing away my governance on some crazy hope that—"

"The Hunters know where Lazarus is," insisted the professor. Back into religion they slipped again, despite the Governess's best efforts. Or—well, not a Governess now, was she? Back to a General again. Debatably. She struggled to reframe her own perception of herself as the human carried on, "Whether resurrection is possible—I'm skeptical, myself. But everybody seems certain Lazarus is a real guy, and I'd give an awful lot to see if he can make a miracle. Prove it or disprove it. Who wouldn't? Since my idiot cousin is so convinced of it, I might as well see for myself."

The dog watched with an occasional wag of its curled tail. She turned from it and asked René, "What happened to you?"

"We were ambushed right while I took a pee break—the reason I survived! The Lamb must have come for us after attacking you."

"I'm sorry."

"It doesn't matter. As long as we have you—and as long as I'm alive, of course!—we'll be in perfect shape."

"Even if you die, don't worry. I'm staking my life that resurrection is real, right?"

Weakly, she returned René's laughter as he once more sealed her into the lazaretto. The border collie turned big blue eyes on her, spicing it up with a hopeful tail wag that carried on until she ruffled its ears.

"I still might eat you, you know." As she spoke, her tongue wiggled into one of the gaps of her stolen cuspids. The replacement, a furry canine, responded with a knowing whine as she lay her head against the ropes that formed her pillow. "Yes," she agreed, "pretty pathetic."

By now, the Internet brimmed with rumors about her. The cracked face of her smartwatch, even with its location functions long disabled, perceived enough to indicate it was 1300 hours in their time zone. More proof to Dominia that the thing's functions were never capable of being disabled. If it was accurate, she had hours before the sun would relieve her from her prison. Most of Europa's highest citizens—certainly those around the Hierophant's preferred castle of Kronborg—had already seen news broadcasts (with subtitles, even) uploaded to every livestream Internet site in which the Hierophant had his fingers: that being, of course, most of them. With a few taps of the watch's digital screen, she picked her own primary source, San-5 News, and found its stream featured an angry, spray-tanned martyr hostess already shouting at the camera with the odd wild gesticulation and, once, the tossing of her pencil.

"It is my personal pleasure to announce the traitor, Governess Dominia di Mephitoli, has been killed by Our Lord the Hierophant while attempting to flee her own municipality of the United Front. I'll remind you that, a mere four months ago, on May Night, Cassandra di Mephitoli had her martyring completed. I think we've all heard enough of the official line by now—but perhaps there's a more sinister story at work." As the General's jaw tightened, the idiot ranted on. "The truth will never be known—rest her soul, the poor woman—but I say, good riddance to the worthless Governess, who let her post corrupt her past the point of no return." There went the pencil. "There's no room among martyrs for traitors, apostates, and liars who intended to bring secret military intelligence to the enemy. Our leader, however, is more generous than I am."

The clip cut to a press conference in what she recognized by the scarlet leather chair and goldenrod drapes to be her own office. Not more than two hours after he'd left her near death, she'd wager. With his beetle eyes the picture of mournful calm, the Hierophant lifted a hand to smooth back his gray-blond hair. He opened his mouth, lost the will, and began to weep.

"My children—" He covered his lips with his fingers, then let those same deft digits dip into his breast pocket for the folded cloth square with which he dabbed those tears. "My children"—he began again—"I apologize. This morning has been one of great emotion for me. It is with profound sorrow that I announce my eldest daughter, Governess Dominia di Mephitoli, had her martyring completed in a confrontation early this morning—owed to an anonymous tip that the Governess intended to flee the United Front for the Empire of the Risen Sun. When we spoke, she remained unreasonable, and I had no choice—though I wish she had given me one. I wish she had given me a choice, my children; oh, my children, my daughter is dead! Sweet Dominia."

His face disappeared behind his hand and his handkerchief. As a camera-decapitated figure rushed to comfort him with a touch upon his shoulder, the Hierophant rose. This forced the camera to pan up and reveal the snot-nosed face of Dominia's baby brother, smug as a pig in shit.

"But, as we all know: in every death, there lies an opportunity for rebirth. Therefore, amid this tragedy, I award stewardship of the United Front to my son, Theodore del Medico. Governor Theodore, please."

The Hierophant swept away with a microsecond's bleak stare into the camera, a look that Dominia sensed to be for her, whenever she would watch the feed repeated in cuts and recuts, news and talk shows, for nights or weeks. Unless something worse happened, anyway. Events unraveled so fast that it was possible for something to steal her unwanted spotlight within hours. She started to zone out into the pain of her eye socket as her tedious brother failed to keep the gloating from his voice. "We will all mourn with heavy hearts the loss of my sister. But I swear, citizens of the United Front: I will do you proud."

Yeah. Proud. Most of the citizens of the Front were human: Europa, especially in the Baltic region and New Scandinavian region, was the area most populated with martyrs. Therefore, martyrs living in the United Front were better off—at least, less likely to know their neighbors, and given to higher odds of success and social advancement. The humans were better off, too, and with much open land made available by migration in and out of cities as the times changed, hopeful mortals struggling to breathe in cramped Eastern countries made the mistake of immigrating, through legal means or otherwise, to the Front. This meant that there was a proliferation of bounty hunters and terrorists hidden among the human population, but it also meant that there were far, far more good, honest, hardworking people who happily withstood the danger of living in proximity to martyr territory if it meant they got ahead. Governance of the region belonged to somebody responsible, somebody who'd govern with compassion for the latter group of humans, which needed looking after if they, and the planet (and, consequently, the martyrs), were to survive. The Hierophant knew that, which was why he'd put Dominia in charge to begin with, and why he put Theodore in charge now. It would agonize her to see. He knew perfectly well that she lived.

"He said he thinks you're dead," observed Ichigawa when she showed him the feed above deck eight hours later. The professor lit a Sterno can with the electric arc of his lighter.

"He's lying so he gets to say later that whoever abetted my escape will merit death."

"Don't you suppose he'll be made a fool of?"

"No. He'll make me look like a cunning terrorist. Not so hard, now that I'll need an eye patch."

"Not necessarily. Your new eye can appear identical to your old one, depending on the features you're after. The fangs, though—those'll be harder. Nobody does fangs in the Risen Sun, for obvious reasons."

"I'd like something more reasonable, anyway. Those surgical fashions... they're practical so long as you're a predator. I'd started to regret mine."

"Trading in your fangs for teeth?"

"For Cassandra. I've given up everything for her. My whole Family, my whole world."

"You still have to give up one more thing before we're able to resurrect your wife."

"Sell my Father and my nations to the Hunters, you mean."

"What does he want?" asked Ichigawa. Dominia lifted her head to the white face of the winsome moon; beyond, semi-terraformed Mars glowed with starry promise. It had been so bright in the sky the night of the meeting—mere weeks after Cassandra's funeral—wherein the Hierophant announced to a room of military geniuses the implementation of a multiphase plan. A lunatic's plan. Project Black Sun, which had, after Cassandra's death, pushed Dominia into final, foolish action.

"He wants to give martyrs the ability to walk in the sun."

"How will he do it?"

"He never said. Only that it's a multiphase effort relying on an assault on Jerusalem. There won't be anyone who knows more if he's not one hundred percent sure they can be trusted."

"How does he know that they can be trusted?"

"How does he know anything? How does he evade bullets, how does he seem capable of traveling vast distances in impossible spans of time? Why does he seem to know everything I do? He'll tell you it's because he's close to God, but I suspect it's the Lamb. He affects probability; he must know something about the future. All he needs to do is say the word to the Hierophant, and your whole plan is kaput. Once a person is equipped with information and therefore has a high probability of betraying them with that information, the Lamb is able to rectify the situation. But there's one person that the Hierophant would trust with anything. Cicero."

With a sickle smile, René lifted his eyebrows. "El Sacerdote. His eldest child, yes?"

"By a hair, though it's said he and the Lamb were martyred at once. And he's not just the eldest: they're the only survivors out of…countless generations. The Hierophant has ruled for two thousand years, and Cicero has been his highest priest and right hand the whole time. My Father acts like I'm the first kid he's ever killed for disobeying him after the age of a hundred, but there have been plenty more. At least six generations I can name. He's taking advantage of short memory spans: the median age for active martyrs is something like three hundred and sixty right now. Martyrs who were alive for his older generations of children are few and far between."

"So Cicero is almost two thousand years old. How old is the Hierophant?"

"Ageless, he says."

"How is it he's so much older?"

"Time lived before his reign, of course, on his planet of origin, where he was the high priest in the way that Cicero is here. The martyr planet, from which he brought his blood and the ways of martyrs. That's the official line, anyway."

Here, Dominia lost the professor, as all martyrs lost any human with whom they discussed the subject of the exoteric trinity and the origins of the Hierophant. It was touchy for them, as it was for René, who shook his head. "That's fine, if goofy, but mixing it up with a bunch of religious nonsense is where I get prickly about it. The last great barrier to sensible living."

Her lip gave the instinctive twitch of someone too long in the practice of suppressing their smirks. "It's one he's tried his best to eliminate. Any religion but his, anyway. Always hard to stamp that spirit out, though."

Lowering his head over the canned stove, Ichigawa probed the roasting potted meat. Hard to digest as what she had told him, that stuff; but the professor took both in stride. "Mankind has, in all fairness, been unified by the martyrs and the Hierophant. Old prejudices of race, language, gender, disability, sexuality—none of it matters now. There are the poor and the rich, but so it will always be, I think. Perhaps one day, religions will be unified. The final prejudice to be destroyed is the prejudice between the living and the dead."

Dominia regarded her hand. Was it really her hand? What once was animated and controlled by cells was now animated and controlled by the sacred protein that had edited those zombie cells, dead but still alive. Preserved for eternity in their ideal physical state by a protein that never ceased its editing. To support the body's state of constant high maintenance, martyrs kept their proteins educated with DNA samples from healthy blood and flesh; otherwise, the protein was liable to overedit, as it was when exposed to the sun. The result of this starvation long-term was not death, but something closer to epilepsy, or, in certain unlucky martyrs, cancer. Ergo, their diets were incompatible with peaceful existence, much as they were incompatible with an average level of vitamin D. Exposure to sunlight resulted in a hyperefficient state wherein the martyr's immune system destroyed itself and the body it inhabited in a matter of ten to twenty minutes, depending on age. If that were to happen to the General, would the sun kill her, or reveal her?

His mind along a similar track, René split the potted meat between himself and the dog head poking out from the lazaretto. "I didn't manage to save any rations more than the Spam in the locker. When was the last time you ate?"

"Twelve hours ago."

"The tremors will start soon."

Yes, the tremors. Then the insomnia. Then the dysarthria. "There's nothing to be done."

"Nothing, yet—but we'll be picked up soon. I hope."

"A fishing vessel out to sea isn't going to have a steady supply of blood." At Ichigawa's blank look, Dominia sucked the gaps in her teeth. "No, René."

"I'm just trying to make suggestions!"

"They're helping us!"

"They're not helping us so you can starve."

"I'm not going to starve." Over the edge of the boat, she stretched her fingers toward the water. Her reflection, disrupted by the churning water and the brooding dark, recalled Cassandra. "I'm not an animal. I can wait."

As if on cue, a ship began to peel itself from the invisible horizon that blended water and sky. "We'll see about that."

Dominia drew her collar high around her face. "How much do they know?"

"As much as you'd tell a cab company. 'One woman, one man, a little luggage.' Didn't mention the dog."

"Or the martyrdom."

"No, didn't mention that, either. Would have been much harder to secure transportation, even with Tenchi's help. These fishermen are used to helping whole families of humans escape martyrs, not helping martyrs escape to East Asia. At any rate, they won't ask many questions when they see—well."

The wind nipped up to splash salt water across her lips. As Dominia's remaining eye trained on the ship, she refused to allow herself to feel trepidation, or pain. Certainly not grief over her eye, the eye that had been with her since her first, human birth and before—the eye whose companion now looked on with agitated acuity, presenting a world that began to her left and ended at the crescent of a nose she noticed more than ever. Another brisk slap of the water licked her mouth, and she allowed this one to conjure the spray of foam that had produced her first look of naked Cassandra while the human emerged, laughing, from the sea. Dominia had taken shelter from the sun in one of a great many coves around the dramatic Pacific beach, and lo! was visited by an angel.

She would forever remember Cassandra's eyes: those fair twin moons rendered crescents as she looked around herself with one hand across her breasts and the other planted between her long legs, bared by the kind ocean for (then mere General) Dominia's astonished scrutiny. Four hours had the General remained in the cove, praising the low tide and waiting for some break in the sun. Now she saw why she had come, why she had been drawn to the ocean and to what hint of light her body could stand. A run seemed it would do well for her distracted mind. That was why she'd come to the shady seaside town in the Pacific Northwest, after all: distraction. It had been as different from Mexico as one might imagine, and a fine place to get lost in thought.

But the dawn that called her to her senses had found her miles from her cabana. The Pacific northwest and its sullen coastlines were known for their morning haze, so where had it gone? She'd felt so stupid, sitting with her coat spread beneath her, hidden in the darkest, driest place she'd managed to find. That foolish feeling remained until sweet Cassandra appeared, her rich honey hair wet to a dark-taupe tangle of curls that streamed over her shoulders and clung to her breasts like the seaweed of a mermaid's fabled locks. Then, this woman with her tumbling hair and her big eyes saw the martyr hidden in the cove and, likewise amazed, let her brassy limbs fall free from her body. In the sun, she almost glowed.

"You're that martyr general." Without a trace of fear. "I know you. Dominia, right?"

Yes, yes, Dominia, yes, general, yes, martyr, yes, yes, many things. Oh, agony! What to say? What trouble, words! "I feel like I'm interrupting something by being here."

"Interrupting? Oh!" Those hands began to move, and so did seated Dominia's, until she conquered instinct—but there was no stopping her voice, which pleaded, "You don't have to," before tapering off in a sad note of embarrassment. At the exquisite stranger's smile and the way her body relaxed, the General's self-consciousness faded.

"It's so hard to get morning sunshine here! I was sunbathing, and just… My name's Cassandra." The human stepped with nimble feet across the rocks, and Dominia sat straighter, heart hammering. "What are you doing here? I thought martyrs couldn't go outside in day."

"We can't, strictly speaking. I went out late for a walk, and I—I thought it would be cloudy."

"Do you live near here?"

"Sort of wish I did." Both laughed, and as the naked woman embanked near Dominia's shelter, the General bit her lip. "You strike me as a local."

"How'd you guess? I love the sea. The soft sound of the waves. They put me to sleep every night." She hovered at the edge of the shade. "Can I— Am I bothering you?"

"No, please." Dominia's voice was as hoarse as her lips were dry; but, oh, how she smiled in that moment. "Please come in, Cassandra. Sit with me."

"Dominia."

René's voice called her back to the present, where salt water heralded only the looming trawler. A flashlight poured into her sensitive eye, and the sound of a barking animal rose over those of waves as the professor shouted, "Are you okay? Did you hear me?"

"What did you say?"

"I asked you, 'How do we move the dog?'"

"I'll take him," she said, shaking herself free of her one moment of joy. "Don't worry."

III

Aboard the Jun'yō

If a refugee wanted to avoid questions when boarding the fishing vessel set to smuggle them to freedom, all they needed do was lose an eye. That, or bring a dog. The McLintock border collie so stole the proverbial show from either Dominia or René that they barely had to do a thing but accept a coarse pair of blankets and watch the comfort-starved men fawn over Fido, who tried his best to pay all sailors equal attention while he pranced around the mess hall. "I'm going to have to come up with a name for that dog," she said as the first mate, a portly, tanned fellow—the Tenchi who was Ichigawa's paternal cousin—came with the ship's doctor. René barely looked up from the lab-grown leather shoes he'd begun to polish the second it was polite. This doctor, a strange and squat fellow who looked less Japanese and more like some sort of gnome, lifted his eyebrows as he examined her socket.

"He says it's a clean job," supplied Tenchi at the doctor's muttered Japanese. "He says if it wasn't for a few bits of glass, it would look like a soft-boiled egg had popped, whole, from its shell."

She asked René, "Whose bedside manner is worse?" The professor laughed while the doctor rifled through the contents of his medical bag. "It's hard to tell with a translator. Is it the doctor, or is it your cousin?"

"Don't blame me," said Tenchi. As the doctor hurried away to wet a sponge and clean the tweezers, he waved a hand at his back. "This guy's used to working with sailors."

Dominia snorted. "What's your excuse?" The doctor, now gloved, returned to wipe the sponge over her nose, cheek, and brow, uncomfortably close to what she'd begun to intellectualize as a depression in her face. Still, she felt her eye like it was there, and feeling her eye made her think of losing her eye. The doctor was right. It had been a tidy job, outside the expected blood. It made her sick to think about, that egg thing, but now it was all she thought—eggs and grapes and her eyeball dipping in and out of the Hierophant's fucking teacup. She shoved the doctor away and ran to the big mess hall sink where she vomited, full of clots and tissue she rushed to rinse away before anyone noticed. "Sorry, I'm sorry."

"You're in shock," said the doctor, aided by his temporary translator, as both men guided her into the nearest seat. René watched, arms crossed while Dominia rested her head against the cool surface of the counter behind her. The bun into which her hair had been placed for the doctor's easier scrutiny had slipped; the inky strands that tumbled down didn't seem like her own, but Cassandra's wet from the ocean, and made her cry.

"Now, try not to do that." The doctor continued plucking splinters of glass from her eyelid without fuss or flinch. "Try not to move."

"I'm sorry; I'm shaking. I'm diabetic." As she lied, she watched the doctor's mouth. Would a fleck of her blood fly in? Would it be enough? Was there a cut on him somewhere? "Have you ever dealt with someone who's lost an eye before?"

"Not for years and years. But it'll be fine. We just have to get you ashore as soon as possible— you'll need eye drops to prevent infection, and a steroid to help your recovery. A conformer, too, for a few weeks while it heals."

She didn't have a few weeks, nor did she need the steroids, but the eye drops would be nice. As the sponge became cotton balls and the motions more delicate and careful, he clicked his tongue, saying in Japanese, "Surgical, surgical," while Tenchi asked, "Who did this to you?"

"Some martyrs," said René, his flat lie the elegant combination of truth and fiction one would expect of a literature professor. "Dominique and I wandered off to take a pee. At the same time, our group was attacked."

"Take a pee, huh," repeated skeptical Tenchi, looking between them with an eye of wry ignorance that must have seemed from within a stroke of genius. "Yeah, I'll bet."

"We're definitely not like that," said Dominia. The doctor understood that English well enough, for he laughed. "René and I are—associates."

"Business partners," supplied René, springing from where he'd sat on the edge of the table with legs swinging to and fro. As his back stretched and his hips gave an audible pop, the professor sighed, then moseyed over to clap his cousin's shoulder. "No need for jealousy, Ten-chan. She's gay."

"What! But she looks so girlie."

"I'll pretend that was a compliment," said Dominia.

The first mate went on with a playful stroke of his multiple chins as his cousin might his beard, "She does have a pretty strong jaw, huh."

"I miss the United Front already."

René jostled his cousin. "Have respect, would you! Dominique is a widow."

"Oh, *gomen*!" The blanching sailor hastened a bow; the doctor, after taking his meaning, sighed and shook his head. "Very sad," said the old fellow in marbled English, throwing away the cotton balls before retrieving bandages. Tenchi went on, his ruddy face further reddened by shame.

"I didn't know."

"It's fine. You never know if you don't try, right?"

The redness now in the tips of his ears, Tenchi nodded again, and the nod turned into a brisk bow. From this bent position, he muttered some excuse and was gone, having so humiliated himself that the only choice was a breezy escape. Despite herself, Dominia smirked, and then, when René also smirked, she laughed, trying not to show the gaps that would betray her in a second. With a twinkle in his eye, René shook his head.

"Man, that guy. He's never been able to keep it together."

"Keep what together?"

"Anything. Life." After dragging over a plastic chair, René flipped it around and sat in it backward; because, Dominia supposed, he felt this made him cool, or edgy, or because it was what Camus did two thousand years before. "How are you feeling?"

"I'm okay."

"I can see. But how are you *feeling*?"

While tightening her trembling hands into better-controlled fists, Dominia licked her lips. "I'm fine. Tired. Dehydrated. How long is it until we reach land?" The doctor answered René's translation of the question.

"Five more days," said the professor, "though our friend here says when he was our age, this journey would take about seven from here. Thanks, modernity."

"When I was his age," Dominia murmured with a hint of a smile and humor hidden in her eye, "it would have taken nine."

René laughed as the serene and oblivious doctor stepped back to assess his work. After showing her a depressing glimpse of her bandaged reflection in the nearest hand mirror, the doctor took up a cotton ball and emphatically mimed the pattern of wiping on his own eye. "He wants you to clean nose to ear, and never the actual socket. Only around it."

"I'll try not to cram it with cotton balls." The doctor passed her the bag of them, then bowed. As she bowed back, she asked René, "Does he expect me to pay?"

"It's part of his job," said Ichigawa. The old man hurried off with his bag, following portly Tenchi the way he'd hustled off. "You're not the only refugee this ship plucked from the ocean. It's no wonder the Hierophant's navy seems so dead set on destroying even the most innocuous Japanese vessel they encounter. The last number I heard Tenchi throw out was a thousand people have been rescued over the life of the operation. Just *this* ship, I mean."

As the dog, tired of affection, extricated itself from the adoring longshoremen, Dominia held out her hand. It lay its massive head in her palm. "That's pretty miraculous, considering how the border is controlled."

"No operation is perfect. If anyone is going to get people out of this place, it's the Empire."

True. Much as, in ancient times, the Japanese had resisted with violence the emergence of Christianity within their culture, so, too, did they resist the (initially spiritual, later forceful) entreaties of the Hierophant, who soon after decided to leave the Empire and most of Asia to their business. As a result, the Asian nations thrived as a bastion of liberty while most of the rest of the world succumbed to the centuries-long power campaign of the Hierophant. The endless fight to maintain existing order while increasing what he already possessed. His greatest ambition was all but impossible: uncontested ownership of the entire Earth. Then, his eye would land on Mars—assuming it had not already, for he spoke of the mistletoe planet often enough, and had contributed enough to the technological developments that allowed its blossoming to feel undue possessiveness. It was natural that, after Earth was in hand, the next step was for martyrs to pack into rockets to explore the vast reaches of space. The thought made Dominia shudder; but maybe that was hunger. Her teeth chattered so viciously she feared she'd off her tongue, and she rose with the support of the dog and René.

"You look pale, even considering."

"I feel exhausted."

"I'm sure. Come on, let's get some sleep."

The prospect sounded wonderful—cool, delicious sleep, soft on her aching, itching eyelid—but was impossible. Sleep would not come. Not on her sad little fisherman's cot, with its wafer-thin mattress pad, and the stained pillow whose stuffing was unknown (rocks? plastic?) but whose exterior was the worn, smooth fabric of something into which years of foreign dirt, sweat, and face oils had been mashed. Eventually she threw the pillow aside and rolled her coat behind her head, a hard support stuffed under the nape of her neck. Ichigawa snored in the bunk above her, her every shift and twist and turn of discomfort lost on the man who had lured her to sleep to steal it all for himself. That was what he seemed like, Ichigawa. A thief. A thief, or a con artist, hands wet with snake oil. It was even hard to discern his age—and not just because it was hard to tell a human's age once they'd gotten into the standard panel of antiaging genetic engineering procedures. He looked thirty, but it was clear to Dominia he was a forty-plus who aged well. If you asked, he'd say twenty-seven, and that was obvious bullshit. Sometimes she got the sense that he lied for lying's sake. That it was a game for him, or a compulsion, or perhaps a result of his identity as a failed writer. Not that she'd known him long: mere weeks. Yet, he had worked from inside the United Front, risked his life as a pivotal doorway by which humans were liberated from the Hierophant, and she believed him when he said he was tired of shuttling people out while putting himself at risk. For all the risk he endured, it was a surprise he looked so young. Maybe it was the lying; he lied himself youthful. Where no one could see it, Dominia cracked a smile.

It wasn't so bad, being awake all night and all day, the rough wool blanket around her body the only source of warmth, her stomach eating itself while her hands shook. Being awake meant that she couldn't awaken further into crushing disappointment. It meant she wouldn't sleep in that deep, deathlike way, plagued with awful dreams: petty, stressful dreams where Cassandra had gone for a walk and wouldn't come back for a long time, or any of the other uncountable images reflecting Dominia's heartache at being left behind. But the dreams were preferable to that second she awoke saying, "No, please," halfway out of bed, expecting Cassandra to sit up with her. To be there, murmuring, "It's okay, you're with me, you're safe." That wouldn't happen anymore. Instead, the memory of her absence and terrible death always flooded back into Dominia's brain, an imitation of the painful moment lived anew each waking.

All that was avoidable if the General never slept. Insomnia wasn't so bad. This tiny room wasn't so bad. She might live here. Starve to death here. How long ago had she last eaten? The day before yesterday, she guessed. The longest she'd gone in ninety years. Since the Battle for the Reclamation of Mexico from the South American Resistance Army, when she'd spent six days and nights as a prisoner of war in a Nogales cell. She still tasted the dirt, sensed its granules up in her gums, all the grit and filth in the air having settled in to make her suffocate. To grind her down. But it didn't. She survived, and she would survive this, too.

Her growing concern, however, was that this could not be said of everyone aboard. On the main deck, the night crew worked their twelve-hour shift. She, wrapped in her blanket, wandered to watch them. Like a woman's cry, the winch squealed the trawl aboard and revealed to the flooding lights of the boat a pulsing tumor of fish bodies, which, quivering with slime, gasped for impossible breath. What were they? She'd never been good at identifying fish. Pollack and flat fish, Tenchi would tell her, later, once the crew was no more. For now, a few of their number working together split open the great net and, after loosening the bundle by pushing a few fish down into the grate to the processing deck, shoved them all in a gross, living pile to mechanical deaths.

IV

The Massacre

Ensuring the crew's survival meant avoiding them. This wasn't because she was some savage animal. Nor was the issue one of self-restraint. She could restrain herself. Starving humans didn't walk around taking bites out of living cows, did they? When a starving man killed an animal, there was butchery involved. Steps were taken between the moment of death and the act of consumption. Thus, Dominia's hesitance to spend time around the crew of the *Jun'yō* was not motivated by insatiable craving. Rather, it arose from the implicit understanding that humans and martyrs had built over the centuries: martyrs were predators, and, like most predators, were considered by most humans a threat worth eliminating. There were humans who had, like the McLintocks, managed to eke out a living by keeping their heads down, and contributing to society in a tangible way; there were also those who, like Ichigawa, took the risk to mingle with martyrs in the name of education, art, and daring social advancement; but then there were those humans who took a dim view of martyrs, their appetites, and what the two had done to the human race.

The men on that powder keg of a ship were the third sort of human. All it would take was one spark to send the whole thing up in flames. She wasn't sure what that spark would be, but she somehow wasn't surprised when it proved the fault of her Family member, Cicero.

Cicero—or the Hierophant, anyway. Both, she supposed, had hands in the speedy orchestration of her funeral, which must have been in the planning since at least Cassandra's death to so hastily tail the incident at McLintock farm. Not surprising. The surprising part of it was that the sailors' network of choice was livestreaming the event. She knew that, for the sake of the intelligence, the Empire of the Risen Sun kept tabs on martyr media, but she didn't expect livestreams of anything but theater: actual broadcasts by the

Hierophant, she'd assumed to be kept for political or military use. Had she known otherwise, she would have disabled their televisions while they slept, and done her best to wreck their Internet. Things could have stayed peaceful.

They were peaceful to start with. She had read somewhere once—several somewheres, several times—that real sailors thought it bad luck to bring women aboard, but these men, she assumed, were used to it with all their rescue work. They kept to their own devices, maintaining the ship and attending to their duties as though she were not there. For the most part, she was indeed not there: rather, she was in her bunk. The dog—trauma-bonded, she supposed—stayed with her, which meant René had to return to feed it sometime midday.

"Have you thought of a name, yet?"

"Bentley?" The dog snorted over its food, a big bowl of dried jerky and rice flavored with some foul-smelling gravy made from the stored grease of many meals. "No?"

"God no. What is he, the member of a country club? 'Bentley,' please. You need a real dog's name. 'Basil,'" suggested Ichigawa. The collie's tail wagged. "You like that?"

"Fine, 'Basil.' What do I know about naming things? If I wanted to name something, Cassandra and I would have had a kid." Lifting her head to regard the canine, which scoffed, eyes toward her, she noted, "Pretty sapient dog."

"It does seem that way." The animal, licking the bottom of the bowl, then stuck its hind leg in the air and contorted to lick its privates. Ichigawa smirked. "Sometimes."

As Dominia's head lowered upon her bunched coat, the professor asked, "So you'll stay inside the whole time? Right here? They'll get suspicious, you know."

"They'll be even more suspicious when they see the way I'm shaking."

"Keep telling them you have low blood sugar. You'll get free sweets."

"The last thing I want is unproductive food."

"Well, I can't help you, I'm afraid."

"Strictly speaking, you could."

"Yeah, so they can notice Chekhov's puncture wound? I won't do it." His arms crossed, and his back went rigid like a woman ill-propositioned in a seedy bar, so Dominia dropped the subject and folded her hands over her ribs.

"We'll have to think of a long-term solution," he admitted while staring off into space. "We still have to take the Light Rail from Kyoto to Shanghai and all the way into Afghanistan. And that's the easy part. When we're bumbling around Kabul trying to find this guy…"

"I thought your Hunters knew where he's preaching."

"Sure, but that doesn't mean he'll be easy to find, or working on a convenient schedule. You're going to need rations, and protection from the sun, if we're going to make concrete progress in a reasonable amount of time."

"You think this guy is real? Lazarus? They're not conflating old biblical stories about Lazarus and Jesus with facts about the Lamb? I always thought it sounded crazy." To say the least. What she had done to the Lazarenes during her two-hundred-year tenure as one of the top generals in the martyr military—and, during rare bouts of peacetime before her governance, head of secret police—was enough to gray the faces of even the most irreligious humans. But, as she told herself, she had done this with cause. Dangerous cults had to be broken up before they corrupted the masses.

"There's at least a guy calling himself 'Lazarus.' I think he named himself after the famous human. He can't be that biblical Lazarus; martyrs didn't exist until 2045 CE— at least, not officially. Cicero and His Ass-Holiness and your beloved Lamb had to be operating for at least a few decades prior to that, since they didn't come out with news about the protein until they made sure they had every big-name politician and tabloid beauty queen in their cannibalistic pockets. Imagine being alive back then! Weird to think about—but the point I'm trying to make is that, based on all the texts I've studied over the past few years, *this* Lazarus starts showing up around that time. As far as the static, historical record is concerned, I mean. The Lady's prophecies kept by the religious higher-ups of the Red Market have predicted his coming since before the Jews predicted a Messiah. Maybe they're one in the same."

Speaking of dangerous cults whose groups she'd many times interrupted over the course of her career. The Lady and the Red Market were a whole other can of Pagan worms; she didn't even want to get into it. "So we know there's a verifiable martyr masquerading as this guy. But why would the Hunters let him live? Abrahamians despise martyrs."

"He's an exception to the rule, because he's valuable to them."

"That immortalizing blood he has, right?" She laughed and rubbed her forehead while contemplating the notion. "The one that makes people live forever without martyring them, or damns them to hell, depending on who you ask."

"I don't think the Hunters are worried about your Father's hell."

"Then why aren't all Hunters immortal?"

"Same reason they're able to track his location but not get him. He won't let them. I've heard he's as fast as your Father, or faster, and disappears in the blink of an eye the same way." At her skeptical look, René lifted his eyebrows and added, "I've also heard that he doesn't partake of meat or blood."

"Then he looks and sounds like a stroke victim." A knock resounded at the door as she added, "If he's even real."

Tenchi's head appeared in the gap, ready with a smile for the dog, his cousin, and then, shyly, for Dominia. "Sorry again about earlier. Won't you join us for lunch? You didn't eat anything when you came aboard, you must be starving!"

"Let me think about it," she said, but to her irritation, René slapped the edge of the bunk.

"That sounds like a great idea. Maybe fresh air, after?"

"It's a bit cloudy," cautioned Tenchi. René, still smiling, nodded.

"All the better, cousin! A spritz of rain is good for the soul. Come along, Dominique." Hand on her elbow, René whisked her out past Tenchi, and the dog followed after, tail wagging with each step to indicate him as the most relaxed member of their group. Outside the cabin, the wet smell of metallic fish grew all the more pungent, and from the decks above and below resounded the shouts and grunts and thumps of men processing the catches to be frozen.

"How large is the crew?" she asked, and Tenchi answered, "Twenty-five, including the doctor and me. Would you believe this thing started life as a fishing trawler, then turned to a battleship? It's a trawler again, obviously, but to have survived that long! Amazing."

"That long?" Now it was René's turn to be skeptical. "You told me this thing was a trawler even before the year 2000! You can't tell me it's the same ship."

"It's been *repaired* through the years," protested Tenchi. "But it's still the same ship."

"Remind me to tell you sometime about the ship of Theseus."

"It's quite a vessel," said Dominia, too tired to suffer their bickering. As they emerged in the mess hall, the General shuffled through every corner of her mind in search of a memory: any sign of whether she had encountered this ship before, during her eastern campaign. She hadn't, she was sure, because most human ships she'd encountered now rested at the bottom of the ocean, although her service in the navy was neither as fulfilling nor as prolific as her time on land. Even so, one might never be too careful, and if she was keen on avoiding the crew before, now she couldn't afford anything more than a millisecond of eye contact and a polite nod of her head before they resumed their variety show. The program, which required live interaction from home audience members' digital devices, had the six crew members on break tapping their watches in hopes of helping their preferred contestant (or victim) reach the other side of a tightrope suspended above a pool of raspberry jelly. From what she discerned, every tap widened the tightrope of the chosen contestant, while diminishing the tightrope of their opponent; thus, it was in the contestants' best interests to appeal to audience members before setting out on their journey, to make themselves seem as personable and beloved as possible. With enough followers, a player won by default. This was one competition of a near-infinite number of them, officiated by a cute young woman, a stern-looking old man, and a well-trained Shiba Inu that sat in a chair with its paws upon the table: the most impassive and least-invested of any of them, yet, the obvious star. Basil gave a bark of excitement.

"He sees his friend." Tenchi placed pair of soup bowls before Dominia and René. "Eat up! You'll need your strength."

She would if she could, and she did sip enough to ease the snarling of her stomach, but in the end, it was a nasty trick to temporarily settle the martyr gut: energy spent on needless digestion would beget no new energy for her to use, so eating food without human components was a surefire way to cause malnutrition. It was the kind of illusory fullness experienced by humans so impoverished they were forced to eat dirt. Yes, her stomach was full. But she was still famished. She felt as she would have after experiencing a full day's sleep of bad dreams, plagued by that bone-deep ache of dread that pushed her nerves against the underside of her skin so that even the leather of her breeches and the fabric of her once-white shirt scratched her into discomfort. She wanted to tear them off, along with her skin, and scream; she remembered in sudden, sharp relief feeling this way when she was first martyred. She would sit at the table, distantly aware of the conversations of others while she, trembling, wanted to fling her plate and blink her life out in a painless instant. Of course, had she flung away a meal at her Father's table, the following instant would have been anything but painless; so, in childhood, she had learned to stay measured, contained, and observant. Those lessons served her long into adulthood, even when her teeth ached and her right eye (socket) itched with phantom pangs. She had learned to swallow her food, to think of it as medicine. To avoid thinking about it. A great many martyrs were selected because they took the same perverse joy in their diet as the Hierophant. Dominia was not one of them.

It still, over three hundred years later, came to her in flashes: rousing from bed at a noise downstairs and hearing, like the sounds of a tahgmahr, a distant voice. The Hierophant. What a different person she was at that time, even with a different name—Morgan—but, no matter how far she plunged into memory, history, and myth, her Father was always the same. That first night she met him, he wasn't her Father. He wasn't anything more than any other boogieman. On awakening, she'd thought her parents had the television up too loud, but soon recognized that, whatever the muffled contents of his speech, her parents responded to him. The cold fear of that instant would never—could never—leave her. She watched the news. She was young, but she was old enough to understand what happened when children woke up to a visit from the Hierophant, or any martyr. Worse than the Krampus.

Tiny heart pounding in her throat, Morgan had crept on bare feet into the bedroom of her parents, and found it empty. From their bath, she took her father's straight razor; then, with this dangerous object folded shut and held between her lips, she wiggled into the closet crawlspace which emerged in their attic. The room's real entrance was the kitchen, and many times she'd taken joy in hiding above the sounds of her mother's cooking, her parents' conversations. Now, her heart pounded. How would she open the trapdoor without being heard? She hadn't thought this far ahead. Or perhaps it was best to wait here, hidden, and hope that he would leave—

The trapdoor opened, and Morgan quite literally fell into the arms of the laughing Hierophant. While her mother cried out in dismay, and the girl, catlike, thrashed to free herself from his grasp, the tall, black-suited man adjusted his hold. "Hello, my doll— Here I thought a raccoon had gotten into your parents' roof. Now, what need has a girl your age of a thing like this?" He plucked the razor from her mouth and showed it to her parents, who hovered at the edge of the kitchen. "Never too young to start getting at that five-o'clock shadow, I suppose."

Then he'd put her down, and when she darted to her parents, he bent to ask questions that seemed strange non sequiturs. "Do you know much about taxes, dear? No? How interesting. Neither do your parents. I intended to make examples of them."

Intend*ed*?

"Now knowing that you're here, that changes things! They weren't reporting you on their census, or their taxes, or even their immigration paperwork. I wonder why?" In that terrifyingly bland way, he smiled up at them. "They are *very lucky* to have a daughter like you. A brave and clever girl— What is your name? 'Morgan.'" He repeated it on her speaking and stared into her face as if seeing through her skin, through her skull—into the substance of her thoughts. "Well, Morgan, I have a question for you: What do you think of me?"

"I think," said the eight-year-old, "that you're a real bastard."

While her parents gasped in stereo horror and scrambled to explain she hadn't meant it (and had never, ever heard anything like that from either one of her parents), the Hierophant burst into a spell of laughter so great it left him on the verge of tears. With a few claps of his hands, the Holy Father exclaimed, "How I love children! Not a churchgoing family, are we." At the reluctant admission of her parents, he said, "That is a pity. But I find myself interested in Morgan's religious education. Perhaps we might discuss it over hot chocolate? My cocoa is top-notch."

The illness came on her much slower than the so-called industry standard one-week-ill/one-week-dying formula that cured martyrs of all ailments in exchange for their humanity. In Morgan's unfortunate case, it wasn't until three weeks later she started shaking; four weeks later, she couldn't write, could barely speak, and her parents couldn't stop crying; five weeks in, and she was sleepless, day and night. No one explained what was wrong. It was the flu, her family repeated—the flu, and pneumonia. Then, one day, she fell asleep in bed, her crying mother holding her hand. She did not dream as one would expect from a fever so severe. Instead, it seemed to her as though she awoke the next instant in a bed four times as large, hidden away in a windowless room while the Hierophant read from some book. For the first time in weeks, she wasn't shaking, or sweating, or in terrible, clattering pain.

"You've come back to the world!" Smiling, he shut his book to take her hand. "My sweet girl. What a tiger you are to have so fought your virus! You will let nothing conquer you, my Dominia."

"Is it the soup?" asked Tenchi. Dominia lifted her hand to hide her tears as she laughed.

"No! It's great, thank you, Tenchi. My compliments to the chef." She lifted the bowl to prove she enjoyed it with a big gulp of the hot liquid. While her mouth and vision were obscured, one of the crew members made an annoyed request in Japanese; amid protestations, the channel was changed to Sun Empire News. This was fine for the first few seconds. The peppy Japanese rambling of the woman on the screen meant nothing to Dominia, and was much less grating than the sound effect–riddled chaos of the variety show. It was also less distracting, until, amid all the foreign words, she recognized her own name, pronounced as though it were a series of musical notes: "Doh-mi-ni-ah."

The trick was not moving too fast, she told herself as she stood. "I think I'm going to go take a nap," she said to Tenchi, trying to modulate her volume so as not to let her words attract attention by the universally suspicious susurrus of whispers. "I'm more exhausted than I am hungry."

"You're exhausted *because* you're hungry," chided the first mate, oblivious to the program that changed to live footage of an ostentatious cathedral in Elsinore. The Church of the Sacred Ram was stuffed with weeping mourners, Cicero already at the altar. Spitting image of the Hierophant, that man—so much so that it was easy to (sometimes) believe the story that the Holy Father was an alien who had, cell by cell, replicated the looks of the man to whom he first appeared with news of the protein. From black eyes to high cheekbones to towering frame, the most notable distinctions between the two, outside El Sacerdote's general preference of the cassock, was age. The Hierophant, clean-shaven, was a far older-looking man than devil-bearded

Cicero, and claimed it was because he had already been so long-lived on his own planet, Acetia.

What did the General believe? The simplest explanation: that they had been relations while human: father and son or brothers much older and younger. But this nonbelief was one of the reasons why she had been forced to flee from the Front, and why she was eager for a life outside her Father's influence. It was important she survive long enough to enjoy said life.

As Dominia lowered her bowl into the sink, she made good use of her roving consciousness by trying to detect what hymn Lavinia sang. In a dress that, to the General, was little more than a wild mess of jet gauze and lace, the girl made her way up the aisle toward the high priest. "Be Washed in Blood," she recognized as, ten feet from the door, three more fishermen bustled into the mess. From the sink, she grabbed a knife and hid it by her thigh. Well, if nothing else, that put nine—ten, including Tenchi—in the room with her. If his math was right, she'd have a mere fifteen more to go. The trick was keeping René alive, and sailing the ship, and all at once there was no time to think, for a great murmur arose among the men. She turned, hand on the door, escape almost good, to see the camera had panned across an array of memorial photographs. Foremost among them stood her and Cassandra's wedding painting, with the General's face, in full view, recognizable no matter the number of eyes.

The air was still on the screen and in the mess hall. As Lavinia stopped before the altar to kiss her brother's hand, then curtsy to the pews of mourners, the sailors vacated their seats. After jamming the nearest mop through the handles of the mess hall doors, Dominia turned in time to see René stuff Tenchi beneath the table. Sweet relief. She wouldn't have to kill him. With the brittle steak knife in her hand, the General faced one of the three late arrivals already arming themselves while repeating the various Japanese appellations for "demon."

The Disgraced Governess was not a monster. She was a ballerina of death, as the Hierophant had taught her to be. He never got her to believe in the Family, or the Faith, or the alleged Freedom in which martyrs told themselves they lived; but he did teach her to believe in herself. Thus, it was not a lack of confidence that made her regard this battle with unease; it was simply that such a battle was the least desirable outcome, and that disappointed her. But it wasn't as though they could talk about it. "*Konnichiwa, watashi wa* Dominia," was all the Japanese she remembered in the heat of that moment. The furthest thing from helpful. Even if she spoke a language they understood, they wouldn't listen.

As a country, the Empire of the Risen Sun had long since decided that beheading was the way to deal with martyrs. Interpreting with the help of

Tenchi and René was out of the question. Time slowed as her body took over for her mind, her motions tumbling with the grace of a river down its ageless path. One thousand battles she had fought, and the first man to charge her, a sink-wet boning knife clutched in his hand, caught the weight of each of those one thousand in the quick in and out of her knife into his lungs while her free hand bent him into the blow. As he cried, she tossed him aside and greeted the next with his comrade's knife: first to gut him like a fish, then to shove him so hard into the stove that the great pot of soup scalded his screaming face. A bare-fisted moron came after her before she descended into regret; from her right, three more rushed over. She was able, with a quick hand, to drop the solitary comer, and was left with only the group.

"Only." It didn't feel like "only" when one of them grabbed her by the hair to smash her face, hard, into the metal of the refrigerator door—the blind spot was already making itself known. Nor did it feel like "only" when she twisted around and got her hand up in time so, thanks to its tremors, it was "only" half impaled. Better than having her throat cut or, somehow, a vertebra severed, though the latter seemed unlikely, given the quality of the kitchen knives. On the rest of the ship, though, where fish were processed day and night, who knew? The men did, like the remaining three television watchers who had lingered behind during the start of the fight. Now, on seeing Dominia occupied, they took their chance to snap the useless broom and burst, screaming, through the mess hall doors. Teeth clenched, the General used her knee to wind one of the men, but thought herself mere seconds from losing her good eye as the most tenacious of the trio, still clutching that knife, pushed it farther through her hand, up toward her face. Martyrs were stronger than humans, but this one was nearly the exception when poised against her hunger-weakened body: this was a sailor carved by years of manual labor, baked hard by the eye of the sun. Knife fights, fistfights, gunfights. The man was ready for anything, except for a dog to run up and bite him on the ass, and, when he wheeled with a howl of pain, the groin.

"Where were you when your family was murdered?" she asked the dog before catching sight, with a snort, of René's shiny shoe as he disappeared through the door with wheezing Tenchi. After yanking the serrated blade from her hand, the Disgraced Governess crammed the tool into the smaller man's eye, impaled the heart of the weedy guy who'd been smart enough to let her go at Basil's approach, then focused on the unlucky muscle head who had thought the next minute would see him a hero instead of a corpse with a slit throat. After a second's consideration for her growling stomach, she grabbed the great man around the neck and hauled him to the half-emptied pot of soup; while he refilled it, gurgling like a caught fish, she attended to the death of the one-eyed man with an apology. Basil watched her drop the body with a wag of his tail and the happy eyes of a dog who knew himself to be a good boy.

"Do dogs like soup?" she asked. When, despite the light of understanding in its eyes, the dog tilted its head, she fetched a pair of fresh bowls, pushed aside the dead sailor, and filled them both with something more suitable to the needs of the quivering martyr. With Basil on the floor beside her, and chaos growing outside the mess hall, Dominia cured her weakness with a meal and watched her own funeral. There was no point in rewinding: she had heard bits and pieces of it, though was distracted by the fight. It hadn't been worth listening to, anyway. All conventional drivel about martyrs being already chosen and saved and having no need to fear death—and about the forgiveness of the Hierophant and the Lamb, the latter being depicted with great, upturned eyes and prayer-clasped hands in the stained-glass window towering behind Cicero. For his part, El Sacerdote watched as the parishioners rose from their kneeling stance for a prayer being spoken in the name of Dominia's soul, that it might find its way home to the bosom of God and not be lost in purgatory. The beard and mustache he wore in the fashion of the fictional devil who provided his name to Dominia's home country did not even wiggle with amusement. He stayed solemn, still. He took no joy in this at all, the goodly priest, but instead delivered up another soul to God. People stood and knelt and sat and he took no relish in it. All standard, until Lavinia rose again from her seat to the side of the altar, then joined Cicero at the pulpit.

"This being, under normal circumstances, the point at which I would refer to thoughts given us by the family of the deceased, I will unconventionally use this moment to give myself a few seconds of grief. She was, after all, my sister. And I—"

Cicero looked askance, his eyes flat with what was, to the General, a sorry attempt at emotion, then shook his head and crossed himself. "She will be missed."

As El Sacerdote claimed Lavinia's seat, she took his place at the pulpit. Dominia was forced to turn up the volume to combat the emergency alert that filled every room of the ship with panicked Japanese. In Elsinore, the youngest of the Hierophant's daughters looked over the crowd, her golden hair pinned in place with a brass tiara, her features warped in sorrow. The Duchess of Florence, Princess of Europa, and Merciful Miracle of the Holy Father lifted her gloved hand to wipe away the only tears Dominia trusted. She, like everyone else, loved Lavinia. In the Princess's case, the official word was that she had been martyred as an infant, most likely by tainted breast milk, and left to die; unlike all other martyrs, the infant did not rise but remained clinically dead, as was to be expected—an additional reason martyrdom was held off until prepubescence. The body seemed best equipped to adapt to the change then, but Dominia knew the primary reason the Hierophant martyred the young came down to psychological malleability. Martyred adults had too many emotions, were too often hampered by human taboos. Children could be more readily indoctrinated in the busy comings and goings of society. Simple as flipping a switch. Most basic preparation for human society was applicable to martyr society; it was a small matter of reorienting the moral and mental compass of the child so that, when they came out the other side, they saw themselves as a species distinct from humankind. Oh, he had tried the occasional experiment, slipping violent or depraved content into otherwise wholesome children's programs as a form of conditioning humans to accept the martyr way of life, for instance. But there was no replication for the change in a child when they were liberated from petty things like human morals. Nothing could prepare them for it.

Lavinia, however, had never had that problem. Lavinia was a miracle because her body grew while she was dead, her cells manipulated by the undead protein inside, each mimicking, say, the antibodies of a living martyr; no human cells muddied the waters. It was not so much that the Princess was being edited as were all the other martyrs. Rather, one could argue her body *was* the sacred protein.

Lavinia had never not been a martyr, because when she gained consciousness in 1930 Anno Lucis, it was the first time since infancy that she had been alive at all. Everyone had expected her to be dead, but the Hierophant had hidden her away to grow, and up she sprang one day, a beautiful golden flower: his Miracle. Proof of faith. Faith in him, faith in martyrdom, all represented by one sweet, innocent girl who now watched the people with sadness. Somehow, at sixty-six, she had lost none of her girlish charm, though she usually composed herself with the grace of her station.

"I intended to read today from the Gospel of Elijah, but I can't. Oh, I can't. I'm so sorry, I—" Her fingers fluttered across her lips, and Dominia fought not to internalize Lavinia's genuine pain at losing her sister. For those long seconds, she wished to send a message: "I'm here! I'm alive! Don't cry." Instead, she had to watch her sister collect herself as Cicero rushed to support her arm. When a look into his stoic face emboldened her, she returned to the microphone.

"This might be wrong of me, but I don't care what she did, or what she tried to do. Of all the people in the world, nobody treated me better than Dominia. I wasn't a curiosity to her, or strange, or even a miracle. I was her little sister. 'Was.'" Lavinia half laughed through her pain. "'Is.' Dead or no, she's still my sister. Please—please don't think of her as dead. She lives on with God, and with her wife. Oh, Dominia—I hope you're happy."

Squeezing shut her good eye, the General pounded back the contents of her bowl, then rose to turn the television off before Lavinia began her reading. There was no time to sit around listening to Bible verses.

"Stay," she told the dog as she rose. It wagged its tail to communicate that it had never possessed any intention of leaving this room for the foreseeable future.

Outside the mess, the ship was eerily quiet. Her focus narrowed for the lightest sound, she crept through the corridor and back to her room. Inside, Tenchi released a squeal of terror before René silenced him with a penknife poked near his face.

"What did I tell you!"

"Don't terrorize him." Dominia waved René away, then took his cousin's pudgy face in her hands. After brief scrutiny in which she found pinpoint pupils of terror and the moist scent of adrenaline but no sign of treachery, she asked, "Can you sail this ship?"

"What?"

"Can you sail this ship? Think hard, Tenchi, because your life depends on the answer, and so does mine, and so does your cousin's. If everyone else on this trawler ends up dead, can you sail the ship?"

"I—Yes. It would be hard with just one person but—maybe."

"'Maybe,' or 'yes'?"

"Yes," he decided, nodding his face out of her hands, then bowing. "Yes! I will sail, I'll do it, anything you ask. Just please, don't kill me. Don't eat me!"

"I don't think I'm at risk of running out of food anytime soon." She turned away and took a deep breath. "What was that announcement before? What's the plan in this scenario?"

"The men have gone below, to the processing areas. Where the fish are gutted and...prepared for freezing." He turned a queasy artichoke shade. "You're not going to— I mean—"

"It's not as if they'll be interested in talking."

Ah, the brief spark of hope in his eyes. "Maybe I could come with you? I could translate!"

René laughed at that, rather cruelly; Dominia pitied Tenchi while his cousin, in routine chastisement, said, "Yes—and slow her down, assuming you don't get killed by one of your own crew members."

"Just stay here, and be quiet." She tried to be gentle as she patted Tenchi's hand but nonetheless elicited a wince. "I'll be back soon; then we can get through the next five nights as painlessly as possible. All right?"

"All right." The first mate looked as reluctant as he surely felt.

As she began for the door, René asked, "Do you have a weapon?"

"It's the processing floor, isn't it?" Somehow, she restrained a spate of dark laughter. "I'm not sure I'll need one."

V

El Sacerdote

TERROR AT SEA!
Fishing ship* Jun'yō *docks with crew dead, security footage destroyed

KYOTO—Terror and tragedy struck more than twenty families Thursday when the fishing trawler Jun'yō *docked in the Port of Kyoto with its entire crew dead, save for its first mate and its doctor. First Mate Ichigawa Tenchi was uninjured aside from psychological damage, but was unable to explain what happened. Police have refused to share Dr. Miku's testimony and have no details to add, except to say that the original security footage seems to have been destroyed in the attack along with all its backups. The men appear to have been dead five days prior to docking. No further facts have been released to the media at this time. Those with information are encouraged to contact their local police.*

For such a horrible event, the article was a footnote in a neglected corner of the *Morning Sun*'s third page. More so the better: the less the people knew, the less the Pontifex knew.

"Soon"—finished reading the article to her, René slapped the paper upon the table of her Kyoto hospital bed—"you'll be able to read this yourself. Damn robot eyes keep us from having to challenge our brains. Why learn any languages when machines will translate our grunts and gestures?"

"Have to learn something to understand the machines, won't we? Anyway, however lazy it makes me: I'm lucky. Thank you, René."

"Don't thank me! Thank the hospital."

"But you called them. Set it up before we'd even left."

"I knew you'd need a checkup; I didn't know you'd need a new eye. As many refugees as they get, it's a miracle they'll be able to perform the operation so soon."

No kidding; but, then, cyborgans were as commonplace and easy to acquire as contact lenses. Easier, when the hospital in question was run by DIOX, the corporation responsible for most of the artificial components on the market. Sure, there was customization to be done—everything had to be built or printed for the individual when you talked body parts, especially for bigger items like hands or limbs—but that was easy as tolerating a couple of doctors who probed and measured and muttered in Japanese before flipping to English to ask what color she wanted. The same as her other eye?

In retrospect, the question had begun to disturb her. "The same, of course," had been her answer at the time. However, it now occurred to her that she could have picked any color. Indigo, chrome, rainbow, cat's. That was a weird fashion among humans: ocular replacements designed to mimic animal or cartoon eyes. The idea had bothered her when she'd read about it years ago in some magazine, but now, having decided "the same color as before," she was forced to live with the decision and ponder what that said about her. She had to talk about something else.

"Did you get our tickets for the Light Rail?"

"So anxious! Don't you trust me?"

"If I'm honest?"

"And after you just thanked me for this appointment! Dominia. You'd better get to the root of that problem. Trust is all we have, you and I. Without it, there's nothing to bind us together, alive, until we complete our task." After stretching to his feet, René moseyed to the window, which he cranked open with a glance for security cameras, holo or otherwise. For the sake of legal liability, the hospital, which primarily serviced refugees, shied away from them. The professor removed from his breast pocket a pack of cigarettes, illegal in Europa and the UF, and Dominia rolled her eye.

Through the cracked window and the inch to which he'd pushed aside the curtain yawned the international orange lightning bolt of Kyoto Tower, a structure built in honor of the Tokyo forebear ruined in a battle, which, centuries ago, had made Dominia's bloody name. Its peaked shape, like an alien mountain, recalled the Eiffel Tower, and how Cassandra couldn't stop eating croissants. How cute she'd looked with crumbs on her cheeks and her eyes brighter than all the lamps of those fair streets! Two weeks they'd been dating, and already, the General had whisked her off to Paris in a jet. A hopeless case from the start.

"This city is so beautiful," her lover had marveled. "Like nothing else."

"Most humans are very afraid to be here." They did get a strange look now and then, but Cassandra's new wardrobe, furnished by Dominia, helped her pass in the chic, shimmering dresses her lover keened to strip; and if that was not enough to shield the human from the occasional bit of unwelcome attention, the identity of Cassandra's companion most certainly did. If anything, since their arrival to Europa a week before, bubbling rumor transformed Cassandra into a whispered extension of the Bitch of Europa. That evening, when the odd daring passerby stopped to beg her (less-sought) Family blessing and she told them the usual "*pax vobiscum*," one in particular stood out. A little old woman, some mother martyred by a sentimental child when faced with their former parent's death by age. She had not wanted the blessing of the General, which was regarded in some circles as an ill omen to the self and, in others, a powerful curse upon one's enemies. Instead, this woman had studied Cassandra with difficulty, then, deciding she was a member of the Holy Family, took the human's hand and kissed its back thrice. The shriveled martyr held this soft hand to her forehead, and said in poor English, "This is how you will give blessings, when you are a Mother of the Church," in a way which made Dominia laugh but which touched (or in retrospect, rattled) gentle Cassandra, who smiled in awkward thanks.

Dominia, moved, said to Cassandra, "See? Everybody already likes you." As if the human had been one-quarter as concerned as Dominia. What a fool she was! She never should have doubted that he would let her have Cassandra, human or no. She never should have doubted that he would let her love, just so he'd have something with which to crush her down the line. Easy as plucking an eye from her socket—or putting one back in.

The primary reason for her hospital stay, the doctors had explained in crisply practiced English, was mental: to her refugee status, and her missing eye. Her refusal to open windows or go outside was seen as evidence of depression, not at all uncommon with her sort of trauma; as for food, René would sneak in packaged rations of human jerky made far too long ago, during the hottest years of the Pacific War. Where he got them, she didn't know, and didn't ask, but it kept her from going hungry. It didn't keep her active, and her lethargy was attributed to grief over her physical condition. Every time the cutest of the nurses came by, her round cheeks glowing with the light of compassion, she would pat the General's hand and say "*Ganbatte, ganbatte*," before helping clean her eye. Three days, this had gone on, and twice in René's presence; the nurse, taking him for Dominia's spouse, would nod and say in Japanese what a brave wife he had.

It wasn't so much that Dominia was brave. It was that she had long since realized she had no choice in where she found herself at any given moment. If she didn't like it, she had the options of waiting for it to change, or changing it herself; and if neither option were possible, there was no point in wasting emotional energy over it. Most patients in her situation were still absorbing the traumatic loss of their eye, but, numb even five months after Cassandra's death, the diamond of ashes cool against her breast, it seemed nothing.

But, ah, how deluded she sometimes felt. Would Dominia see her wife again? She had to believe, had to hang on to hope. After her wealth and station and Family had been taken from her—after she had chosen to take them from herself to better pursue an impossible dream—hope was all she had left. Hope, and a weasel who tossed his cigarette butt out the window while he asked, "Did they prep you on the procedure?"

From the eerie blind spot to her right bloomed occasional sheets of phantom color: blotches of phosphorescent viridian, or a trailing speck of light that quivered around as if consciousness sought for a pupil no longer there and thus perceived itself. Out of this hallucinatory cavern, Dominia's right hand produced a folder from her invisible bedside table, and René strode over to take it. Though it did contain paperwork, the most immediate feature on its opening was the hologram that it projected from its upper edge: upon the folder there stood a convincingly three-dimensional, turquoise-haired cartoon nurse who stood six inches high and spoke in over-enunciated robot English. Its accent was indistinguishable from a human's English, save for a tone best described as "dreamy." While René laughed, the petite hologram clapped, produced a party cracker, and pulled its string with a hop of delight for the excited bang.

"Congratulations, patient, on your ocular replacement surgery! We are so happy to have you with us, and to give you the opportunity to see anew. My name is Mimi Shin, and I am here to explain your procedure! Regardless of whether you will receive a full pair, we will install"—both snorted at the choice of verb—"one eye at a time: the process of receiving an ocular replacement can be traumatic for the body, and though our patented Install Tech is designed to intelligently combat rejection, studies have indicated that receiving two implants at once increases the odds of a problem."

From nowhere, Mimi produced a blackboard and telescoping pointer; she tapped the dark surface as it chalked itself with a drawing of an eye. "The precise nature of the procedure will depend on your condition. Your file tells me you have already experienced a surgical removal!" It was close enough to the truth, anyway; while René pulled paperwork out of the file to skim along, the artificial nurse adjusted her slipping cap in a programmed show of thoughtless habit designed to humanize her. Dominia found this effect alarming as the chalk eye was erased in its illustrative socket while Mimi continued, "This means the procedure will be shorter, and easier!

"Because of the discomfort experienced during the procedure, as well as the psychological trauma experienced by some patients, you will be lightly anesthetized. Just like being at the dentist's office! You will be put under by our caring team of experts, and while you are unconscious, the area around your eye socket will receive topical anesthetic, which helps the muscles to relax. Then"—Mimi stepped "out of camera," and the chalkboard blew to the size of the whole projection, then turned into a cartoony, three-dimensional rendering of a face and the muscles of an empty socket with lid held open—"our on-staff surgeon will place the implant so its connective nerve can find its new home."

Then came the horrible part, played out in holographic cartoons: gloved fingers dangled a vine of wire "nerves" and the realistic eye down into the empty socket. The skin of the face became translucent so viewers might observe that, as the surgeon pressed a tiny button inset in the side of the eye, the cyborgan came to life. First it quivered; then it stretched; then it jammed its tendrils into the brain of the cartoon patient. René grimaced at cheerful Mimi's disembodied voice explaining, "Our artificially intelligent body parts not only consciously soothe the tissues during the post-surgery adjustment phase, but, in most cases, install themselves! This is true of your ocular implant. The procedure is so simple, it could be outpatient! However, as explained, some patients find the process—and the recovery—challenging. For reasons of mental health and emotional adjustment, we at DIOX insist patients remain in the hospital for at least three days to learn all the exciting features of their new implant!"

Again, Mimi reappeared. "Some patients may experience physical discomfort while adapting to their new eye, which is normal. Prolonged swelling may be sign of an infection, in which case—"

"I can't take it." With a heavy sigh, René shut the folder and dissipated the peppy mirage. "She goes on and on."

"You have no idea. I watched the whole thing: it's at least two more minutes."

"Then why'd you let me open it!"

Dominia shrugged. "'Misery loves company,' I guess."

"Well, Misery's going to have to be disappointed"—he checked his watch—"because it's almost time for your procedure, and I have to go."

"You have to go? What do you have planned? We're incognito."

"Of course! I'm not going around waving a banner with a name tag stuck to my chest. 'My name is René Ichigawa, and I am on the run along with Dominia di Mephitoli. Please report me to the nearest Hunter and/or call the Hierophant to arrange my extradition...'"

"I'm not questioning your intelligence, René. I'm paranoid."

"Like I said, you've got to get to the root of that issue. I threw away my life for you, you know."

"You came to *me*, telling *me* stories about this guy."

"To do you a favor! To help you!"

"To help yourself, and your organization. Don't lay responsibility on me. If it weren't for you, I'd be—"

"Struggling to pretend you're still the person you were before Cassandra came into your life, instead of embracing who you've become since her death."The philosopher came out in him and shut her up. His urge for literal finger-wagging satisfied, René left it at, "I'll chalk your ingratitude up to stress."

"Thank you, René," she remembered to say, wondering if she had said it before.

"You're welcome."

The door slid shut behind him to leave Dominia in what resembled a prison. She reached into her dark right side and found the shape of a remote control, which manifested in her vision while she flipped through the stations of the hanging 3-D TV. Without her other eye, the effect was somewhat lost; the old-fashioned 2-D set on the ship had appeared a higher resolution than this one. She paused on the hospital's private channel, and a soft-spoken woman narrated something in placid Japanese that soothed beyond language. The camera panned across beautiful grounds blossoming full of cherry trees, and spent loving time on a knee-height hedge labyrinth for the pleasure of strolling patients. Agony clutched Dominia, not just at that most desirous image of the sun but at the beauty of the grounds. It had been by then at least a week since she had gone for a walk. If she had any idea how much she'd soon be walking, she might not have pined so much. Melancholy, she flipped away, right into the unpleasant smile of Theodore during a speech from her San Valentino office. He said something about how the people needed to "band together in a divisive time such as this, and reach across community boundaries between rich and poor, human and martyr. It is time for martyrs to take a more thorough, compassionate interest in their short-lived friends. I intend to use my new position to reduce within human populations the scourges of poverty and pestilence. Every human being in the United Front will be fed and housed. Every human being will be given work, and the medical support to maintain it. As martyrs, it is our duty to protect our human brethren. None shall be left behind."

Theodore del Medico was prone to bullshit, but this was laying it on thick, even for him. A speech written by the Hierophant? Probably. She'd be surprised if he let Theodore open his mouth in private without scripting it, stupid as her younger brother could be. Or, if not stupid, then so caught up in the euphoric whirlwind of his own ego that he couldn't stop saying stupid things. The problem was that he deluded himself into thinking the stupid things sounded intelligent. This carefully worded mission statement said nothing and everything, and left Dominia with a queasy concern for the humans in her former domain. Pieces of a boy's skull, scattering wetly across the floor. The first death of many during this sabbatical. There was little compassion in her Family for humans. Whenever they pretended they possessed some, it meant something was wrong.

"Dominique?" She hadn't heard the door slide open and jolted at the nurse's voice, to which she turned and nodded and laughed. The girl hurried over to take her blood pressure, then hear her racing heart. With a few short nods, she hit the buttons on Dominia's bedside, and the entire unit detached itself like an electric stretcher; the whole thing, magnetically suspended, she supposed, floated down the hall to the operating theater.

Like all operating theaters, this room resembled less a place in a hospital and more some strange spaceship control room. Try as she might, Dominia could not regard the masked staff members milling about as anything other than alien. Not the best thing for a mind about to undergo anesthesia. She tried to focus on Cassandra: lips, hair, eyelashes, the way she snored sometimes. Especially after drinking. Oh, how the General could have used a drink of her own!

The masked surgeon on the other side of the room inspected the silver tray of tools, particularly a thing that looked like a scoop or a shoehorn. The bed clicked into place upon a silver stand that allowed it to rise and fall at the behest of the surgical team, but he did not turn at the noise. While he picked up the black box containing her new eye, the cute nurse, with smiling eyes above her mask, strapped the martyr down. This bothered her; the nurse's smooth brow furrowed as she worked out Dominia's English concern, and then, with a nod, the girl tapped her own head and said, "In case—ah, seizure. Very rare!"

Oh, right. A mild concern. That was what cartoon Mimi had said, too, during her long spiel on side effects aborted by impatient René: seizure and, in some cases, complete blindness that was temporary and regarded as the psyche's adaptation to the product. It was one thing, after all, when one received a robotic limb. Still eerie, but somehow less confrontational than seeing through a new eye. A robotic eye. Dominia's stomach lurched. Sure, she'd had her teeth done. But this was a bigger deal. In some ways, a virgin territory about to lose its sheen; but, if the untouched state of her body was the qualifier of that, it had not been virgin territory since her proteins refolded, died, and then reanimated as a kind of horrific, cannibalistic parody of antibodies, collagen, keratin. The Hierophant and his servants preached that the proteins—hardly better than prions—were individually intelligent gifts from God, cells inhabited with choosy consciousness. Ironic, in light of the unconsciousness of many martyrs.

With careful hands, her head was lifted and the bandages unwrapped from her socket. The area was cleaned, and, with a syringe missing its needle, an ointment was applied around the surface. When the nurse nodded in satisfaction and said something in Japanese to the surgeon, another woman—the anesthesiologist—hurried over some great cart unseen in the right side of Dominia's world. As a plastic mask was fit over her face, the surgeon bent over her, black eyes a-twinkle so that even before he said in English, "Sister, dear, what are we to do with as wily a woman as you," a white chill of horror paralyzed her limbs with recognition. Cicero tugged down his surgical mask to reveal that immaculate facial hair and explained, "Tragic that no matter what we try to stop you, your rampage continues."

Before Dominia cried out—if she even could, for her tongue was already thick in her mouth and her lungs tasted cotton-tinny with the drug she was forced to inhale—her older brother drew her gun from beneath his scrubs and shot dead all four humans in the room. While she squeezed out a few silent tears and half a squeal, Cicero regarded the gun in his gloved hand, then allowed it to clatter onto the floor. "Fine way to repay your rescuers; but what can they expect? A farmer who rescues a snake had ought to have insurance."

She couldn't move, barely breathed as the mask was lifted away. "I took the liberty of replacing Tomoko-san's cocktail with one of my own, designed for a combination of lucidity and paralysis. Effective, no?"

With a doting hand, which reminded her too much of the Hierophant's, he swept a tear from beneath her eye, then turned back to the table of implements. "I thought it was important you be awake to see what you've done, that you may better grasp what is happening when you awaken—because I do not think you will prove capable of maintaining consciousness throughout the entire procedure. But we shall see! Not every computer program requires the machine to reboot prior to its use. Either way, when you're free, you'll want to take that gun. There aren't many between here and Kabul."

Panic: hot and cold, cold from the sweat and hot from the drug, or from the depth of his knowledge. Dominia tried to focus on her breathing while her brother returned with the miniature silver shoehorn poised between thumb and forefinger. The box rested in his other hand. "Father and I had a long conversation about whether to allow you to have this. We decided it would be unfair not to allow you what you'd spent a voyage anticipating. Not that being down an eye seems to have handicapped your prowess, much to the chagrin of the families of the *Jun'yō*. But it would seem most unsporting if you met your end because of a lost eye. That wouldn't be a victory for us at all!"

Cicero opened the lid of the box and removed the eye, which dangled from his fingers much as Dominia's original had dangled from those of the Hierophant. Though it was gory in naught but implication, missing as it was a coating of blood or tangled ropes of tissue, it was as vile—if not more so—to see a white orb on the end of black and silver wires. These swinging wires, he positioned over their new home.

"Inquisitive a mind as you have, you may wonder why I don't kill you. After all, you're more helpless now than you've ever been, or may ever be again. The answer is twofold. First"—he used the implement to lift the lid of her empty socket—"Father says there is more that you will do for us, whether you mean to, or not. And, second"—with the orb held between his fingers, he used the back of the implement to press the tiny button inset on the eye, which made a noise so subtle it seemed more an adjustment to the air—"well, it would be far less cruel to kill you *now*, wouldn't it?"

The eye was the least culpable of any party involved in this situation and yet, somehow, the one who seemed the most malicious. As the cyborgan booted up, the cords activated, wiggled, and began to burrow into her socket. Paralyzed though she was, her lips parted to allow an exhalation that longed to be a scream, that would have otherwise been a scream, as wires tunneled into tissue that had filled her socket in the absence of an eye. It dug into her brain and found the pathways once used by her optic nerve to reach her visual cortex; there, to her horror, it encountered a wormlike scrap of tissue leftover from the removal by the Hierophant. The DIOX-I reacted to this by using its wires to clutch the leftover nerve and yank it from its place in a way so horrible that, along with the skull-splitting agony, a collection of wavering colors and shapes and lights exploded in her right side. Somewhere above her, Cicero watched, saying, "Fascinating, beautiful," while the cords plunged back to work, sank into the tissue of her brain, and activated. As those hallucinatory blotches began to resolve into a new, crisper world, Dominia proved her brother right, and lost her grip on consciousness.

VI

Escape from Japan

Meadows. Lips. A long-running wave that peaked in a crash of consciousness-by-sound and Dominia running from hounds, the midnight velvet of the womb long gone but never really, the universe expanding out of it like a great balloon, a great breath taken in and let back out. A man who loved her like a daughter and whose face she couldn't see walked her out of paradise, told her something she forgot. Yet, she felt his sentiments in a profound way beyond the grasp of words, so when she awoke with the leather straps loosened around her wrists and a room full of dead bodies, she was somehow euphoric, left with great unconscious catharsis. That euphoria didn't fade as she saw the body of the cute nurse poised in a pool of blood beside Dominia's bed, though it did soften to sorrow, and blacken into the unnamed when the default settings of the new eye—about which she'd forgotten—recognized the object before it as a face, looked up that face's social media profile, and, with a helpful bubble, tagged the cute (now dead) nurse as one Sakaki Kurosawa.

Murph and Carol and Betty McLintock; Sakaki Kurosawa. Dominia didn't like getting to know all these names. When she learned a name, she had to remember it. She thought in shame of Sakaki and the life she might have led in the future; the eye interpreted this as a command to pull up the social media profile of the woman in question. The window filled the right half of Dominia's vision and made her blind with nausea as it flipped full tilt through an entire lifetime of photos, achievements, goals, sound bites, and even short videos. Her relationship status, her favorite foods, her—

Dominia hurried outside the theater to wash her face and clear her head, more rattled by the intangible ruminations of a digital conscience than by the bloody footprints she left behind. While she steadied herself with her grip on the sink, Dominia squinted through the window of the theater:

the eye zoomed in, darting hither and thither in her lack of focus. It raked across all the bodies—Tomoko Ito, Yoshimaru Suzuki, and Kyōka Watanabe. In quiet, postwar times, her preferred tradition was to memorize the names of those deceased by her hand. But now wasn't the time for such a thing, and at that observation, her eye prompted her with the question, "Shall I make a list?" Before she responded, it presented her with a notepad application, its beige window already arranged with the names in helpful bullet points. As she absorbed this, trying to still her mind to keep the eye from reacting in a manner so hypersensitive, another prompt appeared.

"To save this list, DIOX-I requires access to your Halcyon Network Account. Set up now? Y/N."

"Yes." She sighed, rubbed her aching forehead, and then, fighting through her brain fog, located the gun she'd left floating in Sakaki's blood. "Yes, go on."

She'd been given a dummy account to use for the trip, but the dummy account would only work with a device whose data entry was manual. Automatic, reality-augmenting cyborgans couldn't be stopped from information harvesting without practice, of which the General had none. What happened next happened in an invasive eye flash: When prompted, Dominia could not stop her brain from releasing the information in automation, used as it was to privacy in its own space. Username? "LADYDOMINIA_CONFIRMED." Password? "3119191144181." Would she like to receive notifications from— No, God no. She wished the thing had a tutorial.

"Would you like DIOX-I to run the customization wizard," it prompted while she used her hospital gown to towel off her gun. Blearily, she looked toward the clock, then realized there was now always a clock floating in the lower right-hand corner of her vision. Ten past ten. Her procedure had been scheduled for nine: by now, everyone in the hospital was dead, and half the population of Japan knew or was soon to know. This also meant the Special Assault Team was on its way. She would be lucky if she had the opportunity to dress to greet them, and it was hard to focus with her new eye flipping through prompts to her right.

First came the calibration, where the eye asked her to look at a few virtual targets that augmented the hallway before her. Then, it asked her to picture a few basic shapes and think a few basic words. By the time she was near her room, it was asking her whether she wanted it to function by eye blink or by mental commands, the latter being more sensitive and consequently more useful despite its invasion of privacy, decency, and mental health. To this, the General reluctantly consented, though she willed the device to dampen its sensitivity so that only focused, conscious commands would activate its more annoying features.

"Your DIOX-I comes equipped with a wide array of special modes, each calibrated to a specific situation." Outside, a few vans screeched to a halt along with at least one grinding "Tiger" T1-63 Reticulated Vehicle, which became known during the Reclamation as one of many *tanque* varieties—an old model, she suspected, claimed after the Pacific War or delivered as part of the Hierophant's reparations for the ruin of Tokyo. Dominia scrambled into her room and found her armor and clothing arranged upon her bed, the footlocker having been emptied by the same person who'd left a fresh box of bullets. There was even a shirt: crisp, white, and not yet bloodstained. Incredible, how it felt like a slap in the face. All the while, the stupid eye went on. "Your custom settings have been saved under PERSONAL MODE, but be sure to explore other preprogrammed modes as the situation requires."

Stripping away her bloodied hospital gown in favor of her clothes, Dominia asked aloud, "Do you have a battle mode?" and the eye responded with the prompt that, "As a pacifist corporation, DIOX abhors violence."

With another few seconds' consideration and the sound of doors being smashed open three floors below, Dominia yanked on her leather jacket, then loaded the .44 Magnum she thought she'd never see again. So familiar in her hand, that single artifact of normalcy's dead empire, she might have wept over it, had she the time. Instead, she held its cool metal upright against the dexterous side of her face, specifically the puffy temple of her forehead, which was, indeed, aggravated by the foreign eye that had burrowed like a parasite into her brain. "Do you have a hunting mode?" she asked, and the prompt changed faster than she could blink: "HUNTING MODE ACTIVATED."

She expected change in the world, but nothing altered. Not until, back in the hallway, a few bodies were circled and tagged with the word "NEUTRALIZED" in an imperious shade of red. As she marveled, the lights were cut by the team in the basement; the eye responded by adding a neon-green circle next to her clock to indicate it had flipped on its night vision. This effect of night vision in one eye and regular vision in the other was so disconcerting that Dominia, with a shake of her head for the irony, squeezed shut her left eye, her good eye, the eye leftover from the tatters of her humanity, and relied on the invader to do its work.

Many floors below, the team gained ground and confirmed the loss was total. That they thought Dominia was capable of such a thing proved her reputation had survived the march of time. Many, many generations of humans had been born and died since she had last been to Japan; but they never forgot what the Bitch of Europa—the Bitch of the Hierophant—had done to their ancestors, or country. Likewise, no matter how she tried to maintain a moral compass, no matter how she tried to advocate for the humans in the Front, she was forever the General whose bloody banner had portended the deaths of thousands at the heights of multiple wars. It was a banner she forever trailed, no matter how she tried to shake it off. But it was also a banner not without its uses as Dominia tipped carts, arranged tables, and scattered chairs, then picked the southeast corner to crouch in the dark and wait for the first unfortunate cop to pass her by.

The laser sights of guns flashing across the hall, the chartreuse beams of night-vision glasses marking positions: she would have had an easy time locating her quarry without electronic help. Still, the DIOX-I proved its utility—not with its night vision, but with its twelve targets, which encircled each man's head like ill-starred halos. A video game, she thought with rueful humor, rueful humor being the thing with which she maintained her cool as she pressed tighter against the wall. The men split their group in half to begin the sweep. Two slowed behind each party of fellows marching down the hall, and these began clearing rooms. She stilled her breath. Once she moved, her position would be given up, and she'd need to deal with the consequences. So would the men, who, in an attentive group of four, crept past an overturned table. The DIOX-I highlighted their weapons to reveal the positions of a few hidden knives, and she waited, waited, squeezed shut her eyes as an officer neared, sure to blow her cover. But he was not observant enough, and she was protected by the veil of impossibility and rumor, and when the man passed, she raised her gun and took one, two, three, four, five, six shots, and the four men dropped while she, in a movement too quick for a human to emulate, reloaded her revolver to greet the four others who emerged from the rooms, shouting, guns at the ready. These unfortunates died with their fingers on triggers which jerked as consciousness absented itself from four more brains.

Footfalls approached from the distance. Dominia tucked her gun back into its too-long empty holster and swept up the nearest assault rifle, then emitted a disgusted sigh: identity locked. The so-called security only succeeded in promoting tastelessness in battle, as when Dominia dropped to the floor beneath the body with her hand upon its gloved one. As soon as the other units appeared, she squeezed the dead man's finger. The rifle was a powerful one and, from the awkward angle, almost impossible to hold. It took too long for two of the four targets to fall, the other pair having been pelted haphazardly in armor and helmets rendered bullet resistant by an admixture of graphene that didn't seem like a bad idea at a moment like this. Meanwhile, more charged from the hospital's other wings, with other officers surging up floor after floor, or waiting outside with rifles. Then, of course, there was the sun. Glittering bright and hot.

She had to do something stupid.

The bullet-bloodied body draped in her arms until the gun clicked empty, Dominia darted into the nearest cleared room and barred shut the door with the life-support machine of a dead man killed by Cicero and whatever team he'd brought. But what Cicero often failed to take into consideration was that he was unmanageable, and, unlike the calm Hierophant, prone to unpredictable bouts of temper. This was never truer than when he was separated by business or ill fortune from the Lamb, who was more beloved by Cicero than even the populace. El Sacerdote had been in too good a mood to be there alone; surely, that bringer of miracles, that parent who loved her for who she was and not what she could do, was also there. That parent who, at times, looked into the future, and who had, at some point, no doubt foreseen the person Dominia would become. Knowing that, he stopped neither his lifelong partner, Cicero, nor his Holy Father, from bringing her into the Family. She could not understand it now. Dominia had never the faintest idea what a troublemaker she would become: not until Cassandra stood before her. After that, conflict with the Hierophant and the apple of his eye was inevitable. But her quarrel had never been with the Lamb. Never had he been anything to her but gentle and kind: no matter what the Church of the Hierophant had done to him, or forced him to do to others. It was the propensity of the Hierophant to render the Lamb complicit in his crimes, and this propensity was why praying to the Lamb, given her intent at that specific moment, seemed stupid. But there was a reason she had survived so many battles, beyond natural cunning.

As behind the locked door she fell to her knees to pray, Dominia stretched out the limbs of her mind and cried, "Help," as a child for her gentler father. That gentler father responded in immediate kind: the distant roars of men and the thuds of the door slowed, slowed, fell off, and Dominia was inside of herself. Inside and behind her body, a conscious spark: a mere rider of her form, as a body might ride a horse, camel, or elephant. His spirit entered her and she eased her troubled mind. She imagined she glimpsed him standing before her in some formless Void within her mind, the ram's horns around his head—installed to reduce and channel the directions whence he received otherwise-unmanageable psychic input—glowing the soft moonshine silver of stained glass.

"You still answered me. But I guess you don't have a choice. Oh, Rabbi"—the word meant "teacher," but to her it meant "Daddy" and it made her cry all the harder as he took her in his arms—"I think I'm afraid. Maybe it's because I'm so sad. But, please, I need your help."

"There will be consequences," he said. "Greater than those already faced."

"You let me live. You saw this path and let me live, knowing what I'd do. Would you let me come this far and allow me delivered into death's cold hands? Please." Outside the room, the team was close to bursting through the door. She felt numb as she begged, "This once on my journey. Please, lend me your grace. I'll take the consequences that must come, as long as you don't let me meet my end. Not now."

The silent Lamb regarded her face, then bent to kiss a tear from her cheek. It was as though she felt the coarseness of his beard. "My child," he said, and she was in fact a child, standing upon the big feet of her father back in that lost Mephitolian cottage. Outside of herself, Dominia rose on feet commanded by a spirit that was not hers, that was not bounded by time in the way of her own. Though she had but half sense of what happened, being as she was a child learning to dance upon her father's feet, she watched in awe as that good father made her throw open the door so a few unready squad members tumbled in. The trip left them disoriented enough for her to shoot them dead through the throats. She did not know where all the soldiers would be; yet, with the Lamb in her, somehow she did know, and moved all the faster, as if her muscles pounded at their maximum capacity even given a martyr's endurance. The Lamb, like some organic quantum computer ever-calculating at nontemporal rates the amplitudes of an infinity of possibilities, knew in a way beyond knowing the exact position, at every second, of every being on Earth, because he was within all beings, was all beings, as much as he was also himself. As much as he was a slave to the Hierophant. A slave who could only take what petty opportunities he could to rebel, such as this: this fleeting moment when Dominia, bouncing a grenade back to the senders, looked into the face of the Lamb and wondered, "Why are you helping me?"

"Because I believe in you."

"Believe I can do what?"

He didn't say. He just kept dancing, danced her right out into the hall so that she was faced with a pair of specialists holding vibroblades; swords whose high-vibrating frequencies made them as dangerous as they were useful. They required a great deal of experimental armor to operate, but the armor was only a delaying tactic to give the user a second or two in which to cut the blade's power and keep it from sawing through their own flesh. While bullets flew from a distant handful of cinnabar-outlined targets, Dominia focused on the blade wielders, dodged a swiping sword, and was moved by the Lamb to the left. Thus, she narrowly avoided a blade and caused a too-enthusiastic squad member to shoot one of the swordsmen between the eyes. Dominia caught up his sword before he was on the ground. The rest was quick, and clean: in through the gut of the other swordsman, back out, then off, her boots pounding a trail of blood down the hall as she dodged, through sheer providence, the hail of bullets whizzing every way. One snagged her coat as she dove down the stairs and pinned a hapless man to the ground like a butterfly to a display board. His partner's cry of fury was soon silenced by the last bullet in a gun she loaded yet again.

As she snatched up a no-longer-required helmet, it struck her as possible that the Hierophant was aware the Lamb helped her. Maybe even supported the idea. But it didn't matter, in the end, who helped her, or why; even if it was all a scheme to make her look worse than she already did (and it was, she felt in her heart). All that mattered was that she got out alive.

The first-floor lobby was a mess of people when she arrived, and a mess of bodies when she exited. At the Lamb's urging, she dug in her proverbial heels and ran into the sun with the sword still in her hands; sadly, the weapon was quick to slip away from her, as she had to leave it lodged in some poor fellow's chest to dodge roof-mounted snipers. Bullets rained across the pavement while militarized officers screamed orders in Japanese. It didn't matter what they said: the *tanque* was her goal, and no one poised near it was fast enough or stupid enough to stop her as she tore open its door, yanked the driver from his seat, and sent the passenger stumbling out with a gun in his face. She didn't worry about closing the doors before she took off, though she grimaced as the windshield shuddered with a few deflected bullets, then hissed as one lucky shot sliced the edge of her neck. The *tanque* snarled into the closed road and took out the roadblock like it was a wall of hay. At last, she was released into the freedom of a road where all drivers hastened to pull aside for her. "Thank you," she said to the Lamb, out loud, in her head, the white knuckles bared by her driving gloves already pinkened from those seconds under the sun, "thank you, thank you, oh, thank you."

"Please be careful," he said in her heart. "Please be safe. Please, don't pray to me again. Not for a while. I can't keep him from knowing forever."

"I know. I'm sorry I had to ask this of you."

"You don't ever need to apologize: not to me. Go in peace, my daughter."

"And you, Rabbi. Please, stay safe."

Then, her mind was still, and around her, rising traffic noises gripped her consciousness. She felt so alone she almost missed René. With some irritation for the circles that kept indicating pigeons and other potential hunting quarry, Dominia dismissed hunting mode for the "personal" set of features, then used her wristwatch to call Ichigawa.

"You and Basil need to be ready to leave." With a few mental pleas on her part, the DIOX-I pulled up the address of the hotel, which René had given her during his visits. As her new feature mapped it out in a translucent pane that floated in the lower right-hand corner of her vision, she told him, "I'm three minutes away."

"Huh? What's the matter? What have you done?"

"Turn on the news while you pack your bag. Just trust me when I say we needed to be at the LRS half an hour ago."

"*Yare, yare*... What kind of car are you driving?"

"You'll figure it out."

The radio station on which the *tanque* landed played classical music from before even the Hierophant's time, some ancient Japanese artist now dead for almost two thousand years. It struck her as better than the recent stuff, which was all heavy electronic and grinding metal that reminded her too much of the gunfire she'd just evaded. As she rounded the corner before the hotel, a police chopper—or news helicopter, she couldn't be sure—hovered above, but she was undaunted. Beneath the overhang of the hotel's entrance, Basil wagged his tail and barked a few times as he recognized the driver of the massive vehicle that bounced into the parking lot, honked its way past a few short-stopping autos, then screeched to a halt in front of a startled René.

"You weren't kidding about the car," he said, flinging open the door and hustling the dog into the back seat. "This is a European model! Nice, too. They didn't identity-lock it? Pft! The suckers." As he slammed the door shut and Dominia hit the electric, the wail of police sirens encroached on their position. "But how do you expect to make it onto the Light Rail now?"

She hadn't thought that far ahead, living as she was in a minute-to-minute frame of mind. Looking too far ahead would get her into trouble. Thinking too much about the precious gem around her neck, more precious than any diamond anywhere, in this or any world, more precious than the diamonds rained on Jupiter—that would get her into the most trouble of all, because she would think about how easily lost that diamond was, and how she needed to protect it. The more she thought about her duties and the consequences of not completing them while in the line of fire, the clumsier she became, like a person becoming aware of their tongue and no longer finding it suited to their mouth. She tried to focus her consciousness elsewhere, on something productive. She looked into the rearview to see the face of the dog, then asked René, "What's the deal with the tickets?"

"They're universal LR Tickets: good for any one-way ride."

"Under whose names?"

"Your fake one, Dominique LeBlanc. I don't need to hide if I'm not coming back." From his breast pocket, he presented a new watch, cheaper but newer than hers. It was preloaded with information belonging to Dominique LeBlanc, who might even have been a real person: Dominia, for her part, had acquired a few stolen identities for the odd espionage mission over the years, each used once and discarded for some purpose like a mask made of a human (or martyr) life. After programming the vehicle to take the shortest route to the Light Rail, she accepted the watch with skepticism.

"And there's no tracing the tickets back to us?"

"No, no. They're donated. Our organization has many wealthy donors who subsidize or fully fund the Light Rail tickets of refugees who will not be staying in Japan. Far faster and less risky crossing the sea by train than by ship. You're not the only person the Hierophant has gone to great lengths to reacquire."

"I'm not so sure it's an acquisition he's after."

"Then, what?"

"I don't know."

"Well what do you know? You're being tight-lipped about this Black Sun thing." While the dog whined, René slithered into the passenger's seat to admire the thick Kyoto traffic and the glowing skyscrapers enclosing it. Great billboards all around them showed advertisements, but Dominia found to her displeasure that her DIOX-I overlaid existing ads with new, targeted marketing. Normal commercials for toothpaste featuring smiling women through Dominia's left eye became, upon slipping into her right side as they rounded a corner, a Red Market advertisement, which disturbed Dominia because it implied the device had already divined she was a lesbian—perhaps through her Halcyon information, she consoled herself, and not through its access to her literal brain—for purposes of advertisement. It was also rather distasteful, seeing as she was married: but, then, she wasn't now, was she? The recognition came upon her once again with a sad twist while the lingerie model parted her lips and winked at Dominia as if her prerecorded body had been produced just for the former Governess.

"Earth to Dominia," snapped René, his irritation keeping her from projecting Cassandra all over the model. "Come in, come in, I'm talking to you, here."

"Sorry! It's this eye, it's really—" A champagne advertisement, golden fluid showering down, became a tumbling leadfall of bullets asking her to buy from a military surplus website. A blue jean advertisement transmogrified into one for graphene-based armor, which she'd just been admiring. (The one for Lavinia's livestreamed performance in *La Traviata*, however, stayed the same.) "Distracting, showing me all these ads."

"Then turn it off." He stroked his goatee with irritation as he fell against the window. "Didn't you ask the doctor how to use the damn thing before you shot him?"

"You can't think I did that! I tried to keep from discussing it with you until we were on the train— Cicero's in town."

"Cicero," repeated René, his eyebrows lifting high. "What could he want?"

"He was my surgeon"—the glittering gold of the distant rail, visible for a length before it eased down into the Earth, shimmered into sight while they crested the hill—"and he wanted me to know how easily he could have killed me."

"So why didn't he?"

In answer to René's question, advertising on all passing billboards was interrupted, and the radio flipped from music to an emergency news broadcast. While a frantic Japanese man spoke over the radio, a woman paled by urgency introduced on the billboards a clip Dominia struggled to ignore. Camera footage from the masks of the swordsman: her body, steered by the Lamb but herself all the same, slaughtering the unlucky men sent to kill her. Dead, all in a gambit by Cicero to leave her looking—well, like a terrorist, as she said before. One eye, two eyes. It didn't matter, and she grimaced to see her old two-eyed POW mugshot shown as René, sighing, shielded his eyes with his hand to the sound of some woman's scream. As though to add to the clamor, the footage switched to an aerial view of the T1-63 R thundering through hastily parting but still too-thick traffic. So it had been a news helicopter, then. That meant that it didn't have guns like the encroaching sirens, whose noises were now naked amid the news anchor spitting out rapid warnings to the denizens of whatever shopping district through which they plowed. Dozens of people began speeding and worsening the traffic in effort to flee the area, and dozens more, seeing how close they were to the General, opted to abandon their vehicles in the street and run screaming.

"How would you feel about leaving the dog behind?" asked Dominia, looking at Basil in the rearview. While his ears pinned in displeasure at undisguised comprehension of these words, René shrugged. "It was inevitable, right? That, or we would have to portion him between us when we started starving in the desert."

"Right. I'll ask how you plan to keep me alive through that when we get there."

"Yeah, and focus instead on how you're going to keep me alive right now." René lifted his head toward other *tanques*, which, under the control of their proper owners and equipped with gunners, fired down the street of the shopping district. The guns did more to tear up the pavement than penetrate the armor of a machine: most models of *tanques* were designed to survive this scenario under the reasoning that any misappropriated vehicles were better waylaid than destroyed. After all, drivers had to emerge at some point. So did passengers, which was a worrying detail when she considered René. Studying the chaos of the crowd nearby, and how racks of courtesy bicycles offered by the city were emptied in droves, the General careened in that direction. "Grab a bike and get lost in the crowd as fast as you can."

"Ride away," he cried, "with my bags? But we're not even to the station yet!"

"It's five blocks! You can get there from bike paths faster than I can from this mess of a street. Ride away like these people are doing, like you're terrified of me, and do whatever you have to do to get in on the tail of the passenger line."

"What if they're already closed?"

"It would be inhumane of them to turn passengers away from safety with someone like me on the loose. Tell them that."

"And then?"

"And then I'll drive into the station, as near to the train as possible."

"And what happens when I get hit with a bullet? Or when I'm seen and recognized?"

"Then you keep running, or I leave you behind and find Lazarus without you."

"You couldn't manage that on your own!"

"If my only option is to try, then that's what I'll do. I'll draw the gunfire away from you as much as I can, but ultimately"—she shifted the vehicle into its highest gear and allowed it to grind over the sea of vacated cars lining a street that had become decorated by faces pressed against every pane of glass in the flanking buildings—"it's up to you to keep yourself from getting killed."

Scoffing, René pulled his bag into the front seat and threw open his door as Dominia broke to a screeching halt before the packed crowd still fighting for bikes. "You don't have many friends, do you."

"I don't think I have even one," she admitted, but it was with none of the sorrow or pain that had come with the notion when first it arrived in her life. Ichigawa decided to feel that pain for her and shook his head while clambering out. Above the din, he shouted, "That's very sad! If you make it out of this and start treating me decently, I'll be your friend."

"I'll have to think about it."

The door slammed shut; he bolted into the crowd. Sure enough, one or two people winced out of his way for having noticed his association. This gave an advantage, and he was soon on a bike. Meanwhile, in the distant station, passengers crammed their way into the doors. According to history books, Kyoto's Light Rail had been a global wonder when it was opened in 1564. Martyrs across Europa requested special travel visas so they could risk their lives to experience a piece of technology the Hierophant had deemed "a vain and useless show of technical capabilities, though impressive," which was the most cumbersome way to pronounce, "those grapes are sour," Dominia had ever heard.

His sourness arose from the fact that the Light Rail was the finest work of technological art mankind had ever devised, and the world's greatest art collector could never add it to his many claimed museums. Linking Japan, China, India, and the Middle States, the Light Rail's establishment was a process that outlived its initial developers but which would have made them proud. Using the trails upon which far earlier humans had traded silk, tea, and philosophy, tireless engineers had made it possible to get from Kyoto to Istanbul in fourteen hours, with stops in between and quite a few subsidiary lines going far south as Cairo. Istanbul, being as it was one of the most contested cities in the globe and given to a heavy martyr presence, was not a popular destination despite being the end of the line for the primary Light Rail, nor was it Dominia's destination.

Today, they were headed to the center of the Middle States. In its heart awaited the primary cells of the cabal known as the Hunters: René and Tenchi's masters, and the organization behind not only the evacuation of refugees from the UF, but the funding and outfitting of human soldiers in South America, the Middle States, and South Africa. The Hunters had certain standards designed to prevent a martyr from reaching them, and they were not often willing to make exceptions, even for the price of information. Dominia would have no help without René. She had to gamble he'd get on that train.

Kyoto Station, the grandest of the stations and a neighborhood unto itself, was designed for ultra-wealthy humans to make a comfortable life among high-rise town houses. Said town houses were situated overtop a sprawling mall that opened, after many a brick road lain for its quaint European feel, to the station, proper. The Light Rail Station was always closed without a ticket, and in the event of an emergency like this, it was on lockdown. As she and Basil barreled around a corner where the city of technology ended in favor of the city of wealth, Dominia discovered a barred security gate had been pulled across the street to render the glittering wall impassible. Lucky for her, the T1-63 Reticulated was designed for just this situation.

While, elsewhere, René bullied his way onto the train, Dominia pounded the electric. The vehicle slammed into the gate in one, two, three, belligerent attempts to ram it down; after the great machine's onboard computer realized it wasn't going anywhere, it adjusted itself like an enraged predator fixing its posture to fight its way against, through, and over the fence that held it. The vehicle lifted itself from its wheels and, with audible metallic strain, jumped, its front tires used like limbs to drag its bulk over the fence in a series of sharp undulations. In the untrained, this provoked a nasty combo sea- and carsickness. Dominia had long since gotten used to the experience of being shaken around in a *tanque* and neither blinked nor winced as it landed within the station and resumed its forward motion, then brought itself back to speed to tear through the palatial ghost town. Its citizens had managed to move their expensive cars off the road and their expensive selves into their businesses, apartments, and train cars long before Dominia's arrival. This was good: this meant that it was mere seconds and a few blocks until she skidded to a halt before the ticket booth.

The other side of the actual station was, to Dominia's relief, sheer madness, the economy section of the train a lower priority and thus still being filled: here a mother with screaming children, there a few harried businessmen shouting and trying to squeeze on, here the peaked-cap conductors demanding order along with tickets. Their eyes fell on her vehicle, and the shouts began in earnest, all pretense of tickets-taking dropped. Dominia checked her gun, her bullets, then programmed the vehicle to auto-defend the area against assailants, which the other *tanques* had made of themselves in a constant hail of gunfire. Unsure if René had made it, Dominia hoped that he did, told the dog, "Sorry," and scrambled from the vehicle while it wheeled itself around to face its pursuers. A twinge of guilt crossed her mind as she watched it go, and yet—no dog sat in the window, now. Basil should have stood, paws against the glass, pathetic. Perhaps it was a mercy she could not see: she assumed the beast cowered beneath a seat in much the way the passengers, visible in the golden train's temporarily translucent windows, ducked their heads from Dominia's view. As she hopped a turnstile, the conductors cried in panic, and the one within shut the car before his comrades joined him. No doubt they were relieved when she passed them without a second glance, not stupid enough to force her way onto the train through a passenger car. Better to make for the back of the train, where passenger cars disappeared and were replaced with shipping cars. After all, along that ancient path, the Light Rail was as much a mode of commerce as of transportation.

Four, five, six, long cars down, with gunfire rattling behind her, the train began moving and was already entering the tunnel which would propel it faster. Gritting her teeth, the General allowed two cars to roll past before she came to one that, windowless, seemed good a choice as any—and with the massive train picking up speed, no wheels to hamper it and reduced air resistance thanks to its bullet design, the choice slipped further from her hands every nanosecond. Desperate to get out of the sun that burned her forehead, Dominia caught the handle of the great door along the side of a shipping car and forced herself to hang on. She had seconds until the train hit the tunnel: as ever, it was good she was not human, but better that, by some miracle, some oversight (or, she would wonder later, some conspiracy), that great door from which she flapped in the breeze was unlocked. Her foot, braced against the body of the car, pushed the massive thing open with a terrible grind. A second before the shipping cars were in the tunnel, she yanked her leg inside, down upon the floor with her, then forced the groaning door shut.

Miraculous. But she'd expected to be alone. A female porter, her hand upon the door that led to the enclosed gangway from the shipping to the passenger cars, emitted a cry of surprise. The General silenced it with a firm hand upon her mouth. With a warning look, she put away her gun. Then, it was a matter of trying to retrieve Japanese lessons from three hundred years ago.

"*Watashi wa* Dominia—uh, *watashi wa tom*—no, uh...*anata no tomodachi*. Okay? Uh... *Iie himei*, okay?"

The porter, having overcome her surprise, assessed Dominia through a tight pair of dark, cold eyes. The General had to wonder if either were a DIOX-I, now that she was equipped with one of her own. She took for granted the assumption that most people opted to keep their organic eyes. The daring and Internet addicted would immediately see the benefit of replacing their organic models with new ones. She'd begun to, herself. The DIOX-I explained that this girl's name was Romanized as "Miki Soto," which she repeated out loud.

"Yeah," said Miki, in a tone so flat that Dominia flushed, "that's me. What of it?"

"You could have told me you spoke English while I fumbled around."

"Well, I'm telling you now. And?"

"And—and I'm not going to hurt you."

"Congratulations."

The girl moved quick—not as quick as a martyr, but quick all the same, and Dominia reached for her gun until the second plump lips contacted hers. Having foregone any flirting since Cassandra, let alone a kiss, Dominia's brain flicked at rapid-fire pace through available options before accepting the touch, the breath, that soft, wet tongue. Sweet distraction! A kiss every bit as lewd as Cassandra's were sweet and chaste. She was so startled that she didn't feel the electrical baton poised against her ribs: not until the kiss ended and Miki giggled. "But I'm still going to hurt you."

How many times was Dominia going to lose consciousness on the way to Afghanistan? She'd have asked herself that if unconsciousness hadn't come over her like a pop in the back of her skull: a hiccup that left her, on awakening, without Cassandra's diamond.

VII

The Light Rail

Cassandra's absence was not her first discovery. That was her (officially) broken watch, whose blank face reflected her own bleary one. Then came the porter's uniform, folded beside her unconscious body with such tight creases it looked as if it had been ironed: it smelled like the lavender of the woman who had pinned her against the cool metal of the train car to multiply the current's kick. That, plus the ache in her stiff muscles, meant the woman was no hallucination. Dominia had escaped Japan, and now had a whole new level of problems. Who was she? Miki Soto. A card sat atop the uniform, its front embossed with a black-petaled, red-outlined lotus. Familiar symbol, but one she couldn't place in her post-electric haze. She sat up to rub her head and neck with a pained sigh that turned into suffocation as her hand found the necklace gone from her throat.

Her palms were wet with sweat beneath her gloves. She stripped them off to feel around on her chest, then cried out to confirm Cassandra gone. Up the General sprang, then back down on hands and knees in search of her beloved's remains. No trace.

Dominia knew where she was: with that same woman who had left the uniform. A disguise for the train, in exchange for her wife's body. Cassandra! Oh, poor Cassandra, forever dying in Dominia's mind, much as she forever stood in her flowing black dress, whose lace she smoothed while they waited outside the throne room of the Hierophant. Telling her, "You look beautiful, don't worry; you're so smart and funny, everyone will love you."

She had been emboldened by that, all the way into the absurdly long and courtier-filled throne room of Kronborg. The Hierophant, from his great gilded throne modeled after the seats of ancient, greedy Popes, sat forward. "So this is Cassandra!"

"Yes," Dominia had said, "this is Cassandra."

He descended the stairs two at a time to circle like a shark. Dominia, on edge, made panicked eye contact with the Lamb, who stood silent by the empty seat. In truth, she'd been every bit as frightened as she had urged Cassandra not to be.

"You do move fast," he said. Though Dominia had the urge to reply, the comment was for Cassandra, who blushed.

"Excuse me, sir?"

"'Sir.'" He chuckled warmly and shared a glance with the courtiers as for a precocious child. "Please, dear: 'Your Grace' will do." Before Cassandra became embarrassed, he carried on. "I mean to say that you, my girl, have courted our fair General for all of..." At his question, Dominia surrendered the (yes, humiliating) number, "Five weeks." This elicited a few tuts from the audience. The Hierophant made no comment; he lifted his eyebrows at Cassandra.

"A menstrual cycle's worth of romance—plus a few nights—and you would shed your human life to spend eternity with this woman? You know how many she has killed."

Embarrassed (or, in retrospect, threatened) to have it put that way, the human said with an evasive glance at Dominia's shoes, "I love her, Your Grace."

"Oh, and I am quite sure she loves you. Every now and then I find someone I love quite a lot, myself; however, do you see any of them with me now?"

Glancing around a room empty but for sycophants, Cassandra said, "You have the Lamb and Cicero, sir. Your Grace." Dominia sensed that slip was intentional, and strained her ribs trying not to smile. The Hierophant never bothered preventing his.

"Yes. Two thousand years. We are Family, that is why. Do you see these paintings, my dear? Here, here." After taking her arm with a look for Dominia's permission (or to gauge her reaction), the Holy Father guided Cassandra toward a crowd of martyrs who hustled out of the way in an awkward clamor of strange gauzy dresses and the plunging-neckline, techno-chic suits that would, to the General's relief, go out of fashion around the time Lavinia awoke. On their redistribution, they revealed a painting against the obscured wall: "The Martyring of Regulus," depicting the third-generation Family child in question, naked and screaming beside the red waistcoat and merry disposition of the fictional executioner about to toss him into the maw of a great, spiked centrifuge.

"If I wish to avoid tragedy, perhaps I should stop naming my children after tragic figures. But I suppose I cannot help that I see their substance when I martyr them; the Lamb's eternal eye always confirms it. Dear Regulus, he was not as noble a general as his namesake. Instead, he began to think himself a holy man. Of course, he was part of the Holy Family, responsible for blessings, and so forth, but he thought himself holy as me. Holy as the Lamb. And so, he needed putting down, and received a fate appropriate in light of his name. Of course"—he winked—"we did better than a barrel. Here's a fun fact for you: in reality, it was Cicero who did the tossing. The painting was commissioned many years after the event, when we acquired Kronborg in…oh, 1472, I recall…"

As he began to ramble about the castle's history for the forty thousandth time in Dominia's life, the General had relaxed. Hundreds of years and hundreds of girlfriends, short- and long-term, and she had never dared bring anybody home. She had never wanted his opinion about her love life; but for Cassandra, even had she been a martyr from the start, it seemed somehow important that the Holy Father agree Dominia's choice was splendid. This moment, therefore, broke over two hundred years of vague anxiety. He was almost like a real father giving approval to his daughter's girlfriend and taking her on a tour of the house. Oh, sure, there was always a degree of threat implicit in speaking with him. That was the way he was. He didn't do anything violent without telegraphing it in ways increasingly unsubtle until it was too late to turn back; the Regulus thing was boilerplate intimidation for anybody interested in becoming a martyr as an adult. Had his intention been refusal, Dominia would have sensed it right off. There would be one last, standard question, which came as he explained the fire in 416 BL, from which nothing but the chapel was saved. After lulling her into a state of intense boredom, he asked Cassandra, "Have you ever been a Lazarene, my girl?"

Cassandra, who had assessed the painting—which featured a crowd of figures and the Hierophant watching over the proceedings, with him in that silly golden miter he dusted off for holy nights and religious (never political) decrees—lifted her eyes and laughed in that harsh way that the General loved. "Hell no, I've never wanted part of that horseshit. Sir. Your Grace."

In a miraculous turn of events, this proved a rare moment when the courtiers had laughed before the Holy Father. While they tittered, he patted the girl's hand. "No wonder she loves our dear General—they have so much in common. Your friends," he pressed beneath the room's recovery. "Family members?"

"No," she said, firmly.

"Good. Because, when you are transformed, it will become apparent if you are a Lazarene."

"I'm not." Irritation brewed beneath her words. "What happens if a Lazarene is martyred?"

"They are damned to eternal hell and excommunicated from the Church.

It seems an odd problem to have, but there have been instances of martyred Lazarenes. These, I have snuffed myself. The blood of the heretic Lazarus is poison for the soul; depraved humans force it upon their infants, being of the opinion that death is better for them than eternal life. Horrific, the things people will do to their children in the misguided name of protecting them."

Cassandra did not speak, or move, or even blink. Neither did he, until he said, "This is one of the many reasons why it is not in my custom to allow the martyring of adults without special permission."

"That's why Dominia brought me, Your Grace."

"Because she understands there can be so great a many…complications. Psychologically and"—the Hierophant studied her up and down—"physically." He drew nearer, his massive frame shading the human from lights that glowed bright in the ceiling to emulate sunlight without its dangerous effects. When Cassandra's head lowered and a few honey curls fell out of place, he lifted an eerie finger to push them away. "I wonder if you understand those complications. The ramifications of this choice."

"I do."

"Is it immortality you want, Cassandra? Or do you seek this transformation from the purity of your love? What I ask is: Do you think this is a selfish choice, or a selfless one? Of the body, or the soul?"

"I feel…called to it, Father."

With a few seconds' consideration, he patted her cheek, and said to Dominia, "You may martyr her as pleases you, though perhaps sooner than later. Can't have her aging too much before her preservation. Not that she is very old—you cradle robber, you."

Sweet relief washed over Dominia, who exchanged a smile with Cassandra while her Father guided her new fiancée on to the next painting of a tour that wouldn't be finished for at least another hour. Sort of the trouble with his approval: once he decided he wasn't going to kill you, it meant he was going to talk to you. Forever. Luckily, Cassandra was engaging, herself.

"This guy was in the painting of Regulus." The prospect now observed (with admirably unflinching eye, for a human) a painting called "The Castration of Saint Julius." Indeed, the torturer in question was identical, his red waistcoat and gleeful expression a trope in martyr paintings stretching further back into history than was recorded.

"That's San Valentino," explained Dominia. "Saint Valentinian. The fictional saint."

Cassandra made a noise of interest. "I guess I never really thought about how the city got its name."

"Saint Valentinian is the patron saint of death in many of our stories," said the approving Hierophant. "Death, prisoners, slaves—and painters, because he is the only martyr without an historical basis. I liked him so much after his first appearance that I insisted the following painters slip him into official works whenever possible. He is in every painting in this castle, albeit often hidden. One must have one's amusements if one is to live two thousand years."

Laughing in her good-natured way, Cassandra said, "I suppose so. But why pick a fictional martyr to be the patron saint of death?"

"Because, my girl, every martyr has died, and every martyr is responsible for death: every martyr alive or dead has a claim on the patronage of Death. Were it not a fictional martyr responsible for such matters, well, such patronage would become my burden. I've enough responsibilities as it is, don't you think?" Playfully, he nudged her, and though Cassandra restrained her wince, Dominia had been delighted to see that level of familiarity.

Oh! The joy of that night. The joy of sweeping Cassandra up in her arms and feeling for the first time that it was allowed. Now, in the shipping car, amid industrial-size crates of soaps and tea, Dominia tried to hold herself together: tried not to ask herself again and again why he had allowed it. Why hadn't he stopped them?

Not that she didn't, deep down, know the answer, but the asking of the question was somehow a comfort. As if, in the asking and in the refusal to comprehend his motives, she was somehow superior. The feeling was similar to the one she had at the Lamb's failure to intervene in her tragedy. His understanding of probability would have revealed her destiny. Both the gentler Lamb and the not-so-good Father had foreseen all this, and hadn't warned Dominia of anything. Hadn't warned her that, in spite of all her success, her strength, her glory, she would someday be crippled enough by circumstance to weep over the loss of a necklace.

The trick was staying calm. She had made it this far and stayed calm. Would she fall to pieces over some glittering rock? Of course, it was more than that (poor Cassandra's beautiful body, rendered to ashes), but she had to tell herself (in the clutches of some uncaring stranger who thought it a base, mined diamond), for the sake of reason (instead of the General's one chance to see her wife again), that it wasn't. Otherwise, Reason would find itself too poisoned by Emotion to do its work—to raise Dominia to her feet and allow her to ponder, as she dressed, why the woman who knocked her out and stole her diamond would also be kind enough to leave her a disguise. The DIOX-I, at her behest, scrolled through its most recent profile, and Dominia repeated the name out loud as she tucked the bun of her hair beneath the porter cap: "Miki Soto."

Real name? Fake name? Not a porter, whoever she was. Her profile listed no occupation, and no age or relationship, either; but there were self-taken photographs enough to indicate to Dominia that the girl was not a complete construct. It looked like she had spent time all over the world. The human parts of it, anyway. Most of her status updates (the name given by digital social networks of the era to doomed-to-remain-unread blurbs about the user's life) had to do with what bubble tea restaurant she'd visited or where she'd eaten in Hokkaido, and most text posts were high on the ratio of emotive icons to actual words. Dominia's IQ dropped to see such statuses, so she blinked the image of the page away while she tossed away the remnants of her broken watch and examined the dummy. A newer, less-abused device, it had survived the electrocution and would at least serve enough to get "Dominique" into her suite.

Damn good thing. Whoever Miki Soto was or wasn't, she was still on the train. She could be found, and had to be found, before she absconded with the diamond. That meant the General would have to leave her room far more than she'd anticipated. But, of course, before she worried about leaving her room, she had to find it. That was a challenge all its own, and she checked her ticket several times before wrapping her equipment in a parcel made from the paper covering of a crate. Their room was in the Satin Car, with each car of the train named for a kind of fabric as a nod to the Silk Road it traveled. This storage car was not open to the public and, according to the map upon the wall, was positioned behind the kitchen and dining cars. These let out to the Observation Car (the Cotton Car), the Silk Car, and then the Satin Car, with many others to follow until, near the Luggage Car at the front and past Coach, the Burlap trio of ultra-economy cars rushed along, packed with budget travelers.

Though Dominia kept her head down as she navigated through the diners, it was impossible to avoid awe when a room of such elegant design fit in a train car. It seemed not just a restaurant but one modeled after the European aesthetic preferred by martyrs. A great crystal chandelier irregularly swayed from the ceiling, and the frescoed walls were decorated with frosted molding like a well-iced cake. And all the flowing wine! It provoked a twinge of desire. She was thrust back into the Hierophant's parties, right down to the haughty glance of some woman who might have been a courtier had she not been a human on the train. Amid all the luscious fur stoles and tuxedos, Dominia couldn't help but feel out of place; yet, for that reason, she was invisible, the parcel in her hands and the uniform around her better than any cloaking device. A porter she may well have seemed, but the delivery in her hands marked her as unavailable for use, so she was free to cross the scarlet carpet of the Dining Car and emerge on the other side with a soft breath as she made her way across the gangway connector wubbing with the eerie whip of the tunnel outside. The short, glass-enclosed passageway, empty of all other bodies, just her and the dark vacuum outside: she shuddered and moved on.

The Observation Car was a strange affair. With nothing but the tunnel walls to observe, the large glass windows now bore holographic simulations of the vibrant fish and strange, giant creatures beneath and beside which the mega-train rushed. She suspected a similar effect had been installed in the Burlaps, as she had seen so many face-filled windows.

In the next car, a multilevel masterpiece in similar style to the Dining Car, a Japanese conductor emerged from one of the Silk Car's compartments; she strove not to hasten her step. He nodded at her, then did a double take when he did not recognize her face, but she was already on her way out of the car and looked so busy that, surely, she was a person who did what she was supposed to be doing. Yes, she looked busy, was busy. So busy, and in such a hurry, that it took her until halfway across the gangplank to recognize what her sensitive nose had smelled as she'd passed that cracked door. Lavender.

The temptation to turn around was enormous, but porters had special pass cards that allowed them to enter any room. Dominia, not being a real porter, had no such pass card, and had to settle for swiping the digital ticket on the face of her dummy watch at the (difficult-to-find) second floor door of their suite. This same false watch dropped from her hand in surprise as the door slid open to the greetings, not just of René, but a dog.

"Basil!" While the great beast looked up at her, tail still wagging, eyes still bright, coat still black and white and alive, Dominia lowered to her knees and let her parcel of things lay where they'd fallen with the ticket. The door shut behind them while the border collie accepted her embrace with a wagging tail and kisses for her jaw. "Did you smuggle him out somehow? I don't understand. I thought you must have made it in right before the gate closed."

"I wondered the same thing." René muted the television and sat up from where he reclined in the lower bunk. "It was weird, like magic. As soon as you stopped, I got out of the car and biked like a Tour racer—made it without getting shot even carrying my bag, no thanks to you. I slipped in right before the station gate closed. Then, it's a few shoves before I'm on the train, economy boarding, since all the other Satin passengers have been aboard for hours. I go to the economy bathroom to clean up, all well and fine; then, I'm making my way to the room, and I'm alone in the hallway, but all of the sudden I get the feeling that I'm being followed. I look, and bam!" The professor waved a hand at the dog in her arms, who assessed René with much less unconditional affection than he seemed to have for Dominia. "There's Basil, creeping along like he's been there the whole time!"

"What's your deal?" she asked Basil, almost too happy to argue with a being who couldn't argue back—almost. "I don't understand. How did you get out? I left you. I saw—"

No, she didn't. She realized while looking into skeptical dog eyes that she hadn't verified he was still in the T1-63 before she left it. She hadn't been able to look at the animal, so she had spoken to it without looking back, and assumed it was there. Who was to say it had been? Logic, of course, but...her mouth opened and closed. She frowned, squished the dog's fuzzy cheeks, and frowned harder still.

"Border collies have always been my favorite breed of dog," she said. As Basil's tail wagged, René turned up the volume on the television. Her thoughts lost track as Theodore's whiny voice pierced her ears with the explanation that "the new Governor of the United Front will do everything in his power to protect the freedoms humanity enjoyed under Governess Dominia's rule."

"They're bringing back camps," translated Dominia, slipping her cap from her head. René scoffed.

"That could mean anything. Are they going to jump right to that?"

"Watch. First it's ghettos, then it's camps."

Theodore, who had continued droning under their voices, could be heard answering: "—best way to protect these most precious liberties is to band together in a group. Thus, we will be establishing new communities for the Abrahamian spiritualists, and for the descendants of the Risen Sun. It should be easy to migrate them, why, after all—San Valentino looks a bit like China, doesn't it."

His ignorant titter made Dominia say, "Oh, that idiot. Turn it off! I can't watch him anymore. I've had to deal with this simp for almost sixty-seven years. If Cassandra hadn't been enough to ruin my view of the Family, his existence might have done it by itself. Speaking of Cassandra"—she slipped out of the heels and cracked her toes with a sigh, then swept the lotus card from her bundle—"do you know about this?"

"Tsk! Naughty girl." After flipping the card all around, René laughed and stroked his goatee. "I suppose widowhood is lonely."

"What are you babbling about?"

"This is the Red Market! Their calling card." He gave it a waggle before reading its back. "'See you soon'? 'XO, XO'? What did you get up to while you were gone? No wonder it took you so long to show up."

She snatched the card from his hand. "How long have we been on the train?"

"Oh, two hours. Not too long. Lose track of time?"

"Lost track of consciousness." In brief, she told him what happened: the blur of gunfire, swinging her way onto the car before the train was sling-shot all the way into its tunnel, the foxy porter, her missing wife. "I think this Miki's in the Silk Car, but I can't get to her."

"She invited you, didn't she?"

"Don't be stupid. I'm surprised this place isn't on lockdown: I passed a conductor on my way over, and he looked tense. The more often I leave this car, the greater risk I run of bumping into a problem. Besides: I don't know what the hell I'm walking into."

"You'll have to get that diamond back somehow. You want me to go get her?"

"God no. You'll either never come back or repel Miki into keeping her."

While René tittered at her bad humor, Dominia swept up her real clothes. How they stank of sweat and dried blood! Her beloved leather jacket was as good as destroyed. Just as well; most humans along her journey would have been disgusted to realize they interacted with the General while she wore one of them. Examining René's new tie and white shirt, Dominia sucked the gap in her teeth she wished she'd had time to see replaced in Japan. "Did you happen to get me some fresh clothes while you shopped for yourself?"

"You know, I thought about it, but I didn't know your size. Those pants are leather, right? They wash."

With an annoyed look shared by Basil, Dominia strode to his bedside, pulled his bag from beneath his bunk, and, over his shouts of irritation, obtained a shirt and pair of slacks. "I'm taking a tie, too. It'll help me blend if I have to go out."

"Oh, these fussy rich people wouldn't know you from Eve. They don't pay any attention. You want to know why the staff hasn't put the train on lockdown and turned over every car?" René ground his fingers and thumb as if rubbing coins. "Have to keep the people who paid a fortune unaware of danger, lest they never drop the cash again."

As René again turned up the volume, Dominia grimaced to find he had changed to a station reporting the incident in Kyoto. Though the broadcast was Japanese, her DIOX-I transformed hiragana, katakana, and kanji characters into English words. This allowed her to read the scroll beneath the stern reporter. Officials still seemed to be piecing together what happened, but the Hierophant himself was expected to comment on the incident, which leant weight to the international rumor of ties between this incident and the allegedly dead Dominia di Mephitoli.

Dead. She wasn't dead, but seeing news of her death continued to bother her. The urge to right the wrong perception was strong, but that was what they wanted. They wanted her to claim responsibility for her so-called crimes. Jaw clenched, Dominia slipped into the bathroom and sank into the tub.

At some point, she would have to deal with the woman, but not now.

Theodore flitted up into her thoughts like a big-nosed moth bashing itself against a lightbulb. All those citizens of the Front were now in such peril that Dominia was sure her escape from the country would be but herald of others. The government would be prepared for it. It astonished her to see over her three hundred years of life how that vast country that she so loved seemed to dwell in a bizarre cycle of perpetual cognitive dissonance, alternately inviting and castigating (often downright imprisoning and killing) immigrants. The immigrants knew this, and yet they continued pouring in—why? Because of what the region had once been, she supposed, or because they had no choice. When, in one's home country, one was poor and famished, the Hierophant's lure—his universal basic income for the first five years of a human's legal citizenship, and his promises of land and dreams and futures—seemed of greater weight than his threat. This was nowhere truer than in the western UF, around that capital city of San Valentino.

The Western Front often felt its own country from the rest of the continent-spanning empire, and that was due in part to the large Asian population inhabiting the coast: their ancestors or lost relatives had come to the land many years before and joined a panoply of industries, and more immigrants continued enduring the risks with similar hopes of integration. Even though it had once been the cause of war and, ultimately, the ruin of Tokyo, the Empire of the Risen Sun remained protective of Western Front citizens. Martyr military intelligence stretching back to the late 1600s indicated Hunter cells based in Japan often infiltrated United Front lines. The Hierophant had never cared for that, and, after his many attempts to deport dissenters failed due to the wily nature of the human race, he'd turned to Dominia to keep both groups pacified. This had been her duty, lest they consume the Front, and the Empire of the Risen Sun come to believe they own the entire stretch of land, sea to shining sea: north to the Hierophant-controlled Canadian Winterlands, and south to the border of Latin America, filled with humans who sometimes got the idea to press north and contest his occupation of the Mexican Territory. In truth, since the United Front annexed Mexico around 1412 amid spurious mutters of "weapons of mass destruction" and "terrorist cells," it could be argued that the Front was never not at war. Hence its name. Mexico was, so far as the UF was concerned, its 64th Jurisdiction, after Puerto Rico, Washington D.C., the United Kingdom (a controversial single Jurisdiction), and those ten added in the Canadian Deal. Of course—try telling a Mexican that. The UF tried to tell all of them that for good around the turn of the century, and by 1906, it had culminated in the worst loss of the General's career.

Her promotion to Governess after the Reclamation of Mexico had paused a great deal of violence because, feared though the General was, she had also been known for her reasonability. Even before Cassandra's compassionate influence, Dominia had served the Hierophant as a leveling force, and was, one might argue, the most stable member of the Holy Family. Cicero was hungry to sweep up all humanity as though they were game pieces to be dumped in a box and taken out for his amusement. The Lamb was beaten down by years of his husband's abuse and a constant barrage of prayers. Theodore too often whined about his lack of opportunity, and the nebulous plans that he would never have the chance to see to fruition. And Lavinia wasn't even allowed to change her hair without their Father's permission, not after just shy of sixty-seven years of conscious life. Amid this ill assortment of dysfunction, Dominia the Governess had sat at the Hierophant's right hand whenever she slipped past Cicero, and advised Cassandra's routes of compassion: disguised as a General's practicality, of course. The Hierophant agreed to maintain his control of Mexico and descend no further into America once she pointed out how profoundly humans had damaged rain forests and sucked up natural resources before and during his rise to power, from 75 BL to 300 AL Since so many of their descendants worked to restore the environment, was it not sensible to wait, to let them do the fixing, and swoop in when Earth was healthy again?

Yes, that did make sense to him. He had agreed, no doubt knowing she delayed him to spare a few generations of human life. She nursed the hope that his desire to use America like a great, money-filled pitcher plant would depart him, as had many of his more bloodthirsty qualities. Funny though it was to say of the man who had torn out her eye, but the Hierophant had become gentler than he'd been when she was a girl. In those nights, he was more like Cicero, more desirous to claim everything the planet had to offer. That hunger had left him—or at least had relaxed in him—around the time Lavinia appeared.

Hard to explain, Lavinia. She was the Western world's idol, a pure and innocent dove cooped up in the castle for her own protection. Technically, she was the Duchess of Florence, and the owner of several palaces; but that was only as most rich human girls owned their own pony, kept in the stables of their father's summer house. The most troubling aspect of Lavinia's personality was that, in person, she was every bit as innocent and sheltered as that young, horse-loving inheritor—if a bit temperamental, as all spoiled children. She was a novelty in many ways, but the strange tale of her origin and that long coma made her a walking treasure: proof that the protein was a miraculous, life-giving gift from God. Not a burden from which too many martyrs someday sought or met some tragic escape, as had poor Cassandra. Dominia's hand landed upon her clavicle. That space where the diamond should have rested. Miki Soto.

Was it her real name? Probably not. The DIOX-I offered many details available about each translation, a list of virtual footnotes that unfurled when she concentrated on the dot at the corner of each translated phrase. Thus, it was that Dominia discovered the characters of the name "Miki" as it was written on the Halcyon account—美樹—meant "beautiful tree." "Soto" meant "outsider." This was fine, but raised doubt in Dominia's mind as to its veracity when she considered that "Soto"—in addition to being one letter off from "Sato," the "Smith" of Japanese surnames—meant "copse" (as in, "of trees") in Spanish. The eye was eager to give a lot of information about those two details; she could have fallen into a rabbit hole of speculation about more meanings, such as the complex cultural meaning of the word "soto," as she could have on a lazy Noctisatur while browsing her wristwatch. But the most interesting thing to Dominia about the DIOX-I was the accessibility of—well, everything in Japan, so far as the Internet was concerned. In Europa and the United Front, the situation was different. Internet access—to books, in particular—was gated through various insidious means the people had come to accept as normal.

The first barrier was economic. If an individual did not have money to pay fees for the device of their choice and its monthly maintenance, they could count on limited to no Internet access depending on the resources in their neighborhood. This meant they had no Halcyon, which, as the standard profile for every global citizen, martyr or human, was the central network by means of which one accessed all of one's personal accounts, such as banking and electronic mail. Such a "ghost citizen" had no way to find and apply for work, housing, or even, in a cruel twist of irony that Dominia had fought hard to fix, welfare and health care above and beyond the Universal Basic Income—which, in the case of souls so impoverished they had no bank account, was paid into the rent and (government-purchased) food bills of the account-less recipient. Universal Basic Income, therefore, was an illusion. The mere existence of the Halcyon banking and social system made United Front poverty a cyclical trap. A third of the human population was thus disqualified from access to the Internet and to any knowledge that might save them. The second third of potential learners was knocked out by the pay gates for the websites of their choice: most people opted to spend their hard-earned money and precious free time on pornography, movies of a less explicit nature, and video games, rather than the high annual subscription fee of La Biblioteca. And then there was La Biblioteca, itself.

Every book ever created existed within the digital halls of La Biblioteca, in original and translated variations. Organized centuries before her birth, the sum of human knowledge, glorious and shining and difficult to access. La Biblioteca was free to her, being the daughter of the Hierophant, but it was also censored of religious books, a fact about which she'd neither know nor care until centuries later, when she raised an army to turn back upon her Father. In those nights soon after coming to live with her new Family, she was given a tablet: a square of glass she'd heard discussed but never seen before that moment, which in her case accessed La Biblioteca and nothing else. She could read whatever she pleased, whenever she pleased, and so she did. Books became her most desperate means of escape from her strange new reality, that terrible upside-down way of living, which grew, in a sadly observable manner, more normal every day. Gradually, she stopped feeling bad as she thought about the humans who had died for her meals; it wasn't long before she saw one being killed without getting broken up about it, so long as she remembered to detach herself and keep busy, keep reading, when she was later at risk of being alone with her thoughts.

Sometimes she read passive-aggressively, hoping to provoke him, but he was unmovable. Once, at twelve, she lay under the moon in their gardens and consumed Aldous Huxley. She'd just finished Orwell's *1984*, and in Winston's tale found, in foreshadowing of the rebellious teen into which she'd sour, many obvious connections to her Father's regime. But the plight of Oceania only resembled in part the state of affairs experienced by her Father's humans (and, of course, martyrs). Indeed, when she moved to the logical follow-up, she found the truth closer to Huxley's dystopia—even if the saucy text was, to her young mind, quite embarrassing throughout. The more "adult" nature of the text that her Father had negligently allowed her to access was perhaps what inspired her to blurt as the Hierophant trimmed his roses, "I'm reading *Brave New World*."

"Are you?" Far from displeased, he offered a playful shake of his head. "Will you be inspired to whip our world into a frenzy, my little freethinker?"

"I don't understand why you were allowed to get so far when books like this exist."

This further delighted him. "That is the funny thing about such books, my dear. Tired people, as Huxley will tell you, don't want to think: and when they do want to think, they want to think of happy things. Not sad and dreadful things. They want their neighbors to do the thinking for them, and save them from what they must do themselves."

"But why don't you destroy all the books? Like in that Bradbury one."

"Oh, I love books! I would never, ever do that. I love books, and I love to see humans crave knowledge. Never would I deny anyone the right to learn. Instead, I have arranged the system so learning comes at cost; and so that only people of a certain age and a certain education and a certain situation even have the option of certain books. People are more understanding of being denied knowledge when they are told it is distributed based on income.

Even location is an acceptable barrier! Many a member of the Front curious about political texts has seen the disappointing disclaimer, "This Book Is Only Available in Europa." And why would most of them read a book when they've instant access to any movie, any game, any television show once their eight hours of work are done?"

As he resumed clipping his roses, she realized he was right, and returned to *Brave New World* less keen for his approval. Behind her, he said, "We must get you reading Shakespeare, my girl, if you like dear old Aldous."

VIII

Miki Soto

What couldn't a person access from the Japanese Internet? The question inspired Dominia to get out of the bathtub for another look at the card. There was no address, whether web or physical, as there hadn't been an address on the ad floating across that billboard; instead, when she studied the lotus embossed upon the card, the DIOX-I highlighted it as though it were a link. How fascinating, this augmented reality! After fixing the device's settings back to manual control, she "clicked" on the link with an unsteady wink, and her right field of vision was covered by the floating window of a browser. Had she cochlear implants, she would have heard some sort of music, or even a voice accompanying the woman's writhing in and out of the browser's dark: less a whole person, and more a disembodied assortment of lips, fingers, lower backs, and thighs. At last, the vision disappeared to present her with the crimson words, "WELCOME TO THE RED MARKET."

A button appeared: "Connect Your Halcyon for Age Verification." The idea of giving the women of the international and highly loathed illegal organization any information might have stopped her in a simpler time, as it surely stopped 70 percent of potential Red Market customers—the ones able to access the site, anyway, inaccessible from Europa and the Front through traditional routes. That had been all the Hierophant could do to combat in any meaningful way the world's oldest profession-cum-cult. Far trickier than hampering Internet access was controlling in-person transactions in gold or silver, or the off-brand cryptocurrency, Redcoin; and because there were almost no freelance prostitutes left in the world, catching a working girl was difficult.

The Red Market took great pains to train its women, all de facto priestesses, on avoiding martyrs and questionable humans. One of their preventative measures was the Halcyon background check. Though used by almost every human being on Earth who could afford to keep a device and maintain an account, the social network was, in truth, her Father's project, going way back before she was born. It ground his gears to know it was used by the Market, but those very data-securing technologies that allowed the rise of digital currencies also made other forms of data more secure, and easier to spoof. Once the spoofing was discovered, however, it was always too easy for security agents employed by the Holy Father to lock down offending accounts. This was particularly devastating to a citizen of Europa or the Front. In an instant, alleged criminals lost access to everything: not just bank accounts and photographs, but access to other websites, e-mails, bus passes.

All the more reason to use the profile of Dominique LeBlanc: but with the DIOX-I already logged into her previously frozen Halcyon, she was as stuck as she was surprised to see her finances once again liquid. The bank account page showed its seven-digit number in cheerful cerulean, and her stocks were once more available for manipulation. The Holy Father was tracking her transactions, of course—but the mood she was in, let him see his money pour into the coffers of prostitutes. She didn't care anymore.

Dominia gave the website her consent and was approved within five seconds. While she marveled at the ease of access, the DIOX-I opened a new page. This looked more like a fashion website than an application by means of which one ordered a prostitute. A banner featuring a well-off, smiling pair of women rolled across her view, then panned up to reveal their "mission statement," which involved, "Celebrating the sexual liberty of the body," and "Connecting to the core of femininity." What any of that meant to somebody interested in getting laid, Dominia had no idea; but she had the feeling she was on a version of the website meant to appeal to her demographic. In this case, lonely rich women more interested in sexual experimentation or temporary companionship than the quick and dirty lay desired by someone like, say, René.

After selecting "Our Girls" from the site's navigation menu, she was confronted by a page of a great many charming—and clothed—animated images: each girl posing, laughing, clapping like a fashion model before a white background. A few of them waved as though they saw Dominia scrolling past, recalling Mimi Shin and her slipping cap. Each moving image was embossed with a lotus watermark, the girl's name, and a flag demarking her region. There were forty girls on each page, and at least 124 pages that were accessible to her. Rather than shuffling through them one page at a time, she tried the search function and found, relieved, a "GIRLS NEAR ME" feature. Better than sorting them by location, race, and age, as though they were a bunch of jackets. She tried it and watched the lotus cursor load until she was brought to a map that zoomed in to reveal they already neared Beijing. Three dots traveled at her rapid pace, though two were grayed out, meaning the girls in question were either booked up or weren't working. The third dot, however, nearest to the navy dot marking her location, was active tangerine. It resulted in yet another window: a new image of a waving model whose name, "MIKI SOTO," scrolled beneath her feet while she blew Dominia a mocking kiss.

The profile was filled to the brim with statistics, even more than her Halcyon: height, weight, bust, waist, hips; eye and hair color; blood type and birthday horoscopes; education; favorite films; favorite foods; favorite kinks. At the bottom a status read, "Miki is: OCCUPIED" with a frowny face emotive icon, which meant she wasn't open for video chat. The "Book an Appointment" button, however, was promising and bright as candy. When she blinked past it, the appointment page opened with a same-day booking highlighted on its calendar. Even more promising. Though skeptical as to whether it was as easy as making an appointment, Dominia couldn't come up with a better plan. At least, not a more straightforward one. Since she wasn't willing to engage in an unnecessary conflict after suffering through so many already, this seemed the best choice. As her Father had taught her, the courteous path was the correct one. If information could be acquired without violence or tedious espionage, was that not the preferable path? She hoped as she booked the appointment that gentility was even an option, and that Miki was reasonable. When reason failed, violence was all that was left, and the General had wearied of that.

With the request for an appointment one hour out pending in the corner of her vision, Dominia dressed. Undershirt on, she was stopped short by her reflection, and the realization that she now saw herself for the first time since her procedure. Good as new, that eye, and yet it was somehow—wrong. Flatter, perhaps, in its coloring? Not quite the periwinkle of its predecessor and more a soft seawater aqua that depended on ambient lighting to give its colors life. How strange, like a new scar to which she needed adapt. The DIOX-I was already adapting to its new home (according to that peppy anime girl) and, within a few weeks, would be comfortable as if it had always been there. Reliable as her old organic model. Nothing to it, except for all those psychological ramifications.

The eye looked so different to her, was so much a symbol of irrevocable loss, that she could not imagine how, to the outside, it looked normal. To the outside, she looked herself. Dangerously herself. With a frown for the long hair to which she'd been attached all of her life, she shuffled through the drawers until a pair of scissors emerged. With these, she clipped away her still-damp locks. It was as though she heard the Hierophant—and Cicero, for that matter—tsking over her shoulder between every snip, insisting her new hair was, "Fine, if that was how she wanted to look."

"Androgynous stockbroker" was not the look she wanted on a regular basis, strictly speaking, but it was what she needed if she meant to meet a high-paying escort in the Dining Car. It was also going to be necessary at one point or another in the Middle States. Dressing as a man sent a simpler message to Abrahamians than being a strong woman. Of course, try being gay! Most of them understood better now, but there were a few pocket regions of extremists, like the Hunters, who eschewed all homosexual behavior and considered it a sign of degeneracy in human beings: unnatural activity made acceptable by the Hierophant because it was evil. However, as the Hierophant had explained to Dominia, he did not do things because they were evil. He did things because they were sensible. It got the rational people on his side when it seemed he did the opposite of what all history's other dictators had thought to do. So women in history were reviled at worst and, at best, subjugated by means of disenfranchisement or dress code? Good. When the Hierophant came, he loved them and they loved him in return. It was human women and sensitive California liberals who formed the early basis of his political power in the UF and the barren land once known as Russia, before he got the conservatives into his pockets. Abortions? Yes. Homosexuality? Yes. Female priests? Yes, yes, yes. But coveting thy neighbor's wife, or murder? Of course not. The Hierophant was a man of law and order: a higher order. The order of God that escaped the minds of primitives such as the Hunters, who had been relegated to the status of terrorist organization even within their home territories. She would have to deal with them, too, and soon. Dominia might have shattered a mirror for frustration were it not for René outside.

Of course, when she emerged, hacked hair pomaded down with gunk from René's toiletry bag, the professor was already off gambling. She sucked the gaps in her teeth while Basil, ears pinned, assessed her with displeasure. After standing up and sitting down in place a few times, the dog whined.

"You sure you're not mad at me?" She patted the border collie's head while it sighed. "You're a really great dog, you know. I just don't understand how you got out. The timing doesn't make sense. Even if the cops got the *tanque* open..."

Dominia frowned, rolling off into the fog of her thoughts. As the dog tilted its head, a small exclamation point leapt in the corner of her vision. She started as if having perceived a fly dart into her visual field before the notification resolved: the sort of thing she'd see on her watch, if more alarming. Her traumatized brain was ready to flood her body with adrenaline at a second's notice, so as she read a box that said, "Congratulations! Miki has confirmed your appointment," she had to steady her trembling hands by resting them upon the dog.

"It seems like every time I try to ask myself what's going on with you"—she laughed to the wag of his tail—"I get busy with something else. Try to behave, okay?" Then, already nearing that hour to which she'd set the appointment and wishing she'd set it out (as if it mattered, as if this were really an appointment, a "date"!), Dominia glanced into the bathroom, and back to Basil. "You seem like a smart dog. I assume you can figure out the toilet, right? Or something? Tell me?"

To her bizarre relief, the dog pranced into the bathroom. "So well trained," she marveled, trying to tell herself that was the explanation, because any other was too weird. Safe to leave the animal alone, Dominia gathered her wits, her gun, and her pounding pulse, then left the room behind.

The normally comforting revolver concealed in her slacks gave her an odd feeling as she walked down the gold-carpeted hallway of the Satin Car; Dominia smiled lips-closed to herself, rearranging the letters into the "Stain" Car, and, of course, the "Satan" Car. She had to keep herself amused. Had to keep a sense of humor. If she lost it now after all those harrowing and horrific years, well—that was a bad sign. Moreover, she had to look like she was having fun on a train that cost between three thousand and fifty thousand American dollars a ticket. Otherwise, she'd be liable to attract the attention of one of the many helpful conductors and porters nodding and bowing as she passed, eager to see her pleased because she resembled money.

She did have money, a small amount of gold cashed out for the trip and a large amount in her thawed Halcyon; but outside of spending the latter on Miki Soto to rub it in her Father's face, she daren't use a penny. It killed her that René was off spending his cash in the Dragon Car, which merited a non-fabric name because they wanted to draw attention to the casino. Not that Dominia could criticize the professor. She was about to spend a large portion of her finances on a prostitute, whether it was Dominique LeBlanc or Dominia di Mephitoli about to do the spending. The privacy damage would be somewhat mitigated by the purchase of Redcoins for the transaction (the Red Market's legal defense for their activities, since their clients were not paying for sex, but rather an unrecognized form of cryptocurrency not legally exchangeable for goods or services and therefore useless in reimbursing prostitutes). She had to hope René had taken the extra step of acquiring his own off-market cryptocurrency before they set out on their trip, especially if he used those electronic slot machines.

The soft piano and murmur of conversation that filled the Dining Car didn't so much as miss a beat as she entered, her appearance garnering no more than a few glances of acknowledgment. Thank the Lamb. The host, smiling with bright-white teeth and not saying anything at all lest he mis-presume his guest's native language, marked that she expected company and took her to a quiet corner of the gilded car. The man clearly had his job due to a sixth sense for what people needed; or maybe it was the shifty look in her eyes, the anxiety winding tight her jaw, that made him want to get her out of sight. Either way, she was glad to be alone in a quiet, civilized corner of existence with a bottle of wine that was soon to arrive and better, for some reason, than any she'd had in years. Its rich oak fragrance and stinging taste honed her senses to a dagger point so that, when the door opened and Miki stepped in, the General was ready to get some work done.

Much as had Dominia, Miki had made a stark transformation, though less long-term. The escort's dress was scarlet and silver, as fit for a red carpet as the makeup that transformed her shrewd face into that of a porcelain geisha; her lower lip curved like a rose petal and made Dominia remember its taste, made her anticipate the scent of lavender that rolled down to her table. The scent accompanied Miki along with, to Dominia's mild displeasure, a stranger. No doubt for Miki's protection: a body to throw in front of the martyr if things got ugly. Some meek, blushing businessman whose lowered eyes avoided all others in the car as Miki zeroed in on Dominia with complete disregard for the poor host who tried to seat her.

"I wasn't expecting you to bring company," said the General, who, for the benefit of the surrounding passengers, kissed Miki's hand before helping her into the booth. She regarded the businessman, who studied her in nervous return. "Who is this?"

"He's nothing, don't worry about it. Some stupid client. He can't even speak English. *Sōdeshou ka? Kisama wa baka desu.*" The man winced and then, in a way both apologetic and creepy, smiled.

"Does he have to be here?" asked Dominia. Miki laughed.

"No, but then, neither do I." The host arrived with two empty wineglasses; on his leaving, Miki removed a cigarette holder from her embroidered clutch. Now that she was still, it appeared the fabric bunched at her shoulder was the sole non-makeup decoration near the human's neck. No diamond.

"Where is she?"

"You're not in a position to be making demands, Mephitoli-sama." As Dominia tried to hiss her volume down, Miki giggled again, then stomped on the man's foot and snarled something in Japanese. He responded by filling her drink. "Annoying pricks like him like to get lazy, so they'll be punished for their laziness. I don't care for it. If they're going to pay me to dominate them, I'm going to be the one in charge of the whens and the wheres and the whats. Right? Anyway—don't worry so much! No one is listening to us. They're all too obsessed with themselves. I could climb under this table and go down on you"—the blanching martyr scrutinized the lovely fleur-de-lis wallpaper, gold and malachite—"without them noticing a thing."

"How about you return my wife and we'll call it good, before I make this ugly."

"If you want your wife back, you have to play along." Miki had gotten her cigarette lit—by the slave, probably, Dominia hadn't seen—and blew a smoke ring across the table. "Trust me. You'll thank me for all this later."

"Thank you for what? Stealing my wife? The small amount of brain damage I'm still healing from your stunt?"

"Saving you, of course. And your wife."

Somehow able to suppress the roll of her eyes, Dominia refilled her glass and hid her lips behind it. "I hope somebody's able to save you from me."

Giggling, Miki shook her head, and Dominia was amazed that none of the elaborately piled locks fell from the places where they'd been pinned with plum blossoms. "You're not a threat to me, Mephitoli-sama. If you kill me, you will never see your wife again: whether as a diamond, or in the flesh. And that's enough to take the wind right out of your sails, isn't it."

"Maybe you'll explain to me how you know all of this?"

"My boss briefed me on you. She said, 'You'll meet her in the shipping cars of the Light Rail before it embarks on its journey.' Of course, I gave up when it started moving—but wouldn't you know." Catlike, she smiled, and ashed her cigarette into the empty glass of the man. He regarded it with reluctance until she deigned to splash some wine overtop. As he drank it and Dominia tried not to be disgusted, Miki carried on. "I hooked up with idiot over here to get a free ticket and earn us cash for the trip."

"The trip."

"Uh-huh."

"What trip is this?"

"Our trip, of course."

"Of course," she repeated as Miki perched her chin upon the palm of her hand. This action did not smudge her meticulous white makeup, or the vermillion petal of her lip.

"Did you cut your hair since last I saw you? You have to let me fix it. Sort of cute." The laughing prostitute reached across the table and, amid the batting of Dominia's hand, tugged an embarrassing chunk from behind her ear. While the martyr smoothed it back, the human sipped her wine. "I liked your long hair better, though."

"Me, too, but it's conspicuous. I'm conspicuous. People will recognize me." She ran a hand over her forehead. "Stop getting me off the point, please. Everybody's doing that. I can barely think. I'm already on a trip, you may or may not know."

"Of course, but you'll need a companion on your journey. Someone to keep you safe while you sleep. What are they called? Renfields?"

Dominia snorted. "So pejorative. Wouldn't you rather call yourself a 'footman' or something? Anyway, I already have one."

"You want to keep around a weirdo like René Ichigawa? I saw that guy's file. I don't like him."

"Want to explain how your boss has so much information on who I'm with and what I'm doing?"

"And where you're going. I don't think even you know where you're going."

"To Kabul, in the Middle States."

"Yeah, and then? You're going to walk into the Hunters' lodge and say, 'Send me to Lazarus?'"

"That's more or less the plan."

Lifting her eyebrows in a patronizing way, the geisha demanded, "And what will happen when you get Lazarus? You think the Hunters are going to let you walk away with a man they've tried to acquire for the last two thousand years? With your wife? Hunters hate lesbians almost as much as they hate martyrs. They'll let you keep Lazarus busy while they sweep in to get their hands on his blood."

This notion had crossed her mind more than once in both the planning and escape stages of this mission, but she'd been in a one-thing-at-a-time frame of thought. Now here was someone as concerned about the issue as she, despite René's many protests that she need not worry. "How much more do you know?"

"I know more than you know. More than you're willing to admit, at any rate."

"And how does your boss know this?"

"My boss knows everything."

"Does your boss have a name?"

"The Lady's names are taboo to martyrs." Miki snuffed her cigarette with a smile that was sly, or smug—hard to tell with the makeup. "You should know that by now."

The General's eyebrows lifted. Oh, sure, she understood that the Lady was the legendary head of the Red Market; but, much as she once thought of Lazarus, she had always believed the woman a human myth. The stuff cults were made of, not anybody's direct supervisor. This was a notorious enemy of the Hierophant, with many names taboo to martyrs because the words themselves were believed to possess corrupting influence on the soul. This, of course, had bolstered young Dominia's research on this subject—a fruitless effort, since the Hierophant had wisely censored all those religious texts. When he had found out about it by reviewing her tablet's search history, snooping in his Family's private business being his number-one hobby, he had once more disappointed her with his calm desire to educate. He had even told her a particular name of the Lady that she had not found in her cursory research, explaining that it was not the Lady's real name, or even Her oldest one, but that it was still very old and one of her favorites. He loved to mock her pursuits of knowledge by flaunting the depths of his own. "The Lady is your boss," skeptical Dominia repeated to Miki. "I mean to say, your direct—manager?"

"Yeah, she is. She is now, at any rate, since my promotion! She called me to me and said, 'You will be the one to bring her to me. If you do this for me, I'll make you live forever.' The chance of a lifetime."

A likely story. "Because She's a martyr, I'm sure. To have lived since the dawn of time? I mean, She has to be."

This earned a scornful look from the glittering geisha, and while she snapped something in Japanese, the man hurried up to skitter away. Alone, Miki slid to Dominia's side of the table. She pressed the martyr into the corner of the booth where they were shielded by the high seats and the discretion-friendly drapes hung between each set of guests.

"The Lady is no martyr," murmured Miki, lips parted against Dominia's ear to release a voice light as a wisp of cotton. "She controls life and death; She is the seer who gazes into the mirror of the world."

"That sort of nonsense is why the Hierophant calls the Red Market a cult."

"The Lady is a religious leader, whether or not you men will accept it."

Laughing, Dominia began to say, "I'm not a—" but considered her tie—René's tie—with a frown.

"You've spent your whole life controlled by men: losing your eye to men, losing your wife to men, losing your hair"—she tickled long fingernails across the back of Dominia's scalp—"to men. And now you'll go to the Hunter's lodge and expect them to help you? Now you travel with René Ichigawa, and expect him to help you?"

"What do you know about René Ichigawa?"

"I know that someone like you should never trust someone who comes to you of their own volition."

"Didn't you?"

"Of course not. I came because I was told—and because you booked an appointment, remember?"

She supposed Miki was right. Nothing good came of trusting people who came to her. The Hierophant had come to her. So had Cassandra, and look how that had turned out. Now René had come to her, and she expected him to be different? What Miki suggested was not a new idea. This was why she had trust issues, why she'd never settled into her friendship with the professor.

It was all so convenient that he should come to her with this story of resurrection, no matter what rescue organizations with which he worked, or which groups had him in their pockets. Not that those groups didn't have good reason to seek her out in a time of need if they thought they might use her, but…

Was she being paranoid? Were these feelings of mistrust the result of being in a situation where, more than ever before in her unstable life, she was surrounded by strangers possessing their own malicious agendas? Were these feelings because she had lost the last good thing in her life and now floated around, clinging to absurd dreams and waiting to die?

As Dominia drifted into thought, Miki lowered her eyes. "I see you're a woman who needs more convincing than logical persuasion. Some evidence of treachery will be necessary before you see the truth, won't it? Well, don't worry: it won't take long, I'm sure."

From her clutch, she removed a business card that on one side featured an embossed lotus. Another link, Dominia observed, to Miki's profile. The prostitute's name and private number were printed on the reverse. "If you want to make another appointment," she said, a coy smile on her lips as she scribbled a four-number code with a pen from her purse, "or, if you just want to come by my suite, this is the guest pass code."

"You aren't afraid I'll break in and kill you in your sleep? We have at least ten more hours on this train. That's plenty of time for something to happen."

"Too messy, too much attention. Besides, you know I have my own friend with me: he might not be good for much, but he'll take bullets enough for me to run screaming down the hall."

Smirking, Dominia accepted the card and memorized its 7162 code. As she looked back up, Miki snapped shut her purse and slid out of the seat. "Think about my offer of friendship."

"You'll take me to Lazarus, will you?"

"We'll find him together, if you promise to come with me to see the Lady after."

"What does the Lady want with me?"

Sporting that sly expression, Miki bent and gave Dominia a glimpse into the plunging depths of her décolletage. "If you want to know that, I suppose you'll have to come to your senses about me."

Those lips pressed to hers once more, along with that insidious tongue. Dominia could not relax as last time but all the same accepted, her eyes falling closed to fool her brain into believing it was Cassandra on the other side of their shut lids. "Hail Amaterasu," crooned Miki, who pulled away to breathe the illegal word. "I'd have thought a martyr's lips to feel cold, like stone."

"I'd have thought your makeup to taste like paste, but I guess we're both wrong. Don't do that again."

With a laugh in her voice and a wiggle in her step, Miki left the Dining Car; Dominia, alone with her thoughts, finished her wine under a cloud of paranoia. Why did she need to believe in René? Dominia had no attachment to the man himself, but in what he represented. Miki put her finger on it with her troubling insight into Dominia's trust issues. The martyr wanted to prove to herself that not everyone who came to her did so with poisonous hearts. With a great wall of lies erected to mitigate the chance of true connection. The kind of wall Cassandra had erected in secret before they'd ever met.

That wasn't fair, of course. Or maybe it was—when their relationship was founded on false pretenses, how could Dominia but grapple with betrayal? Even close to a century after their meeting, it still stung. But there wasn't anything to be done. She hadn't been about to end their marriage—not once they'd eloped and Cassandra was martyred—and the illness had claimed her in three days, which came a mere eight weeks after their meeting. So stupid! But it had seemed more romantic than stupid at the time. The woman had thrown away her whole life for Dominia, to be with Dominia: or so Dominia had thought. Too soon, she learned she could never trust the motivations of others to be quite so pure as her own.

A few nights after being martyred, Cassandra started getting sick again. That wasn't right. Once a martyr's transformation was complete, they should have felt healthier than ever. Stronger, faster, smarter. Instead, on night three, Dominia awoke from their brief state of matrimonial bliss to fine their honeymoon aborted. Cassandra shivered in the bathroom, her body around the porcelain toilet like it was the first hour of the illness over again.

Dominia forever remembered that conversation in fragmented images: the cold tile floor; the strand of hair sticking to her wife's damp cheek; her own voice saying over and over, "Are you okay? Are you okay? Oh, Cassandra, oh, sweetheart, oh, honey, are you okay?"

Cassandra's terrible red vomit. The sticky sensation of her forehead and shoulders; the acid stench of the bathroom as the new martyr's quivering body recoiled against the sink. Her great doe eyes, lined with sleepless shadows, landing fearfully on Dominia's.

"I should have told you. Oh, I should have told you— I'm so sorry."

Her hand on her stomach. The pallid skin of her face. Cassandra lurched to vomit again, gasping for air between horrible wretches, while a million tiny things clicked into place for Dominia. The powder-soft fragrance of her bride's skin, the perfect glow of her face, the comforting pillow of her body. A perfect kind of softness found in the swells of maternal breasts and thighs thickened just so. The thunder of terrible understanding propelled Dominia from the room until she came to her senses at the door.

"You can't be pregnant. How can you be pregnant?" Dominia's brain tried to make sense of this and found perfect sense in their whirlwind romance that had felt so destined, so beautiful and pure and true. She knew the truth without having to be told as Cassandra lifted her gasping head and from behind shaking shoulders wept, "I'm sorry, I'm sorry: I was pregnant when I came to you. I wanted to save my baby. It was all I had left— He was shipped off to the war, Dominia—"

"You lied to me."

"I never lied to you! I just never knew how to tell you. I knew after I told you, nothing could be the same."

"Because you knew I never would have let this happen! I would have made you—wait, at least."

"That's why I couldn't tell you."

Dominia had ground the heels of her palms into her eyes as if she then wished to hasten her future blindness along. Oh, Lamb, the *pain*. To discover their love artificial! "No wonder we rushed. No wonder it was so serendipitous and urgent. That was how you wanted it."

"I'm sorry." Cassandra uttered a sob that was muted by the back of the hand she pressed to her mouth. "I'm so sorry. I'm so in love with you: I would never lie about that."

Like a broken automaton, the General paced the hall. "Why would you do this? Why would you do this to me? I thought you loved me."

"Please, I do love you. Dominia—" But more vomiting came, and with it, more weeping. Even in memory, Dominia's ribs ached to see Cassandra suffering so. In seconds, she was by her wife's side, hands on her shoulders as Cassandra righted herself. Carefully, the new martyr said, "I do love you. It's true that I came to you at first because of who and what you were. But I didn't expect—feeling the way I do. Loving you the way I do. I didn't want to tell you. I didn't want to hurt you. I wanted to hide it, to have the baby in secret, and then…I don't know. Find some place for it to go. I didn't realize it would be like this, that I would feel like this."

"Of course! Do you understand why? Do you understand what's happening? Your baby is eating you from the inside. Your body is feeding itself to your baby. You know why pregnant women aren't martyred? Because they *die*, Cassandra. The mothers and their babies, they both die." Dominia took a sharp breath and, fire in her watering eyes, gasped, "But I won't let you."

"Even though I hid this?"

"No. Because you've made this my baby, too. And I—I have to handle this."

The delirium of that moment. She had put Cassandra back to sleep and excused herself to get a bottle of wine; her wife still slept when she returned. Then, as now, her lips trembled to think that their happy synchronicity, that beautiful and romantic moment on the beach, was some lure to trap her forever: But what good had been her feelings when her wife suffered? At any rate, she believed Cassandra. When she said that she loved Dominia, it was true. The General felt it then, and felt it still almost a full century later as she let herself into the empty Satin Car room. She felt it, much as she felt the weight of her failed responsibility to keep her good wife, her kind wife, safe from the world's many harms. She was glad René hadn't returned, because only Basil saw her cry.

IX

The Dog and the Rat

René's extended absence would not be cause for Dominia's concern until almost too late. Without Basil, the professor might well have maintained his tenuous control of the situation. Frankly, without Basil, her journey would have been shorter and messier, but she wouldn't realize that for several nights; and it would take far longer before she came to understand why this was. For the moment, she was occupied with a storm of distressing problems, like the absence of Cassandra's diamond, and the thought of what happened in the United Front, which rose back every so often. All those suffering people. Or people who were, at any rate, about to suffer. She lay catatonic in the top bunk, Basil asleep on the floor and the television the solitary glow of a room, which, lacking open windows or active lights, recalled a mausoleum. The Light Rail raced the sun and always lost, but it made an impressive effort, and was a cause of major disorientation in most travelers. She would hurtle through about four time zones and emerge in Kabul before the city saw dawn. When that happened, in what condition would she be? How many eyes would she have? From minute to minute, her life was a tahgmahr such that she couldn't keep up. The distractions of media were, for her, no more distracting from her problems than newspapers for a schizophrenic: every headline, pregnant with a threat. This was a more objective situation, however, as she watched the Hierophant's statement on the events in Japan. The man on the old-fashioned two-dimensional set absolutely addressed her. He was thin with lack of food, had probably eschewed sleep to make himself look extra haggard. His hair looked whiter than usual, lacked sheen, and reminded her that Basil needed to eat something proper.

"My children," began the sorrowful Holy Father, "it has come to my attention that Kyoto has been the site of a tragic terrorist attack." While Dominia suppressed her annoyance, the Hierophant heaved a sigh. "An error was made in my most recent press conference: Dominia di Mephitoli, thought dead, is alive and well. I am sorry to say I have proof. If you have children, please remove them from the room."

There followed footage already overplayed by the Japanese news: Dominia cringed to see herself sweeping out of the fog of war. The guns, the blades, the blood, the horror. Her hand rested against her forehead as she endured the scene. Why did this feel so much worse than all those military nights? Not to say those nights didn't plague her—there was a reason she, with three-quarters of a bottle of wine in her system, already thought of ordering another while she still had the luxury. Those nights did plague her. Had plagued her. They had driven her out to the seaside to meet Cassandra that day.

It was her wife's softening influence that had made the vicious General into such a compassionate Governess. It wasn't hard to appear kinder than the previous governor, Dominia's late (very late) second cousin, Trimalchio of California, who was assassinated by a South American Hunter cell early in the twenty-year conflict. In this war's aftermath, her Father had placed her on the North American throne; the Family then began to prod her into reinstating Trimalchio's camp system, which had, in their estimate, streamlined both labor and food production processes.

Dominia disagreed. She saw the Front as a model for how martyrs and humans might live together. The notion inspired her all the more now, nursing as she did memories of that month in which she and Cassandra were happiest. Happiest as human and martyr, prey and predator. All the problems started when Cassandra became a martyr. Yet, being martyred never changed Dominia's wife: her heart was, in the end, the greatest burden the poor woman was forced to endure. Martyred as an adult, she had retained intact her conscience, morals, and ethics; she had struggled to eat; and she had begged Dominia, from the instant the General was appointed Governess, to rule kindly, if only to ease Cassandra's mind.

"Imagine all those humans are me," she would plead.

Impossible. No other human being could be such a unique combination of heart-wrenching and heartbreaking, of inflaming and infuriating. But all those pleas over time had worked, and Dominia had been able, with her wife's support, to stay strong on the issue of camps, of labor laws, of human health care and a real brand of universal income, which, in the General's experience, did an excellent job of attracting large swathes of free, mobile immigrants to allow a more sporting, hunt-based system of food acquisition. The game was fairer when humans knew they'd ought not to be out at night. They were defenseless without the government streamlining undesirables into grocery stores.

Of course, not all humans were defenseless. On the train, Dominia was drawn back to reality not by the words of her Father but by the whine of the dog. Basil sat by the door with his big eyes turned to Dominia, sometimes easing up on hindquarters as though reaching for the handle.

"I was just thinking about how hungry you must be."

As the Hierophant went on to say, "Even now, I am taking extreme measures to ensure the hasty capture and extradition of my daughter," she rifled through René's bag in pursuit of a necktie, the best option for a leash in a place that would never abide an unrestrained dog. All the while, Basil's whines grew more urgent, and rose to such a frequency that they almost drowned out her Father. "Though her whereabouts are yet uncertain, I have some intelligence regarding her destination, and her means of transportation. And my instincts inform me she watches this broadcast even now."

"I'm working on it, buddy, just a minute. I don't know how this is going to work out...that's a pretty nice Dining Car. Are you sure you want to— Hey!"

Incredibly, she'd caught him stretching on his hind legs, every ounce of his canine weight used to force the handle with both paws to trigger the door. The second it slid open, he was out. Teeth clenched, Dominia tossed the tie away and darted in pursuit rather than remaining to hear the words of her Father. She didn't have to: they followed her into the hall. "If you are indeed watching this, Dominia, I beg you: please, come home. No more killing. The time in which we live is already so fraught with misunderstanding between martyr and mankind. Add not to fear, but come back home. All will be forgiven."

The car outside was empty. Considering the hour, most people digested in the simulated beauty of the Observation Car. The rest whiled away their boredom in front of televisions, playing on phones, or gambling in the Dragon Car. Thank the Lamb for that—nobody to disturb. The dog was in a panic about something, barking as he pawed at the automatic door to the Silk Car. Though she almost caught him, he sprang like he knew where he was headed. Dominia suffered a twinge of maternal anxiety as the door slid open and they emerged upon the gangway with the transparent walls of the giant pneumatic tube all around them. Wouldn't most animals be terrified? But Basil seemed more competent than even her. Not scared at all. What a strange animal—and stranger still because he went not after the source of distant food smell but straight to Miki Soto's door. He gave one urgent, muted bark, then danced from leg to leg while hopping to indicate the keypad.

"Stuck in a well, is she? You're not even pretending anymore." With a shake of her head, the General tapped the code that allowed them into a foyer with a marble floor, a small chandelier, and an artificial ivory-lined telephone table. As if she had stepped into a scaled-down mansion. The dog, without Dominia's amazement, charged through, and she snapped from her momentary befuddlement to follow that which Basil pursued: sounds of violence.

Through the door to the left and past the tiny dining room, a miniature living area stood in terrible disarray. A coffee table covered in takeout had been upended, but it hardly obscured the dead businessman who'd just wanted to suffer at the hands of a beautiful woman. Poor guy. Who didn't? While Dominia tutted in sympathy, she turned her attention to the struggling humans and might have felt more like an adult breaking up a couple of children if she weren't so pissed at René, the apparent assailant, who was on top of—and throttling—Miki. For her part, the smaller human appeared as if her brain was about to go out of commission. While the dog barked in a panic, René looked up in time to see himself yanked off of Miki. He made another grab for her, but too late: blood flooded back into her brain as oxygen rushed back to her lungs, leaving the escort to gasp and cough back to consciousness while Dominia shook René by the collar.

"What the fuck is wrong with you? You lying bastard, what is this? Who sent you?"

"It's not what it looks like, Dominia," he said, but the prostitute spoke, or tried: wheezing words, over and over. They sounded like "hiss size" or "his sighs" until, with a great cough and a clearing breath that came as Dominia worked it out on her own, Miki bellowed, "His eyes!"

The martyr's mouth opened and shut in terrible comprehension. For the first time, she really looked into René's eyes: and, perhaps because Dominia knew what to look for after having seen her own (a porcelain, creamy flatness), she realized Miki was right. René's eyes, all this time, had been cyborgans made to upload video streams to the Hierophant.

The human in her grip winced when asked, "How could you?"

Whatever explanation he had drifted away. He tried being pathetic instead of making excuses. "You don't understand, Dominia. He came to me. He forced me."

"Of course he did. You would have to be stupid to go to him on your own. I'm not saying you aren't stupid, of course. But anybody with half a survival instinct is going to stay far, far away from the Hierophant—and from me."

"Not the Hierophant," breathed René. "Cicero. You think what your old man did to you was bad? My eyes were normal before I met him—before I was busted for involvement with the refugees and the Hunters. The Hierophant was apologetic. He promised me that he would see me taken care of if I did this favor, but I—I didn't want to do it, Dominia. You understand, don't you? Like you said, no person would choose to do this. I was a good man, once. I *ran* a rescue operation, risked myself in a double life funneling refugees out of the country. But he found me. He threatened my whole operation. Threatened me. Please, Dominia, please! You're a good woman. I hoped—I wanted to get you to Lazarus."

"That's what the Hierophant wants, too." Miki clambered to her feet and smoothed the silk of her disheveled gown. Her hair, beyond repair, fell in velvet curtains as she loosed pin on hidden pin. "The Hierophant, and the Hunters. Poor Dominia's not a tool to scoop up Mr. Popularity."

"But I wanted to help her from the goodness of my heart." The pleading man turned those recording eyes again upon the General "It's true. Once I met you and learned about you, I wanted to bring you to Lazarus. To find a way to..." His expression strained. "I am sorry about your wife. I think it's sad."

Barely breathing, Dominia stepped away from René and half tossed him toward the door. "Did you kill that man?" She jerked her head in the body's direction.

"It was self-defense."

"Because he broke in," Miki explained. "The Hierophant probably gave him access to your DIOX-I's stream; I'm sure he's had ready access to it the whole time that thing's been in your head. Both he and René must have watched us while we were in the Dining Car. At least, I'd bet that's how he got my pass code. Then, while I visited the Dragon Car, he killed my man and waited for me. If I weren't quick as I am, I wouldn't have escaped with my life."

"If I decide I need to kill you," Dominia told him while he backed to the door, "I know where to find you. And if I decide I need to kill everyone on this train—"

"I won't say a word to any of the staff, Dominia, believe me. I'm turning my eyes off right now, I promise!" The eerie phrase bothered her, but not as much as the notion that she had no way to verify he'd turned them off. "Oh, thank you, thank you for leaving me alive. I don't deserve it."

"You're a thousand times more repulsive than him," said Miki, nudging the corpse, then hurling a sharp-looking hair comb in René's direction. "Get out of here if she's not going to kill you."

Before Basil snapped his ankle, René tried saying, "I wouldn't have done anything to you if you hadn't—"

A yelp—and not by any means the dog's yelp—interrupted him, and the professor hurried out the door while Miki turned furious eyes to Dominia.

"Why are you letting him go? You really are stupid."

"He's harmless."

The human, much shorter without her heels, raised her chin to show the bruises. "You've got to be kidding. Talk about damaging the merchandise! This is why beautiful vases are put behind glass."

Dominia used an index finger to steer Miki's chin back and forth under the light. Yeah, it was bad, but she had seen plenty worse; and from the look of it, René hadn't known that the goal of strangulation was to cut off blood, rather than oxygen. Any progress was incidental. "You'll be fine."

"Easy for you to say, martyr. Get away from my neck." With a slap for Dominia's hand, Miki lowered her jaw, looked around in a huff, and began to straighten. "I don't mean to be rude, or prejudiced"—a certain pleased pup pranced back into the room and received a pat from Dominia—"but I'm on edge at the moment."

"I'm sure you are. Tell me again what happened?"

As the women slipped the body upon a tablecloth to be whisked into the suite bathroom, she did. After her appointment with Dominia, Miki had taken the Redcoins automatically deducted from the General's virtual wallet once the appointed time had been met and, after exchanging the fake currency for a standard one, laundered their finances in the casino by buying chips, gambling for a few minutes, then cashing out. "Gambling for a few minutes," however, apparently meant "spending an hour playing cards and another hour getting blitzed at the bar," the latter being evident in the flush across her cheeks and the brusque way she scoffed, "What's it to you if I did? Do you judge everyone you meet, Preachy?" in response to Dominia's innocent query about whether she had gambled away the money.

"I ask because, if you're going to travel with me, we might need it. They've thawed my account for the moment but might freeze it again anytime. That means René and the dummy account he gave me made up most of my wallet." Now that the professor was revealed as a servant of the Hierophant, though, didn't that make Dominique LeBlanc's account as suspect as her own? She frowned while Miki went on.

"Not anymore. As a matter of fact, I *made* money in the Dragon today. Ten thousand yen—that's almost a hundred bucks, UF—and furthermore, what are you? My husband?"

"You're a pretty mean drunk," observed Dominia, cheerful as she stood before the bathtub-cradled body with her hands on her hips. Despite the betrayal, she felt lighter. Perhaps on some level, she had known René was a traitor who needed to be expelled like an ingrown hair.

"You're in a pretty good mood," rebutted Miki, observing this lightness.

"Well, I'm sorry that this guy died, but— Hey"—she assessed the fellow's features again—"you know, the eye doesn't pick up on his face." Nor had it on René's.

"He must pay a privacy fee to Halcyon. Keeps you out of search engines and facial recognition databases." Not too bent out of shape over the corpse, herself, Miki turned away to wash her hands, then removed a bottle of golden oil from the drawer of the ivory-inlaid sink whose dead-eyed cherubs made Dominia a little homesick. While Miki wiped the makeup off her face and scrubbed it with some comically bubbling wash, Dominia watched her in the mirror.

"You mean to say that you, a prostitute, don't value privacy enough to pay the privacy subscription?"

"On the contrary, it's in my interest to maintain an accessible public profile. Especially—well, I haven't for some time, but I used to work in hostess clubs after I got out of being a geisha."

"You were a real geisha." Dominia laughed.

"Are you surprised? Please, nobody spends hours doing this makeup on a regular basis if they aren't trained to endure it. You need, like, therapy and shit."

"You seem more...crass than I would expect from a geisha, I guess. And I didn't think they existed much anymore."

"Well, we're rare. I was. I'm not one anymore. Anyway, the hostess clubs were less involved, but similar, in a way. Sort of like being a geisha, you know, where I would come to a table and be their hostess, get them to spend money on drinks and all. But there's no art to it. Mindless work, stupid and boring. So"—she turned her now-bare face and big, bright, organic eyes to Dominia—"I promoted myself."

"You mean, you became a prostitute."

"I don't feel there is much difference between promotion and prostitution. Not when you're a geisha. When I was young and stuffy, of course I did. I used to think that the pure and icy living dolls only bought in pressing circumstances by top-dollar lovers were the epitome of the divine feminine. Anyone easier was classless to me. But I sort of told you before. A woman came to me one day." Miki slipped past Dominia to right the upended table, then busied herself in the pouring of wine, an act that highlighted the delicate beauty of her hands. "A beautiful woman. She asked me to come with her, to serve Ishtar"—that most popular appellation of the Lady—"with her. And what woman wouldn't take an opportunity to meet the creator of the Red Market?"

"Quite a few. Most." Dominia lowered into the couch and Miki flopped beside her. "Most people don't want to meet the queen of prostitutes."

"She's not the queen of prostitutes!" Miki's tone was as sharp as her clout of Dominia's head. "She's the mother of the world. And that's capital: the Mother of the World. She's also the Queen of Springtime, of Youth and—cows. Bees." The already-drunk prostitute made herself drunker between objects, and the General wondered if that wasn't how she had gotten through most of her life. Not that Dominia couldn't relate. "Lots of other things, too, but it's pearls before swine, talking to you about it. Oh...pearls are sacred to her, too, I think."

"And swine?"

"No, that's your Father." Miki laughed at her own joke until she snorted, looking like a schoolgirl. Most humans looked somehow fresh, childlike to ancient martyr eyes (or, depressingly, eye). Even without the sacred protein, they modified themselves to hell, and experienced a pretty extended shelf life given money and diligence. Miki was probably in reality more of a late thirty-, early fortysomething, but Dominia looked at her and saw, at best, a twenty-year-old when she wasn't burdened by makeup. Her age became visible when her eyes narrowed and she got a stern, serious look. "Have you turned off that DIOX-I? Its recording capabilities, I mean. He's for sure watching us right now, you realize—you think it's just René's data he's got?"

"I hadn't had a chance to think about it until now. I've been trying not to."

With a curse, Miki threw back the contents of her glass, wiped her lips with the back of her hand, and leaned toward Dominia's right eye, her lips over-forming the words to allow easy lip-reading. "Then I'll take this opportunity to say, 'Fuck you, you snooping pieces of shit. And your rat, René.'"

"Which, for the record—"

"No more talking. First, go into your eye's settings and turn off its data transmission to all places—storage clouds, DIOX error teams, anything."

Dominia blinked. "What?"

"It's a front-line precaution at best, if you know what I mean. There's probably software still embedded in the eye that's inaccessible to the user: something that streams data to the Hierophant's offices no matter what we do, especially if the eye was originally leased to him. But we can keep DIOX from delivering it over the table. You don't know how to shut it off? Don't you care about computer security?"

Still startled by the woman's chiding, Dominia tried to find some excuse, but was forced to admit, "Computers and—anything more than a cell isn't popular with my people. Even fancy phones and watches aren't popular. They're frowned upon. E-readers are about as high-tech as we get."

"What? Why the hell are you guys such Luddites?"

"It's the blue light. The blue light of the sun is what causes our reaction to it; the blue light of electronics isn't as bad, but studies have indicated it impacts a martyr's motivation and, in some cases, digestion." Never mind that she and Cassandra had once made frequent fun of goofy martyr housewives who claimed to have any number of nebulous issues thanks to the glow of their neighbor's holo-corner as seen through a curtained window. Miki, as though sensing this, snorted, and forced Dominia to struggle on. "I think my Father has a point when he says that people don't learn anything when they rely on computers." That justification seemed ironclad to the General, as it was one of the few "common sense" beliefs she had always thought exceptions to the rule of her Family's backward evil. Nevertheless, Miki laughed.

"How do you have room to create anything when you're wasting your mental space remembering junk you could store on a computer? Doesn't a computer run faster when it isn't bogged down by nonsense? Of course it's important to learn, but it's more important to discern."

"Was that a poster on the wall of some depressing school of yours? No wonder you humans are in the shape you are."

"Sassy. But I mean what I said. And for the record"—Miki's eyes blazed bright—"humans will always come out on top. That's *because* we're willing to rely on tools outside ourselves. You can tell an animal over a human because the animal has too much pride in its physical traits to condescend to the use of a tool."

Dominia blustered without meaning before stringing together a wounded conclusion of their debate. "You're a fine one to speak of condescension. Just help me with this stupid eye, okay?"

Rather than taking offense, Miki laughed, and proceeded to walk her through the process of turning off things like forced software updates and data backups from her eye to the cloud. "The cloud" was a term for data virtually stored in (often insecure) servers, rather than more controllable personal hardware. Somewhere along the line, her Father had helped convince everybody this was a good idea, like Halcyon; it might have continued to seem like a good idea until martyrs showed up, and even for a while after, when people still believed there was no way he could access their private information. But, long before Dominia's birth, the digital line between "personal" data and "government" data became blurry. Privacy meant keeping one's data in one's personal possession, which meant scouring a new device for any sign of uploading software, malicious or otherwise. Basil, bored, wandered off, and Dominia admitted during their work, "I suppose it is pretty stupid to refuse to use something out of pride. That's probably why I got stuck with this eye now. Karma, right?"

"That's almost how karma works," agreed Miki, impressed. "Is it off?"

"All off, I think."

"Good. You should still be able to use the Internet, but—hasn't he frozen your Halcyon account, yet?"

"Well—no. The eye nabbed my real information from my brain before I could stop it, and everything was frozen at first, but by the time I was on the train, it seemed to have been released again. I'm going to toss the dummy watch René gave me—not like I need the ticket anymore." Despite this sensibility, annoyance tensed the human's face.

"You need to delete your should-be-frozen account, if you still can. He's for sure using that to track you, too. Accessing your brain— Ugh! Stuff is evil these days. All these details!" The prostitute raised her hands from where they'd rested on her hips. "You have to take care of them."

"I will. But, as far as details are concerned, there's one I'm worried a... bout." Dominia's thoughts trailed off as she became aware of the horrific, wet sounds of a dog eating. The women shared a sidelong look of disgust before they peeked into the cramped bathroom with its undefended corpse. Basil, tail wagging, lifted his head to smile with a gory muzzle, eyes brighter and coat shinier by the minute.

Eating him had crossed her mind, but it was hard to prepare such a large body in such a small space. She had to admit she was a little jealous. Dominia's mouth opened and shut in silence before she found her question, at which Miki scoffed. "Is this dog a martyr?"

"What? No, stupid, of course not. Dogs eat flesh all the time. This one's been eating poorly, running around with you. No wonder he's hungry. *Sukuramu, sukuramu.*" The human waved the dog away so that it scrambled between their legs and out of the room like a more innocently mischievous hound caught in garbage.

"Right," cautioned Dominia, but Basil's innocent look stayed her from further discourse. Right, of course. Dogs ate flesh all the time. That was what her Father had suggested to her, right? That she leave the door open so the dog wouldn't starve once he'd eaten his humans. And their own dogs in Europa: some of them were trained to eat human flesh, too. The hunting hounds, and all. Of course, dogs ate flesh. It was just— Basil was so...*intelligent.* So...

"So, what are we going to do about him, huh? You're daydreaming." Miki snapped her fingers in front of Dominia's face while standing between the General and the dog; the pup behind her appeared oblivious to the dollop of blood gathering at his lip, about to drop upon the spiraling pattern of the lilac-moss carpet. "I can't take care of all this by myself. It's your man who did this, so it's you who should clean it up."

"There's only so much I can do."

"You need to at least keep him out of sight of the porters for the next few hours. And keep the smell down, too."

"It won't be that bad that fast," said Dominia, observing the gaping stomach wound carved by Basil's hungry jaws. "But you're right. We have to keep this from getting out, and we have to keep other people from getting in. For all we know, René could make a noise complaint. Maybe somebody's already lodged one."

"Too impolite. These people mind their business to a fault. It's a matter of keeping our volume polite and quiet between here and Kabul. Easier said than done"—the human rolled her shoulders in a shrug—"but all we can do is try."

The prostitute wove past Dominia, past the bloody dog, and tumbled into her bed: not a bunk like the arrangement in Dominia's room, but not near as wide as most would wish and barely comfortable for two. Alone for the space of a second, she studied the corpse and wondered if her Father watched through her eye even with its backup features disabled. If it was true what Miki said about programs for some reason delivering information to the Family, wasn't it possible that the Hierophant had potential access to every pair of DIOX-Is available? That was paranoid thinking, but if anyone was capable of such a thing, it was him. How? He couldn't manage it. He owned Halcyon, but DIOX and their cyborgans were an enterprise of mostly human clientele. Why would he fund their medical technology?

She had to hope he wouldn't. If that was the case, it didn't matter if she had a DIOX-I of her own. Walking down the street, she would be exposed to thousands of streams recorded by passing strangers, and the Hierophant could observe any or all. Horrible. This thought lulled the General into a trance from which Miki drew her with the pluck of a shamisen string.

"That's a pretty old-fashioned instrument," said the martyr, coming to sit in the awkward, armless white chair in the corner. "I've always liked it."

"You martyrs love human culture. You just hate humans. At least, you don't think that we're as good as you." While Miki's slender fingers produced twangs that filled the air like incense, she talked away. "He's convinced himself—and everybody else—that you're all so much better than us. That you're different from us, at all. How is a martyr different from a genetically engineered human?"

For an ugly second, she was back on McLintock farm. "I've begun to ask that, myself. I always asked that. I...ignored it." Dominia frowned at her hands, at her hungry stomach. Soon she needed to eat, and she regretted letting the dog get dibs on the businessman. "You have to ignore things to survive sometimes."

"When your nervous system tells you a situation is bad, you should listen."

"Of course, but what's a kid supposed to do?"

Miki's lips twisted in the shred of a sympathetic frown as her face lowered to her instrument. "That is the tragic part about this. Things would be different if martyrs were not so convinced of their own righteous nature. But your Father is good with children. Give him an infant, and blue will be red in a few centuries."

Too true. The martyr rested her face against the cool wood of the door and listened to the instrument, let it quiver into her while she said, "I wanted to protest. I did, often, but I was afraid to take action."

"What changed? Why have you taken action now? Not because some rat came to you. Not because your wife died."

"But it *was* Cassandra. Cassandra changed me." In the back of Dominia's head, she saw her, pale at the table, the adult version of the girl that the General had once been. So reluctant—so terrified—to exchange humanity for immortality. Every bite of food Cassandra consumed for the next six months were for her child; after the birth, they were for Dominia. Now, Dominia regretted that fact more than any. "She never let anyone make her forget that what she did was wrong. That shame kept her human, but it also kept her apart from us. It kept her so unhappy."

"Better to be unhappy and repentant than an ignorant sinner," said Miki. Dominia laughed.

"You believe in sin?"

"I might not worship your Father, but I'm a very religious person."

"Ishtar, the Lady?" At Dominia's question, the human's dark eyes fluttered in surprise. The General smiled. "I'm not concerned anymore with the illegality of— It's just a word."

"Nothing is 'just' a word. Nothing is a word. Words have power; words bind, conceal, illuminate, and curse. So, too, can they free. The Lady is older than the word that is Her name; older than the word 'Lady,' older than the concept of 'man' and 'woman.' Older than the world."

Over the plucking of the shamisen, against the closed lids of her eyes, great imaginings of near-psychedelic variety played out against the warm madder backdrop—some formless Lady with the world in her arms. Miki went on. "The world has been created many times over: so believe the Lady's priestesses, those in the marketplace who have been initiated into its higher echelons of truth. But we are not the only ones who believe that. Many religions—all of them, if you pay attention—say the world has been created again and again. All of this has happened again and again."

"That's a depressing thought."

"Then let that be motivation to live a pure life. That way, you can minimize the amount of pain you endure for eternity." While Miki chuckled cheerlessly, the shamisen carried Dominia away with the sound of the human's low voice. "The Lady is the one who creates the world each time it is destroyed. She was not present in the universe when it first began. Rather, She was created by the first destruction."

"What destroys it?"

"The death of Lazarus. Lazarus is the sun around which the Earth of the Lady rotates, and when his light is snuffed, She has no means by which to see, so he must be made again. But, to make him again, She has to make the universe."

"Lazarus is really a person?" asked Dominia, unable to open her eyes against her fatigue, but conscious enough to be distressed by the fleeting notion that maybe René had lied to her about everything. Maybe all the old murmured human legends were the stories she'd believed them to be. Miki, however, soothed her.

"Lazarus is a person, yes: but he is also a pillar for the world. It is said he was only human once, the first time the universe was created. It is said that your Father stole the protein from him and used it to his own, unholy ends. That Lazarus is the Protomartyr, and the one to whom the people should have always looked. He has not been a human since the first time the world was new. Created a martyr, he dies a martyr, too; and when he dies, the world begins again. It is why he stays so far from mainstream humanity—why he is capable of such great miracles but has allowed his name to slip into obscurity, echoed on the sidelines of the Abrahamic books and worshiped by the cult of the Lazerenes."

"But why? Why is Lazarus tied to the death of the universe?"

"Lazarus is a miracle worker. This Lazarus of whom we speak is a great man, but humble, and so he took his name from one who was saved by a messiah, rather than one who did the saving. The miracle of Lazarus is that he saved even himself from death: saved himself through Her. The first time he died, the Lady emerged from his blood to revive him, and She seeks to make from him Her King. She seeks to purify the world of martyrs and set all things right again. For, much as he was responsible for the release of martyrdom upon the world, so, too, must he be the one to end it."

"Then why hasn't he ended it already?"

"That, I cannot answer. Perhaps because he has seen it all before, and knows that the Lady's way is not the true solution to the problem."

"Because it will all happen again, the next time he dies and the universe is created?"

"Aren't you a wise woman." The shamisen's twanging stopped and a light flickered off; Dominia, too tired to lift her head from the wall, accepted the blanket that Miki draped over her. "Only Lazarus knows why he does what he does; only the Lady knows why She does what She does; only you know, Dominia, why you do what you do. Worry about yourself, and let the gods handle themselves."

X

Mass Hysteria

Dominia must have been tired: that night was the first time in over a month she managed to sleep longer than three or four hours. And that included those spells of unconsciousness. Best, it was a concrete block of sleep that hosted no bad dreams. Almost strange to come to under the comforter feeling refreshed, instead of panicked. No traumatic memories unfolded themselves in a rapid fractal of pain. Yet, a weird shame lurked in that. Half of her wished to never think of Cassandra at all, ever again; the other half was desperate to keep her alive or re-invoke her being through sheer willpower, however impossible this might have been. But it was all impossible, wasn't it? Even the dog, who twitched in his sleep, was impossible. Miki snored on her bed, tangled in her sheets and sweaty with the alcohol processed by her human body. There was Cassandra's far sweatier forehead, her sweaty palms, as she waited in the Family doctor office— the Family doctor, of course, being Cicero, as partial to playing doctor as to playing priest.

"A rather naughty girl, aren't you." He checked Cassandra's pulse under Dominia's hawkish scrutiny.

"Has anybody ever told you how creepy you are?" the new martyr asked. Cicero laughed, the spitting image, sight and sound, of the Hierophant.

"Try not to take offense. I think of you as a child, of sorts. You would do well to think of yourself as such, too."

As Cassandra shot Dominia's amused expression a far more rueful look, Cicero selected a tube of gel for the ultrasound. "You are, though, quite ill-behaved to have brought an unwitting party for the ride. Lie back, there we are." While Cassandra obeyed, her hand stretched out, and Dominia realized belatedly that her wife wanted her to hold it. Many long days the General had been up, dealing with Cassandra's sickness and talking about the circumstances that had brought them to that point. Cassandra's lover had been killed by a martyr, and she then learned (through the miracles of that same over-the-counter pregnancy test that had informed her of the bittersweet conception) that the baby had a genetic defect: a particularly unfriendly one that would leave the child dead in utero and threaten the mother's life without unaffordable genetic treatments. Even with those treatments, no amount of money would have guaranteed the infant. The baby was all she had left of her lover—all she had in her life—and she had nothing to lose in martyrdom. Everything to gain.

Cicero swept up the small wireless wand of the portable ultrasound device. "How has your nausea been?"

"Violent," answered Cassandra; Dominia added, "She can't keep anything down."

"Well, she will need to try. She is, as they say, 'eating for two.'"

In one sweet second, Cassandra's eyes lit, her head lifted, and she asked, "It's alive?"

Even Cicero's smile was genuine enough to crinkle his features. "Yes, she's fine."

"Oh, 'she'! A girl." Those beautiful eyes welled up in tears, and Cassandra shone with a smile that inspired a matching one in Dominia. As though it were her child. "I'm so glad she's okay. Thank God, thank God—alive."

"Yes, the blood test showed her to be a girl; physical differences should just be developing. Your instinct to turn toward martyrdom rather than flee east for refugee medical care, as so many women do, is quite interesting. Has Dominia told you the true history"—he glanced from the screen—"of the sacred protein? We keep it at the 'gift from God' level for the common man. Humans and martyrs who only go to Church to receive the stabilizing blood of the Lamb."

Cassandra shook her head, and Cicero spoke without looking up from the laptop with which he printed pictures. "Quite a long time ago, there was no such thing as genetic modification. This was when I and my brother, Elijah, were mere humans. As men of science, we saw the world's problems and wished to solve them. Foremost among these problems were mortality, cancer, genetic defects—all those things handled in the medical field, which, it became apparent in time, could be fought with a combination gene editing and various other therapies. He and I studied a protein that compares the DNA of foreign bacteria to stored RNA to better identify and eliminate biological threats—a miracle of a thing, a genetic pair of scissors still used to treat humans unwilling to take the steps to immortality. But it was mortality that we sought to cure through the protein. There were, after all, animals in the natural world that went without aging. Animals that survived in the vacuum of space. There was a cure for everything, given the protein and the correct RNA. We were on the cusp of something most grand; and then, one day, the Hierophant came knocking on our door. He looked frighteningly like me, and explained he had come from Acetia, a world far away, to bring us the answer for which my brother and I, of the whole human race, had most feverishly searched. He martyred us that day. Humans prefer to teach that the protein was developed in some lab, and it is true that my brother and I never would have become the first martyrs of Earth without our scientific background; but, you see, we had to rely on the grace of God for the answer we required."

"I had always heard that the Hierophant brought the protein from his alien world," said skeptical Cassandra, accepting her first—and only—baby pictures with a soft smile. "I guess I thought it sounded kind of…odd."

"He was attracted by our discovery. The martyrs of his world knew Earth was ready for the protein, and may have discovered it alone if not for the intervention of the Lord's highest servants. The Hierophant, His high priest on Acetia, was sent to instruct us in its use. That is why the blood of Lazarenes is forbidden; his protein was synthesized in a lab. It is not a gift from God but a base creation of the world."

"And—you, and Elijah—you thought this was worthwhile when the Hierophant told you that you'd need to resort to cannibalism?"

"Oh, I seldom *resort* to it, as I am always within my brother's comforting proximity. But I choose to engage in it, because it is the highest pleasure that our Father's world may offer." While Cassandra shuddered at the merriment in his black eyes, he added, "Most martyrs, as we did at that time, consider it a small price to pay for salvation. You must also agree, Cassandra, or I would not find you thus."

"You weren't put off by the alien business?"

"Certainly not. How thrilling! What vindication it was to meet him, evidence that our paths were divinely inspired! Like having a child who stood up right away, walking and talking on day one. We had never considered the existence of aliens, let alone that they should be servants of the divine; but it only makes sense that higher intelligence should have a higher standing of Eternity."

While Dominia's wife frowned at the images of her baby, Cicero patted her arm. "I think you should be proud, and excited. Two thousand years is a long time, and this has never been allowed to happen. The occasions that almost slipped through the cracks have not started this well."

Dominia, irritated, slipped in with, "She's puking day and night. You call that 'starting well'?"

"Pregnancy is a difficult time. I recommend eating a lot of crackers, drinking something carbonated, staying off your feet. Aren't you lucky to have such a doting wife!"

"I am— So, the protein is fixing my baby?"

"Editing her as we speak: clipping here, rearranging there, adding this and that."

The mother-to-be found, after brief struggle, a way to phrase a difficult question. "Will she still be my baby?"

"Your baby, a dead man's baby, and the Lord's baby." Cicero crossed himself, chuckling, on his way out of the office.

Yes. A dead man's baby. Now, having lost her, Dominia understood why Cassandra had been so desperate to hold on to one thing—anything—that contained part of the person she'd loved. It was why she now stood in Miki's tiny suite and quietly shifted the lid of some luggage in hopes of finding the diamond. Somehow, though Dominia's sigh on waking, her stretch on standing, and her footsteps across the room had not been enough to awaken the prostitute, the rustle of her clothes in foreign hands proved better than an alarm. Miki bolted upright and shoved away the blanket without a thought for her modesty, then recognized the General.

"Oh, it's you." She fell once more and yanked her coverings back while tucking her drool-soaked pillow into the crook of her neck. "You're not going to find it."

"'Her.'" The General grimaced at her reflexive correction, but doubled down. "You don't even know what I'm looking for. I might be trying to rob you. Maybe I already found it."

"Of course you're trying to rob me, but you won't find it, and you haven't found it already because the diamond hasn't even been in this room."

"Where is she?"

"Beats me." Her rear wiggled for an emphasis lost on the fuming martyr.

"You mean you don't even know where she is?"

"Actually"—she smacked dry lips and cracked her arid eyes open enough to look at the clock—"I don't think she's even on this train anymore."

A chill whipped over Dominia at the skipping of her heart. "Did you sell her?"

"No, no, of course not. I sent her somewhere for safekeeping. She's on her way to the Lady."

Impotent adrenaline flooded her trembling limbs, but that may have been the protein going to town on her DNA as her body entered starvation mode. Whatever it was, Dominia barely heard Miki's words over the intrusive images of Cassandra's remains in the negligent hands of some stranger, headed someplace Dominia didn't even know, for purposes occult in every definition of the word. She remembered the unavailable prostitutes she had seen near her location when making the appointment with Miki. Cassandra was with one or both; the inactive dots would be gone if she looked now. Losing grip on her temper, the martyr strode to the bedside of the human and gave her shoulders such a shake that Basil awoke with a soft bark. "Why would you do that? What the fuck were you thinking?"

"It's the only way to guarantee you'll bring Lazarus to the Lady. She's being treated with the utmost respect, don't worry. Do you think remains belong swinging around your neck while you run all over creation?"

"Now's not the time to develop a sense of moral decency. Who's to say I don't just kill you?" She examined the bruises developed on Miki's throat and narrowed her eyes. "Finish the job René started. I'm a fool to trade him for you, anyway: the Hunters don't deal with women. René's intimacy with them was integral to finding Lazarus."

"We'll find him."

"How?"

"You just *think* the Hunters don't deal with women. The truth is, they're more than a secret club of jihadists sitting in a bunch of tents outside of Jerusalem, in the jungles of Brazil, and working with yakuza. They're *everywhere*. Why do you think you were headed to Kabul in the first place? There are less-extreme extremists who are part of their stupid brigade, and those less-extreme extremists are more flexible when it comes to talking like a civilized human…or putting down money to get laid." As Dominia relaxed her hold, Miki stumbled up in search of her robe. "I know a guy who can tell us where Lazarus is. At the least, he has the resources to find out."

"And he'll do this because…"

"As I said, his bosses are way more extremist than he is. You think it would sail with them if they found out he'd solicited a prostitute? You're half right about that sort and women. To the Hunters, Red Market workers are as bad as a martyr." With a scoff of derision, Miki lifted her arms and sent her hair pluming in great jet-colored streams from the maroon cotton of her *yukata*. "It's like, the tiny penis club, or something. Look at René! Whining like that to save himself. Makes me sick. I'm sure he's going to tattle to the Hunters— We need to find Lazarus as soon as possible."

The General felt almost bad, but Miki was right: René was, for lack of a more eloquent phrase, a little shit. Responsible for the flight of a great many refugees or no, he could only be considered so noble when associating with even the lowest echelons of a terrorist organization. It wasn't so much that he deserved was he got; it was that what he got was such a straight-line consequence of his spineless nature that an excess of empathy for him was out of the question. "Maybe you were right, and we should have put him out of his misery. If they buy into the story that I'm a rogue terrorist responsible for the atrocities on the ship and in the hospital, some loose martyr mass-murdering humans across the globe, any agreement we might have had to peacefully exchange information is as good as ruined. If they don't, well—there was nothing in the first place to stop them from betraying me, and there isn't anything now."

"But, with the power of technology, anything is possible! Like I said, my guy's a better solution than risking a conversation with the Hunters' higher-ups. Kahlil's okay, you'll see. A bit misogynistic, but all Hunters are. He doesn't mean it; I'm reeducating him. Anyway, if he's going to keep my mouth shut"—she shrugged slim shoulders as Basil scrambled up and, apropos of apparently nothing, wandered into the hall—"he's going to have to do me a favor. We should be there in an hour: I told him we'd take a cab from the station."

"What's he do?"

"Oh, he helped found one of the biggest tech start-ups in Kabul—for whatever that's worth, fast as that industry moves!—but a couple years ago—Sh." The human lifted a hand almost pale as her face while the front door of the suite slid open. Her dark eyes highlighted by alertness, Miki glanced into Dominia's face, then let her gaze slide toward the bathroom—and the corpse inside. Dominia's brain churned. Was the dog's face clean? She hadn't paid attention since waking up. Why had a porter ignored the "Do Not Disturb" light? Had some complaint been lodged? If so, why hadn't they called over the intercom and asked to be let in? Why did her heart beat with the fast insistence that it was someone she knew and didn't want to see? Not Cicero, please. But Basil barked a happy note, and the familiar, carefully cultivated chime of an airy voice sang, "Oh, aren't you a handsome boy!" And Dominia felt a deep kind of horror.

It seemed ever more that the General lived in the worst possible scenario. She almost would have preferred Cicero. Saint Valentinian, himself. Anyone, really, but Lavinia.

With a grim expression designed to anchor Miki in place, Dominia edged down the short hall. Its tiny length increased to an incomprehensible stretch that revealed, second by Zeno's subdivided second, the tip of Basil's curling tail; then it unveiled his fuzzy black haunch, which was matched, by pure chance, to the lace of the elaborate gown worn by the woman who petted him. The smile on her pearly face and the unyielding gold of her hair seemed bright as those portions of the border collie's fur that were white, and the DIOX-I's box resembled less a digital affectation than a halo. Dear Lavinia—now was not the time.

"Oh, Dominia, I'm very happy you're alive, but I'm just as pleased to meet this handsome chap! Yes, hello, yes, hello, aren't you sweet, how are you." While the dog's tail beat a delighted rhythm against the marble floor and once or twice threatened to upend the telephone stand, Lavinia turned her

Marianas eyes toward her older sister and hugged him to her breast. "But, oh, Dominia, I *am* so happy you're alive."

"So am I, mostly. Did he send you here?"

"Yes and no. I've *begged* Daddy to tell me where you were! I pestered him and pestered him ever since that ship ran aground in the Port of Kyoto, and finally he told me you were on the Light Rail, and I've never *been* on the Light Rail before!" Her vast child's eyes sparkled bright with her breathless delight as she released the dog to spread her hands. "It's so *beautiful*, isn't it, Dominia? Like a big gold snake popping in and out of its tunnel. And it's funny to see how the foreigners think we dress and act."

"They've got it pretty close. Have you seen the Dining Car?"

"No, not yet—I came straight here! I wanted to see you. Oh, Ninny, Daddy told me about your eye, and I'm *sorry*. Does it hurt?"

"No, it doesn't hurt, it's fine. Look—you want to go to the Dining Car with me? Maybe we can have a bite to eat? Nothing real, but—"

"I can't, Ninny. I've come to deliver an important message and then hurry off posthaste: I don't have much time to dally."

Snorting, Dominia glanced down at Basil. "Can't let you out for too long; you might start getting ideas."

"Ideas like yours! But Daddy sent me to say that he wants you to come home, Ninny. And so do I." Lavinia threw the pout of a twelve-year-old, rather than the solemn expression of a near-centennial Princess as worn for official broadcasts. "I miss you. I was so scared when I thought something had happened to you. And whatever's gone on with your *hair*?"

"People were going to recognize me."

"Well, yes, but you wouldn't have to worry about people recognizing you if you'd come home. I've never seen you without your long hair, how funny! You'd make a pretty boy, if you were a boy."

Trying not to cast any anxious glances down the hall where Miki was blessedly silent, Dominia laughed in as normal a manner as she managed. "Thanks, I guess. I kind of like it. But I can't go home. Not after what he did to Cassandra."

"Daddy didn't do anything to her! Why would you say that?"

"You don't know what happened."

"She was such a dreary lady." Lavinia sighed at the thought, as oblivious to the sting as any child. "I always heard she made an awful fuss about being a martyr, even though she chose it! She was nice enough, I suppose, but since her baby died, after all, I mean—the whole thing was pointless, wasn't it? Holding on to that for ninety years…weren't you enough for her? And now she's causing you so much grief. Why don't you meet a nice, new girl? A proper martyr?"

She wasn't going to get angry. She had to maintain reason. The girl didn't understand. How could the Eternal Virgin of Europa understand anything about love? "It wasn't pointless, Lavinia." A thousand kisses and sighs and touches and smiles and lazy evenings and good nights and bad nights and seeing her there, asleep. "There's so much I would never trade, even for all the pain. The pain was worth it."

"If the pain was worth it, you wouldn't have run away clinging to the false hope some liar put into your head."

Was it worth trying to convince her that the Hierophant had sent René, and had therefore been the one to tempt her into running away? "If the hope is false, then what does the Hierophant want with Lazarus? He could have killed René and me in the Front—but he didn't."

"Of course he didn't. Did you see his broadcast? He's been so sad, Dominia, he barely eats or sleeps. He looks so tired. I hate everyone *fighting* like this. Aren't we supposed to get along? We're a family."

"Families fight."

"They don't have to!" Optimistic Lavinia's perception of family life had always been half what the Hierophant told her and half what she selectively gleaned from books, preferring ancient works like the exhausting *Anne of Green Gables* while ignoring *Anna Karenina*. "Families can be happy."

"Or deeply unhappy."

Frowning, an unpracticed expression on her gentle face, Lavinia looked like she was beginning to understand something long hidden. "Are you unhappy, Ninny? Don't you love us?"

Dangerous territory. "I love *you*, Lavinia. Isn't that enough? Look: part of the reason I left is because of the way he treats you."

"What—Daddy? He spoils me! I don't know what you mean, 'the way he treats me.'"

"Keeping you like…this." Dominia waved a helpless hand without finding a word gentle enough. Nonetheless, Lavinia's face fell further. "Not that there's anything wrong with you! You're a sweet girl, but it's the way he—shelters you, and denies you so much of your own life. You must see that sometimes."

"If I wanted to go into the world, I'd go. I don't because our cities"—she lowered her voice—"well, a place like Denmark, Old Elsinore—it's *safe* for me, isn't it? Instead of doing something like this."

"I didn't say you had to take the fu—fudging Light Rail your first time out on your own. Just, you know, try living your own life. Away from him, and Cicero. You like our cities, so get an apartment in New Elsinore in the Front and live like one of the young poets there; Brooklyn's a nice neighborhood. Or hang out in your duchy! I lived an anonymous life in Canada for about twenty years…didn't talk to anybody from the Family until the final years of the South American Conflict." She relished the thought. "What a nice vacation."

"I couldn't do that! I love Daddy and Cicero. And what about the Lamb? Why do you act like they're such horrible people? All they've done for you! Given you!" It was like listening to a feminine clone of the Hierophant. Dominia shut off in a way so visceral that Lavinia noticed; she changed tack, and her features softened. "I know you're sad for Cassandra, but—"

"Please: I think you've done enough damage there. I'm not coming home."

The girl's tone dropped to a note of warning. "You really want more people to die?"

"It's them or me," she said with a pathetic attempt at a smile. Her little sister didn't find that funny, from the looks of it, and official worry vibrated in Dominia's skull. There were other reasons why the Hierophant kept Lavinia away from the world—why she was a walking, talking, singing argument against unregistered martyrings and the martyring of adults, the latter being ironic since she was found as a baby. But because she awoke as an adult, and had, in a vague and technical way, the right to an adult's agency, she served as paradoxical warning for both cases in one person. Dominia glanced at Miki, who briefly appeared down the hall, now dressed in a chic suit and looking as mundane a professional as anybody else on the train. Though Lavinia's head turned with the sound of movement, Dominia stepped closer to distract her sister by taking up her hand.

"I don't want anyone to die, Lavinia. I don't want to be doing this. You think I wanted to upend my life? Lose my position and power, everything I had? I wrestled with the choice to leave. But the best choice for me—the healthiest choice—was to leave."

"Daddy said some scummy human offered you a deal."

"Because the Hierophant *sent* him," insisted Dominia at last, in fruitless—and fatal—agitation. As predicted, Lavinia looked offended by the notion. Once, she stomped her foot. Twice, she tapped it. Horror filled Dominia and she scrambled to placate the girl. "But he only sent René because—because—"

"Daddy would never send some gross creep to trick you." The tapping of her foot became the beat of a metronome. Miki, who had continued peeking (with what she must have thought to be subtlety) from the bedroom, began to move her foot to the rhythm. Everything was lost if Dominia didn't calm her sister down. Was it possible to escape from a train in a hyperloop tunnel alive? How about with a dog under one arm and a prostitute under the other? That was, assuming said possessed prostitute survived. Lavinia insisted something about the Hierophant's integrity, and Dominia, fear-deafened, forced herself to tune back in as Lavinia said, "And that's why Daddy sent me.

Because he was worried about you, and sad that you let some human tempt you off the righteous path."

"I don't think there is a righteous path," the General suggested. Her sister sniffed.

"I'm sorry you're depressed, Ninny. But when we get you home, you can see a doctor! Cicero will help you. He gives me pills to help me sleep all the time!"

Gritting her teeth, Dominia let slip, "If I never see Cicero again, it will be too soon," which darkened Lavinia's face more than even aspersions against the Hierophant.

"I guess you'd rather hang out with your garbage friends like René and the prostitute. Is she here?" Now graceless as a bossy toddler, Lavinia shoved Dominia aside with a shocking amount of force. Before the dog even barked, the martyr strolled around the corner, her steps marching to the beat she'd tapped: the beat that possessed Miki, whose knee and hip now wiggled with the pace, and whose expression brightened without regard for the threat represented as Lavinia appeared, cheery as ever, her own body moving to a silent dance.

"There you are! Do you know who I am?"

"Lavinia di Forenzzi," said Miki, unable to stop smiling or, for that matter, dial back the way her legs moved her into the hall. "The Duchess of Florence and the Princess of Europa and like twenty other things, too, right? Do you know what humans call you? Satan's Pet."

"Daddy's not Satan." Lavinia cheesily mimed tossing a lasso to the inaudible beat, which caused Miki to mime being pulled toward the martyr. "What's your name?"

"Miki Soto." The prostituted came to a stop in which she danced, hips and shoulders and chest wiggling in time with the moves of the martyr.

"Do you like to dance, Miki?"

"When I choose."

Giggling in that soft, condescending way, Lavinia said, "Nobody chooses to do anything, Miki! You didn't choose to be born. You didn't choose the life you've lived. And you don't get to choose how you die, either."

"I'll never die." Miki laughed, inappropriately gay, given the circumstances, but unable to help herself when her extremities forced her to do the hustle. "Ishtar will protect me."

Lavinia's pupils shrank with alarming speed while Dominia asked the dog, "Can't you do something?"

"That's a dirty word." Lavinia's dancing stopped, but her foot-tapping continued as Miki wiggled past, bent to the martyr's will. "You shouldn't say words like that. If you do, your tongue will fall out."

"Ishtar, Ishtar, Ishtar," repeated the prostitute, singing it to the sound of the beat until Lavinia gave a murderous banshee cry of distaste. After a few more inaudible bars, Miki lifted her hand to her own wide-eyed mouth and stuck out her tongue while saying around it, "No, wait!"

Before Miki began yanking out her own tongue, Dominia was upon her, martyr hands clamping down on delicate wrists and then, with profanity, dropping away to hold the human's jaw as it shut to gnaw the organ off.

"I don't ever want to hear you say that word again." Lavinia's face was a mask of porcelain fury. "I don't ever want to hear you *speak* again! Ninny, what dirty friends you keep!"

While Miki and Dominia wrestled with Miki's body and Lavinia ranted over the whining of the dog, the General tried to think of a way to solve the problem. The high priority of keeping mass hysteria under control struck Dominia when the front door slid open. An oblivious porter, reading off his paperwork, stepped into the foyer.

"So sorry to disturb, but I was sent to tell you that we are almost to—"

He had looked up: his eyes landed on the struggling women, then on the one who watched. Dominia could only cry, "No!" as Lavinia, with her sunshiny grin, kept up the tapping of her heels and lifted her hands to clap in time. The porter, weaker than Miki and requiring much less exposure to fall under Lavinia's so-called spell, dropped his papers to clap with her.

"This is going to be so fun! I wish we had music— I'll call Cicero! He should be in the engineer's cab by now, I bet he can do it!"

This month was getting worse all the time. The porter danced back to the train car's hallway and Dominia knew what happened out there. It had happened a few times before, albeit in isolated human villages, and mostly when Lavinia, just awoken, dealt with emotions in a (partially) conscious way for the first time. The effects of her powers had been reported as "outbreaks of mass hysteria, delusion, and paranoia," and cited as examples of the human brain's capacity to be controlled by others. More alarmingly, some (Cicero) interpreted it as evidence of the human's implicit desire for relief from self-control. An almost fair assessment, as the effects of Lavinia's powers always seemed at first glance to be fun.

Laughter was a common effect. A whole village, starting with one person, would burst into hilarious uproar. The first man's neighbor would catch it; and that neighbor's kids and wife would crack up at that; that wife inevitably laughed all the way to the market; and in a matter of no time, every man, woman, and child in town rolled on the floor, asphyxiated by guffaws of sourceless amusement. Dominia and her Family pieced together the cause not that first time, when Lavinia had herself first descended into hysterics as an amazed messenger fell from his bicycle and into the mud on seeing the

Holy Family. Rather, it was the second instance that had clarified Lavinia's influence over the human nervous system. As now, she had caused a different village of humans to forego their jobs and lives for the pleasure of a spontaneous, seemingly choreographed dance, which did not stop until everyone in town dropped dead of exhaustion several days later.

Those were the charming instances. The zany, wacky ones that made every girl on Earth think Lavinia's life was a fairy-tale adventure. When Dominia thought about the sheer number of sharp objects in the Dining Car, let alone all the candles for mood lighting, electrical outlets, and countless other means of death...she grimaced as Miki's body tried gnawing off the General's fingers to get to the tongue that was its target.

"Don't bite me! If you swallow my blood, you'll end up one of us."

Incoherent with her mouth full, Miki insisted something to the effect of, "I'm not trying to," then gagged as the suite loudspeakers crackled with a catchy human pop song. Lavinia bounced in place and clapped her hands the way most ill-informed children might on seeing her.

"He heard me, Cicero heard me! Yay!"

Caught up in her own excitement at the possibility of seeing a dance number just for her, Lavinia charged through the front door of the suite and made an immediate right for the Dining Car.

Was it appropriate to thank Cicero for anything, let alone this? She was tempted. Dominia took a breath and, with a free hand, slipped off the belt stolen from René. Through a quick apology and a bevy of protests, the martyr gagged Miki—not to keep her quiet, though that was sort of a bonus. Rather, with the belt angled between her teeth and buckled in the back of her head, she couldn't bite off her tongue. When her hands lifted to undo Dominia's work, the General took the human's wrists, dragged her down the hall, and searched her massive collection of luggage for the handcuffs the prostitute was sure to have. As they clicked in place, Miki demonstrated control of her faculties enough to offer a lascivious eyebrow waggle. Dominia pulled her out of the room, insisting, "Now's not the time," then paused at the great fuss the woman kicked up. "What? What's wrong?"

Her great dark eyes waggled toward her bag, then down the hall, and Dominia took her meaning after a few seconds but shook her head. Her voice raised over the thundering music. "You want us to haul that massive thing with us? There's no time." Fleeting panic that Miki had lied about Cassandra's diamond being off the train filled her, but she saw in the prostitute's urgent and angry look that the concern was not for the sake of her duty but for her attachment to the many dresses, makeup pots, and Lamb-knew-what sex toys she'd (for some reason) brought along with her. "All that stuff had its purpose," consoled the martyr as she hauled the whining, dancing human down the hall, "but that purpose has been served. Look, I need new clothes, too! We can get clothes when we get to Kabul. If," she added, frowning, "we get to Kabul."

The porter had come to alert them to the half hour, it seemed, and she had to assume for the sake of her sanity that Cicero was either not planning to conduct the train at all, or was not conducting it yet. If he was, they were in trouble, because it was likely he wouldn't stop at Kabul and would instead keep going on to wherever it was he was supposed to drop his victims off. And where was the Lamb? Never far from Cicero: his brother, his husband, and his keeper. She daren't think too much on him, either. And if Lavinia was here, then the Hierophant...

One thing at a time. Before the Holy Family killed them, everyone aboard would die in a choreographed frenzy of self-mutilation. There was precious little she could do about the latter; even diverting Lavinia's conscious attention would do no good once the proverbial party ramped up. After a certain point, the memetic infection was a self-perpetuating mechanism. A poisonous thought-virus that would sweep every car and compartment it touched. It would not guarantee death, but if Lavinia felt evil enough, it might. Even martyrs could, under some circumstances, become subject to it. This meant Dominia was going the opposite way, which meant dragging a squealing, kicking, gagged, possessed, and angry Miki Soto to the front car with her; making damn sure the train stopped in Kabul; and keeping everybody, if possible, from dying.

Except Cicero. She was almost fine with that fatality. But if she made it up there without any others—any human ones—that would be appreciated. This was possible if she capitalized on her infamy. A great many things were possible thanks to her reputation. Thanks to the Hierophant. She'd might as well take advantage of what he'd done to her already dark name.

"Look"—she glanced between the human and the dog—"this is going to look bad. I've accepted that. Sometimes you have to dirty your hands. But that doesn't mean I feel good about it. Try to remember: I'm a good person, okay? I actually really like people."

Three minutes later, Dominia stood on a table in the red-carpeted Dragon Car, her revolver having been fired through several rows of machines to keep from puncturing the precious hull of the far larger bullet within which they hurtled. Attention gathered, she brandished Miki like a hostage while the world's least menacing dog barked and the whole room of people screamed themselves to hushed silence. Amid all the faces, the Disgraced Governess of the United Front roared, "Listen to me, you stuck-up pieces of shit. My name is Dominia di Mephitoli. Yes"—she pointed the gun in the direction of the gasp—"by now some of you have heard rumors that I'm on this train. Yet, you're still surprised. Do you know why?"

The car was still. Miki did her best to resemble a helpless pinup model while Dominia pointed the gun at her head. "It's because half of you didn't think I was real, and the other half of you have been praying I'm not. I'm sorry to say that I am real, and in possession of what I imagine to be one of the only guns on the Light Rail—if not *the* only. I am not, however, needlessly cruel. With that in mind, will all passengers class C or lower please leave the casino."

A few people tarried to say the name of the God they worshiped; a handful of others dashed, mostly shabby, tired-looking people but one or two better-dressed, probable class Bs smart enough to get while the getting was good. She let them go, because those who were smart enough deserved to be rewarded, and those who stayed behind had opted the route of donation. "The rest of you"—she took the oversize purse of some wealthy lady wearing a fox-fur hat, who gasped as if she had been slighted at a party rather than robbed of her possession—"hand over your cash, your rings, necklaces, and watches."

A thrill passed through Dominia, who found herself the sort of figure she'd admired in spirited stories of the Front's ancient Old West days. Only the tiniest thrill, understand. As much as she dared. She had always dreamed herself more the lawman-hero type, but beggars couldn't be choosers when living on the fringes of normalcy—if this was still a shade of normalcy at all. One brave (stupid) porter released a childish war cry and charged for her. She let him run his nose into the butt of her gun and land, crying, on the floor.

"Any more questions?" she asked.

The queue which formed was more orderly than any she'd seen. She had to temper thrill with a healthy, quasi-religious sense of naughtiness. Otherwise, there was too much temptation to dive into the abyss of amorality and come out the other side a warlord of esteem more terrible than that of her preexisting reputation. Better to stay Robin Hood than Genghis Khan: but, if the Sheriff of Nottingham pinned her with false accusations, he deserved something to blame her for.

Not five minutes later, the bag was full of riches enough to make Miki's eyes bug when Dominia, having dragged her from the car, showed her the contents. "There. Feel better?"

The girl shrugged, and through teeth that sought to gnaw the belt to get her tongue, made a noise resembling, "Well..." Her hands had stopped clutching a tongue they could not reach and now seemed to be struggling to enact a choreography in which they could not engage; Dominia was relieved to see Lavinia wasn't feeling very homicidal.

Behind them, Basil's tail wagged, accompaniment to his joyful bark. The trio marched onward with Dominia's gun leading the way, aimed (playfully) at Miki while they beat their long and ragged path through the many cars of coach. In a kind break, they were beset by no more heroic porters or passengers, and were left to their own devices by people who quite rightly did not want to risk their lives. It was relief enough that no passengers from the Dining Car had made their way up, but that did make perfect sense, since they were busy dancing along to the beat that pumped through the cars like some sort of stupid music video. Grating, that. It was almost a relief when they reached the first of the Burlap Economy cars and the music paused with a bing-bong electronic chime to set the stage for Cicero's announcement.

"Good morning! This is your emergency engineer speaking. As most of you are by now aware, we have a special guest on our train today: the terrorist Dominia di Mephitoli." Dominia clenched her teeth so hard she thought the remaining ones might shatter; she hauled the human at a faster pace. "You may all remember the Disgraced Governess for such battlefield exploits as the Reclamation of Mexico"—many around her gave a cry of terror or sob of recognition, with some hissing as though she were a theater villain—"that infamous, single-handed sweep through a sleeping barracks known as the Nogales Rampage; and her integral part in what humans refer to as 'the Black Night.' But you know, I believe I once heard Dominia call it"—"No," she shouted at the intercom, but Cicero had already said—"Garbage Day."

The martyr winced. English speakers and those with cochlear implants translating for them screamed in outrage; even Miki gave Dominia a hard look from the corner of her eye. She was almost through the door by the time the first shoe hit the back of her head. Then came another, and then, because she had to shelter Miki with her body, she took quite a few other strange objects. Nothing expensive like a book or a leather bag, but a lot of garbage like phones and tablets, cheap in the East where such devices were plentiful. The hard amalgamations of metal and glass bounced off her head and back to skid across the floor in a clatter almost sufficient to drown Cicero's words. "You know the one. All those poor people in Trimalchio's camps! Just because the old man was killed—which worked out for her in the end, anyway! No amount of gentle governance makes up for that war crime. She'd like you to think she's changed, but she hasn't. Not in almost a hundred years. That's right—this is only what she did in the last hundred years, to your friends and relatives in the Front…I don't need to remind my Japanese passengers of what she did to Tokyo, since your classrooms have reminded you since infancy. If any of you would like to shake the hand of such a famous military figure, I recommend you take the opportunity now, as she makes her way through Burlap Economy–class Cars C through A. And"—his tone, which had already been bright, cheered further—"those passengers interested in having a good time on the way to their destination are encouraged to visit the Dining Car, where I can assure you, you won't be disappointed. If you like dancing, good music, and fast friends, be sure to drop by. We are now five minutes from Kabul. As always: thank you for choosing the LRT."

Between the cars, Dominia tried to catch her breath, but Basil surged forward with purpose. This automatic door slid open to a far more savage booing and throwing of objects. Car B, having had time to coordinate their effort, assaulted her with wads of paper, phones, shoes, and once an old lady's umbrella. Their hate had been given time to boil like a teapot; now it whistled out at her, and she could only hurry along and take it, to her shame. It was all true. If she was honest, she deserved this, and worse. When Trimalchio was assassinated by South American Hunters for what he'd done by encamping those vast swaths of humans, the vengeful General Dominia's knee-jerk suggestion to her Father had been the mass slaughter of every last human in those camps. It wasn't so much that she cared about Trimalchio; she barely knew the man. But she had made the suggestion because it was what she thought her Father wanted to hear. They had not been real people to her at the time, those souls in the camps. There was no point in her life other than violence; therefore, the lives of others deserved to have the mere possibility of point violently wrenched from them. The awful, awful things she had done—the awful person she had been. After Nogales, she was forced to face it. And the day she started to face it, Cassandra showed up.

Did Cassandra change her? Or was her love of Cassandra mere manifestation of her own desire to change? Maybe she was still that same awful person she had been all those years before. The same shameful person who had enacted genocide with the flippant disrespect of a child kicking through a sibling's army men. She was ashamed, and that shame turned into fear to imagine what the last batch of humans would do to her.

Of course, as trepidation for the anger of the class A passengers melted into horror when the door opened to a terrible stillness, she considered that, for as bad as she was, she was far from the worst member of the Holy Family. Miki let out a terrible cry but couldn't shut her eyes against the gory sight because, of course, what proper dancer kept their eyes closed? All Dominia could do was shield the human's head against her shoulder while the dog went ahead, sniffing the blood dripping from the hands of slumped passengers and, once or twice, giving it a lick. The windows with their digital images flickered and buzzed, some of them broken and at least one passenger's skull attended by holographic birds that skipped forever between the same three positions. Grimacing, Dominia nudged Basil along with her boot, pushed him through to the baggage car, and walked the gangway suspended across the stacks of bags. Miki trembled, silent tears rolling down her cheeks at the horror of so much death. More death than the poor human had ever seen at once.

The door to the engineer's cabin was unlocked. In United Front trains, these areas were different, and the job of the engineer was more involved. The LRT required less effort in some ways and more effort in others: timing was the most urgent concern of a Light Rail engineer, followed by the watching of a great many scales, monitors, dials, and the Lamb knew what else. Dominia would have taken more time to look around were it not for the engineer slumped in the corner, and the sight of Cicero wearing the dead man's hat. While El Sacerdote looked over the dials in his stead, Dominia tried to lay Miki down and found her body yet moved with too much strength to be stilled, even bound and exhausted. Cicero spoke without looking from the security camera footage on the screen below the map.

"You know, sister, I didn't think they'd have the gumption to take me up on my offer. Now I think it rather a pity Lavinia and I exterminated Car A: they would have thrilled for a chance to detest you to your face! Ah, humans. They get so excited to be part of a mob."

"Why would you kill all those people, Cicero?" Annoyed, Dominia freed one of Miki's hands and slapped the empty cuff around a rail welded to the wall—presumably for when the engineer had to pull the brakes on a giant train traveling excess of six hundred miles per hour. While the human protested and her now-free arm began to engage in a series of choreographed gestures resembling semaphore, Dominia continued, "This is unnecessary. Bringing Lavinia…you could have just found me."

"Yes, well, no one planned to bother you on your train adventure, but unfortunately your…companion"—he offered a sneer in the direction of the prostitute—"was too canny when it came to René Ichigawa's sight. It became apparent that the whole Family needed to get involved. Lavinia will be collapsed with exhaustion by the end of this! Do you know the poor girl was shipped by jet to Almaty just to get on the train to Kabul! She didn't even have a look around. A fine first trip to the Middle States—and for such a pitiful reason. I must say, Dominia, I'm disappointed you would turn on a friend over something so simple as his being blackmailed by Father. That rules out a quarter of the adult martyr population from your pool of potential friends. Anyone in politics, for certain."

She barely listened, too busy rolling up her sleeves and emptying her gun of bullets. "I guess it wouldn't have been a concern if this particular blackmail didn't put me at risk. Sort of funny how that works."

"You always have been sensitive."

Before the butt of her Remington made contact with the back of Cicero's head, his hand caught hers with such speed that it seemed it had always been there, crushing her wrist. By this wrist, Cicero whipped her around to slam her head against the glass with an audible thud, but wasted time trying to aim her unloaded gun at her own head. When he'd made it click, she had managed to twist her knee hard up into his groin while her free hand landed a nasty jab to his throat. Hat askew, Cicero wheeled back with a noise that was as much a laugh as a wheeze; Dominia righted herself, then her fists.

"Trying to keep me from Kabul? From meeting Lazarus?" A few swift jabs were ducked by Cicero, who fought with as jolly an attitude as if the scene had occurred two hundred, three hundred, years before. Back when he still seemed Family. "You thought if you brought Lavinia on board, I'd be faced with a moral dilemma."

"I thought you would try to 'rescue' her," admitted Cicero with a laugh. He took a wide hook in the jaw but managed to fend off the trailing uppercut. While his hand lifted to his cheek, then came away in a fist that jabbed (almost) quick as the Hierophant's, he tutted. "Terrible shame you'll let those people in the Dining Car meet their ends. Such a terrible way, too. Although I may suggest Lavinia draw it out for them, give them time to disembark in Kabul, assuming we stop at all. Have you ever seen an entire *city* overtaken by mass hysteria? I mean, one the size of San Valentino?"

Once, twice, thrice, she tried to punch the smug light out of his eyes. Each time, she missed. Cicero glanced behind her with a smile while he countered her strikes, landing a few sharp jabs in her sternum while he said, "At last, here we are! But what a pity that it seems we'll overshoot it. I do so hope you weren't planning on meeting anyone—"

Was as much as Cicero got out before he was interrupted by the bark of a dog: the boxers paused to look in the direction of the noise. Basil, tail wagging, stood on his hind legs in all his canine glory. To Dominia's astonishment—and Cicero's humiliation—the border collie made defiant eye contact with El Sacerdote while, with a paw too deliberate to be accidental, he applied sufficient pressure to drag the brake lever down into gear.

"Did that dog"—was as much more as Cicero managed before Miki (sweet Miki!) used her one free hand, some understanding of the pattern of her dance, and the butt of Dominia's fumbled gun to crack the Holy Family member twice in the back of the skull. To the General's profound relief, Cicero fell, unconscious, to the floor.

"I could kiss both of you," said Dominia. Amid a great deal of squealing and grinding, the train sought for purchase, found it in the bottom of its translucent tunnel, and slowed as they emerged from their belowground track to the distant silver pool of Kabul's elaborate buildings. Even with the brakes on, the sweet vision grew larger, building itself out of the desert to swallow them in welcome. "But we don't have time."

She didn't have time because Cicero, as usual, was right. All they needed was for one dancer to disembark at Kabul. Then there could be a real problem on her hands, as well as the hands of the human officials running the city. She had to hurry: but the train offered a real advantage in distributing a cure. The intercom system. She was quick to find and activate its fuchsia button, which banished the stupid music by its happy chime. On air, as it were, Dominia cleared her throat. Outside, the buildings whipping by did so at an incrementally slowing pace. Through a great deal of research, the Holy Family had discovered one way to consistently cure the effects of Lavinia's hysteria, and enacting said cure made Dominia self-conscious. However, now was not the time to doubt her capacity for recitation.

"Shall I compare thee to a summer's day?" While Miki arched a skeptical brow that waggled in time with her dance, Dominia tried not to smile and stared out the windshield. "Thou are more lovely and more temperate. Rough winds do shake the darling buds of May, and summer's lease hath all too short a date."

It always seemed like magic. Lavinia's memetic virus could be definitively cured in even the weakest minds given sufficient exposure to quality art. To thinking art. The experience of reading or hearing Shakespeare was always effective, but afflicted humans had been given tours of the Louvre or, in less time-sensitive cases, brought to a Wagner opera to equal success. As Dominia recited sonnet eighteen, Miki's eyes brightened, and her body's movements stopped; as Dominia recited the second piece which popped into her head, Cassandra's favorite, which began, "When I do count the clock that tells the time, and see the brave day sunk in hideous night," the train slowed past an industrial district and cruised home into the shopping center that was its station. Miki's dancing and gnawing had stopped, and instead she laughed with joy. Basil, tail a-wag, put his forepaws upon the nearest window to bark at the people passing. Miki was her gauge for how the Dining Car looked without bothering to flip through the security feed, and by the time sonnet twelve was over, that living gauge was still. As their bodies swayed with the slowing train, Dominia unbuckled the belt around Miki's mouth and winced at the deep indents at the corners of her lips, about to apologize when the human exclaimed, "That is *bitchin'*, dude!"

"I don't mean to sound like a preachy three-hundred-year-old, but if more humans read Shakespeare rather than playing with their phones, Lavinia wouldn't have so much power." After accepting the gun from her friend, Dominia frowned at her brother. What was that about Cicero and fatalities?

"You should kill him now and save us trouble later," said Miki, but Dominia shook her head.

"I can't do it. If I did, I'd be everything they said I am. A terrorist. Then he'd really be a martyr"—she smirked—"and I would have no hope. They'd throw everything they have at me. The Hierophant loves Cicero too much." As did the Lamb, who was surely on the train. A shot into Cicero's head would cause the gun to backfire; or she would discover the remaining bullets were somehow blanks; or another improbable event would be elicited. El Sacerdote would live to fight another day.

"Who loves such a creep?"

"More people than you'd expect."

"Well"—Miki snatched the plundered bag to assess its contents with a petulant sigh—"I can't believe I'm saying this, but you were right to leave that luggage behind. All those years of clothes, though! Oh, my shamisen. My mother gave me that."

"I'm sorry, Miki, but—"

"It's fine." The girl shook her head before straightening her power suit and smoothing the bun of her hair. "Once we pawn all this stuff, there'll be enough money for twenty shamisen, and I know just the guy."

"And how will we get there?"

"The same way anybody gets anywhere," said Miki, laughing while she ducked back through the baggage car. "We'll get a cab."

XI

Welcome to Kabul

After all they'd endured, Dominia had not expected getting a taxi to be simple, but they were soon well away from the train thanks to a driver who didn't look twice at the disheveled, suitcaseless women and their dog. He had seen weirder tourists—probably ones more criminal, too, since he didn't bat an eye as Miki guided him, in brisk Arabic, to her choice pawnshop. Dominia, still buzzing with adrenaline, barely registered the city outside; yet, even to her distracted eye, how it resembled San Valentino as it was when she was young! The San Valentino with which she'd fallen in love, before she'd fallen in love with Cassandra. All the tight-clustered shops: so many shops that even the DIOX-I could not comprehend the many passing signs. There was the market district, disrupting like a cock's crow the sleepy morn with vendors shouting a chant to hypnotize listeners into purchase. (This, perhaps, was the meaning of "enchantment." No wonder she didn't trust Mass anymore!) There were the glittering spires and massive towers and all-over busyness of construction, of doing, of being and seeing. Kabul had stolen the achievement once held by San Valentino, and did so in a manner somehow more glorious. The sunlit mirage of a megacity glittered its defiance against the martyrs in a collective cry of humankind: *We are still here, we will never leave, we will never die.*

Something soft rested on her hand; the dog had lowered his chin.

"You are such a good boy," she said. Though the animal's tail wagged, the praise felt condescending for a creature so intelligent. This wasn't like shaking hands or rolling over. How did you thank a dog for stopping a train? How did a dog know to stop a train, and with such precision? *Was* Basil even a dog?

Now, that was a weird thought. She recalled the game show aboard the ship: its well-trained Shiba Inu, conditioned to press a random button. Basic Pavlov. But Basil seemed a mite more advanced. Her head hurt as she considered it, and she stoked memories of cell phones thrown at her skull, the hisses of the angry people, and the horrible thought that, if Miki was right, she was, in a way, having that experience eternally. Not that she didn't deserve it. Dominia glanced at the human, who had lapsed into silence with the driver to count the cash and coins in their bag.

Dominia licked her lips. "What he said about the Black Night—"

"I don't want to talk about it here." Soto didn't look up from her count.

"Does he speak English?"

"I don't think so, but, to be honest, I don't want to talk about it anywhere. 'Garbage Day'?"

The General could only bear to face the city. "It was a different time, I was a different person. When I believed—"

"That humans are trash? That Asian people don't deserve to live in the United Front?"

"That my Father was right," said Dominia helplessly. "That my Father was right, that he was close to God, and that if I did something like this, I could finally get his real approval. Maybe for five seconds of my life I would feel like I was better than my brothers and that I hadn't been martyred to be the black sheep of a dysfunctional Family."

Miki paused her counting with a sigh and a look not lacking in sympathy.

"Look"—the human folded the cash over and tucked it into her blouse—"all kids believe stupid things because of their parents. That's part of growing up: realizing half of what they taught you is flat-out contrary to the person you are. I already told you my old beliefs on sex. That was my mother's doing. She implanted those beliefs in me. The wronger and harsher our parents, the more powerful and pure we'll be when we overcome the beliefs they've ground into our souls. But that doesn't mean people around us now have to accept the people we were then."

That didn't make her feel any better. "What does the Lady teach about forgiveness?"

"Depends. Usually, that it comes from within. Have you forgiven yourself?"

"Not entirely."

"Then you can't expect me to forgive you, right?" At Dominia's frown, Miki patted her hand. "But I'll tell you: I had a great-great-great-uncle or something who was exterminated in the Black Night, and my mother talked about it like she'd been there to watch him die. She said that we could never forgive the martyrs for what they did to our family—so, based on her track record, I'm bound to forgive you, right?"

The General smiled as much as she allowed herself, though it was true. She hadn't forgiven herself for what she had come to view in recent years as crimes against humanity—no more than she forgave herself for her crimes against Cassandra. That, however, was a dangerous line of thought. After all, she couldn't see how she could ever forgive herself for Cassandra—but that was because grief for Cassandra provided a focus for the otherwise free-floating grief over her own existence, having killed so many.

A swinging pendulum of violence and shame, her thoughts. She shielded her face against the atomic dawn growing across the city and longed for shelter. Above the traffic noises sang birds who met the sun with greater cheer. There were ravens in Kabul, just like home. Just like everywhere she traveled in the world. Always ravens, and tidy onyx crows. A few sat upon a lamppost, flew off with that dawn. The skipping record of her mind produced the final lines of a poem she once loved, read a hundred thousand times, memorized with an eagerness surpassing even that for the Bard. The lines—to a little girl, so intriguing and beautiful—were, to Dominia, harrowing reminders of loss represented, for the ancient poem's protagonist, by its eponymous black bird.

And the Raven, never flitting, still is sitting, still *is sitting*
On the pallid bust of Pallas just above my chamber door;
And his eyes have all the seeming of a demon's that is dreaming,
And the lamp-light o'er him streaming throws his shadow on the floor;
And my soul from out that shadow that lies floating on the floor
Shall be lifted—nevermore!

The last time she'd heard that poem, during Cicero's annual Walpurgisnacht recitation, Cassandra had burst into tears well before the end, and Dominia had been forced to pursue her. The next night, she was dead. The silken, sad, uncertain rustling of each purple curtain that had once thrilled Dominia was now forever linked with Cassandra's pain, and her own. Well now did she understand that deep crest of loss attached to the word "nevermore." Behind her hand, she closed her eyes, and Cassandra's face, beautiful and pale, emerged: pale as the walls of the hospital room in those early nights of their romance. Cassandra had been in-patient since month five because her body fed itself to her baby too quickly to maintain her health without constant nutrients and supervision. She had to be given drips for fluids and for pain, but nothing stopped her nausea. In response to this, she was given blood transfusions from healthy martyrs—largely, her wife—and put on a steady diet of bland soups.

Her room, meanwhile, overflowed with Dominia's flowers as though it were a garden: a place of life and life's beginnings, rather than a place where most healed from illness or died trying. The hospital was in the mystical city of Venezia, the star of Mephitoli that had once been drowned by man-made climate change and that, resuscitated by the Hierophant's bottomless bank account, was a territory under control of the woman not yet promoted to Governess. Until giving up her Mephitolian territory on her promotion, she had an exquisite palazzo there: a paradisiacal Roman villa. She had not once visited it since coming into town. Instead, she would sit and talk to Cassandra, hold her hand, and droop to sleep in her chair while her lover watched some benign sitcom whose formulaic nature was designed to inspire maximum comfort (and, consequently, limitless boredom). Themes focused on family; Dominia always winced at that, because if she were in Cassandra's position, that subject would be the least desirable locus of thought. But Cassandra wanted to dream, and often Dominia awoke to find her wife still glued to the old television, shadowed eyes bright with better humor than the General could have felt. With one hand, she would hold Dominia's right, while her other clutched one of the many stuffed animals that littered the room, supposedly for the baby.

Then, one morning, something small but beautiful happened. Dozing Dominia, who had gotten a chance to slip off for a moment, awoke to Cassandra pulling on her arm with those eyes big and beautiful and wide and wet while her mouth cried the words, "She's alive, she's kicking, she really *is* alive!"

The General's hand leapt upon the ballooned stomach Cassandra couldn't have hidden had her pregnancy gone well enough for her to remain home. Yes, there she was. The kick of tiny feet, like someone thudding the opposite side of a great drum. Dominia was more awake then than she'd been for any battle. She stood with wild-eyed laughter: first, to listen to the sound with an ear to that soft stomach; then, to kiss her weeping wife. Her sobs indistinguishable from hiccupping laughs, Cassandra shut her eyes, leaned her head against Dominia's breast, and listened to the sound of her heart.

Then, as now, the General's eyes welled in silent tears. Then, she had been able to weep into Cassandra's hair. Now, she had nobody. She had a dog, who gazed at her with melancholy eyes. As if he knew her every thought. Basil wagged his tail at that silent supposition, or seemed to.

Let that be coincidence!

The absurdity of a telepathic—certainly sapient—dog distracted her enough that she lifted herself from out that shadow. Fine timing, too, for the cab driver pulled in front of a pawnshop. The district in which it was located seemed... less than kosher, given its general uncleanliness, multiplied by the density of wig shops and adult arcades to actual businesses. Her guess was this was spurred by the presence of the corner theater. Everybody who attended the Elsinore Theater Festival knew theaters attracted a strange group: in testament to this, the distant lampposts marking entry to the borough were enlivened by red flags, each dotted by a black lotus.

"Isn't that the Red Market symbol?" asked Dominia.

Miki, with reluctance, removed the cash wad from her bosom and slipped a few bills free for the cabbie. He doffed his hat while his passengers piled out and the prostitute said, "I guess it would seem pretty remarkable to you, that we have locations friendly to us. You—your Family is so stuck-up." They both had to dance around the word "martyrs" in public. Some English words were universal.

With a grimace for the slow-rising sting beneath the growing light of dawn, Dominia took shelter within the entrance of the shop. Miki made sure the cab door had shut itself and hurried to the store's security gate while the cabbie squealed off for his next mark. Though the prostitute's hand dipped into her purse, she stopped with a furious gasp of displeasure.

"That's right! Since you insisted on leaving my stuff there, I'm missing my key. God dammit." On instinct, Miki lifted her hand to lay a slap on the back of Dominia's head, but the General had been getting enough of that action and caught the human's wrist. Though startled, Miki whipped up a lascivious grin. "Learn to pick a better moment. People are going to start filling this street!"

"I'm not messing around." Dominia released the human, who slipped with a laugh down the alley on the building's west side.

"Neither am I. Come on!"

As the geisha mounted the shadowed fire escape with annoyance, Dominia and the dog followed along. The martyr asked, "Are you allowed to operate here?"

"Here? Technically, no, but the Market...exists, at least, as an entity. There are some Middle States even worse than your Father when it comes to prostitution; I've never even visited New Persia, which is too bad, since it looks like a beautiful country and I'd love to see Mecca. But we're fortunate that Kabul has gotten even to this point—like, Red Market girls can go to doctors and stuff and legally can't be turned away because of their profession."

"What a privilege," said the General, her tone dry as the air. Miki snorted.

"Right? Even toleration here isn't like where we'll be going."

"Which is?"

"Cairo—the real Babylon. At least, where the Lady's center of operations moved after Babylon's fall."

More words that would have made Lavinia wince but gave Dominia a twinge of naughty pleasure to remember murmuring to Cassandra that she was a hot little Babylonian harlot, which was some pretty filthy talk by martyr standards. To hide her flush, or at least reroute it, she gave a huff as though from exertion. "So it's still a real place? I thought it was just a legend that the Lady had a city."

"Of course it's a legend"—Miki glanced west as they emerged atop the roof—"as much as Jerusalem. But that's the difference between legends and myths. Legends have historical basis. The Lady has to live somewhere, man. She's real. And She keeps Her city a lot nicer than the Abrahamians' deadbeat dad."

Dominia always had a weird time with references to God, because the Triune was still so tied to her Father's mythos that she barely separated the original intentions of the deity from his corrupted variant. She compromised in her conversation with something nonconfrontational: "That's nice. I don't care how great whose city is, unless we'll find Lazarus there. Cairo, Jerusalem. Doesn't matter."

"You wouldn't find him anywhere near that garbage dump. It's controlled by the Hunters—they're its skeleton, at any rate, and the skeleton can't help but pollute the whole body when it's full of poison." Miki frowned at the shabby padlock sealing the rooftop door. After a glance at the martyr, the human stepped away and let the General's foot shatter the rusted knob. Miki sighed and shook her head.

"Why Kahlil spends as much as he does on girlfriends like me without paying a lick for security..."

They descended down the grimy stairs, the flat, unwashed oil smell that came with stores dealing in used goods so plaguing Dominia's sensitive martyr nose that she bumped into Miki when the human stopped at the first landing to rap upon the door. The reason for the lack of security was that Kahlil thought he had enough in the form of the assault rifle that he thrust in their faces on answering; but the tremble to the gun's barrel and the softness to the face behind his glasses, which somehow escaped the masculinity beards afforded other men, indicated the General had nothing to fear. Indeed, on recognizing Miki's scornful face, Kahlil lowered his gun with an exhalation of surprise, relief, and mild humiliation.

"Miki, what the fuck!" It came out in English; the boy glanced toward the martyr with one hand atop his taqiyah as if surprise's aftermath might blow it off. "I thought you said you'd call me. And come in through the front."

"It's a long story. And, I'm going to need money. Real, digital currency: none of this useless paper shit. What a pain it is to convert it to Redcoins! You do it for me. It'll make me look like I'm the saleswoman of the month when you transfer it all into my account."

As she spoke, she dumped the contents of the bag on the undusted coffee table askew in the center of the room. In an instant, Kahlil looked torn between blocking the martyr's way and attending to the wealth of objects awaiting his attention. After a careful glance past the man's head for the dusty bookshelves within, Dominia studied the nervous fellow and tried to make him comfortable. "Kahlil? Like Kahlil Gibran, right? Are you Lebanese?"

"No." His frown deepened as he was forced to make an intellectual connection with the martyr. "My mom liked his poetry. Come in, I guess, but if I see you move funny—"

"Why are you so hostile?" Miki collapsed into the couch and kicked off her business flats in a way that made both Dominia and their host give a tsk. "You knew I was bringing her! I told you. You probably saved the chat, even though it's supposed to self-destruct."

"I save everything you send me." The chestnut of his face further colored as he stooped to collect her shoes; Dominia's brow knit to see telltale signs of some poor schmo in love with a working girl, then smoothed it over when he righted himself. "I'm not sure I'm comfortable hosting her after what they've reported!"

"You're the last person who should be listening to rumors." Miki rubbed her palm over her left eye and snuggled in against the couch cushions, yawning as she spoke, worn out by her dance recital. "What are they saying she did? Because what she did was save a whole train of people, and possibly all of Kabul. That's pretty great, no matter what she did before." It was gratifying, that glance from Miki.

Outside the room, Basil politely wagged his tail. Kahlil, annoyed, said, "Well! Come on, bring him in. Look at the place, it's haram as it is. A prostitute and a martyr, what am I doing to myself…"

As he spoke, Dominia shut the door behind Basil, and Kahlil lowered his voice with a shifty look around. "I've got a couple of tenants downstairs, so keep quiet. They heard on the news that she massacred an entire car of people and were already up here talking about it— I haven't even had breakfast."

Miki, bless her, did the talking. "Car A? Cicero did that. I saw—well, I didn't see him do it, but Dominia couldn't have done it. Mostly because she was with me the whole time, and I was occupied."

"They said Cicero was sent by Iblis," said Kahlil, who spat in the corner at his use of the Hierophant's epithet. (Small wonder about his bachelorhood, if that was his custom.) "That he was to retrieve ad-Dajjal"—this was a new term to her, but it made Miki roll her eyes as he went on—"and was defeated by her sheer strength."

While deigning to stand, Miki crossed her arms and exclaimed, "Really, 'ad-Dajjal'? I thought that was what they called the Lamb."

Now Dominia spoke up, curiosity piqued. "What does it mean?"

"It's the anti-Christ in some branches of Abrahamian faith." Miki rubbed the bridge of her nose while triumphant Kahlil declared, "Everybody is saying it's her. The prophet Muhammad, peace be upon him, said ad-Dajjal would be blind in his right eye."

But that amplified Miki to full blast, the girl being versed enough in this particular branch of Abrahamianism to correct on her fingers, "'His' right eye, *and* it's a metaphor, *and* didn't your Prophet (*peacebeuponhim*) *also* say something about eyes that bulged like grapes? And all kinds of stuff about miracles, and whatever ridiculous nonsense? I haven't seen her do a miracle. As far as I've been able to tell, her greatest power is poetry recitation—and running Family therapy sessions, based on her conversation with Lavinia."

"Hey," tried Dominia, but Miki waved a dismissive hand. "You know you sounded like a social worker. Anyway, her special—skill, or whatever, is her ability in combat. She's not one of these crazy people like the rest of the un-Holy Family and other powerful martyrs who can do messed-up stuff to your head. I don't know why everybody acts like martyrs are so much better because they have talents. Humans have individual talents, too. Like you have a talent for being a real pain in my ass."

Dominia fell silent while Kahlil rebutted, "Me, in *your* ass!"

A sly smirk crossed Miki's face and Kahlil looked horrified, as if he had made a terrible mistake. Instead of making a joke that she was visibly pained to resist, Miki tapped her foot. "Yeah, a pain in my ass: since I brought you a whole bunch of new stock for your pawnshop, and you're also getting plenty of favors in exchange for the imposition."

Did she need to cover the dog's ears? Was this inappropriate for Basil? His fuzzy mouth opened in a canine grin that turned into a yawn, and she was unconvinced that the yawn was not put in place to cover his reaction to her thoughts. Lamb! She'd become so paranoid! Dogs, reading her thoughts, hell. Sapient dogs, hell. She was starving from the trip, or tired from the fight, or both.

Dominia wandered to the cramped and unclean kitchen while the humans quarreled. In the dirty refrigerator, she discovered the pleasant surprise of several pints of blood. Miki had thought of everything—or maybe Kahlil had. Either way, the dog left the living room to prance down the hall once she turned around. She followed, blood bag in her hand like a juice box, and found Basil circling a spot on the floor of a guest bedroom crammed with two sorry twin beds and a lot of crap. A vanity with a broken, inexcusably dusty mirror once very nice; a nightstand with a crooked drawer she wasn't interested in trying to fix. As she fell into one of the mattresses, the dog sneezed at the dust kicked up from the bedclothes, and Dominia noted that the singular window was sealed against police raids.

She had a feeling it had been like this before they were on their way. The Hunters, who were also known in this area as the Caliphate, al-Siyadun, and al-Saalihin, (or, to their opponents, al-Mawta), posed huge political and legal danger to the states they inhabited. It wasn't enough for them to act as vigilantes who killed any stray martyr wandering into the area. The official position of the Hunters was that the only acceptable course of action, from a moral standpoint, was for human governments to wage total war upon all martyrs until one side or the other was destroyed to the man. Any government not fighting active war against the species was opposed to the human race and worthy of overthrow. Their presence in South Africa rendered that entire continent highly unstable, and although areas farther north were at greater risk of playing host to the odd tourist martyr (or even, in the Hierophant's friskier years, an invading army from Europa), living there was still a safer bet than anyplace south or east. The Hunters were scattered across Africa and the Middle States, and though they elicited much turmoil in the region, they also struggled to maintain reasonable foothold. Consensus was that it was better for a human to risk being eaten by somebody on vacation to see the Fertile Crescent than to allow the Hunters power. Martyr tourists were far more reasonable and predictable than the Caliphate.

All this made Dominia wonder again what she was doing there: terrorist organizations aside, every human city held for her limitless danger. It was true that the presence of the Hunters in the Middle States put the region at risk, but since signing the Constitution in 1260, the union had held strong against both martyrs and extremists. The States, though independent and often in disagreement, were able to maintain order enough to serve as stronghold for generations of Abrahamians driven from Europa. This harmony was a defense to support spiritual humans as much as a move against the Hierophant, who had bloodlessly claimed the former human state of Italy, and changed its name, a mere ten years before. Often, he had tried the boundaries of the Middle States, and even after they had banded together, he still sometimes sidled up against them. He forever awaited the time he might penetrate their boundaries. One thing that kept him out was the sun, but if he had means to blacken it, no pocket of civilization would be free of martyr control. Then, the humans would have no choice but to turn to the Hunters for help.

That assumed, of course, there could still be a world after the sun went black. Did the blackening of the sun not mean the death of Earth? She had once, long ago, read the story of an unwilling man, a torturer, who journeyed to renew the sun of his world, and became a man of God: but there could be no renewal here. Not of this world. Further, if Miki was right, and the blackening of the sun meant the death of Lazarus, and the creation of a new iteration of the universe, did it matter if it, everyone, everything, died? Hadn't they all done it before? Hadn't Cassandra died before? Hadn't her baby, also, died before? Died twice over each iteration: once with her mother's martyring, and once on her own, not long after those delayed first kicks. Not long after Dominia, in equal maternal joy at tangible evidence of life, rushed to furnish a former guest apartment in the palazzo with a gilded crib, and a real ivory changing table, and sweet little cashmere socks, and far more stuffed animals than even comforted the sick mother through each day's restless sleep. The kicking continued, night by night, and Cassandra's nausea worsened: but then, at the apex of that sickness, the kicking stopped. Cicero was on a plane from Europa that same night. The next, he sat at Cassandra's bedside in the midst of another ultrasound, lips narrowed in a frown behind his mustache while the expectant mothers asked in stereo, "What, what is it, what's wrong?"

"Cassandra"—the words rolled from his lips after an agonizing moment of thought—"I am sorry, but this is one of a great many reasons why this sort of thing is ill-advised."

Pale Cassandra began to sit up, only to be pinned by Dominia. The General demanded, "What are you talking about?"

"The baby's heart has stopped."

The silence carried its own sound: a ringing experienced by both open-mouthed women. Cassandra, of course, felt the weight of the words more intensely than Dominia ever could. Cicero went on explaining, "It is too early to tell, of course, but I would suspect it to be a result of the protein's interaction with her particular anomaly."

"What do you mean, 'it's too early to tell'?" Numbed by the notion that her wife's pain had been for nothing, Dominia realized the question had come from her own lips once Cicero looked at her.

"I mean—unpleasant as this may be—your wife shall have to carry the fetus to term."

"Oh, no, please," Cassandra now forced herself upright, tears filling her eyes. "Please, can't something be done? Oh, God, if she's dead, I can't—I can't, I can't, I can't." She was unable to vocalize the words "carry her to term," her lips and cheeks wet with the tears of a rising panic attack. Dominia pushed onto the bed and folded heaving Cassandra into her arms.

"Can't you induce and let her deliver it early? Won't it calcify?"

"We are on the barest cusp of eight months now, Dominia." As her brother slid away and packed his equipment, wailing Cassandra was forced to bury her face in Dominia's breast if anyone was to hear. Cicero continued as if deaf. "Blood clots would be the biggest risk facing your wife, but the protein would never allow that to occur in a martyr. These situations clear up after two weeks, but if she requires the full four to come to term, we should not be alarmed."

In the end, of course, it took five weeks. Five miserable, painful weeks of Cassandra knowing each evening, each morning, that her baby was dead inside of her. That she would have to give birth like it lived. When the day arrived, there was a strange, almost complete disinterest on the part of the staff in seeing to her, as if she had disappointed the nurses by her failure to keep the baby alive. It was far from her responsibility, of course. Neither would Cicero arrive in time for the labor; a replacement doctor had to oversee, and in the midst of all the disinterest and confusion, despite repeated pleas from both Cassandra and Dominia, by the time said replacement arrived, he announced it was too late to give an epidural. Cassandra had to deliver the corpse naturally.

All the screaming, and the blood, and the joyless, alien silence of the staff. The silence of the baby. The silence of Cassandra when her screaming stopped and she slipped into unconsciousness, a blissful break for which Dominia was glad when she saw the infant. She had always been skeptical, when people—usually humans—referred to sleeping children as "perfect" or "angelic." Yet, in that second, she understood. A perfect porcelain cherub: wrapped in a pink blanket, then shipped away. Oh, Cassandra's face when she learned she wouldn't be able to see her baby, that she was already being prepped for burial. How she cried, and cried, and carried on with her crying while her breasts wept, also, with gifts for an unreceiving baby.

"I keep feeling like she's alive," repeated Cassandra, sobbing into her hand, into Dominia's neck, into the pillows of her recovery bed. "I keep forgetting. Oh, God, I wish I could hold her."

Once, Dominia thought she could never comprehend her wife's heartbreak; now, she only hoped hers would not take ninety years to fade.

XII

Filling in the Gaps

Wherever Dominia went, she seemed to end up in the hands of medical professionals. Funny, in an unfunny way. Twenty-four hours after arriving in Kabul, she lay in the chair of a dentist with a booming laugh, a Nigerian accent, and a face that filled her vision like a great blob rendered square by the lines of that same DIOX-I that tagged him "Doctor Tobias Akachi." The dark flesh of his face left his perfect smile all the whiter, and Dominia found herself thinking of the man as a talking set of disembodied teeth. "You know, I've never worked on a martyr before! What a crazy world we live in. But people's mouths are all the same, no matter who they are."

When was the last time she'd been to the dentist for more than a cleaning? When she got her artificial teeth, she supposed. She barely remembered the occasion, since, at the time, she'd been put under anesthetic and had woken up with a pair of fangs. Her Father had done her a favor by yanking them out; she increasingly felt toward them what a fortysomething businessperson felt toward a regrettable lower back tattoo. Since they were gone, the step of removing them was saved. She'd ought to write a thank-you note.

"I'm surprised you were willing to see me at all," she admitted when the man swiveled to examine the x-rays of her mouth, fine aside from absent cuspids.

"You mean after the train? Miki told me you saved those people!"

"And the destroyed hospital in Japan, and the ship, and…"

"I know bullshit when I hear it." The man chortled in a booming bass while he rolled from her vision to root through a tray of tools. "Even if you were a terrorist, I mean…the whole hospital? Come on."

"That's what I've been saying." She felt motivated to talk by the vague sense of dread instilled upon finding herself at the mercy of anyone, no matter how friendly; Cicero's fault, to be sure. "It's so over the top. Don't people think it's absurd?"

"Always easier to assume the other person is wrong and that our own opinions are right—that there is no conspiracy and that mankind is fighting a battle against itself, instead of playing a game for God."

Beyond the window, Kabul glowed in a neon rainbow by even those earliest hours of the evening. "I thought 'God' was 'Allah' in these parts."

He rolled back, now holding a device resembling a mechanical pencil, mouth hidden behind a blue mask. "Only when my patients discuss Him. I am an English-speaking Christian, myself."

These Abrahamians! Jewish, Christian, Muslim. You couldn't tell them apart for trying—at least, martyrs couldn't—yet they were touchy about getting mixed up. Their petty distinctions made little sense to her, and this must have been communicated by the near roll of her eyes as the dentist opened her jaw and began using the small water drill. Though less cruel than its prehistoric metal counterparts, it still made her wince deeper into the uncomfortable chair. As he cleaned, the dentist continued above the whine of water, maybe imagining her responses.

"You probably don't know much of our faiths, soldier as you are, but we Abrahamians are quite different from one another. Even Christians are different from one another! You know that, don't you?" She tried to nod, but he carried on, using another implement to vacuum spittle from her gums while he lectured. "As it happens, none of us used to get along. Even before your Father showed up, and for many generations after, there was much struggle about 'the right faith.' That was what helped him rise to power. But, as he took control of North America, we realized we all fought the same enemy; and when we were abandoned in the Rapture by the wealthy and the elite, a new era of cooperation began on Earth."

Ah, yes. Dominia had been so young those nights: not quite hopeful for the future anymore, but not as bleak a woman as she would become. Martyrs had been open about their presence for almost seventeen thousand years at the time of Dominia's human birth as Morgan, but the species had begun to close their iron grip decades before that fateful day in which the wealthy fled. This had mostly to do with the failed attempt to conquer Japan, regarded as a victorious maintenance of the boundaries of the UF in much the same way that the harrowing destruction of Moscow and the inhabitability of much of Russia was forever regarded as an opportunity to experiment with terraformation technology—and further evidence that martyrs were a cruelly maligned, unfairly detested people.

He had given society so much, the Hierophant: by the time Russia's terrain was at all recovered, he donated the many technologies established in its healing alongside tech developed for asteroid miners to support the first living colonies of Mars. These were quick to die, of course, but every generation after died slower; and while humans on Earth were busy fighting among themselves and keeping their heads down to avoid Hierophant attention, Martian humans slaved to make their planet habitable. By the time 1700 rolled around, it was in impressive shape; come 1744, the wealthy multitudes, whose human life spans shielded them from the knowledge that the Hierophant had begun the terraforming effort in the first place, were ready to flee to the stars. Her Father had gladly let them go: more land for him. The impoverished of Earth, however, hardly realized they had been abandoned until too late. They seldom realized anything until too late. As Dr. Akachi pointed out, this was because they had been under the thumb of the Devil.

"You Father would like nothing more than for us to continue the old ways—persecuting one another while crying over our own persecution. So, we have done the opposite, and brought ourselves together!"

When Dominia gagged at her ill-advised attempt to speak, the dentist removed his hands enough to let her sputter, "Except the Hunters," before he dove back to work.

"Well, I can tell *you*, miss, that their mouths look like yours. Maybe they would like their mouths to look different! But no. The same. Only"—he dropped his voice to a conspiratorial whisper—"they are bad about brushing. And try getting one to floss. Gum disease! It's rampant with that sort. Which reminds me—are you being sure to brush your gums? You'd ought to take your time. I notice you haven't been in the habit lately."

"I've been busy," she said, her tone sufficient to tan a hide. The man laughed.

"So I understand. This process takes a few weeks, but Miki told me we do not have that luxury. I can see why she insists it needs doing. Rather indiscreet, eh? If one of the Caliphate saw your missing teeth, you would be good as dead. We'll have to install both your titanium implants and the crowns that lock into them, all four in the same appointment. I don't care for that, even if it can be done on a martyr, but we have no choice. I'll still need a day to prepare the crowns; those, I can print at my apartment. Are you comfortable waiting that long?"

"Do I have a choice?"

With a hearty chuckle, he lowered his mask and offered a cup of pink mouthwash. "Of course! You have many choices. You could go running in the street and get hit by a car. Fine a choice as any. You could go home. Or, you could choose to carry on. And since it seems to me like you're making that last choice, I have to say, I am pretty impressed."

"Thanks," said Dominia, who fell silent as the dentist carried on.

"We'll put you under light anesthetic, and when you come out of it, you'll be good as new!"

At this statement, her brain replayed the cartoon nurse's assurance that her eye installation would be, "Just like going to the dentist." As Tobias turned away, she snatched his arm. His understandable wince passing by, the man met Dominia's blazing eyes with curiosity.

"Can you remove DIOX-Is? Or—uninstall them, I guess."

The dentist regarded her face, his own a cautious mask in the wake of his fright. "I could, but I hardly see why you would want such a thing. After going to all the trouble of having it installed…isn't that why you were in the hospital?"

"Yes, but"—she considered how unwise it was to confess to the man, whose face was labeled by an azure box, that the Hierophant may have watched her every movement because he owned her eye—"it's a terrible distraction. The features are outweighed by—everything. The ads, for example."

"You would rather be blind in one eye than see a few targeted commercials!" The earnestness in her expression faltered the humor in his. With gravity, he pressed, "Have you given this much thought?"

"Well, no…this idea came to me right now. But I hate having this thing in my head. And I hate how I got it. I hate how I look in the mirror, and it looks like my old eye, but I know that it's not my old eye. It's not even *my* eye. I didn't buy it. The refugee operation provided it pro bono. Best case, it's the company's. Worst, Cicero's, or the Hierophant's. I don't know; I'm not sure how they manage to get into my device's software if it's not somehow leased to them. It was awful when he installed it, and"—she took a sharp breath and loosened her grip on the dentist—"I want it taken out."

Brows knit in sympathy, Tobias removed his gloves to pat her hand. "Please give it more consideration," he said while rising from his seat. "I do not know how comfortable I am with this idea, but we can decide when you return for your implants. It is possible. I have done it before, for patients with ill-functioning, jailbroken DIOX-Is or small cyborgans who could not afford to go to a real clinic. But when there are so many who would kill for such sight, Miss Mephitoli, would you throw it away?"

It was a question she'd asked herself for a few nights, since before the train, or before Kabul. The DIOX-I was invaluable for purposes of battle, but the merest possibility that her Father might use it to record her comings and goings made her ill. What she had said about the ads was true, too. As she emerged into Kabul's yet-warm evening with Miki, who had been slouched over a dented magazine e-reader in the waiting room chair, the right side of Dominia's vision populated buildings with digital billboards not present in her sinister eye. Wholesale liquor, cheap (virus-loaded) pornography, cigarettes, fitness tips, new books, plus more weird spam about weight loss and digitally altered pictures than she absorbed. And try to tell the digital ones from those *actually* there! It made her crazy. She focused on the dentist, and asked Miki, "Where did you find that guy?"

"Oh, he's an old client. Actually, I met him through Kahlil when we were having a sandwich one day with this super-hard bread, and—long story, anyway I needed a fake tooth, and 'Bias hooked it up. No money down."

"Is there anyone in Kabul—in the world—you haven't fucked?"

In response to that, Miki gave her ass a shake, brandishing like a weapon the short-shorts purchased while Dominia had slept that day. "Only you, *senpai*."

"I thought a *senpai* was supposed to be a kind of mentor." The martyr lifted her blushing face to the light-polluted sky.

"Well, aren't you? You're my upperclassman in the school of life, *oba-san*."

Dominia cleared her throat as Miki wandered in the direction of a food stand. "You're going to blow our cover if you keep calling me things like that."

"And you're going to blow our cover if you don't try to look like you're having fun. Come on! So serious." After jabbering in Arabic with the huge man running the food stand, both laughed, and he assembled a falafel for Dominia while Miki said, "Eat that, you'll lighten up."

To her credit, the falafel was damn fine: even though it lacked the basic nutritional components which Dominia's body required, it didn't lack the taste requirements. She found herself overjoyed to eat after her procedure, since taste was the final sensory frontier when it came to DIOX corporation's replacements. Taste was still pure. Taste, unlike sight and sound and even touch, was not yet marketable by their standards. But once the first super-tongue or digital nose was on the market, rest assured, everyone would be a gourmand in the way everybody was trilingual thanks to audio implants.

She was crotchety, Dominia. Another reason she so missed Cassandra. Her wife had been there to soften her, to make the General seem kinder than she was. But there was also something to be said for the leveling influence of her new friend. Miki wasn't interested in soothing Dominia's ego or making her feel like a good person. Miki was interested in...being Miki, the martyr supposed. Even now the girl bopped down the street while savaging the sandwich whose cardboard tray she had already trashed.

"Hey," said Miki through her full mouth, as if confirming Dominia's thoughts while, with a free, un-sauced hand, she gestured to something down the block. "It's the Hie-Race! I didn't even think about it."

Squinting and then troubled (and disoriented into closing her good eye) to find the DIOX-I zoomed in for her, Dominia watched a crew of yellow-geared workers setting up barriers and signs that translated to state that the street would be closed the next morning. "The what?"

"It's a thing they do here. Like a special marathon where people dress up in costumes and stuff to make fun of—uh." Miki coughed as she almost choked on her bite. "Your folks."

At seeing that Dominia's expression was not offended so much as flabbergasted, Miki felt free to continue. "It's super fun! We have to lighten the mood somehow, right? And this city can be so uptight—it's like, half serious tech businessmen and a quarter religious families. It's up to the last quarter, people like us, to cheer them up, so we do it with fun things like this!"

"'People like us,'" repeated Dominia. Miki giggled.

"Yeah, 'us'! Weirdos! Anyway"—the human turned away as Dominia caught a chilling glimpse of chrome upon a rooftop overseeing the preparations—"we should head back. I'm—"

"You go." The General pushed her trash into Miki's hand, oblivious to the girl's noise of protest. "I'll meet you there."

"Hey"—the human waved after her—"where are you going?"

There was no delaying. She knew the Lamb when she saw him; it didn't matter how far away. Those horns were distinct. Always the first things she saw of him. Often, the only things that stuck in her memory after a conversation with him. Warm words and loving reassurances all got lost in his horns. Or in the arrival of Cicero. But until then, those times when, sent to her room for inability to adapt to her new reality, she had wished her windows unbarred to accommodate suicide— Ah, how often he appeared in her doorway! He'd sit at the edge of her bed, his knee a pillow to her tear-stained face, as she struggled to make verbal sense of the new and violent shift in moral expectation. She would try to explain how it made her feel every time she was forced to eat human flesh, struggling to articulate how awful it was that she wasn't allowed to treat humans like people; more often, she burst into a new crest of tears and explained that what hurt her most was the loss of her parents, and the thought that they were in the world without her.

"I'm sure they think the same about you," the Lamb told her, gentle, patient. Or: "Just because you can't be friends with the humans working around the castle doesn't mean you have to be cruel to them the way Cicero is." And: "Nobody reasonable likes eating human, sweetheart."

"Daddy does," she would sometimes accuse. "And Cicero, and the people who follow them around at parties."

"True; but they're exceptions. I don't like eating human. Thankfully, I don't have to."

"Then why do I have to do it?"

"Because that's the way your Father and Cicero decided the world would be when they released the protein to the public. It's important for you to be able to eat if you can't receive my blood some week, for some reason; and you'll be miserable if all you're having is my blood at services. Trust me."

"But we could make fake people, in labs, the way they make beef and poultry? I read in school—real school—"

"Martyr school is real school."

She hadn't been in the mood to argue that point. "People used to eat cows and chickens, too. Then they were rescued because people developed fake meat that was like the real thing. Why can't we do that with people?"

"They tried that with people," explained Elijah, "which is something you'll learn in fake school during next year's history class, but I digress... it didn't work, is my point. Eating lab-grown people was good as starving."

"But why? Why does it have to be this way? Why does everything have to be so violent and ugly?"

"Because that's the way the world is. This physical world."

"It doesn't have to be," she insisted at the time, eliciting a wan smile from the Lamb.

"Please, don't ever think otherwise."

"But why didn't you stop them from releasing the protein? You were there."

"And so was your Father. But even if he hadn't been there..."

"You'd still let Cicero push you around." The flippant accusation gave way to immediate guilt, but she refused to take it back, and he didn't make her. The hand petting through her hair never even stilled.

"I didn't stop them because, once they infected me with the protein, I saw all things. All possible things. Not in a way I could control as much as I can now, which isn't much. I saw that if we didn't release the protein, someone would, and I wouldn't be able to do anything about it that time. But, most of all, I saw you."

"You did?"

"Yes. And I couldn't find it in me to stop him when he would someday give me a daughter like you, right?"

What a stupid reason. She knew at the time he had only been trying to comfort her. In the unit that was her Family, the Lamb may well have been the good cop: but he was still a cop. And wherever the Lamb was, Cicero was never far behind, possessive as any psychopathic husband. Between that quality, and the Lamb's duty to be carted from church to church throughout martyr territories and symbolically sacrificed every Noctisdomin—rather close to a literal sacrifice, which, given a martyr's healing abilities, always recovered itself by Noctismartin—the brothers rarely separated in body or in mind. If the Lamb was given the courtesy of time with his daughter, or the privilege to comfort her without interruption, it was because Cicero willed it.

Cicero, or the Hierophant. This last notion arose as, atop the fire escape of the building whereupon she'd seen the glitter of his horn, her stomach lurched to see not just the Lamb but, pleased and dapper as ever, her Father. Beetle eyes glittering, he assessed her head to toe and crowed, "My girl! At last! Here you are. How happy I am. I do so love your new hair. Did you do it yourself?"

"Here I thought you'd hate it. And"—she recalled the broadcast watched aboard the train a few nights before—"that you were back in Kronborg."

"Oh, for a jot—but I had to catch up to the Family at some point. I can't leave your welfare in their hands, or vice versa. A man has to be responsible for his child; any parent is responsible for their child. Cassandra knew that very well."

Lamb, keep her temper in check. "Starting early, are we? I thought you'd try soft-balling before you riled me up."

"I'm sure you know well as I do that the time for soft-balling passed—if there ever was such a time for you, my hard-hearted daughter. What trouble you make of yourself! As if you did not spend nearly a hundred happy years as Governess of the Front."

"I wouldn't say 'happy.'"

"Neither would Cassandra."

"You don't know anything about our lives."

"I know enough. Its rocky start and questionable end, and quite a few moments in between. Or are you forgetting that I was as devoted to Cassandra, my spiritual daughter, as you were to Cassandra, your wife?"

How sick she was of his childish jabs in her open wound. Her eyes narrowed at the silent Lamb, whose expression remained placid as ever. "And here you are as usual, letting him say whatever comes into his head while you look sorry for yourself."

"Sorry for you," corrected unflappable Elijah.

"We are not here to abuse your emotions." The Hierophant crossed to lay a hand upon the Lamb's shoulder. "We are here to plead that you come home."

"I won't. You would do anything for Cicero, wouldn't you?" This, to Elijah, who did not respond as Dominia placed an instinctive hand upon a diamond not there. "I would do anything for Cassandra. I would die to see her live again, to make up for the mistakes I made. Letting these awful things happen to her. Letting her die."

"You didn't let her die," the Lamb assured her, but her eyes welled up in furious tears.

"I did. I failed her."

"You are failing yourself, my girl," said the Hierophant, not unkindly. "You would throw away your whole existence—three hundred years of a well-built life—to spend time with humans of the worst sort, in pursuit of a false hope."

"Lazarus is not a false hope." The General was weak in her conviction on this matter but unwilling to admit that she was even potentially wrong. "I've already been brought back from the dead once. So have you both. Probably," she added, with respect to her Father. "Is it that insane to think it can happen again?"

The Hierophant's tone remained oh-so gentle. "All things are as God made them in this world, my daughter; the river of time will never flow backward. The protein is the gift of eternal life, and those who would reject that are rejecting God and life, as did Cassandra."

"Cassandra rejected you," Dominia insisted. "You and your hideous world."

"It breaks my heart to see you so wounded by her cruelty that you cannot admit who is to blame for your poor wife's death. Will you fight me to the end over mistakes you made? Over your own choice to hand your heart to a stranger who abused your good nature?"

"Why don't you kill me here? It would be quicker for all of us. Cleaner, too."

With his thinnest smile, the Hierophant lifted his eyebrows. "And force you to miss the marathon? That would be a shame. We intend to meet you there; there, you'll deliver Lazarus."

Oh! Now, that was funny. Laughing, the General covered her mouth at her own surprise on the abrupt noise, and exclaimed, "Give you Lazarus? And why would I do something like that?"

With a sympathetic glance to the Lamb, the Hierophant shook his head. "Perhaps, my dear, you had ought to tell her why we have come by; we will argue ourselves in circles, trying to reason without getting to the bottom line. You know how she can be."

"Your Father brought me here to tell you the probabilities, Dominia."

"He brought you to scare me back home."

"He brought me to tell you that, no matter how long this continues, or what direction events flow, the ending is the same. Your death. I have seen that this is true." Bracing herself against his words as though against a physical onslaught of truth, the General let him carry on. "Cassandra won't come back. She can't. Even if she weren't cremated, it wouldn't be possible. You're throwing your life away."

"It's a lie." Dominia covered her eyes, then shifted to her ears. "It's a lie, and I won't hear it."

"You will die, my child," assured the Hierophant, his expression solemn. "You will die, and I will be the one to kill you. I do not want that."

"Can't dirty your holy hands."

In the thud of a single heartbeat, the Hierophant appeared centimeters before Dominia: she had not seen him move. He did that now and again. Uncanny every time, as though he teleported through the air so the object of his prey might spend their last seconds in terror. As this terror passed and the General was in the process of stepping away, he caught with a stonelike hand the fist raised in self-defense; but, rather than tossing her to the ground to initiate a boxing match as might have been Cicero's aim, the Hierophant pulled her into his arms and crushed her with the force of his embrace.

"Please think on this, my girl." He relaxed his hold enough to take her shocked face in his hands and tilt it toward his, so she was forced to see his earnest expression. "We have brought this offer out of love. It will not come a second time. If you continue down this path, you shall be an enemy, not just to man- and martyr-kind alike, but to your own immortal soul. I could not bear to see you throw that away."

Every word she spoke caused an unnerving tension of her face against the grip of his hands. "You can already see me doing everything, anyway. I'm surprised it matters to you what I do when you can see through my eye. I'm getting the thing taken out. Not that that's news to you."

"So I have seen, I do admit. But I wouldn't worry about that. Don't you understand, my daughter? I run Halcyon, I provided the technology for the terraforming of Mars—I *am* the DIOX corporation."

Startled, she at last managed to yank her face out of his hands. "The CEO?"

"Answers to me. I would never publicly reveal my position at the top of the corporation, my dear; not without good reason. What trouble it would have caused me if you knew that going in! But now, you understand the futility of all of this. The *pain* it causes me! So many people in this city have augmentations—praise God, for, to lay eyes upon my dear daughter, I must steal their sight! To hear you speak, I must invade their ears!" As her mind raced, the Hierophant made a pained noise, and covered his shutting eyes. "Oh, my child. If you knew the agony this causes me! Your soul—your poor soul."

As those manipulative tears sprang in skyward-turning eyes, the General was able to dart to the fire escape. When she turned to see if he pursued, her Father had disappeared without so much as the scrape of his shoe upon the rooftop. The Lamb, still there, lingered but a few seconds to study his daughter's expression; then he, too, abandoned Dominia by exiting through the building's door with a harsh metallic slam.

XIII

Trust / Issues

What a fool she'd been! The owner of the DIOX Corporation. Of course. Wasn't he everywhere? Dominia's stomach remained rancid all the way back to pawnshop, a path she couldn't have recalled if the DIOX-I didn't light the way with a floating aureolin line that plunged ahead to decapitate passersby. So, the Family was traveling together. Good to know. Also good to know that Cicero was at greater length than arm's reach from the Lamb, which put a skip into every third or fourth step. Had Miki made it home? Dominia couldn't risk trying a call. Who knew how much data was always being transmitted to the Hierophant at a given moment? Who knew what she would find when she returned to Kahlil's? Maybe Soto was already dead, along with their host.

Even after all these years, her Family terrified her. That was why the idea of a marathon designed to poke fun at them didn't stir her offense: she needed it more than any human did. Her Father, in particular, was always popping up to startle her. What had just happened was such a common occurrence that she should have grown to anticipate it.

Take, for instance, the day the Hierophant visited Cassandra after the disastrous birth of her child. Dominia would never forget the jolt when, tray of food and coffee cautiously balanced in her hands, she nudged open the door of her wife's hospital room to find the Hierophant holding her Cassandra's delicate hand in his big, spidery own. The yet-new martyr choked on her tears.

"I was so hopeful. I believed so much— I believed, I believed."

"I know, my dear. I know. But there are times when belief is not enough. Times when the will of God, mysterious as it is, must be accepted. All tragedies that arise do so to strengthen the faith of Man."

"My faith is so shaken. My faith—"

She hiccupped and stopped herself to follow the Hierophant's eyes as he acknowledged Dominia's presence. Grieving Cassandra looked right through her, released a sob, and ducked her head to study the Holy Father's hands. "I wish I had never done this. I love Dominia, but for this? For all of this…"

The sting! It was natural to be hurt, Dominia told herself, as natural as it was for Cassandra to think such a thing. Her gentle eyes, after all, had skipped over the lunch tray. While she put away the offending human-based meal and lowered upon her wife's bedside, the Hierophant tutted.

"That is no way to think. The Lord called you to His service for a purpose. No martyr is expendable. No martyr is without value. Your baby"—the Hierophant bent to kiss the back of Cassandra's hands as she burst into tears on the words; she had to be consoled by both the Holy Father and her wife before she was able to accept his repetition of the phrase—"your baby did not suffer, although you did. But through her absence, and your suffering, how close you've come to God! How blessed you are with a loyal wife, a loving Family, a wealth and privilege unheard of by any but those few I call my true children."

"But I want my baby." Cassandra's lips trembled with the same suppressed sobs wracking her shoulders. "I just want her to be alive. I wanted to name her 'Lucy.' Is that a stupid name? It was his mom's name." Her eyes met Dominia's red-ringed own with guilt, but the General stroked her hair.

"It would have been cute," the future widow assured her grieving wife. "A sweet name, for a sweet girl."

Something in this paused Cassandra's tears. Dominia felt exposed until the woman shut her eyes and said through trembling lips, "I wish you would hate me."

Alarm plunged from the top of her skull to the base of her spine. How was she to feel on such words? At her (perhaps sharp) demand to know why Cassandra would say such a thing, the woman lamented, "Because then I'd have no reason to live, and I could die. I could be at peace, alone, with him."

"What was his name?" asked the Hierophant.

The query calmed Cassandra by its tone enough to say, "Ben—Benedict. He was also—he—" Cassandra trailed off, unable to bear the look on the General's face as poisonous recognition flowed in. "He was in the military, too."

Yes. Benedict Miller, with a mother named Lucy. She remembered that name like all the names of the remembered dead (easier before the DIOX-I revealed so many). But Benedict, she remembered better than the others. The Battle for the Reclamation of Mexico was a fresh wound in those nights; her time spent as a POW still stuck in her teeth like the grit of Nogales.

If the suspicion that she had killed Cassandra's lover had ever crossed her mind before, it was tucked beneath more relevant thoughts. Confronted plainly, the Holy Father's black eyes drilling into her from Cassandra's other side in that cramped hospital room, Dominia understood at last the depth of her responsibility. The nature of her bond with her wife. What strength of spirit it took for Cassandra to love her at all, even if, at first, she'd but pretended! Ben Miller: the young, impromptu soldier and even more impromptu jailer she had befriended, then used like a doorway by murdering and escaping in the midst of a momentary lapse of the human's judgment. His death had bothered her more than the average because he was a young guy shipped from home to serve as backup, and because she had discovered on his person a photo of his mother. Humans had an ugly habit of sending kids to war: especially in emergency situations, which the Reclamation had been. It had been a dark fortnight for Dominia, and for many others. When the dust was washed from her scalp, the battle remained.

That damned spot. A symbol of how bad things were. Its memories drove her day after day to the seaside, unaware that Cassandra had learned of her travels on news stations that (in the most literal sense) religiously announced the comings and goings of the Family across the globe. Cassandra turned her hatred for Dominia into a doorway of her own. One which was exit only.

"I think I meant to kill you," her wife confessed, lips twisted with wet despair. "But the way you looked at me the first time you saw me…oh, Dominia."

"I'm so sorry," was all the General could say; Cassandra shut her eyes.

"I didn't want to tell you because I didn't want to hear you lie. You're not sorry. He was any other dead man to you. He's only important to you now because he was important to me. And if you hadn't killed him, you would have been killed, yourself. So, you don't regret it. I'm the only one here who has anything to regret."

"But"—the Hierophant stroked her hand—"you have everything to gain."

Her lips were back to trembling again. "All I ever wanted was a family."

Magnanimous as ever, the Holy Father lifted his eyebrows. "My girl, be glad: you have one."

Afterward, he took the General aside in the hall and asked how she would like to be Governess of the United Front. Fine time to ask. Finer time to accept. No doubt his ability to pull a stunt like that and still get an affirmative response was the reason he showed up now, his presence a threat not just to Dominia and her friends, but all Kabul. Kabul, which was supposedly protected by the Hunters. In a world where cameras were everywhere, even in the eyes of passersby, was Dominia to believe her Father was the only one with omnipotent access to every device? That the Hunters didn't know her Father was there? That she was there?

That they didn't know Kahlil abetted them?

As her legs pumped with the pace of her run, she couldn't help but think something here was wrong—and not, necessarily, Miki. All the major players—at least, her Father and the Lamb—seemed in on the game; why wouldn't the Hunters be? That was what all this seemed more and more, in truth. What Tobias had said. A game. She wished she could flip the board, but she supposed that meant suicide in this context, so she wiped the metaphor from her mind as she stood before the pawnshop. Miki's back door was still open; the General's entrance was silent, but that silence proved needless when she arrived at Kahlil's apartment to find the prostitute and the Hunter already having a too-loud fight.

"I think you could have warned us!" Miki's sharp tone resolved when Dominia pushed open the front door and laid eyes on the man who, beneath his beard and olive skin, nonetheless paled to macabre slate. Somehow, Miki had discovered the news of the day, and agreed that her friend should have been wise to it. Never a good sign. The martyr was upon Kahlil before he so much as moved, holding the human foot above the floor to be shaken in one brisk whip of his head. Amid the uproar, Basil barked for joy.

"Is there something you'd like to tell us, Kahlil?"

"I didn't know your Family was here! I swear, I swear, I didn't know, oh, Allah. You think I sit around switching between security feeds all day long? Huh? You think al-Saalihin would actually tell me anything?" While trying to extricate himself from the martyr's fists with one hand, he used the other to straighten his crooked glasses. "They can't stand my guts! I'm their tech support. I run their Halcyon accounts. I'm PR! They used to bully guys like me—well, not in *school*, but in the crappy neighborhoods where they grew up."

"Then you'd better start doing your job and spin your story."

"You tell 'im, boss." Miki, arms crossed and foot propped against the wall, did not look as belligerent as intended due to her short-shorts. "I have a hard time believing your bosses didn't send out some kind of high-priority emergency alert as soon as the Hierophant set foot on Kabul's soil. You let us walk out of this place knowing those creeps are out there wandering around!"

"I swear, Miki, I didn't. I'm their cleanup crew! They don't tell me anything. Do you remember—remember when they tried that coup in Iran a couple of years ago? That was my first year on the job! How do you think I felt, having to handle the social-media backlash?"

"How do you think *they* felt?" asked Dominia, rattling him once more for good measure. "The people who lost their lives, their families—how did they feel? How do you think they *will* feel when whatever violent conflict brought to this city spends more lives today? You're responsible by failing to tell me these important details."

Fear vanished from Kahlil's face, and his expression hardened to a steel mask that came from somewhere else. Some divine source, she thought in ironic tone. "How about all the people you killed, huh? All the humans killed in all the wars you've fought, all the things you've done. War crimes."

"War crimes," scoffed Dominia. The man sneered.

"Yeah, war crimes. Torture, genocide, enslavement, who knows what else. And then there's your so-called legitimate battles."

"All my battles are, by definition, legitimate battles. Battles with soldiers who signed up to be there."

"I guess those people murdered in the Black Night volunteered for camp?"

Miki averted her gaze. Nostrils flaring, the martyr lowered the human to the floor. After he had put the couch between himself and the General, Kahlil cleared his throat, straightened his shirt, and said, "Every human being is a soldier in the war against you, your Father, and your so-called people."

"So why didn't you tell me he was here?"

"I haven't been debriefed yet."

"Miki"—eyes blazing, Dominia turned to assess the prostitute—"why are we wasting our time with this idiot?"

"Because he's going to have information on the Lazarenes. *Right*, Kahlil?" The prostitute stared the man down with a devilish look.

"When my computer has finished decrypting his location for the week." The man stepped toward the humming collection of screens and towers so old as to practically be artifacts. Somehow, these constituted one device, though said "one device" took up a quarter of his living room. "It's not instantaneous. This is how he protects himself, and why the Hunters and your Family get only a slim window of opportunity to acquire him. Every Friday night at nine o'clock, wherever he is, he releases a message in a few secret digital channels—mostly via direct messages to his priests, but also in one of two Lazarene chat rooms with forever-changing addresses. This message is encrypted, and the instructions for the computer on how to derive the key are also encrypted, but known to those who use the chat rooms, and to worshipers. It's not dissimilar to blockchain, the basis for most digital currencies, but it's lighter, and instead of crunching problems to mine for digital coins, computers are crunching problems to mine Lazarus's encryption. Like digging out of a cave, instead of mining."

"Reminds me of the protein somehow," mused the martyr, glancing into the bright eyes of the dog. "If everybody in the world is trying to get ahold of him for one reason or another, why is he releasing information on his location?"

Miki, annoyed by Dominia's ignorance, said, "Because he's got people to save."

This was a controversial topic. Ask her Father and the Church, and Lazarus's blood was a one-way ticket to permanent excommunication—the condemnation of the soul to eternal hell. Miki, however, was one of a great many people who seemed to believe the opposite, the subject of Lazarus being the point where the common cultist joined with the Red Market priestess. Indeed, they sometimes seemed part of the same faith. This was so well veiled from Dominia for over three hundred years that, seeing so now, she hardly understood. "So Lazarus travels the world like Cicero and the Lamb, distributing his location of the week to humans who believe in him. The Abrahamian Hunters intercept these codes in hopes of capturing him, and using him to…what?"

"What do *you* want him for?" asked Kahlil with a shrug and an adjustment of his glasses. "Whether or not he's a martyr, he's a useful one if he can resurrect the dead."

For her own benefit, the General pressed, "Do you believe he can?"

The young man turned his back on the martyr to study his computer's progress. "Why does it matter? Like I said. I'm tech support at worst, PR at best."

"I guess I wanted you to clap your hands for Tinkerbell." From behind the human's shoulder, the muttering General studied the screen. She had to admit, the eye's translation of Arabic to English was useful. "Get me the second this is done. How much longer?"

"Even the fastest computers can only manage to decrypt the code by Saturday night, and mine's the fastest in Kabul. It's been at it for twenty hours already. Any minute now, it will be finished."

After translating "Saturday night" to "Noctisatur" in her head, she nodded. "And the rest of the Hunters will lag behind us?"

"Better," insisted Miki, her grin ear to ear. "Kahlil is the one who gets them the information every week! He's going to have a computer problem tonight, right?" This, with a cheesy wink to her friend, who rolled eyes that landed on the General.

"Yeah. I'm willing to hold the information back for Miki's sake because, well…my career is ruined either way." His annoyance was directed to the prostitute. "But this way, there's a chance I can salvage it by making it seem like a computer problem. It's not the end of the world to them if they miss one Lazarene ceremony, since even if they're able to interrupt it, they're not going to catch him."

"Why not?"

At Dominia's question, Kahlil offered an answer that reminded her chillingly of her Father's uncanny movements earlier that evening. "I don't know. I've heard he just disappears."

Shaking her head, the General made her way down the cluttered hall and let herself into the cramped guest bathroom. Miki was not more than a few steps behind as the martyr washed her face in the sooty-looking sink. After flipping on a single lightbulb whose pale fluorescence amplified the depressing state of the broken tile floor, the human rustled through all visible drawers. Dominia watched her shameless snooping with fond relief.

"I'm glad I made you stay behind."

As Miki straightened with a pair of tarnished scissors in hand, the human exclaimed, "What *was* that with you? You see something, or what?"

"Not just the Lamb, but the Hierophant." The General allowed herself steered to a seat upon the toilet lid.

"I gathered from what you said in there...are you all right?"

"Fine. I was surprised. He tried to convince me to come home." Memories of her discussion with her Father reminded her that she had walked in on Kahlil and Miki having an argument, which she had thought to be about her Family—but perhaps she'd been wrong. "What were you and Kahlil fighting about when I came back?"

"Oh"—Miki turned to close the door but for a crack—"I was pissed because he wouldn't try to find you on a camera feed. I didn't know where you were! What if I needed to help you?"

She was a good kid. "You're a kinder friend than I deserve. When I talk to my Father, I always walk away feeling like there is no real way to change. Like I'll always be the same evil person he taught me to be."

"You're being too harsh on yourself! Look, hey!" When her eyes remained lowered, the scissors tapped Dominia's ear, and the cold contact sent them springing up. "I mean it. I already told you that nobody has to forgive or accept what you were before, but the worthy will be able to see that who you are now is different. You have to see yourself as different. But, if you can't forgive yourself, at least try to learn. Look"—she glanced slyly toward the cracked door, with the dog waiting outside and the unbreaking flow of distant keystrokes—"if I tell you something to make you feel better, will you keep it secret? It's bad for business. Well...this business. Sometimes it's *great* for business, you wouldn't believe."

Embarrassing how quickly Dominia's self-pity morphed into burning curiosity: she waited, the picture of childlike impatience as Miki leaned in and whispered, clipping the air with her scissors. "I was born with a penis."

"Really!" Astonished, Dominia found herself reacting in the stupidest way possible: a way that made her think of blushing, flustered Tenchi sticking his foot in his mouth on the *Jun'yō* only after she realized she'd said, "But you're so hot!"

Luckily, Miki had a good enough sense of humor to raise her head in a cackle. As she resumed snipping the stray hairs of twice-embarrassed Dominia's 'do, she exclaimed, "I know, right? Modern medicine, it's a miracle! All thanks to gene therapy, hormones, and one great surgeon." Like an all-business hair stylist, Miki directed Dominia's head this way and that. "But none of that matters, see? I mean, look at me."

Before Dominia said, "No," Miki slipped down shorts and skivvies, and grinned to see Dominia's furious blush. "See? A sputtering lesbian is praise from Caesar."

"It's—very organic looking."

"You want to touch it?" asked the leering human while Dominia averted her gaze.

"Um, no! Not—"

"You're right, this bathroom is gross, and that dope will be back before we get anywhere. When we're alone, *senpai*." To Dominia's relief, she slipped her bottoms back up, and Dominia looked down to make eye contact with Basil, whose tail wagged through the crack of the door. *Pervert*, she told him in her head, and his mouth opened in a big doggie grin that made her smirk. Miki, redressed and back to clipping, missed this.

"Anyway, who we really are is living consciousness. Light on the inside and out. What do our bodies matter? I wanted to be a girl since I was little! I was a regular hoodlum, getting into my mother's gowns and makeup. So many beautiful kimono, smeared with white paste…it makes me want to die to think about them. Sigh"—she said the word "sigh" out loud, and the martyr laughed, earning a nick on the ear that instantly healed—"I could have inherited those someday. Theoretically."

"Was she mad?"

"About the dresses? You should have seen my ass!"

"No, about—"

"Oh, no way. Are you kidding? She was always disappointed that I was born a boy! I was almost eight when I admitted to her that I was a girl, and it was like, we were at the doctor two days later." She told the story laughing, but Dominia couldn't help sadness for the small child forced to endure eight years of life in tortured secrecy. At least young Morgan had been granted a sweet sliver of Eden before life unveiled its unjust face and delivered her to her fate among the Holy Family. "Part of the reason I look so good now is because we were able to make small adjustments while I was young. You can at least feel *these*!" No boundaries, the woman: she snatched up Dominia's hands and settled them on the warm breasts beneath her shirt. For her part, the General tried to maintain the objective and studious look of someone, say, at an art gallery, or perhaps a doctor looking for lumps. She even threw in a bit of, "Oh, mm-hmm? Ah, I see," which cracked Miki up.

"You're so *shy*! This is hilarious. I always heard you martyrs were super-depraved S and M freaks. Anyway, yeah, these are real, see? The doctors couldn't do anything at first, of course, because I was small, so Mom overhauled my wardrobe, started treating me like a human being, and taught me how to be a proper woman. Then, when I hit puberty, the hormonal therapies started. It was a long road, but I was cured by the time I was in my early twenties. No better way to take it all for a ride than to leave work as a geisha and apply my talents elsewhere! Hah, she was way more pissed off about that! But, see?" She caught Dominia's chin. "It doesn't matter who we were before. None of who I was would have mattered if I hadn't told you. None of what you've done matters now that you have this chance to free yourself through change."

"Thank you," said the martyr as Miki clipped and arranged one last lock that was allowed by the stylist to hang upon the General's pale forehead.

"Any time, cutie. Come to me first, next time you need a haircut." Kahlil appeared in the doorway and drew her attention. "There are a few chunks I wasn't able to save...what's up?"

"You guys are going to want to take a look at this."

Always fatal words. Sensing the weight of what she was about to observe, Dominia followed Miki, Basil, and their maligned host to the proverbial command center. There, a paused video buffered. She recognized it before he said anything at all, because she had seen it, quite literally, with her own eye.

"You wanted it, you got it. This stream was obtained by a friend of mine in Jerusalem, a guy who has access to some serious martyr information. They've had this stream's link for the past couple of days."

That fucking DIOX-I. The fucking Hierophant. There it was, her conversation with her Father on the rooftop of Kabul, recorded in perfect silence. Everything she had done, everything she had seen: watched not just by her Father, but by the Hunters, and every human government in the world. She would have gouged it out right there if she wasn't sure it would try to cram itself back in.

Calmly, she asked, "The stream was leaked by whom?"

"A confidential source."

Still reeling from before, she almost speculated aloud, "the Hierophant," but refrained as he went on. "If they don't already know you're here with me, they will when they've caught up. And that's assuming they aren't getting live reports from its GPS, anyway."

Oh, yeah. This thing was coming out of her skull. In retrospect, of course it tracked her location: it had a map feature, didn't it? What was the world coming to!

"Do you happen to have an eye patch lying around?"

Kahlil offered the kind of expression that made even Dominia feel stupid. "Do I look like a pirate?"

"A little," said Miki, earning an irritated look she exchanged for a grin. "With the beard, and all. A software pirate, at least."

Muttering something in Arabic that got him slapped in the head, Kahlil minimized the video stream with a tap of his touch screen. "Look, Miki...I've got a lot of equipment here to interfere with recording devices and unauthorized uploads while people are in my house, but this...you can't stay here. I'm sorry. I broke the encryption, but I can't help you beyond that. The Lazarene ceremony is in the basement of a music store, at"—he paused, looked at Dominia in irritation, and covered his mouth to prevent lip-reading efforts while he shared the address.

"This is bullshit," said the prostitute; their host rose from his seat to defend himself.

"What do you want me to do, Miki? I'm stupid. I'm stupid to have taken your money. With the Caliphate—and probably the government—aware that you're here, I'm as good as dead."

"This is a risk you knew when you agreed to put us up," Miki began, but Dominia shook her head.

"He's right. He's done enough for us. There's no reason another human has to die because I'm here."

"They'll be dying because the Hierophant came," said Miki.

"And he came because I did." She thought of the lifelong suffering of the patient Lamb, who never wished for anything but to be with his brother. How she struggled against the urge to admit defeat against suffering; how she grappled with inevitability! The calm, rational General forced herself to say, "We can go elsewhere."

"Thank you." The man's voice relaxed with a heave of gratitude. "I'm sorry. I wouldn't be this inhospitable. But—"

"We understand. At least, I do. Thank you for keeping us this long. I hope"—she frowned and decided not to carry on with that particular line of thought, opting instead to say—"I hope we'll meet again, in better circumstances."

Then, with a glance down the hall, the sighing General added, "At least we don't have a lot of luggage."

They did, however, have a dog. A dog who was found in the bedroom with his head upon his paws, ears pinning back and forth upon his tuxedoed head like fuzzy satellite dishes. A dog who, when called, "Basil, we have to go," decided he was now as stupid as all other dogs in the world. He got up in place, dashed in fast circles, then settled back down with a pre-nap huff.

Somehow, this action gave Dominia the idea that she'd done something wrong.

"Come on." Miki pushed the mongrel with her toe while the dog peeped up at her from one eye. "We'll get you some bacon or—oh, wrong town. Do dogs like falafel?"

"Lamb," the martyr profaned, stooping to the level of the dog. "I'm missing something, aren't I? There's something…something I'm not doing. Or maybe..."

"Are you seriously talking to the dog?"

"Thinking out loud to it," she tried, which was blatantly false, because the border collie deigned to lift his head and wag his tail in some kind of indicator. She was, in fact, talking to the dog. Miki's tongue expressed her displeasure with a click against the roof of her mouth.

"Primitive man—I mean, before the primary Western calendar flipped from CE to AL—used to just, like, murder each other for fun. You know that, right? Not only gladiators in Roman times, I mean, but serial killers—and this *one* dude talked to his dog. Or his neighbor's dog. I don't remember."

"And Caligula promoted his horse. Why do you know this?"

"It's a requirement for Red Market women to learn the savage nature of mankind because now the savage, murder-for-fun types are you. I just mean to say, when I see you talking to a dog, my palms start to sweat."

"That's a kind of profiling I don't appreciate." Dominia struggled to keep a straight face and failed when she turned her attention back to Basil. He stared intently at the gun concealed in her waistband: that emergency-only device that seemed ever more chain than tool. "But maybe you're right. I mean, it looks like he's staring at my gun right now."

"Hey," said Miki, "it kind of does."

At the time, what Dominia did next seemed to be a small mistake: as an experiment, she removed the gun and held it out to see if it was the dog's focal point. His gaze remained plastered to the weapon. The General was about to comment on the strangeness of it, amused that in all her years of working with military dogs she had never seen an animal interested in guns; Miki appeared on the verge of a similar conclusion; but none of that happened, because Kahlil opened the door without knocking, saying as he entered, "Look, guys, I feel bad about turning you out, and—"

No dog had moved faster; no martyr, slower. It was the sheer surprise of having the dog move in a way so sudden and directed. Not for her hand or her arm or her body or even Kahlil, but for the gun. The next five seconds abstracted: sheer surprise, the scramble of movement, black-and-white blur, the clatter of metal, and the urgent *no-no-no* of thought followed by the inevitable crack of the gun. All this chaos released into a new kind of order, which took the form of the scream of their unfortunate host and his string of Arabic profanity. While the man clutched his hip and cried, "What the fuck, what did you shoot me for," Dominia exchanged with Miki a startled look.

Both women turned this incredulity down upon the dog; Basil, for his part, wagged his tail, laid the big, sweet doggie eyes on extra thick, and stepped away from the weapon.

Feeling somehow apart from this tableau as much as she felt a part of it, Dominia considered that this was what her Father must have felt all the time: vague amusement. That, or the palpable sense of being the butt of some intangible joke. She cracked a smile that let show the gaps the Hierophant had made in her teeth.

"Well…we do know one medical professional in Kabul."

XIV

Communication Skills

In many ways, Tobias Akachi seemed too good to be true. Dominia first thought this was because she had not known many humans in anything other than a bureaucratic sense, as when they came into her San Valentino office to appeal to her for grants, favors, stays of execution, etc. Humans, therefore, seemed increasingly to be an otherwise defenseless group in need of a compassionate hand—though she had always felt that way, even while slaying them. The bloody course of her final war arose from a deep admixture of love and hate, in which love found but recent consideration. Somehow, love was more painful for the General. Was that a symptom of evil? Humans, after all, seemed to express love with ease. Not having seen them in their own environment since her aborted childhood, she had not recognized how their kindness, their prevailing belief in the basic decency of conscious individuals, drove some to help even martyrs. And martyrs, well...perhaps it was wrong to call her kind inherently selfish, but what else could be said of a cannibal race? Her Father had, since before their human births, drilled the message of martyr superiority: How could humanity but believe it? How could martyrs but act with those beliefs lodged in their hearts? If, in the martyr world, Dominia had called a friend for help at a strange hour, would she have received any friendship? Any help? Martyrs were to be hospitable to other martyrs, of course. But they were also taught it was understandable to refuse the phone call of an absurd hour, and acceptable to find a solution other than inviting a general, a prostitute, a wounded man, and a dog over for unlicensed emergency surgery. Dr. Akachi had a different approach, about which he discoursed while tending the thrashing patient.

"One should leap at the opportunity to help one's fellow man." The dentist used one great hand to hold Kahlil while the other manipulated a pair of silver tweezers in a way topical anesthetic and slow-acting opiates wouldn't help. "And, with love in the heart! If you do not have love in your heart, you'd might as well do nothing at all."

"I don't know." Miki pinned Kahlil's shoulders to the silver surface of the dentist's chic dining room table, sometimes grimacing through her friend's struggles. "A lot of great charities were founded from a sense of obligation. Lots of old people have been helped. My country has a whole system of elder care—and why? Because old people are so good at guilt!"

"Obligation breeds mutual resentment. I help because I am happy to! Because I was put on God's Earth to help my fellow man. To help you, Kahlil, get this nasty fellow out of you!"

With a glance for the martyr, then the dog, who observed from the living room couch, Miki said, "This is a great argument for ID-locking all guns."

"This is an antique," protested Dominia, who lifted the hem of her shirt to show the handle. Kahlil hissed.

"Put it away! Didn't you learn your lesson? That stupid dog— Ow!"

While lifting into the light a bloodied bullet that made Miki wince, Tobias laughed. "Relax. You won't die! Maybe limp a bit. Some long-term aches. You'll get a good idea of when it's going to rain!"

"You should be grateful." Dominia adjusted with a snap the band of her drugstore eye patch, procured at a clerkless convenience store to blind the DIOX-I to their conversations. "That dog saved your life by forcing you to leave your house. You think your Caliphate would have been understanding?"

"Oh, Allah." Kahlil tried to sit up until Miki shoved him back. "Do you need to mention my—affiliations?"

"I do not care. Much." The winking dentist brandished a hooked suture needle intended for stitches in gums. "After all, I have a martyr who can testify to my impartiality! That is high praise, I think."

"You should have destroyed her brain while she was in your office," said Kahlil, who swore as Miki slammed him down into the table. "Shit— Well? Can you blame me?"

"Yeah, asshole, I can blame you. It's your own fault you got shot, the way you barged in." Sniffing, Miki looked over at the dog. "Poor boy was startled. Weren't you, boy? Who's a good boy?"

"He *shot* me!"

"He doesn't know that!"

Dominia wasn't so sure, but there was no point in arguing. Better to play along, to smirk and say, "Holding a grudge against a dog is kind of petty, Kahlil."

"So maybe I hold one against you."

As Dominia pointed to her own chest in a *who, me?* way, Tobias rinsed the closed wound with distilled water and daubed on some hiss-provoking antibiotic cream. "Good as new!"

"Great. Can I go home, now?"

Dominia's hand on his chest rendered his effort to sit up humorously futile.

"Actually," she said, "since we have you here, maybe you could do us a favor. I've been thinking…two can play this hacker game, right?"

"What do you mean?"

"I'm not the only one who's been blinded by the Family."

Miki took her meaning right away. "Yeah—yeah, that's a great idea! That idiot, René…he's probably making the mistake of appealing to the Hunters as we speak! About to lose his life, too."

"Then what are you hoping to gain?" Kahlil's voice reached a high pitch of annoyance. "He'll be dead soon! All of us— *I'm* going to be dead soon! You have to let me get back to my apartment."

Eye narrowing, Dominia demanded, "What's so urgent?"

"You heard me before. In spite of my security efforts, your stream is going to lead the Hunters—even the government—straight to my house."

"Then you should make yourself scarce," said Miki, but he didn't agree.

"They'll think I'm colluding with you. If I was in my apartment, I'd have a chance to explain myself and protect my possessions. Now they're going to rifle through everything, and they're going to find Miki's information, and that will be that. Either the government realizes I'm part of the Hunters, or the Hunters realize I've been running around with a woman of ill repute."

"Looks like you're going to have to find a new business," suggested the aforementioned working girl, who looked amused as anybody might in the given circumstances. "I'm sure we could use someone like you for our own tech stuff. Ever thought about joining the Red Market?"

"And join a bunch of heathen prostitutes?"

"Whom you *solicit*," Miki emphasized, much to the visible chagrin of Kahlil. Clear on the source of his offense, she waved a hand. "Oh, nobody here cares. Hell, you introduced Tobias to me."

"To fix your *teeth*."

"And, of course, I did." Akachi remained shameless and jolly as he'd be for any other subject. "She is a very fine woman! Perhaps an exception among the usual Red Market sort. The Bible says, my brother, that the sin in prostitution is upon the shoulders of the customer—not upon the prostitute, as such."

"And the Prophet said that the finances made through prostitution are as haram as that made from soothsaying. And the sale of dogs. No fucking wonder! All this is happening to me because I've been a bad Muslim."

Rolling her eyes, Miki said, "I love how men are all happy to stick their dicks into a whore, and then judge their character as soon as their boners are gone…be as stupid about this as you want, Kahlil, but you're going to end up dead if you stay in this city. Look"—she made sure Dominia's eye remained covered—"we're going to Cairo after we meet up with Lazarus. It's safe there. At least, the Red Market isn't going to kill you in cold blood because you hosted us. They might even reward you for it. And if it's religion you're worried about, nobody cares! You won't be forced to worship, or even meet the Lady. But I'm telling you, Kahlil…you stay here, you're dead."

"Fuck," said Kahlil; then, in a higher and more tearful pitch: "Fuck! Miki, why would you do this to me? You've ruined my life!"

"Oh, buddy"—the prostitute patted his shoulder—"I didn't ruin your life. I saved it. Sometimes your old life has to be ruined before you can start the next. Like bankruptcy!"

Looking between the two of them, Dominia was in the process of asking, "Now I have to take two humans to Cairo—" when Kahlil, not in the rightest of minds, made an angry, stupid, and sluggish lurch for the gun in the General's waistband. She got to it long before him and used its handle to crack him on the back of the skull much as Miki had Cicero, whereupon the human dropped against the table with a theatrical clang.

"Shit," cried Miki while the much-startled dentist, who had retreated against the midnight marble of his kitchen counter, now hurried to study the young man's well-being. Dominia lifted her free hand to her good eye—to rub it, its brow, the bridge of her nose.

"Sorry. It was instinctive."

With a look of disapproval, Akachi said, "Resorting to violence is never the right choice…he will live, as you did not break the skin, but I would be concerned about a concussion."

Miki nodded. "All the more reason to get him to Cairo as soon as possible. Red Market medical care is top notch."

The subject of Cairo was what had agitated the General, and was, in retrospect, a contributing factor to poor Kahlil's head wound. That, and her starvation. Four bags of donated blood over the course of her stay did not a full stomach make—no more than it helped her recover from the fast of her train journey. Among her problems, tremors were somehow both the least and the greatest of her worries. While Miki continued Tobias's conversation in Arabic, Dominia tried to reduce her trembling through sheer force of will. That wasn't successful with the adrenaline of conflict flowing through her limbs. It was Kahlil's own fault for trying something so stupid on a rattled martyr who was ready for many things: for a meal; for a bed; for a therapist; but, most of all, for somebody to do something stupid. And because she was so ready for the latter, she had "resorted" to violence. So? So what. Violence was her art form, wasn't it? Violence was her life.

But that was her Father's influence. She tamped it away, cleansed herself of the notion that he had permeated even the human world. Dominia hid the gun once more on her person while Miki said in English, "What the fuck are we going to do about René now, wise guy? That was an important detail you thought of, and you fucked it up, yourself! We're blind. *And*, if we're going to get him checked out, we don't have time to wait around for your teeth."

Tobias looked up in an offer that seemed, at the time, altruistic. "I can work through the night, if necessary. The most difficult portions of creating the implants are already complete."

"I would be in your debt." To Miki, the General said, "It'll take my body all of thirty minutes to recover from the procedure. The Lazarene ceremony starts before dawn?" At Miki's single nod, Dominia said, "We'll be cutting it close."

"A good day for it. Everybody will be busy with the marathon." The prostitute's statement reminded the almost-grimacing martyr of her Father's promise. She would deliver Lazarus to him during the race. Dominia tuned out as her friend continued, "The odds of police raids, or even Hunter interference, are pretty low."

"Even so..." The General studied the unconscious man, whose head Akachi supported with his hand. "I don't think it's safe for you guys to come with me. Especially if he's in need of recovery."

"Remember I have your diamond," sang Miki, wearing that sly expression. "At least, the Lady does."

"I'm not trying to get out of going to Cairo. But I'm going to have to meet you there. When I saw my Father"—Tobias's gaze flickered up in brief attention—"he made a threat about Lazarus, and about the marathon. About meeting me during the race."

"Did he say where?" When the General shook her head, the prostitute crossed her arms. "Probably near the start, in front of that big hotel. At least, that's the most logical spot. That or the end, out by Hashmat Khan Lake. Otherwise, it runs through the whole city, so I can't imagine where you'd find him."

"Staying in the hotel's penthouse," speculated the General with a snort before turning away from the humans. "Can you handle the car situation, Miki?"

"For me, or for you?"

"For yourself, and Kahlil."

"Yeah, I can do that. We have enough 'Coins from our stunt on the train that it won't be a problem. But how will *you* get to Cairo?"

She hadn't stopped to think about it. After all, her next step was emergency surgery. While a simple procedure would not normally bother her, the idea now stuck in her craw after her experience with Cicero. Her mild preoccupation with the forthcoming removal of her eye and replacement of her teeth was more irritating than the actual event would prove to be. But perhaps it was the principle. Could there never be a moment of peace? A moment when the tide of her thoughts didn't turn to crush her beneath their loathsome waves?

If she went home, perhaps. Perhaps, given time, she'd get over her pain and her moments of doubt. With enough effort, she could return to that numb half-life in which she dwelled before Cassandra's arrival. That security of unfeeling. The more Dominia observed herself, the more she recognized an upsetting pattern of dichotomy. Perhaps she had created it. The world was more complex than a binary of goodness and badness; yet, she could no longer use that complexity to justify evil acts. Now she was forced to admit that evil—the truest evil—would be a knowing return into the bosom of evil out of sheer, pitiful fear.

But how easy it would be, going home! How safe. How comfortable. Normal. Not like this, her life destroyed, her body displaced in some human's (admittedly classy) high-rise apartment, where she washed her face and tried to convince herself she wasn't a complete fool.

This inner division traced to the issue of her parentage. The discovery of a parent's imperfection was a natural (indeed, pivotal) point in a child's development so far as the General observed, but that opportunity was swept from her—she thought—when the Hierophant stole her away. That made the initial divide neat and tidy. Morgan's parents remained forever pure and good and helpless. A couple deprived of their only daughter, into whom they had poured no small amount of love and care, by the wickedest man in all the land. It sounded like a fairy tale, because Dominia insisted on a child's way of thinking about the matter for almost ten years; until, at sixteen, the ever-surly girl and all-the-surlier teenager spotted, by total happenstance, a quartet of out-of-towners gone for a day trip to the Vatican. Two of the tourists, she recognized in an instant: beside their grief-grayed hairs, her parents could never be that changed. Ah, that second of joy! Of thrill! What small odds that they should both visit Rome at once! Her Father rarely brought her back to Mephitoli in those teen years. Yet, this week he had surprised her. She had been optimistic that, for once, the trip might be pleasant—and then, this vision.

This was a sign from the God her Father was always babbling about. Her heart raced as she pulled away from the Hierophant with whom she walked. She took two steps forward, and stupidly called out (if she had but waited a few strides, until there was no escape for them!), "Mamma! Papá!"

Words she had thought that would never use again. Words she would forever wish she had never used again when her father's head lifted, and terror filled his eyes. Terror, or sorrow. Whatever they contained, he tapped his wife on the shoulder. Morgan's mother looked at Dominia with a kind of coldness that made the girl think the human looked at the Hierophant.

No. This woman, turning away, gripped the hand of the little girl with whom she walked, and yanked her along so fast that the child's pigtails snapped in the wind. While Dominia stood, dumbfounded and making excuses (they hadn't recognized her; or were afraid of the Hierophant; or, the saddest excuse of all, they were too busy to speak to her), Morgan's father lowered his shamed eyes and tugged attention out of his son's shirt collar. Then, with another pained flicker toward his lost child, and what might have been something akin to the subtle wave of his left hand, he and the boy he guided disappeared into the crowd.

The Hierophant appeared at pale Dominia's elbow.

"What is it, princess?" His great hand lay on her shoulder. "What did you see?"

Nothing, of course. She had seen nothing. Eating was easier after that moment because before she had held out secret hope that someday, somehow, her condition would be cured, and her parents would be her parents again. How silly she'd been. What a child. In that moment, she understood that the emptiness of a martyr would be with her forever. The one thing to do was to try to fill it with flesh.

That abject emptiness that plagued her at the thought of family was what made it so easy to be home with Cassandra while her mourning wife reclined upon the favored couch of their new San Valentino estate. She looked like a painting from the Holy Father's galleries. Sometimes she would lay, unspeaking, for hours; Dominia spent that time reading, sipping wine. Just looking at her. An hour seemed much shorter to the Governess, who'd lived far longer than Cassandra. In the scale of her life, an hour was good as a minute, or less. Yet, those hours with Cassandra had seemed an exquisite eternity in which Dominia forever watched sleet waves of the Pacific in the picture window behind her wife's head, the image framed by gauzy curtains that, sail-like, bloomed with wind creeping through the patio door. That same wind stroked Cassandra's hair until, as the starry night gave way to the viscous fog of coastal morning, Dominia, jealous of that wind, kissed her wife, and coaxed her off to bed, and gave her the opportunity for the smallness and safety that came with being in a lover's arms. That same safety Dominia felt in holding her. She refused to believe she would never feel that safety again—perhaps with the same stupidity by which she once believed her parents would return. But she had to cling to something. The notion that memory was now her only respite weighed too much to bear.

Even in that respite, after all, she had no real peace. Emerging from the bathroom to find Miki flinging herself upon the guest bed, Dominia adjusted the awkward band of her eye patch and studied, with her organic orb, the tasteful decoration of the slick room. A palace beside Kahlil's, with a lot of in-built storage and bookshelves curiously empty of books, but ornamented with a few fake orchids. "I'm surprised Dr. Akachi is so accommodating."

"That's why I brought you to him! He's been my client for about two years. Pretty good guy. Does good cleanings. Lets me pay him in—"

"Okay," interrupted Dominia. "But, I mean, I'm a martyr. You think that would stop him."

"You're not going to bite him when he sticks his fingers in your mouth, for Lady's sake. He's a good, Christian man, but he's not—well, of course he's an idiot. All people are idiots. But he's not a *complete* idiot."

"You can't think all people are idiots."

"I'm an idiot! You're an idiot. Even—especially—Basil here." Finished unpeeling her socks from her feet, she tossed one over the dog's nose, then sprang to squish his fuzzy face. "Yes! Yes, especially Basil, you're so cute and stupid."

As Miki sang to the dog, Dominia made smirking eye contact with the animal that, despite its tail wags, strove to communicate something with its hilariously dry expression. The General laughed, then turned to study their view of Kabul when she recognized the distinct shape jutting inside the duffel bag to which Miki went when done harassing the hound. One patched eye meant she couldn't watch the human from her periphery, and had to wait: had to listen for the sound of the zipper when Miki, sure the martyr wasn't watching, opened the duffel bag to reveal the shamisen within.

Thoughts whipped at rapid clip across Dominia's consciousness, a chain unfolding in the order of shamisen, train, Cicero: by the time her brother's smug face entered her mind, she was already upon the human, who emitted a shocked cry as the martyr pinned her to the wall with a hand to her mouth.

"That was your mother's shamisen. It was special, you said." The licorice lacquer, the cherry blossoms: yes, it was the same. "Where'd this new one come from, Miki? The pawnshop? I thought it was strange you were already fighting with Kahlil by the time I got back from seeing my fathers, but you managed to keep me occupied until something else came up. You were angry with him for the same reason as me. Just like he didn't tell me they were in town, he didn't tell you, either, and you met one on your way back to the pawnshop."

As the martyr lowered her hand for the human to speak, Miki said, "Shit, dude, listen, I wanted to tell you, but we've been—busy. You need to relax."

"Where'd you get the instrument?"

"You said it yourself. When you ran off, I made my way back to the shop, but on the way, I—" The prostitute laughed, a high-pitched noise that indicated high levels of anxiety enfolded within her comic layers of brazen self-defense. "I thought I was dead, for sure!"

"Cicero."

After glancing at the eye patch blinding Dominia's DIOX-I, she uttered the word, "Yes."

Dominia swore through the broad window that overlooked the glowing city, perhaps more active for sake of tomorrow's race. "I guess you'll betray me, too, huh? He returned your shamisen as a bribe? Or did he give you something else?"

"This was why I didn't tell you. I knew you wouldn't trust me to be better than that!" At the martyr's skeptical look, the human's temper reached such a pitch that Dominia grew more inclined to believe her. "Of course he tried to get information out of me, to get me to spy on you or whatever. But they only have chump shit to offer me. Cicero, the Hierophant—none of your Family can give me what I want."

"What will it take to get you to betray me?"

Here came a slap, which caused the martyr to study with new, ringing perception the scowling human. "You bitch! I'm not some rat, and I don't appreciate your assumption that I am. Did I bump into Cicero? Yes. Did he offer me money to report to him because he was 'concerned'"—the girl made air quotes—"about you? Yes. But I didn't take it. I'd be getting in my own way. Ishtar's way."

Miki then went on to describe their interaction, but Dominia didn't need her story, because she could picture it. How deferential Cicero was, how quick to assure Miki need not worry about the crack in the head. He'd tell her he was fine and just impressed that she'd force of will enough to pick up the gun, with her state at the time. Well Dominia saw how he'd have gotten into Miki's personal space while handing her the instrument. After draping an arm around her, he'd start walking her back to the pawnshop to show her he knew where they stayed. All the while, he'd say something to the effect of, "My poor sister has lost control of herself in the wake of her wife's death. We've discussed paying a caretaker. Would you be interested?"

And when Miki, politely as she could, refused his offer, he listened to her with that frigid priest's air, patted her shoulder, and said, "If that's how you insist things must be."

"Then he left me, and I was already at the pawnshop. Creep." Miki frowned down at the shamisen. "I had time to put it away and get into an argument with Kahlil before you showed up. Sorry I didn't mention it sooner, but, like I said…we've all been busy."

"Did you check the shamisen for recording devices? Tracking devices?"

"Of course. There's nothing, it's unmolested."

Naturally. Cicero would never hurt an instrument. "And did you remember to thank him? For bringing you the instrument, I mean."

"Yes, of course. I'm not stupid, Dominia. I've seen the public service announcements since I was a toddler."

Ah, the PSAs: ads in television and magazines and Internet videos that explained to humans how they should behave if they ever met a martyr. Most humans went their whole lifetimes without needing the information—those who lived in Asia might never see a martyr at all, let alone merit one's attention—but, much as all people knew from early on that, in the event of immolation, they were to "stop, drop, and roll," so, too, did they know that being alone with a martyr meant staying calm, friendly, and respectful. Particular emphasis was placed on the last directive, as certain subsets of martyr populations were arrogant and prone to quick offense. Cicero, as it happened, was often cited as the textbook example of this quality, for El Sacerdote made it clear that the world owed him reverence for his position in the Church, and that humans were totally subservient animals beside the martyr race. He was also well-known as the most violent Family member, and in any poll would have been recognized as the one most likely to take liberties with local laws. It was that temper of his. For instance, had Miki forgotten to thank him, he might have cited this as a form of entitlement on the girl's part; worse, he might have seen it as a deliberate slight. The Lamb's company helped, in large part, to keep him relaxed, his love of his brother being the single thing that might be said to humanize him. They were never apart for long. It should not have surprised Dominia that the entire Family had stopped at Kabul together.

"Isn't it a nice Family vacation," said the General to herself, calculating with relative certainty that Cicero and the Lamb had gotten on the Light Rail in Kyoto and been on the train the entire time. Lavinia and the Hierophant only joined them at martyr-ambivalent Almaty, as the girl was no more allowed to travel alone than was the Lamb. Now all of them were here. Waiting for her.

Let them. They could wait until the sun came up. In a few hours, she would be in possession of what seemed to all the world a full, normal set of human teeth. And the General would be missing an eye, but if that sacrifice was what it took to shake herself free of her Family's influence, she gave it with a glad heart. Especially if she could meet Lazarus without interference.

Now the question was whether Lazarus wanted to meet her.

XV

The Blood of Lazarus

Miki, like most children, possessed the miraculous ability to expunge all recent trauma when given a toy. Thus, upon her early-morning airport acquisition of the rental car while Akachi spent an hour replacing Dominia's teeth, the human returned to collect the General and the semiconscious (former) IT whiz with an attitude that indicated she had put her frightful meeting with Cicero—along with Dominia's reaction—from her mind.

"I can buy songs straight from this thing's dashboard! Did you know all vehicles have access to J-Sing? What a wild world!" She wiggled to the beat in the driver's seat of the cherry-colored, human-operated coupé; in the General's opinion, not the most discrete getaway vehicle around these parts. "I haven't ever owned a car, you know. They're so *expensive*! All the licenses and taxes and insurance—give me a break. I let other people drive me around."

"I'm sure there's no shortage," muttered Kahlil from the back seat, one wary eye always on the dog that, happy for a car ride, panted away while the city passed.

"Are you jealous?" Miki asked with a wrinkled nose. Dominia, trying not to be annoyed, checked her face in the mirror of the sun visor. The swelling beneath her eye patch had reduced to mild irritation. And her mouth, well—that was already healed, and had been since moments before they left Akachi's. The dentist had marveled over the speed with which the martyr body recovered. Such recovery was commonplace to the General, but she had to admit she was particularly grateful for the enhancement at a time like this, in a place like this, where there was no safety or sanity to be had.

Her regret was that her recovery speed meant she had no reason to linger and thank Akachi as profusely as she'd have preferred. The world as wide as it was, she would surely never see him again.

Too bad.

After folding up the visor, Dominia contorted in the passenger's seat to don the black niqab that would hide her face from Kabul's early risers along with its most bright and punctual one. Moving through the city on her own was bound to be challenging anytime, but it was set to be a downright tahgmahr in the sun. Her only advantage was that marathon, which would, she'd been told, tie up most of the city.

It was always good to see serious people coming together for fun. Too bad it had to be against her Family, though she appreciated that aspect now. She could use a bit of levity, knowing that the Hierophant floated around the city, haunting the start of the race. Waiting for her. As if she would bring him Lazarus! She supposed it had been worth a try—nothing ventured, nothing gained, as they said—but he had to understand that she was in no mood to be subservient to him. He had to know he wasted his time.

Yet—if it was absurd, why was she so bothered?

"You're awfully quiet over there, dude." Miki glanced at the hooded General. "You okay?"

"Thinking. Is there a password or something, Kahlil?"

"No. He knows who's acceptable and who isn't. If you're supposed to be let into a Lazarene ceremony, he'll let you in."

Annoyed to hear that, Dominia demanded, "Then he has to consent to seeing me at all, let alone coming with me?"

"Better hope he wants to see you." The Hunter lifted his eyebrows with a certain theatrical disdain. "I don't know why this is hard for you to grasp. The Hunters have operated in various forms for almost two thousand years: if it were possible for anyone on Earth to catch Lazarus, my people would have him by now. You don't stand any more chance than they do. Far less. You're going to have to hope he wants to see you as much as you want to see him."

"I'm sure he will," said optimistic Miki, who never missed an opportunity to cheerlead. "He's got to! That's how the world gets saved. Lazarus comes to Cairo and together he and the Lady lead an army that brings about the final battle with the Hierophant."

To think, martyrs thought of the Abrahamians as a cult! Though, as cults went, Abrahamians were considered the most charming. An infantile permutation of the martyrs' own "true" faith, which the Hierophant brought with him from that (certainly fictional) planet called Acetia where martyrs ruled the land. She had, sometime in her centuries, been in frequent contact with all manner of human contraband for various roles in the military police; during this time, she discovered a positively ancient (positively filthy, positively illegal) United Front comic book series about a female vampire in scant clothes who came from a similar planet. Glancing through that by accident (because who read such trash, ha-ha), she had felt certain that this particular bit of his backstory was a myth; but even her skepticism about her Father's origin could not spur her into questioning his many opinions about God, and about other religions. It was as if something in his mythos had to be provably false to assure her the rest of it was true. That was the power of the Hierophant. He could wave a truth—a horrific truth—before the eyes of anyone, and in so doing render them silent by complicity. All martyrs were cannibals. Therefore, it was in the martyr interest to believe what the Holy Father said when he explained martyrs were the true master race, made in the image of God.

In fairness, their prejudice was more interesting than most human standards. It was not the color or the creed or even the moral character of a person that counted to the divine: it was possession of the sacred protein, which had raised them from the dead. The already metaphorical Bible was rendered in the martyr Church a massive series of metaphors for the protein, whose arrival was embodied in the second coming of Christ. This second coming was never outright stated to be the Lamb, for no true second coming would announce Himself, of course. But it was implied to the point that certain disdained human cults that had once been called Christian turned their prayers, instead, to the Lamb; and even some less-devout fringe Muslims and Jews confused the martyr Elijah with his namesake. These sects, appearing across the United Front and Europa, were not just left unmolested by the martyr government but held to the rest of the human world as shining examples of proper attitude. Subservience to martyrs was key to a long, semi-safe life.

Other, real Abrahamians despised this sort, whether they distinguished themselves as Jewish, Christian, or Muslim. Dominia had never cared for such groveling humans, preferring those Abrahamians such as Kahlil and Tobias. They insisted on maintaining a certain purity of their faith, keeping it all as martyr free as it had always been—except to acknowledge the obvious fact that, if there could be said to be an earthly embodiment of the figure of Satan, the Hierophant was he. The martyrs were hardly more than demons: real devil worshipers who needed, from the popular perspective, extermination. This was where the Hunters came in. This was also where Dominia sometimes came in, because—not always, but sometimes—Abrahamian houses of worship, whether church or mosque or synagogue, became hubs of anti-martyr terrorist activity. These needed shutting down. Most attendants of such places were good citizens. These, the General sought to protect while Governess; but she had long since learned how to tell the difference between the two groups of humans, based on a lifetime spent campaigning against their violent variations. She had broken up more than a few Hunter cells attempting to operate across her Father's territories, but never during an Abrahamian service.

Lazarene services, however, were a different matter. Dominia had never been privy to Lazarus's coming and goings and had always considered him as fictional a character as the Lady, or her Father's martyr planet. However, she now knew that after Lazarus visited an area, his followers kept the ceremonies running in secret: so Miki explained to Dominia on the way to the actual, physical music storefront (a rarity in those nights) where the ceremony was to be hosted. The whole thing was not dissimilar to the Lamb, who bled out every Noctisdomin; the local priests would collect every drop, for Elijah's blood was as sacred as it was physiologically vital to martyrs who were not engaging in nightly cannibalism. Such martyrs had no choice but attend Mass, yet houses were always packed with irregular worshippers when El Sacerdote and his sacred brother rolled on through.

Those Lazarene ceremonies that the General had broken up over the years were almost certainly not ones at which the man himself had been present; all the same, they always seemed outrageously crowded to her. He had probably passed through some years before and left his message, along with some of his blood, with a person he trusted to keep the ceremonies going in private until he could risk coming through the area again. Nobody knew which ceremony would be blessed by a personal appearance until the encryption was broken, at which time it was usually impossible for anyone nefarious to mobilize in sufficient time to reach him. There was no detectable pattern. He seemed to travel miles in the blink of an eye. Today he was in Kabul; last week, he had appeared in some obscure corner of South America after manifesting nowhere for a fortnight, which sometimes happened. Where would he end up next, if Dominia didn't lure him to Cairo?

"If he's supposed to be the Lady's partner, why doesn't he present himself to Her? I'm sure he knows where She is."

"He can't just waltz into Her house without bothering to help humanity! You're pretty selfish sometimes." As the martyr blushed, Miki laughed at her. "Humans can't be saved from martyrs and your Father's world without the blood of Lazarus."

"No wonder Christians can't play nice with you guys." The General checked her gun as Miki pulled the car to a stop along a line of shops tucked beneath a broad overpass, the sort of architectural feature that made her pine for San Valentino. "They must get offended when you talk about it."

"Some of them. Christian-identifying Hunters, especially. But it's true! Watch, you'll see. You'll drink his blood and something crazy will happen."

"I'm not going to drink his blood," scoffed the General, while Miki rolled her eyes and slid open the passenger door with the press of a button.

"Still stuck in your freaky-deaky martyr ways? Whatever. You have to get over it soon. You've spent all this time acting like we're a bunch of cults with messed-up beliefs, but why don't you look at yourself? If it weren't for Tobias, you'd have leftover skin cells in your teeth."

At Dominia's humbled silence, Miki sighed, released her seat belt, and leaned over to hug her martyr friend. "Look, I'm sorry."

"Don't be. You're right. I have to admit that my Father and my people are wrong. I have to change deep down inside—not what I'm doing, but what I believe. I just don't know if I can. Or if I'll be able to live with myself once I do."

"You have to live, idiot! I don't think we'll manage to save the world without you. We need an inside man, right? Somebody with knowledge of your Father's world. You can help us. And we can give you Cassandra."

Those words rolled over her with such cool promise that Dominia closed her eye, exhaling against the fabric of her veil. "Yes," she said as Miki patted her cheek and released her from the embrace.

"You'll be fine! Remember: if the legends are true, Lazarus has done all this before. Listen to him, and you'll end up at Cairo in no time."

"I will. Kahlil"—into the back seat, she thought to say—"I'm sorry."

"Don't worry about it." He lifted a hand to wave her away, along with her concerns. "It was time for a change in career, anyway. People who know too much can be dangerous to the Hunters…I'm sure you know how it is."

Did she ever. Basil had edged forward in his seat and now wagged his tail expectantly. "I suppose you want to come?"

The animal sprang over the center console, across her lap, and upon the pavement of the city.

"What *is* the deal with that dog?" asked Kahlil. Dominia slipped out of the car to shrug as the door shut.

"I'll let you know if I figure it out. See you around." With a pang of sorrow, the General waved to Miki through the window, and the woman who had become her friend waved back with a purse of her lips and a furrow of her glassy brow. Then, boldly, the Red Market priestess turned up her radio and hit the electric. The car whizzed off, destined for Cairo.

Alone with the dog before a storefront whose Arabic letters she could no longer read, Dominia squinted at the time of a distant clocktower: 0400 hours, almost on the dot. The ceremony was supposed to start at four thirty, but she'd secretly hoped (selfishly hoped, according to Miki) to lure him away before it began. They could somehow acquire a vehicle of their own and get out of the sun before it rose. The marathon had already started, and the racers would be weaving through the city for several hours. Running until the dawn, and after. Something martyrs could never do. Attention would be focused on said race, so it wouldn't be impossible to steal a car, or…

The dog looked at her. She sighed, caught. "Why is my first thought always a criminal one?"

You know why, Basil's face seemed to say. Free to stop pretending he was ordinary, he shut his happy mouth and pranced in the direction of the store. To Dominia's surprise, the front door was open, and the pair emerged in the dusty store of antique and new records to find it empty. Aside from her footsteps upon the carpeted floor, she was most keenly aware of music. The choice of song was an old Front one, more popular with humans than with martyrs for the obvious reason that the theme of the song was the love of the singer's eponymous "Lady." Even so, it got the occasional cover in the Americas; therefore, she recognized it, but not this version, or this accent. It might well have been the original. Had it been a new version, one of the heavily mixed, grinding bass modern songs, she might not have heard the soft drone of a familiar voice before she noticed the blue light of the holo-vision emitting in the otherwise unbroken dark. That nasal tone made her skin crawl with irritation no matter where she heard it: but to hear Theodore here? Her baby brother was in the middle of saying: "—times, we must come together as one nation: one people beneath the brilliant banner of the United Front, and the Hierophant."

She cringed. There he was, floating behind the counter, no doubt left on for her. Lo and behold, his doll-size hologram sat behind the desk of her office. She would never adjust to seeing that simp sitting there.

"But there are those who do not believe in the cause: who wish to divide our great nation amid this tenuous transition of power. This is why I am tightening border security in and out of the Front, and am issuing a temporary stay of applications for travel visas. Those of you who had legitimate reasons to leave the country on business or even pleasure, I'm sorry to say a certain former Governess and her terrorist organization ruined it for the rest of us. As for said terrorist organization"—he must have meant René's refugee ring and the Hunters behind it—"we are doing all we can within our borders to detain and punish every member for his or her part in this sordid effort to undermine our nation's unity."

Theodore was, by far, the newest addition to the Holy Family. In his human life, he had been a doctor of some small acclaim who had, in a turn of apparent luck, been selected to watch over young Lavinia, whose first twenty-four years of existence resembled death in all ways, including lack of pulse or organ function, but for one: she grew. When she was around ten, Theodore graduated medical school, and a few years later, he had kissed enough asses to catch the attention of the wrongest right people one could hope to know. Thus, he found himself overseer of a sleeping princess for over ten years, and when she awoke, his service was rewarded by martyrdom, and, the greatest honor possible, adoption into the Family. He had been there when she awoke, and that miracle of all miracles that a once-tiny body should have grown while dead was overshadowed by the greater miracle: that twenty-four years of clinical death might end in sudden life. Why Theodore reaped the reward for this achievement of the protein, Dominia would never understand. As he exclaimed with joy, "With that in mind, I'm pleased to announce the initiation of our long-term space reallocation program!" she could not help but think his reward should have been the ending of his life.

Ghettos were the first step to genocide. She had known them to be coming but had not anticipated them so soon and could not stand to hear of them now. She kept up with snatches of Theodore's babbling explanation but found her mind drifted off; she turned off the holo-vision, because she didn't need to hear him to know what he would say. The rationalizations would be the same as they'd ever been: something about how the most recent wave of immigrant humans represented a dangerous trend in immigration, where, rather than good, hardworking human families coming to contribute to civilized society or labor as the servants of martyrs, people flooding through the borders came to incite rebellion amid their human compatriots. Yet, now that they were there, they could not leave. Ones already in the country needed to be contained, though this was a concept always delivered in terms as whitewashed as possible. People were sensitive.

Dominia, however, was not sensitive. She knew what would happen and recited it in the silence of the shop as Basil led her around the counter to the poster-hidden door that revealed the basement stairs. Humans would be herded like chattel into ghettos, then camps, with healthier ones slaughtered and distributed for food to United Front population centers where martyrs thrived in happy neighborhoods the way humans once had. Many immigrant humans had worked hard amid their neighbors to earn and maintain their homes, their lives, and their families; martyrs hungered to steal that away. Those nice houses would be redistributed to more deserving hands by Theodore as he played favorites in his term as UF governor; those lives would be ended and used to sustain the lives of so-called higher beings; and those pretty, talented children who had once been the future of humanity in the Front (a flicker of hope that Dominia had inspired by the notion that things could change, and humans and martyrs could both work together to meet the future in an optimistic way) would become martyr children. Martyr children who, like Dominia, would grow up to hate the parents they felt abandoned them, either by getting themselves murdered, or by accepting their child's fate and moving on. To a developing and confused mind, a crime nonpareil.

This life was unsustainable. Small wonder she had snapped, albeit slowly, with the death of her wife. After all, it was not so much the death of her wife that had crippled her. Rather, in the midst of that hurricane of absolute emptiness, after René had approached her with promises of Lazarus, she had been invited to a military conference hosted by her Father. The military conference wherein he had announced Project Black Sun.

"Can you remember warmth on your face," he had asked the room packed with high-ranking generals, seeming, as ever, to ask Dominia in particular. "Remember what it was to live and move in the world without fear of the sun? We may be the children of God, but that is why we are hampered by His greatest creation. Without the danger the sun presents, we would be gods, ourselves."

There was a way, he claimed. A way martyrs could walk in the sun. "It seems like a fantasy from where we stand, but the means exist. Humans are in possession of it, and do not even know! Over the next two years, Cicero and I will roll out a plan to acquire these means: and the fine men and women in this room will help me. The world is ours. We need to take it."

A whole world of ghettos. A planet, at constant risk of people like her. The horrors humans endured in the Front paled beside those the world would see if martyrs moved freely. The thought terrified even the General. It had driven her here, and it found her now, along with a dog, knocking at the heavy locked door into which the hidden stairs terminated. A peephole was revealed, then snapped shut. She was close to annoyed when the door opened and there, exactly as she had pictured him, stood Lazarus: a resemblance to imagination so unexpected that she almost fell back against the narrow steps while Basil bolted past her, into the room.

"There you are, Dominia," said the man, a stranger she nonetheless knew. His eyes, pale blue as Basil's, crinkled despite his crabby tone. "Take that damn thing off. You're not fooling anybody."

"I—" Faltering to find he had already turned away, the General removed the niqab and bundled it beneath her arm. The room into which she followed him looked more like an addiction support group than a church. Sweet incense was replaced by humid mold, and pews were nowhere to be seen. Folding chairs had been arranged in the tight space, and a rickety podium served for a pulpit upon which the thickly bearded man resumed arranging a bowl, a dagger, and some napkins. "Do you know me?" she asked, and he said without looking, "Of course I do."

Though she studied his face and felt the familiarity of imagination in his features, she no more truly recognized him than she could divine what race he might have been while human, or his age. For a martyr to achieve grayed hair was an impressive feat: accomplished, to the General's knowledge, only by her Father. But Lazarus looked older than even he, face lined with deep furrows doubtless caused by centuries of nomadic living and, if Miki's stories were true, infinite lifetimes' worth of knowledge. However, old or no, no one lived forever, and she had a hard time buying the story that the world ran itself on repeat. If he did know her, it was from the news.

"If you know me, do you know why I'm here?"

"I know why you think you're here, and I know you're going to be disappointed. Do *you* know why you're *actually* here?"

At her blank look, he lifted the dagger and said, "You're going to help me," while slitting the forearm beneath his robe. Even the battle-hardened General winced to see such an abrupt spray of blood. Basil, who had been sniffing all around the room, bounded to the holy man's side. "Hey, kiddo," he said to the dog, and Dominia asked, "Do you know him, too?"

"Of course I know my good-for-nothing son." He bled into the bowl with a casual expression, unmoved by the bafflement that bloomed in Dominia's voice.

"Your *son*," she clarified, as if it would make any more sense coming from her own mouth. It did not. As the holy man grunted the affirmative, she studied Basil with a kind of grim clarity.

It shouldn't surprise her the old man was crazy, she supposed. It was just—well, it made her job more difficult, didn't it? She already saw herself trying to drag a lunatic to Cairo and wondered if it wouldn't be better (certainly easier) to drop him off with her Father after all. But, before she followed that train of thought to its depressing station, he had tied off his arm and dabbed at the blood with the napkins. "You need a daub of this blood before you can join the ceremony, or they'll never accept your being here."

Almost laughing, brows lifting above her remaining eye, she asked, "Can't we tell them that we did?"

"Sure we can, but you can't tell me." As her laughter faded, she realized he stared at her mouth. "Show me your teeth."

"What—"

He was around the podium and reaching for her with hands almost certainly unwashed. Grimacing, Dominia leaned away until Basil leapt behind her and, paws against her back, shoved her into Lazarus's path. Like he checked a horse, the mystic lifted her upper lip, then shoved her away with a sigh of agitation and a flurry of motion from his hands. The meaning was apparent after a few repetitions.

You know sign language, don't you? For slaves, right?

Yeah, she signed, as displeased to acknowledge that as she was to have had her gums probed by some homeless guy's grubby finger. *Don't you sign at* me *like I'm the one who decided to start muting and deafening uppity gossips.*

I'm not. I know that was Cicero, and way before your time. Anyway—his hands fluttered together in a dismissive wave and he edged back to the podium—*sorry. I saw the eye patch and forgot for a few minutes that just because you've made one good decision doesn't mean you've made two. Sometimes I get sentimental when I see you again.*

"I've never seen you in my life," she exclaimed aloud, echoing her sentiments with hand gestures and a roll of her eye at the severity of his look. *Never in my life.*

Not in this one, he agreed. *You never remember anything. Consider yourself lucky.*

And you?

Every time I'm martyred, I remember everything again. It's my blood.

The blood you want me to drink, she signed with an arched brow of skepticism for the rust-stained basin. *The blood that my Father says is a sin. The blood that humans sometimes kill each other for, that we kill humans for even speaking about. The blood that works miracles.*

Yeah. Imagine being full of it.

Unable to resist her wry smirk, she signed, *Oh, I imagine you're full of it, all right,* and Lazarus cracked something of a grin beneath that unkempt beard. *So why aren't we speaking?* she asked as another knock rang against the door. Her muscles tensed. Before responding to it, Lazarus lingered to deliver a disturbing explanation.

It's Dr. Akachi, he signed before indicating they word-shorten the man's name to a gesture that indicated either the sign for an elephant, or somebody who spent a lot of time ingesting parts of male anatomy. *He's listening through those nice, new teeth of yours.*

Oh, yeah.

This Lazarus guy was certifiable.

Right?

She still reeled from this schizophrenic accusation when the old man opened the door and the first worshiper, the store owner, stepped into the room, chatting in Arabic, then crying out when he saw the General. Before he got too deep into what universally read as a plea for them to escape with their lives, Lazarus stopped him and said something that left his host's expression, at best, dubious. While the men had a conversation, Dominia turned to lay Basil with an annoyed look. Did the dog sign, too?

What is this shit about Akachi? Can't you see this guy is nuts? You're not his son, you're a dog. Why don't you do something?

With those too-cute eyes turned up at her, Basil's tail gave just one wag. The animal was too polite to point out that she was as crazy as Lazarus, signing at a border collie as though it understood. Yet, it was too obvious that it *did* understand. Wasn't it?

Oh, she needed real help. Cassandra's death had done something to her, that was for sure. Miki was right to be worried; she'd started to feel concerned, herself.

"Hey." Lazarus caught her attention once more. *Mehrang here wants proof that you mean to join the Lazarenes for good. It's been almost a thousand years since the last martyr converted. Can't say I blame him for his concern. Looks like you're going to have to do something to prove you're trustworthy, huh?*

Lamb, she signed, glancing over at the bowl.

Lazarus, he corrected on his way to the podium. *It's painless, I promise. Get over the taboos of your culture. If you're going to hell, it won't be because you drank my blood.*

Is *there a hell?* she asked, reluctantly edging toward the podium, as anxious as she'd been when, at fifteen, she was first forced to take full part in a martyr service and have the blood of the Lamb.

If there is a hell, it's almost certainly this world. Calling in Arabic, Lazarus waved the man over to witness Dominia's conversion. The human was as uncomfortable standing near the martyr as the martyr was uncomfortable with what was about to happen. Would she experience something tangible? Would she feel a shift in her own spirit? Surely no. Surely she was just repulsed because, well—it was an intimate thing between martyrs, the sharing of blood. She wasn't eager to taste this random man's. But even the dog studied her. The General pursed her lips.

What was she doing, hesitating like this meant anything at all? There was no point. It was a tiny gesture to make them trust her. Take a dot of blood and talk Lazarus into Cairo. Simple enough. Bracing herself, she dipped a fingertip into the crimson meniscus, and lifted it, stained, to her lips.

Not even the taste was extraordinary! An average martyr's blood, the same as any other. Intriguingly impotent, which was why so many humans ingested it without being martyred—but, aside from that, the same as any man's.

There, signed Lazarus, gesturing toward Dominia. After the human expressed something in Arabic, Lazarus nodded: Mehrang did, too, and offered Dominia his hand.

What did he say? asked the General. Lazarus smiled.

He asked if you would be assisting me today. I told him "of course."

Of course, signed Dominia with irritation. The next knock resounded upon the door.

To what had she agreed?

XVI

Prisoners' Mass

An hour later, Dominia was no longer clear on what she'd expected from the Lazarene ceremony. Some great miracle, she supposed. Some sign of power. Yet, in a way, she had expected this, too: this grinding hour of an old man using sign language to preach to his ramshackle parishioners while in her former periphery. She was forced to turn her head if she wished to see him sign, but he had assigned her the task of holding the bowl of his blood and greeting those (understandably reluctant but incredibly bold) men and women who, in the hurry to kiss Lazarus and taste his blood, looked past all the horrors the General had committed—or had, of late, been accused of committing. Therefore, her understanding of the sermon's start was limited to those glances she stole, but not limited by language. Universal Sign Language had been taught in almost all human schools regardless of nationality since 1200 AL or so, right alongside arithmetic, history, and all the others. Some of these people, she suspected, had not gone to school, and some were children too young to keep up with his words. All told, about thirty followers were in attendance, and those who were not rapt to the motions of the old fellow were riveted by the interpretive whispers of their companions. They watched from the line that led to the bowl, then from their seats, hands folded and faces eager with hope. Those listeners not interpreting were so silent they might have been dead. A few kids too small for even the explanations of their parents had accepted with distaste the bitter substance, then been allowed to gather around the happy dog in the corner; even they seemed to sense the need for silence. Perhaps Basil told them so himself, the General thought as the last worshiper tapped a fingertip of blood upon their tongue and hurried to the edges of the insufficient seats.

Now, Dominia was free to turn her attention to the service. She had caught pieces: the theme, she'd discerned, was forgiveness.

If there's a singular, personal, almighty sentience to the divine forces running the cosmos, I don't think I've met Him: but I know I've met all of you tonight. And when I look into the eyes of the people in this room, I see walking, talking, conscious fragments of the divine, because nature is divine. You are divine. And nature that has evolved to the point of consciousness is true divinity. It is a god that has emerged from a tree, or a statue that has sprung to life. When that emerged consciousness becomes conscious of its own divinity, that consciousness may heal itself, and its body, and its world. When that soul emerges, it is immortal: and that which is immortal is so eternally. I am called a martyr, but my blood will not martyr you. If it did, it would offer a false immortality. An extension on your prison sentence in this world. But prison should not be a place of punishment: it should be a place of reformation. And a prison does not contain prisoners, alone. It has guards, and wardens; janitors, cooks, and nurses. It has holy men to save the battered souls of the living prisoners, and to placate the ghosts of the victims that have followed them to their cells—for the prison also needs the victims of crimes, without which it would have no prisoners. The building of the prison takes much time and planning and many hands, and all those employed for the purpose have been given wealth and good lives in return. They have since died, for a prison requires many generations if it is to be established long-term.

He looked at Dominia. *And a prison also has visitors. Those who stay, even for a short time, to comfort the condemned. They do this generous act through a combination of circumstance, free will, and love; after all, they would never visit such a place if their loved ones were not within. When their visit is terminated, it causes the prisoner great pain. But we martyred prisoners carry their company with us forever.*

Cassandra flashed through the General's mind in such a painful manner that her eye filled with hot tears, and she was forced to weep in front of a room full of humans if she wanted to see what this ragged bastard rambled about. And, oh, *what* a bastard! Making her cry. His mission accomplished, he focused on the crowd again.

Humans are not prisoners. Martyrs are. You all agreed to be here, though you do not remember it. Even the martyrs agreed to be here. Even I, tired as I am, agreed to be here. I am here for you. I am here, not because my blood is a key to your prison cell, but because my blood will reveal that never will you be prisoner unless or until you make the choice to become one. When you choose a life of misery and violence, when you inflict pain on others, when you take from their mouths or bodies to satiate yourself, it is you who will suffer most. You will be made a prisoner of this world and blinded to all that is higher. You will seek and seek and never find, like thirsty, starving Tantalus. But when you choose a life of joy and love, and heal your brothers, and allow the world to feed you, you will never starve or thirst. You will never die. You will be free: and you will see upon your passage to a higher state someday that you have never not been free, and never not been divine.

The sun is a blessing, he summarized. *It is a gift that brings all life and all things. But a prisoner never sees the sun. Not without good behavior, and the help of a guard.*

His hand landed on Dominia's shoulder. She started, even though she'd seen him reach for her. With one hand, in common Arabic, in dying Farsi, in universal English, he said, "Never forget. Though they be terrifying, though they may rape the nurses who heal them and stab the guards who protect them from themselves: none in the prison suffer more than the prisoner."

This was nothing like a martyr ceremony. Where was the unfeeling pomp? The prayer-bruised knees? The acrid incense? The gilded icons and bright stained glass? Where were those moments for her to get lost in her own thoughts and feel nothing? That was what she missed. Where was the emptiness that came with a martyr service? Where was the freedom from looking so closely at her own inner substance that she had to cover her eye, lest her weeping be observed more than it already had? The hand Lazarus still rested upon her shoulder patted, then lifted to her head to draw it to his heart.

"It has been over three hundred years since Dominia has seen the sun without fear," said the old man in English, signing around her for those Arabic speakers who did not understand. "But the sun gives life. The sun gives power. It has always given us power—it has always given us everything. What you have now is the ability to access this power, though it is harder for humans to see without willful practice, meditation, and prayer. When you are in duress, you may well understand. You, all of you, have within you now that substance that allows the body to transcend this place as much as the soul. You possess that which has protected me from danger all this time." He released Dominia and stared hard into her eye.

"If you follow me, and are a careful student, you will learn how to achieve this bodily escape. Even the prisoners among you will bask in the glory of the sun. I will show you how it is I've come to do all this."

She might have asked him what "this" was, if it did not become self-evident the second he disappeared.

Dominia's gasp was but one of a chorus that rose soon rose into climactic clamor. As heads whipped toward those of neighbors to ask what happened in tones no longer hushed, a flurry of movement drew the General's attention. Basil bounded through his circle of admirers, past the shocked worshipers, and to the door at which he pawed. He was unable to work the round knob, but he was able to demonstrate urgency. Her motions swift as those of the animal, she rushed down the makeshift aisle and regretted how a few humans uncomfortable with the martyr's company winced away. No time to linger for apologies: she threw open the door, and the border collie sprang four stairs at a time, confident that Dominia scrambled behind. She had not exchanged a word with the dog, yet was positive of its intentions. Could a dog be the son of a martyr? Lazarus's blood was impotent for means of martyring, or so she'd heard over the years. It was not a metaphor for the dog's suspected martyred condition. What did it mean?

Upstairs, the storefront remained empty, with the front door still locked from within: but raucous sounds pervaded the room as though a thousand marchers streamed through its aisles— caused, Dominia thought, by the holo-vision. It had been turned on again, and switched from Theodore's smarmy face to a far more graphic scene. An Arabic broadcaster, safe in his station, spoke with hurried gravity in words Dominia did not understand, but the gruesome models of light did the translating for her. Before her eye, and those of the cameras, a river of joyous runners ran through Kabul's streets. The first group of "serious" racers had already finished, and now a great mass stumbled through, looking better fit for Halloween than a marathon. Cow costumes, mermaid costumes, bee costumes, djinn and ghost and zombie costumes, naked runners: but, most especially, runners dressed up as parodies of the Hierophant who, in their oversize suits and various states of decomposition, sparked an age-old, ingrained sense of sacrilegious offense until she remembered she could laugh. The Hierophant probably also viewed it with a good sense of humor—superficially, anyway. Every action he took was formulated for its ambiguity, and his doings were so consistently patient, good-natured, and generous that, when it came to complaining about him, no one who knew him could vocalize the distinct root of their mistrust. By the time they had a clear reason, it was too late—as late as it had been for Cassandra. Oh! Opening the door that night: that night after ninety years of love. Ninety years, unable to prevent or expunge one moment's tragedy.

Yet, the images before her cleared her spell of self-pity, for they were perhaps worse than even that odious discovery. The runners, shots of whom were absent any journalists, smiled, laughed, and were frequently joined by those who stood watching the race on the sidelines: people in casual clothes, sometimes even business clothes, despite the weekend, ran in dozens between their costumed fellows. They ran, and ran, and the camera feed cut to their destination, Hashmat Kahn Lake, where floated the bodies of all those winners who had drowned themselves in waters ankle deep. Smiling followers pursued with merry laughter, floating the bodies of serious runners off to the center of the lake so as to kneel facedown in the shallows. A few intrepid marathoners sprinted through the water, to its center, in search of a deeper patch in which to drown effectively.

Her brain almost failed to comprehend the scene. Then, a racer in a curly blonde wig hefted a rock from the water to crush her own skull in particular savagery. Lavinia's doing. Dominia turned toward a noise at the door and found Lazarus standing before it.

"We have twenty minutes to sunrise," said the mystic over the drumbeat of feet amplified hundreds of times by the open door. The marathon's route (perhaps thanks to Lavinia) included the overpass under which the music store was tucked. "Do you understand? That means we have fifteen minutes to save Kabul from your Family."

"They'll be forced inside by the sun, too. Whatever we start can be finished in their hotel."

"We won't be going inside when the sun comes today. At least, you won't."

"Where will I go?"

"Same place the dog's going." The old man stepped out of the store, and once more disappeared when Dominia pursued him onto the noisy street. Cursing, she studied the riotous overpass, then turned around to ask Basil—herself, she supposed—what she'd ought to do—

But the dog, too, was gone.

"Basil," she called in the silence of the shop. "Here, boy, we don't have... Lamb." The title crossed her lips in the wind of a heavy sigh that marked the moment she turned heel and ran as fast as she could in the direction opposite the marathon.

To be fair, marathons were rather less impressive when one was a martyr. Everything from increased reflexes, to improved metabolic efficiency, to simple muscle mass differences, meant that martyr was to man what cougar was to house cat. Consequently, humans tended to favor athletics as a hobby more than martyrs did. It was more impressive and more vital that a human maintain their endurance. As active as she was, Dominia had always resided among that niche of martyrs partial to watching the human Olympics. This made her something of a nerd in her culture, but she had never been ashamed to like what she liked, and she had always been interested to see the physical development of mankind as chronicled in their Olympic statistics. Even in her life, the time it took the best of the best trained human Olympiads to run a mile had shaved off so many seconds that it had begun to approach the three-minute mark, hovering somewhere around 3:34.89, if she recalled the women's record—men had pushed their number down into the two-minute-something region.

A martyr's physical capabilities, meanwhile, were in excess of even those top Olympiads (which meant that they were unwelcome at the games, much to the General's profound dismay as a young girl). Of these, Dominia's physical capabilities were within the top percentile. Most acknowledged that the only martyrs capable of besting her in a brawl or match of wits were Cicero and, of course, the Holy Father. But a race? The General could outrace them any day. At her absolute physical peak, she could clear a mile in one minute and fifteen seconds; she was forever aggravated that she couldn't get it down to a clean minute, to render herself good as a low-speed self-driving buggy of the sort in gated communities established by those rare wealthy human families remaining in martyr territories. Granted, when she was running more than one mile, there was a significant drop-off with each subsequent. Add to that the fact that, though she was far from out of shape, neither had her third century of governance left her quite so honed as she'd been in her dual centuries.

This was all to say that she had to hope she was no more than five miles from the start of the race, if Lazarus's cryptic declaration was to be believed; if she was to have sufficient time to handle her Family and cure the racers before sunrise, it would be best if she had less than five miles. On top of her aggrieved emotional and physical condition, she was forced to run upstream, against that happy crowd so eager for her to join that sometimes they tried to turn her by the shoulders to get her going in the right direction. Well-meaning folks, these hypnotized sorts.

Another problem: she paused at the corner of one block when she recognized a storefront from the broadcast, feeling obligated to destroy a holo-camera set long since abandoned by its infected crew. The more sets she destroyed, the better. The memetic virus was much stronger in person than over a medium like television or radio—so far as the Family's experiments on the matter had discerned—but that did not mean it was without effect. People rushed down the street to join the race, having seen it on television in their apartments. These infected were obliged to take part in a happy mass suicide, motivated by Lavinia's fury. The General was ashamed she had failed to predict this result the instant Miki had explained the marathon's premise. Of course saintly Lavinia would react this way after one look at all these sacrilegious racers: these gross humans mocking her beloved "Daddy" and good uncles and poor, corrupted older sister. Of course this was the result of their presence in Kabul.

Of course this was the result of her running away.

A nearby electronics store, across a panoply of screens and holographic figures, demonstrated that the bodies had begun to pile up. Above her, even the light poisoning of the dense city could not hide the intensifying blue tint of the coming sun. She fancied her skin already burned, for mere knowledge that the blue wavelength of sunlight had such profound effects seemed sufficient to sicken her. It may have seemed silly that the tiny amount of light from electronics—enough to impact a human's sleep—could do a martyr harm, but that small amount of artificial blue wavelengths were good as shade compared to those belched by the unforgiving sun. Enough to kill a martyr frighteningly quick, especially with UV involved; even these predawn minutes were known to be dangerous. When Dominia had reached the cove in which she was destined to meet Cassandra, she'd already felt the gentle sting of spotty sunburn avoided. Now she was as concerned about her ability to endure the path to the marathon's origin as she was about how seared she'd be. All Cicero would have to do was slap her in the face, she mused, trying to make herself laugh amid her deep duress, and failing. As she paused to destroy another camera set, Lazarus appeared from the depths of the crowd and grabbed her arm.

"We don't have time for that." As he drew her forward, he urged, "Come on," and flung her through a space that didn't exist.

What a strange lurch! The world flickered. For a skipped beat, not a racer remained in sight. In the second during which she stumbled, it was through a strange velvet place whose darkness was not so much interrupted or overlaid by light, as it was embossed by vast bands of bent colors that emanated from the slats between her ribs and from elsewhere, too. They tugged her forward by the solar plexus, yet showed her so many other ways that she might go. She only recognized the tug as a sense of direction—and only recognized they weren't alone—when pulled out of that strange space by Lazarus, who ran, as normal, through the marathoners that made themselves once again present.

"What was that?" cried the General.

"Patience, please."

Hindsight exhibited hints of what her mind had experienced but not perceived: a carmine waistcoat, and the bitter scent of cigarettes. "I saw a man there."

"Right," he said. "My son."

Dominia could not find words to articulate her questions—*concepts* to articulate her questions. Her mind now struggled to parse from the ground great obstructions between which the racers were funneled, and she was shocked to recognize the grandstands rising at the head of the race. In that eerie flicker of reality, Lazarus had drawn her steps sufficient to take her several miles. She trembled in his grasp, so overwhelmed by her comprehension and her added confusion that, at best, she half saw the Family. They had assembled themselves to watch the chaos of a race that was now infinite, surpassing the boundaries of its starting line and stretching as far through Kabul as there lived people to be infected. Yet, she paid the tragedy no mind: she asked, voice hoarse, "How powerful are you, Your Holiness?"

"Don't get weird and religious on me! No titles, please. I'm a fraction as powerful as you. Now, get out there."

With one, sharp shove, Lazarus pushed her through the crowd and left her exposed beside the grandstand opposite that of her Family. Her eye met Cicero's; he rose in those same seconds in which she snatched the gun from her waistband. While veiled Lavinia cried out from beneath the Hierophant's parasol, Dominia expended bullets, but the effort was futile when the Lamb, also, rose from his seat. The first one missed El Sacerdote's shoe, polished for the occasion and matched to a suit that, still collared, was less garish than the Father's but by no means one of his typical cumbersome religious uniform; as he stripped off his jacket in preparation for the fist fight, a marathoner, by some stroke of the Lamb's ill luck, tripped over an untied shoelace and knocked the General's firing arm askance with such force that she did not just waste the bullet she had been aiming, but also its follower. The next shot, by likewise remarkable luck when she decided to shift her target, ricocheted from the Hierophant's fat golden ring, and he uttered a noise of distaste audible even over Lavinia's shriek.

"Are you finished," called Cicero while the Lamb accepted his jacket and waded with him into the crowd. "Put down that gun! It's the weapon of the craven and the lazy. Fight me like a real woman and the Lamb won't need to be involved."

"I'll fight you whatever way it takes to kill you if you won't stop while you're alive."

"All for these?" The Family's priest waved about him, and in so doing, avoided taking a shot to the shoulder. "For these weak-willed fools manipulated into suicide with the words of a livid child in a grown woman's body? You would abandon your Family for *these*?"

"This was never about you! This was never about the Family, or treason, or terrorism. It was about Cassandra."

Sneering, Cicero thrust aside a few racers. While Dominia gritted her teeth and flipped her gun to use as a cudgel, the priest asked, "You would return her to life; is that right? Depend on the madness of pagans to accomplish what you know to be impossible? The protein is the only route by which we may have eternal life in this world. If that is scorned—"

"Cassandra didn't scorn the protein. She scorned this way of life." The handle of the pistol was meant to whip across Cicero's face, but with his most beloved brother there, he was close to unstoppable: he ducked with a full second to spare and tackled Dominia with such force that her head slammed against the metal bleachers. Garnet sparks burst in the eye still there. As she thought, with sympathy, of Kahlil, the priest forced her to the ground and slammed her skull once more—this time, against the concrete.

"Ninety years she lived this life, my sister, without complaint. You mean to say that you are free of sin in this? You don't think you had the slightest hand in how she died?"

"It was this Family." The words were hissed through a jaw clenched by Cicero's hand until he caught her fist. "It was this way of life, this Family, this whole fucking world! It was Father!"

"It was *you*, Dominia," snarled Cicero, as his free hand caught her gun in effort to break her fingers against it. "A healthy woman, satisfied with ninety years of marriage—"

"You don't know anything about our lives."

"Do you think such a woman would commit suicide?"

The word made Dominia ill. She had succeeded in not thinking on Cassandra's exact method of death so long that it came on her like it had the first time. That brutal surprise as the sound of the door's opening gave way to the discharge of her own gun.

All the shame in Cassandra's regretful eyes, locked forever on hers.

"It was Father." She had to say it through a layer of misting tears. "What he said to her that night, at Lavinia's party—I know that it was about."

"And you know"—he relaxed his grip on her hands—"Father is far from the only one culpable."

A third voice interrupted from across the clamor of madness. "Maybe not; but he deserves a lot of credit."

It was not the voice of the Lamb, but the voice of Lazarus. Heads turned to the source; in the distance, the Hierophant's eyes lit. The holy man stood with his ceremonial dagger poised against the throat of the Lamb.

"Sorry, Elijah," said Lazarus, tone causal, "but you should be used to this by now, right?"

The Lamb did not speak. Cicero showed his teeth, perfect and white and free of augmentation, but nonetheless sharp enough to elicit a lupine aspect. "So, Father was right. You brought your heretic to play."

"I brought her. Let the General go, or this dagger goes in his heart, and not his throat."

"You wouldn't." Cicero's pitch rose to that of uncharacteristic fear, and his body, in instinct's mistake, lifted toward his brother enough that the thrashing General freed the empty hand that he held by the wrist. As he looked back to her, his face written in layers of rage, the General clenched her teeth and, with the satisfying pop-and-splatter of gore, put out her brother's right eye.

Cicero's scream pierced the eardrums of those around, such that a few racers, even through their hypnosis, thrust hands over their ears with deep grimaces. A plethora of cameras formed a perimeter, all intended to capture the race, all transmitting a virus across Kabul, and now, all transmitting more evidence of Dominia's terrorism to the world at large. The Hierophant, wearing that same look of disgust worn when Dominia had shot Murph McLintock, handed Lavinia the parasol. Lazarus, meanwhile, seemed to have disappeared, leaving the Lamb standing there as calm as—

Well.

With her Father coming down the grandstand stairs, now was hardly the time to think in clichés. But what time was it? When was sunrise? Was this to be the moment of her death? What would it feel like? A thousand thoughts rushed through her mind as the Hierophant blipped out of existence (in a manner identical to Lazarus, it was worth noting) and appeared before her as if he'd been there the whole time. All those harried questions were laden with terror, and froze in that terror on his appearance; but, rather than tear out Dominia's remaining eye in return for Cicero's, or take her gun, or strike her in any way, he picked up his gasping son and slung the man, a few inches shorter than he, over his massive shoulder.

"It's always the same with you two, isn't it, Dominia? You and your brother have never gotten along."

"I always thought of him as more of an uncle."

"A matter of perspective, I suppose. Uncle, or brother: I will need your help to get him out of peril. And I shall require your help in protecting Lavinia."

The question was so strange, in this place, in this circumstance, that the General could not understand the words. "My help?"

Before he answered, the blast wrenched a hole through reality and responded for him.

XVII

Saint Valentinian

Until that moment, Dominia was sure she'd heard her life's loudest sound. A gunshot might not seem that loud. But it could be. One single discharge, looping in her mind in the world's most painful eternal recursion, blocking out all other noise, blowing out the world. That was loud.

How loud had Cassandra perceived that sound to be? Dominia pondered this when masochistic, and made herself sick in wondering. From within her wife's mouth, the discharge of the antique barrel's slender phallus must have sounded as loud as the explosion in Kabul, which, sufficient to rattle the ground for several blocks, shattered the street the way the gun had devastated the back of Cassandra's skull. But she never imagined what happened after that moment of death—that moment around which her mind swirled ever closer if she drifted too near the vortex of her sorrow. She did not contemplate any notion of eternity, for better or worse. It seemed from the General's jaded perspective that Cassandra's entire existence ended in that moment, when Dominia opened the door too late. Always a second too late.

There had been nothing in this physical world for Cassandra after that awful second of sonic disruption that marked the destruction of her brain. Martyrs had two irrecoverable organs: the heart, and the brain. Everything else grew back, or could be replaced with a cyborgan. But nothing could be done about those two physical mainstays of martyrs. A basic biological fact known the world around.

This had not been a cry for help. This had been a calculated decision that left Dominia as disoriented as now. Both times, she survived the tahgmahrish noise, and now, in Kabul, stood amid the screams of this *massa confusa* that might have been, for all she knew, her own charging back from the past. They must have been, at least partially: the screams of the humans were loud; yet, muted like a socked phonograph amid her Father's collection of antiques, they could have been miles away. It was the motion of the Hierophant's lips that drew her attention back to the present, and that helped her keen senses pierce the dense ringing to compile the meaning of his sounds. "We have a car," he was saying. She struggled to divine what he was getting at in the haze of the explosion; when it clicked as he said, "Come with us," she laughed.

"You want me to help you? I have to save these people from Lavinia's virus."

"You claimed before your quarrel was not with us; then, it cannot be with Lavinia." The spray of a semiautomatic weapon in the distance did not deter unharmed (even wounded) racers from resuming their run as if nothing had happened, with more ignoring the debilitated amid the rubble of the blast zone by the distant podium and most prominent camera set. The Hierophant placed a compatriot's hand upon her shoulder. "Will you help us?"

Before she spoke, the feedback of a microphone echoed through Kabul: the city's emergency alert system had been co-opted to announce the marathon. Now, it had been co-opted again, by a familiar voice whose inappropriate jolliness exceeded even that of the Hierophant.

"Ladies and gentlemen, there is no need to fear." Tobias Akachi didn't even bother to switch to Arabic, the prick. "The Hunters have heard your call of alarm. While your police waste their time at Lake Hashmat and the martyr terrorist runs rampant in your city, the source of the problem has presented itself for the slaughter! Miss Mephitoli? May I see you for a moment?"

Dominia leaned around the grandstand that had sheltered her from debris. Tobias lowered the microphone from where he stood surrounded by a bunch of armed and armored soldiers. With those perfect white teeth, he smiled, then called across the rubble- (and body-) filled pit that smoked with energy from the explosion. "I am sorry to see you have not secured Lazarus for us, but I am pleased, as I said, to see the bad teeth making up your Family are all here for the extraction. Even infamous Miss Lavinia! I suppose it is no use asking her to come along with us."

"What do you want with Lavinia," asked the General as the Hierophant set Cicero on his feet and rendered him, as usual, the responsibility of the Lamb, upon whom he leaned his bloodied face and caught his staggered breath. The drama queen.

Akachi, as though they were not present, enthused, "What does anyone want with Lavinia? As powerful as your sister is, a man could control the world. But I have so many questions—perhaps you could answer them for me."

"Go to hell." Dominia ducked back around the grandstand for a safe place to reload her gun. At that, the Hierophant spread his arms in a show of helplessness.

"How sorry I am to say, Tobias, that my daughter may be a troubled girl, but she is not a fool."

"You two know each other?" asked the aggrieved General. Her Father chuckled.

"I know him better than he does me, but we have some small association in this life, I admit. We have quite a lot in common, so far as I can tell."

"Then"—Tobias drew a gun from the tan fabric of his cloak—"perhaps it is a pity this will be the moment our association ends."

She had seen many people disappear that morning, but it was still uncanny to see the Hierophant blink out of existence and back into it five centimeters behind Tobias. As the dentist registered the event, he winked out of existence to the sounds of open fire.

Through clenched teeth—two of which were, indeed, designed to listen in on her private conversations—the General swore. She swore, not just for the observation that Akachi, head of the Hunters in Kabul and maybe all the Middle States, was also in possession of that same power as Lazarus and her Father. No: she swore because, after all the pain he had caused her, all the disgrace to her name and his responsibility in pushing Cassandra to suicide, she would greet dawn fighting by her Father's side.

The tone of the sky and the singe of her cheeks alerted her that they had, at best, five minutes. Darting around the corner, the General unloaded (by luck of the Lamb) three rounds and killed four men while the Hierophant snapped the neck of one, acquired his weapon, and put down three more. This much gunfire hadn't filled the air around her since Nogales, and it sent her into a conditioned response so efficient in open terrain that the DIOX-I couldn't have kept up. Before, she had needed the influence of the Lamb to clear the building due to problems of tight quarters and a clear outmatch in numbers and equipment: here, she was free. Here, she sang, first acquiring the ceremonial dagger that Lazarus had let tumble at the feet of the Lamb. With this, she meant to charge into the fray, but her Father called, "No," and, "Your sister."

The densely skirted girl crouched in a panic against the shelter of the grandstand. After ending the lives of some Hunters who charged around a corner, Dominia dashed to the side of her sister and caught her by the arm.

"Are you all right?"

The girl, paler than Dominia had ever seen her, shook with such violence that her older sister ached beneath the immensity of guilt. "I wanted to see the world with Daddy," Lavinia said, her pupils pinpoints. "I wanted to bring you home."

The poor girl. A soft heart was clay to the Hierophant. "Stay close to me and I'll keep you safe, all right?"

"Yes, Ninny, please."

Tearful, the Family's alleged superweapon clutched Dominia's forearm, and the General shifted her to reload. "Why would you do that to these people, Lavinia?"

"Didn't you see their awful costumes? It was terrible! They're disrespecting Daddy, and because they're disrespecting Daddy, they're disrespecting God."

"Our Father is not God."

"Of course not, Ninny. But he's closest to God on the whole Earth. He knows God."

"Your Father"—Tobias appeared in a blink before them and provoked a shriek from Lavinia—"is a liar."

"Why don't you join the race," hissed the girl, but the dentist laughed.

"I have taken the blood of Lazarus, thank you, and while I do not go in for the sacrilegious nature of his efforts to explain the phenomenon of his blood, the effects upon the body and the mind are undeniable. Your filthy pagan magic means nothing to me, witch."

While Lavinia squawked in indignation, Dominia leveled her gun with his face. "Why don't you show me how fast you can disappear."

The answer was "faster than a bullet." In her blind periphery, he reappeared, and she whipped right on Lavinia's scream to find him already pointing a gun at the General's face.

"Do you martyrs have time to drag this battle out? Dawn is minutes from breaking over the city's horizon. When the sun shows his golden face, where will your sister be? We can offer her immediate shelter if you'll send her with us. And if you hand her over, General, I am sure you and I can meet at some reasonable compromise."

"My daughters belong at home with their Family, Akachi." The Hierophant appeared behind him and pressed a rifle into the back of his head, for whatever good that might do. "Let them be."

"You are making a mistake by going with him." Tobias once more flickered out of existence; Lavinia, with a cry of relief, flung herself into her Father's arms to weep.

"There, there, princess, we'll have you home soon enough."

"I wish I'd never left," she lamented as he swept her off, the General racing alongside them and picking off scattered insurgents before accepting the assault rifle from her Father to act as their proper escort. While she continued mowing down anyone with a gun, keeping her bursts of fire short and even to prevent civilian casualties among the runners, the Hierophant did not seem inclined to stop shaming her to Lavinia.

"In all fairness to the big, bad world from which I have shielded you, it *is* often bad—but not often this bad. It takes a character wild as our dear Dominia to bring about this level of chaos."

"It's not my fault you followed me! And it's not my fault that Lavinia infected these people."

Their protector nailed a few snipers poised on fire escapes while the trio darted down an alley in pursuit of the Lamb and Cicero, who were already about to emerge on the other side; nonetheless, Lavinia insisted, "They deserved it!"

Dominia could have screamed, and almost had to over the battle. "No one deserves this! These are good people!"

With a pettish noise of disgust, the Hierophant ducked a spray of gunfire from behind and hurried Lavinia before him to hasten their escape. "Yes: humans are such good people, my girl! That is why they are trying to kill us because we are martyrs. Why they maligned us with the insulting marathon to which your sister took offense."

The alley's exit was close, but behind them it had filled with Hunters. Dominia wheeled about to dash backward amid her wild firing while she shouted, "That doesn't mean they all deserve to die."

"And they will not," answered the Hierophant, as, in a moment that seemed choreographed, the emergency alert system again booted up with the sound of feedback. No longer the voice of Tobias Akachi: to Dominia's relief, it was the voice of Lazarus, who'd taken advantage of a podium emptied by Hunters in pursuit of the escaping Family.

"To be, or not to be," his voice announced, "that is the question."

"You see," asked the Hierophant, smiling over his shoulder. "No harm done."

Throughout the city of Kabul rang the melancholy speech of Prince Hamlet, its English words capable of curing even those who knew no English. The effects were the same with reading the Japanese *Tale of Genji* to Spanish speakers, or even, in one remarkable instance, forcing an ailing human to look at a QR code that would have decrypted into an image of the "Mona Lisa" for a computer or digital implant—to a normal eye, was the same as any bar code, but it had some effect. The format in which the information of the fine art was represented did not seem to matter when it came to curing the memetic virus; so long as the information was presented to the ailing mind in any form, for any sufficient length of time, the will would be restored. A brain desperate for a cultural palette cleanse seemed to take what coherent information it got; or perhaps there was a deeper reason at work on another level, as Dominia would someday suppose.

As Lazarus continued on, "Whether 'tis nobler in the mind to suffer the slings and arrows of outrageous fortune, or to take arms against a sea of troubles and by opposing end them… To die," and Dominia shot down men, those many running citizens of Kabul began to slow, and stop; those watching from other countries who had felt compelled to drive or even fly to Kabul now found themselves in their cars or at the airport, baffled as to their own intent; and those earliest to heal, those quickest to regain consciousness, responded to the realization of what had happened with a citywide wail louder than any siren.

As the speech slipped into the subject of dreams, Dominia, Lavinia, and their Father emerged from the alley. Time was up. Sunrise stretched across Kabul, and as the *tanque* driven by the Lamb snarled to a halt before the ragged trio, the Hierophant turned to his former Governess. Studying the gun and deciding that forcing her into their car was not a valid option, he settled on his usual weapon: reason.

"Come with us, my girl. Come home now, and spare us this heartache. Are your false hopes worth this? Don't you see none of this would have happened—no one would have died—if you would have stayed at home? Come back, Dominia. Leave with us now, and it will be like nothing ever happened."

Lavinia's tear-stained, debris-smudged face gazing up at her, her Father's expectant, all-knowing black eyes barreling into her.

The empty spot upon her breast where Cassandra's diamond should have been.

"I can't." Her words were hoarse as she stepped away. "I'm sorry."

"You would rather meet the sun than admit you were wrong," shouted Cicero from within the vehicle, even as the Holy Father stuffed protesting, crying, and pleading Lavinia into the *tanque*. All the while, the girl screamed, "But Ninny! She'll die!"

"It is her choice," said the Hierophant, pulling the door shut behind him. "Drive."

Her Family peeled through the streets of Kabul; stomach in knots, Dominia faced the alley down which she'd come.

Save for corpses, it was empty. The remaining insurgents had seen they walked into a death trap and turned tail, either to run, or to try and acquire Lazarus, whose words came to their abrupt end with the phrase "Thus conscience does make cowards of us all," and another, swift-to-end hail of gunfire.

The General dropped her stolen gun and hovered in the shadow of the building as dawn glowed across the cured—but not yet near healed—city. What was she to do? Where was she to go? How was she to find Lazarus?

"Follow me," he had urged her.

She would see the sun, he had promised her.

She studied her own body with a wretched feeling and wondered, again, what it was like to die. "And thus the native hue of resolution is sicklied o'er with the pale cast of thought"—her voice was tight and humorless as her soft laughter—"and enterprises of great pitch and moment with this regard their currents, turn awry, and lose the name of action."

Although she laughed, laughed at herself and the (in)appropriateness of the soliloquy amid the citywide grief of Kabul, she could not make herself step into the sun. She could not believe that she was not reading into his words, that it was not all wishful thinking on her part. Yet, as Tobias Akachi appeared before her while his men called from the distance, she could not deny her eye.

"Alone at last, eh, Miss Mephitoli?" She no more bothered to level her revolver at him than she usually would have at her Father, and he smiled at that. "I am sorry to see you were abandoned by so many: first, Miki and Kahlil; then, Lazarus and your dog; now, your Family."

"I'll be meeting at least one of the pairs you mentioned elsewhere. For the others…I don't know what to say about them."

"You do not need to defend the actions of those who have abused you, General. We all must reach our breaking points, and rise against our traitors and slavers. If we do not, we are as good as dead!"

"I'm already as good as dead, whatever I do." She studied the hardening edge of the building's shadow and pressed against the clay bricks behind her. "You and your men seemed pretty comfortable with the idea of killing me a few minutes ago."

"When you tried to kill us, we needed to defend ourselves! It was your Father who began the fight, remember." She made no comment. "I see you are cross about the teeth."

"You're the most stunning hypocrite I've ever met. The Hunters are terrorists."

"To your people, perhaps."

"And yours. Don't play games. Your organization has killed more humans than martyrs over the years."

"All in the name of higher justice. The most important thing is that your species is wiped off the map. The cost required to achieve this goal does not matter to God."

"Met Him, have you?"

"I know nothing more of God than any other Christian man; but I will say that I know more than your blasphemous Father, who profanes the Word at every turn he may. He has so profaned the Word of God that he has dropped a veil before your eyes, and the eyes of all your people."

"My eyes are—" She fought back an expression of annoyance. "My eye is open." Although, it was rather obvious she did not believe it, and she was not at all surprised by Tobias's look of distaste down the death-filled alley behind her.

"Then perhaps you had better put it to use, General. Do you suppose those men you killed to be nothing more than dreams? Is that how you won your thousand battles?"

This blistered her, and had she not been restrained both by the increasingly spectacular sunlight and Akachi's supernatural capacity to blink out of sight, she would have killed him then and there to show him how she'd made so many victories. But that was what he wanted, wasn't it? Wanted to goad her into striking him so he could mock her. She almost hoped so; because, if she was just projecting her own expectations upon him, well, maybe Miki was right. Dominia needed to adjust her attitude toward herself before she learned to get along with anyone else. With forceful calm, she shaped the words. "I remember the men and women I've killed. If not their names, then their faces. How many faces do you remember?"

The son of a bitch laughed at her. "Why do you bother, Miss Mephitoli? Do you think that your remembering them makes up for what you have done? Think of all their mothers."

"Did you come here to shame me, Tobias?"

"No, my friend. I came to speak reason to you. I am concerned about what will happen if you will not be reasonable." Around the corner of a distant mosque flooded a troop of Tobias's men; Dominia rolled her eye along with her shoulders. "We cannot afford to let you die at this juncture—and it will cost a great many men, I suspect, to take you alive."

Her lips curled into a spray of her own bitter laughter. "So you need me for something? Want to find out about my Father's Project Black Sun?"

"My friend, I know all about your Father's project." This shocked her, until he went on with a pleased lift of his brows: "Monsieur Ichigawa was compliant."

"I didn't tell him anything of value."

"You didn't have to. You told him that your Father had a plan to allow martyrs to walk in the sun. That was all I needed to hear to know his intentions."

"Know him that well, do you?"

"No." The dentist's glasses, which had darkened with the rising of the sun, did not hide the way his eyebrows lifted to the top of his glittering bald head. "But I do know Lazarus that well. At least, better than you."

Dominia glanced into a cyan sky that her eye, blinded by that glare, collaged with great shards of noncolor. "You mean to say that Lazarus is going to help my Father?" She heard, as she spoke, the echo of her Father's commandment—declaration, prophecy—that she would bring Lazarus to him during the marathon. It had been the other way around, in the end—but Akachi's next supposition provided a particle of relief.

"No, Dominia. I do not proclaim to know the future as does your profane Father, for only God may know that. I do know that Lazarus is not the type to help your Father. You, however, may be."

"So why not kill me?"

His men assembled behind him, awaiting his word to attack or subdue her. "Because without you, there will be no one to kill your Father. If you are not alive, the magician will depart to a world where you yet live, and the martyr stranglehold on this world will never find relief."

"'Magician,'" repeated the baffled General while he ignored her and barreled on. "I cannot seem to discern the exact nature of his role. But he has made it most clear to me—as I have always believed—that this era in which we find ourselves is a tipping point. The mass panic in Kabul today is but a symbol for the state of this world: and when the chaos calms, either martyrs will have closed their stranglehold on the planet, or humans will shrug them off and rise to dominance once more. The cowards of humanity's past valued an uncertain future in an uncertain world above solving a problem that has grown worse by the year. But we have a duty to this world, Miss Mephitoli. We humans, that is."

"I'm a martyr," she admitted, "but I'm not like the rest."

"No: you are not like the rest. You are much more important. If the magician is to be believed, we would all do well to keep you alive. Your death, he has insisted to me, shall mean the end of the human world. Even if you live, you may yet choose to bring it on. A true apocalypse."

She tried to laugh in the face of his superstition, but she found she could not when she thought of the Red Market and the Lazarene belief in the cyclical nature of time in the universe. "I would never help my Father with his designs against humanity." Best to play it dumb. "I've changed."

"You have not changed, General. Had you changed, you would have apprehended your Father and come with us without spilling human blood. You are the same mass murderer you were before."

"You don't know anything about me. It's not up to you to say whether I've changed."

"Until you can admit that you are no better"—Tobias drew his gun, and the General readied hers—"you are a liability. I understand you lost your wife? That she killed herself." She did not speak, for she could not untense her jaw, and the dentist went on to explain, "She did that because she retained her conscience. If more martyrs would but follow her example! This world would be a safer, holier place."

Nostrils flaring, Dominia glanced at the ground, then in the direction of a dog's short bark. From the shadows of an alley, Basil made eye contact with her, stepped into the sunlight, and appeared to dissolve on its contact. While seeing this, Dominia admitted for the first time in months, "That wasn't why she killed herself."

"You know, do you? Yet here you are, trying to resurrect her—not only against the will of God but also her own will. Do you expect you shall flee to Cairo, reproduce her body, and live happily ever after in your Father's world? In the human world? If she took her own life and you give it back, will she be anything but resentful?"

"We'll make our own world. Wherever we go, whatever we do: it won't matter, because we'll be together."

"When all this is said and done, Miss Mephitoli, and you have helped us to kill your Father, I promise"—his men moved forward on some subtle signal of his head—"I will see to it that you and your wife are reunited forever."

"I'd rather see her right now than look at you another minute," said the General. As the insurgents closed in, she holstered her gun and dashed, not into battle with the men, but into that one thing that might save her: the risen sun.

Much as with the Lazarene ceremony, she had not known what to expect—but what she expected was, nevertheless, not quite this. In the instant that her body hit the sun and she expected her skin to burn under the intensity of its unhampered blue light, time appeared to freeze. Tobias and his moving men jolted to a halt, and so did the morning pigeons in the air, and so did the General's own body, which was frozen for seconds in the act of stepping until it seemed that all of this, like some vast shell, shattered away, then compressed into a pinpoint within her solar plexus that stole her breath and imploded every limb. This implosion, which she thought meant her death that first time, dissolved her body and left her ears ringing. Those great colored bands she had glimpsed during the race presented themselves once more, expanding from her core and meeting others that bent from the cardinal directions. Electromagnetic fields, she somehow knew. Behind her, the world altered: there was no more city but a vast ebony landscape with distant mountains, a sky the violet of a contusion, and a sun that burned like an outraged obsidian. But, most fascinating of all, this strange black sun did not sear her skin.

Mouth agape, the General touched her chest to find it there yet somehow different: but it was the sway of long hair before her face that shocked her more, perhaps, than even her environment. As she reached up to touch it, feeling in a dream, the ringing in her ears gave way to the sounds of a distant argument in a dialect she recognized as old, old English. She did not recognize the language until picking out her own name led to the picking out of the words "fucking dentist," although "dentist" was a much flatter and stranger sound than she was used to hearing in English as it was in 1997 AL. Much of the rest of the conversation was lost on her.

She turned in its direction, amazed to find the fields emanating from her center to be weighted in a direction she presumed north. In the distance, two figures were in the midst of a complex argument. One, she recognized; one, she did not. Not until her steps, uneasy and somehow broader in this echoing place, brought her close enough to make out a red waistcoat amid the starlike magnetic ribbons that flexed and parted for her vision as she drew nearer. This red waistcoat triggered memories of the glimpse she'd gotten before, yes, but more than that. Astonishment struck the General: she was not thrust back to Kronborg with Cassandra while the Hierophant finished his tour of the throne room paintings. Rather, she was thrust to that moment's diametric opposite. Still at Kronborg, where she had flown for Cassandra's memorial, her Father called her to his office. As a girl sitting across his great oak desk and wingback chair, amid all those books and portraits, she always felt so small. At that moment as an adult, she felt nonexistent, and had not so much studied the covered painting in the corner as absorbed it, unconsciously, along with the rest of the room.

"I thought about having your wife's cremains inurned in the Family catacombs of Rome," he began. Dominia listened numbly, having wanted nothing to do with the arrangements and having asked him to take care of them, but not to tell her about them until she had been given a year or two of relief. Typical of him to ignore that wish. "But Rome was not her home, even if the name she took from you marked her as Mephitolian. Nor could it be said that San Valentino was ever her home, no matter how many children she taught there, or how many good works the both of you did in the Front."

"Did you call me here to remind me I could never make her happy?" Her voice brittle from private weeping, the Governess's impudent words elicited an expression that, from the Hierophant, recalled a kind of sympathy. He reached out to hold her hand and pressed something cold into her palm.

"No, my girl. I mean to say that her real home—the only home that could give her any joy—was in your heart."

His hand lifted away, and there she was: a beautiful diamond, lying in the Governess's palm. Though she had expected to, she did not weep. Not in that moment, although she would often weep over the diamond later, day on day while other martyrs slept, Dominia edging ever closer toward contacting the René Ichigawa who had not yet come to her with promises of resurrection by the time she sat, there, in her Father's office.

In that moment, she perceived nothing except a chill in her cheeks, and a brief contemplation as to how much this amounted to desecration of Cassandra's corpse. But she had left the choice to him. She had to live with it now.

"Thank you." Her eyes passed his many books to land on that covered painting. She raised her chin in its direction. "Is that her martyring painting?"

"She will be the patron saint of childbirth—of grief and suicides."

"May I see it." Not a request, but a resignation.

"Are you sure?"

After staring into her exhausted eyes, awaiting some protest, he rose. Centimeter by centimeter, the sheet of burgundy velvet drew away.

Reproduced in a richness of oil work like few had the privilege of viewing up close, was Cassandra: not with that gun in her mouth and her eyes full of fear, but kneeling down to pray at the bedside of their UF mansion while Dominia's gun rested upon the nightstand. The red of the painting was not of the blood and brain matter that had shattered, chunked with skull and matted with scalp, across their marriage bed. The red of the painting marked the waistcoat of the fictional saint who, with a most sorrowful expression, touched Cassandra's shoulder with one hand and, with the other, gestured off frame to indicate the time had come for their departure. It would be some weeks before Dominia awoke from a dead sleep with the epiphany that the painting's oil medium indicated it must have been commissioned months before the suicide. At the time, she did not think on it.

At the time, the Governess wept.

"You're Saint Valentinian," marveled the General now, interrupting his argument with Lazarus so that both men turned with a look of relief at the sound of her voice. As her approach ended before them, the bands marking fields that appeared as one with the two of them standing close flexed to accept her like a larger water droplet accepting a smaller one. While she overcame the brief vertigo this inspired, her vision cleared of color to allow both men to be easily seen. "I thought you weren't real. Am I dead?"

"Please, just 'Valentinian.' And you're not dead. Not right now. No more than anybody else here, anyway."

"Do you know each other?" she asked Lazarus. His taller companion laughed, then searched his waistcoat for a silver cigarette case.

"Some people! We've been halfway around the world together, and you don't even recognize me."

A few beats passed in which the General studied the tall man's pale-sapphire eyes. Somehow, she did know him. "*Basil?*" she asked in a tone almost accusatory.

"Woof." After bending to light his cigarette, the fictional martyr made to disappear the Tesla coil lighter that had emerged from his palm in sleight-of-hand demonstration. "It's more complicated than that, of course, but what isn't?"

A damn good question. The General's reeling mind raced through a thousand queries, almost all impossible to articulate. "Where *are* we, though?"

"That's not any less complicated than the dog question," said the useless saint. Dominia turned her agitated eye to Lazarus.

"I told you in the ceremony. You are liberated. Your Father's world? The material world? It's one way of viewing the information of the universe. And it's not the most accurate way."

"Your blood did this," she marveled.

The holy man nodded. "My blood does not deliver pseudo-immortality to the flesh. Rather, it gives the flesh—especially the flesh of martyrs—the opportunity to recognize it is already immortal. All things are already immortal."

"Welcome to Nirvana, kid," summarized Valentinian. "Rest assured, it's nothing like you dreamed."

XVIII

To Sleep

Whether Morgan or Dominia, General di Mephitoli had never done well with unanswered questions. Today, as she trudged through a desert dry without heat and visible without light save for colored bands warping her perception, she could not help but wonder how long her many, many questions had gone unanswered. One week? Two? Impossible—though she sensed it would be that long, or longer, before she had any measure of satisfaction. The black sun abuzz in the sky like a great, aching pit had not set during their journey, and not once had she hungered or even tired enough for rest, and never had those distant peaks drawn into greater detail than that of far-off thorns.

Yet something in her insisted no less than a week had passed since the men began their argument, which had been spurned by Dominia's simple observation. It had been an observation directed for the man who was, for his fictional nature, a source of exceeding curiosity to the General. To her mind, her observation was fair enough, though when it exited her lips, it sounded something more like an insult.

"You never seemed like a dog."

"I've never been a convincing liar," said Valentinian.

Lazarus spoke up: "You do it often enough."

"Still bent out of shape, are we?" asked the former dog with a bat of his eyes. She wasn't about to let them slip into a dialogue without her and cut in before Lazarus responded.

"Now, what's going on?" She tapped her hand as though a list of questions was written upon it. Of Valentinian, she asked, "Are you a martyr?"

"Yes, of course."

Dominia studied the icy-blue eyes he turned upon her single, resolute one. "But you've been in the sun." Old martyrs in particular began to leather in an instant under the sun's rays. The man arched a brow.

"Assuming it even matters once you have the blood of Lazarus: *Have* I been in the sun? Really? Even when you met us at the hotel, we were beneath an overhang."

The frowning General tried to sort her memory for an instance of this. She came up with nothing. It was true: the dog had been in the sun no longer than she. Basil had shown an almost exclusive appetite for human flesh, so much so that she had speculated herself that the dog was a martyr—but she had not speculated anything quite along these lines. Now, with a slap upon her own forehead, Dominia remembered, "The train! When René boarded the train and found you already there!"

"Now that's the ticket! You're so smart." Valentinian moved to pinch her cheek, but Dominia ducked away.

"You teleported then, the way my Father and Akachi and Lazarus..." Her thoughts trailed off and she pursed her lips. "All this time, you've been a man disguised as a dog so as to...what, exactly?"

"Nothing weird," promised the thin man, and the bearded nomad snorted from Dominia's good side.

"Yes, nothing weird. Not even of his own volition."

"It's a complicated story." Valentinian ran a hand over the eternal shadow of close stubble across his jaw. "I'll tell you sometime. At any rate, don't worry too much about me. We need to keep you focused, here."

"Where *is* 'here'?" she demanded again. Lazarus answered, beginning to turn away.

"Nowhere, really. It's sort of a pre-place. Not another dimension, so much. More a higher manifestation of the same universe. A higher frequency."

"So, another dimension," said Valentinian in a smart-assed way. Lazarus rolled his eyes.

"Different ways of saying the same thing. Some ways are better than others." After patting the invisible pockets of his ashen robe, which in this space seemed formless and shifting as everything else upon which Dominia tried to focus, the True Protomartyr withdrew from his pocket a white pebble. He had a whole palmful, and the one loaded in his thumb pinged like a bead from a slingshot into the distance. When she tried peering through the bubble of their collective magnetic field, the concept of depth had not seemed existent: not until the pebble indicated it. As the men began toward it, Dominia followed, and Lazarus carried on.

"This place is without static shape. It is where mind rules over matter: where imagination holds sway over the environment. Thoughts are information, like any material manifestation of energy. It's just that here, thought is given prevalence over matter."

"This can be a good thing," said Valentinian, slowing to match the General's pace. "It can also be a bad thing if you're, say, distressed, or dying, or if you arrive here without somebody to guide you or knowledge of what's going on."

Lazarus nodded. "In those cases, you're on a lower frequency instead of a higher one. But you don't have to worry about that much."

"We're moving within the electromagnetic spectrum," Dominia at last gathered.

"That's the axis along which we're traveling when we come here from Earth. Time is stripped away at higher and lower frequencies...the edges of matter become indistinct. This can be good or bad. Like Valentinian said, it can be bad if you drop to the lower, sub-radio frequencies. Or, if you're unfocused." They had reached the pebble and continued, though it drew Dominia's attention as they passed it; she was redirected by the sound of the second pebble skittering across the floor. "Focus is important here, because if your mind wanders, you can get lost."

"You can disappear," cautioned the waistcoated man. "But that's not likely to happen when somebody's there to observe you. One reason of many why we're here. Of course, I'm always here. Sort of."

The General's eye narrowed in scrutiny. "So you're not a dog? Really, all the time, you're a man?"

"Yes, and no. I'm here at the same time I'm there, of course—aren't we all—and this is arguably a higher truth of what I am. But the physical shadow I cast is mangled. I have lost my old one, the earthly one I had when the universe was first set into motion. All physical selves are mangled, in truth. Your physical self is mangled. Have you noticed your hair?"

She had, and once more reached up to touch the long locks shorn to make a fast disguise on the Light Rail. Still amazed to feel them again, she asked, "How is this so?"

"It's how you're used to thinking of yourself, isn't it? How you picture yourself in your mind, in your dreams. That's who you are all the time, but here it's visible."

"But my eye?" She realized she had not removed the patch, and began to reach for it. Valentinian stayed her hand.

"The damage incurred by your physical eye is symbolic of higher truth. You do have a sort of eye here, but the magnitude of its powers means it must be hidden. Leave it shut: when it opens, it'll end the world."

"You can't just be telling her these things." Lazarus, about to toss a third pebble into the distance, offered Valentinian a resentful glance which was bounced back to him in the form of an eyeroll.

"People have already started hinting stuff about her end-of-the-world responsibilities! It's worse to tell somebody a bit of something without telling them the hows and whys. Like keeping a gun around a kid and telling them not to touch it, but not specifying which end is dangerous." Dominia sickened at the metaphor, but Lazarus blustered off in immediate response, not noticing the expression, or the chill that wracked her to remember that odious moment in this place where thought was naked.

"It's *all* dangerous, which is why it's better the kid should know the gun is going to kill them if they touch it. Leave it at that."

Valentinian scoffed. "You're hardly an expert on child-rearing."

"And you are?" Lazarus laughed, his language shifting, then, to that old English variation. It had frustrated her the first time she'd heard it, like listening to characters in a dream babble in made-up languages only the unconscious understood: but, by the final time she would hear its words bandied between the two men, she would come to wonder if this was not how prelingual children perceived the chatter of adults. For now, trailing behind them, she observed by tone as the conversation escalated into argument. Though she knew a great many languages, Dominia found this one beyond her grasp; and she was used to being around many other people who spoke in foreign tongues, but she never appreciated when others had private conversations in front of her. This was how she began to assail her own brain, each thought punctuated by the irritating ping of a pebble as she came up with a great list of questions that seemed without number, and that were impossible to flesh out with the pinging of the pebbles separating each thought. By the time she managed to articulate a question, ping! Another pebble scurried across the textureless ground like the full stop at the end of a sentence, a period, a point audible with each stone flicked away. How long had they marched? Ping! Where were they? Ping! Who was Valentinian? Ping! How a dog, why a dog? Ping! What was beneath her eye patch now, and what did it have to do with the world, its end, anything at all?

Having thoughts in this place seemed futile as collecting water in one's cupped hand. Or perhaps it felt like sitting at the edge of a (pinging) fountain and trying to will it to collect itself into the form of a cup, without having a cup or a means by which to direct the liquid. Ping went a pebble, and Dominia was almost grateful for it, now. She became afraid of what might happen should she indeed follow a thought to the point of getting lost. The men chattered among themselves, their backs to her, and her body leadened at the absurd worry that they would forget her. Might she vanish while their backs were turned?

On the edge of quavering anxiety that felt it might be deadly, Dominia interrupted their conversation. "Are there other people here? Are we ever going to meet anybody else? What's going on?"

Their argument paused (for now), the men turned to look at her. While gentle relief flooded her mind to confirm that she, if nothing else, still existed,

Valentinian said, "We'll meet some other people eventually. Lots of other people, but not for a while."

"We're going to Cairo," answered Lazarus. "It's a shortcut. Kind of. The walk won't be quite as bad as you're thinking."

"But we've been walking such a long time."

"It's been about"—Valentinian paused to check his pocket watch, and Dominia discerned a wing-cloaked tetramorph etched into the metal—"oh, six days or so."

"The sun will set soon." Lazarus gazed at the great mole that hadn't shown any signs, so far as Dominia had seen, of moving an inch, west or east, whatever good such directions did in a place like this, where she sensed—and where the fields around them seemed to indicate—that there were more than four cardinal directions. "We'll have to make a camp."

"We can go farther," insisted Valentinian, snapping shut his watch and studying Dominia with eyes that would be glacial were they not crinkled with cheer. "How's it going, kiddo? Can you keep it up? You're not tired, are you?"

"No, it's not that. I don't understand how we've traveled so long when the sun hasn't moved."

Lazarus seemed inclined to let the magician field these questions. "Time works differently here. Not only that, but the flow of time back on Earth—so far as our own perceptions are concerned, anyway—is more related to perceived distance traveled here than actual earthly time spent. If we spent three days hanging around the same place, like, say, a town, or a ship, or anything else one might find in this place, we wouldn't notice much of a difference when we came back, and we also wouldn't find ourselves having experienced a significant change in our relative space compared to that of other Earthlings.

"Think of it like a film strip." Valentinian rolled back his sleeves and from his empty hands produced an antique strip of movie film. As he ran it through his fingers, light projected from them to terminate in a moving image at an arbitrary point in space: a simple show, played upon a screen unobserved. "As the physical film moves in space, the images and sounds it's projecting carry forward in time and perceived space—though, of course, the film itself never leaves the boundaries of the projector, and the movie watched never leaves the screen on which it's being played. Unless it's stopped. But when the film stops moving, the image on the screen also stops. Strictly speaking, when we're at the movie and unaware of the film on which it's printed, we're still simultaneously viewing the physical print and the motion picture: but when we become aware of the prints, we're able to manipulate them, and our position in them, by operating solely on that level. Instead of being a viewer, we become a projectionist."

Somehow, perhaps because of the dreamscape the trio inhabited, the man's production of the film seemed so natural that she was not surprised by it. She decided he must be some sort of magician since he knew so much about the fabric of reality. It struck her then: Valentinian was that magician to which Akachi had referred. As she watched but did not see the image of a woman walking, the General asked, "Is it possible to run the film strip backward? If we walked back to the point where we started—assuming we even could—"

"Would time go backward? Well, yes and no. Think about the movie again. There's multiple perceptions at work: first, the character's in-world perception—that's everybody else, everybody we left behind, Miki Soto and René Ichigawa—all the people in the world. Everybody who hasn't entered this space. If I stop the movie and rewind"—he pulled the film backward through his fingers, so that the woman's wobbling stride reversed its motion as though she beat hasty retreat from some threat that left her expression bland—"what is this lady going to notice when I start it running again?"

"Nothing," said Dominia. "From her perspective, she never even got to the point from which you rewound it."

"Okay. How about from your perspective, as an audience member? That is to say, someone who knows the movie's a movie, but who also has the potential to walk up to the booth where the projectionist works? Now that you've seen the black sun once, you can call on it again any time that you need it, like how a person awakened to the existence of a projectionist can go knock on his door. What happens from your perspective when you're watching the movie and it rewinds, then starts again from a point not at the beginning?"

"Well, I get annoyed."

"Because you can't unknow what's already happened, and it's not going to change. It's filmed and already on a track, so your chances of having a new experience are reduced. In fact, you can't have a new experience. And since the present is nothing but new experiences, once you have crystalized reality by experiencing it—by rendering the abstract information around us the physical space of reality—it is impossible to go back. The projectionist can't rewind his film because the audience can't unsee what they've watched. He only rewinds it"—Valentinian let the film slip from his fingers, and the light vanished along with its walking woman—"when the whole thing's done, and it's time to show the movie over again."

"In other words, we can only really fast-forward."

"That's true when you've made contact with the material plane, or crossed paths with a visitor who isn't in your group; but when you're in this place, if you go too far or get lost and you haven't met any strangers to confuse your field, you can get back to your original position and no harm will be done. It will be like you never even left the spot where you stood in reality. All places you initially walk represent forward motion in time and space toward one of many potential ends, depending on which direction you pick and what intention you have; however, all places you backtrack represent backward motion along those same lines. Think of it like this: until you are forced to make up your mind by returning to Earth, you're free to change it as often or as much as you please. Like our projectionist searching the film strip, frame by frame—the movie can't start until he locks it into position."

"So I can do this any time? Come here?"

Lazarus said, "If a person, even a human, has had my blood once in their life, they can come here any time. Be here forever, if they wanted. But, please—don't do that."

"We need you too much," said Valentinian, laughing. "So, does that satisfy you?"

Enough, she supposed. There was no satisfying her in a situation like this, but there had not been any satisfying her since the Hierophant pulled out her eye, or before—since Cassandra died.

Cassandra. She had not thought of her wife in what was technically a week. The setting of the black sun banished the embroidery of their colored fields and Valentinian stood before the final pebble. As a fire blazed to life, seemingly sourced in the stone, she found herself thinking of her poor wife with stabs of sadness—and bitter disappointment that the vast space afforded no true backward motion. The darkness enclosing the circle of their fire, without benefit of their rays, was thick like tar. In day, the landscape had been already bleak under the dark un-light. Now, in this night that lacked a moon, the rest of existence had vanished, and Dominia failed to prove to herself that it had ever been there to start. Memories of Cassandra were her tether to reality, for they were the only memories of which Dominia could be sure.

There was something to be said for that place when it came to the subject of memories. Perhaps that was because, while lying beside the fire, she felt weightless. As if the ground upon which she lay was not ground, or even water, but a vacuum. Thus, with nothing to look at, nothing to feel, and nothing to contain her rampant memories, she dreamed. Hypnotized by the sound of shuffling cards Valentinian had produced from his pocket, it seemed to her the warmth of the fire now was the warmth of their estate's fire then, all those years ago, not that long after Cassandra had first appeared. Not all that long, either, after she had lost her baby. Night after night, her wife sat immobile by that fire.

At the time, Dominia feared Cassandra would never recover from her depression. She still felt that fear, ninety years later, and wondered if her wife ever did recover in a way that mattered. But, one night, in an effort to see some change in demeanor—and to prove it was possible to find moments of joy after a storm of loss—she took Cassandra to the zoo. San Valentino had many zoos, of course, but the San Diego Zoo was known as one of the best, and most compassionate—they subscribed to a strict anti-alteration policy when it came to the genetic code of cloned animals, and showed consistent preference for the acquisition and breeding of organic ones. Especially endangered species, which were legion, thanks to the long-lasting climate changes of industrialization. Most of the world's more fascinating animals, like its rhinos, its elephants, its tigers and its lions, would have only survived immortalized as weapons were it not for the noble cloning operations that had made their rebirth possible.

Cassandra had never seen a live elephant before—or a tiger, for that matter. Ocelots, parakeets, markhors: all were mythical animals to the twentysomething, who appeared a giddy girl dashing from cage to cage. The prohibitive cost of zoos meant they were predominantly attended by martyrs; humans who wished to see them often found the easiest way was to get a career as a keeper. That was a good, safe job for a human. No martyr was inclined to hurt a zookeeper.

Yet, as cherished an opportunity as this had been, and as bright as Cassandra had become in their hours wandering from exhibit to exhibit, the animals paled beside the moment her wife laid eyes on a trail of schoolchildren, aged eight to ten, forced to hold hands as they navigated the zoo. While Dominia had tried to turn down another path to save her wife's emotional state and to avoid wading through a crowd, Cassandra tugged her to a halt.

"Is that a school?"

"Bible school, I think." The Governess studied the uniforms, then tried to draw attention to the map. "Look—"

"Like Sunday school, you mean? Martyrs have that?"

"Sure we do. But remember, sweetheart, it's Noctisdomin."

While Cassandra substituted a bland stare for the eye rolls that she had learned were an insult to the Governess, she primly agreed, "Noctisdomin school. Cumbersome."

"Makes more sense than a bunch of nocturnal people talking about the *days* of the week. And, anyway, it sounds better in Mephitolian." At her wife's continued look, Dominia began to worry they would have a fight there, in the zoo, in front of the now-passing stream of kids; they'd been having a lot of fights around that time, weird fights, due to Cassandra's emotional state and—well, to be frank, the Governess's inability to empathize. She didn't want to be around kids, herself. That's why it amazed her so when Cassandra, with an abrupt flip to her bright expression again, strolled to the pretty Filipina martyr who seemed to be one of their three teachers, and asked for a moment of her time. Ten minutes later, she was back with a phone number written on her wrist, and—oh, Dominia's poor heart, just to remember it—a big, real smile on her face.

"She said I should call her sometime, and she can tell me more about how to get certified."

"You're going to teach Bible school?" Dominia laughed gently. "You haven't even been to Mass since we got married."

"It's creepy, that's why." Away from other people, they spoke of her Father's culture and their opinions on it. On everything. Together, they strolled hand in hand past aviaries of sleeping tropical birds. "If I taught Bible school, it would be *during* Mass. I wouldn't have to go."

"But you have to learn the material you're going to teach, is what I'm trying to say."

"I can learn it. You think I can, don't you?"

At her wife's anxious expression, Dominia's own had filled with pain. She had pulled Cassandra close, into a kiss. "I think you can do anything."

Oh, Cassandra! Ah, memory! But what was memory in this boundless place? There they were now, those lips, those soft lips, those hands, that—

"What are you doing," cried Valentinian above the scattering of fifty-two cards. Or, maybe the cry came as he shook her back to her senses: hard to tell, with half of her dreaming of Cassandra's mouth, from which she was unwilling to be torn away. "Hey, wake up, look at me!"

But she was with Cassandra, who said, so gently, "I love you, Dominia—oh, Dominia, I'm so glad I have you. Dominia, you're all that I have."

Those words! That woman who clutched her and looked up at her with such sweet, big eyes. That woman who needed her love and protection, who stood now by the fireside.

Yes, by the fireside, at its edge. Her form, dark in the unholy night, yet discernible as Cassandra's. But, oh, cruelty! The shouting men (Lazarus having awoken) would not let Dominia near the lover whose name she repeated in a chant. That name that rang across the thick night of formless space. "Come here," she cried, "come here, Cassandra, please— Oh, won't you *stop*! Let me see her!"

"It's not Cassandra," shouted Valentinian. Lazarus stooped for the king of hearts and ace of spades, which he caught in the fire. As the General tried to extricate herself from the magician's grip, the mystic tossed the flaming cards at the apparition. Light singed the shadow's face to reveal features much like Cassandra's—but not hers. Those eyes—bleak and flat rather than the great, emotional, haunted ones of her wife—awoke Dominia, who also found brassy hair to be a tarry lie. This entity was not her love.

"What is it?" Dominia asked. The shadow resumed its watch from the other side of the fire's circumference.

"Call it a thoughtform." Valentinian collected the rest of his cards. "It won't come into the light. It can't, without showing us how it looks. But that's the problem with this place, with remembering things too vividly here. There's a lot of...stuff...hanging around. Think of it as sentient negative thoughts: an active type of information that, given sufficient energy, looks for the best way to harvest more energy from you, for better or worse."

Cold, the General watched the odious thing. To think anything could be so sick, so cruel, as this which mocked her wife! "Why?"

The magician shrugged, tapped the incomplete deck of cards, snapped his fingers, and produced from the stack a new king of hearts, another ace of spades. "Why does anything do anything? It wants to eat. Biological viruses are the closest metaphor I have for you, but even that's not accurate."

"It's close." Lazarus lowered upon his haunches and warmed his hands by the fire, one eye upon the thoughtform's silhouette. "Viruses are programmed to evolve like anything else, and this thing is desperate to evolve. In this case, the evolution isn't genetic. It's an evolution from a state of near total abstraction, to physical representation. That's why we refrain from giving these things a real name or definition. Even calling it, say, '*tulpa*' like they do in Tibet, or '*egregore*' like they do in occult texts, gives it a preexisting form and eases its ability to manifest in reality. If it can collect enough energy, it might be able to manifest in real life—return attached to us, or attached to your energy—and that isn't a good thing for you."

"Not necessarily," cautioned Valentinian. "But there are good thoughtforms."

"Good thoughtforms don't need to drain you of psychic, emotional, or memory energy to manifest. They are parts of established patterns that exist in large varieties of information and help the person with whom they connect."

"Argumentative!"

"Just being specific. But do you get it?" Lazarus turned his attention to Dominia now, who touched her head, embarrassed.

"Yes, of course. As much as anybody can 'get' something like this, anyway...now that I'm awake, I know that's not Cassandra. Of course that's not Cassandra. But it was like I was almost...sleeping, before. Not here."

Valentinian nodded. "That's why you have to keep focused. I meant it when I said that, about getting lost in your thoughts. If you find yourself getting too deep into a memory here, you need to ground yourself—I mean, literally, make yourself aware of the ground." He patted it as he sat. "It'll put you in the present and keep you from attracting other...parasites."

"It'll be better if she gets something to do." Lazarus, upon his stomach, tucked his arm beneath his chin in lieu of pillow. "Give her your cards, '*Basil*.'"

"Why not give her your rocks?"

"Because she doesn't know how to keep time."

Dominia shivered under the stolen eyes of the thing wearing Cassandra's face. "How long do the nights last around here?"

"A while," answered the magician, handing his deck to Dominia. "It's better to sleep."

Bitterly, she laughed. "What if I dream while I sleep?"

"When the whole world is a state of dreaming"—Lazarus's voice was muffled by his half-curled position in the firelight—"sleep is the last place you should expect to dream."

"But how am I supposed to go to sleep without thinking of anything?" She clutched the cards in her right hand like an angular stuffed animal, and tucked the deck beneath her miserable arms. Lazarus's tone was less sympathetic than Valentinian's: largely because he was on the verge of sleep. "Ask yourself how a bluebird does it, and you'll fall right to sleep."

"Is he always like this," whispered the General to the magician. He patted her shoulder.

"It comes from a loving place."

His hand lingered with a brother's weight, his eyes no doubt the same place Dominia's singular orb found tense focus. That vacuous silhouette had edged along the light and now seemed all too near the General for comfort. The bands of color having vanished with the light, she had not even the psychological, imaginary barrier of their electromagnetic field. As Dominia ran her thumb back and forth along the edge of the cards, she murmured, "How am I supposed to sleep with that thing watching me?"

"It can't hurt you with the fire going. And it can't hurt you when I'm nearby." This sentiment was paired with a playful jostle that made her think of the dog she better knew. As though reading her thoughts—and she was certain, based on history, he could—the magician noted, "It's nice you trust me after the whole...you know, 'surprise person' thing."

The General laughed. "Out of everyone I've met this past two weeks, you've been the entity I've trusted the most, and even you've had a secret!"

"Yeah, but I tried to make it clear I was strange. I mean, all dogs are great, but stopping the train? Shooting Kahlil?"

"Thanks for that, by the way. The train, I mean, not Kahlil."

"Well, thanks for the food! And for the company, and for everything you've done for me in all those past attempts. Don't worry. This time, we get it right."

As strange as the world had become, she had somehow lost all doubt that existence was cyclical. She didn't bother asking how much he remembered about their lives before, or how he had survived, or what the future was like, because there would be no getting a straight answer out of him, and she was certain knowing all those things would prove a dreadful weight. The burden she held by virtue of being responsible for the world's destruction, whether proverbial or real, was dreadful enough. She had quite a few questions about that, but Lazarus would strangle her at this rate. Anyway, delirious as this place made the circles of her thoughts, she dared not spare much consideration for the suggestion. Instead, she turned back to see Valentinian staring down the silhouette, and caught his eye to ask, "How do you know we'll get it right?"

"I can feel it." He cast a twinkling glance into space, as though reading there the words of some invisible book. "And I can see it. There are a great many truths yet to be revealed, Dominia."

Was it the first time he'd said her name? Perhaps not—but for some reason, it felt as such, and she turned back to tuck her arm beneath her head in a fashion not dissimilar from that position into which Lazarus had curled. The magician continued speaking while he lifted his hand from her shoulder to reach into his waistcoat's pocket.

"Our success in ending this cycle is dependent on the number and proportion of truths revealed, in a way. The truth will set you free, or so says your Father's raggedy old book stolen from the humans, but I prefer, 'The amount and momentum of surprise information within the truth will help our consciousnesses achieve the escape velocity required to keep all this from ever having happened in the first place.'"

"But if none of this happened"—the General's throat tightened—"will I have existed?"

"You will have existed more than ever before!" He laughed, and leaned over her. Before she realized what he was doing, something—a dust or a powder or a sand—was scattered across her eye, and he murmured, "These are questions for reality, when they'll seem less oppressive. Now go to sleep, kiddo."

Magically compelled as she was, she did. For hours, it felt, Dominia plunged into a sleep in which one moment she lay upon her arm, and the next she did not exist: neither to dream a dream nor think a thought. It was like having her eye and spirit washed in the Lamb's blood, soothing a sleep as it was. So soothing, it induced brief delirium. When Dominia awoke, unsure of what had awoken her, she thought it to be morning by the profusion of light; then, she remembered the light of the sun here was not like any she'd known on Earth. It could not be day by any means.

As the tinkling of music reached her consciousness, she lifted her head and found Valentinian and Lazarus both sound asleep. During their inattention, it seemed the light of the fire had multiplied. Like trees instantly grown, torches had sprung in the darkened night. These thin rods of gold towered over the General, who was of no short height for a woman, and the blue-hearted fires atop them formed a chain through the darkness by the pools of light that licked the perimeters of their fellows. This light was clean, yet somehow false in comparison to the magician's. Her colored field still had not returned—would not, she sensed, until the day.

The most curious thing was not, however, the appearance of the torches, or the hue of the fire, or the late-noted disappearance of Cassandra's doppelgänger. It was Dominia's lack of fear. Not often a woman given to fear, she had of late been inundated; now, on being alone in this alien plane, with music streaming from an unknown source to tempt her down this new-laid path, Dominia looked back on those moments in reality where fear had visited her. She marveled that she had ever, in that place, been afraid. Reality had grown less real. Valentinian himself had said that this place was a dream, and now, without the thing watching her from the edges of the light, she remembered nothing could hurt her in dreams. Thus assured of her safety, she padded beneath the lights as if following a stream to its source.

A great many torches passed her by—she supposed she should have been counting in anticipation of her return—but, soon enough in comparison to that day's walk, she noted a far greater light in the distance. An island, amid all that watery darkness. The closer she drew, the better she discerned that the light formed a study with no walls: only a door carved in an extraordinary forest tableau, and a few bookshelves lining the enclosures of a room that, like Valentinian's screen, was implied. The music increased in volume and clarity, and now she recognized it (an ancient composer named Berlioz), along with two chairs resting beside the orange-blue fireplace. The unanchored door obstructed her view of the filled armchair, but she knew what she would find well before she knocked—well before she heard the words, "It's open," and touched the knob. She knew what she would find well before that door yawned wide: yet, she did not stop herself from letting it swing open to reveal, wine in hand, the Hierophant.

"How glad I am you've accepted the invitation, my eternal General. Please: won't you come in?"

The men might tell her whatever they wanted to gloss the truth for her, but in that moment, Dominia confirmed her instincts had been right.

She was in for one long walk to Cairo.

[ed.: The following requests to Saint Valentinian, originally written in Modern Mephitolian circa 3670 CE, come from prayer cards said to belong to Dominia di Mephitoli in her childhood and first two centuries of life. As they began public circulation in Nogales, Arizona, this is a strong possibility.]

PRAYER TO SAINT VALENTINIAN

For the Dying

Saint Valentinian! The Lord, in His wisdom, has seen you, above all His saints, fit to guide all souls, damned and righteous, to eternity. Through the Father's works, you know the trials through which beings strive. Pray now on the trials of *[the dying]* and relieve, somewhat, the burdens of their sins. You, who were too wise to be made real; for whom God has made home of eternity; who knew all things before Wisdom was revealed to mankind: your knowledge raised you high above all spheres and to the bosom of the Lord, into whose ear you speak. As pleasing as your wisdom is to Him, surely you will see to it that *[dying]* is granted that knowledge by means of which souls enter the next life not in fear, but peace and love of God. Amen.

PRAYER TO SAINT VALENTINIAN

For the Success of a Creative Venture

O Saint Valentinian, master of all arts and wise attendant of the Lord, by your works of death you know the nature of Creation. See from your heavenly abode the struggles of the Father's beloved artists and pray they be delivered to greatness. Let their divinely granted gifts purify the world, and flood its land with the wonders of eternity. With your generous prayers, draw God's blessing upon all who would create in His name, and allow *[artist's]* works, models for that Greatest Work, to thrive as golden crops sewn beneath the shining sun. Amen.

A Timeline of Events

CONCERNING THE RISE OF THE HIEROPHANT

[ed.: As this document was transmitted non-temporally, concerns exist about the impact of foreknowledge upon future events. Therefore, certain names irrelevant to the story of General Dominia di Mephitoli have been redacted, in the hopes of preventing willful future atrocity. Names and events related to the Rise of the Hierophant or predating this book's first printing in CE 2019 (BL 25) have been left as is.]

CE 1974 / BL 70

American science-fiction author, Philip K. Dick, has a visionary experience with an entity that he calls VALIS: Vast Active Living Intelligence System

The Hierophant arrives on Earth

Paris radio station, France Inter, is subject to a break-in; the burglar is said to have carried off tapes waiting to be broadcast as part of a series about UFOs, with the missing recordings relating to the theory that UFOs are not extraterrestrial, but supra-physical

American neuroscientist, Dr. John C. Lilly, receives a warning about a nefarious entity called the SSI, or "Solid State Intelligence", delivered by an extraterrestrial organization that he calls ECCO: Earth Coincidence Control Office

While on tour in Detroit, alien-fascinated British superstar David Bowie happens to catch a local television report of a "verified" UFO landing; later reports deny the incident

US President Richard Nixon resigns in disgrace following the Watergate scandal

His replacement, President Gerald Ford, is quick to pardon him

American author and Playboy *magazine editor, Robert Anton Wilson, "enters into a belief system" concerning telepathic contact between himself entities residing on a planet of the double star, Sirius; Sirius A, the brightest star in the sky, is wildly known as "the Dog Star"*

CE 1976 / BL 68

The Man Who Fell to Earth, *a film starring and largely orchestrated by David Bowie, is released in theaters*

The film will provide vital contributions in Philip K. Dick's efforts to develop a frame of reference intellectualizing his VALIS experience

CE 1978 / BL 66

Pope John Paul I dies 33 days after election in the first Year of Three Popes since 1605 CE; his death proves the genesis of many conspiracy theories

CE 1980 / BL 64

An international cabal of prostitutes known as the Red Market is formally founded

American movie star, Ronald Wilson Reagan, is elected president; Robert Anton Wilson, among others, later notes this name to be an anagram for "Insane Anglo Warlord"

British musician and advocate for peace, John Lennon, is shot dead by Mark David Chapman as the result of a series of strange coincidences

CE 2005 / BL 39

Pope John Paul II dies and is succeeded by Pope Benedict XVI

CE 2011 / BL 33

The Hierophant reveals the sacred protein to researchers, Elijah, and Cicero

Lazarus goes into hiding after being martyred

CE 2013 / BL 31

DIOX Corporation is founded by Cicero and Elijah, with private funding from the Hierophant

Pope Benedict XVI announces his abrupt resignation and is succeeded by Pope Francis, 266th sovereign of the Vatican City State; Francis immediately proves a divisive authority among modern Catholics

CE 2020 / BL 24

The Hierophant works to quietly spread martyrdom to the hyper-elite of Russia

The Church of the Lamb is founded in California by a pair of eccentric brothers; it soon fails to maintain more than a small gathering, and will be reworked over the years into a proper organization

CE 2029 / BL 15

The newfound Holy Martyr Church is a more successful attempt than Cicero's previous effort, due in part to a number of fresh-martyred celebrities blackmailed into public support: ████ *and* ████

The organization's patriarch, the Hierophant, is thought to be a former politician due to those who begin joining the HMC, but he refuses to give his name and cannot be identified; until initiation into the Church is complete, most regard the Hierophant as a likely relative of Cicero's

However, official members also seem to transform into true believers overnight; many lose friends and family members to the strange group, which promotes, among other things, a nocturnal lifestyle resulting in isolation from one's former life

Due to the strange behavior, mild tremors, and pale countenance of many members, outsiders speculate their sacraments may involve the use of drugs; the Hierophant routinely decries these accusations and invites reporters to observe the services

These reporters eventually pervade the erroneous—and dangerous—conclusion that the Holy Martyr Church is merely an offshoot of the Catholic Church

The HMC's holy text is a book called The Post-Testament, *which the Hierophant claims to have recreated from a combination of memory and divine messages from his home world of Acetia*

Many outside the Church speculate that tales of extraterrestrial origin are mere fabrication, and the HMC is routinely mocked in pop culture

Nevertheless, by CE 2041, the organization boasts an impressive 10 Churches and 5000 worshippers in the United States: Elijah, now called the Lamb and thought by Churchgoers to be a prophet, travels between what is later identified as the fastest-growing cult in American history with the help of his brother and only priest, Cicero

CE 2045 / AL 1

Martyrs go public after one of the Church's celebrity supporters is indicted on murder charges

The species is considered the result of religious delusion until ████ *dies in the custody of officers while forced to wait outside the courthouse for his transportation*

Blood tests volunteered by the Hierophant confirm that the proteins of martyrs are biologically different from those of humans, and that this trait is infectious

Many human beings refuse to believe in martyrs, but those that do fail to react well

CE 2046 / AL 2 – CE 2150 / AL 105

A dark time in martyr history where the species is relegated to the shadows, and many martyrs are killed on the discovery of their identity; some governments go so far as to render them "non-people"

Russia, home of the Hierophant and several martyr politicians for many years, extends itself as a safe haven of the "maligned" group suffering "religious" persecution

Defenders of martyrs point to the Lamb, the savior of the group; consumption of his blood makes it possible for a martyr to survive up to one week without consumption of human proteins

Detractors argue that the Lamb cannot be everywhere at once, and martyrdom is a disease which cannot be controlled

CE 2150 / AL 105

Senator █████ of Vermont is the first American politician to be outed as a martyr, sparking numerous gubernatorial debates about everything from the ability of martyrs to run for office to the number of terms they should be allowed

For the first time in human history, a government recognizes the martyrs as a legitimate race: the United States of America

The American Registry of Martyrs is created in AL 120, which results in several decades of backlash wherein the list is used for discrimination, rather than to curb it

Martyrs are given the vote in AL 147, thanks in large part to the compassionate efforts of their human proponents

CE 2240 / AL 195

The Hierophant is formally elected president of the Russian Federation following the untimely death of his predecessor, █████

In a terrible shock to the Russian people, █████'s cause of death is listed as suicide; the Hierophant nobly swears to guide the people through this time of crisis

The Italian city of Venice is declared uninhabitable due to rising sea levels

CE 2310 / AL 265

British and Canadian martyrs win personage

Senator ████████ is arrested for murder after it is discovered he has not been subsisting exclusively on donated blood, as he has led the people to believe

While the United States has gone back and forth on the issue of martyr rights, the species has taken particular hold in Europe; China begins to demonstrate anxiety about its small martyr population

The Holy Martyr Church gains alarming claim to Apostolic Succession following the revelation that Bishop ████████ of Verona was martyred before his episcopal consecration; the bishop officially converts to the HMC soon after the public revelation

The Roman Catholic Church responds with the blanket excommunication of all martyrs, thus voiding the false claim to succession; the Holy Martyr Church claims, as ever, to be victims of persecution

CE 2400 / AL 355

When the slaughter of the Hierophant's second generation of children provokes dissent in Europe, China surreptitiously foments rebellion and funds the nascent Hunters

The Hierophant survives his sixth recorded assassination attempt, provoking World War III: Britain, Canada, Turkey, and Russia are soon awarded the support of the United States, which is increasingly regarded as a martyr nation; China manages to win the support of Japan, India, and small portions of Europe

CE 2401 / AL 356 – CE 2415 / AL 370

Over the course of fifteen years, World War III stretches global resources past their breaking point

Outside of densely populated countries, martyrs are at constant threat of hate crimes, which the Hierophant claims to be the result of war, religious bigotry, and racism

Russian annexes Poland during the war in what the country claims to be defensive action

High-tech drone warfare and the rapid speed at which information travels keeps the conflict limited to a series of skirmishes and intermittent bombings until Turkey joins Russia in an abrupt assault on Kazakhstan; it becomes apparent that the Hierophant's real goal in the war is to gain land

Desperate to end the conflict, the Chinese military makes the decision to drop an atomic bomb on the city of Moscow following a series of warnings to evacuate the city

For reasons unknown, the warnings fail to reach the populace in time; even those martyrs not killed in the blast die from radiation poisoning

Evidence later indicates a mass power outage gripped Moscow hours before the bomb was dropped

The Hierophant, in Rome for an unannounced business trip, is unharmed

Following the bombing, a vast swath of Russia is rendered uninhabitable; the Chinese government, having been provoked into a war crime, reluctantly admits defeat and pays reparations while firmly denying, now or ever, rights to martyrs in their country

CE 2545 / AL 500

After the war, the subject of martyrs and martyr rights becomes an important subject worldwide: in 50 years, 63 countries pass legislation either for or against their citizenship

Every country in Europe recognizes martyr citizens

Environmental repair of Russia begins in earnest

CE 2650 / AL 605

The Hierophant, on surviving yet another assassination attempt, appeals to the Pope; the official Catholic position soon becomes pro-martyr, an arguable contradiction of the Church's respect for all life

Despite amending their official position to assure their followers that martyrs deserve the dignity of life as much as any other living thing, the Catholic Church still believes members of the Holy Martyr Church to be heretical, and martyrs are still considered excommunicated upon their martyrdom

A series of small wars are fought between anti-martyr and pro-martyr European states; this loosely connected series of conflicts earns the name "the European Civil War" and stretches until 705 AL

CE 2770 / AL 725

The Second European Union is established; due to human majority leadership, the motion to conglomerate the separate nations into one country fails to pass

Nonetheless, the Hierophant is elected speaker of the Union, a position comparable to president of the United States

CE 2845 / AL 800 – CE 3045 / AL 1000

Russia, though considered once more habitable, is widely regarded as the most undesirable place in the planet, second only to the ultrahot island nation of Australia

Using technology created to save Russia, the drowned city of Venice is raised from the sea

The Hierophant turns his attention to the notion of a Martian colony

Hunter activities grow more prominent throughout South America and the Middle East, while the martyr population of the United States is deliberately grown; a terror attack in Washington, DC, leads not only to a change of capital city, but to war

American declares war on Afghanistan without sufficient proof that their citizens were involved in the attack; the European Union, now frequently shortened to Europa, provides military and fiscal support

CE 3060 / AL 1015

A series of wars with America rocks the Middle East while martyrs worldwide play the victim; every time a Hunter cell is disbanded, another pops up

America is eventually urged by its own people to end the conflicts and pay reparations; devastated, the Middle East struggles to rebuild

CE 3295 / AL 1250

After an escalating series of violent acts by Hunter cells advocating against martyr rights, Pope ██████ is assassinated; the Catholic world mourns, as do martyrs, who consider the Holy See to be a religious authority

In the wake of the violence, the Vatican offers a stunning response: Cardinal ██████ I is elected the first martyr Pope

The schism this creates in the Church is unprecedented

To celebrate this union of Catholics and martyrdom, Italy's name is changed to Mephitoli

CE 3305 / AL 1260

After much struggle, the constitution of the Middle States is ratified; those states ravaged by the Hierophant band together in the fashion of Europa and form a home for displaced humans

Supporters of the traditional Roman Catholic Church flood the new union's borders; Jerusalem is established as the new Holy See by the Council of Bathsheba in 1262

While the Vatican declares a merger of the RCC and the HMC, the congregation in Jerusalem formally denies the apostolic succession of the martyr church and expands the doctrine of excommunication to all martyrs, as well as human attendants of the martyr church

Millions of superficial Catholics, failing to understand the difference, continue attending their old churches and are, with varying degrees of awareness and concern, excommunicated

CE 3411 / AL 1366

After determining enough generations have passed since the merger of faiths, patriarchs call to order the Thirty-Third Ecumenical Council of the Catholic Church

Following the meeting, informally called Vatican III, Pope █████ *steps down, and martyr doctrine is seamlessly integrated into Church teachings*

The Hierophant is formally elected Pope ad vitam aeternam *after the shortest conclave in history: 20 minutes*

CE 3445 / AL 1400

Following Vatican III, Asian countries begin rejecting martyr (and even Lazarene) influence more violently than before

By the year 3445, it is the official position of the Catholic Church that the Hierophant and his organization are the beings described in the Book of Revelations, heretofore considered symbolism: Jerusalem quietly calls its own Vatican III to establish the new position

In the United States of America, violence against humans proves on the rise; the Hierophant makes many special trips to advise the president on how to handle such trying times

Upon the release of a number of large-scale studies that indicate mankind's technological development has been drastically impacted by needless wars with the Hierophant, a coalition is formed between Japan, China, India, and the Middle States to develop the first global mass-transit system

Japanese Engineer, █████*, names this transit system "The Light Rail"; in celebration of this achievement, the Land of the Rising Sun becomes known as the Empire of the Risen Sun*

In AL 1412, a terrorist attack which military intelligence claims to be from Mexican soil leads to the annexation of Mexico: the world knows better than to respond to the Hierophant's attempts to provoke them into war, and Mexico's pleas for assistance go unanswered

CE 3495 / AL 1450

With more than 50 percent of the Senate and 30 percent of the House seats now held by openly martyr politicians in the United States, the first martyr president is elected

Two years later, the New Constitution is proposed, and the United States agrees to rejoin Britain due to "concerns" over expanding Eastern Hemisphere technology

CE 3517 / AL 1472

Through skillful tax maneuvering and no small amount of intimidation, the Hierophant acquires his dream castle of Kronborg, located in Elsinore, Denmark; the already martyr-heavy town becomes the political capital to the Vatican's religious one, and martyrs flood in, giving way to a new social structure that will spread out across most of Europa

New York's name is changed to New Elsinore to celebrate this achievement

CE 3560 / AL 1515

Most US citizens who were upset about America's rejoining have either been martyred, grown old, or died; the new generations raised with this reality accepts it as simple fact

They also accept as simple fact the notion that, as an extension of the British Empire, the Hierophant has complete sovereignty over their domain

Protests are launched when the term limits of American presidents are formally abolished; these same protests are soon squelched, and lifelong term limits for presidents become the norm for the next generation

Accusations of poor working conditions on the part of some humans in the employ of martyrs, especially the hyper-wealthy variety found in the Denmark city of Elsinore, echo accusations of slavery both in the European courts and in American factories and farms

Arguments about humans being murdered for food have long since become so rote that only a few countries, namely Japan, China, and a handful of African states, seem to care about the subject at all

CE 3609 / AL 1564

The Light Rail officially opens; one year later, the United States proposes unifications with Canada and Mexico, with the latter formally declared property of the United States

Mexico retaliates by declaring (civil) war on the United States in 1570

Turkey's president is outed as a martyr after a suspicious centennial term; he declares allegiance to the Holy Martyr Church, and to the Hierophant

After the death of US president [redacted] *of Virginia, Holy Family member Trimalchio is elected president*

He humbly signs a document formalizing Church powers over the government of the United Front, and grants the Hierophant the authority to install future presidents, hereafter to be referred to as "governors"

In a gesture almost certainly intended to be mocking, Trimalchio allows the measure to be submitted for a vote; the people pass it, even without the surreptitious influence of Hierophant-employed hackers over the electronic voting machines

CE 3666 / AL 1621

Under Trimalchio's controversial reign, new measures are put into place walking back the crimes of murder, assault, and kidnapping for martyrs in the Front

Many European countries follow suit, while increasing sentences for humans who commit the same crimes against martyrs

Humans lose the right to vote on anything more than local measures around 1650

Concerned about its citizens still flooding into America—lured by the universal basic income, which Trimalchio and the Hierophant work to establish in 1654—Japan begins to earnestly fund the terrorist organization known as the Hunters, and begins to engage in a series of sanctions against the Front, which inspires some countries to follow suit

The Hierophant's response to this is to encourage martyrs to vacation in or move to Japan, and to find a nice Japanese child to martyr

A small wave of martyr immigration in Japan is swiftly and violently halted, which provides the Hierophant a fine excuse to start another series of conflicts

Trimalchio isolates Asian and Mexican citizens into specialized neighborhoods, citing concerns of terrorism and spying; by 1658, proper concentration camps have been developed in Canadian Jurisdictions, Montana, and a few isolated spots in the Mexican desert

Horrible rumors about the treatment and slaughter of humans circulate quickly in an age where DIOX cyborgans equipped with Internet access and usable reality-augmentation features have begun to hit the market

By 1662, Japan and the martyrs are once more at war: the First Invasion of Japan leads to catastrophic loss of martyr life and the subsequent invasion of California

CE 3711 / AL 1666

The Hierophant martyrs an eight-year-old girl named Morgan in a small Mephitolian Jurisdiction; he changes her name, as is tradition

The child, Dominia di Mephitoli, will grow up to become the single most formidable—and frightening—general that the world has ever seen

CE 3731 / AL 1686

By the age of 28, Dominia has become well known for her particular capacity for violence and strategic warfare; after joining the military at 20 and being sent to the Southwestern theater to engage invaders in California and Mexico and achieving the rank of lieutenant colonel, the plight of the navy at the hands of the Japanese becomes woefully apparent

At the Hierophant's request, Dominia is transferred across military branches, and is forced to endure a brief stint in the navy; such transfers are common in the long-lived species of martyrs, but Lieutenant Colonel Mephitoli is personally unhappy in the new role, as well as disgusted to see so many of her comrades die

Believing a new, more serious strategy is needed than allowing the Japanese to play Battleship with them for the next twenty years, Dominia convinces her Father to stage a Second Invasion of Japan

Under Mephitoli's command, the operation proves so successful it leads to the Ruin of Tokyo, and her promotion to general; however, the deaths of many citizens means that Japan has formal evidence of war crimes

Strictly speaking, the Front loses the war, and is forced to dismantle its camps, pay reparations, and extradite Governor Trimalchio for trial in Japan

The Hierophant politely refuses this third demand, and Trimalchio will never leave the United Front again

Throughout the rest of her Earthly life, until her promotion to governess of the Front, the General will be shipped between wars, with any peacetime filled with an on-again, off-again career in the military police

CE 3845 / AL 1800

The increasingly paranoid governor, convinced humans are planning to murder him and that Japan is planning to invade just to capture him, has to be forced by the Hierophant to allow electric threshold technology in his country

The electric barriers only do so much good; human citizens are still at constant risk, and human immigrants are in particular danger

The Hunters are happy to oblige Trimalchio's paranoid fantasies and begin a long-term campaign of ideological subversion in the Front

Over the course of eighty years, multiple generations of Front citizens are warmed into dissent through subtle countercultural motifs worked into art, music, literature, and the platforms of those few human politicians still with money and security enough to run for office

The Internet makes this process, once practiced by the Hierophant for the sake of martyrs, very easy

CE 3905 / AL 1860

In response to an increase in violence against martyrs, a booming martyr population in need of ready food, and evidence indicating willful conspiracies of ideological subversion, Trimalchio quietly reinstates his camp policy; all humans may potentially be encamped for any number of crimes, and most city-dwelling humans receiving universal basic income are relocated into organized neighborhoods to allow for ease of their control

By 1875, the world is once more aware of what is happening in the Front, but the dangerous nation, having cut ties to every non-martyr country, refuses to yield in a folie à deux linked to the mental illness of its leader

Most humans agree that the removal of Trimalchio is the only way to make any progress in diplomatic relations with the Front

The Jurisdiction of Mexico, refusing to recognize his sovereignty, dismantles its camps and declares war on the United Front; it claims it has no need to secede, as it never accepted being made a Jurisdiction in the first place

Those freed from the Mexican camps form the first basis of the South American Resistance Army

Citizens all across the Front join secret local militias in support of SARA, which swiftly becomes associated with—and funded by—the Hunters

CE 3929 / AL 1884

UF governor and Holy Family member, Trimalchio of California, is assassinated by SARA extremists; the Hierophant becomes de facto governor until the war's conclusion

In retaliation, General Dominia di Mephitoli orchestrates the mass slaughter of encamped humans in an event which will come to be known as "the Black Night"

Soon after, the General enters seclusion in the Canadian Jurisdictions for 20 years; the reasons for this are broadly related to threats on her life following the Black Night, but the real reasons remain a mystery

CE 3948 / AL 1903

General di Mephitoli is ordered back from her sabbatical to engage in the ongoing South American Conflict, in hopes that her presence will end the thirty-year struggle

CE 3951 / AL 1906

The Battle for the Reclamation of Mexico, the final battle of the South American Conflict, begins as the bloodiest loss of the General's career; she is captured and spends six nights as a POW before making good her escape in what becomes known as "the Nogales Rampage"

The bloody path Cicero and his company carve to rendezvous with her in Tucson puts a brutal end one of the most horrific wars the planet has yet seen

On a Pacific Northwest beach following the war, the General meets her future wife, Cassandra

Six months later, General di Mephitoli is promoted to governess of the United Front

CE 3952 / AL 1907

A strange announcement is made: thanks to a tip from the Lamb, the Hierophant discovers an abandoned baby girl, which he claims to have been infected by tainted breast milk; however, through the mercy of God, the baby will rise again despite the fact that introduction of the protein into an infant body tends to kill the child permanently, rather than transmute it into a martyr

Therefore, although the baby dies soon after the Hierophant's discovery, he places the dead body under the care of a team of doctors

Incredibly, the abandoned child grows during death, and over the next twenty years, will develop into a physically normal adult; the reasons are unknown, and efforts to replicate the effect can lead only to permanent infant mortality

CE 3975 / AL 1930

Santa Lavinia di Firenze, Sacred Princess of Europa, Merciful Miracle of the Holy Father, and Blessed Virgin of the Holy Family, awakens after a twenty-four-year-long period of clinical death; a heartbeat begins in February and brain activity starts in March, leaving the girl in a comatose state until the year's end

She awakens for the first time in her life that December

For his efforts in maintaining watch for signs of vitals over the past decade, her doctor, Theodore, is martyred by the Hierophant, and awarded the title, "del Medico," as well as a large sum of land he tends to spurn in favor of following Lavinia's transportation between the Holy Father's many castles

CE 4036 / AL 1991

In an effort to increase the martyr population, which is still struggling to renew itself after the war, the Hierophant issues a blanket writ of permission: for the next twenty years, all martyrs looking to become parents may martyr any child under the age of 10 without an interview by a Holy Family member

Particularly in the Front cities of San Valentino and New Elsinore, martyring rates skyrocket

On a farm in the Jurisdiction of California, a border collie gives birth to a litter of puppies; one finds its way into a neighboring farmhouse, belonging to the McLintock family

CE 4041 / AL 1996

Santa Lavinia di Firenze celebrates her 66th Feast Day

CE 4042 / AL 1997

Cassandra di Mephitoli dies on the First of May, aged 113

The Governess of the United Front attempts to flee her post for reasons unknown to the public

She is branded a traitor, a terrorist, and the most wanted woman in the world

THE GENERAL'S BRIDE

At that he seized the bowl and tossed it off
And the heady wine pleased him immensely. "More"—
He demanded a second bowl—"a hearty helping!
And tell me your name, now, quickly,
So I can hand my guest a gift to warm his *heart.*
Our soil yields the Cyclops powerful, full-bodied wine
And the rains from Zeus build its strength. But this,
This is nectar, ambrosia—this flows from heaven!"

So he declared. I poured him another fiery bowl—
Three bowls I brimmed and three he drank to the last drop,
The fool, and then, when the wine was swirling round his brain,
I approached my host with a cordial, winning word:
"So, you ask me the name I'm known by, Cyclops?
I will tell you. But you must give me a guest-gift
As you've promised. Nobody—that's my name. Nobody—
So my mother and father call me, all my friends."

—Homer's *Odyssey*, Book IX,
Lines 396–411

I

Perchance to Dream

The Hierophant was everywhere. Every door she opened. Every place she ran. Even in this Void: a place she'd never meant to visit! A place she'd never known to exist until an incalculable time before. Dominia found it impossible to discern hallucination from thought from objective experience, and wondered if they differed in this place. Was this some dream? Her wife, fair Cassandra, seemed distant memory, dream, terror—sleep's chimera from many days prior, when confronted by this much more pressing tahgmahr before her.

In a half-formed study suspended upon nothing, she had found her Father. That man who had stolen her right eye from its socket as she'd fled in search of the mystic who might restore life to her wife. Dear Cassandra, who so suffered at the hands of the world. At his hands.

Hearing the voice and seeing the shape of her Father proved more powerful than either sense alone, and her thoughts skittered between the stimuli: him; his wineglass; the magnificent strings of Berlioz piping into the vast space from an artifact record player at his elbow; a profusion of memories that scattered across her eye like so many mis-shuffled playing cards. Dominia focused on the oriental rug that slithered even once her body settled into its surroundings. The Hierophant uttered a sympathetic (and condescending) tut as she swayed with obvious vertigo.

"'Be not afeard.'" He set his glass beside the gramophone while rising to his feet. "'The isle is full of noises, sounds, and sweet airs, that give delight and hurt not.'"

Caliban's speech, drawn from the finest of Shakespeare's plays, proved better anchor for consciousness than Valentinian's advice of remembering the ground, tossing stones, or shuffling cards. Everything snapped into simple clarity. Lucid as the real world.

"The real world." She almost laughed at the concept until she realized she was responding aloud to her own thoughts and managed to ask while edging across the threshold, "Are you real?"

He smiled, and filled a second glass of burgundy fluid from the keroid decanter. "As real as you; more real than my wine. Yet"—he approached to hand her the glass; his eyes crinkled as she accepted it—"unreal though it may be, it has quite the effect in this strange place."

Now she saw him close, and he appeared younger than she'd ever known him to be. The tension of flesh against bones, a certain sleekness of body brought on by hyper-advanced age's loss in muscle mass, had been reversed. All that had faded from his features after so prolonged—possibly eternal—a lifespan had returned with new glow, and fit the Hierophant with increased resemblance to Cicero. The clearest visible difference was the Pontifex lacked his son's Mephistophelian goatee.

Cicero! The General had not thought on the Holy Family's unhinged priest since taking his eye; an event which felt simultaneously moments and months before. No doubt he had no knowledge of this place; otherwise, she would have known about it, partial to bragging as he was. Cicero's discovery of such a thing would only disturb their Father's peace. El Sacerdote was a gnat, and particularly loathsome when something could be gained in the way of knowledge or power. Dominia, also, hungered for knowledge, but showed patience in learning and less cruelty in its use. In her own opinion, at least. Thus, it made some sense she was welcome in an imaginary study of her Father's where even the Eternal Son was not invited, but not by much; after all, as she insisted, "You tried to kill me. Or let Cicero try, at any rate."

"And you took his eye!" Said with a twinkle in both his dark ones. "My dear. You have waited quite a long time to teach your brother that lesson, haven't you?"

"Call me 'inspired.'" Her free hand lifted to her eye patch. "Lest we forget, this started with you pulling out my eye."

"It actually started with poor Casandra's death. Speaking of—why don't you come out, darling?" The Hierophant looked at a bookshelf against the farthest implied wall. "We are alone. No one will hurt you here."

Cold sweat prickled across Dominia's palms well before that vile thief of Cassandra's form stepped from where she—it—listened. Panic overwhelmed the General. She turned her eyes away, to the fireplace, in a look her Father followed. The creature twitched through her periphery in an effort at walking that seemed that of an alien recreating a description heard secondhand, perhaps through translation. Something within the body walked, but the body did not. As cramps of nausea clutched the General's ribs, the martyr permitted her Father to take her free hand. She allowed him kiss and pat it in that doting manner he demonstrated when he felt like supplicating his children into something, rather than ordering or threatening them. She tolerated the sound of his voice as he said, "You should know better than to think I would let true harm come to you. That I do not want to return Cassandra to you."

She almost laughed; but there again for a wink of the mind was the first appearance of the thing, outside the fire she'd shared with Lazarus and the formerly fictional Saint Valentinian. "I was told it wouldn't be able to come into the light."

"Not normal light, no. This light—my light—is much superior. All God's creatures may enter it without harm: I am like the black sun, in that respect. Please"—he released her hand to gesture toward the armchair seated across from his—"won't you sit down?"

With effort, Dominia set eye upon the vulgar recreation of Cassandra. Visible in her Father's blue firelight and standing statue still, the likeness almost passed: but Cassandra's hair was not the ink of this creature's, nor were her eyes dun and half lidded. Lifeless. Still, as the Hierophant did not wait for her to fulfill his invitation before settling into his crimson armchair, she felt obliged. In that vacuous space, any sensation was as comforting as the doppelgänger was disconcerting. She lowered herself into the empty seat and winced when that copy jerked to her side, where it knelt at her arm in perversion of Cassandra's occasional custom.

"She has a gift for you," said the Hierophant. The General grit her teeth as it brandished a crown of lush sapphire flowers once held behind its back.

"Dominia," the thing recited, trying the name and a smile. Both actions were ill-suited and ill-advised. The creature showed its beautiful teeth in a cold, mechanical way that did not alter its eyes or brows one whit. It held the crown in expectation, waiting; but when, after a time, it asked, "Don't you love me," Dominia slapped the so-called gift out of the pirated hands. The thing emitted a cry in hollow replica of her dead wife's voice that only made the General down a mouthful of wine. While it scrambled to collect the ruined crown and crouch by the side of the Hierophant, her Father clucked like the old hen he was.

"You're hurting the poor girl's feelings!"

"What does it want from me?" She stared the uncanny thing down and it shrank against the Hierophant's chair, mouth pressed to the upholstery. Its jaw warped under the pressure as though its bones were rubber while the Holy Father regarded Dominia with bland innocence.

"What does *she* want from you? Only that you should love her! If only Cassandra had so pure a motive in life."

That stung her back into her wineglass. After the burning liquid sprang her taste buds into work and tightened her jaw, she said, "That thing's not Cassandra."

"She is. She is Cassandra, and more than Cassandra."

"It's a monster. Some kind of—formless, abstract thing." What was the word Lazarus had used? "A *tulpa*."

The Hierophant rolled his eyes. "I would not put much stock into what Valentinian tells you." She did not correct him as he carried on: "The word you have just used is of Tibetan origin and means, quite simply, 'thoughtform.' Look around you! Everything here is a thoughtform. The wine you drink, your chair, each book upon my shelves, the fire that lights the room! Even our bodies here are sorts of thoughtforms, suspended upon our own unconscious understanding of ourselves."

At his words, she studied the books. The titles remained legible despite how, on a second, harder glance, the individual letters forming these words made little sense. What registered to her mind as the spine of the *Odyssey* yielded, upon closer inspection, a word spelled "TÆ CΦDVUKΘP." As her mind tangled in cognitive dissonance to marvel at such mechanics, the Hierophant carried on. "The origin of this Cassandra, within the cauldron of your memories, makes her no less real than the woman you once called your darling wife; if anything, this memory-borne bride could prove more real than your last, if you would let her."

"Now you're just lying. This thing isn't Cassandra. Cassandra doesn't move like that, doesn't even look that way. It's wrong."

"She is wrong because you have not yet invested energy into making her right. She is like an infant, newborn. Why, she would not even know how to say the name of her adored Dominia, had I not spent this whole night teaching her."

"Dominia," repeated the thing in a sullen voice that made the General's skin crawl.

"I wish you hadn't. I wish you'd kept that thing in the darkness, where it belongs."

"How cruel you are! How forgetful of all those years of love." While the terrible thing wept Cassandra's tears, the General pushed herself from her chair and paced around the bookshelves. On second pass, the nonsense titles were different in either lettering or meaning. "Forgetful of your love of Cassandra as you are forgetful of your love of me."

"I never loved you. You stole me."

"I saved you from certain death. I gave you a destiny." His pale-blond eyebrows lifted as she spared him a withering glance. "And you did love me at times, against your better judgment. You love me even now, or you would not be here. Would you?"

Dominia did not speak. When she was a teenager and he had taught her how to draw, Berlioz had played in the background then, too. It was a natural cross-discipline for a fighter in martyr culture; thanks to Saint Valentinian, patron saint of death as well as artists, any form of visual art was by and large considered the domain of soldiers, executioners, and other individuals of violent inclination. These classes to foster a creative hobby in a girl whose only interest was fighting represented a rare few times where, yes, wrapped in the moment, she looked up and realized she'd been forgetting to hate him. It made her eye sting to remember. She covered it and the patch with one hand. "I wish I'd stayed with Valentinian and Lazarus."

The Hierophant drained his glass and set it aside. "Confront the root of your dark feelings toward this poor, sweet child of a woman. Why do you hate her?"

"Please don't."

"Is it because she is a Cassandra you may safely hate? Into whom you can pour all your resentments, all those old feelings of having been used and manipulated? When she came to you at the beach, it was, for you, a pure moment, but the purity was cheapened by her intent. Perhaps this dark-haired Cassandra pulled from your thoughts is that base intent of hers brought into shape. That is why you hate her so."

"It's a thing attracted by my energy, my emotions. It has nothing to do with Cassandra. Cassandra is dead."

"And yet, she yet lives."

"No, damn you! She's dead!"

"Dominia." The thing lifted reddened eyes from its tear-wet fingers. "Why, Dominia?"

"Oh, shut up."

It resumed weeping. The Hierophant stroked its hair as though petting a cat. "Perhaps your resentment toward our poor Cassandra is meant for yourself. Perhaps you do not feel deserving of a second chance with her, after the way things happened."

On furious instinct, she took a step toward him. The arctic heart of the fire flared against its tangerine edge, and her shadow fluttered like the wings of a gargantuan black moth. "What happened to Cassandra was your fault. Cicero's fault. This Family drove her insane. She never forgot we're just a bunch of cannibal monsters."

Symphonie Fantastique, in its final ten minutes, took its sudden somber turn, and the Hierophant let his lips curl in his calmest smile. "Another truth turned Cassandra toward your unlocked gun, but I suppose it's true she might have killed herself any old way. Surely it was convenience. Not some symbol."

The gun at her hip, whether dream or no, seared her thigh through her trousers as her Father rose. His long shadow quite dwarfed hers. As she stood her ground before the towering man, she insisted, "Her final choice didn't have to do with me. The gun was something she knew. It was handy."

"It was also the gun of the woman who killed the father of Cassandra's child. The gun of the woman who killed her the first time by martyring her, thus sealing the fate of her baby."

Dominia began to storm away, but the Hierophant snatched her arm with such viselike grip she had to remind herself she could not be hurt in this place. As he drew her back to him, he continued, "The Cassandra you loved is different from the Cassandra you knew. The one you knew—the one you refused to see—never moved beyond her human life. This is why martyring adults is so dangerous. It only brings heartbreak. But, my girl: this Cassandra is new. She has become as a little child"—there he went with that fucking book—"and from the purity of her meek and humble heart grows the love for which you've pined. The kind of love you never had with the old Cassandra, despite what you told yourself."

"You're lying! Cassandra loved me. She came to me for her own reasons; but in the end, she loved me."

"Then why did she kill herself that way?"

Over and over, five times in one second, Dominia walked into their room at the exact point in time Cassandra pulled the trigger. Over and over, her wife's eyes met hers with shock to find the Governess had woken up early. Over and over, it was too late to do anything but watch.

"It took some planning, princess. It was not a split-second decision."

Oh! The impossibly soft feeling of her wife's lips as the Governess had comforted her the morning before, when she had been so unexpectedly devastated during the Walpurgisnacht Party. That powder-soft femininity and mint and warmth. Finally, Cassandra had calmed and dozed off on the sitting-room couch. Dominia had thought they could sleep in safety. She had not wished to move her wife. She had fallen asleep beside her, still in her clothes, gun not put away.

"I am sorry to say this, but she was deeply unhappy."

The cold panic on waking from a tahgmahr—no, a real day terror, a replay of her escape from her Nogales cell—to find herself alone. Her racing heart. The memory looped: calling her wife's name, clambering up, seeing the gun was gone and knowing her second of intuition had been justified, running through the halls, checking every room in their vast estate until reaching their bedroom, and there was the door, the door, so close, so close—but never close enough.

The Hierophant touched Dominia's cheek, and she came back to herself to realize she wept. Her Father wiped away her tears and held her as, forgetting herself, she collapsed into sobs. As if the past month had never happened—as if the past lifetime was erased and she was a girl again—she allowed herself to be rocked against his chest, to cry there and say, "I just wish she would have talked to me."

"There are some pains too deep to express. She did not hide it because her heart was stone. She hid it because, though she may have loved her late soldier, she also loved you, her living soldier, much as she could. And she knew the pain of her lasting grief would hurt you, in turn."

The first true thing he'd said in some time inspired a sharp breath by which she steadied her nerves. This gaslighting was insane: he was a pendulum. She pushed away from him to clear her throat. "You're right. She loved me more than you would know. Pain or no, she loved me."

"So will you cling to the intangible memory of love? Or will you come to your senses and see it waits before you even now?"

Behind him, the standing thing had shambled forth a few steps. One hand kept its balance against the General's empty seat. Still ill at the mere sight, she insisted of her Father, "That thing is a lie. A false creation proceeding from my hopes, my memories, my feelings. It's a predator. Fake."

"She can be real. And she is far less a lie than those Lazarus and his friend tell you."

Though her ears burned with fury, and denial boiled on the tip of her tongue, Dominia still nursed doubt enough to withhold comment. Her Father insisted, "Those nonsense stories of resurrection, of the stream of consciousness you knew as 'Cassandra' finding bodily resurrection in this world—they are lies."

"The only liar here is you."

"My poor, sweet angel! So trusting of your friends you will not listen to your own Father's words. I tell you, they lie. Lazarus will not help you."

"There's someone," she began, stopping because he said, "They will lead you to Cairo, and you will be disappointed."

Her stomach tightened. She stepped away, toward a fire that emitted no warmth. "How do you know about Cairo?"

"Do you think Lazarus and Valentinian are the only ones who have been through all this bad business before?" The Hierophant returned to his seat while smoothing the fabric of his suit. "'I do not know everything, but I am aware of much,' as a great devil once said; and I am aware Cassandra will not be resurrected in the way you hope. But *I* can give you Cassandra."

"You can give me a lie."

"A lie becomes the truth if told enough. Cassandra's love for you was, in the first place, a lie that became the truth. Why would it be different were it to happen again, this way?"

Somehow, the question staggered her more than any he'd posited. The simpering doppelgänger gazed through tear-matted eyelashes, lower lip trembling, as the stalwart General nonetheless insisted, "She's not real."

At her Father's smile, the General bore her teeth to realize she'd slipped by calling the thing "she." As if it were a person! It even responded. Brightened around the eyes. Dominia shuddered and folded her arms, more eerily afloat than ever in her life. Every word she spoke seemed more futile than the last. Horribly, sooner or later, she would have to acknowledge this thing in a way not dismissive.

But then—praise God, or damn Him—they were interrupted by a knock. The General held her breath.

II

The Magician and the General

"*Entrez*," called the Hierophant, his tone reminiscent of teatime conversation. (Though it did always seem such with him, didn't it?) When the broad oak door through which she'd entered swung wide, Dominia exhaled. Relief mingled with anxiety in the way it had when, in too deep at a party as a too-young girl turning toward substances and trying to pretend she wasn't a Holy Family member, she had urgently called for a driver. Instead, her Father had knocked at the party's door. Though she was all of fourteen and much, much too high, and he'd found it all ill-advised, he had arrived to save her—and embarrass her. Now, salvation and embarrassment arose to find the doorway filled not by her Father but the lithe frame of Valentinian, who leaned with his elbow propped against the jamb.

"Leave her alone." The General studied her Father's reaction to the saint's impudent tone and found His Holiness illegible as ever. "We've got a long way to go. She doesn't need you distracting her."

"I'm connecting with my daughter the only way I can! Every time I see her in real life, she runs away." A merry twinkle lit the Hierophant's eyes as he picked up his decanter. "May I pour you a drink?"

"No, thanks." Valentinian strolled over the threshold, hands in his pockets and eyes sliding around the room until he noticed Dominia's empty glass. With his scoff of annoyance, bold eyebrows lifted high and his hands flew once more into sight. "Don't tell me you drank his wine. Fairyland rules! Do they mean nothing to you?"

She was assailed by a thousand myths, fables, and legends about stupid people eating stupid things and facing stupid consequences. Oh, no. "I don't have to stay here forever now, do I?"

"What? No—I don't mean *that* level of fairyland rules. I just mean, don't eat or drink things you're given here unless we clear it. For one thing, when you're drinking his wine, you're reinforcing his reality and his power in this place even more than I could. This is new to you. You've got an impressionable mind at this phase; he could convince you of anything, no matter how levelheaded you usually are. And when you're drinking his wine, you're... connecting with him. Accepting him into you. You're drinking his thoughts, after all."

Dominia wasn't sure of the concrete harm, aside from the abstract sense of violation, but she wasn't sure she wanted to learn. It was bad enough knowing his blood flowed through her veins. His influence was inseparable from her present self, even if that self felt so removed from the woman who had been, among other things, architect and tool of genocide. As she edged toward the door, Valentinian extended his hand, and she took it without second thought. A childish impulse, she considered after. Perhaps he was right about how impressionable she was in this place, this early in her exposure. Perhaps it was his perception of that same trait that made him say, with a nod toward the melancholic replica of Cassandra, "You didn't touch it, did you?"

"Only to slap its 'gift' out of its hands," she admitted. The mage nodded.

"Good. The surest way to strengthen a thoughtform is by touch."

Though he began to lead her away, Valentinian stopped short when Dominia refused to move. "What would happen," she asked in the absent way of forced innocence, "if it did manifest in reality?"

"We'd lose," he said with a cold glance at the Hierophant. "If it manifested, Cassandra would have no hope of coming back—you would be willing to settle." Her lip twitched in an untenable defense that went unspoken; he continued in a gentler tone, "But that won't happen. This is the time we win."

"I love your optimism," said the Hierophant, black eyes curled with nasty levity. "Every time."

"Cute." The magician half laughed in his own nasty way, showing his teeth, then let the mirth drop when his expression was visible only to Dominia. "If it weren't for this place, somebody would have murdered him long ago. And I'm not talking about me; there'd be a line."

Too true. No wonder no bullet hit him, and why his speed was in excess of even martyr dexterity. Now she understood how it was he and Lazarus and Tobias had flickered in and out of existence like hallucinations. Much as this place accounted for the legend of Lazarus—that those martyrs who partook of his blood would never again need to eat human flesh and would, in exchange, never burn in the sun—so, too, did it explain her Father. Many traits, however, remained unaccounted for, and Dominia could not wrap her head around the mechanics of reality's oscillations. The idea of someone like Valentinian or the Hierophant moving between high amplitudes, rather than dwelling within them...

"I hope you will visit me again, Dominia." Her Father smiled such that perhaps he had his own form of telepathy here. Mere paranoia. "We still have much to discuss. Thank you for picking her up, Valentinian."

"Yeah, yeah." The magician was now successful in his efforts to shepherd her through the threshold; she took but a quick glance at the duplicate as the door shut, and her friend told the Hierophant, "See you tomorrow."

Valentinian did not look back, but Dominia was hung up on the Hierophant's phrasing. Like divorced parents, exchanging a daughter.

"You knew I'd go to him?"

The magician released her hand. "I had to sleep sometime, and Lazarus has been up for days... He's more bothered than I am—that you go to see the Hierophant while we're here—but, hell, I visit him all the time, too."

"You do?"

"Look around. Who else is there to talk to? I mean, sure, there are—people, some places, depending where you look. But nobody on my level. I don't have a choice. If I want to have a conversation with somebody without constantly explaining myself, my options are limited. No offense. Anyway, there's no real damage capable of being done here—not to one another's bodies—so I swing by to play cards. He's got a chess set. You have no idea how sick I am of chess."

"I can't imagine." With every step, the richness of the dark anti-landscape paled into what passed for dawn, and it was not long before those electromagnetic bands of color began to once more twist into relief. "You must be lonely. How long have you spent here, stuck as a dog on Earth with only Lazarus and thoughtforms in this place to keep you company?"

"Only about two thousand reality years," he said with cheer before adding to a flabbergasted Dominia, "this cycle."

"Two *thousand* years?"

"Yeah, well, time moves differently here. It's flown by like four hundred years to me, as much time as I spend hanging out between dimensions. See? Only a bit older than you. If you're talking the real total, though, I'm not even sure I know. How many times have I watched the world go around? How many times has the game been played in this particular fashion, with these pieces, with this set? I can't rightly say, but I can tell you this—we will win this time. Because he may be aware of much: but I know everything."

For whatever reason, Dominia believed that. She was willing to believe it, at any rate. Whether it was truth, she wasn't sure, but she was desperate to think that the magician who was also a dog had answers. That was why she was glad when he stopped and turned to speak seriously to her. The black sun, on the verge of creating the peaked horizon by breaking it, paused with them.

"He's a deceiver, Dominia. He's easy to like, and the things he does are superficially good, and it's a fact he wants you to know the truth. But he wants you to know the truth in a way that perverts it, and makes it good as a lie."

From the corner of her eye, Dominia noticed two things with a distinct chill of terror: the path of torches disappeared behind them, one at a time, two back from the one beneath which they stood; and the doppelgänger, having stalked them, was now still as one of those torches. It stood in the darkness, from which it observed in eerie silence through owlish eyes that had grown. As if the thing had learned how to hold its expression to emulate its forebear but naively exaggerated certain features to make itself more attractive. The effect failed spectacularly, into total uncanny horror. Valentinian gazed also at the silent creature, whose violet dress and long black hair—not Cassandra's at all, bearing so slim resemblance it enraged the eye—hung motionless. Dominia realized only when the magus spoke that the thing drew no breath.

"No matter how well you tell a lie," said the magician, "it can never be the truth."

"I know." Miserable, she turned from that ugly thing founded on beautiful memory.

Valentinian clapped the General upon the shoulder, then resumed his brisk pace to their camp. The sun, to their right, resumed rising. "You know better than anybody, kid. The man can spin the truth the way athletes spin their balls."

"Then why are you letting me see him?"

"Complicated answer; save my pride by boiling it down to, 'I can't stop you.'" At her silence, he noted her expression of skepticism and touched his chest. "Look, kiddo, I'm not the miracle person. I mean—I am in the end, but somebody else is in charge of making big, profound, Earth-moving miracles manifest in reality."

"Is that Lazarus?" asked Dominia. Valentinian did not answer.

"What I'm trying to say is, short of producing a miracle of some kind, I can't stop you from going to him during the night. That's just the way it is. Fish gotta swim; birds gotta fly; your Father's gotta be a huge pain in my ass. Excuse me for a second."

He ignored her to pat around the pockets of his waistcoat. As if he needed to find things, rather than manifest them like a walking Higgs boson! After a few pats, he withdrew a pack of cigarettes that couldn't have fit into his waistcoat without disrupting its silhouette. Yet, as he stuck one in his mouth and put the rest away, no sign of a box-shaped outline remained visible against the man's ribs. He didn't bother to hide that he lit it with an electrical spark cresting between his fingers, rather than his lighter.

"Smoking's bad, kids," said the fictional martyr while lifting his head. The puff of smoke he exhaled formed a bisected circle of nonentry. "But Lazarus has his stones, and I'm not exactly going to get imaginary cancer in my astral body. Not that somebody couldn't if they believed they could." He regarded the cigarette before resuming it with a shrug. "Anyway, it sticks in your dad's craw he can't reason me into quitting, so you'll have to pardon my smoke."

"How do you know each other, exactly?"

"He's the asshole who's got me stuck as a dog, among other things. I mean, *really* 'other' things. Basil is just one of many. This one incarnation many centuries ago, I somehow got hooked into an aquarium of sea monkeys." The magician shuddered. "That family's cat had it in for us. Stuff like that's why I spend so much time here until you show up."

"But how is it you *know* each other?" The General tried to study his face, but it was difficult with the both of them moving and the black sun warping all it revealed. This space seemed different from where they'd been yesterday; distant mountains were replaced by the elevated planes of mesas, and a vast gorge now split the distant world, east (if she correctly read the fields) of where far-off Lazarus smote the night's flames. There was resemblance between the men, between Lazarus and Valentinian, as though they were of the same stock; but it was not so strong a resemblance as, say, between the Hierophant and Cicero. If anything, such resemblance elevated to a kind of twinship on seeing her Father with so young and spry a form. Valentinian and Lazarus shared features: shapes echoed in noses and eyes and the magician's high-cut cheekbones, the likes of which were hidden in Lazarus by agéd beard and tangled old-man eyebrows. Yet, overall differences of stock and build—the broad old mystic looked as if he had a background of pit fighting and had nothing of the lean, middle-aged magician's wiry frame—indicated they were not so closely related as the Hierophant and his Eternal Son. "Who are you?"

With a coy smile, the man answered, "I'm nobody."

Dominia tried to shake off what seemed not so much a lie as a reference to the *Odyssey*: as though he teased her with knowledge of the books she had studied. Her face burning to wonder if this was how it felt to be schizophrenic, the General cleared her throat.

"Why won't you tell me anything?"

His look grew somewhat stern. "Because if I tell you the truth about anything, you won't believe me. You'll decide I'm lying, you'll go into the future with unnecessary predispositions, or you'll try to test me."

"More than I'm testing your patience?" she asked, brow arched.

The magician, who had been gesturing with his cigarette, coughed himself into a laughing smirk. "All right, wise guy. Let's hurry up. The old man looks impatient."

So he did: Lazarus stood in the distance, hands on his hips. As they approached, Dominia made out the tapping of his foot—and the clouds of dust puffing around his foot, as if some dirt, some real ground, had developed overnight.

"Well," the old man barked when they were within range, "did she touch it?"

"Not tonight," answered the magician. The mystic nodded as the General tried to avoid distraction from her initial question—one she cemented in the depths of her mind so as to never forget: Who was Valentinian?

"Then we still have a chance, though it's going to follow us." The thing at which she had deliberately not looked was now quite a distance away, perhaps as distant from them as Lazarus was when first she'd noticed his figure; yet, because she knew Cassandra's features so well, she saw every false freckle upon the doppelgänger's sallow cheek. With a sigh of disgust for the thing, the mystic reached into his pocket for his rocks. "Let's move this train along, folks." The day's first pebble pinged along the growing gorge. "Still thirty-three more real days to pass, and a lot of ground to cover."

"But, wait." The men ignored her, walking on, which blistered her entire being. "Hey! If you know me so well, you know I hate being ignored."

"We've never tried ignoring you before," admitted Valentinian.

"Military ego," explained the mystic without looking back. That military ego flared in real indignation while she made no move to march. They kept walking; like a pair of bubbles splitting off, the greater compass shared by the men parted from that of the General and left her with not only a poorer sense of confidence but the nauseating discovery her compass pointed back in the direction of her Father's study. In time, she would find his study always manifested north of her location: in those irritating seconds of scorn at the hands of her so-called comrades, however, the glowing tori that swept in his direction provided a suggestion, rather than an objective marker of magnetic (or other) poles.

"Have I ever refused to go on before?"

With a sigh of irritation, Valentinian paused to do her the decency of looking at her. "Once or twice. Under similar conditions."

"What conditions are those?"

"Our refusal to tell you anything. But if I tell you anything now, like I keep saying—"

"Dominia." Lazarus, who had also stopped, drew her hostile attention and watched it melt away, for the old man had a kind of infinite patience about his face and being. It was difficult here to maintain indignation before him; or perhaps being in this place clarified the pointlessness of indignation.

"This same free will that lets you stand in place and stop all three of us is the same free will that makes you such a valuable treasure. You like to think on a decision before you make it, and make it with care. I understand it's frustrating to know so little. We've already told you almost everything; we'll keep telling you. But all you have to know is that you are going to save the world, and kill your Father."

"Like you said when we got here. But save *what* world?"

"All of them," said Valentinian.

"Humans *and* martyrs," she pressed. The men exchanged a reluctant glance.

Through some spurious form of telepathy (or Valentinian's puppy-dog eyes, which recalled Basil), the men decided Lazarus would be their spokesperson. "Do you remember, Dominia, when I explained to you Earth is a prison, and martyrs, its prisoners?"

A most painful kind of beauty—something like what Miki Soto, Red Market prostitute and Dominia's only real friend, would have called *mono no aware*—arose in Dominia's throat at the memory of the sermon. "Yes," she said. The old man approached her to rest a warm hand upon a shoulder she would have otherwise forgotten.

"It does not always have to be like this. Martyrs are people, too. But they are not people meant for Earth."

"Acetia?" The planet from which her Father claimed to herald, and which would not develop life for millions, possibly billions, of years. In its present state, circling the distant star of Procyon A near sacred Sirius, it remained in noxious and primeval condition. Deadly. "I never believed in it before."

"It's possible, in a sense. But only without your Father." Valentinian glanced in silence at Lazarus, then turned away to light another foul cigarette while the mystic said, "Humans and martyrs can never live together, it's true. But that doesn't mean one or the other has to die. It just means martyrs have to change. They have to be willing to leave."

"Sort of like an intergalactic Australia," suggested the exhaling magician, "before it was turned into a prison camp in half the state, and a nuclear waste and garbage dump in the other half. You know, way back when it was just a prison colony, after the Aboriginal people were horribly subjugated but before the place became prohibitively hot and most who could afford it skipped town."

"Hot Siberia, with superpowers." The irritation in Lazarus's mutter was not just for the human race but all sapient life. "Anyway, it's true. What I'm suggesting for the martyr race is scary, but you have the irresponsible pleasure of not having to worry about it."

Her mind now open (possibly for the first time in her life) to the concept that her Father was an alien martyr from the future who had somehow copied Cicero's features, Dominia asked, "Why is that?"

"Because you are our military ego," said the old man with a wry smile. "By the time the war is over, you'll already be at home with Cassandra."

Whether or not he told the truth, Dominia had to give it to him: Lazarus knew how to get her marching again.

III

Attention Deficit

The General had endured many a long march. Indeed, she'd led more than she'd endured! Though her Father's army had always been technologically well equipped, there were those locations, those battles, those infiltrations that required substantial walk and some hastily constructed encampments. Mexico was still covered in her boot prints. But, for her thousand battles and thousand-plus marches, she had known in her life no march quite like this. Not one so long. The conventional secret to marching was placing focus on anything but what was happening and what would continue to happen—as if, in not acknowledging the road, one would suddenly find oneself at the destination.

In this case, imagining was dangerous. Her coping mechanism for marches was gone, but she'd lost far more than that. Imagination was how she dealt with trauma, and, at times, how she dealt with killing—though she needed that coping mechanism less now than she had as a young woman learning the arts of hunting or war. And, in modern nights, her usual figure of distraction was a memory whose name she feared to think lest it feed the thing behind her. She dared not think of anything now. Not for a prolonged stretch, and nothing of her dead wife.

So, as the gorge broadened with the march upon their untiring legs, she instead thought how the unflagging nature of her dream-legs was a torture of its own. With the black sun still in the yet-dark sky, time froze, and though there was now more to look upon than "nothing," there was still not much. Perilous thoughts marched to the beat of her feet: her unanswered questions, her dread for the length of the trip, Cass—

No. Back to her feet. Remember the ground and the pinging of pebbles. But what about her Father? How did these people know her Father? Many questions filtered through her head, the doctrine of martyrs clashing with what she'd heard from Miki of Red Market legends. The only way the General would gain clarity was by hoping somebody told the truth.

"Is it true"—she hurried to Lazarus's side while he spared a glance her way—"my Father is an alien? Are you an alien, too?"

"Do you believe everything you hear? Do we look like extraterrestrials?"

"Neither does my Father."

"I wonder why," Lazarus dryly asked of laughing Valentinian.

The magician spread his hands. "We're all aliens, in a way."

That night, when they would camp near the opposite end of that gorge and settle in for the night, the torches would once more appear, and the doppelgänger would be gone, and Dominia would find herself drawn down this nighttime path to the study. This occasion, the mobile room sat on the gorge's opposite side. She would remark on the earlier, extraterrestrial conversation to her Father while refusing his wine politely as possible. In response to this refusal, he would say, "No offense taken, my dear: I understand your hesitance. Who knows what was said to you! But take a seat, at least."

Likely as bad as drinking his wine; but, her sitting made him comfortable to say, "You asked me of Lazarus, and Valentinian—yes, I knew them when I arrived on Earth. As to whether I stole the protein from Lazarus, as you say your Red Market friend suggests"—wry smile—"how could I have done that when I brought it from my world?"

That day, Lazarus will have said, "Cicero and I were genetic engineers together in the earliest world I recall. Him, me, and his brother, Elijah." The name of the Lamb, her ram-horned, gentler Family member, somehow alarmed Dominia to hear. "The same night I was martyred, the Hierophant swooped in to martyr the brothers with his inferior blood."

"I was originally involved, too," was Valentinian's addition, which had earned glances from both Lazarus and the General.

"Yeah," the mystic had allowed, "but I don't remember it."

"Why not?"

Dominia would ask this question twice; only the Hierophant, that night, would give her something resembling a straight answer.

"Valentinian was never born into this crest of the universe because of a wish gone bad."

There was no maintaining a straight face. "A wish? Now you're being childish."

"Don't tell me you don't believe in wishes! I've fouled up somewhere in raising you, haven't I?"

"Valentinian has no body," Lazarus explained before that moment, in those careful words, "because your Father trapped him."

"How?"

"The same way he turned me into a dog." The alleged saint, having tarried to grind a cigarette beneath his shoe, hastened to catch up. "By magic, basically."

Because of that, Dominia would later think to ask her Father, "Are you a magician in the way Valentinian is?"

"Every man is a magician in this place. What Valentinian does is not so impressive."

"But, if he were back in reality, would he still be a magician? More than you are, I mean."

The Hierophant studied her, hands folded upon his knee, the specter of Cassandra leaning its head against the arm of his chair. It had been that way since Dominia's arrival, plaintive eyes plastered upon the widow's steeled expression with all the emptiness of a statue's hollow gaze. "If every man is a magician in this place," the Pontifex decided, "then every man is also a magician when on Earth. It is a question of his means in producing magic, and how powerful he is—that is, how much energy he uses to produce how drastic of a change. A drastic miracle—or wish, if you'd rather—is something that would normally require a complex, energy-costly series of transmogrifications, but which the magician elicits with a tap of the finger." He lifted his glass to his lips. "Turning water into wine. Rudimentary business here.

"'Magic' in reality is another word for 'influence.' One uses magic to influence events, whether personally, locally, or at an even larger scale; magic often consciously utilizes science, but science never seems capable of acknowledging its magical potential. The magical man is such because of his connection to this place, among other things. Our bodies here are like the dark star of Sirius B—the occult twin of its bright-shining brother, who keeps close watch on Acetia and its procyonid sun. Once the individual reaches a level of self-awareness high enough to detect that black star and utilize its secret light, anything is possible."

"Like what?"

"Anything at all."

"Anything" was such a staggering notion she dared not think on it, for the only thing she wanted was something(one) too easily corrupted. Something(one) she could not give herself, could not manifest from nothingness. Not that same Cassandra who killed herself, who she knew and loved. Not in the reality she knew. She had accepted that fact well enough for the doppelgänger to seem less an opportunity to move forward and more a bleak reminder of all the ways the General had gone wrong. But the tiniest sliver of her heart—the tiniest spark—wondered at the replica, abominable deception though it was. She longed in sporadic moments, fraught with shame, to lay her hand upon the softness of Cassandra's cheek and feel it emulated, however false the emulation. In such fleeing moments of—yes, wishing—the creature's eyes glittered, and Dominia spurned those hopes that fed its vapid existence.

The Hierophant asked in a mild tone, "Did you inquire about their ability to resurrect Cassandra?"

"Valentinian assures me you're a liar, which my personal experience confirms."

"I never lie, certainly not in so crass a fashion. Neither one has the power to resurrect her."

"They know who does."

"You are on a fool's errand. The men lead you astray from what your intuition warns: something is not right. You do not even know half the truth."

"Why don't you enlighten me?"

Across the room from her smirking Father, the fire spent shivering light upon a glossy floor that had appeared overday as a base for the study. These tiles, alternating shades of wood, were arranged in the pattern of a chessboard and did, in fairness, render the space visually warm. This did not negate the disturbing effect of such a drastic change being engendered with no effort. After the General had sufficient time to ponder this, her Father spoke up.

"Any truth I say is bound to be dismissed by them as lie; therefore, I dare not share the way of things with you just yet, lest my honesty implant some sense of falsehood in your mind. But Cairo will see you leaving empty-handed, without your lover. All after is violence. They are keeping you upon a certain track and draining you of your free will."

There was that first time she'd met Lazarus, before the service, after Miki and the wounded (ex-)Hunter hacker, Kahlil, had dropped her off and left for Cairo. So long ago to her mind—or perhaps '*nous*' was a better word in this place of no-mind, no-time, no-thing. "Lazarus said my free will gives me power."

"It gives *him* power, too, if he goads you into making choices in service to his cause, rather than yours." His pale brows lifted toward slicked hair. "You deny your senses and lean on faith—hope!—when a solution is before you. You deny their ill intent when they've kept you here so long! Have they even told you how to leave?"

That expertly aimed question startled the General. They had not; but she insisted, "No, because we're going to Cairo."

"And going to Cairo is your choice?" At the purse of her lips, he smiled. "I have watched the footage from your DIOX-I, Dominia. I wish you had not taken it out." She grimaced to relive, in brief, the horrible surgery wherein Cicero had installed it. Would she could take it out a second time! "While I still saw your comings and goings, however, I noticed the same thing you noticed upon waking aboard that train to Kabul. The same thing I notice now: your missing diamond. Your missing wife."

Dominia's hand lay upon her breast with bitter longing for the absent stone. It had already been many terrestrial days since Miki shipped the compressed body of the General's wife to Cairo on orders of her goddess, the Lady. At the unspoken title, jasmine and lavender flowed through the study as if on a breeze not felt. The Hierophant turned his nose toward the scent as his daughter said, "We need to go to Cairo for Cassandra, yes. Your point?"

"You would need not do that at all, were it not for the actions of that prostitute who somehow befriended you. Indeed, were it not for Miki's actions, you would have the components necessary for the alleged resurrection. If nothing else, you would have the ability to seriously consider my proposals. I know you won't, as things stand now."

She hated when he told her what she was and wasn't going to do, and knew he thrived on that hatred. There was never any telling if what he said was what he honestly felt or another hollow manipulation. She forced herself to remain silent.

"You might yet leave that false diamond, all those unfulfillable promises, far behind. You are here with me—with me, and more precious a Cassandra than you might ever hope to know." His hand lay against the doppelgänger's shoulder, and it leaned toward Dominia, hands clasped between familiar, pale knees that peeked beneath its short violet dress and made the General think of how much higher up they went, those legs—of when they became thighs, and where those thighs terminated. As she returned struggling attention to her Father, he asked, "Have they described to you how space here represents space, time, and, to a certain extent, probability in the 'real' world?"

As the General nodded, he went on. "If you continue to follow them, you will find yourself in Cairo when they generously share the means of awakening. You will have made a choice about the future of our relationship, the future of this world—and you will have sealed your fate, much to my regret."

The weight of significance borne by his look pressed down upon her chest. He continued. "But you are here with me. In my study. And I could tell you how to awaken this instant, if you like. Wake up at home, Dominia, and it shall be as if nothing ever happened. Your Family will be back; I'll restore your governance of the United Front and help you bring your wife back to true life. I'll help you exercise your valuable free will. Whatsoever you desire, I'll see the world manifests it one way or another. Or perhaps you would rather continue on your own. Regardless, I would be happy to inform you of the means to leave this place. I hate to think of you stranded here, should something happen to them, or should you run afoul of one another."

"You expect me to trust you after all you've done to me?"

"Can you trust them any more than you can trust me?" was what the Hiereophant asked as Valentinian knocked on the door to collect her the second time. Both inhabitants of the study paused while its owner invited him in, and the mage entered with an uneasy but satisfied look toward the still-crouched doppelgänger. His gaze soon shifted to the new floor with a snort.

"Nice work."

"Do you like it?" asked the Hierophant in his gayest manner, terrifying, boyish mischief in his face. "I thought the place deserved some sprucing up, and Cassandra, sweet thing, reminded me of your love of chess."

"A deep love," agreed the magician dryly, offering Dominia a hand. She accepted it without thinking, preoccupied by her efforts to avoid mental recollection of the conversation just had; at any rate, she suspected it didn't matter whether she touched the magician. Between the boundaryless nature of the space and Valentinian's magical talents, there was no means of hiding information. Not from him, at any rate. "Come on, Dominia. Time's up."

As ever, her Father was gagging to leave her with questions. He insisted on adding as she was tugged toward the doorway, "Valentinian would have you believe this world is more real than reality, and with good reason: he is, in reality, a dog."

Yes, in fact, he was. Basil, the border collie. It was difficult to look at Valentinian and see a border collie; but she had often looked at the border collie and seen Saint Valentinian. That incanine, inhuman determination in his eyes as he put a stop to the rocketing train. Those moments of wry mirth and silent validation: when he saved Miki from traitorous René Ichigawa, blinded spy of her Father; shooting poor Kahlil, who had never been so much a member of the terrorist society as a kid with an easily manipulated ideology (and/or penchant for ladies of the evening). Not unlike Dominia, only less successful, and with a technological emphasis rather than the General's physical one. Indeed, it might have been said Dominia was more like the violent and sometimes base members of the infamous anti-martyr coalition than Kahlil: yet, he had been shot, and naturally reacted with more violence. Understandable—as it was understandable that she reacted with violence by cracking him over the skull. But it haunted her with guilt, that mindless crack. When would the violence end? It was all too bloody: from the moment humans were born in a screaming mess, it was a parade of violence, loss, betrayal, fear, death, Cassandra, Cassandra—anything but Cassandra.

Dominia hurried herself over the threshold that second night, her Father's words stuck in her like venomous darts. She and the magician spoke little until they reached Lazarus, who confirmed she had not touched the thing, and again said, "Then we still have a chance." Off they set again, to a day the same as before less the gorge, and less a degree of trust.

It was not their fault she mistrusted them. It was her Father's fault, whether he had spoken the truth. No scrap of information could be garnered from him unless he meant for it to be used against someone else, or (best case) to his gentler benefit. Thus, she couldn't give his words much credit. At the same time, there was marginal truth to all he'd said, and more he had yet to reveal.

Knowledge was a tempting thing. Knowledge had been Cassandra's undoing. Though she strove to forget, Dominia was plagued by the six months of increasingly erratic behavior that crescendoed in the death of her wife. This had all begun during the winter of 1996, during Lavinia's sixty-sixth Feast Night—a commemoration of the night she awakened at the physical age of twenty-four, rather than the anniversary of her birth, as it was explained to inquiring children. The Governess and her wife had flown into Europa to visit for the first time in ages.

Dominia had thought it all a perfectly lovely time while it happened. Though she was not a party person, even she admitted the fete was grand. Her sister turned ninety that night, all years counted. Therefore, the gala had been a most important and busy occasion, populated by barons, the European governors, journalists, judges and barristers, military men and women. All of them were there with their adorable, spit-shined children, half of whom looked miserable and terrified as one might expect, and half of whom—blossoming sociopaths handpicked for their "charm"—circled a punch bowl kept cold by a few cheerful frozen eyeballs. This latter group required frequent interception by servants, lest their grubby fingers muddle dirt into the pomegranate and blood of the punch. Cassandra studied the former class of frightened squibs with a half-suppressed sigh, and leaned her artfully decorated head against her wife's besuited shoulder.

Dominia laughed. "You spent an hour on your makeup and hair. Are you going to mess it all up?"

Cassandra's eyes, lashes tinted with glittering powder and lids more colorful than any parrot, lifted toward Dominia and warmed the Governess's soul. "I like the way it looks after you've been kissing me."

Oh! Her heart. She kissed her mouth, that chin, the corners of those lips. The taste of makeup sat on her tongue even still, the powder-soft clay recalling a far-off childhood, a mother applying makeup at a mirror, a time of peaceful stasis and safety existing in a separate dimension from all of this. Endless. Dominia would so often be inclined to leave after touching that soft mouth—Cassandra's safe, reassuring lips—just one time. That night, at Lavinia's party, she came near to such an abrupt exit. If only she had! If only she had...but she hadn't. The Hierophant had found them. When Dominia lifted her head, there he was with his warmest smile, having emerged from the profusion of people.

"The most beautiful couple this family has ever produced." Their Father bent to kiss both their cheeks, Cassandra more accepting and smiling to see him than Dominia, who stiffly presented her cheekbone like a succumbing cat. As she stared out into the crowd, she located Lavinia, who greeted people in the company of the somber Lamb with her blonde hair in elaborate ringlets and white ribbons. Her dress for the night was a furling, white-and-azure assortment of petticoats; the Princess looked more like a woman from the Southern United Front in ancient BL times than European royalty. Not that it wasn't charming, and not Lavinia didn't obviously love every second of the silly dress.

"Livy looks like she's having a nice time," said Dominia. The pleased Hierophant placed a hand upon Cassandra's shoulder while he watched the scene.

"I certainly hope so! We've put hours of preparation into this party. You wouldn't believe what trouble we went to, acquiring the centerpiece of this gala!"

The banquet table was decorated with quite a statement-making centerpiece, though why it was such trouble to acquire, Dominia was not sure. A delicate arm had been arranged to hold a quail-egg diamond and a slew of other stones, the slender wrist emerging like one of many exotic flowers that spilled around the offering to the guest of honor. Amid all the floral sprays, sumptuous fruit avalanches, and gaudy cakes, the delicate "centerpiece" was easy to miss. "Was it so hard to get here in Elsinore, of all places? The butchers across North America are fewer and farther between, but they always have plenty of whatever cut I want. I'd think your shops overflow, Father."

"The perfect pair of arms is impossible to find among humans. How we had to search!" Shaking his head, the Hierophant added, "But, nothing is too good for my girls. And see that smile?" Lavinia noticed her sisters and, beaming, sprang through the crowd.

"Her Father's smile, no matter whose she was to start." The Hierophant said this with a broad smile of his own before releasing Cassandra.

Perhaps it was only in memory she recognized, while turning her head, the way her wife's face fell. She certainly didn't notice it then, because Lavinia was upon Dominia for a hug, and all was forgotten by the Governess amid the girl's babbling insistence they come and see the mare Lavinia had been allowed to ride into the ballroom—hadn't she a *lovely* mane! Dominia agreed, but the three-hundred-something-year-old curmudgeon in her felt a noose's tension every time the shod equine brought its metal-lined hooves down upon the lovely marble floor. The floor, the floor!

The floor.

Dominia remembered she was remembering when she remembered the floor, because then she remembered the magician urging her to remember the floor, and then she remembered her body and found herself standing at a concrete fountain amid short weeds. Before her, Valentinian punctuated something with the phrase, "You know what I mean?"

Her mouth open, she glanced, helpless, at Lazarus. She looked, too, at the black sun blazing overhead, and sensed the day had ticked away much of its time. "I'm sorry—" She laughed at herself and then, unable to help the terror contorting the edges of her lips, looked between them. "How did we get here?"

"Oh my God." Valentinian slapped himself on the forehead. "Were you seriously not listening?"

"I don't know what's going on. How far have we walked? Please." She grasped Lazarus's arm, and he, usual inscrutable expression softening, held her hand. "I'm so sorry. I got lost in thought."

"Explains why it's closer," said Valentinian, rubbing the bridge of his nose, then stopping her from turning around with a quick, "No! Trust me. It'll be worse if you see how close it is."

"That's not going to help." With sudden patience, Lazarus looked deep into Dominia's good eye. "What's the last thing you remember?"

"I remember Valentinian arriving. The Hierophant...he's all I remember. Then I started thinking and I got caught up and I remembered the floor, finally."

Fingers working over his temples, the magician perched upon the chipped edge of the fountain, which emitted, from the mouths of alternating cherubs and fish, eight streams of glittering water. "We've walked half a day already. We just spent an hour explaining the operations of Fortune to you."

"I'm so sorry." All she managed was a fluster of apologies, embarrassed to have missed a cosmic lecture for which most mortals might have killed. "I didn't even realize we were walking. It was like I fell asleep."

"You're already asleep here." Lazarus released her; she seemed steadier, despite her alarm. "The problem is the same as the benefit: you're dreaming. Your attention got caught up in another dream. Reality is malleable for the observer in a place like this. Speaking of, *magician*."

The mystic extended his hand expectantly, and the sighing magus slapped the open palm. As his hand bounced up, a clay sphere manifested between them: a cup with a circular lid that Lazarus unscrewed with care. As he filled it from the nearest fish, Dominia looked around and, tinted by the alarming notion she dreamed, began to see the landscape in an even more menacing light.

Perhaps it was the effect of that landscape's new feature. Solitary amid a desert of nothing, the sole source of water, the only sign of life they'd seen in this disorienting place with that thing so close, the fountain was no comfort to look upon. It was a man-made fountain; they had seen no people. No one she knew had created the landscape. Who, or what, had made the fountain? She dared not think on it in so unanchored a place as this.

"If I'm dreaming"—her heart pounded in her ears as she sat to take Valentinian's hands—"can't you tell me how to wake up?"

"Kiddo," began the magician, but she gripped his hands so tightly he winced.

"Please, Valentinian. Tell me, just so I know."

"If you know, you might try it."

"What would be wrong with that? Couldn't I come back?" Her eye leapt between the men, Lazarus no longer looking at her but studying the cup. "That's the way it works, isn't it?"

"Yes, but you need training to come back and forth reliably, and to find your way around. At least, you have to come in and out a few times on your own to experiment a little, gauge distances. You could awaken in the middle of some trap, or at a bad time and place. And it's not possible to get back here when you're panicking, or when it's night—not without some creativity."

"Who said anything about me being panicked? Me, being panicked—can you imagine! Do you know who I am?"

"Buddy," said the magician, "your hands are shaking."

Gritting her teeth, Dominia released her grip and shot from her seat. "Fine. Yes, I'm afraid! Nobody tells me a thing, and when they do, it's conveniently while I'm getting wrapped up in memories of—the past." A sheen of tears glossed the General's eye; she covered it while bowing her head. "I'm afraid because I have no idea where I am. I have no control or knowledge of the situation. I've lost my life and my Family, and I mean more than one family. I've been in accidents. I watched my wife *kill* herself." The sentence, which she had never said out loud in quite so many words, solidified the event in a way that curled her lips back from her teeth like wilting flower petals. She sobbed, and because Valentinian stood to put his hand upon her shoulder, she stepped away. "I've been a prisoner of war! My own Father...my Father. I'm more afraid of him than I am of anything in the world. But I've never—*never* been afraid like this. That was all on Earth. This—I still don't understand what this place *is*. What *is* it? Where *are* we?"

"New people always insist a thing has to have a name before they understand it. Call it what you want." Lazarus screwed the lid upon the cup. "It's not hell, but it's not exactly heaven, either. Valentinian called it 'Nirvana,' but it's more like the Bardos. Catholics and martyrs call it 'purgatory,' science calls it something else. I like to think of it as similar to the Wyrd."

"Like the Norse fates," asked Dominia, hyperconscious of her eye patch while Valentinian nodded and resumed his forgotten lecture.

"In short—to redescribe to you what I've been describing—this place is a web of probability in addition to space and time. We are experiencing consciousness from a wave form instead of a particle form, and when we perceive everything else to also be information interpreted as waves, reality is malleable."

"I don't see waves, or anything except for our electromagnetic fields. I see a landscape."

"People who have made it this far while retaining a sense of self and bodily tie to reality tend to experience static images, especially at first. The more time you spend here, the more you're able to abstract it all. Hell, sometimes when I stop concentrating, all of existence is just a geometrical lattice. Like a kaleidoscope, in dimensions even I can't explain! But when people experience their final death and have no more ties to physical reality, that's their first time here if they don't have some kind of esoteric dream experience or a few drops of Lazarus's blood. With no context, all bets are off. It could look like anything. A parade of demons, a series of bodily transformations, a vast plane of nothingness. Worse, they might be trapped in the lower frequencies; VLFs and ELFs are like a prison for the crystalized soul that can change no further, can draw no closer to liberation. People who think they hear ghosts on the radio aren't always wrong. Over time, though, less crystalized people wandering here learn they can do things. Then, they can move on, or look at the data in another way. Some people can abstract all the data of reality down to the experience of a sound. When Elijah manipulates the probability of events to grant prayers—low-grade wishes, but sometimes pretty powerful ones—he's manipulating this place while remaining present in the physical interpretation."

"Will we find the Lamb here, too?" She wouldn't be able to handle both her fathers coming to guilt her night after night. Luckily, Lazarus shook his head and answered for the long-winded magician.

"Cicero keeps too close a lock on the Lamb for him to acquire my blood and physically ascend, which means the position of Elijah's shade in this place is most often tied to his position in reality. Just like the Hierophant keeps Cicero grounded because he'd lose control of El Sacerdote within five minutes of this discovery, he also keeps the Lamb from utilizing this place to its fullest extent."

Understandable. The Lamb was never far from Cicero, out of a blend of love and something ancients called "Stockholm syndrome." Martyrs called this "family ties." But it was also true the Lamb kept as much of an eye on Cicero as Cicero did on the near-omnipotent Lamb. It was entirely possible the Lamb sacrificed the extent of his powers for two thousand years simply to keep his brother from catching a whiff of this place; no doubt, the Hierophant approved. The mystic, with his own strong opinions on the matter, went on. "Better to keep him trapped in the material world, where he can be corrupted into minor tweaks to reality, than let him come here, where he can make significant changes that might solve the problems his brother caused." Lazarus slipped the clay canteen into his robe, just over his heart, and turned away. "If it were up to me, I would have given the Lamb my blood a long time ago."

"What's stopping you from showing up in his closet?"

"The horns, for one. Electromagnetic effects are warped near him so if you can find him here at all, you can't drop in on him as closely as you can with somebody else—not if he doesn't want you to. Also, I hate to admit, but I'm not as talented as Houdini over there when it comes to rearranging how I perceive this place's information. That means—for me, anyway—it's hard to find *any* person's precise location, here or in reality. It doesn't help that Cicero and the Lamb are a traveling carnival of sacrilege, going from martyr church to martyr church and taking his false blood along with them. With each day here being about a week in reality, it's extremely hard to pinpoint and intersect the physical location of a far-off moving person through any means other than chance or elaborate design. The magician, though, or the Lamb, or somebody less set in their ways than I am—they can find their way to specific people or places based on energy patterns like the electromagnetic field of our collective presence. But...even then, it can be hard to sort one person from another."

Lazarus waved at the colorful bands, which, accommodating as they did the combined space of the trio, faded enough into the edge of Dominia's visible perception that she had grown accustomed to it. "People give off similar patterns of emotional, physical, or even psychological expression. A magician like Valentinian learns how to read the spark of individuality hidden there. But, for example, the Lamb's physical brain is a receiver for all prayers of the world, whether human or martyr, and he knows their identities even if they don't. He's half in this world and half out of it all the time, so unlike those whose thought-bodies are absent because they're on Earth, his phantom is always around here somewhere. If his physical body was free of those metal horns, he'd be pretty easy to find on this plane, bodily presence or no. Normally, his spirit is a conglomeration of pleas. That's one of the reasons your Father has become such a big fan of artificial enhancements. Helping the Lamb deaden the sounds of prayers and disguise his presence here.

"And, frankly"—Lazarus resumed tossing the stones, and Dominia wondered just how many pebbles he had—"the consequences to my capture are far too vast to risk. Elijah is a gentle person in a bad position, but there's nothing I can do about his situation with things the way they are. Your Father uses all kinds of fail-safes to keep interference on this plane from getting anywhere near him, his castle, and his business."

"How is *he* coming and going? Why does he only come at night? How does his study move with him?"

"Please, will you drop this," the magician begged. Dominia was in no mood to relent.

"I've agreed to go with you to Cairo. It's in my best interest to go to Cairo; I want Cassandra back." She winced at the rattling exhalation of the thing behind her. The General redoubled her will to go without looking over her shoulder. "That means getting the diamond back from Miki, which means I have to stay here. But it would give me—psychological comfort to know the way out of here, even if I never use it."

"It won't."

"It will," she insisted, with such force that Lazarus stopped, heaved a sigh of disgust, and once more faced her.

"You want to know how to leave this place? You have two easy options. First is, get to where you want to be and let the black sun take you back—just stare into it for long enough and it will be a door for you. You want to try it? Go back now? Huh?" He waved his hand toward the sky, and she, taken aback, sputtered some useless noise while his hand lowered. "That's what I thought."

As he turned away, she thought of her Father's study, and how it—and he—appeared only at night. "What if the sun isn't out," she asked in meeker tone.

Lazarus spoke without looking back. "What's the easiest way to awaken from a dream? Kill yourself."

The General's mouth opened and shut in silent horror. Valentinian, realizing she still stood frozen, paused to shrug.

"Or let someone else kill you," the magician added. "Either way...better to wait for the daytime, right?"

Fair point.

IV

Two Souls, Alas

Death could not be the only means of awakening. That night, as she gazed into the blue heart of the fire, the Hierophant studied her face with a half-suppressed smile.

"You look tired."

"Only four more nights." The words felt miserable aloud. "Pretty easy for you, showing up where and when you please. Otherwise, you're safe at home."

"It's as though you never should have left."

While she tried not to snort, she focused on the spot where awaited the new-sprung, green-felted pool table. Arguing with him was pointless. He was too adept, and too annoying. Better to keep focused on topics in line with his one use: as an echo chamber for frustrations she otherwise locked within herself. If nothing else, her Father gave half answers, as opposed to the nonanswers of Valentinian and Lazarus.

"This place is so creepy. Why is it so dark? Where's the moon?"

"It is all around us, in a way. All things are, in this place." The Hierophant's gaze fixed upon his fireplace. He crossed to stoke it with the poker above its mantle. "Yet, all things are not."

For some reason, the thought of the absent moon evoked Miki's thousand-named goddess. Ishtar, Amaterasu, who knew what else. Those words were taboo, along with all Her other names, among self-respecting martyrs. "Couldn't there be a moon in this sky, if somebody thought of it? At least, over your study?"

"Anything might be made here. You might recreate every star in the sky." His tone was too approving for her comfort.

"You'd like that, wouldn't you? What would those thoughtforms do?"

"Only light up the night, and make it a more palatable time to travel. You might arrive at Cairo faster; perhaps your friends would thank you."

"Don't treat me like I'm stupid." As he batted innocent eyes, she turned toward the thing wearing Cassandra's face. Tonight it sat using her wife's hands to numbly manipulate a book through which it gazed as though pretending to read. Fear to foment it turned Dominia away, back to the nauseating dark. "I'm not sure of the harm, but I'm sure there would be some. I know they wouldn't be happy with me."

"Perhaps. But if they are unhappy, the root of their unhappiness will lie in displeasure at knowing you've nurtured your powers. You, Dominia, have a grand capacity for so-called magic. It is a capacity of which you have been kept ignorant. I admit I've had a hand in this, but with the secret out, I feel responsible for helping hone your abilities. These forces can cause harm when allowed to go untempered. Powerful as you are, the world might be at stake."

While rubbing her forehead, she laughed without joy. "Funny you should say that. I've been tasked, according to them, with ending the war, and seeing the martyr race off to Acetia."

"They said that?" asked her Father in near-incredulous tone, the corner of his mouth giving a twitch.

"Sort of. Why?"

"I'm only surprised. They're not often so forthright." Without batting an eye at his daughter's questioning, the Hierophant replaced the poker and began to use his pool table as if hoping she would join. She would not. "What a terrific burden to lay upon your tired mind! Have they no idea what I've put you through over the past few weeks?"

"Nice that you're honest seventy percent of the time."

He racked up the colored balls in a series of clacks that flashed her to times in barracks and bars, earning the respect of her soldiers and impressing far more than a handful of beautiful women. Cassandra, of course, had been the last—oh, teaching her to play it properly! The deerlike bend of her body! The smell of her neck—

Dominia gripped the chair to refocus her thoughts from dangerous sorrow. What had they been speaking of? Yes—her obligations to humanity and martyrdom. "It's pretty exhausting."

"Then I'm glad I need not point out that your companions intend to bring the apocalypse for our people. They would jettison us into space without so much as a return address!" After whisking away the triangular frame, he circled the rectangular table, brows lifted high in significance. She was not sure when the cue stick had gotten into his hand, and she had watched him the whole time. "I, my girl, strive only to prevent the horrors of entropy."

At the crack of his cue, the balls thundered apart, and both a stripe and a solid wheeled into opposites corners. As the rest arranged themselves, the

Hierophant adjusted his tie, loosed the buttons of his jacket, then resumed his prowl around the table.

"You think I am bad. Think of them! My efforts at culling human populations are for their own good, the good of the planet—most of all, for the good of our religion. For God, my girl!" *Crack!* A solid whirled into a side pocket. "Fair Earth cannot sustain the human race when it balloons to such extents as the past would have encouraged. At one point, it was necessary to spread one's genes through as many heirs as possible; now we must think of the Earth, for the humans do not. Why else would the Lord have put us on her face, were we not to control her population? Martyrs manage the human population, and I manage the martyr population."

"And who manages you, again?"

"The divine wisdom of the Lord. You should know that by now." *Crack!*

He was a fine one to talk of his God-given responsibility toward the environment. Much of the technology responsible for wrecking the planet had been pushed into development by him, even before his public appearance alongside Cicero and Elijah in 2045 CE, otherwise known as AL 1. He alternately reveled in destroying and rebuilding—perhaps because when something was rebuilt by him, he did so in his own image. That was what he did with people, after all. Still, she did not want to waste time arguing tangents. Another ball cracked off into a pocket's void. In the corner of her good eye, the doppelgänger sat in her Father's chair, rapt as they spoke. "I don't know." She glanced from the ugly sight. "They have a point. I think the humans were better off managing themselves."

"This guilt over your own existence is unhealthy. Martyrs are necessary. You are necessary. But what is not necessary is the end of the world. Not at this point in time."

Annoyed he mixed a valid point about her emotional state into an unrelated one about the conflict at hand, she nonetheless decided to play the Hierophant's advocate enough to extricate his opinion. "I don't know. I haven't made up my mind about any of this. They've hardly told me anything, aside from my responsibility. I mean, what happens if we stay on Earth? We'll colonize space eventually no matter what. Humans continue to perfect and spread the terraformed state of Mars, and with technology you paid to develop."

"But your friends would see every martyr wiped from Earth's surface. It is not a matter of colonizing other worlds; it is a matter of exiling an entire species before it is ready."

"Why not bring them here?"

"I admit: one reason I have encouraged population growth for the past several years is the vain hope we will find another mutation like Lazarus."

"A Lazarus you can control." At his mild smile, she pressed, "You teach his blood is the damnation of martyrs."

"It always is. I have never met a martyr who does not taste of his blood and wish to overthrow me straightaway. This is the real story of Regulus. But perhaps, if the Family had a child with blood as extraordinary as that of Lazarus who remained loyal to the cause, I might guide the initiation of my more educated children. This is fruitless, but one never does know."

"So you really have lived through all this before? Lived through this war, then gone on to colonize Acetia just to come back and start it again?"

"Yes."

"How many times?"

"Once." *Crack!*

He scratched. The white ball bounced around, twirled into the corner pocket, and took nothing with it. Dominia smirked as her Father offered the stick. "Care for a turn?"

With a glance for the too-close doppelgänger, the General made her way to the table. The Hierophant's smile as she accepted hovered between mocking and paternal even more than usual, and she strove to ignore it as she turned her attention to the game. Eight balls left—no, six. Every time she looked, the number changed: the order, the colors. She tried to focus her wandering eye and force her muscle memory to work.

As she arranged herself, her Father said, "Your abilities are far vaster in scope and possibility than merely bringing about the end of the martyr world. I told you I could give you anything you liked, but the fact is I would only be showing you how to get it, yourself."

"I know how to get what I want on my own." She pocketed two balls at once, in side and corner pockets. As she worked her way around, she refused to look at him, lest the order change again. "I don't need your help."

"You do if you're to keep yourself from being corrupted. From devouring lies. They hide so much from you! Why, they have even forbidden you to take advantage of your own, holy body! They have encouraged you to think it would be some crime against your wife to make love to her shadow—"

"Corner pocket," she interrupted, waving the cue to indicate the four ball and her target.

"—when in fact it would honor her. Bring fair Cassandra closer to reunion with you."

The announced ball propelled home with a gunshot's crack. "It wouldn't be the real Cassandra."

"What defines the real Cassandra? What is real here? You said yourself, you might well create the stars. Your body, too, is a thoughtform, as is mine. Here, you are as real as Cassandra."

"I'm always as real as Cassandra." She didn't bother calling the next and pocketed it while saying, "That thing's not Cassandra."

"By that logic, Valentinian has little to do with his canine counterpart."

"I'm not sure I follow."

"My dear girl"—he put heavy emphasis on his next words—"everything here is a thoughtform. What has a dog to do with a man? Nothing. But a dog might be imagined to have the *spirit* of a man, and be reflected as a man."

Now, it was her turn to scratch, though rather more dramatically than had her Father. Her cue ball, propelled by too much force, leapt from the table to bounce across that nice chessboard floor. While the General grimaced, the false-Cassandra-thing hurried after it with a laugh and the disgusting chide "Dominia!" from a hostage voice.

She shoved the cue stick to her Father. "What are you babbling about?"

"Only what I have tried to tell you for some nights." The doppelgänger returned the ball, smiling dumbly as it did, and her Father set it on the table. "You are being deceived, lest you should realize the truth and see what fool you've been for listening to their lies. They will not even tell you the truth about your eye, will not let you lift your patch!" She had forgotten about her missing eye in this place where she barely felt the body parts she had. Her left hand tightened. The eye had not mattered as she played pool, but, now reminded of it, the weight of the elastic band dominated her consciousness. Her depth perception, as though remembering it was supposed to falter, did. As with all strange things here, she fought to ignore it.

"So, then: What's the truth?"

"Valentinian is as much, or more, a thoughtform as your dear Cassandra here—and equally created by you."

Crack!

The General did not see if the ball had sunk; she did not care. A strangeness overcame her. She insisted, "That's stupid, of course he's not," even as his words evoked the first night Valentinian had collected her from the Hierophant. When he'd asked her, on touching her, if she had touched the doppelgänger. As she recalled all those times in which he'd laid on her a comforting hand or she'd gripped his arm for support, her Father continued speaking, continued shooting on a table whose number of balls returned to eight when the cue was passed between players.

"It makes less sense that a man should be turned into a dog. I told you Valentinian was trapped here for the sake of a wish gone awry, did I not?"

"Yes. I've also heard Valentinian is trapped here because you tricked him."

The Hierophant turned so she might see his dubious expression. "You mean to say I turned a man into a dog? My girl"—he laughed, and her face burned as, with relish, he resumed shooting—"we have talked from time to time of magic, but let's not be absurd. The amount of energy required *alone* would be cataclysmic. Nuclear. It is as vain a hope as the hope your Cassandra could rise from the dead. Yet how easily one talented in magic might accidentally imagine a dog as a man, lest they be alone with a mad old mystic!"

"Lazarus is supposed to be his father, though, or something. Originally. Right? Didn't they work with Cicero and Elijah the first time you came to them?"

"Mere fantasy. I have never seen Saint Valentinian in the waking world, not in all my many nights. Not in this world, or any other. When an imaginary being cannot reveal it is imaginary, it must concoct an elaborate backstory to earn its host's support."

"If he's imaginary, and from *my* imagination, then why have you put him into paintings all these years?"

With a pitiful look, the Hierophant leaned his hip against the table. "He has done such a number on your mind you cannot see you have it backward. Saint Valentinian is a symbol of *death* to the martyr. He is a fictional saint, a false star crafted to fill a hole in our culture's spiritual constellation. This place is a place of death, and your soul knows it. Therefore, though you may not be physically dead, to be here is to accept a visionary experience that shares many of death's qualities. It is only logical a thoughtform in the shape of Death should greet and guide you."

"No, that's wrong. He's taking me to Cairo—they both are. Lazarus wouldn't support his story—"

"Unless Lazarus, who remembers more than even I, feels Valentinian serves his ends. What could a thoughtform of death want more than a mass sacrifice in war's bloody climax? What could he crave more than the deaths of seven million helpless martyrs—for, my child, it seems we are many, but that *is* the true number of our populace, I remind you. A speck beside the bacteria colony of mankind! And what of those many servants"—de facto slaves who signed away human rights for cushy paychecks as the result of a lifetime of social brainwashing—"who depend on us for food, shelter, their entire social infrastructure? For *these* make up the majority of martyr-controlled towns and cities. Their livelihoods would dry up, and many would not be accepted back into human society after working with us for so long. What are they to do—follow us to the stars? Helpless women and men and children sent to uncertain fate in the vicissitudes of space? The premature birth of an entire species? Indeed, perhaps *then* he would have the energy to craft his physical body."

"We could go to Mars." Her eye glassed with tears of doubt while the Hierophant waved his hand in dismissal.

"Then when they have finished ruining the first marbled planet of which we were once custodians, they shall come to defile the new one, and chase us from *that*. You do not understand what humans are like, Dominia, because you have never seen them have free rein. They are *violent*. They are *savage*. They are apes, unevolved and unconscious animals hooting and shitting in the Garden of Eden." His use of profanity always shocked her into attention. "We must not just be gardeners but zookeepers. Of course they resent us. They call us depraved and evil and insist we are better off floating among the stars because they have been 'left behind' with us and their sin in a Rapture not even described in the human Bible—a Protestant invention, a device with which to question our claim to the throne of the Lord. But we are the children of God, and they are larvae beside the glory of our imago. To think you have allowed yourself lured off the righteous path by some imaginary fiend." Disgusted, her Father resumed his game. "I tried to save you from all this, you know."

Despite knowing better, she mentally succumbed to his talent for shaming ungrateful children. Despite knowing better, she tried to explain to herself why Valentinian couldn't be a thoughtform. "But he could have turned himself into a dog, if he's..." She couldn't bring herself to say the words, "a magician," because the sentence still sounded absurd. She looked, embarrassed, at the table. The eight ball sat alone.

What if she was wrong? What if, all this time, she had been quite literally letting her imagination run away with her, and because of that, she now found herself on the opposite side of—what? Rightness? Decency? Divinity? What was God in a place like this, in a world like this?

"Whose wish was it that trapped him here?"

"Yours." The Hierophant took aim, savored the moment, then mis-struck and sent the white ball askew when a knock reverberated the heavy door. Dominia lacked the schadenfreude she reserved for such things. The usual semi-relief of Valentinian's arrival was displaced by unaskable questions.

The doppelgänger shambled to get the door, and the magician stepped inside with a look of displeasure. "Ugh! It's opening doors, now." This, punctuated with a pointed look that expressed uncomfortable knowledge of Dominia's thoughts.

"'Speak of the devil and he shall appear.'" The Hierophant transmuted his displeasure for the unmoved eight ball into a wry glance at Dominia. Head bent to light a cigarette, the magician loped to the table and ignored her Father's sniffs of puritanical disdain. "Need you do that in here?"

"What are you talking about, 'in here'? In where? There's no ceiling, no walls. We're not inside anything, except the miasma of imagination. Goddamn." He stopped by the table with his blue eyes bright, treacherous cigarette dangling from the corner of his mouth as he rolled his dark sleeves to his elbows. "I love a good game of pool. About time you got something new! Something new and decent, I mean. May I?"

Forcing himself to smile, an effort evident in the quick-upturned, then relaxed corners of his still-shut lips, the Hierophant passed the cue to the magician. Valentinian rolled his shoulders, balanced his cigarette upon the edge of the table (Dominia felt her Father's eyes upon it), and bent forward.

"The key to a good pool shot is all in the breath." He exhaled, that exhalation guiding his stick into the cue ball into the black-eyed eight, which bounced in playful fashion against the nearest edge to spin into the opposite side pocket. "That"—he handed back the cue with a (doggish?) grin—"and the ability to ignore distractions. You ready to go, Dominia?"

She wasn't eager after that conversation, and glanced at her Father with a mind that whirred from thought to thought in a useless effort to evade questions. "Run along, my girl," said the clairvoyant Hierophant. "We can resume our conversation tomorrow night."

"Unfortunately, he's right." The magician waved. "Come on."

The General had anticipated Valentinian would try to take her hand, as usual; but this time, he went to the door, cementing his obtrusive study of her inner thoughts as obvious fact. Suppressing her irritation to the fullest extent possible (not much, in truth), she strode through the door, then winced as the thing in the study called, "Goodbye, Dominia."

"Why the fuck are you telling me goodbye?" She paused on the threshold to narrow her eye in the profane thing's cringing direction. "You're going to stalk us all day, aren't you?"

"Actually, I will be keeping her behind. We have some lessons, I think."

"That's great." Valentinian attempted to guide Dominia out by the shoulder and was left rolling his eyes when she stormed down the path of the Hierophant's torches. "People get so touchy."

"I'd be less touchy if you'd stay out of my head."

A certifiable statement of the mentally ill, considering she might be speaking to her imaginary perception of a border collie—specifically, her projection of the patron saint of death upon said border collie, assuming Valentinian even had anything to do with Basil in the first place. Could be he was just a smart dog, and she'd made a false connection. Or, if it was true Valentinian was a disembodied spirit from the first iteration of the world, had Valentinian's martyr spirit attached to the dog's material body specifically to direct the course of events? She tumbled through an infinity of paranoid thoughts and considered his mention of previous incarnations during even this cycle of reality. What else had he been in her life? A tiger at the zoo that led to Cassandra's job teaching Noctisdomin school? The job that gave her wife a reason to live as long as she did in the wake of a series of unfortunate choices leading to undesirable immortality?

It was almost *more* logical Valentinian should be a thoughtform, though short of serious mental gymnastics, it was nigh unimaginable she could have ever created him. But it might make sense if things happened again and again, and thoughtforms got more power with every interaction. In that case, it was possible Valentinian was a thoughtform created—summoned, manifested, whatever—in a repetition long ago. From that point on, he could have existed in linear fashion from the start of many other universes, each time perpetuating some bullshit claims even Lazarus couldn't remember about a life he probably didn't live as a researcher alongside the mystic, the Lamb, and Cicero. With all this talk of lies becoming real, it was impossible to tell what might have been truth: and when everyone's truth was so incomplete, she wondered if they weren't petitioning her with their versions of reality, rather than trying to deceive her.

"Which place is more real"—she decided to ask of the magician—"this place? Or reality?"

"Consensus, material reality is real by definition. As close to 'real' as you're going to get. But you have to real-ize—ha-ha—after you reach a certain point of understanding that one is untenable without the other. Both this place and reality are the same amount of real." Dominia could have screamed for such nebulous answers piling around her, and he knew it. "It's not helpful. I'm sorry. Think back on our film analogy. Is the series of static images making up the reel of film more real than the movie projected? More appropriately, which is more real when you're reading a novel? The individual words your brain decodes into experience? Or that experience of the story, undergone by your consciousness?"

There again were the books in the study, "TÆ CΦDVUKΘP" somehow unstable in its own existence but nonetheless emblazoned gold upon the side of a lapis-blue tome. She had since seen the *Odyssey* upon his shelves twice, and neither time had the title resembled its prior arrangement; yet, each time she registered the meaning of the text as if it were spelled the expected way. The most recent appearance was in nonsense-full Greek, and still she comprehended it; but it seemed a falser representation of the word than the variant before. This, she recounted to the nodding magician.

"A good metaphor. Ultimately, the arrangement of letters underlying the words you see don't matter as much as the overall meaning. The less observed something is, the more abstract and true to itself it is, because it contains a wide swath of possibilities. Infinite. But, the more you observe something, the tighter it becomes. The more crystalized. You understand it in a comprehensible way—maybe you're even able to take it into the real world with you. But the thing is then less true to its highest self because your observation has tuned its frequency to the band necessary to render the experience of it static. The Greeks had a three-faced goddess, Hekate—one of the ways Ishtar manifests, or vice versa, if you'd like. Her name means 'far-darting one,' and the arrangement of Her body and faces mean the most men can hope is to see two at a time. We can never see all three, like a Heisenberg uncertainty principle of metaphysics and creativity. There is always some information lost in translation from abstract to concrete: yet the abstract cannot be wholly comprehended by the three-dimensional perspective, so, to the human and martyr mind, the abstract is less real, even though it contains a perhaps higher truth."

"And to your mind?"

He shrugged. "I've spent a long time here. It's all the same to me. But I pine—oh, how much!—to walk with my own body through the world."

"Have you, ever?"

"In this world, this time? No. But many times, I have, and after all this... Your Father is a liar." He punctuated his abrupt turn by tossing his finished cigarette in the direction of the black sun, which had hefted most of its body above the horizon. "I keep telling you, yet you keep listening. It's always this way. Why? What can I do to get you to listen to me like that?"

"Try telling me the truth. Who you really are and what this is, and why you want to jettison my people into space." When Valentinian offered no response, she scoffed. "You can't even admit that. Even after Lazarus told me before, you still can't bring yourself to talk about it! What is it with you?" The blister of her fury swollen sufficiently to burst, Dominia grabbed his shirt.

"Why am I here? Why all of this, why me? Why won't you tell me the truth about my eye?"

"Because if you take off your eye patch one second before I tell you to, everything we've worked for is lost."

"But why?"

"If I'm not back to myself in the world before your eye here opens—and especially if the Lady isn't restored—there's no way for me to help you, and I have to move on to the next Dominia."

"Sounds like more bullshit to me."

"It's the truth. Your Father claimed sending martyrs into space sooner rather than later would be like giving premature birth to a world; real premature birth is removing your eye patch." While she was baffled by this, he blew right on without explanation. "You know what happens when you open your eye? You wake up. You *really* wake up. You wake up so hard, in a way beyond waking, that the truth itself creates a new world. You can't open a portal to a new world if you aren't ready to move through it. Rifts like that only have the energy to sustain the movement of one body through their substance, and even *that* is dependent on there being an empty space for the body to go. If they don't have an empty space, they'll have to make one, or risk destroying the whole system. Guess who's ready to jump through a universal rift *and* happy to make himself an empty space?" The agitated magician waved his hand in the direction of her Father's study, a path empty of doppelgängers for the first, blissful morning. She could not appreciate that absence with the magician mad at her, because she couldn't follow his babbling. "You don't understand how any of this works, do you?"

"Of course not! You won't explain it to me!"

"Because every time I have, you've fucked it up!" The normally composed magician raised his voice, and Dominia was so surprised she released him. While he straightened himself out, he continued, "You fuck it up again, and again, and again. Well over forty times, a hundred times I remember, you have fucked it up! I hate to break it to you, kid, but you fuck up a lot. Big, unfixable fuckups. And each time one happens, guess what else happens? Everything! Every-fucking-thing happens over, and over, and over again. And you know why? Because you take off your eye patch too early, or because you manifest Cassandra's *tulpa*, or because you decide to go along with your shitty dad, or because of forty-something other reasons I don't even want to remember! You fuck up *repeatedly*. Because of that, Lazarus and I have lived an eternity and you have to keep doing this again, and again. Have to keep living your miserable life again."

At the pain that crossed her face, Valentinian's tone and expression softened, but he was not deterred from saying, "You have to watch her die again."

"Why would you say something like that?"

"It's true."

She slapped away the hand that tried to comfort her. Briskly, she turned toward the study of the Hierophant. The sun did not sink with her, perhaps because Valentinian did not pursue. He merely called with a sigh, "Kiddo, come on, come back. We should go."

"What, can't you come after me?"

"There's no point if you don't want me near you."

"Why? Because a thoughtform has to be wanted?"

"Yeah, okay." The sighing magician turned from the General with a wave of that slapped hand. "Do what you want. So this is the clichéd part of your journey where we have a falling out? I can take it. I've got a thick skin, to use another cliché. But if you get lost—"

"If I get lost, you've got more to worry about than I do."

Dominia hastened her retreat to the Hierophant's study and away, as far and fast as possible, from Valentinian. The rising black sun revealed a distant, shadowy river that went unappreciated, for she was as annoyed by herself—

and by the magician's refusal to follow her—as she was by his cruel points. No matter how accurate. The thought of eternally walking into their spoiled bedroom, shame in Cassandra's eyes, a second too late, the silver barrel in her mouth, *Crack! Crack! Crack!* forever—it made her too sick, and her conversation with the Hierophant left her too disoriented. She felt like she had as a girl hanging upside down for an extended length of time. When she straightened, she found a new surreality, and wondered for a strange moment which way was "up." The mere thought made her slow her steps and spare a reluctant glance in the direction of her friend, who waited to see if she would return.

Perhaps because he waited, she decided she wouldn't, and dashed on until he was far from sight.

V

Are the Stars Out Tonight?

This childish habit of running away emerged from childish pain, and Dominia grew more aware of her own inescapably embarrassing motivation every meter her legs dragged across the dark ground. Valentinian seemed trustworthy after his actions as Basil, but now she could not be sure. She could not be sure of anything they'd told her. Oh, yes, her Father was a most notorious liar among those who were not sheep gamboling about his bloody flock. But he told the truth with pleasure when it benefited him; and Valentinian had not appeared interested in or able to refute the planted ideas, assuming he knew what was discussed. Yet she harbored a certainty, deep-rooted as a United Front redwood, that both men had told as many truths as they had lies. It would be far simpler were things clear-cut into the black-and-white lines of liars and honest beings. Instead, truth was not just veiled: the notion assumed a different shape behind those veils, depending on who did the talking.

Of course, the ambiguity of truth didn't justify running away: so she felt with greater acuity each step farther from the magician. All the while, the sun rose. The torches of her Father had disappeared, and horror dropped a mocking hand upon her shoulder to remind her she wandered alone in an alien desert with no path to guide her back. No trail of bread crumbs or Lazarus's stones—nothing but her lonely set of fields, claustrophobic without the cumulative space of three people. Maybe she should have been leaving playing cards behind. However, as she dug into the ammo pouch for the deck given her by the magician that first night beside the fire, the Hierophant's office presented itself as a distant speck. Unfortunately.

Dread tightened the General's jaw even as relief tried to loosen it, for she couldn't bear to listen to the Hierophant pontificate for an entire day. On what, Lamb only knew; however, neither could she bear to return to Valentinian. She braced for her Father's smug expression when she knocked upon the disembodied door. No answer came, and she opened it to find the study empty.

Not just empty: a still life. Remarkably static without his presence. As if she'd penetrated the hollow shedding of a cicada. Like that husk, the dimmed books upon unsteady shelves seemed brittle. Not only was it intensely eerie to observe the study by herself—was it not somehow worse reinforcement when she observed it independently of him? Did that make the location more concrete, as it drew upon her fields to form her perception of her Father's thoughtform study? They vanished as she crossed that threshold, their daytime colors flexing against the invisible walls and fading into the bookshelves. Did they render her Father's reality more, as Valentinian put it, "consensual"?

Still: with the doppelgänger also missing, and some of the comforts of home (a sense of space and the illusion of depth), she could not resist. Could not help but think if her so-called friends wanted her back so badly, well... they could come and get her.

She pretended the source of her bitterness was unaccountable as she sank into her seat and assessed the postmodern wine decanter arching like the neck of a lily. Two glasses, hers still empty from the prior night, waited to be filled. She squinted at them to see if they were smudged by prior activities, yet they were clean, as if some metaphysical maid had swept through the unoccupied study to make its contents fresh again. Somehow, this infuriated her. A mockery, this spurning of detail and causality.

Her frustration was not the exclusive fault of the thing walking in Cassandra's skin. That honor lay with the burden. The sheer, unimaginable burden that her Father hastened to clarify. To decide what to do with her own people! To decide whether they should live on Earth and make others suffer, or alleviate that suffering and threaten the life of her entire species! Old friends who now thought her an enemy of the state; ex-girlfriends who'd once read her military exploits in the paper and had sometimes sent longing Halcyon account messages at one in the afternoon; children who'd never had a say and wouldn't hurt a human being for many years. All of them, up in a rocket gunning for nowhere, deluded into believing a nubile planet awaited guiding hands.

Real or fake, wine was wine. That desperation driving consciousness to escape present circumstances was never particular in its means of evacuation. The glass of wine Dominia poured contained every glass of wine she'd ever poured herself, from tacky disposable cups imbibed at teenage parties to those many flasks of whiskey downed during her military career. Most of all, it was that first glass of wine with Cassandra, in that wonderful house on the coast where Dominia went to escape herself and what she'd done after her last military campaign. That beautiful house, where she had never expected to bring a woman so gentle, so beautiful and human. So un-self-conscious. Natural. Always laughing. Gazing at Dominia with such adoring eyes.

How that had changed after her child's death! Cassandra's flowerlike way of blossoming with joy hollowed through the years, no matter how she loved the children she taught. Dominia had never become conscious of that loss—not in almost a century, until she looked back in pain. Then it was all so obvious.

The Governess's drinking had been proportionate with her wife's unhappiness, though Dominia never blamed her for being depressed. Drinking wasn't a problem as far as her hyperefficient martyr liver was concerned, so Cassandra never found a decent argument against something in which she herself engaged on Noctisfreis and holy nights. Alcohol poisoning for a human meant drunkenness for the so-called master species, which was good, because most martyrs found it somewhere between desirable and necessary to be drunk as often as possible. But this drinking Dominia did in her Father's dream-study swiftly became a bit much even for her. The decanter never emptied, though its amount fluctuated whenever she returned from her thoughts for fear of falling too deep into any memory, any fancy, any idea. Her foot tapped in the empty room to keep her from thinking too much about anything, especially Cassandra—

Obviously, she needed music.

Wine upon the end table, she knelt to flip through the assortment of albums in the nearby bookshelf. How heavy each movement was! As if she sat in a bath of tar. The square cardboard sleeves containing large vinyl pancakes were difficult to move and more difficult still to read: far more difficult than the spines of books. Perhaps just because her limbs felt heavy.

The wine sat beside her elbow. Had she put it there? She took a sip, resumed her work, and at last read "Mozart"—muddied with some Cyrillic, but legible. Instantly, she stood before the record player to find her prize the composer's Requiem. Had it been there because she expected to find it in his collection, or had it been there because it was there? Because her Father put it there, by will or imagination? The wine sat beside the record player. She took a sip and carried it back to the chair; if it was going to follow her, she might as well consciously bring it along.

Now that she considered it, that had been her reaction to Basil, the cute dog Valentinian had been. Or the cute dog he remained, when one met him upon Earth. She lifted a hand to her patch; if only this world were more real than its counterpart. Then again, how could she be sure it wasn't? She felt this was where she came in her dreams. Perhaps she had even glimpsed these moments in her waking, and only now experienced them in linear condition.

The sound of Mozart's Introitus rang more powerfully in her ears and chest than ever before, the force of the music flushing her face as much, or more, than the wine—as much as any lover. Her head tipped back and she fell deep into its flow, forgetting even her own body.

Not unlike being pierced by the sound. As if her flesh were stripped away and her consciousness, purely contacted by the psychedelic experience of the art. Her lips parted. Somehow, she sipped her wine. No wonder her Father spent so much time listening to music! No wonder human and martyr flesh so craved music when it afflicted the soul thus. It inspired a heat, a hot and furious anti-sexuality, founded in deep-set nerves she had never before felt and which the uninitiated might never understand. Behind closed eye, the world was naught but color, the formless texture of music more real than a body. Her fingertips did not exist, yet they filled with sublime delight. *Were* sublime delight. Perhaps it was the nature of the music, written for its composer's own mortality: a grand celebration of life and a humble genuflection to the awe-inspiring power of death. She had already died once she knew of; how many times had she died eternally? How many times had Valentinian skipped from Dominia to Dominia? Who knew! She kept drinking.

All was well and fine until she reached the Benedictus. Then arose logical memories of Nogales, which had been, at the time, the worst experience of her life. The Battle for the Reclamation of Mexico had been horrific: one of the most profound wastes of martyr life in all military history. It proved a mark upon the lives of many humans, too. She never let herself forget that. Being a helpless prisoner changed her; or maybe it was her jailer, Benedict, a bright-eyed kid barely twenty-one who had been amazed to see that his charge—not only the infamous General but the only survivor of her ill-fated unit that dark night—looked all of twenty-six years old.

"I'm two hundred and forty," was her curt response from behind the wood-and-iron door. Primitive, but its reinforcement served to trap her in that stone room reeking of shit and piss and rancid meat and base, animal sorrow. Too frequent a visitor in dreams, that room.

"Oh, gosh"—the boy laughed at himself—"I'm sorry."

At the time, his laughter seemed mocking. "You're going to apologize for that?" There was no humor for her while she huddled upon her bench, forced to stay awake all day to navigate her cell lest her flesh encounter that square of sunlight her captors refused to cover. A sleepless prisoner now mocked by a child, she snapped, "Don't insult me. You killed my people. Good men and women with families whose children have already been orphaned or abandoned by one set of parents. Now you've orphaned them again, you keep me here like an animal, and you apologize for thinking I'm twenty-six? Like I give a shit how old you infants think I am."

The boy blanched. "I don't mean to apologize, it's just—I'm real sorry, ma'am."

If only something throw-able had been left in her possession. In reality, she was lucky they'd left her with shirt and pants—were she a man, they wouldn't have. "Don't call me that, and don't apologize to me." She pressed against the cell door, having strode through the patch of sunlight that the boy apparently thought impassible: so quick, he barely had time to jump. "I could rip your tongue out through this window. I don't want to hear another apology. Frankly, I don't want to hear the sound of your voice, but if you don't talk to me, I'm just stuck here listening to you breathe, and that's worse. Since you mongoloids are going to put me on trial instead of killing me right now, we've got a lot of time to fill. That's a lot of wet mouth-breathing—"

"Mouth-breathing," repeated the flabbergasted young man while the General railed on.

"—I'm forced to hear without interruption. So do me a favor and, if you insist on talking to me, talk to me about something—anything!—that isn't an apology."

With his brows knit in an expression that initially recalled worry, the boy slipped his hand through the tight-fit bars of the antique cell and startled her by touching the hand that gripped her window. "You're right. I guess it's disingenuous to apologize to you, since I didn't have a hand in the battle and I'm only here to defend the things I care about. I just got here yesterday!" The boy laughed nervously and released her hand, sliding his own dampened palm back to safety with a glance down the hall. "They're desperate for men. There's a bunch of us here and more on the way, so don't get any ideas...but you did a number on us, too."

The boy had looked back at her with a hard, significant glance, one hand lifting his feldgrau rebel's cap while the other scratched his blond hair. It occurred to her, despite his deep tan, he was from nowhere near Nogales, or even Mexico. The 64th Jurisdiction of the Front had long been a subject of conflict, and the seat of terrorist activities whose impacts stretched not quite as far as the Jurisdictions of the Canadian Winterlands—this was why the General had stayed in those generously dark and quiet states during her twenty-year sabbatical, until Operation Sole Sovereign was put into motion and the Hierophant ordered her return. During her absence, hundreds of citizen militias had popped up across the Front, and all of them champed for an opportunity to slaughter their martyr oppressors. The idea had been to abandon unsuccessful drone tactics and take Mexico City by city, the good old-fashioned Roman way; and there was no one to lead such an assault but Dominia di Mephitoli.

The problem was intelligence about human military capacity proved wrong, time and time again. While things had started well and many target locations were secured, the martyr army—more brainwashed human slaves than martyr overseers, truth be told—was harmed by its own prior efforts to deny Mexico necessary supplies. What supplies the Mexican citizens had were funneled by the South American Resistance Army troops and various other Hunter cells; the same could be said of the weapons, which were easily passed along routes built to exchange precious goods. All that was to say: martyrs had expected a primitive and scrambling group of testy animals, and were met with many waves of well-armed fighters, guerilla or otherwise, who so wore the General's army down over the four-year campaign that, by the time the strike was launched on Mexico City, defeat was inevitable. Four years they had marched around in circles, and their human troops were stymied by malnutrition. Of her sizable unit drawn from the whole during the Battle for the Reclamation of Mexico, Dominia was the only one shipped to long-since ruined Nogales—the only survivor. She was shipped up, and Benedict, down, to a location that had become a storehouse for the tiny smattering of living martyr soldiers captured alive. She deserved it. Benedict, decidedly, did not.

Dominia drained her glass and filled it again, and wondered how many times she had repeated the motion. How many times had the record skipped, waiting for her to pick its successor? How long had the doppelgänger leaned against the bookshelf far behind her Father's empty seat, pale cheek pressed to the cherry wood? It looked more physical: a more compelling rendition of her deceased wife. With that horrific thought, the thing bit its lip as though acting coy.

The General's eye narrowed. "What do you want?"

The thing continued staring, the hand not braced against the bookshelf lifting to play with the dark curls tumbling down its neck. They were lighter in color today, those curls; the neck they surrounded seemed so like Cassandra's fragrant one that Dominia felt herself kissing it. She took a burning swallow of wine.

"Don't look at me." Her faltering words strengthened. "Don't look at me, you thief."

The parody did not move, though it did smile in that horrible shark's way. So unlike Cassandra's it sent a shiver down the spine. As she rose, the General demanded, "Did you hear me? Do you understand what I'm saying?"

"Dominia," it whispered.

The wine was on the verge of backing up her throat. "Don't use her voice."

Gaze unfaltering, the abomination took a step. Did it ever blink?

"Don't you love me, Dominia?"

The question ended in a shriek as the General hurled her glass past the thing, which lifted its arms over its face and cowered against the bookshelf. Dominia approached it for the first time, to grip the front of its dress and rattle it as a wolf might a rabbit.

"You bitch," she said into the vacantly fearful face. As Dominia spoke, she reexperienced all the times Cassandra had called her the same: their most violent fights, times of fury and panic early in their marriage. Those first few troubled years, when Cassandra had pushed her and slapped her and accused Dominia of ruining her life. Of taking everything from her. All accusations from which Dominia could not possibly defend herself, because they were true. What was she to say to things like, "You killed the man who should have been my husband," or, "If it weren't for you I wouldn't have to stay alive," or, the worst: "I wish I hated you, so I'd have a reason to leave you."

How had those fights come about? Dominia had never been able to discern. She once ceased drinking in hopes it would help them get along, but when the fights didn't stop, she doubled her previous alcohol consumption. All those failed attempts to make her wife happy—to get her to move past what seemed increasingly to Dominia like a blip near the start of Cassandra's otherwise beautiful life of ninety martyred years—made the General a miserable wretch. Every time her wife wept over life not lived and death not died, the Governess felt so inadequate she often wished she might just disappear. But things had improved with time, and distance, and love, and patience, and communication: until one day, many years later, it became apparent they weren't communicating at all in the necessary ways. After all, Cassandra would rather be the confidant of a bullet than the then-Governess.

It had not been Dominia's fault. She had told herself that, and so had everyone else, but it was hard to believe. Hard to ignore the resentment now that she held this false Cassandra. This lying Cassandra. Her Father had a point when he said Cassandra had always been a liar. This was merely the amalgamation of her lies, or perhaps her lies as personified by Dominia. This thing stared through a convincing recreation of Cassandra's largest, most terrified eyes, and the General laid a heavy slap across its face.

This was not the first slap she had laid across Cassandra's face, but it was the first that felt good. She did it again, and as it cried her name, she grasped its delicate jaw as though to shatter it.

"You're not Cassandra. You'll never be Cassandra, and if you keep talking to me like you're Cassandra, I'll kill you."

"Dominia," the thing sighed, half whining, squirming in her grip and against her body. She glanced down and saw its own, naked beneath the thin fabric of its violet dress. The General might have let her fingers push new holes through its pale cheeks had she not noticed the motions of its hand, pinned between thighs she knew too well, had missed so much, were not real, were not there. Yet—

Her hand was there, too, like it was one hand. The General's kisses lay bruises on those lips as she dragged the vile thing, writhing, to the floor where she pinned it. There, it keened at and reached for and begged of her in ways Cassandra never had. Cassandra had been more inclined to make sure Dominia watched her undress. Her motions would slow to sensual drag, and cream shoulders came rolling out of her blouse like the soft hills of breasts already spilling from the chocolate lace bra. The hair would come down, followed by the panties. Then she'd recline upon the couch, the bed, the floor, and look at Dominia in nude expectation that reminded her so much of the first time, so much, oh...the General never had any choice but crawl to her side in devotion. How she had loved Cassandra! She had hated their fights, but craved their tenderness!

But: this thing. She loved abusing it and hated it more than ever now that it rolled her over with its sex-hungry body and pulled its dress over its head. There she was. Every bit of her. Tragic, beautiful memory, profaned. The thing bent its head over the General's belt, over the stolen, fumbling fingers. Dominia wondered if this was less or more a betrayal of her late wife than would have been a jaunt with Miki in the train or the pawnshop or the dentist's apartment. As she winced, then relaxed into the caress of the thing's cold tongue, she became aware of her Father's distant voice, and felt she sat again in the chair across from his now-filled one. Around the edge of his seat, there was herself, lying on the floor with the doppelgänger's head between her legs. Incredible, to be so out-of-body: yet, from time to time, she felt its mouth.

"Sexual fantasies"—he spoke as if in answer to some query and was either oblivious to the activity behind him or, more likely, felt toward it the distant interest any alien scientist might reserve for a pair of coupling subjects—"are a misapplication of the creative libido down into the sexual drive, rather than upward, toward God."

From her position sprawled upon the floor, she turned her head to watch with her good eye herself in that velvet chair. Her Father, on rising, took the skipping needle from the record, then withdrew from the sleeve collection an album she could not see. As the black sun sank and with it night cooled all remaining definitions of environment, the cobalt fire spontaneously emerged in the fireplace, and the thing between her legs redoubled its efforts for her attention; efforts that, undeniably, had effect, so Dominia panted and struggled to divine the lyrics of the ancient United Front ballad she'd heard more than a few times growing up. It went almost unrecognized in the wet heat of pleasure. The whole world was muted by the long curls of dark hair that tangled around the General's fingers while she pushed ever tighter the creature's jaw against the apex of her thighs. All the while, the Hierophant talked on. "The average man is incapable of salvation because he is so wrapped up in the material world that he cannot see that his own lust for flesh is truly a lust for a higher power. The average martyr, even, cannot be saved, and the best he can hope for is a close connection with his community in the form of the living Church."

The song was one the Holy Father had sang playfully to her so many times. Its eerie tune, its themes of eyes and stars and the moon in a superposition of existence and nonexistence, were a playful paternal melody in those nights. She even turned around and sung it to Cassandra! Now she knew the song of devotion for what it was: a teasing promise of that fateful night at the McLintock farm. As her Father poured wine, then abruptly reappeared in his seat, his voice carried on: "When we find our lover manifested in the flesh, we derive from them a surge of inspiration because the soul is liberated from the surly bonds of lust. Our fantasies are revealed as the poisonous wastes of time they have always been. Idle hands are the Devil's playthings." He lifted his glass in toast to her.

"You really are the Devil." She marveled to watch herself, eyes glassy, stomach churning at the thought of more wine but brain unable to stop the movement of her hand to the glass to her lips. Her Father smiled, onyx eyes as burning as his fireplace while darkness ended its descent.

"Labels like that seem such primitive notions in this place, don't they? 'You' and 'I,' 'Valentinian' and 'Basil,' 'Cassandra' and 'it'"—for the first time he acknowledged the scene behind him with a glance and, from the floor, Dominia met his black eyes and looked away, not embarrassed so much as furious he would interrupt this moment of what was supposed to be private shame. The Dominia of the chair was calmer: perhaps because of the wine, or the conversation, or the way her Father said—"'God' and 'the Devil.'"

She was capable of only mechanical motion while the Dominia upon the chessboard floor, exhaling, forbade exaltation of her pleasure. The thing carried on, carried on, carried her away. The darkness around the study quivered. She chronicled its motions through one hazy eye that dissolved into a burst of color and pleasure along with the rest of her, then recollected to discover a new ceiling upon which was painted quite a fresco. An old religious story called the Assumption of Mary. A primitive, pre-Hierophant interpretation of the Truth, but a small part of the story after the addition of the Post Testament. The music had also changed. She recognized neither it, nor its lyrics, but she heard a distant keyboard and saw from her chair that her Father had moved. Now, he tended the fire.

"You have been alone so long, and refused yourself an outlet lest you offend your dead wife. All this time you've clung to the hope she'll return as once you knew her. But would she want that? If you brought her back, would you ever find peace? All these questions, poisoning your mind. What relief awaits you, if only you'd accept your pet!"

On the floor, the thing crawled the length of Dominia's body to kiss her mouth. She gritted her teeth but nonetheless found herself absorbed into its kisses while her Father carried on. "This pursuit of fantasy has been the ultimate in distractions. A lesson on the life-ruining power of inaction, of lust. Poor child, poor girl, poor daughter! I cannot stand to see you throw away your life on so fruitless a cause. My tragic angel; your hopes are being manipulated by cruel and greedy forces. You are trapped in a dream—a tahgmahr such you cannot remember the girl you were."

He was back in the seat across from her; the poker, abandoned, leaned against the marble of the fireplace. "My girl, first plagued by bad dreams, as so many young martyrs—who then one evening looked so prideful, victorious, over breakfast."

And she was that girl, sitting in that too-big, ornate wooden chair at the expansive dining room table of their Vatican home (where they stayed frequently to bribe her into good behavior, for the child was always in a better temper when upon Mephitolian soil), silver spoon grasped in her hand as was the wineglass pinched in her fingers. Had she not broken it? Had it not shattered behind the cringing *tulpa*? Even now, it fell from her hand to break once more upon the floor: in the Vatican, her Father asked, "What's pleased my princess this fine evening?"

"I figured how to stop my night—tahgmahrs." At his curious "Oh," she nodded. "First, I realize I'm having a dream. Then, I decide to open my eyes."

"Of course, of course!" The Hierophant laughed and exchanged smiles with the other adults at the table, his beloved Cicero and adored Lamb and a few transitory favorites from the Mephitolian court. "How simple. Would all problems had such easy solutions."

Was he saying those words then, or now? While she was in the chair, or on the floor? She struggled to orient herself against the mouth of the thing until its fingers edged up her face: for a fraction of a second, it attempted to caress her cheek. Then the black band of her eye patch shifted against her ear.

Her drunken, dissociated head cleared as if by the ringing of a bell that focused her consciousness to one point. She grasped that hand and, with a grip automatic as it was steely, broke two fingers. It cried against her mouth in a voice so terrible, so unreal, that the General no longer recognized it as any way related to Cassandra. As she shoved the creature away, she glimpsed its true form, and cried out at the edge of one horrific gray mandible while midturn for the poker. By scrambling to her feet and twice nearly falling, she reached her goal and was ready to fight: it had fixed itself by the time she turned back, though the Cassandra-flesh it wore rippled as if ants crawled beneath. The General saw in it nothing of the terrible bulging eyes and profusion of teeth floating in the adrenaline-drenched recesses of her mind. Her chair was empty. She had collected herself. The only Dominia to be seen stood with her back to the fireplace, brandishing the poker against the thing, which, naked and weeping, retreated behind the Hierophant's chair.

Someone knocked upon the door. Edging to throw it open without taking eye from the scene, Dominia found herself more ashamed than ever when the man who entered was not Valentinian but Lazarus. He observed the room, then Dominia, his expression tight.

"I take it you touched it?" When she managed a reluctant nod, he sighed. "Well...there's still a chance. I'm glad you were honest."

"How could I have hidden it?" Her voice shook as she glanced down. To her surprise, her clothes were in perfect order. Belt and all.

"The truth renders us naked," the Hierophant said, reaching behind his seat to pat the shoulder of the doppelgänger. "Poor Cassandra's fingers! It will take her a whole day to recover. I hope you're happy."

"I know I am." Lazarus glanced at the poker Dominia forgot she held. As he removed it from her hand, she felt more like a sullen child than ever. "Come on. Let's get back on track."

"But it's not morning yet." No one had ever told her she couldn't leave her Father's study before the morning came. Even so, the idea of leaving it prematurely numbed her every limb. Lazarus shook his head.

"It's soon to be."

"That can't be—the sun's just set."

"The time you spend here is in what you do, not how many minutes you spend doing it. Other measurements are more important."

Eye watering, Dominia struggled to avoid seeing the doppelgänger. "I didn't screw up, did I? This isn't an unfixable fuckup?"

"Nothing's unfixable as long as we're friends. Are we still friends?"

"Of course."

Just slightly, Lazarus smiled. "Valentinian will be glad to hear that, I'm sure. He's waiting: come on."

"Actions have consequences, Dominia." She turned back to watch the Hierophant as she allowed herself led down the path of lights. "How many times will you slap my offered hands?"

"As many times as it takes for you to get the message," Lazarus responded. Over the threshold, he released Dominia and doubled his stride.

Relieved to escape that place of stasis and surreality, she hurried along with one last glance over her shoulder. "Will it follow us again?"

"Probably not today, not since you damaged it. But you'll see it tomorrow, I'm sure, good as new."

Her bones lurched at the thought of what had happened, of more days and nights wandering through this desolate place. She stopped, the back of her neck breaking out in the putrid sweat of a hangover. "Do I have to keep going back there? Why? Why can't I just stay with you all night?"

"I told you already about time. It's doing things that makes the morning come. Otherwise, we would have to wander in the dark; and whether you believe it or not, that's more dangerous than enduring a nightly visit with him."

"How could that be more dangerous?"

"You could completely forget who and what you are—or, worse, drop to lower frequencies. It's easy for any of that to happen in this place no matter what, especially for somebody unprepared or with no will of their own. But in the darkness, when you can't see your body or anything else, you can forget what you are. Become something else."

"Something like what?"

"It's one thing for a man's physical body to be swapped with a dog's. It's another thing if the soul thinks itself a dog. The same is possible for you. Get caught up in a flight of fancy, and with no body to act as a frame of reference, you could become anything: a dragon, an eagle, a tiger. It sounds great, but when you're doing it, you forget to enjoy it. You forget that it was ever any other way, and become so caught up in being that thing you could live a whole lifetime. Trust me: your Father would love that."

Worrying her tongue against her teeth, the General asked, "About what happened before—"

"You don't have to talk about it if you don't want."

"But what have I done? I got drunk and it just...things happened, but I didn't mean—"

"Gazelle don't mean to be eaten by lions. But you still fed it, and reinforced it *and* your Father's study. Valentinian talked to you about the wine."

Yes, the wine. It hadn't felt like any alcohol she'd had—like any drug. So heavy and strange to imbibe; yet, its effects had already disappeared. The mystic nodded at that.

"You're drinking his spirit. His thoughts, his ill intent...it's poisonous. The more you drink his wine, the more you'll accept his way of thinking, and the more you'll be tempted by his servant. But it only has power over you while you're engaging with it in his reality bubble." Her own luminous bands, their edges fading in with the graying morning light, were evoked at that term. The furniture and the space of the study had been formed by her Father's fields, *were* her Father's fields—and her fields, too, while she visited. All other fields, by virtue of the observer, were drawn into the system of the imaginary object. And, as with the thoughtform, it reflected the inner essence of that observer.

It was more than a visible demonstration of electromagnetic fields, this series of neon streaks encircling them. It *was* them in so many ways; ways she could not articulate; ways that so stirred her she migrated the subject back the conversation at hand, and the mystic's description of the memory bride as her Father's servant.

"Did he send that doppelgänger? It seems...close to him."

"No. You attracted it without knowing. But your Father likes to think himself compassionate toward all things, thoughtforms included; he doesn't care that it's a compassion that comes at the expense of compassion to humans, and even martyrs."

For the first time, Lazarus hit a nerve he himself had exposed. "You're a fine one to talk about compassion to martyrs. Wanting to shoot a whole species into space."

"I'm not talking tomorrow," said the old man, looking as annoyed as she felt. "And you're jumping to conclusions. I never said anything about outer space. That was *your* idea. Not mine." At her astonished expression, he barged on: "Look: when your Father is killed, there will be a schism among your people. However you slice it, his death will cause so many problems that martyrs will lose their grip on the power structure of the planet. You know that. You also know that your Father needs to die."

She lost any hope of adequate response, and chose to linger in troubled silence as he continued. "You know things can't proceed as they have. All this suffering is unnatural: you know it, the good martyrs hidden among the population know it. Those good martyrs, and the good martyr we choose as their leader, will see that it is not only in the benefit of humans to depart Earth. It is in the benefit of martyrs."

"How will we eat? What will we do for all those centuries of travel? Surely you don't want *me* for leader after him, right?" Now, it was Lazarus's turn to remain silent. Finally, her lips pressed thin, Dominia tried one more nagging question. "Please. Is Valentinian real? A martyr? Or is he just some dog, some fictional character, who only exists because I've convinced myself he does?"

After studying the General, the mystic admitted, "As long as I've known Valentinian, I have been personally unable to remember when I met him, or how I knew him. Valentinian says he was once my son, and that he regrets not salvaging my consciousness from that first world."

"I thought it was your blood that caused your memory to come back—why wouldn't it contain the memory of that first time?"

"The blood allows it, but I think he's responsible for it somehow. He won't admit it. I've sort of given up caring. He seems lonely. It's one of the reasons why he makes me suffer this eternal existence, I guess: so I don't forget him again. Apparently, his mother in that place was the woman who became, in all universes thereafter, the current manifestation of the entity known as the Lady. I *do* know her. Trisha," he said with longing. "But we never had children. Hell, we never had more than one date before she sort of fell off the map, and I was too embarrassed over a misunderstanding to track her down. Now, I see that misunderstanding wasn't a coincidence. It was designed so she and I wouldn't be together: so she could become the Lady, and Valentinian could never be born."

So that was the space her Father had made for himself. "Do you believe him about his parentage?"

Lazarus shrugged, which was becoming the physical expression of choice around those parts. "Someone has to be responsible for all this. This conflict, this eternal loop, this struggle against your Father. If he wants to take credit, I'm happy to let him."

"But if he can extract your consciousness and restore it to your new body, why can't he do that for me?"

"Do you *want* him to do it for you?" At her grimace, he nodded. "We did try that once, actually."

"How did it go?"

Following an ominous pause, he answered, "We decided it was better you don't remember your past...attempts."

She shuddered, and tried one more point: "If he's a magician, can't he turn himself into a martyr instead of staying stuck as a dog?"

The old man chuckled. "The material world is, by definition, more concrete and static than this one. It takes a higher power than that of mind alone to change something as vast as the molecules of a being's body, or to replace one being with another. Valentinian is a great magician, it's true, and he has tremendous power, but...let's say it is prohibitively difficult for a man operating the body of a dog to upgrade to bipedal, sapient primate."

"Is there a way to help him?"

"Yes." In the distance, the red-and-black figure of the magician appeared to be packing his true fire as though coaxing it into an invisible kennel. "But if you want to help him, you'll have to make a choice."

"What choice is that?"

"When we get to Cairo, there will be an opportunity for a miracle. You can have a wish granted: something restored. But you only get one wish, so you have to choose."

Beneath the anchor of his meaning, her heart began to sink. "Restore Cassandra, or help Valentinian?"

Lazarus turned toward the magician, who noticed them, and waved. "Sometimes," the mystic said, "the fastest way is not the best."

VI

Tyger Tyger

Valentinian's mood had so improved by the time they reunited that the General was forced to consider she had been the only one upset. She even felt she was the only one in a tizzy about the *tulpa* business, though it was possible they only pretended not to be upset, lest the emotional energy remotely heal it. On reaching his side at the shadow-gray apotheosis of dawn, the magician asked in the knowing tone of a bosom buddy recovering from his own night on the town, "Good morning! Did you have a fun night?"

She somehow felt the only appropriate answer was, "It was great."

"Good!" The twinkle in Valentinian's blue eyes was so different from the one in her Father's, yet so much the same. "Let's get a move on."

"We haven't lost a day, have we?"

"What did I just tell you twice over about time?" asked Lazarus. "You sort of did us a favor."

"Yeah, we basically partied all day. I won four hundred bucks. You know, theoretically. Eventually. When I have a body with a wallet again."

"Does this bum even know how to use money?"

"I've been running the stock markets since before you were born," grumbled the old man.

"That's just informed gambling," she said, and he answered, "Not if you know what's going to happen." Dominia considered this was true, and thought, with a faint pang of sadness, not just of gambling Miki Soto but of René Ichigawa. He seemed the gambling type and surprised her with something worse. A big brick in the foundation of her trust issues with Valentinian and Lazarus, that professor. They hadn't done anything untrustworthy outside withholding information; but Lazarus had a point. It would be horrific to remember every possible (and definite past) method of death. What a paralytic notion! On top of that, knowing all the times she had failed Cassandra...all the Cassandras out there, dead forever. It ached her.

And she ached more to consider she might need to leave Cassandra dead forever, even if for the good of the world. Of the human race, and the martyr one. Oh! Who could be asked to make such a choice? Who dared even call it a choice? Only the most selfish soul would entertain it: but she must have made the choice once or twice, in her litany of unseen mistakes. The phantom weight of a familiar body pressed her arms. She dismissed it, lest it produce a second, more horrible duplicate. She focused on where she was: following the men as they trudged through a barren landscape whose hues gained saturation, for what was once black and white warmed into sepia. Or perhaps, having been there so long, her mind gave the grit at her feet an artful flaxen cast generously shared with the day-gray sky. When—at last!—some distinction emerged in the distance, Dominia cried out and dashed beyond her friends.

From a distance, this protrusion in the landscape resembled a gangly tree; but, on her approach, it resolved into a signpost whose two roots furled roughly south by southwest and north by northwest in the form of long paths laid in clay brick. The marker at this juncture, hand-carved of teal- and bright-pink-painted wood (though Dominia had seen no real trees), was marked with characters that appeared that same combination of readable and unreadable as her Father's books: here, mysteriously, the characters appeared a kind of dream-Arabic. Though she did not know the language in real life, she read the signs just fine. The left-hand one declared "CAIRO," while the one pointing right indicated "JERUSALEM."

"Not much farther," said the relieved mystic. "I'm always happy to see this sign."

The General was pretty amped, herself. "How much longer? It should only be a few more night cycles now, right?"

"About two." Valentinian crushed another cigarette filter. "Just a while to wait. Then, you can have Cassandra. If you want."

He watched as if waiting for her to broach Lazarus's warning, but she could not yet speak on it. Her face turned away, toward Jerusalem. "Earthly cities appear here?"

"No, no. This just puts you in the right direction. Like Lazarus told you before, you can leave this place by looking at the black sun for long enough; it'll take you to a specific point in Earth's space-time based on where you're standing and the sorts of things you've done. However, that takes practice, so kindly magicians such as yours truly make signs."

"Magicians such as you? I wouldn't call you 'kindly.'"

"For all I do to help you," asked the man in a mock-wounded tone while the mystic sighed in disgust to which neither of them paid attention. "To help you save the world and your wife!"

"If you're such an amazing magician, why haven't you helped me to the finish line before?"

"Ouch! There's just so many ways to go wrong. It's hard—impossible—to know what any given iteration of the universe will hold for us. Your Father remembers it as well as we do, so he's liable to tweak his strategy each time. We just have to do the best we can at piecing together past experiences, and hope we know enough to get through this time."

The weight of her patch seemed almost painful against the right side of her face. "If I'm such a threat to the Hierophant's world, and he knows the future, why did he martyr me at all?"

A jolly bass voice emanated from the blind spot that hid Jerusalem's path. "Because you, Miss Mephitoli, are too valuable a commodity to be passed by: no matter the risk."

Dominia and Valentinian turned toward the disruption Lazarus had long since noticed. The approaching figure drew his hood from his face, and there he was in all his white-toothed glory: Dr. Tobias Akachi, the dentist who fixed her teeth and removed her DIOX-I, then betrayed her by assaulting her Family during the tragic Kabul marathon. He tried to win the General to his side; worse, he showed interest in acquiring her powerful sister, Lavinia, whose memetic curse brought many marathoners to their mortal end—before the bomb detonated by the dentists' men murdered more.

Her chest tightened along with her itching fist. "What are you doing here?"

"Looking for you! Do you know how long you were missing when I came here to find you? Nearly an entire lunar cycle! Almost a month!"

"You're al-Mawta. Hunter trash—and the king of the trash heap, at that." To Lazarus, she said, "At least one cell of Hunters stole some of your blood, didn't they? Their most initiated members come here?"

The mystic, rubbing the temple of his forehead, managed, "Yeah, they come here all right. Come here and annoy me."

"Our founder was a man first tricked by the Lazerene faith, who then saw the light. He recognized the cult was but a means of pacifying humans into perpetuating the endless struggle against martyrs, rather than destroying them. One of these days"—the cheerful dentist looked to Lazarus, dark cheeks creased by the breadth of his grin—"I am going to catch you. Then all my men, and all worthy humans of the world, will come and go from this place as they please. It will be nothing to destroy the martyrs."

"You're the leader of *all* the Hunters." Dominia corrected her misperception in astonishment as Valentinian, crossing his arms, shifted his weight so both men—rather unnecessarily—stood between her and the dentist. Then again, she supposed it was for the human's good, no matter how impermanent death was in this place.

"You're wasting your time, Tobias. She's not going to Jerusalem with you. Run home to the rest of the Hunters."

"Oh, I know Miss Mephitoli will not be going to Jerusalem with me today. But I have come to extend the option, because she may change her mind in the future. It would be immoral if I did not give her a way out of what she must otherwise face!"

That a Hunter—their leader!—should lecture on morality was laughable, but what got her attention was something else. Talk of the future in any context alarmed her these nights. "Don't tell me you've also been through all this before?" she asked. That provoked a hardy laugh.

"No, no, my friend, oh, my, no. Why, compared to your single lifetime, I am practically a boy! A mere fifty-three years old. But even at my young age, I have learned much of the workings of the world, of martyrs, and of you. I know the path down which you trek"—said with the slightest ironic grin for the bricks beneath their feet—"is a shortsighted and petty one. If you think your people will ever submit to starvation floating around the void of space, you are a fool. If your Father is the only martyr to die, it will begin an unceasing war. Your friends would destroy the whole world to cure the blight of martyrdom. One does not kill the body to extract an abscessed tooth."

"The only shortsighted one is you," Valentinian insisted, but the human didn't stop for breath.

"This place exists for a reason, and it is not to shelter martyrs as your Father would see fit to use it; nor is it a means to manipulate the world, as would this heretical magician. This place exists to protect humanity from martyrs! Lazarus holds the key to salvation, but hoards it!"

Disgust rose in the General's heart. Though she'd had her share of hypocritical moments, she would never be as blatantly false in self-representation as Tobias. "For someone who professes to hold such love for humanity, you never mind when your terrorists kill humans by the hundreds. What about that marathon bombing? My family didn't get a scratch; a *pile* of human corpses filled that crater. For that matter, how often do your people pray to the Lamb for help conquering cities or destroying innocent lives in the name of your so-called mission? You have no problem appealing to the saints of the Holy Martyr Church when it serves."

There was no use in logic. Everybody in this place had an answer for everything, and the dentist was no exception. "Those individual lives must be forfeit for the sake of the whole. It is indeed a tragedy, but when Iblis stoops to genocide, what can be done? We play by his rules."

"'Iblis'—that's the Islamic term. I thought you were Christian."

"Oh, yes, of course. But our organization is full of people who understand that the cause of eliminating martyrs is the *true* holy war, and when a Christian works with a Muslim, he soon realizes that 'Allah' and 'Iblis' are simply another language's names for 'God' and 'the Devil.'" Dominia fought against the chill that crawled through her to remember her Father's words. "We are Muslims, Christians, Jews, and men of all Eastern faiths: even Buddhists join our cause, so it must be righteous, for they are peaceful and hold the destruction of all life as sin! But the faith of the leader at the top does not matter to those who join our cause. It matters only that he possess the vial of Lazarus's blood, and prove capable of seeing this place and living on. This is all very secret, you see. I only became involved with the Hunters while attending a school for those humans lucky enough to buy their way into safety by serving martyrs, working in vocations your idle people refuse to perform. A slave, yes? Only given the opportunity because Iblis refuses to enlist the help of artificial intelligence like the rest of the sentient world. Not that our artificial intelligence is anywhere near the quality it should be, given the amount of time and resources we've spent at war with your Father for the last two thousand years!

"You can imagine, Miss Mephitoli: during my so-called European internship, I saw much suffering. What terrible pains your Father inflicts upon the Earth, upon humankind! I could not stand for it. I escaped to join the Hunters. When it comes to the issue of martyrs, you see, there is no such thing as 'Muslim' or 'Christian' or 'Jew.' Not even 'Buddhist' or 'Hindu'!"

Dominia's irritation was on the verge of boiling over. "Of course not. Because they're just bodies to you. Tools to be used as you see fit."

"You act as though I am as bad as your Father. I assure you, Miss Mephitoli: I am the one who will be legislating in the wake of war. Not him. If even a Buddhist will join our cause, your life must be worth less than a tick's; martyrs are worse than subhuman. They are entropic. A species of primitive apes without the decency to develop the concept of cultural taboo."

"You and the rest of the Hunters"—Valentinian draped an arm around Dominia's tensed shoulders to steer her toward Cairo, away from the man she trembled to punch—"think that because you're a bunch of modern primitives, so you see primitivism everywhere. Hooting in your stolen *tanques* and tossing bombs like cartoon villains. Wastes of space!"

"I cannot bring myself to lie to you," Tobias called after them, still near the signpost. "I cannot promise you the life of your dead wife, as so many others have: that is something only the Lord can give, and He can only give it on the Day of Judgment. Nor can I promise you any particular power, for that, again, is a matter of God. But I can promise you two things. I can promise you exception from the doings that need done against your people, that you might keep your martyr life under fulfillment of certain conditions; and I can promise you, Dominia, that you will be doing what is right. You will be doing what is good by all humankind and by God if you come with me now, to Jerusalem. Your soul might still be saved."

"And if I continue with them?" She jerked free of Valentinian. "What'll you do?"

Akachi's eyebrows lifted and his expression remained humorous; but a new, rotten tone curdled his words. "Then you are as much an enemy of mankind as your Father, and I will see you killed."

Still as an ice sculpture, the infamous General assessed the dentist and said in her own warning tone, "You know what's disappointing about you? Everybody I meet lately has some ulterior motive. I guess I was stupid for hoping you were an altruistic person."

"Ah, Miss Mephitoli. You speak of disappointment, but I assure you: the feeling is mutual." Tightly, the dentist smiled, then turned away while pulling up his hood. "I shall see you in Cairo, my dear."

"I hate that guy." Valentinian made an obscene gesture with his forearm while Lazarus resumed tossing pebbles.

"What do you expect? Humans who get a taste of the black sun are insufferable know-it-alls. Anybody who spends all their time in this place has to be a pain in the ass."

"Yeah," said Valentinian absently. Dominia's laughter got him listening too late, and he caught on with a sullen, "Hey," while the mystic offered a sly grin.

"Even I have a sense of humor," said Lazarus. The magician rolled his eyes.

"Yeah? Where'd you leave it?"

In that moment of genuine mirth, the stirrings of the Hierophant between her and her friends lay so far away. It occurred to her she had hardly batted an eye when it was Tobias's chance to manipulate her. Chalk that up to the men's reaction to her brush with the doppelgänger. They treated her as if nothing at all had happened. She had to believe they were worth trusting—had to believe that the spirit of that good dog was her friend, and not one of the imaginary kind. Thus, alone with Valentinian while Lazarus went to early sleep that night, Dominia watched the magician tend the fire and, after a time, said, "I'm sorry."

"I should be sorry! I lost my temper. I try to be patient with you, but you've got a pretty short fuse yourself, buddy. Easy for one spark to light another." After watching her from over his shoulder, the magician returned attention to the crackling blaze. "Something you want to talk about?"

"It'll all be okay, right? I mean…won't it?" She felt like a child again, a sad girl trying to find some sign from the universe that the world was not cruel as she'd come to fear. Upon the blanket the magician had unfurled for her, Dominia pushed long strands of dream-hair back into the ponytail corralling them. "I haven't done something unfixable, have I?"

"With the doppelgänger? No, not yet. If you keep going back to it, maybe. But if you can help yourself, we'll be okay."

"What about Tobias?" For some reason, she had not anticipated meeting a Hunter here; and this specific Hunter stirred other thoughts. "Did Miki know about him?"

"No, but the Red Market does. They use their girls like spies and distribute them accordingly, whether the RM agents in question are aware or not. You thought your eye was streaming a lot of information? Hah! Every phone that's had Miki Soto's ID number in it has been a recording device since 4031."

"If you're a dog in the flesh, how do you know so much about Miki? I mean, I know you've lived many times, but—"

"That, and eternity is a long time—so long it's 'always.' From this space I've gotten much information. Even people—read the fields and atmosphere correctly, and you can find anybody. There really are a lot of people here, although"—he chuckled into the darkness—"it doesn't seem that way. But, it's better to walk seven days here with no people and no sun exposure than forty days on Earth with the profound threat of Hunters."

"What about here? Aren't they a threat here?"

"Everything is and isn't a threat here. I told you before: get killed, wake up. It's disorienting, but it's not so bad except for the lost time and the difficulty of precisely finding your way back."

Satisfied enough, Dominia closed her eye against the eerie dark. "What do we do if he follows us?"

"We'll deal with him. Look, General: I know you're used to planning. You want to have control of the situation. Don't we all! But now's not the time. Now, just go to sleep. You want to know if everything will be okay? Well, I promise. You have a hard time putting faith into other people's words, but believe me: I wouldn't have invested so much time and effort helping you if you weren't the key to a grand and terrible prison. If I didn't like you as a person and think you worth helping. There are a lot of 'yous' who haven't made it this far…who don't think to ask the questions you're asking, or put them together in the way you're putting them together. Because of that, you're the only 'you' that will make the right series of decisions."

That was all well and fine, and comforting—or would have been. But, after the events of the night prior, her nerves were on edge in the dark. Valentinian applied the same dust he had each night, and like each night, she tumbled off to deep, velvet sleep: but she continued tumbling again and again, for many times she awoke and thrashed upon the blanket only to fall back unconscious. It was as though she fought off some virus, though the only virus that plagued her was one of her thoughts. Not even the magician's sand might keep her from fear of herself, fear of her own lust, fear of Cassandra's disappointment. From thoughts of Cassandra, dead and unable to feel anything, let alone disappointment.

Good point: when (if?) she eventually returned, surely Dominia's wife would not be so broken by the General's loneliness- and pain-motivated infidelity. Not as much as her ego imagined. It was not Cassandra's disappointment she needed fear, but her own. She thought of the book in the Hierophant's study while awaiting his torches; of Odysseus, returning to Penelope after years in the arms of Circe and Calypso. Surely the wife of that man skilled in all ways of contending did not begrudge him those caresses transpiring at the whims of goddesses! But surely also, as Dominia once had heard Cicero joke to the Lamb, there were two versions of the *Odyssey*: the version Odysseus told Penelope, and the version he told fellows in the bars. Would there were but one truth! Would she were pure enough, good enough, to carry only one back to her vivified bride.

Eventually, muscles aching with tension she was unused to feeling in this space—and perhaps only felt because her sleepless mind expected as much of its restless body—Dominia sat up to assess the sleeping men. Valentinian snored into his arm and Lazarus lay like a corpse, mouth hanging open and no observable breath disrupting his chest. Even so, and even though she had slept as "long" as nights before, the path of the Hierophant had not appeared.

This should have proven relief. As if she cared to see him, or that thing! She tried to assure herself that her passing scorn was misplaced. Her Father mentioned it would take time for the doppelgänger to repair. Perhaps he and it had taken the night off? Too good to be true.

Something was wrong. No path would be forthcoming, she felt. Perhaps if the path did not come, day would never break. She considered waking Valentinian but knew without having to try he would not awaken. Like the day, he would not rise until she had gone to the Hierophant, or accomplished some other strange task. As long as she lay doing nothing, the light would not come.

Anxiety filled her with the truth. The only way to reach his study tonight was to find it, herself. After some delay in the hope Valentinian would spontaneously awaken, she placed a foot into the black Void beyond the firelight.

For days, her mind had wondered at the substance of that darkness. Was it a true void, like outer space? Some unknown, tarry matter? Or, would she would step into the darkness and stop existing? She expected all those things to varying degrees, but as it happened, none occurred. She remained herself: she was simply now herself standing outside the circle of light, in a type of dark that cooled the muscles of her body, the overdriven thoughts of her brain. More alone at the edge of the light than she'd been with the sleeping men, she closed her eye to think of the Hierophant's study. Where might it be located? She could not see the ropes of her compass, that marvelous diffusion of not just light but perhaps all the electromagnetic spectrum, including regions then unknown, unmeasured, by man. But there had to be some way. The men had indicated several times that one could find one's way by tracing some sort of energy pattern, but the General saw nothing in the dark. What about the concept of attraction, though? Her electromagnetic field was not absent, just invisible. A compass you couldn't read was no good as a compass, but what about the magnetic component of the device? Was she not a walking magnet? The mortal coil through which a current of consciousness ran?

If she had attracted the thoughtform, could she attract the study?

She tried envisioning it, its checkerboard floor and broad, filled shelves springing out of space. The music replayed in her head. The more she ruminated on the study, however, the more ill at ease she became. Perhaps thinking of the study would create a false variation: her own perspective of his study, rather than the actual thoughtform. Maybe this false study would even house a *tulpa* of her Father. Then there would be two of them. Dear Lamb, how could she prove there weren't already? Was that something breathing in the distant dark? Pray for her, Elijah!

With utmost caution, she thought on her Father. There were times in the real world when thoughts of him made her brain crawl in specific regions, mostly around the amygdala. She needed care in turning down those slippery slopes of thought. Instead of thinking concretely about him, she evoked the feeling she experienced when she did, tried to feel as if she already sat in his study, talking to him, lungs full of sandalwood and cloves while his sickly fire licked its chops within its marble cage. There was the cold floor on her back and the taste of the wine and not the doppelgänger—not Cassandra. Instead, the clacking of pool balls, and the velvet of the crimson chair beneath her hands. Feeling small in that chair, like a child; feeling like a child again; feeling memory cut a different path: her hands flexing past that velvet, into fists, the Hierophant laughing to watch her box with Cicero in one of Mnemosyne's gap-filling flashes. Above the huffs and puffs of a girl fighting her brother like she wanted to kill him, her Father said to the Lamb, "She is my little tiger, isn't she."

That word echoed as if spoken aloud. "Tiger." The slide through her memories and the association of her consciousness terminated there. Like a mind on the cusp of sleep, it grasped that final cogent thought, and rolled into it with a different kind of momentum than the one Valentinian had described. This was not the escape velocity by which a consciousness might slip free the surly bonds of Earth. This was more like falling: ecstatic falling. With the word "tiger" came all the associations of tigers, of being a tiger, of fur and teeth and claws. Facts: the tiger was the world's most vengeful animal, could crush a skull with the swipe of a paw, went extinct due to poachers and climate problems in 2093 and was artificially renewed in 3545, 113 years before Morgan, unlucky human prototype Dominia, was born. But who was Morgan? She was not even sure of Dominia.

Her mind was predisposed to seek the energy of a thing imagined, being in search of her Father's study: with her heart so open, her ribs unfolded, and she turned inside out. The General lost sense of herself to her memories, then to her thoughts, and soon had so faint a notion of body it seemed perfectly reasonable she was a tiger, yes, a tiger, a beast of hot breaths and tremendous, heaving muscles that thundered into the darkness like an embodied storm, its shoulders, paws, jaws ready to strike with a might shaming the very lightning for their fury. To be a tiger was to be the physical condition of hunger, and that running hunger craved to be filled: sought the invisible meat it felt in the darkness. There arose the sensational hope of satiation to hear the breathing of a distant other, then the sound of that other's feet upon the formless earth. Neon body flickering like a candle, this tiger rocketed through the black air into which its dark stripes melted until its eyes found that which it sought, a broad-soled and double-tusked beast that shook its long gray snout and galloped into the dark. After, after! Her heart pounded in her ears. There was no existence but for muscles, and the movement of muscles. She had no fear of getting lost, no sense of running farther from the fire, from her friends, from the Father for whom she had wandered into the dark before forgetting. There was no sense of self for her, this tiger. Only the hunt, the prey, so close she tasted it—

"Dominia."

The familiar sound was so unexpected that, in the context in which the tiger heard it, the syllables seemed the foreign voice of the sail-eared beast it chased. Only on second repetition did it falter the cat, who paused to study the shape of the call in its ears. This sound was not the deep and breathless grunts of predator animals, nor of the prey that she lost as it vanished into the darkness. This sound gave some sense of self and context and space outside "this" and "that," outside the arrow drive of primeval hunger. Indeed, it spoke to a deeper hunger: a deeper craving. The tiger thundered after that deeper craving, while within it Dominia stirred at the sound of her own name. She felt again the word "tiger" and recalled an ancient poet whose utterance,

"Tyger! Tyger! Burning bright" repeated in her head. A vibrating mantra in her Father's voice, the deceptive humanity of which shaped her back into a woman as the poem ran its course.

Perhaps it was the memory of her Father: of how, as he recited the poem while tucking her into bed, he would put such growling emphasis on the word "dare" that she would giggle despite herself. Because, to children who knew better, he was yet so playful and charming and kind that one never hated him as much as one wished. Even now, she heard his words: felt him closing up her ribs with tickling hands that restored a body she knew.

"What immortal hand or eye *dare* frame thy fearful symmetry?"

A woman, she tripped in the darkness as if she'd reached the edge of some invisible cliff. Perhaps she had; she seemed to be hurtling as such. The General fell such a length, at such exhilarating speed, she had no time to be afraid: only to marvel at the sound of wind whipping past her ears. The blackness plunged into her skull after the sound, filling it with immense pressure. Would her head explode?

The farther she descended, the slower she fell, and the more the darkness assumed newer, colder embrace. It was impossible to tell at what point "darkness" became "water," or if there had ever been a difference. Perhaps it was a matter of changed depth, viscosity, and perception. The difference was not a concern that came to Dominia's mind, nor did thoughts of drowning trouble her until she considered she ought to be drowning. Light, though, began to grow in the water before her, for at some point, "down" had become "up"; in that same quantum sphere where "darkness" tangled with "water," so, too, did these lack discernment. There was only the goal toward which she pumped her burning limbs until, with a violent splash, Dominia emerged from the water, gasping and coughing, good eye too blinded to see until well after she discerned amid her sputters for air the hush of feminine whispers. After a good wiping with her wrist, her eye opened, and the General was taken aback—though far from disappointed—to find herself surrounded by a coterie of exquisite women. Two of them nude, and one draped in wet cloth (which was somehow better)—plus two more pricked their heads from the bushes at the bank. Who knew how many more yet unseen. Odysseus, indeed!

"Excuse me, ladies." The General tried not to take too much advantage of her own femininity and looked politely at the nearby trees. "Sorry to bother you, but I have no idea where I am. Or"—she grew aware she stood in a lake no more than waist deep, the way she'd come having been, evidently, closed off—"how I got here."

"You are in the True West, although it seems that, to you, this is the East." The clothed woman rested a hand upon her shielded breast; another sought to smooth the speaker's hair until one of her sorority also helped. "You are a stranger here."

"No kidding." As Dominia's eye adjusted, it became apparent that these were not human women, for they were beyond the pale of earthly—or mortal—perfection. Some breed of nymph? Their hair, through of golden luster in the sun (the sun! The golden sun! The General only now registered it as it glowed unburning in the straw and chocolate tangles of the hair that haloed them) revealed the seafoam sheen of algae, and certain regions of flesh where most women's skin grew darker carmine or dusky brown were here illustrated in the same fragile ivies as the luscious flora surrounding their clear spring. She could not think to speak, but the creatures appeared as content to study her until their clothed leader asked, "You are a woman?"

"Of course."

"It is not often women find our pool. Women with your needs do not often come."

Marveling past the beautiful creatures, at the distant golden orb that did not burn, the martyr said, "Well, I'm here, though I don't know what needs you mean, or where 'here' is."

They so laughed that Dominia blushed. The water splashing around the limber legs of the clothed nymph rose to her hips; she waded to meet the General, who remained fixed to the spot.

"I know you now. How did I fail to recognize you? Because you did not recognize me, perhaps?" The girl's glistening lips parted in a smile. "How pleased we would have been for a woman's touch! But how pleased I will be, General, to lead you."

"Are you thoughtforms?" tried Dominia, somewhat weakly. The nymph before her paused to laugh, that gay, sweet ringing further burning her face until the giggling offender turned back to see her displeasure with a click of the tongue.

"We are older than thought. We are older than form."

With a hand as cool as the darkness from which still-delirious Dominia emerged, the nymph touched the General's face, lifted her palm, tried to draw her from the water. "Excuse me." Dominia's efforts to pull away were foiled, the ethereal woman's grip deceptively strong. She marveled as she was tugged past the unclothed nymphs and to the bank of the pond. "Where are we going? Who are you? Do I know you?"

"Not yet. My name is Gethsemane." The smiling nymph stepped up to the grass, and as the water beaded upon her skin to be dried, dot for dot, by the sun, the color of the woman's flesh resolved from celadon tinges to more human tones. That strange beauty, however, remained. "My sisters and I are the Water Bearers. We are here to aid you."

"Me?"

"Yes, you. Lady Dominia di Mephitoli, Governess of the United Front, General of the Hierophant, Bitch of Europa, and Serpent of the Southwest." The girl embraced a slender tree, which, to Dominia's astonishment, bent its boughs as though to return the affection. When they lifted away, the nymph stood in light armor of bark, with a skirt resembling leaves. "I have awaited you an eternity: you, after all, are the one who crafts the eternity in which I wait."

VII

The True West

Dominia's people did not approve of drugs, but that had not prevented teenage experimentation. In the end, she was always partial to liquor, but she dabbled in tobacco, tiptoed into reefer, and, as a young woman during slivers of peacetime, gone through a phase of psychedelics that lost her more friends than it earned spiritual revelations. She had done enough substances to know out-of-body experiences and hallucinations of this degree were, to put it mildly, rare: the closest she had come to something like this was dimethyltryptamine, but even that tended to reduce reality to the pattern of a Persian rug and enhance her imagination rather than take her to any true faraway place and convince her she was awake while it happened.

This place made her awake and whole as she might have felt on Earth, or more. Yes, more awake than awake—if that last place had been a dark place of dreaming, this land, bursting in hues more exquisite than those she knew, was a land of hyperconsciousness. It was decidedly not Earth. Beneath the merry sun (a wholesome star whiter than Sol, with his angry sheen of city smog and summertime wildfire smoke in the UF), grass reflected an emerald she had seen nowhere on the face of her beloved planet, and the wind whistled a song through every blade. With it carried a fabulous scent, as if to indicate the walkers of this world breathed not some lesser gas like oxygen but rather sweet perfume. Yet, for all the glories of nature that assailed her as she was led from the spring to a distant road that curled along an unmade bed of hills, that most glorious was the spirit guiding her by the hand.

"Gethsemane." The General repeated the name and was rewarded with the lifting eyes of the nymph. Now she had to find something to say. She cleared her throat. "So—did somebody tell you to collect me?"

"Yes. We have long awaited your arrival. I am sorry I did not recognize you at first; most humans look the same to me."

"Oh, I'm not—"

"There are no martyrs here," Gethsemane corrected before Dominia made her mistake. "There is no one for the sun to burn; there is no need to shed another's blood. Not unless it is the will of the king."

"A king, huh?" Dominia eyed the girl's armor and felt for a moment she had fallen into the song of an ancient crew of earthly composers named for an outmoded style of dirigible. "Was he the one who told you to wait for me?"

"I wait for you because it is my duty. But, no. The king and his queen are on vacation in the East."

"I thought you said this was the East."

"Your East. We are the West, properly called the True Western Kingdom in the Time of Felicity. It is much easier to say 'West,' however, or 'Kingdom.' At any rate, no matter where you are, General, there is always an East."

"I suppose...uh"—coming out of a daze, or the spell of her dreamily chattering new companion, Dominia thought to ask—"where are you taking me?"

"To the City, to meet the magician called Valentinian."

With perked ears and sweet relief for the familiar name, Dominia said, "Valentinian! He's here?"

"If not already, he will be soon, because you are here."

"So, he knew we were coming... I'm still not sure how I got here. Is this the same place as before? The dark one, I mean, where I came from."

"In a sense. Everything that surrounded you before surrounds you. It has been rearranged."

Quite an understatement! To compare this place to the Void was an impossible task. They did not seem in any way the same, and Dominia was certain that mapping them (if mapping the Void was possible) would elicit two different geographies. "It was so dark there; it's hard to believe this is the same place. I feel as if I've been dreaming, and I've just woken up."

"You have, if it was night's darkness in which you wandered. The mind dreams in that darkness, which is filled with formless spirits."

And formed spirits. Her mind struggled to reconstruct the beast in that darkness, that snorting thing that watched her even before she'd wandered off and lost track of her body. Glimpses of gray, and long horns—no, tusks. "I saw an animal while I—dreamed. I thought I was an animal, too. Then I heard my name." Spoken by whose voice? In the manner of an interrupted dream, the memories refused to resolve into a functional image.

"Someone prayed for you, General." Gethsemane's explanation was so matter-of-fact that Dominia barked out a laugh.

"Prayed for me?" A thousand stuffy sermons swept to the forefront of her mind. "I never thought that did any good."

"If one is not connected with the spirit, it may not, except by accident; and it has no material use but to bolster the self in the waking day. But you must learn the benefits of prayer if you are to aid in the Lady's cause."

"The Lady...you serve the Lady."

"I am Her Bearer."

"Then—do you know Miki Soto?"

"Not in this place, at this time. In a different place, and in a different time, yes."

Someday, someplace, Dominia would meet a person who gave straight answers. For now, she'd given up worrying about it. Failing to keep sarcasm from her voice, she asked, "So, what are the...*benefits* of prayer?"

"You've felt the real benefit. It reinforces the souls of those who pray and those for whom they pray. One must be in the Unspoken to observe the impact of thoughts and speech upon Earth."

The Void, the Unspoken, the Bardo, Purgatory! Pick a name! "Does that place have anything approaching an agreed-upon title?"

"No," said Gethsemane, in a tone flat enough that the General once more laughed. The nymph smiled slightly at the sound. "Your holy books tell a story called 'the Tower of Babel'...that place is like the tower. It cannot be directly communicated one way for all to understand because your people speak so many different languages, and each believe only one of those languages correct. I speak of spiritual symbolism, General. Not true language. It is hard to find a neutral word that can describe something across all tongues without ire, just as it is hard to find a neutral symbol that can describe something across all faiths. But there is a man in the East—*our* East, General—who is a very wise man: the Wisest in the World. When he is in the West, he must labor to repent for crimes he committed out of arrogance. But, when he is in the East and has worked off his burden, he is called the Engineer, and he is as good to his people as any king. I have spoken to him many times before, and he once told me Earth's globally preferred term for the Void. He said learnéd men believe it is what they call 'the Ergosphere.'"

"The Ergosphere," repeated Dominia. "Isn't that—isn't that the area around a black hole?"

"A rotating black hole of the sort once a sun; yes, those are the words that people of Earth prefer to describe these places."

"We were in a *black hole*," enthused the General, mouth opened, hand releasing Gethsemane's in surprise. The girl, without any sense of wonder, looked plainly up at her.

"No, General. We are currently in it, or, at least, upon what you would call its event horizon, where all the information of eternity is stored. The black hole that waits at the end of time for all life to return home is existent in your time, has been existent since the creation of Sol, and before. It does not seem as such, because time's illusion has hidden it; if you viewed all things from the black hole's perspective, you would understand all things simply are."

Her hands upon the top of her head as though to contain its contents, Dominia marveled up and around. "But there's a *sun* in the sky," she tried. The nymph nodded.

"The sun exists, General. Therefore, the sun must be here. Long, long ago, your scientists corrected the notion that black holes are mouths made to devour reality. They are mouths that *speak* it: holding all words upon their tongues until the moment they must manifest as sound, yet containing them even once they have been spoken so as to use them again in a different way, during a future conversation."

It took some fantasy naiad to tell her a science fact that would have made her understand the Void weeks ago! "Why didn't Valentinian and Lazarus just explain that to me?"

"Such a notion is frightful to those who fear standing at the end of eternity; and while in that space where the Ergosphere has exposed the malleable field of the universe that magicians call 'aether' and scientists call 'the Higgs field,' misunderstanding this revelation can cause total destruction of the body and mind. Anything one thinks may become reality there. Even brief thoughts of total annihilation can be deadly. Therefore, one must come to understand the nature of the space when they are upon solid ground of one form or another; it keeps them from being carried away." With another look at the sun, Gethsemane extended her hand. "If you please, General. We have some ways to walk, and the day here passes as it does on Earth: regardless of how we spend its minutes."

Pretty embarrassing, to have spent so much time in the Ergosphere that basic facts of reality needed re-explained. "But if we're in a black hole now and when we're in that—Ergosphere, what is the black sun in the sky?"

"It is Earth, General, standing at the end of time, at the outer edge of the Ergosphere along whose inner edge you walk. When you look up into the black orb, you are putting your attention back on your home planet and time: 'coming down to Earth,' you could call it."

Behind the nearest hill sprawled a vast and well-manicured orchard. Seeing it, Gethsemane cut off the main path. The house was so large it seemed not a home but an inn; Dominia suspected this was so based on the two sets of sprawling stables. Amid the trees, she was back begging for help from the ill-fated McLintocks; but the parallels only increased when Gethsemane, rather than using the orchard for a shortcut and passing by the house, stopped to knock upon the front door. After a moment, a gentle-looking woman lined by middle age answered them, smiling pleasantly, her "Yes?" becoming an "Oh!" when she recognized the General. "Oh, *my*," said the lady, and Gethsemane smiled.

"Please, miss?" The Bearer seemed to be asking something implied, and the woman inside looked delighted by her unexpected guests.

"I didn't know they were *my* horses... Eric"—the woman called to a boy unseen—"would you watch the pot? I have to take care of something."

The woman, wiping her hands upon her apron, stepped outside and shut the door behind her. As Dominia tried to find something recognizable in her face and found nothing—to her relief, as she'd half expected Carol McLintock at the door—the smiling woman assessed her in return.

"*Well*," said the stranger. "Well, would you look at this!"

"I'm sorry...do I know you?" It was becoming the question of Dominia's lifetime.

"Oh, everybody knows everybody when they come to live here." With a wave of her hand, the woman led them to the smaller set of stables. "You just don't remember that, because you haven't come to stay. Though you'd ought to consider it sometime."

"She will," said the nymph. "Eventually, in a long time. She cannot, not until—"

"Oh, of course. That certainly would keep her from settling down in comfort..." Behind the doors of the structure painted merry pinks and blues like no stables Dominia had seen (but akin to the magician's signpost, she noticed), a humdrum of conversation buzzed; but, as the woman pushed open the doors, a few whispered noises hurried the others to silence, and the hinges swung wide to reveal a perfectly mute, normal collection of horses. More stocky and primitive—older models, say—than the ones to which she'd grown accustomed, and doubtless slower than the mechanical variety favored by animal-rights activists—but horses nonetheless, and fine ones, at that.

"Take whichever two you need. I'll just have Eric pop into town and pick them up from the hotel tomorrow. Have you eaten?" she asked Dominia, then turned to Gethsemane. "Has she eaten?"

"Not since coming," the girl answered for the General, which elicited a maternal click of the woman's tongue.

"Take some fruit on your way out. And why don't I get you bread—"

Remembering Valentinian's warning about "fairyland rules," Dominia tried to politely decline by saying, "Please, don't trouble yourself," but the lady had already darted for her house, perfectly comfortable leaving two strangers alone with her horses.

"If everybody here is so friendly," said the General, "I might be tempted to stay after all."

"Everyone who visits is tempted; but no one ever does before the time is right. It would not be the same if you had another calling elsewhere."

Maybe so. Still, she remained tempted, for, yes, everyone *was* as friendly as the woman whose name Dominia realized she hadn't gotten while they rode away. As they resumed along the main road, now seated upon a pair of marble mares who knew the route, she found new license to marvel around her. Passing vast fields of colorful crops and pens of docile oxen, she found these no more extraordinary than the animals to which she was accustomed; and it was safe to say the startled bird that just went screeching from the nearby tree was a redheaded woodpecker and not some miniature dragon.

Yet the General sensed an ancient magic about the place—or perhaps projected such qualities upon it, since she had spent so long navigating the Ergosphere with a magician and a mystic. Stunning to think herself upon its other side, walking the surface of a black hole as convincing a planet as any other—yet a kinder, gentler planet than the one she knew. Upon that road, they began to pass friendly person after friendly person, and Dominia was astonished by every smile and wave and doff of a cap. Humans in her world had been so long terrorized that, passing a stranger, one tended to avoid all eye contact and hurry one's pace in case that stranger was a martyr.

There were no martyrs here, Gethsemane had said. But were there humans here? Were these people human? Was *she* human while visiting here? She could not rightly say; but she sensed it was somehow improper to describe these people as anything, let alone "human." From her experience in the Ergosphere, she had retained most poignantly the notion that it was useless to try to name or discern anything. She had asked more questions than she could remember, and their answers did no good. Even the satisfaction of achieving a model compatible with her preferred worldviews (that her Father was no closer to God or Eternity or anything than anybody else, among other aspects) did her no good, per se. It did not teach her *how* to do anything; it did not tell her *why*. She could ask forever "what" and "but" and never be satisfied, and not because she was not asking the right questions. There were no right questions to *ask*. The experience was communicated piecemeal, over—and by—time.

And how loath was the curious General to accept that notion!

Still, it was good to be where one could think on anything, and the world around would remain in physical place. Good to listen to the birds, and not the constant chatter of the men. And pleasant to do so in the company of a beautiful woman, who studied the General from time to time, riding respectfully along her left side. Yet, the blonde curls of that woman—

"Stop, General." Dominia leapt as Gethsemane stirred her from thought with a hand upon her wrist. "I do not mean to intrude upon your meditations, but I hear their ripples in the Waters and know the shade does, also."

"Oh," said Dominia, her tone bitter enough to curl her lip. "Even here?"

"Even on Earth, though in a muted and indirect way. But here, it is clear; the medium by which we move now is not mass, but potentiality, who, fleet-footed, carries information in a wink."

"And in the Ergosphere?"

"Light," answered the girl.

"So Valentinian is using light to read my thoughts. Like the red eye that reflects out in a photograph; that's somehow carrying information from my brain, into the Ergosphere?"

"All mediums of energy are also mediums of thought; it is a matter of the thoughts being communicated in different ways. When thoughts are given sluggish mass in the material world, they must communicate over time and through more obvious means. You must give your thoughts energy of their own, whether by speech or by giving them physical form. But in the Ergosphere and in the Kingdom, those who are sensitive and who know the secrets of the Water can hear much if they listen. And those who *are* the Water, as is the shade of your wife, cannot help but hear all communications, subtle or otherwise."

"So you're saying it can't help but torment me," said Dominia, disappointed to feel such an ugly way in such a beautiful place. The girl, her affect as muted as it had been since they'd met, nonetheless looked upon her with a particular gentleness. Taking the General's hand, she lifted it to her lips and kissed its knuckles.

"In a sense, this is so. But to it, it is not tormenting you. It seeks you, as you seek your wife. If you are to find her, however, you must not be so pained and regretful. I hope to make you less so."

Flustered into a thudding heart and annoyed by her fluster, the gruff General slipped her hand out of the girl's and primly took her own horse's reins. "Thanks for being honest. Can you lay off the thought-reading, please?"

"Certainly, but I will not need to read your mind to know your next set of thoughts."

"Oh?" asked Dominia, not seconds before her stomach growled. The girl laughed, and the General recognized that the sensation of vague nausea that had been growing since her arrival was not nausea but hunger. Normal hunger: for food, not for flesh. With a muffled, alien cheer, the nymph slipped her hand into the picnic basket packed against the saddle and withdrew a handkerchief full of jerky along with a chunk of dense, soft bread.

"You will be shy about eating, perhaps, but you must not be. You have to eat while you stay here, or else you will starve, just as you would starve on Earth were you a human."

"These aren't some creep's evil thoughts?" This elicited a small smile from the girl, who removed a hunk of soft cheese and a bright ruby apple from the pack.

"As much as any other foodstuff. I must also eat if I wish to stay on land, though I will not starve; I will evaporate. Food keeps us grounded here, you see?"

As if through the thickest of fogs.

"Fog," Dominia said aloud. "Water Bearers. You serve the Lady. She actually exists, huh?"

"Even after all this time, you have not believed."

"I've been skeptical. Lazarus is a known quantity—and criminal—to m...y people, but the Lady is fictional."

"To you, and, as you said, to your people. She is real to everyone else; even the people here know of the Lady, although She does not walk about this place. Her avatars do, as any other person here. But the Lady is the substance of this place."

Kind of a weird thought. "So I won't meet Her here?"

"One of Her avatars," answered the girl, gaze caught by something glinting in the distance that also drew Dominia's eye. As if punched in the solar plexus, the General gripped the reins of the horse and observed the distant disk of the glittering City.

"Incredible." This, from the woman who had seen a thousand towns and decimated half as many. But for those many glorious cities, there were none so radiant as this: circles within circles, twisting spokes like the rays of a sun lapping upon itself, or an egg dividing in the womb, or perhaps a spiral flower. The marble of its buildings glistened in the distance and seemed to breathe with life. A thin cornflower ribbon of river trailed through its center yet didn't break the pattern of buildings so much as highlight them. With a smile, Gethsemane admired her stunned face, turning away only when the General returned to herself well enough to look over.

"You should see it at night. All the candlelit and gaslit quarters look so soft...and there are a few electric quarters, but they are tucked deeper, so they cannot poison the sky. *They* see the sky, of course; but the City is built so it spirals within itself forever, and the more unsightly quarters therefore rest within its coils."

"Sounds like a terrible place to get lost."

"The best place. If you become lost in the City, it means it has a surprise for you: a gift, or a lesson, or even a friend that you never would have given to yourself."

Dominia knew only one thing she wanted, so it wasn't hard to give her something she wouldn't consider. Yet, she sensed it wasn't the usual flimflam peddled by "psychics" and snake-oil salesman; perhaps this place was more causal than the Ergosphere, but she sensed it was just as much ruled by synchronicity, or more.

Many people milled along the slope of the final hill between them and this extraordinary fractal, some pausing to wait for friends, some chatting along their way to join the line through the gate that seemed mere formality. There, a chipper guard in silver armor recognized the Bearer—and, after a moment of consideration, Dominia.

"Aha! She came. Thank goodness! The magician's been on my back about you for a week."

Oh, her friend! "He's been here for a week?"

"Well, I don't know I can rightly say *that*... He tends to come and go without the gate, so I can't keep track of him." This irked the fellow but mildly, and he adjusted his helmet with a hearty laugh. "Not that what he gets up to is any of my business, but, well, it *is* my job to keep track of folks coming in and out. Just for census purposes, mind."

Behind them, someone politely coughed, and he appeared to remember there was a line of people extending quite far along the road behind the women; he chuckled. "But look at me, yammering on! Go on, ladies. Good to see you now, Gethsemane."

"And you, Martin." With a wave, the girl urged her horse down the populated main street.

There was no place like this—not in all the world. Though she supposed it *was* the world, if Gethsemane had spoken truth. Her world, and all other worlds. Even Acetia, if it wasn't fictional—or even if it was. This much was revealed as true when she saw not the Renaissance fair she expected but a dreamlike mishmash of cultures, peoples, and *times*. That, perhaps, was the most startling thing. Some guy wearing goofy neon shorts and carrying a big black box playing ancient music passed a gentleman whose clothes resembled the pre-martyr era known to humans as "Victorian," whose style Dominia recognized because Lavinia was obsessed. Yet she spied plenty of sport coats, T-shirts, and many woman wearing pants; there was no shortage of varieties and no telling upon whom or what one might lay eye. And all of that did not begin to touch the buildings! So many facades, of an extraordinary variety of styles that only distinguished themselves as more than generic but beautiful buildings of ultra-white stone when one drew near enough, or viewed them from straight on—as if an effect of light shaped the building's purpose. Were it not for the horses, Dominia surely would have been bumping into passersby. The nymph smiled at her inattention, and the thoughtful furrow of her brow.

"You are bothered, General?"

"Nothing here is what I expected...not even the clothes. I guess I had a certain...vision. When I saw you, and your outfit."

"The City has a way of defying that. It is an interesting place! There are many who dress like me—in simpler cloth or silk, not bark. These are native Westerners."

Born in a black hole? Her mind reeled but the girl hardly paused. "Some are born in the City, but perhaps more are born in the Country without it, as was the queen of this Era. Often, these move here after waiting their whole lives, and they are more excited than anyone to be here, more curious about everything they see. These tend to make friends with their neighbors because they want to know all about them and the times they are from. And then there are many, many in the City who are refugees; all these are the ones in strange clothing."

"Refugees?"

"They do not belong here originally, but the City has taken them in. Our world, this black hole. It is"—the girl frowned in irresistible thought—"like a storage space. I do not know..."

"Like a hard drive?"

"Yes, General, perhaps; the Engineer would tell you, even while still the Doorman. I do not think we will see him today, though that is for the best... He can be long-winded."

"I know someone like that," said Dominia, thinking of her Father. Her lips quirked in a smirk the girl echoed.

As usual, the General's stream of questions may well have carried on without end all the way to the hotel: but, near the arched entrance of the marketplace—passed beyond the bridge over that sweet, crystal stream—a shout and commotion let up from her blind spot. Jerking her horse to a stop on instant defense, Dominia reached for her gun and hoped it had not been waterlogged into uselessness. No sooner had she turned her good eye to the noise's source, however, than she recognized the sound of her name on the lips of a certain breathless *Jun'yō* first mate: and there he was, running up to meet her. The chubby sailor, Tenchi Ichigawa.

Would you get out of town.

VIII

Bumps in the Night

Throughout her long career, Dominia had encountered more than a few people she'd previously victimized. Survivors thereof, at least. Of all these, the survivor of the *Jun'yō* massacre was by far happiest. "Dominia"—he cried her name while tripping down an aesthetically modern curb and only barely found his feet upon the cobblestones—"oh, wow, Miss Mephitoli! How are you?"

He halted before her, swabbing his forehead while huffing for breath, and bowed a few enthusiastic times she returned in awkward manner from atop the horse. "I didn't know I'd see you here! Not so soon, anyway. I'm sorry about my cousin. You know what a coward he can be..."

"It's all right." Dominia tried to smile. "You can't control René, and neither can anybody else... Anyway, I never expected to see you here."

Though confusion darted through the man's pursing lips, it soon resolved. "Oh, I see! My goodness—what a thing, time!" As he laughed, Dominia turned a look of concern to Gethsemane. While Tenchi had been a rather cheerful, almost dopey fellow, he now seemed to be rather, well... "doped up." That didn't concern the nymph.

"You are from the General's future." She stroked the neck of her shifting mare while the sailor nodded. "I urge you, hold your tongue."

"Yes, ma'am! I wouldn't say anything. Only...ah, I'm so happy to see you, Dominia!"

Not her Tenchi—the Tenchi she'd known—but the Tenchi of the future. A disturbing notion. Oh, she'd gathered the eternal nature of the City from the clothes of its inhabitants, but she hadn't stopped to think that eternity included all future as well as all past. Which passing faces would be familiar in some future visit?

"You are a refugee," observed the nymph of Tenchi, drawing the General from her thoughts as her companion took up the reins of her impatient mount.

While she spoke, she urged the animal forward, and Dominia's followed. "I was explaining the hotel—about to, at any rate."

"Oh, you haven't checked in yet? You'll love the hotel, Dominia. I'm the courier!"

"You work here?" she asked as the man fell into stride with her good side.

"You have to work someplace if you're going to stay." His eyes glowed with the earnest depth of his words. "Contribute to society as a helpful member! I guess on Earth they'd call this place 'communist,' huh? But it's not like that... I mean, it's true, I just got through delivering Mrs. McLintock's paycheck, and she'll just give it back to the—"

"Mrs. McLintock?" The name shocked her so to hear that Dominia practically felt her own pupil shrink. Tenchi didn't notice.

"Yes: she's a barker at one of the vegetable stands. A refugee like me...a little different, though."

The nauseating snap of Carol's neck, seconds after the quieter one of her daughter's. Dominia trembled with horror and shame, her fingers tightening around the reins. Horror and shame—yet, hope.

"Mrs. McLintock was a Lazarene?" asked Dominia of Tenchi, whose eyes sprang in the direction of the nymph's back. "Is her son here, too?"

"Well—that is, I don't—"

Gethsemane, hiding her annoyance for the babbling sailor, turned to say, "Mrs. McLintock was made a Lazarene in childhood; her son and daughter were not inducted into the philosophy, as she never entirely believed, and her husband did not trust even a martyr such as Lazarus."

That hope dissolved into nothing; Dominia sat back upon her saddle. "Forced to be here without her children? She can't want that."

"No one is forced to be here," Tenchi blurted, his voice a defensive pitch. "If she is here, it's because she wants to be."

"Yet this place is supposed to be a black hole encompassing everything?"

"All space, General, all time. All things are here—all planets, all stars. Ours is not the mere black hole of an ordinary galaxy; when one is upon its event horizon, one understands all black holes are the same black hole, for they will eventually all submit to their own dismissal. Like a slate wiped clean."

So where was the McLintock boy? She couldn't stand to go into the marketplace and ask Carol in person. Not after she had shot the child in front of the harried mother, whether Dominia had a reason or no. The General dared not contemplate what would happen then, what had happened after the boy died, no more than she could contemplate what had happened before the boy, before she, before anyone, was born. She had tried to conceptualize that state while on her journey and found it almost impossible. How could something emerge from nothing? Consciousness from unconsciousness, matter from space? How did the magician create something from nothing? The Higgs fields responsible for giving particles mass was a fine explanation, but what was that field? What, really? God? Then what had Dominia to do with the oscillations of reality? She could not think on it too much. Could not think that all things happened in patterns, that she eternally put a bullet into the head of Mrs. McLintock's son, just as Cassandra had done to herself. That was surely why, when Tenchi said, "Maybe I can introduce you, and you can see she's happy," Dominia forced a polite smile.

"I don't think that we'll have time today. Soon. But what about the innkeeper? Or—hotel clerk." It was hard to think of this place having a hotel rather than an inn, but she tried to erase the preconceived notions of language. "Who sent you to pay Mrs. McLintock?"

An important question, because sending this courier at this time to that woman was not anything close to coincidence. Perhaps it was the synchronistic nature of the City, but this smelled deliberate. Gethsemane all but confirmed this when, in response to Tenchi's exclamation that, "She's a great lady," the nymph corrected, "*the* Lady."

Was it rude to snort? She couldn't help it. "Your goddess is an inn—a hotel clerk here?"

"My goddess's avatar...or, rather, the spirit of the woman displaced when the goddess possessed her body. This old soul of the vessel does good works in the City to pay for her stay, like everyone else; she is responsible for managing the refugees."

"This was Lazarus's girlfriend?" asked the General.

"Not for many cycles, not since she first birthed the magician. But the magician has since become a self-created man with no need for a mother, so his mother is liberated to achieve her true potential as an individual."

"Sounds like she's anything but an individual. She submitted her body to an alien consciousness."

"No. She discovered the divine within."

Any further questions were silenced by the ringing of the crystal clock tower towering above the busy market. Startled, Tenchi looked at a watch he didn't have, patted his head as if in search of a hat, and said with an apologetic bow, "Is that the time? I should go, Dominia, but I'm happy to see you! Please come to stay soon."

"Okay." Off he dashed, at a pretty brisk pace for his size. "Bye for now, Tenchi."

As he disappeared around a corner, Dominia realized Gethsemane had stopped before a building whose anachronistic facade was still rather disorienting to behold. It resembled an historic San Valentino high-rise, built of that same ultrafine substance (a kind of post-white stone that glowed like marble, resembled sandstone, and felt like silk) the rest of the City had used. But, compared to the split-level roads rolling past quaint shops and spiraling in all directions to reveal more lovely white buildings, the yawning hotel resembled an invasive species. Even its gargoyles, hanging animatedly from their pedestals in the midst of acrobatic tricks, were a design feature apparently unique to this neighborhood.

Yet no matter how interesting its exterior, Tenchi was right: little compared to its insides. If a tall building without, within it was infinite, and made no effort at disguise. Upon entrance to the gilded lobby, the General spent so long with her head craned in search of a miles-distant ceiling that she almost bumped into one of an immaculate pair of chiseled lions that, flanking the entrance, lifted their paws in greeting from the fronds of sumptuous ferns. The sprays of orchids, a perfect aqua like none she'd seen, startled her with the revelation that she *had* seen the color before: woven into a crown in the hands of the *tulpa*, and sprinkled around the pond of the Bearers. She was then drawn to examine the quartet of gold-and-marble columns disappearing into the distant heights of that infinite ceiling. Everywhere she looked, another stunning objet d'art awaited, and that included the woman at the counter: she looked from her paperwork with a brusque sigh, which blew from her lips a flaming lock of hair.

"Another new guest." She spoke more to herself than to them as she turned to consult a wall of keys stretching beyond reach, or reason. "And staying how long?"

Gethsemane folded her hands upon the edge of the pearl counter. "Only one night, and with me."

"You have a room here?" asked Dominia of the nymph, who nodded.

"I am a creature of water, but also of land, and when I come to land, I must have a place to stay here in the City... It would not be right of me to keep a house if I did not use it every day."

While Dominia's brain tried to work out the amphibious nature of her companion, the hotel clerk lifted her scarlet cap to tuck that obtrusive hair, only a few shades less red, beneath. "That's good," she said with a relieved glance at the General. "I was getting tired just looking at you. You're a perfectly fine woman, Dominia, but you wouldn't believe the paperwork required when somebody needs a new room."

"I'm sure," she said, not surprised that the woman whose name tag read "Trisha" knew her name. "I don't know you, right?"

"Do you know anyone, anymore?"

With a small smirk, the General tried, "Will I ever know you?"

"Not as you are, and not in a personal way. But maybe in a Biblical way." She winked at the blushing General and added, "If you play your cards right."

"Aha." Dominia laughed and coughed, her brain whirring for focus. "Well...what's our—uh, our room number? Gethsemane?"

"606," answered the nymph, who accepted their key from Trisha. Free, the chuckling clerk merrily tapped her fingers along what Dominia recognized as an invisible keyboard of the sort popular when she was young, when the "in" thing was to have a computer so unobtrusive you could easily forget where it was and wind up knocking it from your desk.

"Breakfast is at five in the morning and runs for four hours." While she explained the rules, Trisha sometimes raised a delicate finger to tap the almost extra-dimensionally thin screen only visible from her side of the desk. "Leave your dirty towels on the bathroom floor and, please, try to keep it down after eight in the evening. We have a lot of older guests, and a lot of unwell guests who need their rest."

"We'll be good," answered Gethsemane, which may have been the first not-serious thing Dominia had ever heard her say. The laughing porter wiggled her fingers as the nymph made her way to the elevator.

"Aren't you always." Then, noting the General hesitated to leave her desk: "Is there something else you needed?"

The name "Carol McLintock" sat on the tip of her tongue, but for whatever reason, she could not make herself say it. Not that, or anything else about Tenchi. But, Tenchi did bring to mind his work; so, forced to come up with something to say, she asked, "Do I need some sort of job?" When that elicited a blank look, she pressed, "To stay here? People need to work, right?"

"Oh!" With a glance at Gethsemane's back, then at the General, she said again, "Oh!" and laughed. "You don't *know*! Goodness, I remember those days...kept like a mushroom, as my grandfather used to say. 'In the dark and covered in horseshit.'" Trisha waved her away. "No, darling, you don't need to work. You already have a job! It's perfectly fine."

"Is that job 'ending the martyr world'?" she asked grimly. The woman smiled in a way that flattered its host more than its recipient.

"It's rather more complicated than that, dear, but yes. Will you be needing the workout room's location?"

"No," grumbled the General, who made her way over as Gethsemane hit the brass elevator call button. "I think we'll be fine."

Only once the polished doors closed to sweep them to their sixth-floor room did Dominia think on her own hesitance to so much as speak of the McLintocks. She had killed many people, and Tenchi's presence positioned that thought in the forefront of her mind even before considerations of the boy. But this child's death sat poorly with Dominia. Children had been killed by her before, indirectly. The Black Night had been about 20 percent children in the final statistical reckoning. She had decimated whole cities in Japan and

Mexico until the Hunter cells they sought could be called "eliminated." But, like most cancerous cells, they only receded, mutated, and awaited a day they blossomed again. Akachi was their tumor. But, Akachi was also human.

"You know"—the elevator opened to their floor with a joyous chime—"I would like to make Tobias Akachi the last human being I ever kill."

The nymph held the door for Dominia. "That is a very nice idea."

"Do you think it's possible?"

"For you, General, anything is possible; but, please, don't be disappointed if things do not work out that way."

In a room less modern than the lobby (or even the plushly carpeted hallway down which they'd moved in silence), Dominia's attention remained tuned elsewhere. For instance: What had Carol McLintock looked like? As she wandered into the nymph's room, the General tried so hard to remember that she barely noticed the thin deerskin upholstery of the chair into which she slipped, or the dark-wooded interior which matched the "rustic" frame of the shabby-if-large bed across the room. At the time of the tragedy in the outskirts of the almost Jurisdiction-wide San Valentino, the General had been rather distracted; but she almost pieced together those aspects she'd failed to absorb. There was that tired beauty glimpsed as it fled through the house to please the Hierophant like a bird bashing against the bars of its cage. There was the edge of a plump lip, the glint of a mossy eye; but there was no whole, which, for some reason, filled the General with regret.

The nymph, having sparked a light in the glass lamp by the bed, drew her from her thoughts by resting upon the arm of her chair. "You are in most intense mourning, General."

"How do you commune with your goddess here"—her voice was hoarse as she unbuckled the Bearer's curious bark boots—"if the woman downstairs is the woman She inhabits, and She's supposed to be the substance of everything?"

"You know her." The milky curve of a perfect calf left the General shuddering while she worked free the next boot. "The Lady is found in every woman. As much in you as in me, or more."

"Okay," said the General, usually willing to agree with anything said by a cultist to end conversation, and always, for obvious reasons, willing to agree with anything said by a woman edging into her lap. There was as much self-flagellation among the religious martyrs of her barracks as mutual flagellation in any bedroom of Dominia's. It was as if, in the absence of any meaningful God, her deity had become violence, and that violence suffused everything about her. Cassandra had known that violence, though not always (and not always consensually, either); she had known it implicitly, like Benedict's skeleton enclosed in the foundation of their relationship.

But her wife had found pleasure in those small acts of violence, too, and Dominia had enjoyed her share of love-laced agonies. Perhaps it was just that when she thought of Cassandra, Gethsemane slapped her face.

"Shit," said the General as the Bearer clutched her restored hair.

"Miki Soto is right: you are a man, as much as any I have met. Your troubles are a man's troubles."

"They're a person's troubles," protested Dominia while struggling to extricate herself. "But I've heard I fight like a man, too, if you want to find out."

As she attempted to twist away, she confirmed herself no stronger in this place than an extraordinarily athletic human—not that she minded, when she noticed the free hand of the nymph had unzipped her jacket and now slipped a cold set of fingers beneath her cotton shirt.

"I am not concerned if you fight like a man, General, but I am curious if you fuck like one."

Scandalized, somehow, to hear such a word from this illustrious entity's Cupid's-bow mouth, the General turned her blushing face away and found no escape when the nymph straddled her lap. "I'm married."

"And if your wife were here, I would have her, too." Oh! Those lips! How soft they were: impossibly plush, so much so that Dominia sagged hers open at the lightest touch of them upon her jaw, her cheek, her mouth. "I told you when first I saw you and mistook you for a stranger that it is not often women of your needs arrive to us."

"And when we do?"

"We drown them, as we do the men." At the horrified sputtering this elicited, the nymph loosened the buckle of Dominia's belt. "Never fear, General. We are on land now; the bathtub is not large enough to drown you in, I think."

"Why do you drown them?"

"Why?" The nymph, who had knelt between the General's splayed legs in effort to better unzip her trousers, now looked up with pure curiosity filling the eyes beneath her golden curls. "No one has ever asked us that, General. Most just assume we eat them...but I suppose we do it because they are so happy when we have all played together, they submit to being drowned because they do not wish to tarnish the moment by allowing it to recede to memory. They would rather dwell there forever and allow us to dissolve their energies back into the pool of the Lady. Perhaps you will understand why."

"But my wife—"

"Will not be upset." Gethsemane lifted that wandering right hand to touch Dominia's good cheek. "Would she wish you to be so restless? So ascetic? Lonely?"

"Lonely." What a horrible word. Oh, Lamb, what a horrible word! Pain welled in the General's breast, and in her good eye. She shut it against the nymph's touch and turned her face away. All this time, surrounded by people, she had never had time to think of herself as lonely, but she was. She had been lonely since that final, horrible moment of Cassandra's life. She had been empty. No more the smell of sidewalk chalk on wholesome hands after school nights; never again the light in her eyes while extolling her new favorite book; lost was the way she looked at Dominia, sometimes, when she thought the General slept. The way Gethsemane looked at her now, with adoring innocence and deep concern.

"The gun stays close," she said, minding the holstered weapon clipped to her belt. "And the eye patch stays on."

"I would never dream of touching them, General."

Mysterious. The idea of sex had been repellent since Cassandra's death, and now in the space of—well, a few days, from her perspective—she had succumbed twice. No doubt the doppelgänger had sensed her weakness, and that was why so much nothing had so quickly swooped in to mock her with her dead wife's face. The guilt, too, played a hand. There was no way of knowing why the creature found her so quickly that first time: but it was easier to detect the cause this time, when the thought of repellent sexuality provoked immediate thoughts of the fiend. Thoughts unavoidable no matter what her limbs, tangled with Gethsemane's, got up to in the bed of the City's hotel. Yet the nymph, lips against the General's jaw, spoke no admonishments. She did not urge the General, as before, to turn her thoughts from that semi-formed study where it seemed she remained, nauseous, drunk on false wine and shame.

"Dominia." The voice of that thing, rooted in her memory, yet emerged from that memory to float, sourceless, within the room.

"It's here," breathed the General, turning through the haze of pleasure in search of the naiad's eyes. "Gethsemane—"

"Sh." Those lips planted upon Dominia's. "This hotel is its own space. Closer, perhaps, to the Ergosphere than to the Kingdom; yet the Kingdom leads to it more easily than the Ergosphere. It is the function of the attendant to repel pests that slip into the hotel from that place, you see, General—and to keep them from leaving the hotel at full strength. Once it is wounded, it is free to leave, for the guardsmen can eject it easily."

"But this pest?"

"Dominia," whispered Cassandra's voice. The General recognized with a clench of infantile terror that it emanated from under the bed.

"Surely there's something we can do." She turned her face in the silence of terror to regard with her good eye the edge of the bed and the leather jacket left upon the chair across the room. At least she had trousers to pull up. "What will it do if we try to get down?"

Gethsemane, unconcerned by her nudity, shrugged. "It will try to devour us."

Shock, cold and white, streaked through the General's body. "Valentinian said it can't kill us," she protested, though she heard him appending the words "in the Void" at the same time the nymph appended, "There. Here, it's more desperate to couple with you than ever. This place is a space of high density, eternity: you are more physical than you were in the Ergosphere, where falsity and reality are meaningless distinctions. You are of even higher density here than you are on Earth, though you could not possibly measure or perceive this effect. There is gravity to everything. Here, terms do have meaning. Here, General, words are everything. The thing in pursuit of you wishes to take advantage of that meaning. It wishes to reach you in a place from which it can easily slip into the real world and take on physical presence. Wouldn't you, if the alternative was a life of shadows and darkness?"

As Dominia reached for her gun, still at hand, Gethsemane stayed her. "Do not forget what the attendant said, please. We mustn't trouble the other guests."

Teeth clenched, she instead tore part of the pillowcase away and sprang neatly upon the floor four feet from the bed, a simple matter to any former child afraid for their life every bedtime. As her bare feet landed upon the wooden boards, an intake of breath like a lover's gasp hissed from beneath the box spring and left shuddering Dominia to dart far from the noise. With her eye set upon it, she backed toward the armchair, and the darkness beneath the bed breathed at the pace of the thing concealed. That thing sometimes twitched: a motion that, with Valentinian's light (as was all light in that place), illustrated mere glints of its bulbous gray shape. She cracked the coatrack over her knee in a grimacing act a deal harder than anticipated, which also left her glad she took care to exercise in her nightly life. Many martyrs relied on their advanced metabolism to increase their speed and strength, like her useless brother Theodore, or (she presumed) skinny Valentinian. In a place like this, without the endurance from actual training, they'd be as physically weak as kittens. Even Dominia bruised herself in the process of trying to snap the rack and came to the final solution of shattering it over the armchair, which also shattered—and yielded a more desirable proto-torch than anything she might have crafted with the precious seconds given her. After selecting an upholstered piece of wood for the nasty spring protruding from its tip, the General edged toward the nightstand and its waiting lamp.

With a howl, the horror whirled from beneath the bed; Dominia cried out along with previously unflappable Gethsemane, who bolted upright as the odious thing received a gouge across the—face?—courtesy of the General's weapon. Infuriatingly, the thing wheeled in the direction of that precious glass lamp. Jostled from position, it shattered on the floor.

The dark room shuddered as the laughing creature slithered off to regroup in some far corner. As the General clambered upon the nightstand, the nymph whispered, "Are you all right?"

She received no answer. Dominia's toe bumped the pack of matches with which Gethsemane had lit the lamp. In silence punctuated only by the arrhythmic sound of infected lungs rattling after moist breath, the General bent, took them in her hand, and struck a match.

Mixed feelings bloomed in that second of light. Relief, namely, because had she struck that match but half a second later, it would have been upon her. However, it was hard to deny the sheer terror that poisoned her body as that blipped image revealed it mere centimeters from her: the clearest and most fang-filled vision of its hanging, tattered flesh she'd yet to receive. A visage like that made even the General scream. The thing screamed, too, and, blinded, retreated beneath the bed. Jaw set, Dominia struck a second match and, deciding her torch to be too unfeasible a proposition, set the edge of the bed ablaze. Gethsemane cried out on instinct, for she still sat upon the mattress, and moved to quell it, but she recoiled when she saw that lurching, six-eyed fiend that, with a shriek out of time and space, threw odious gray arms above its writhing mandibles to retreat from the light into the shrinking shadows of the room.

"We have to kill it," Dominia insisted again. "I think we've made plenty of noise by now."

She drew her gun, and wondered how long—and how well—it had dried since her emergence from the pond. She feared its ability to fire, but, as always, human engineering impressed the martyr General, who shot a trio of bullets into the shape. It screamed in a duet of agonized voices: that of her dead wife, and that of something else.

"It found you by your grief and shame," said Gethsemane while sliding from the bed to back against the wall. In the shadows, the thing's blood oozed with unearthly viscosity. "But it would have always found you in your guilt, anywhere. By bringing it here, we can cripple it."

"Can we?" she was forced to ask, for it began to stagger up: but it did so from its position behind the door, which, thank the Lamb, flew open. Light from the gold-carpeted hallway streamed in to reveal, in glorious silhouette, that miraculous Lady named Trisha.

"I thought I told you girls about our noise policy. And I thought, Gethsemane, that we discussed our visitor policy already."

Ruby heels clicking with every step she took after the thing that fled her light, the attendant stooped to collect a piece of shattered coatrack. After regarding its heft, she used it to impale the screeching beast.

"All visitors must enter through the front and register with the desk.

Absolutely no exceptions! Can you imagine what kind of loony bin this place would be if I allowed my clients to run roughshod over me like that?"

The thing howled; the porter edged it closer to the dust-caked window, heedless of its efforts to pull itself the length of the stake. Indeed, Trisha emitted a pettish noise at that, and with a mighty shove baptized the thing in the flames of the bed. Its cries rose to alarming pitch, and the otherworldly *tulpa* thrashed in agony: while it lost control, the redhead stuck it through the dusty window as though the glass were made of plastic wrap, and the creature she expelled like a prosciutto-wrapped date upon a toothpick. She was not some toned woman of military or other physical might, yet the act was so careless Dominia was flabbergasted—more shocked, perhaps at the column of moonlight unleashed by the act, for she had not realized night was upon the city. She dashed to the window to watch her wife's profane imitation fall, screaming her name in thirty horrible voices, a final few feet before its deformed body shattered on the pavement.

Far from victorious, the General felt ill at the sight. Trisha dusted off her hands in theatrical symbol of victory and said, "There! No harm, no foul. I understand how these things can happen. This place is...special."

"I told her," Gethsemane said, pounding the blaze that started to overtake the bed. The General, still near the window, insisted, "Not soon enough."

Outside, the thing's pelvis twitched to kick its legs into a horrific mimicry of activity. These twisted limbs tried to drag its walking body east until its yet-unruined arm had to get in on the job. The forearm looked shattered, but the elbow, judging by the uncanny, crustacean pace and method of movement, remained intact.

"Shouldn't we go kill it?" asked Dominia.

With low urgency, the porter returned to the hall for a fire extinguisher she used to aid the nymph. "That's someone else's job now, dear. The guards will come and sweep it away, and that'll be that. Just try not to attract another one."

Grimly, Dominia stuck her head out the window to track the thing until it disappeared down some nondescript alleyway. Would they really find it?

"There." The blaze managed, Trisha planted hands upon her hips and pursed her lips to blow aside a lock of hair. As it moved, her expression flipped into a smile she allotted between her guests. "Aren't you glad we have such a strict noise policy?"

"Thank you for your help," Dominia finally remembered to say. The woman, a twinkle in her eye, doffed her cap.

"If I can give some friendly advice: guilt and sex never mix." As the General blushed, the porter laughed, and even Gethsemane smiled. "Neither do feelings of hopelessness and sex. Sex should be fun!"

"I'll try to keep that in mind." At Dominia's visible embarrassment, Trisha laughed.

"She's *very* shy for a military lady, isn't she."

"Very," agreed Gethsemane, who looked quite attractive draped nude upon the unsinged side of the bed. "And loyal as any. I hope you are not hurt, General, that our activities were meant to summon the thing; and I hope you are not hurt for the sake of your wife."

"Oh, now, there's no shame in fun! I'm sure Cassandra would know that." The name twisted Dominia's stomach as it came unexpectedly from the mouth of Trisha, this woman who the General had only met an hour or so before. "This is a different sort of thing, after all. Spiritual, for one."

"Our love was spiritual," said defensive Dominia. Gently, the porter laughed, glanced at her watch, then strode over to peek down the hall.

"Of course. I didn't mean to imply otherwise." Satisfied the way was empty, she leaned back into the room and, causing another, different flutter in Dominia's stomach, locked the door. "But there's spiritual love between two people; then, there's...well. Something else. Something just as deep, in the opposite direction. Honest, naked physicality"—the first few buttons of her top opened at the slight touch of her hand—"can be as deep a route to the divine as any profound, self-sacrificing love."

Dominia opened her mouth to object but found that she could not, because she had never opened her mind to the notion before. For no real reason, she remembered Cicero's stupidest catchphrase: "If one opens one's mind too wide, people will throw garbage into it." Maybe that was because Cicero couldn't distinguish garbage from jewelry. As the porter crossed the room to kiss the Bearer of that goddess both her new friends served, Dominia found her own line between trash and gems perfectly clear.

IX

The Orbit of **Dominia**$_0$

There was no more thinking of Cassandra that night, except in narrow corridors of thought between starbursts. Yes: beautiful, carefree fireworks. Dominia didn't know how close she felt to any divinity, but there did seem something liberating in renewed ability to surrender to someone who had nothing to do with Cassandra. Gethsemane alone had not allowed this surrender, and the General had resisted Miki's playful come-ons due to the seriousness of her quest. But, perhaps because the horror had (for now) been purged, she nearly floated above the ruined bed. The nymph dozed at the foot, curled like a cat, to make room for the porter. Body contorted around the burned spot, Trisha dreamily traced the lines of the General's palm.

"Is this place heaven?" Dominia asked, and her lucid bedfellow chuckled.

"I suppose it might be for some, but there are more heavenly places than this. It is a fine place, though."

"Where do souls fly on death, if not the event horizon of the black hole?"

"Oh, it depends. Some go in the direction of earthly Jerusalem, but as its substance in the Void—its interference pattern, if you'd like. Valentinian likes his movie theater metaphors, but I prefer holograms, because it's more accurate. That's what the Lady, the black hole at the end of time, is doing to us. Projecting us back to the beginning of time—creating time. Within the Ergosphere is the interference pattern of reality. Therefore, the interference pattern of Jerusalem is the same as physical Jerusalem, and the souls sense it. Much confusion has been caused by ignorance. Exoteric teachings of any church, taken without thought for the true profundity of the encoded metaphors, pose danger to the soul and cannot free it from the hologram. Whether they're part of the projected image, or the interference pattern, if they cannot rise above it and reenter it willingly, it's all the same. Mecca has the same problem, as does any holy city... Irreligious souls—the souls of materialists who don't believe in anything, for instance—

tend to float around, waste away, if they haven't developed their own frame of reference to get themselves someplace like this. Some never even became conscious enough to experience death, and these don't even notice they've died... they generally don't have souls, though, except in some cases."

"What do you mean, they don't have souls?"

"Just that. The soul is a product of sentient consciousness mated with the ego, the sense of self, whatever you want to call it. If somebody only has an ego and never achieves this consciousness, they're in something of a pickle. One can't exactly sail the seas without *some* vessel. Even a barrel will do in a pinch. The blood of Lazarus is physiologically triggering the production of a soul through manipulation of the genome; in fact, a theory I developed before I hosted the Lady—never published, understand—was that the successful development of an individual's soul could be indicated based on the associated genetic markers triggered by the process, but you understand why it would be hard to convince the materialist scientist crowd to see the pattern if they don't believe in souls. Goodness knows I used to be one, myself!"

She could relate. Did Cassandra have a soul? The General had long since taken the nonexistence of souls for granted, but now she was bothered. "What about reincarnation?"

"I suppose that exists, but not in the way you mean it." As she spoke, she pressed her lips to the General's knuckles, then rose to re-dress. Dominia pursed her lips.

"You mean it in the sense of living the same life, over and over again."

"Until you become conscious, yes. Trying to escape that hologram, aren't we, dear."

"Doesn't that seem torturous?"

"That's what the Bible means when it talks about hell, or what the Buddhists call *saṃsāra*. Only the material world that your Father grossly claims to be his is so full of pointless death, pain, and boring restrictions on metaphysical truths. Real hell is being stuck living in his cycles forever without ever becoming conscious enough to pull yourself out." She bent to reclaim her abandoned undies, and Dominia struggled to focus on the conversation. "But even that isn't so bad...after all, you used to be one of the unconscious horde"—she slid the panties over those creamy thighs while the General sighed—"and you don't remember it, do you?"

"No, but it's frightening. So nihilistic. The idea that I'll experience it again."

"If you're actually conscious, you'll never have to." The porter crept around the room while engaging in her reverse striptease, her words a murmur. "I understand why death seems frightening—I felt much the same—but these days, I understand it better. It's not as bad as we all make it out to be; I mean, it's not as if they don't still exist, those members of the soulless dead."

"Where are they, then? If without a soul they drown—I guess, *are* the black grounds of the Ergosphere—then how could they be saved?"

"What do I look like," asked Trisha, buttoning her blouse, "the Lady?"

"But I thought—"

A sharp knock rapped upon the door. Annoyed (but, due to her career, used to being interrupted after, or even during, intimate moments), the General draped a blanket over stirring Gethsemane, then retrieved her shirt and pants. "Just a moment," Trisha called, one lascivious eye upon Dominia.

When it was appropriate, the demi-dog came trotting in upon the porter's say. "Didn't mean to interrupt your sleepover, ladies." Typical that Valentinian's first sentence to her in what felt like too long should have been a half-assed apology. "Refreshed?"

Behind the bed, Dominia zipped her leather jacket. "I could have used some time to rest."

"There's time to rest when you're dead, as my grandmother always said." Valentinian turned to Trisha with a lecherous quirk to his smile—wasn't she supposed to have been his mother? A long time ago, Dominia supposed. He was a martyr, after all; the Lamb and El Sacerdote, lest she forget, had once been brothers. A few hundred years passing by changes your mind, and breeding is never a concern; what was some extra friendliness among flesh-eating relatives, then? So most rationalized, but Dominia stubbornly maintained that, rather than some bizarre sign of superiority, incest was gross even in cases of adoption. Maybe she just felt that way because she hated her Family, or because the Hierophant was aggressively asexual and hammered the point that all sex was ultimately the same fruitless time waster among his violent people. Therefore, she had to take the opposite stance by drawing a line somewhere, and she wasn't alone, because about 40 percent of martyrs in any given poll of the populace stood right there with her.

That didn't stop Valentinian, though. For once ignoring her thoughts, he dug out his smokes and waggled a brow. "You want a cigarette, Trish?"

"Oh, no, darling." She laughed and patted his chest, sliding past him in a weird way that gave Dominia the creeps. "You know I quit smoking."

"I still have questions for you," the General called after her. The porter paused to listen. "Is it true you were Valentinian's mother?"

"Once, the first time, a long time ago. But he's a self-made man, now. I don't think we'd be passing any DNA tests on the subject."

"Sorry, babe. Lots of mutations, traveling through all those dimensions and all those worlds. Not to mention all those animals!"

Dominia laughed at him, but kept pressing. "What about the McLintocks? What do you have to do with them?"

With a giggling glance at her watch, stylishly positioned to face her inner wrist, the porter adjusted her hat. "You'll have to address that to Mrs. McLintock." A sassy wiggle in her hips, Trisha strolled from sight, and the magician watched her go before turning his arched brow to Dominia.

"A-plus, am I right?"

"Please." The General pinched the bridge of her nose, her eye squeezing shut. "I'm sure you've, like...transcended mortal values, or something, because you've spent so much time in either the—Ergosphere, or the bodies of animals, but...you've got to know how creepy you are."

"Ah, things are different here. The information is organized differently. Didn't Gethsemane tell you that? Hey, kiddo." He acknowledged the sleepy nymph, who lifted her head to force open heavy eyelids. "Thanks for collecting her."

"It is my honor, sire." That head lowered back and disappeared beneath the blanket. "The General is a hero."

"She sure is."

"Well, she *feels* like a fool." Arms crossed, Dominia glanced over her shoulder at the shattered panes. A breeze trickled in to sweeten the room and prove that not even a broken window was an objectively unpleasant experience here. "I'm sorry I wandered off into the dark like that. I didn't mean—"

"You didn't do anything wrong." The magus crossed to examine the frame. "The night had to pass somehow."

"You might have warned me, though." The annoyed General accepted one of the cigarettes he withdrew; after considering she might be smoking his thoughts, she let him light it, anyway. "I was worried I'd never see you again. That I'd never see *me* again."

"That'll never happen, buddy. I'm sorry you were afraid, but I'm glad you made it here."

"I'm still not *sure* what happened." When she struggled to recall the wandering, she still felt her body's muscles were those of that otherworldly predator. "I was lost in the dark, and then the dark was the water."

"I told you, General," insisted Gethsemane's soft voice beneath the blanket. "Someone was praying for you."

"Probably Miki," agreed Valentinian. "She's a pious girl. You should ask her!"

The idea of Miki Soto as some pious nun made Dominia laugh. Valentinian smiled in perfect patience.

"You'll see her soon enough...ready to go?"

"Where to?"

"Earth! Sweet relief." A tinkling sound caught Dominia's attention, and she looked in time to see what her brain first mistook for rain. Broken glass refilled the window frame as though the magician rewound time. Once the pane sat as good as new, he pushed the window open to finish his cigarette.

For a funny moment, Dominia felt the window had only been put there in the first place because of his courtesy. That the City and the man were somehow the same. Such a thing was easier to fathom in the Ergosphere, where the concept of definition was nothing but a meaningless hamper on thinking. That the Hierophant and his study should be one was less incredible than the idea that Valentinian—this goofy, lazy, chain-smoking (of tobacco and pot, it seemed) martyr saint trapped in a dog's body—was somehow inextricably tied to this strange place tucked within the event horizon of oblivion.

Yet, as he turned, and those electric eyes set upon her, they provoked a crackle in her blood. She felt obliged to tell him, "That thing followed us here, or was summoned by us, or something. I'm sorry. Hopefully the City's men will be able to control it."

"It was bound to show up eventually. Now that it's crippled, it'll need lots of time to recover, and won't be able to follow you around. Certainly not to reality."

Squinting through the smoke of her cigarette, the General asked, "Did you tell Gethsemane to do this?"

"What"—he touched his ear with one hand and flicked his cigarette out the window with the other—"who? Me? Huh? I can't hear you."

"You really are a terrible liar."

"Still can't hear you."

"You heard me," she said, trying not to laugh.

He raised his voice to ask, "Why don't you try speaking up?"

"Did you—" began the General loudly, eliciting a shush from the nymph.

"General! Noise policy!"

The magician had used this time to beat it to the hallway, of course. In a combination of irritation and wry amusement, Dominia considered her own half-burned "herbal" cigarette, then drew the covers from the nymph's curly head. With a smoky kiss upon those soft lips, the General asked, "Will you come back to Earth with us?"

"I am already there." Gethsemane patted Dominia's cheek, then rested that delicate hand upon her shoulder. "You will be so surprised when you see me, General."

"How is it possible for you to be in two places at once without leaving here?"

"Everyone on Earth is in two places at once, General, all the time. The Kingdom is Eternal. The most amazing thing is what you and all those Lazarenes do: you can choose at any moment to reside only in Eternity, then change your mind. Most can never change their mind."

With one last study of the delicate woman's beauty, Dominia placed the cigarette in the corner of Gethsemane's mouth, patted her pert little rear, then exited the room with only one pang of regret. Surprisingly, not regret for what she had done, but for leaving the nymph behind.

It was naïve, considering her age, but Dominia had never understood the mechanics of casual sex. Granted, she'd had plenty of it. Women (sometimes literally) tripped in front of the infamous General for a chance to visit her bed, and more than a few had courted, coaxed, and coddled her in hopes of becoming a member of the Holy Family. Only Cassandra had ever been worth that, but Dominia had enjoyed the attention before that fateful seaside meeting. What she had not enjoyed, however, was the procession of selfishness, hurt, and loss that came with every woman who wanted less than she did. She'd always felt the painful need to know the insides of another person as well as she knew her own, and to be known in kind—as if that knowing made her more real than her historic record. It *was* the real, tender side of her. Not the violent side of her.

But was there a real side of her? Were both real? Did she only dream her tender side was the "real" side, or did her violent impact upon so many lives make her existence as servant of death the truer Dominia? Without the bridge of another being, she feared she was destined to drift along, unknowing, trapped within the cell of her own body.

When trapped in a real cell and given the opportunity to make a platonic connection, she'd wasted it. Her interactions with Benedict—this young man fresh-shipped far from his home, his mother, and the girlfriend he didn't know to be pregnant—must have seemed, to the human, a kind of friendship. To her, it was a slow, careful, conscious manipulation that she could plan twenty-four hours a day/night cycle, every cycle, until she blacked out or got free. She had sensed from their first meeting the depths of his innocence, that innocence that sparked in him a silent but obvious hope he might somehow redeem her with his friendship. One too many United Front movies about the goodness of people, perhaps. Fine by her; small wonder her Father paid to produce so much shlock when it brainwashed them into delusional mercy.

First, she demonstrated a need. Easy enough to pretend to be lonely. She let him hear frequent sighs and made sure he was around to watch her wander the cell. As she paused by the door, she'd gaze out its little window with the most somber expression manageable, then wander out of view. It did not take many repetitions—two or three of his shifts—before she noticed him reading, and asked him about the book.

"Just my mom's old Bible. She gave it to me when I left, and I've been trying to make it through this thing my whole life, so I thought I'd give it a shot while I was here, but...it's a pretty heavy book. Fourteen pages of 'And

So-And-So begat Such-And-Such, and Such-And-Such begat What's-His-Name...' No offense." He offered a meek smile. "I know martyrs are religious."

"I'm not. Not really." For instance, she had to wrack her brain for a book from the human Old and New Testaments, rather than the more important martyr Post Testament. "But I always did like the Book of Tobit. It's short."

Then, after a second's recognition for the suitability of the text and the suggestion it would place in his mind, she lifted her eyebrows. "It's a fairy tale, about a young man who frees a woman from a demon."

There it was: that light of transference, of false hope sparking so bright from his irises their afterimages floated, ghostly, upon the cell wall. He would make his mistake when he returned to yammer excitedly about the story the next day, to talk to her all about the adventures of Tobit and his friend, the disguised archangel Raphael—and the dog, there, in the background.

She hadn't thought about that dog in years. On the way down the golden elevator, she wondered about it the same way she wondered about Valentinian. What was the point of the dog in that story? What was the real goal of the magician? By his own admission, he was a kind of thoughtform. With no earthly body, he could say, "I used to be real," until his face turned blue. That didn't mean he was real now, so far as it concerned Dominia and the world where she lived. Yet, he was real as anybody or anything here, and was clearly *known*, as by Trisha, who tapped the invisible keys of her computer and blandly tolerated the flirting of the magician leaning with his elbow propped against the desk. A man as any man, albeit several degrees smugger. Like a man with a great poker hand and a terrible poker face—or a terrible hand and a great face. Impossible to say.

"Here she is. Checking out?" Outside a hat left askew and a naughty edge to her smile for Dominia, the porter acted as if nothing had happened. The General coughed.

"Sorry about the room."

"Don't fret. You wouldn't believe the things that happen in this place. And most people don't tip me nearly that well." With a saucy calendar-girl wink, Trisha turned the screen in Dominia's direction, which had the odd effect of looking like she summoned it from space by spreading it between her hands. "Sign here"—she indicated—"and here, and here."

"What am I signing?"

"You know"—with an attractive frown, Trisha turned the screen back in her own direction and nibbled the inside of her cheek—"I can't say I know the answer to that."

"Eternity in a black hole, yet nobody has time to read fine print." The laughing magician leaned across the counter to kiss the porter's cheek. "All right, Trisha, have fun, be safe."

"I should be telling *you* that, shouldn't I?"

"Nah. Age doesn't matter in a timeless space, but if it's a contest...I still win."

To be sure, the magician had lived forever if he had lived a day. Flat-out reading her mind, he said, "Same goes for everyone. Shall we?"

"What?"

If she was annoyed when he responded, not with words, but by dropping his hands on her shoulders and turning her around, her annoyance melted into awe as she noticed what she had missed the first time: a square fountain in the center of the lobby shielded—along with rows of ferns and begonias that she'd thought to be the entirety of the centerpiece—a tranquil sitting area with black leather benches and a firepit waiting empty like the mouth of a cauldron.

"We're going home," he said.

"And what does a nice sitting area have to do with getting us home?"

"You remember when we had that conversation about projectors? And Trish talked to you about holograms, right. You understand it all better now, I think. If, in reality and the Ergosphere, we're in the movie and the film—"

"The hologram and the interference pattern"—called the porter, to his eye roll.

"—then this is arguably the '*real* real world' of images being filmed, scanned, super translated, whatever. And not just for this film, but every scrap of footage that was ever shot for any film: back in reality, we'll become editors of our one film again. Or you will, at any rate." With a grin and a pat on her back, he strolled to the sitting area and expected her to follow. "I'm just a supporting actor."

"Are you saying I'm the editor, the actor, or the projector?" He ignored her question and stood with his hands in his pockets, chin craned high and eyes angled as if in search of the ceiling. He gestured she should do the same, and she did, but failed to see. "Okay. What are we looking at?"

"The ceiling."

"I thought we were supposed to stare at the sun to get home. There's no way you can see the ceiling from here! Aren't there infinite floors in this place? Look at it up there!"

"You remember how you got here?"

"I remember walking into the sun." As she started to look down or at him, he urged her, "Just keep looking. Tell me about it."

"Well, I was—I was about to be captured by Akachi and his men. Then I saw you. Or...Basil. Out across the street, in the shade." She frowned. Her eye, struggling for purchase throughout the infinite floors, must have constructed one, for she now imagined she did see a ceiling: so far away, it appeared a pixel. "Is that—"

"Then what happened?"

Annoyed, she answered, "Well, you walked out into the sun, didn't you? That's how you get back and forth, from reality to the Ergosphere. You and Lazarus told me that." Yes, that was definitely a ceiling. And growing. Or descending?

"Consciousness is all about momentum, vibrational states and the electromagnetic spectrum. However, all things, including consciousness, are subject to the principle of inertia; that goes for creativity, too. If information is the basis of reality, you can understand how information that already exists requires certain conditions—certain levels and types of energy input into the system—in order to reach an appropriate escape velocity from unconsciousness to consciousness. You're a logical woman, General, you were all right with higher level math in sixteenth grade. Think of it in purely numeric form, with the Mandelbrot set, otherwise known as the first fractal."

"That creepy, black beetle fractal?" It discomforted her just to think on it.

"Reminds you of your old man, right?" While they both laughed, he said, "Because it's an appropriate mathematical symbol for how you escape his world. Stop me if you've heard this one before—the Mandelbrot set is generated by iteration, or the repetition of a process, in this case, quadratic polynomials." The numbers of the floor at the lowest level of her vision, printed across the columns by the stairs (who could take the stairs in such a place!) changed from a real number into the example form $z_{n+1} = z^2 + C$. "In the Mandelbrot set, $z_0 = C$, so if $C = 1$, so does the first iteration of z. You are our cheeky variable of z, and Lazarus is our constant of C. You started off as z_0—$Dominia_0$, if you'd prefer—and applying the function of reality to you yielded $Dominia_1$...which we iterated again."

The floor numbers flashed from $z_1 = z_0^2 + C$ to $z_2 = z_1^2 + C$ to $z_3 = z_2^2 + C$, and trailed beyond at a pace outmatching her capacity to observe. They were passing those floors by: this whole time, they'd moved. He had stopped her from looking down because she would have seen how far they already were above the floor. Over her astonished gasp, he continued, "The list of generated numbers is called 'the orbit' of z_0 under iteration of $z^2 + C$. You can use this function for a mind-blowing amount of models, including reality itself, you now understand. There are two primary results with iteration: in the case of a positive constant in the example I just gave, the orbit tends to infinity by growing larger each iteration. But with a constant of zero—no constant, no blood of Lazarus, no hope, no soul—the orbit remains fixed for all iterations. Snore! You Father just keeps winning, and winning, and winning."

"You're as responsible for controlling probability as the Lamb, aren't you? You've been altering the odds in Lazarus's favor and keeping him on the right side every time."

"And keeping that sweet, sweet blood of his available to you and all the others in need of a way out of the loop." Yes, they flew: the floors whipped past, a thudding wind that accompanied the shifting of colors as layer on colorful layer whirled by, peeled away, dissolved into the next. "That mutated blood activates the CRY gene; in humans and normal martyrs, it isn't fully functional. Fruit flies and birds, among other beings, use that gene to perceive magnetic fields and so much more. Activated in a human or a martyr by Lazarus's blood, we see the same but struggle to put names to them as other beings don't. Yet, we are able to use the blood of Lazarus, through the lens of the gene, as other beings don't. When high-frequency wavelengths—like those of blue and ultraviolet light—interact with the mutated CRY in our eyes, our molecules are excited to such extent that it becomes possible to travel through those frequencies of light and beyond the Plancks of reality. Light travels through the optic nerve, into the brain and down into the nerves of the solar plexus, which is where we perceive the source of our fields. They indicate far more than direction, by the by. They measure the electromagnetic spectrum and connect you with devices and people sensitive to it. The Ergosphere itself is not radioactive, but individuals who have returned from it briefly are, because they have traveled at frequencies unrecorded by Earth's populace; their bodies, and their realities, have been reconstructed by what a great man once termed "Hawking radiation," the electromagnetic field around black holes that is responsible for their diminishing mass. It's pulling information back out to be constructed elsewhere, realized by the Higgs field: a result of the constant activities of souls in and around the black hole, backward across time."

"And when this black hole's mass is completely diminished?"

"An almost infinite amount of time from now? Don't worry...it's all the same black hole, anyway. If I'm being honest, the black hole itself is just a door to the highest reality there is...but this nesting doll of metaphors has to stop somewhere for your three-dimensional brain, right?"

As Valentinian spoke, that distant ceiling grew ever larger, ever closer, and at such speed that her bones felt on the verge of bursting. They moved so fast, a hundred floors passed them in a second. What a speed at which to fly! It was almost more like... "Wait," she cried, "are we *falling*?"

She took his lack of response as confirmation. "The blood of Lazarus creates a spiritual yearning in those who take it, because it has created a soul with or without their knowing. It takes a soul to experience the Ergosphere; most people never consciously experience it, even with the blood of Lazarus, because they never learn to mount that soul. But when the body knows it's but an organ of the soul, well...your organs have to come along, too, right?"

Clutching his arm, Dominia screamed, and tried to indicate that the ceiling—decorated with a mosaic depicting the swirling rays of a sun—prepared to crush them. As if to indicate these highest floors were somehow larger than the ones below, the work of tile stretched the length of a North American football field and was intent on growing. Grinning, the magician pointed to something black upon the face of that ceiling: a sunspot, the pixel's width the whole mosaic had been at first glimpse. While this black dot grew, the magician said, "You can go anywhere, and even humans will be unaffected by their own body's radioactivity... They should take a shower before visiting with friends and neighbors, though. And it's not instant teleportation when it's a chemical reaction within the body, but it's better than nothing. It could be engineered to give the answers to actual teleportation, though, if men look."

To Dominia's relief, the mole resolved into an open skylight and the night beyond. She relaxed her grip on her friend's arm, and asked, "I can do this from anywhere? Go back and forth, up and down, the electromagnetic spectrum?"

"It's safer to come to the Ergosphere from the earthly day, but you can leave it at any time. And the trip from the Ergosphere back to the planet is, from our perspective, faster than this one. From Earth's perspective, it doesn't matter."

Close though they were to home, and Cassandra's diamond, and what she hoped would be the end of her journey, Dominia was nonetheless seized by a wave of sorrow. "Will I be able to see you with my own eye? Is there really a way?"

"Of course, buddy. You'll see Basil."

"But, I mean—as you are now. A person I can talk to. Sometimes." They shared a grin and she turned her face toward the skylight that had grown so close and so large it pushed away the golden tiles of the sun. The cosmos beyond swirled so clear that the General was chilled by the sight. She had never seen such stars: swirling columns of gas beckoned them close, and sweeps of color tantalized with iridescent glimpses of neighboring galaxies. She still had too many questions. "Are you real?"

"Is anybody?"

"Are you really Death?"

"Your Father says I am. Pretty flattering."

Turning to see him with her good eye, she pressed, "Are you God?"

"Who, me?" With a cheeky grin, the magician turned a sparkling eye her way. "I'm just some dog."

She didn't manage to catch that Planck wherein he transitioned into the mangy-but-adorable shepherd dog. As he spoke, the skylight leapt for them—closed that last gap, itself—and on its other side, the General found herself adrift in outer space with Basil. It was all so abrupt she gasped. Tried to, anyway: her airless mouth, mere information being recompiled into her physical body with a new location associated—thanks, she supposed, to Hawking radiation, the Higgs field and Valentinian-only-knew-what mechanics, produced no sound in the vacuum of space. It was Basil's softly wagging tail that galvanized her resulting fright into exhilaration. She sensed no harm could come to her in this transition period, and suspected that she flew through time as much as space. In particular, the planet Mercury formed seconds before she was hurled past it. Miles and millennia passed in microseconds, and the tail of a timely comet revealed, like a curtain drawn away, the distant face of blue-green Earth swirling in a more beautiful—and more astonishing—vision of home than any she'd seen.

Legs paddling through the void, the dog twitched its ears with a look of such pure animal delight that she almost forgot—that quickly—he had ever been a man. But she would stubbornly hold on to everything learned from this place. She would take every scrap of knowledge and make it another component in the weapon she forged of herself. A weapon meant to destroy not just Tobias Akachi but her arrogant Father as well.

If it was possible to go any faster, the pull of Earth's gravity did it. On instinct, Dominia lifted her hands above her head, but, in turning her face away, was astonished by the source of her journey. Still floating at the edge of space, she rolled upon her back and looked the way they'd come. In the distance burned the naked face of the sun, which propelled them, its little sunbeams, the eight minutes and twenty seconds it took to get to Earth.

Her throat tightened. She imagined Cassandra's radiant face and looked away, urging her eye not to leak half-real tears lest they freeze to her face, or boil when they regained physical form on contact with the atmosphere. Incredibly, against all logic or rule of physics, they slowed. Dominia had undergone a palpable shift in dimensions experienced only by her sensory relationship to her own body, which grew solid enough to establish a clear difference between a thought-body and a real one. Vertigo twisted her renewed stomach as she turned back to Earth and saw they plummeted for the continent of Africa at increasing—but material, and therefore somehow comforting—speed.

Who could waste time being terrified by a sight so marvelous? Free to bark, Basil did, and Dominia grinned against the whipping air. Home! Home! Oh, her beautiful planet. She had never been to Cairo, but every part of Earth was home to her now, and as she fell to its good grounds, she let that tear escape.

The speed with which the skylight leapt to meet them was as quick as the bustling city of Cairo—more dense with highways, bullet trains, and sky-scrapers than its ancient founders ever envisioned—distinguished itself from the landscape. Like most cities, Cairo stretched to such an extent that even its mighty pyramids, dwarfed by mega high-rises, resembled children's toys. Astonishing to think that, from the black hole at the beginning of reality, they could hone in on an exact point in space-time: yet, she saw the indigo diamond of the Lady's temple well before they hit it, apparently not quite solid as she'd anticipated. The General and the dog whizzed with harmless grace through several closed floors before they landed, as if always there, upon the crimson carpet of Miki Soto's bedroom.

X

There's No Place Like Home

The notion that this was Miki's bedroom took a bit of doing to puzzle together. Her ears, once filled with the high-pressure "welcome home" scream of sweet oxygen, clamored with feminine voices, a shouting man, a barking dog, and a woman saying, "What the fuck? What the—Dominia? Holy—"

Her eyes resolved hints of bronze tapestries, which distinguished the crimson walls of an octagonal room. Its door was impossible to find amid the ornately dressed women whose sabers and halberds were drawn from veils so translucent it was amazing they concealed anything. All the while, a voice she recognized as Miki's called, "Stand down! Stand down, would you people just relax? She was probably the point of this thing, right? Right? I don't know, *you* guys are supposed to know this. You're the priestesses or something, right?"

On the round bed that was the room's centerpiece, Miki's glowing face hovered between curtains of gauzy silver and emitted a high-pitched squeal. As the baffled women began to (almost) relax, Basil was so overcome with delight that he chased his tail. Glad to be on Earth, herself, the General laughed. "I never thought I'd be so relieved to see you," she said. "Or so confused."

"Not as confused as you're about to be." Lazarus, of all people, sat up behind Miki's painted face to reveal a trimmed beard and a hairstyle that had been moderately managed. "Glad you made it back."

As if reaching his own escape velocity, the dog plunged past the armed women to leap upon the bed and dash in small circles around giggling Miki. "Basil! Basil! There's my Basil! Who's a good boy?"

"Definitely not the dog running all over the bed." The naked old man grumbled his way up and stooped to collect his pants while a grimacing

Dominia shielded her eye. As he covered himself, he said something in Arabic, and the women stood down. Miki crossed her arms over her loosely closed gold kimono with an indelicate snort.

"Real nice. I thought you were supposed to listen to women! To *me*! Not some dude."

"Some dude who knows more about all this than you," Lazarus said. "No offense, Miki, but just because you're the next Lady doesn't mean you know anything now. For all you know, this is Dominia's doppelgänger."

The General rubbed her forehead. "Don't say that word," she pled, almost too exhausted to consciously integrate the piece of information Lazarus had slipped in. (And too distracted by her missing hair—heartbreak!) Miki, the next Lady? Miki *Soto*, serving as the avatar of some trans-dimensional goddess best interpreted, maybe, as a pool of water upon the event horizon of a black hole, or even the substance of the black hole and therefore the basis of both reality and eternity? Soto Miki-chan, cramming her mouth full of falafel, shaking her short-shorts, and swearing like Tenchi Ichigawa never could, the next head of the Red Market and its global cult of pagan women for two thousand years?

It was easier to focus on the *tulpa*.

"It can't come here, right?" she asked Lazarus, who strode over, she presumed, to shake her hand. "I mean, to Earth."

"Not without your help, it can't. The physical body is like a portal to those things."

Then, he did reach for her—but kept reaching past her hand, up into her mouth, where, like a grandfather yanking a baby tooth, he popped her recently implanted right canine out of her mouth.

"Elijah," she screamed; the old man investigated the thing while Miki shouted similarly.

"No"—he showed her the speaker before he crushed it between his martyr fingers—"Lazarus. You want me to do the other one, too?"

Oh, how she'd hoped he was crazy when she'd met him in the basement of that record shop where he told her Akachi listened through her teeth! Removed from earthly concerns as she'd been, she had all but forgotten about those things, and was now forced to pull the remaining device with a terrible series of eye-watering cracks. Much worse than the one Lazarus had pulled; she should have had him do it. As, gasping, she tore it free, Miki's horrified face emitted the word, "*Sugoi...*"

"Uh-oh." Lazarus frowned, investigating the tooth. "This one doesn't have—"

Dominia's shriek of fury quickly crumbled his facade into laughter. "I'm kidding. Good God, I'm kidding! Don't look at me like that... Everybody's so serious around here." After demonstrating to Dominia's tear-filled eye that this tooth was a location-tracking device, Lazarus crushed the thing, and said, "How about we get you some new ones?"

"Before or after somebody tells me what I walked into?"

"Just, like, a ritual," said Miki, as if that explained everything. "You know."

"That explains the plum incense, but not..." She couldn't bring herself to vocalize—or even form the thought—and instead waved vaguely in Lazarus's direction. The Lady-to-be grinned.

"*Well*, it's like, like a sacred marriage? Lazarus is symbolic of the energy that's supposed to be entering me, and—"

"Okay," said the General, "I've heard plenty." While trying to erase the last few seconds of her memory, she forced a bloody smile for Lazarus. "New teeth, you said?"

"Better: your *real* teeth." Having slung the neat white robe of a spiritualist over his shoulders and adjusted its high collar, he marched for one of the tapestries. Miki whined.

"I was just about to tell you all to buzz off so I can talk to my"—her voice lilted into singsong—"best-friend-in-the-world, because-she-has-been-gone-too-long."

A smile quirked the General's swelling upper lip, but, from the cluster of rearranged guards, a low voice spoke in a cadence familiar even if the tone was not.

"Neither the General, nor the magician, may see the Lady while unclean."

Heads turned, Miki looked annoyed, and Dominia tried not to reveal her abject embarrassment at the thought of meeting Gethsemane's physical persona with a swollen, bleeding mouth. It was impossible to hide the shock, however, or perhaps the delight of finding her to be so *different* in this place. The fair nymph with lips so pale they were almost sapphire and hair as blonde as Lavinia's curls had been replaced by a slender ebony Amazon, who, though dressed as the other priestesses in the room, seemed to Dominia's eye a thousand times more flattered by the sky-colored bodice and those many flowing veils. Ignoring or missing Dominia in the act of picking her jaw off the floor, Miki snuggled the tail-wagging mutt with an expression of motherly defense.

"Basil is a clean dog!"

"I don't know about that," muttered Dominia, watching an animal that accepted belly rubs in so convincing a way that she might have doubted Valentinian's existence had the memory of his arm not remained so real in her hand. From the door, Lazarus snorted right along with her.

"Even if I could begin to tell you how wrong you are, Gethsemane is right. He's mildly radioactive at the moment." Miki's hand jerked away and her lip curled with a little "ew" while the mystic shrugged. "Doesn't matter since you're going to be resistant in about an hour and immortal soon anyway, but rituals exist for a reason."

"He is correct." Gethsemane slipped past her peers and took Dominia's hand with her gloved one. "The General is much the same. She has returned from eternity, and its energies have followed her as well as Basil. Even Lazarus required purification before entering this holy room. They should not be allowed to touch the new Lady until they have been cleaned."

The woman nearest Miki hefted the border collie, struggling to hold the wiggling dog and evade its cheek-seeking kisses. As Dominia took a protective step forward, so, too, did another pair of women, but Gethsemane calmly tightened her grip.

"There is no need for conflict, General. Please: Nein takes him for a bath, as I take you."

Just like that, she was much less concerned about Basil. Dominia grinned crookedly. "Should we be talking about this in front of everybody?"

This elicited a slap from the Bearer, the pain on her bloody mouth an unimaginable fire in her long-missed body. "Please, General," said Gethsemane above the giggles of the other women and the ringing of the martyr's cheek, "this is a holy room."

Just slightly, the woman cracked a smile, and Dominia repressed her own smirk as she allowed herself led out. "What about Kahlil?" she called before exiting. Miki rolled her eyes.

"Oh, he's around." Her tone told Dominia more about the interactions of her friends over the past weeks than they would tell her, themselves. "Probably in the gardens."

The General would have to ask him what he thought about all this when she got the chance. Or not—she didn't want to rub it in, after all. But she couldn't imagine Kahlil was thrilled by the thought of Miki, at whom he looked with obvious and ill-fated stars, engaging in ritual sex or sacrificing her body to some goddess. Dominia wasn't sure about that, herself. But there wasn't anything he could do about it; it was Miki's body, and though he may have been able to talk her down to Earth if given time alone, the future avatar had surely spent every waking moment attended to since their arrival in Cairo, and no doubt didn't want to be talked down at all.

In the hallways, Dominia was stunned again—not by Gethsemane's beauty in the brighter light but by the light itself, doubled by the rosy marble of lapis-accented columns that served as canvases for many murals: from what the General glimpsed, of life, the afterlife, and the worship of the Lady, but it was hard to make out details as she was being hurried to the baths. There was a lot of emphasis on the numbers seven, eight, and nine, if she was counting right—and colors. Many colors. Specifically, arrays of colors she recognized as a rudimentary depiction of the electromagnetic field that had bent from her ribs. Still bent from her ribs, her mind, though she couldn't see it with her eyes. Seeing this depiction, this rainbow of stripes (like wings, she thought as she was whisked past a large image of an ascended soul) only heightened the beauty of what she had seen, but which could not be grasped by memory, because there were no words to describe the colors there, nor cones in physical eyes sufficient to translate them to sight. Perhaps in the fabulous mantis shrimps, with their bullet claws and magical eyes: she had always loved those creatures. Always wondered what it was like to be one, and now she knew. She wanted to reminisce, but even memory, when bound to her mind, failed to reproduce in true strokes the tori of her spectrum. Somehow, rudimentary though the exquisite images were in comparison, looking upon the murals of the temple brought those memories to clear, almost tangible life. Had she known how quickly everything would unfold, she might have urged Gethsemane to wait, and let her take time to examine the beauty of scenes that would not exist much longer upon the planet.

Instead, she studied the profile of the woman who guided her—who had technically guided her from the first moment she'd emerged in the event horizon. "I knew you for Gethsemane the second I saw you, somehow."

"I am amazed you recognized me, General... I have dreamed of the woman I am bound to in that other place, and she is not like me."

No, not at all. Just as beautiful, but a completely different kind of beauty. If the nymph's beauty bore whispered resemblance to the name "Cassandra," the beauty of her aligned human was the elegant compound word of a foreign language. What language that might be was impossible to discern, and somehow pleasing to keep a mystery. Without the attachment of heritage, she still seemed a pure, dreamy beauty, as all things in the Ergosphere and event horizon seemed the purest versions of themselves. Gethsemane's earthly form was so perfect to Dominia's eye that the priestess was a walking rift by which one glimpsed that other world where boundaries dissolved.

Yet, that rift reminded her she was not in that other world. Technically she was, the magician or the mystic might lecture her. But that was just it—she couldn't hear the magician lecture her in this world. Ergo, it was different. Only a few moments after she had fallen to Earth alongside a dog who in that other place was a man, the memories of her experience in the Ergosphere possessed that obscured quality particular to memories of dreams, rather than of real events. She bore a certain guilt for what she had done there, but those mistakes felt understandable now in her actual, causally bound body, hair cropped disappointingly short against her head and clothes notably more ragged than they had been in that other environment. Not to mention starkly different. As happened in dreams, she had forgotten the ruin of her leather coat; René's tattered jacket and shirt had also been abandoned. But even this crisp white button-down Miki had bought her in Kabul was soaked with Hunter blood—not dried, she noted. As if she had just been at the battle with the Hunters and her Family. And, boy, did she ever feel like it! Her body ached for rest.

Wasn't it pleasing, though, to be exhausted again? Connected to her senses, she was once more in control of her thought process and reassured nothing "magical" could happen without extraordinary circumstances—and by the Lamb, she appreciated it.

The General cleared her throat as they entered the baths, and those (mostly) controlled thought processes wandered to a different place. The steam-thickened room was dense with the cloying aroma of honey—and lavender, that scent that followed Miki Soto everywhere she went. All of it—the scent, the steam, the air she breathed—formed to the General some kind of protection from the beautiful woman who shut the door to seal them alone in the wide pool room. One of several in the complex, Dominia assumed.

"Have you never been to the Ergosphere?"

The woman shook her head at the General's question while arranging all number of towels and weird froufrou oils whose mere bottles aggravated the martyr's sinuses. "No, General. Bearers are not meant to travel to the Ergosphere unless urgent circumstances require. The Lady's attendants there are too pure, too powerful; if we discover firsthand our true selves, all the human in us will be subsumed by them and the beauty of the Kingdom. We will forget why we ever came to Earth, and our aligned spirits must start again many years later with a new body. Just being in the Ergosphere may cause this, but the first time I enter the event horizon, I will never again leave. I will not desire to. Not all are made to come and go as you, General. But I dream of it often, and have sometimes seen it in waking, as one sees through an open window."

"What do you do here that's so important? Not to be rude, I just mean—I understand why you'd want to stay in the Kingdom. I guess I'd ruin things if I did it, since I'm—annoyingly—integral to this...function"—she remembered Valentinian's formula, perhaps the clearest detail from her entire journey, and promised herself she wouldn't forget it—"but what's stopping you?"

"Our duty is to carry our Lady. Most cannot even touch Her. But we Bearers have adapted to suit Her, or, rather, have been adapted by our contact with our higher selves. Therefore, I have no concern for your physical state."

Here Dominia and Basil had been accused of radioactivity: if the Lady was a black hole contained in the body of a woman, She must have been a walking atom bomb. "Why doesn't She walk around Herself, if people can't touch her? Genetic mutations that make you and other women radiation-resistant are fantastic, but wouldn't it be easier if—"

"Because the day that She is forced to walk, General, the world will end. The same is said of Her voice. If She used Her mouth to speak, we would remember we have no ears."

As the woman turned to undress Dominia, the martyr lifted a staying hand. "It's for the best you don't remember what happened between us. That place was like a weird dream. I'm a married woman, and here..."

Cassandra waited. The thought rose in her with a giddy flash, the bird of her heart fluttering once to prove itself not completely dead. Yes, sweet Cassandra, or what was left of her: that diamond of ashes, stolen by Miki. Soon, she would be reunited with the precious gem. And maybe—oh, fairest of words—maybe she would hold her wife in her arms that night!

She dared not dream such a thing. The thought made her more sorrowful than happy, and she stowed it away at Gethsemane's soft smile. "Yes, General: and here, were my kisses to stray from this mouth"—the priestess brushed the martyr's lips and provoked a shudder—"I would be a martyr within a few days without self-control. But I must treat you; what we said is true. This is a holy place, and all within are to be purified. Especially for the Lady's wedding to Her new host."

"Well"—wary Dominia watched the priestess unbutton her shirt, much as the nymph had unzipped her jacket only a few hours before—"I guess it's been a while since I actually relaxed."

Not that this bath proved actually relaxing. Stripped of her clothes and the eye patch, which, in this world, was not some key or metaphysical symbol whose removal had strange consequences not yet comprehensible, Dominia was dunked into the pool. The human soon joined her, then began to scrub her as brutally as a human grandmother scrubbing a child. There was, sadly for Dominia, nothing sexy about the experience: but, just as well. The Ergosphere may have felt a dream, but in its last moments it had become a refreshing, pleasing one. As a result, the General felt quite shagged and a bit baked, an effect impossible to receive from dream alone. To keep her mind off the feeling of her skin being buffed in water so hot it dehydrated her, Dominia asked about the temple.

"I'd think a worldly General would know more of it...but, the theaters of your Father's wars have not yet extended to Africa, so you've had no cause to visit. He is wise to avoid the continent and make peace with the people upon it, trading through the waypoint of Malta as he does; he knows the land will do his people less good than someplace far to the north, and knows our own northernmost countries would be quick to punish any slight by crushing Malta before moving into Mephitoli. I think he only refrains from taking the land and improving its climate for his people because he has other priorities: if he could but have his Jerusalem along with that pesky (true) branch of the Catholic Church that fled his acquisition of the Vatican, he'd sweep from there across the Middle States. A systematic conquest of the African nations would be his next move...perhaps you will see the continent then."

"I will never be his general again."

"Then whose general are you, General?"

She did not know how to answer that question, and pressed on, "But this temple. I've heard of the pyramids, but—"

"Why would your Father let your people know of the Lady's temple? Cairo has always been a heart of religious tradition. This place was built by the now-fading Lady when first She took the throne two thousand years ago. It was this Lady who centralized our faith and founded the Red Market as we know it; before, Her worshipers only loosely connected with one another, and the only ones who followed Her bodily avatar were those who had met the Bearers, or who were the Bearers. Even now, our services are practiced in secret, and are more often than not private visitations between the priestesses and those who pursue our brand of divine connection."

Sacred prostitution had once sounded to her like a goofy excuse for paying to fuck, but she had to admit that after her visitation in the Kingdom, she wasn't sure anymore. At least, the General was open-minded enough about it now to seriously compare it to her childhood faith. "Sort of like the early years of the Holy Martyr Church...it began underground, the way the Lazarenes are now. Cicero and the Lamb preached the faith and had this...cabal of groupies, I guess, musicians and artists and famous actors. Martyrs came out because one of them was prosecuted for murder and the Hierophant went public to defend him under an assumed name, though he was living in Russia at the time, spreading the faith there while pretending to be a Catholic missionary, so he wasn't in danger like all the martyrs living in North America. He loves to tell stories from those nights, when martyrs could kill with abandon because that was what people expected of them." She remembered her audience and tried to change to a lighter memory. "Sometimes he'd pretend to be Slavic, sometimes flat-out Russian, but then he'd imply he was Italian, or he'd talk about being raised in France...nobody could figure out where he was from or even who he was."

"Many books have been written, General, speculating on the nature of his identity."

"Have they?" She laughed to think there was something she didn't know—another type of book censored from her, outside of holy books. Ill-fated scholarly works striving to debunk her Father and his Church! "How funny...I guess we all take it for granted that he's from his alien planet, or in some way divine." To say such a thing now seemed shockingly rotten in her mouth: Was this a growing sense of sacrilege? "I don't know if I should talk to a human about our period of persecution, because it was natural, and we deserved it, but during that time, those groupies fled across Europa and the United Front—States, then. They carried on the Mass in secret...martyrdom used to be passed through the faith, not parenting. That changed when the HMC took possession of the Vatican, and the souls of superficial people who thought it was all variations of the same thing."

"That is why the Lady and the Lazarenes are both so important. They save as many as they can, not just in body, but in soul."

When the (disappointing) ritual bath was deemed finished, Dominia was hauled out of the pool, dried, and anointed with heady frankincense oil. To her surprise, however, she was redressed in a broad-shouldered man's kimono of forest-green cotton. "Isn't this Cairo?"

"Her Majesty-to-be is Japanese. It is the bride who designs the wedding."

She supposed that was true, but it was funny to think of Miki as a bride, let alone the stereotypical harried version arranging an over-the-top ball. Miki was a tomboy, which led Dominia down another byway of consideration. Did the Red Market women know that the geisha selected as their next Lady hadn't always been a lady externally? Perhaps that was what had factored into their selection. But, more than likely, it didn't matter, and nobody cared. It was far from Dominia's place to ask, and guilt stirred in her for even wondering, though there was no rational reason for that guilt. Curiosity was natural when it came to the particulars of this occult business. If what she assumed to be an...incarnate, multidimensional pool needed a body, and wanted to make that body into a woman, and it had all the powers of a goddess, well, who was anyone to limit the original biological sex of the host?

Other pieces began to fall together, like Miki's insistence on getting Dominia to Cairo despite the prostitute's total lack of firsthand knowledge about the location of Lazarus. Her motivation for doing anything at all, come to think of it, was clearly rooted in this. Would her body be altered by the possession? Furthermore, what would Kahlil think? The General was sure he had never known about Miki's past, and sure he was crushed by the idea of losing her to a religion in which he didn't believe.

As it happened, Dominia saw him on the way back to Miki's room, but not in the gardens. Kahlil came sulking around a corner, arms crossed over his poorly fit kimono, *taqiyah* slightly askew upon his head, and was utterly unprepared to run into the woman who had once allowed him to be shot by the antique gun now concealed in the convenient sleeve pocket of her kimono—safety on. Though, she could have sworn the safety was on when Basil shot him; but that was a different conversation.

Regardless, given that—and the concussion with which she'd left him after his foiled attempt to claim that gun—Kahlil resembled a cat upon the sudden appearance of a dog. "Dominia!" His voice leapt to the high tone of a man trying make terror resemble pleasant surprise. "You're back?"

"I just got back," she said, nodding as Gethsemane offered to take her clothes to be washed. As the priestess vanished around the same corner from which Kahlil appeared, Dominia jerked a thumb after her. "She's a nymph in the place where I was."

"All...right." The man studied her face in search of some visible evidence of insanity. Instead, he noticed, "You lost your teeth."

"They were bugged," she said, which did not make her sound much less insane, and provoked a short laugh from the human.

"Bugged? What? By that dentist? No way."

"Way. Turns out he runs the Hunters. Didn't you know?" Kahlil had gotten his back up about mentioning his line of work in front of Akachi, but that could have been a charade. Nonetheless, irritation tightened the human's face at the mere mention.

"Please. I've been pestered with this for weeks already. Before my concussion, I didn't know anything worth knowing; I'm a low-level tech guy. I've told you this before. Tobias told me who he was while he was treating my head wound and tried to get me on his side before we went to Cairo, tried to say he'd 'forgive' me for helping you—but I had the feeling he was selling me a load, and when we heard about the bombing on the radio after Miki got sick of her music a few hours later, turned out we were right."

Dominia hadn't even thought about that, the car's connection to the music store: that would have kept Miki from overhearing any radio broadcast hijacked by Lavinia's virus in the early part of the marathon. What a fascinating lucky break: the boy went on. "Anyway, I don't think anybody but the highest higher-ups really know who's in charge of the Hunters. If they let people know who was in charge, human governments would have him. And, I mean—a dentist? If the peons knew, they wouldn't listen to anything he had to say."

"How do you think he got into power?" He had fed her some story about being set to be a slave to her people and joining the Hunters but had left out the part about his ascent to the throne.

Shrugging, Kahlil said, "I guess he impressed the right people at the right time. Or killed them. I don't know—you know more about violence than I do."

Wincing at the bitterness of his words, Dominia folded her arms in semiconscious mirroring of his body language. "How's your head? I'm sorry about before, I...I'm sorry."

"It's fine," he said, clearly aggrieved by the memory. "They've got a bunch of doctors here. They checked me out while trying to interrogate me about the Hunters way more intensely than you just were."

"Can't say I blame them."

"I can! They've been harassing me. Watching me. The only way I can feel like I'm not being watched is by going on walks, because they can't keep track of me without obviously tailing me all over this crazy temple. I've been here forty days"—the number startled Dominia to hear, though she abstractly knew it—"but it took them two or three to make it clear I'm prisoner."

"Come on, I'm sure they've treated you well." She felt the weakness of her argument even before she lamely pressed on. "Clothing you, feeding you, I'm sure you have plenty of opportunities to be with beautiful women..."

"Oh, I've slept with, like, twelve of them since I've been here." While Dominia laughed, Kahlil grinned in a way that was clearly despite himself. "I don't care about that." His smile faded into an expression of absent darkness. "You heard about Miki, right?"

"I was just thinking about that."

"She's making a huge mistake. These cultists—I guess I shouldn't be throwing stones, since I'm part of the Hunters, and they can attract some real crazies, but I'm not one of those nuts. All I've ever tried to do is be a good Muslim, and a good human. That was why I joined them. Because I thought it was the human thing to do, defending ourselves against you. I sacrificed a law-abiding, secure life for what I thought was right. But Miki...she's sacrificing her existence. She's talking crazy. You know what she told me the other day?"

The boy's eyes had assumed a soft tint. "'I know you think you love me, Kahlil, but after the ceremony, there won't be a 'me' to love.'" His face strained with a combination of horror and incredulity, his posture relaxed enough for him to spread his arms in demonstration of these feelings. "Would you tell me what that's supposed to mean, Dominia? Look—can I ask you something... personal?"

With a shifty look, Kahlil folded his arms and focused his gaze somewhere around the belt of Dominia's robe. "You don't have to tell me if you don't want to talk about it, but when your...wife"—it was admittedly bold for the man to even acknowledge her wife, considering the homophobic culture of the Hunters, which only widened her mind's openness to his concern—"died, did you...I guess—do you think you'll ever get over it? Losing her? Allah, I'm so stupid to ask... You won't. You're on a journey to resurrect her, right?" They both laughed together, hollowly; the boy removed his glasses to rub the bridge of his nose, to hide the red of his closing eyes. "But how do you go on? How do you even wake up in the morning?"

"I don't," she teased. "I wake up in the evening."

In one tearful note that jerked his shoulders, Kahlil laughed behind his hand, and sympathetic Dominia considered touching him before she thought better of it. "I wake up because I have to," she said. "Because it's what Cassandra would want for me."

"I don't think Miki ever wanted anything for me... Hell, she never wanted *me*."

A horrible feeling, that. "You can't let yourself think something like that. She's a prostitute, but she's also a person, and it seems like she spent a lot of time with you. She talks fondly about you to me, anyway. You don't know what she's thought, what she's wanted, while visiting you. I'll bet she was just as happy to be with you as you were with her. But it's not about you, what she's doing. It's about herself—what she believes, what she wants." The General faltered, and realized she spoke to herself. Kahlil's eyes had opened, and he watched her now from behind replaced glasses. Quietly, she told him, "You can't let her decision to do this to herself ruin your whole life."

"Probably too late." The young man chuckled. Down the broad hall, the Lady-to-be rounded a corner with a trio of Bearers. On seeing Dominia, she gave a cry of delight. With a snort toward the sound, Kahlil turned back to the General and lowered his voice.

"I feel culpable in this, you know. She's been brainwashed. She's going to let these psycho women keep her captive and brainwash her more and more—take her whole life away, even cause her death. Are you going to let that happen? Am I?"

"Ultimately"—the martyr adjusted her tone and expression to reflect excitement on Miki's high-speed approach—"it's her religion, her body, her decision... Hey, Miki!"

"Hey, girl, hey," squealed the future Lady, blasting past Kahlil to throw her arms around the General's neck. "Damn, you look fine in that kimono! What's up, Kahlil?" She turned, still clinging to Dominia, to nod at the man.

"Just welcoming Dominia. I'll let you two catch up. Be careful on your stay, General...who knows what these people will convince you to do." With a disdainful glance for the Bearers, three older women who openly watched the Hunter's tech guy as if at any second he might assault Miki, Kahlil ducked away from them and went down the hall from which Dominia had come.

"He's just bitter"—Miki whispered to Dominia—"because he feels like I spurned him... He doesn't understand. The problem with long-term clients. They always want to save you."

Yeah: that was all Kahlil wanted. Just to save Miki, and to have that salvation rewarded by her love. Those shards of herself that the General found in him and his hopeless love inspired natural pity. What was infinitely more desirable about a woman whose love was somehow tainted? Why was that woman always worth so much more than all the honest women in the world, those gained at lesser cost? The General would never understand it, not in all the time she lived.

Maybe it was because a complicated woman knew she was complicated, and had to take better care of herself than a woman who was sane, straight-laced, and harbored no tragic secrets. Had to put on a more alluring front or pay greater attention in areas of self-care: Miki's makeup-whitened face looked pure as the plumage of the snowy herons and cranes that patterned her shimmering kimono. Even as she yammered at the frenetic pace of a chatty person denied adequate conversation for more than a month, the effect was doll-like. "Dude," this doll exclaimed, "I've been *dying* here without you! I was driving away from that antique music store—who uses records, anyway, I mean, what?—and Kahlil was up in the front seat and he looked and me and was just, like, 'Are you crying,' and I was like, 'What? No way, stupid, I don't cry,' but of course it turned out I was and I cried for, like, twenty minutes, so that Kahlil had to drive for a while, and—"

"Why were you crying?" asked Dominia, to the prostitute's exasperation.

"Because I was afraid I would never see you again! Idiot." Falling back upon her own two legs, Miki began to fan herself with the long sleeve of her glorious robe while her two huge eyes rolled toward the ceiling. "If you make me cry again, I'm going to have my servants whip you."

"We don't do that," said one of the Bearers.

"We're not servants," said the second.

The third qualified, "Not yours, not yet."

"Quit spoiling my power fantasy," shrieked Miki, hands balled into invisible fists while the General laughed. "If you're going to follow me around like a bunch of baby ducks, just play along!"

"I missed you, too," said Dominia to the little woman, who regained her grin as if it had never gone. "But I'm happy to see you now, and I'm glad I'm back in time for your—wedding." Only barely missed that beat.

"Oh, I knew you'd make it! The Lady said the wedding was scheduled based on your arrival, not the other way around. Anyway, you want to walk in the gardens with me? I'm not going to be allowed to walk on unconsecrated ground anymore after the marriage. The next time it happens will be in two thousand years, when the next avatar accepts my body—unless the world ends, in which case, I'll walk much sooner!"

"You knew what you signed up for with this gig, right?" Dominia thought specifically of Trisha the hotel porter, with a background of Kahlil's (frankly, valid) concerns about Miki's retention of self-identity.

With another wave of that vast *furisode* sleeve, the devotee of the Lady said, "Sure, I knew! I mean, this past forty days, I've had everything I've ever wanted! Forty days of servants, getting my face stuffed..." She was, as it happened, looking "softer" since last they'd met, and Dominia smiled; Miki grimaced. "Dude, we have to get you new teeth today." That smile vanished. "Sorry, just...needs another few minutes of healing, looks like. Anyway...I've been allowed to basically do whatever I want, other than be alone. Honestly...I'm tired of it. But it won't be my problem much longer, right? This way!"

It was amazing to Dominia how brave the woman was. Perhaps unaware of her fate, or perhaps imbued with divine valor, Miki led the way to the gardens while going on like a magpie about all the things she'd done and seen in Cairo over the past few weeks. Everyone here felt a reverence to some abstract goddess—the substance of darkness, itself—but Dominia felt a reverence for Miki, who had come far from the place she started in life and now rested at the cusp of a long dream's fulfillment. That reverence only doubled as the girl chattered on: "And I've just become—*super* religious over the past few weeks, like...praying every night"—memory stirred in Dominia even before Miki continued—"for you, too! Especially for you. You're why I started praying again at all. I haven't since I was a kid."

The prostitute's self-conscious laughter for her emerging spirituality was ended by the General's embrace. "I heard you," she said, to Miki's wide-eyed surprise. "You saved me while I was there. Thank you."

"Oh...oh..." Visibly unsure how to respond to this kind of emotion from Dominia, Miki stiffened up, breathed with a hiccup, then began to sharply pull away. "Well...well, don't get all—all soppy about it, stupid! And don't hug me so tightly...you'll—smear my face..."

Miki's tears were bound to do that on their own. Springing from the martyr with the haste of hidden emotions, the avatar-to-be pushed up her long sleeves and pointed forward. "Let's go!"

Beneath the rising moon, Dominia took her first breath of fresh air—air from her home and her world—in far too long. The temple was thick with the humid scent of women, beautiful in its tapestry of perfume, sex, and powders, but the martyr's senses, hyper-tuned to smell flesh on account of her natural hunger for it, were as relieved by the gentle aromas of innocent nature as her eye was relieved by the low light of the torchlit garden. She hadn't seen landscaping like this since her last trip to Europa: something at Kronborg or Versailles, maybe. Yet, she might go so far as to say Cairo's garden was more beautiful than either of those. The effect of rolling hills and a kind of mystical forest had been achieved within an enclosed palace courtyard. A thousand plants flourished, exotic flowers and vines artificially engineered to resemble the impossible plants of the Kingdom within the event horizon. Not even these matched that beauty, but they came close with cotton-candy-pink flowers springing in clots among orchids resembling the crystalline petals with which the Memory Bride wove her crown.

But the extraordinary element was not the flowers. Dominia was most enamored by the arrangement of its walking paths, which reminded the General of the contemplative labyrinth advertised for the patients of the Kyoto hospital. Far from a maze designed to confuse, this arrangement of open paths nonetheless tangled into what Dominia perceived would be, if viewed from above, a decorative knot of Celtic origin. The chords of the knot were distinguished from one another by low-set hedges, much like the hospital labyrinth, and were crossed with similar ease should the fancy to move to another path come to the mind. Yet even this beautiful design was not the most striking feature, for as they drew close, her eye resolved the four paths that led into the knot were guarded by statues: images of goddesses, whose marble gowns pooled about their feet with such liquidity that mere material garments dared not approach their grace.

At first glance, they were but marvelous artifacts of ancient time, these lovely statues: on the left, a maiden bent to wash clothes in an invisible stream, her hair in one thick braid that tumbled down the cloak upon her back, her head eternally lifted in alert at the approach of fleshly visitors; on the right, a madwoman, who gripped some hallucinated adversary by the throat while a trio of ravens in flight tore her age-thinned locks; but ah, the center! That helmeted Valkyrie who gripped a halberd with one taloned hand while the other, low by the armor of her hip, beckoned to the path at her right: a detail almost missed by Dominia against the background of the raven's wings unfurling from the deity's back.

"Who is that?" asked Dominia, her hush giving way to synchronicity's chill when her friend answered, "Oh, Her? That's the Morrigan."

She had never heard that word before, because it was, like all other epithets of the Lady, illegal for martyrs to speak.

Miki then went on, so excited to chat that she missed both Dominia's visible fright, and its increase as the martyr's eye neared the statue. The face beneath the partially opened helmet plainly resembled her own; the General felt exposed as must have Valentinian when first he saw, through whatever animal's beady eyes, that the Hierophant rendered his likeness in paintings. Desperate to pretend this was a coincidence and to keep Miki from noticing, she tried to devote her attention to the conversation at hand.

The garden was arranged in honor of Trisha's predecessor, way back when the now-departing Lady claimed the throne in 1974. Or when She began the process of claiming Her throne, anyway. "The transference takes a few years," Miki said. "I've thought about it lately, and it's been happening slowly, a bit at a time, my whole life. It's just now, I'm approaching the epicenter, and things are happening so fast..."

With a sad hiccup, she laughed, and Dominia took her hand. The human smiled, looking genuinely bashful for what the martyr suspected to be the first time in her life. "I don't have anything to say that could comfort you." The General felt queasy about it, herself. "But I'll be by your side for as long as I'm allowed."

"Thank you... Anyway, it's said on the eve of her coronation, this Lady saw into the future until the end of time, and demanded the creation of this, the finest garden ever seen on Earth, because of your Father." As Dominia laughed, the human protested, "It's true! It was impossible to keep him from knowing where they were located, She saw; but She also knows him as well as you do. He could never bring himself to destroy a thing as beautiful as this garden. It's said he's even invited to walk in it, if he comes alone. The legend is the invitation pacifies him into leaving Africa in peace; he's never taken us up on the walk through it, either. Good thing, because this is where"—she dropped her voice because of the trailing Bearers—"we keep the encrypted hard drives with the Red Market data on it. Hidden in these statues." While the General tried not to laugh at the ease with which her friend spilled state secrets, the human went on at normal volume. "Let's all pray he never comes."

"Not in this life," Dominia said as they passed the hooked claw of that warrior Morrigan.

Within the maze, the only difference in the paths was the order in which one encountered the statues. At each juncture rose another piece featuring one of many figures she did not recognize. Miki took joy in their naming: Venus, Minerva, Juno, these, the General recognized from their prevalence in the artifacts, plays, paintings, and myths that her Father prized. As the skeleton of the Western world ever decayed to a more hollow state, these goddesses had been so overwhelmed by their male counterparts they must have felt, to the Hierophant, "safe." Robbed of any liberating meaning. The same could be said of the Virgin Mary and Mary Magdalene, who stood and knelt on the left and right-hand side of a juncture near the center of the maze. But many other names had escaped even Dominia's well-read knowledge due to her Father's curated electronic library, which censored many books from her digital accounts over the course of her three-hundred-year life. Ishtar, she had known only because it was a dirty word, one let slip into the public presumably to keep them from wanting to know more. But there were more permutations than the General could have anticipated. Inanna, Isis, Izanami, Astarte, Nuit, and more than even Miki could identify when you got into the plethora of faces given Her by the Hindu or Buddhist societies. Not even all the Greeks had been in Dominia's education. She had not known of

Hekate except in Valentinian's passing reference and references in different folios of *Macbeth*, nor long meditated on pale Persephone, whose appearance (moon-whitened marble hair tumbling over one winsome, bare shoulder, with aching doe eyes turned sadly toward the viewer) recalled, to her pain, fair Cassandra.

In her enthusiasm, as ever, Miki did not notice Dominia's moments of introspection. "Hekate is the Greek Lady of crossroads, in three parts, like the Morrigan. Or three-faced, at any rate. Crossroads are also sacred to Izanami"—she waved as they passed the divided goddess, whose proud and elegant appearance held the leash of a ghoulish duplicate crouched in the middle of birthing a heinous monster—"but I prefer her stepdaughter!"

With an imitation of a trumpet's fanfare, Miki raised her arms as they rounded the corner and found themselves before a statue most beautiful, indeed: a woman whose Rapunzelian hair, trailing down her back, was nearly long as the kimono that pooled so far down the pedestal it trailed behind, as if the goddess had been exploring and made it back to her place just in time to be viewed. "Amaterasu," said Miki, who, even in her own beautiful *furisode*, did not hesitate to kneel and kiss the statue's hem. "The sun goddess. *My* sun goddess."

Who seemed to shower her languid smile upon Dominia. The General noticed this when she looked up from her study of the incredible detail of the goddess's delicate hand, clutching as it did the marble-bamboo handle of her parasol, and found that beatific expression waiting for her. The goddess's gaze focused on the white orb cradled in the statue's other hand. This, for some reason, summoned in the General the uncanny notion that she prepared to drop the sun into Dominia's hands. Despite the silliness of it, the martyr moved from the way as Miki said, "Her story was what brought me here. Why I started to wake up all those years ago... I saw her." She searched Dominia's face for skepticism and was emboldened by its absence. "She woke me up and told me I could be whoever I wanted to be. That she would help me, and I would help her."

When Dominia looked away from her second, safer scrutiny of the statue, Miki intensely studied not the goddess but the martyr; the human looked away, but the General pondered the look's true meaning as her friend carried on. "Amaterasu's best story is about how she was driven by her shitty brother to hide away in a cave, so all the other gods had to lure her out by throwing a party. The goddess of dawn and dancing threw off her clothes and put on such a goofy show that all the gods were in a hilarious uproar, and Amaterasu had to peek out of her cave to see what the hubbub was about. Lo and behold, they'd set a copper mirror outside, and she was dazzled by her own reflection! She saw herself, see? The sun."

"And then?"

Lamely, Miki shrugged. "Then they yank her out and cut off her brother's nose or something. It's a fairy tale, you know how it ends."

"Happily ever after," Lazarus answered. His voice so startled Miki that, with a cry, she sprang in the direction of her meandering Bearers only to trip over the hem of her kimono; the man was forced to skip over a hedge to join their path and catch her. He had emerged from the Norse Fates, but who knew where he had started? Dominia sensed she hadn't seen a quarter of the statues here. A peacock, likewise startled by the sudden noises, shrieked past as Lazarus set Miki upright, then adjusted the saffron fabric of his own kimono. "Good thing the Lady doesn't have to walk," he joked.

"You surprised me, you dope! You can't surprise people in a messed-up world like this one."

"Then we better get around to fixing it, because I hate walking on eggshells."

"Why did I get put in a man's kimono, again?" Dominia asked of Miki, noting as she had the fabric and texture of Kahlil's and having the difference brought to mind by Lazarus's appearance. With a sniff, Miki said, "Because you're a man."

As Dominia rolled her eyes, the girl insisted, "Well? There are two types of people allowed at the wedding and the coronation: Red Market women, and men they've slept with. And you're not a Red Market woman, so you must be a man!"

While Miki laughed at her, the General pinched her butt with a discrete hand and elicited a squawk so similar to the startled peacock that, in the distance, the bird answered. As if she had done nothing, Dominia asked, "Where's Basil?"

"Inside, waiting for you with the Lady." While Dominia's pulse skipped, Lazarus said, "I'm here to bring you to Her."

"Is this it," she murmured, afraid to hope. "Do we get to—Cassandra—"

"You can have her back," assured Lazarus, "but I'd like to talk to you first, if you don't mind."

Anything at all, just to see that diamond again. "I'll see you later, okay, Miki?"

"You'll sleep in my room," said the girl with a cheeky grin. "There won't be any escape from me, don't worry!"

On their return along the path, Lazarus fell into slight lead, and was silent until out of earshot of the Bearers. When sure they were alone, he said, "You know what's weird: there are often lots of differences between iterations, like how things are done or said or formatted. But no matter how many times I've lived this life, this garden is always the same. All the statues in the same place, all the chords intersecting into knots at the same points. How is that possible? Even throwing dice, they'll fall differently every time if it's a nonfatal roll. The chords of this garden are not fatal in their format, yet every time they appear in the same manner, the same order. The same statues."

"Maybe their order means something," observed Dominia, following, from the corner of her eye, the earnest face and clasped hands of kneeling Mary Magdalene before she passed from view. "Like a sentence for the initiated."

"Could be. Probably is. I guess I never think to ask them about it."

"Sort of surprises me that you don't know."

"Why should I know the Red Market's specific esoteric symbol set? I already know what they're driving at. You're the one who needs the symbols. All you people who haven't lived what I've lived and seen what I've seen."

"I suppose that's true."

As they emerged from the labyrinth, Lazarus took a breath and turned, frowning, to Dominia. "There are many other things that do not change. Fatal things. History-altering events. Vital moments in games and war: these do not change once a track is picked, so this is the only chance I get to speak to you before certain events occur. I urge you, Dominia. Please don't forget about Valentinian."

The joyful promise of Cassandra's diamond still fresh in her mind, the General had indeed forgotten the way the men had, in that dream-space, urged her to choose the magician over her wife. Mirth fell from her face, and from behind her deflating spirit, she assessed Lazarus with an eye not just wary but weary.

"Cassandra is the whole reason I looked for you in the first place."

"I know." The old man's tone was as miserable as she felt. "I know. I wish I could help you the way you were told that I could. But you know how these legends go. They turn into lies very easily, through nothing but simple misunderstanding. I can't give you anything. The Lady can. But She can only give you one thing, and only one thing is the right thing."

Bitterly, Dominia asked the question she had asked at least once in that Void, but in her head a thousand times. "If the magician is so powerful, why can't he do it? You can talk to me all you want about closed systems, and my Father denied him a body, and whatever: if it's possible for the Lady to do it, why isn't it possible for some magician?"

"Because the Lady can hardly do it, Herself. You said it: once the world is set into motion and a cycle has started, it's a closed system. Like a human being born into the human race, made up of hundreds of atoms replacing themselves over time and brought to the body from places far away: that seems like something new is being created, but it's just an emergence of life within existing units of matter in the system. You can't add to the total number of these units, which means interferences with the physical body are mostly entropic in form. It takes willful intercession from another force, antibiotics or a surgeon or whatever, to add some needed element back into the game, and it is neither good nor possible that such operations should be frequently engaged; even that isn't adding something that doesn't exist. But in the material sense of what can actually happen, something has to be traded for healing. For the human body, that might be money, or vitality, or time. On this world, the transference of the Lady from one body to another is a lateral transference of energy; during this transfer, other energies can be traded up or down, if you'd like to think of it in basic three-dimensional terms.

"The distortion during the moments where the Lady's true appearance is exposed makes it possible to bend the rules of entropy the way they're bent in the Ergosphere, because the Higgs field is being exposed in the same way: and the more people who are around to observe the distortion, the more powerful it is, and the more drastic the vertical transformation that can be made. Miracles are easier to observe when they happen in private, but they are much, much more powerful when they are accomplished in the presence of multiple people at once—infinitely more powerful when such an event occurs before a temple of fervent worshipers. What you trade up doesn't have to match what you're trading down, in that instance. If you have enough additional energy from a mass of witnesses, you could trade lead for gold, a diamond for a woman, or a dog for a man. But you can't have multiple miracles at once. Not this way."

As he spoke, they had reentered the temple and made their way through its halls, but the General had not even realized it. A sickness claimed her. Lazarus watched from the corner of his eye and turned at a juncture that revealed a pair of crimson doors decorated by that infamous lotus, here emblazoned gold. "It is true Valentinian is potentially powerful enough to restore your wife from death. To find her spirit in the dark—for, had she a soul to keep her from getting lost, she never would have killed herself." So unnecessary an addendum that Dominia's throat tightened in hot displeasure and her batting eye welled up. "But the information about her existence is still available; her spirit exists yet. From that spirit, her body might again be derived by operation of the Higgs field, but it could only be derived in the place and time and way you wish it during the distortion caused by the Lady's possession of Miki."

"But I could have her back forever because of that rift."

"Yes," answered Lazarus, tiredly.

Those lips, soft, gentle, already so close: close as the honey of her hair, the feathery touch of her fingers. The General's mouth tightened. "Is there anyone else who can help her? Any other way?"

"In this world, this life? No. But there are potentials for future disruptions. And then, there's you."

"How can I bring her back?" asked Dominia, wretched. One of the women guarding the double doors slipped within to announce their presence. "How can I help her?"

"With patience." Lazarus folded his hands politely before him, his expression apologetic for his unhelpful response. "Trust me, please. Don't ever trust your Father. Don't try to bring Cassandra back on your own just yet. And don't forget about Valentinian."

XI

Gratia Plena

As the daughter of the Hierophant, and an (arguable) only child throughout most of her life, Dominia had been exposed to much grandeur. Yet, as those towering doors yawned apart to reveal the Lady's throne room, she felt her Father, never shy in demonstrations of wealth, would blush to see such ostentatious architecture. Almost. In fact, its gilded glory deliberately recalled that of the hotel lobby, which had been a garish masterpiece of marble and gold. This, somehow, was far more marvelous, and farther stretching, the path of crimson carpet that unfurled its length marking, after the halfway point, the width of a bridge crossing the low pool inset before the throne. The throne itself sat atop a platform, which, accessible only from the flight of stairs marked by the carpet and the theatrical curtain behind the massive seat, had the effect of stranding its sovereign on a beautiful island. Upon this glamorous throne sat a woman. Though shriveled by the profundity of her age and struggling to breathe, let alone sit up, she was nonetheless as bejeweled as her temple and richly dressed in fine, thin linens that clutched the wheezing bones of her ribs.

This, after all, was Trisha: the body of Trisha. Like trying to connect Valentinian to Basil (who sat, tail wagging, at the Lady's shriveled side) or the nymph to earthly Gethsemane, the buxom redhead's appearance refused to conform to that of the dying avatar. Indeed, to avoid looking too closely and having her visit with the porter ruined by images of cobwebs upon a patchy scalp, Dominia bowed as soon as she and Lazarus stopped at the foot of the stairs.

The Lady's voice was a choir of voices that contained most prominently that of Trisha, vibrant despite her body's age, and crisp despite its immobile lips. *Our prodigal daughter returns home.*

Trying to discern the source of the voice only derived the strange notion it emerged from her own central nervous system; she tried not to question it too deeply after that. "I wasn't aware I had been Your daughter before," she said, trying to be polite, then relenting in a wan smile at the Lady's laughter.

All children stolen by your Father were Our children, first.

As the General lifted her gaze to better admire her surroundings, she instead found her eye drawn irrevocably toward the Lady. It seemed some black hole vibrated in that seat, stealing all light, absorbing all information. In reality, this was a tiny woman. How could such a body contain so much power? How could this body, upon which Dominia could hardly bear to look, be in any way linked to the creation or destruction of reality?

You cannot stand to look upon Us because this body is old and wretched: and you, like all mortals, fear death. Perhaps more than most.

Embarrassed to have her mind read in front of the room (as she glanced away, she noticed Gethsemane standing stock straight before the nearest pillar, and found that each pillar now had a Bearer stationed before it), the martyr began to apologize, but the Lady's voices rose. *Some look into life and see only death. Man must see in three dimensions, because if he saw in the fourth, he would see nothing but his fate, which otherwise he can but intuit. Yet most do not see either life or death. They do not see at all. You understand that, don't you?*

Dominia assessed those priestesses waiting like the garden statues, faces unveiled and vestments different. These new clothes resembled the uniforms of those female martyrs who took Holy Orders and joined the Church, but with a higher white collar, and no sign of a hood. This lack of a hood allowed for another second of searing eye contact with Gethsemane, which inspired the General to say to the Lady, "Some of us do not see death or life because we are not of this world, I think—not because we are not conscious."

Just slightly, the body upon the ill-size throne smiled. *Who is truly of this world? We have taken many forms. We have had many homes. We have borne many names and been born a hundred thousand times. Yet, We are not of this world.*

"Clearly."

You are not, either. Not anymore.

She hesitated. "Not entirely."

Do you think you were ever of this world, if you are able to become not of it?

"I suppose not."

None are truly of this world. Death exists only in the fears of mortals who lie awake in the dark of night and wonder if that darkness bears similarity to a future which is, in truth, incomprehensible. Do you dream Cassandra sleeps, to be roused by the life-giving kiss of her gallant trobairitz?

A white sag of sadness raced through Dominia's body: not to hear her wife's name or think of her death, but to think of her without a soul by which to navigate that after-space. "I cannot imagine how it is that she exists at all, now that she's dead."

She exists. She has trapped herself in an eternity of suffering. The reality was not delivered unkindly, but there was no kindness in reality. *By taking her own life, she has committed herself to repeating the experience forever, and shunned the possibility of redemption. But that does not mean that she cannot be redeemed. Come to Us.*

Sadness mixed with gentle horror as, degree by painful degree, the body lifted its right arm. Blinking away her eye's mist, Dominia glanced to Lazarus, cleared her throat, and reluctantly strode to kneel before the ruby-encrusted arm of the throne. There, her nose filled with the woman's breath, reeking to martyr faculties of damp dust and rotten age. In her struggle to be polite by finding some place to put her gaze, her focus fell to the mounds of jewels draped upon the avatar's visible sternum. From these, Dominia recognized in a half second that most beautiful and perfect of diamonds hanging amid her inferior siblings. As though they dared compare!

You worked so hard to avoid seeing Us that you did not even notice your bride among Our jewels. Take her back: you came all this way for her, after all.

With itching fingertips and anxiety caused by Gethsemane's warning that most could not even touch the Lady, Dominia felt only a heartbeat of concern before she once more caressed the cool surface of that diamond: the compacted ashes, hand-delivered by the Hierophant several weeks after the funeral. Nothing had mattered after her initial receipt of that diamond, and nothing would ever matter again. As she slipped the necklace over the Lady's head, the old woman's lips softened into a smile.

It was that thought that made all this possible, wasn't it? That nothing would ever matter to you again, not in this world.

Desperate to steer away from the subject, or regain some ground, Dominia held Cassandra to her heart and reveled in the relieving cocktail of dopamine and oxytocin. "Why don't You speak? Your body, I mean. I've heard Your voice will destroy the world, but will it? Why?"

Because Our body has been gifted Our true voice, which speaks only true words: and true words are truer than reality. Mortal bodies who hear them are not equipped to comprehend them here, and may go mad, or perish, depending upon the word spoken. True words can only be safely spoken in the Ergosphere, or in moments where that other place is in contact with this one. True words are the objects they symbolize; therefore, speaking these true words will bring their objects into being. Shall We speak for you the true word, the universal word meant when earthly men speak of "madness," so you can understand?

"No." The General's words were thin as she slipped the diamond over her own head. "That's fine."

Relief! That slight weight. Her wife bounced upon her heart and at passing speculation on the true word for "diamond," a revelation came upon her. She turned her widened eye toward Basil, whose tail wagged in giddy confirmation as she spoke. "True words—that's how you make fire! Or the playing cards! You're not *making* anything—you're speaking! Oh my God. Or—uh—" She laughed, feeling she'd committed some faux pas. "Sorry."

The Lady, not poised to take offense, chuckled in Dominia's heart. *Very good, General. Perhaps you will be ready for the whole truth, yet.*

"I'm ready to know anything you'll deign to tell me."

Yet you would not hear Us speak true madness, would you? While the General faltered, the Lady's legion carried on. *You are not prepared for all truth. Mortals so fear the truth that they would rather wander in the dark. We see you wish to protest: but you do not realize you have died many times, been lost in the dark many times, upon your death. Many times, you have died without a soul. Worse, you have often died with a corrupted soul. In the past, you have brought your wife's abomination into Our Earth and let it roam free, or opted to resume your place at your Father's side. Or you have forgotten it is by the grace of the magician you are here at all.*

"And will Cassandra have the opportunity to be here?"

She had one. She wasted it.

"That's bullshit." The General was shocked at herself but couldn't stop. "What about all the people who have ever died? People who didn't know anything and didn't have the opportunity to know anything? The illiterate, the isolated, the atheist? You're telling me all those people are condemned to wander around, not knowing anymore who or what they are, or where, or why? Is that just?"

Would We could craft it all another way, agreed the patient goddess, a kind of merriment stirring in Her body's milky eyes to the resentment of the General. *Would a goodly Redeemer sweep those souls together and set them right. But We are hardly more than one of the many columns in Our chamber—the lowly support of a palace made of Our same substance, though far grander in scale. We took no part in its building. We are simply here as its support.*

"Everybody loves to shuffle off responsibility," Dominia muttered, more to the diamond whose facets she stroked than anyone in the room. "Whose fault is it, then, that all those people are lost?" She studied the dog, who acted like an actual dog for the first time in their acquaintance, seated at the side of his mistress. "Valentinian's? God's?"

It is the fault of your Father, because that is the order he has chosen to maintain in his world. He has mastered the art of rendering his flock docile while keeping his neighbors too busy fighting among themselves to see how he steals, one by one, their own poor lambs. None of them have hope of surviving death, so long as they believe his is the only way.

"And it's somehow my responsibility to fix this?"

You are the Hierophant's daughter, and his only liberated child. Therefore, you are the only one in a position to accomplish his death. It is not necessary that you fix his world alone, however. You have already begun to collect many friends.

The General assessed the deity with a new brand of impudence that arose, perhaps, from the comfort given her by Cassandra's cold weight. "And one of those friends, you'll be keeping."

It is Miki Soto's destiny—her dream—to become Our avatar. She has never not been Our body. She had forgotten: recently, she remembered.

"So she has to stay here forever, alone, in this palace?"

With a stiff turn of Her head that was supposed to amount to a wry glance, the Lady suggested, *We are seldom alone, child.*

"Yes, but—"

Miki will not exist as you know her much longer. Not in this place. You will see her again, but not here. You already know that.

As Lazarus laid his hand upon her shoulder, Dominia softly asked, "Miki's not going to die, is she?"

Quiet Basil wagged his tail. The bearded mystic answered while drawing the General down the steps, away from the throne. "Her consciousness—her soul—will fly far from here, like the porter's."

"Then she'd might as well be dead." Misery tightening her throat, Dominia ground her thumb into the sharp edge of the gem and wondered if this trade had been worth delivering Miki to her end—or allowing Miki to deliver herself.

Without Miki's sacrifice, assured the eavesdropping goddess, *the integrity of reality could not be maintained. We are that which must have some presence, or else the world may not exist; yet, were We to reveal all of Our holy self, the world may cease to exist then, also. But the women in whom We live, child, live forever. Miki's voice shall be lifted among Ours, but her soul will fly freer than it ever has. And she will be given a rich treasure: something she has prayed for every night, imagined every second of her life. She will become a biological woman.*

What other promise could inspire such self-sacrificial religious devotion in a girl so materialistic she had almost cried over abandoning clothes on the train? Good thing they held off allowing her to—uh, absorb any of Lazarus's genetic material until recently, because if the body of the Ergosphere demonstrated the soul's personal truth, Miki would have discovered her femininity there and never returned. The whole world would have collapsed while she found her way to the City to party as the person she really was; or maybe she would have tried to find her way, and gotten lost. Far worse, in Dominia's opinion.

Yes. It is treacherous to navigate existence unbounded to materiality. Too many directions to go, too much to do, too much for the untrained mind to affect in themselves as well as in others. But that is for another night. This body is most easily exhausted, and how We long for one not quite so delicate! Be glad yours is so resilient. And gladder, still, of Our gift to it.

"What gift?" Even as she asked, Lazarus withdrew a silver flask from the sleeve of his kimono. Her attention, drawn to this, could not counter the finger he extended to flip the patch from her right eye socket; though she tried too late to jerk from the sudden intrusion, she could do no more than wince as the old man splashed the flask's contents beneath her eyelid and then, much against her will, past the upper lip whose swelling had abated mere moments before. The Lady's words muted the General's sputtering.

The Observer gives you Our water, which he has brought from the Ergosphere. It is precious: abide its workings. You shall need time for the restoration, and there is little before they arrive. Before, a treacherous snake gave you two false teeth: one to track your movements, and one to listen to your conversations. Now, your Mother returns your real teeth, which you gave up so long ago.

Response was impossible. As much pain as had surged through her at Lazarus's abrupt removal of her teeth, this pain was far beyond that. Not to mention totally foreign. The terrible, salivating itch began in her gums; its tear-provoking cousin emitted from her sinus cavity to consume the entire right half of her face in a quake of pain whose epicenter was her eye socket. As she thrashed free of the old man amid the terrible confusion of presumed betrayal, the General could not even reach for a weapon over the fiery screams of her nerves, and would only have thought to shoot herself to end the agony, anyway. She touched her gums, home of that pain with which she dared interfere—and the hard buds of new teeth cut through the tissue to meet her touch. Mouth widening in astonishment, the General rolled the gaze of her good eye toward Lazarus while the Lady, with gentle amusement, observed, *How afraid she is.*

The mystic nodded. "Like a cat, at the veterinarian." Basil added a soft bark, a laugh.

Somehow, Dominia had ended up on her knees, and as she accepted the old man's hand to be helped up, the pain ebbed into numbing endorphins. She dared not—not just yet—open that right eye, for a strange but welcome pressure increased as an orb bloomed within that too-long empty socket like fruit from the branch of a tree. "This will be my old eye," she asked. "My eye from before? These are my real teeth?"

You already know. All information is present upon the surface of a black hole, just as all that you are is reflected within the blueprint of your DNA. Our waters contain your eyes, your teeth, because they are Our eyes and teeth. We have loaned them to you, spirit, to do your duties in the world. Everything you have ever received has only been a loan. In truth, you have no body. In truth, you have only one eye.

In truth, the Truth was an apt name for the Ergosphere, and it was one that followed her back to Miki's quarters. Truth could set one free, or be weaponized. Her Father was an expert at using the truth to collar slaves and sow doubt, as he had about Valentinian. The truth had killed Cassandra. The truth had driven Dominia from her home. The Truth, yes, was that her wife, her life, and her eye had been taken from her—and it all seemed fantasy when she looked into the mirror of sleeping Miki's vanity and her teeth reflected back. Those were fine enough that she laughed to see them: but when, with the easy pace of a burlesque act, she unveiled her long-absent right eye, it glossed in instant tears of joy to find itself back home. Her own eye. Not some artificial toy, some spy developed by the Hierophant. Her own flesh-and-blood eye.

Or the Lady's eye, she supposed. Lazarus had stayed behind to speak with Her; otherwise Dominia would have plied him with questions. The only one she had to show was the dog, who had followed her back to the room, and over whom she now bent. "Look," she said, pointing at her prizes, then laughing softly. At the excited light in the dog's eyes, she worried he might bark, but the wise animal sat up to kiss her cheek and then, gently, paw the diamond around her neck. Again, the dog looked at her—now with more significance, though his joy was undeterred.

"Yeah," said Dominia, "isn't it wonderful?"

What else could she say when there was still so much to think about? Basil opened his mouth in that agreeable canine smile, then let the expression fade as he hopped upon the foot of Miki's bed. The Bearers, who slept in rooms adjacent, had made a cot for the General, and her things had been piled neatly beside. For a time, the General tossed and turned, the chain around her neck something to which she once more needed adapt—especially when she tried to sleep outside her normal circadian rhythm. Unconscious bliss had come with such ease in the Ergosphere, with the help of Valentinian. If only she managed to bring him back with her, as Lazarus had retrieved the water! Dominia had all but forgotten that short stop by the fountain—so early in their trip it seemed a century ago. Why was it possible for the water to come to Earth, or a *tulpa*, but not a lost soul? Why was it not possible for her to bring Valentinian into the world and save it, but also, for her own selfish interests, have Cassandra?

Sorrow tightened her throat, and the General relented. She slipped the diamond over her head to place it safely in her satchel. Although it was good to have her wife close again, thoughts of her and concerns for her well-being kept Dominia awake. Were Cassandra there, she would want Dominia to sleep more than she would want her wearing the diamond all night. As she reached within to tuck her wife into bed, the General's knuckles brushed something cold and hard that she did not recognize. For this, she traded the diamond, and withdrew her hand to see Valentinian's deck of playing cards.

As if those would help her sleep! They made her mind rove even wilder, fill with guilt and embarrassment; but, somehow, the hard rectangle of the pack was better than a sleeping pill, exuding from its place beneath her crossed arms a sense of safety. A reassurance that the magician was, in fact, not some dream. That reassurance evoked his voice, which she imagined chastising her: "How could anyone dream up somebody as great as me?"

Or did he actually chide her? Speak into her ear from the Ergosphere? She had felt the Lady's voice originated within her own nervous system. Perhaps all experiences with the divine, the otherworldly, were the same. It was all so strange; yet, thinking of the Ergosphere lured her off until, in the predawn hours, the General (who, for the record, was almost certainly struggling with undiagnosed PTSD from her many military experiences) awoke to the frantic shaking of Miki. This left the martyr thrashing about and so violently trying to clutch her perceived attacker that she tumbled from the cot to land face-first upon the floor.

Hilariously, Miki asked if she was awake. "Well, yes," she said into the antique rug.

"Then come to my bed and talk to me! I woke up an hour ago and I can't get back to sleep. Wait"—she gasped as the General righted herself—"is that your eye?"

"The Lady fixed it. And Lazarus. Long story. I'm surprised you saw it at all; I can't keep it open right now." Drawn to her feet and given a shove in the direction of the real bed, the martyr flopped upon it and somehow did not disturb the dog who snored in enviable peace. "Don't you want to try to sleep?"

"I've tried. I'm lonely! I'm scared." The human climbed back into the right side of the bed whose entire surface had been disturbed by fitful tossing. "You know how long it's been since I was scared of anything?"

"From what I can tell, I'd be nervous, too." Not that the martyr would ever do a thing like this. It was an unimaginable level of self-sacrifice: she was already being pressured into sacrificing the one thing that meant anything to her, and even the lives of all her people. To sacrifice herself? She couldn't picture it.

As both women ruminated, Miki's lower lip disappeared. "Will I still exist?"

The General's neurons dreamed of the porter's red hair tickling her neck. "I think you will." She told Miki about the hotel, and Trisha's appearance there; the prostitute wrinkled her nose in displeasure after Dominia had finished, whitewashing, of course, the "visitation."

"I have to work for eternity? As a desk monkey? I don't know if I like the sound of that."

"I don't know, she seemed to like it. I think she was the boss. Or she didn't care what her boss would think. And I wouldn't call it 'work,' what she was doing."

Although Miki smiled slightly at that, the smile was quick to fade. "What if it isn't like that for me, though? What if I lose myself completely? Like, what if I don't even know who I am anymore? I won't even know there's a me that's afraid...that's the scariest thought of all!"

Remembering how, as she wandered in a tiger's skin, the sound of Dominia's name on Miki's lips brought her to her senses, she took her friend's hand. "I'll pray for you," she said. "And you'll hear me, the way I heard you."

"You really heard me," marveled the human, unbelieving even now. "It's all so strange."

"Cosmic radio signals," Dominia suggested, positing a metaphor likely to be used by the man pretending to be a dog pretending to be asleep. Her head against the silk pillow, she said, "I used to worry death would be that way. That the final one would be a whole lot of nothing. Especially since I didn't remember the first one—I was afraid it would be like that again. Nonexistence. But now...I'm not sure." Darkly, she smiled. "Maybe it's wishful thinking."

All those people she had killed over the years! More nameless than named, but the named still too great in number for her sense of shame. She imagined them, all of them, wandering in the dark because of her. Those many victims of cities sieged, like the many starved to death in Tokyo before the last horrific blitz. It was all made up when, in reparations, the Hierophant donated the technology required to move the radio tower, and poured money into the Japanese branches of the DIOX Corporation as if he weren't just moving investments from one account to another. Everybody won: DIOX had a surge of orders for artificial parts following the war, which was around the time such items first came into mainstream fashion; the Hierophant, Dominia now knew, had his investment returned threefold; and the people of Japan, well, they earned the global right to kill or expel any flesh-eating demon discovered on their soil. They could suit themselves. The martyrs may have been expelled from Japan, but the tentacles of the DIOX company plunged deeper into the brains of the populace with each passing year.

Dominia had been the misdirection in his sleight-of-hand trick. While the Bitch of Europa turned her eyes on Hunters based in South America and Mexico, and the Family used this as justification to make their way south, DIOX products steadily slithered into the homes and bodies of everyone in the Far East to such extent that Dominia wondered if there was an electronic in the world to which her Father did not have instant access. She had killed many people, but he had control of so many more, and all of them were churned through his system of violence like grain in a mill. She was not a part of his mill, the General: she was his scythe.

But wasn't the fate of cut wheat, after the milling, to serve as the bread of higher beings? He had tried to convince her of that. Had tried to claim she was doing the right thing by leading his armies, by striving to please him. That futile striving led to the Black Night, an act of genocide that still haunted infamous Dominia. But that same futile striving led, also, to the moment when she began to question everything she had ever done in the name of her Father. This moment came a couple of decades before Cassandra, and was so simple it seemed nothing—was nothing, for certain, to the Hierophant. That nothing moment had been near the climax of the party after the Black Night, when a raucous feast was prepared with some of the slaughter and food was distributed for free to the rest of the masses. Dominia was several drinks in soon into the affair, which was why, perhaps, when she was finally able to get her Father's ear near the balcony, she had looked around through all the crowd and asked him, sincerely, "Are you proud of me?"

He blinked, as if either unprepared for the question, or unwilling to answer it. "For?"

For! She almost laughed. "For the idea—the South Americans are furious. They're already planning to strike Mexican soil, just like you want. You'll have your proper war. I thought it was a good idea."

"Perhaps it was—time will tell."

He turned away, and she, forgetting herself in all the drinks and the shock of his snub, grabbed his forearm. People nearby turned to look while she implored, "Hey! Can't you—" Now she did laugh, more a hollow exhalation that ended on a hopeful, high note. "Can't you tell me, just this once, 'Good job'?"

"Good job inspiring me to have all those people killed, Dominia. You didn't do anything yourself, you know—why, Cicero had more to do with enacting the operation than you. You may be my muse, my dear, my architect, my genius: but if there's a child I'm proudest of, it would be him."

Her mouth had fallen wide as her hand in that second. Now free of her grip, the Hierophant patted her cheek and said, "This is why we don't pressure our parents to play favorites, princess."

There went his back, into the depths of the party. There went Dominia's delusions about her place in the Family, and her hope that her Father might see her as something more than a grunt. All she had done, all the people she had killed to please him—all to accomplish an impossible task. To please an evil man who had kidnapped her from her home and trained her to throw her life away for him, acting like a doting Father but never quite letting anybody (except his precious priest) get any concrete approval.

Yes, a tiny straw, but the next night she filed her sabbatical paperwork, and the night after that she was on the plane to Quebec. What a stupid child she'd remained, for two hundred years! But that was testament to her Father's power. She couldn't blame herself when she had been so expertly trapped and brainwashed by him; Miki wouldn't.

Dominia rubbed her face, then turned over to see her human friend watching her with near-luminous eyes.

"I don't think you'll vanish into nothing," was what she settled on. The geisha nodded once, tucking her arm beneath her comically oversize pillow.

"I hope you're right. I'm so afraid! Maybe I'm egotistical." While the human laughed, her voice cracked and Dominia realized she wept. "After all, what am I compared to the whole world? I've seen too much of it to think I'm more valuable than all those places, all those people. All those people! My people." The General felt a strange electrical discharge, as if the Lady already welled in Miki's bosom; but her mortal tears kept the martyr grounded enough to reach for the human, to pat her, then wheeze as Miki threw herself against Dominia's rib cage.

"It's a lot of responsibility, isn't it! I feel so small. It's like when you're a kid, really little, and you think it'll be this way forever, you know—staying home with Mom, playing when you want. Even if she can be cross sometimes. Then, one day, you realize you have to go to school, and this is the *new* way it is—the way life *really* is—forever. Then school becomes work becomes volunteering for the board of your stupid HOA to keep yourself busy so you don't notice you're dying. I could see it, all of it, as soon as I discovered what the world was like, and I got scared then, too. Like I am now, but...worse. I put up such a fit on my way to kindergarten! I cried and cried. That was before Mom realized I was a girl so she'd hit me and say, 'Quit acting like a girl,' and, of course, I'd cry more. I was jealous of real girls! They got to feel whatever they needed. But I don't want to feel like this anymore, Dominia! I don't want to be so afraid. I wish tomorrow would hurry up and come."

Lowering her voice in case the Bearers listened somewhere (and, surely, they did), the General said, "You don't have to do this," but earned a hiccup of Miki's displeasure.

"I do! I've waited all my life for this. The world needs it. Me. And I can't stand the alternative, that nightmare I saw the first morning I was dragged to school. I'm going to die eventually, somehow, anyway. But I guess...this isn't really death."

Thinking of the fresco on her Father's ceiling, of that blue-clad woman, arms extended, attended by a choir of angels, Dominia said, "It's assumption. Immortality. Things can't be immortal here, so that which is destined for immortality has to go...elsewhere."

"Yes." Miki wiped away her tears. "Yes, I guess so. But...I don't want to forget." She hiccupped again, and laughed, squeezing shut her reddened eyes. "I don't want to forget my stupid mom. That bitch."

Laughing, Dominia kissed her friend atop her head. "I'm sure you won't."

"I don't want to forget you. Or"—her lips trembled—"you to forget me."

"Nobody," said the General, trying to stuff away her own emotions to tend to Miki's, "is going to forget anybody. Least of all you."

With a sniff and an emboldened nod, the human calmed at those words as she had been soothed by nothing else. From within the frightened girl, the regular, bossy version peeked out. "You better make sure you get it right this time, idiot." She flipped on her other side to back against Dominia for what was, at best, semi-consensual spooning. "Every time the cycle repeats, I have to go through all this fear again."

Yes, sad to say. Every time the unobservable cycle repeated itself, all of this would happen again. Dominia would remeet Miki every time the world was new, and every time, Miki would sacrifice herself. Most times, anyway. The General was sure there had been occasions where the girl prematurely entered her thought-body, or ran away with Dominia, or was somehow killed. And what happened to those worlds? How did they end? It was hopeless, surely. What a terrible thing to imagine, a hopeless world! And what a terrible burden to rest on Miki.

They had both been unfairly chosen to shoulder these tasks. By the arbitrary cruelty of the universe, Miki had been given the duty of maintaining reality, and Dominia had been given the duty of destroying it. At least, of altering it drastically. Of purging the world of her people, thereby ending it for them. Why was this not the task of someone better equipped? Of Valentinian, the Saint of Death? Perhaps all this was Dominia's responsibility only because of her originating decision: to choose between him, or Cassandra.

Now, it was the General's turn to lay awake. While Miki snored, Dominia turned and, in a bedside mirror strategically positioned across the room from its cousin, saw infinite selves engaging the same turn in an infinity of bedside mirrors. An infinity of Dominias: an infinity of wars, of sieges, of crimes against humanity. Infinite mistakes. How many times had she walked into that room and seen Cassandra blowing out her brains, the same crimson jelly of all the brains the General had bashed from human skulls? That same she'd bashed out of Benedict's skull, that day he'd come to her with the bright, sky-colored eyes of an innocent boy sent to war and said, "What a book, Tobit!"

He spoke while opening the steel plate installed in the door, through which she was expected to stick her arms to be cuffed for blood infusions delivered, insultingly, via intranasal drip rather than a glass. "You were so right. I got sucked right into it; read it all in one sitting! Well, kind of. I had a lot of duties last night, so I had to come back to it a couple of times, but—you weren't kidding! It was beautiful. Made a whole lot more sense to me than all that stuff about begetting..."

The poor boy. So excited to talk about that book. Probably even more excited to have some way to bond with his prisoner, to redeem himself in her eyes. Baffling, that desperation for approval. After her twenty years in Canada, she had been called back for a war that culminated in this, this moment, wherein she had a choice to make. Her own desperation for the approval of a hollow, evil person had put her there to begin with. Maybe that was why she did what she did, killing the private instead of just knocking him unconscious, or threatening him into silence. She saw a part of herself in him that she hated—a part of herself she wanted to kill. When his excitement over his opportunity to bond with her mixed with inexperience in just the right way, it kept him from fully ratcheting into place the cuff around Dominia's left wrist. It hung just a little loose as she lowered her hand; he hadn't done it properly at all, busy as he'd been talking about the angel, Raphael, who instructed Tobit in the use of fish whose organs could cure anything from demonic possession to physical blindness. That same miracle fish was the cause of Benedict's death in the end, when he opened the door and found that, in the seconds of its opening, the General had already jerked her slender fingers from the cuff, bending the metal to do it: he'd left as much give as a martyr needed, which was not much.

After six nights of being guarded by an overgrown boy, Dominia walked free while painted in his blood, and the blood of the two men who'd come to oversee her meal. Then she had gone on to kill every man in the ragtag encampment, silent as night, and had not thought again during the Nogales Rampage of poor Benedict, who ended his life twitching in her cell, short blond hair smeared in the same blood coloring her. The same blood with which she had manhandled his possessions in search of his gun and instead found a photograph of his mother, the town of his birth labeled on the back. She tossed it aside and took another man's gun because it was already in his dead hand.

She next thought of her jailer in Cassandra's hospital room, in the presence of the Hierophant. From that point on, Benedict's death was a trigger—the starting link in an inevitable chain of thoughts, which, like his endless "begets," led shame by deeper shame to the first human life she ever took under her Father's watchful eye as a teenager undergoing a rite of passage like any in her world: attending to the deaths of humans during Mass. Now, outside that world, her whole life was a horror.

As her thoughts reached a peak of sorrow, the dog emitted a soft "boof," eyes still innocently closed. Drawn from her unfortunate mental cycles to look at the beast, he appeared for all the world as if he'd barked at something in his dream. She knew better. With the same hand that stretched to pat the animal's side, the General wiped the tears from her face and lay back down in search of a few more precious hours of sleep.

XII

The Assumption of Miki

Those few hours of sleep Dominia managed proved vital. The ceremony was scheduled to begin shortly after the martyr normally roused; but, running on Miki's human schedule, she awoke at the stiflingly early hour of eleven in the morning. Truly back at war!

But, it was worth it. Worth it to spend Miki's last afternoon keeping her spellbound with stories of what Dominia had seen and done in that strange and sometimes terrible place where forty days had passed as a week's long march. Miki wanted to hear about the Kingdom, so Dominia tried to tell her, but she was at a loss to describe such a glorious place when, while seeing it, the General had lacked one eye, been sleep-deprived, and was overwhelmed by sensory bombardment after a long period of next to nothing. Dominia endeavored to comfort her friend, and to explain that, from what she had seen, the Kingdom was, well—heavenly. The human did her best to be reassured.

Not long after they awoke, they were brought breakfast: Miki received a platter entirely of fruits and vegetables, which meant that Dominia's thoughtful steak and eggs and (graphic) bloody Mary elicited the same envious cartoon eyes in the bride-to-be as they did in the dog. Although the General offered her a bite, Miki sagged.

"I can't. I gave up everything delicious forty-one days ago, when Kahlil and I arrived. I haven't even smelled meat since! But the Lady can't enter me if I've so much as touched it."

Vaguely, Dominia sensed this had something to do with the effects of protein on the spirit or soul inhabiting the body, but she could not articulate why or how. Somehow, it made her reluctant to sip her drink or finish the thick steak, which was, astonishingly, a natural side of beef rather than artificial. Not ideal—not human—but she was not sure she could bear to eat such a thing again, and not sure she needed to with the blood of

Lazarus flowing in her veins. Whatever the substance, she was glad to eat normal, material food again—and the fine, buttery, almost sweet flavor of the otherwise intensely umami steak was a welcome way to start. Funny how mass quantities of beer paired with idle living made both cows and humans much more delicious.

Miki downed a big swig of her mimosa, then refilled the glass from a pitcher-size container; Dominia eyed the thing. "But booze is fine?"

"Shit, are you kidding me? It's required. I'm pretty sure the incense here is mostly cannabis, anyway." While Dominia thought about the cigarette the magician had given her, Miki shrugged. "Who knows what they'll be pumping into the air during the ceremony? Maybe pheromones." She tacked on a goofy eyebrow waggle, which made Dominia laugh.

They would probably require pheromones to get the General believing in anything scheduled to happen that evening. Though she may have been to the Ergosphere and met Trisha, the struggle to find direct correspondence between that world and the one she knew was as fruitless as expecting a dream to manifest in physical reality. Oh, sure, her Father's religion was also adamant miracles were possible: but his religion centered around convincing its worshipers that only the chosen—the highest and mightiest and very, very few—could hope to wield those powers of the divine that mankind called "miraculous." Now confronted with a religion focusing on the open display of divine miracles, the skeptical, spiritually jaded martyr wasn't sure how to react. Yes, she had been given her eye and her teeth, but lurking beneath the layers of mysticism was surely a scientific explanation: maybe exposure to the substance brought from the Ergosphere activated her genetic code or sent her stem cells into overdrive to recreate old missing parts exactly as they were. Whatever the explanation, the spiritual trappings over it made her uncomfortable, and left her dubious anything would happen at all.

Yet, when the time came to wrap up the stories of her Void march and leave the future avatar to her early-evening preparations, the General found herself reluctant to go. She waited for some protest from Miki; but her friend's face revealed no trace of that fear that, in the early hours, had awoken Dominia, and that was exhaled in one long sigh that left the human still and perfect. A dove, meditating in her nest.

"I guess it's time for me to start getting ready." A Bearer waited in the doorway. Miki laughed for no real reason and then, quieted, reached for Dominia, only to wheeze with surprise as the martyr crushed her with the force of her embrace. "Dominia"—the human made a noise like a hiccup, and turned her face against the martyr's heart—"thank you."

"Don't thank me for this." The General fought the trembling of her lips and moved to push away hair not there anymore, for it had been sheared off a month ago. She smoothed back what remained as she said, "If I were any kind of friend, I'd save you."

"Now you sound like Kahlil. There's nothing to save me from." Her eyes blazing, Miki turned her reddened face up toward Dominia. "I'm the one saving you."

As Dominia hurried toward Basil and those guards who were too excited to act authoritative, it was with one last kiss on the cheek for a girl who, strictly speaking, had caused nothing but trouble from the first moment she'd electrocuted the General into unconsciousness. How strange, to think they parted as friends! She could not even discern the moment they'd *become* friends. But the world was a strange place, and the heart, far stranger. The heart was open to as much change as it had love; and of all the people she'd ever met, Miki was most full of love for life and other beings. The only one with more—or the potential for more—had been Cassandra, but that capacity for love, if not shattered, had been damaged in two parts: the loss of Benedict, and the loss of Benedict's child. Yes, there were always the schoolchildren, but Dominia saw early on it would never be the same. Not the same as a child of Cassandra's own who she could love and raise and teach to be good, despite their surroundings. Despite what they were. And Dominia, meanwhile, felt for over two hundred years before her wife that she'd endured too much, lost too much, seen too much, to love another person in a full, soulful way. Cassandra's death confirmed it: what love she had was not enough, or, worse, was poison.

This scarcity of love in Dominia's heart made the love radiating from Miki that much more precious. The General had long since closed herself off from trust: from feeling. Once that brief golden window had closed to her for good, she thought of love as an organ—attached to her, but useless and dead, or perhaps entirely missing. A phantom limb. But here, led down the hall by a bounding dog intent on a direct path to the gardens, the General felt that dead organ pulse again. Alive with love for the world through which she walked: a donation from Miki's bottomless resources.

The gardens that night were a sight to behold, more than any other night for the past two thousand years. On first emergence, the exquisite statues seemed to have multiplied, animated, begun to talk and laugh and sing with all the gaiety of birds: only the priestesses, relieved of their duties and given run of the liquor stores for Lamb-knew-how-many hours by the time Dominia joined in. Though the General paused upon the threshold with an anxious glance for the faint veil of sunlight still sharpening the edges of Cairo's skyscrapers and cell-phone towers, Basil gave a supportive bark and charged outside. Her body tense with the three-hundred-year instinct of pain, and the forty-/seven-day instinct of being swept into the heart of Sol, she crossed the threshold and found both her fears to be, at best, wastes of energy. If anything, she felt refreshed and alive—more than she'd felt in years. But the most remarkable effect of standing in the sun for those few seconds, in her own, real world, was the purity of it. In her mind, and her body. She didn't need to ask Lazarus or Valentinian: she felt in the base of her heart, as Cassandra must have felt those first inklings of pregnancy, that the normal food and bovine blood given her earlier, in concert with the sunlight, would keep her proteins from structural collapse. Perhaps a Lazarene martyr who chose to live at night still required blood. She hoped she would never have to test that theory, though felt as if, in the hoping, she had invited the experience by clumsy accident.

No matter. That was the sun, the real, earthly sun upon her face so long denied, and she was relieved that it sparkled through the trees, intent on sinking past the roofline of the courtyard; when she gazed toward the source of its light (as uninitiated humans were taught never to do under any circumstances, for fear of burned retinas), the boundaries of her body began to dissolve. The edges of her vision flickered with darkness, and against her skin rose the slightest vacuum pull—

Basil's bark tore her vision from the sun as if she had been but musing, deep in meditation. Had the orange trees spreading their leaves above not obscured the light, her untrained mind certainly would have whisked off to the Ergosphere. Ahead, the dog flirted merrily from woman to woman, taking advantage of his fuzzy appearance to receive the giddy embraces of perfumed arms and squealing kisses mashed upon his fur by so many pairs of painted lips that the white portions of his forehead bore the rainbow refraction of a prism by the time he halted at Kahlil. The young man's pensive study of the warrior Morrigan was interrupted by a pair of paws that, planted upon his back, shoved him forward. If he'd held a wineglass like everybody else, he'd have left both himself and the dog drenched. While the General tried to restrain her laughter so as to whistle for the border collie, Kahlil looked upon them both with bleak annoyance.

"Now there's a face I hoped I'd never see again," the man grumbled at the dog who'd shot him. "Tobias was right. If it's going to rain in Cairo, I'll bet I could tell you."

"Good thing that doesn't happen often. Other than that, you healing all right?"

Blandly, the man shrugged, then noticed Dominia's own empty hands. "You don't drink?"

Only all the time, as often as she could, for the past three hundred thirtyish years. "I've already had three or four this evening." Kahlil's vaguely impressed look transformed to one of religious scorn. "Just thought it was time for a break."

"How long ago?" On his asking, she was so baffled by the question that he had to repeat it. "How long ago was your last drink?"

"I don't know—they laid off a while, then brought me the last one about... an hour ago? I guess because they knew my time with Miki was wrapping up. Why, are we going swimming?"

"No, you—" Annoyed, Kahlil's voice dropped as he neared the General. "There's acid in the liquor." She almost laughed before he qualified: "Lysergic acid."

"What," the martyr practically shouted. "No, I've been drinking all day—"

And those first drinks hadn't left her quite like this. The lovey feelings; the hyperacuity rising over her; now that he mentioned it, she'd attributed that strange vibration in her feet to the sunlight, but she could place it now. Kahlil looked furiously up at her, a few curls of hair springing into disarray as his hands waved with his words.

"They started doping everybody two hours ago. I'm telling you, the women here are crazy. It's a cult! I *knew* they weren't going to tell you—I should have mentioned it yesterday when I saw you, but I...I had other things on my mind."

"How did you discover this?"

Annoyed to have to admit it, he said, "I looked around the place a bit, when I could shake them off my trail. They're up to no good; I've known it from the start. Then, last week, they were making a big fuss about something, and after I probed around with the girls I've been—hanging out with, and it turns out they have a lab to synthesize their own psychedelics. They have—basically gallons of it."

The phrase "gallons of LSD" may have been thrilling dirty talk to a certain breed of counterculture artist—she suspected it was to Valentinian, the way Basil's tail went nuts—but to the General, who still absorbed the fact that her brain currently processed its first molecules of lysergic acid since 1709 AL, the phrase was something out of a tahgmahr. Was this how the so-called miracles of the ceremony were accomplished? Where was the divinity in a base, drug-inspired hallucination? Oh, she'd dabbled acid and liked it fine, but then she came down and got back to her life like the rest of the world. Then, there were the bad trips, which made her stop for good: LSD, notorious for its self-insight, was not the best drug for cannibals dealing with the trauma of their first twenty-year war. It was one thing to try it a few times as a fortysomething kid. It was another thing to be given it nonconsensually as a centuries-lived General responsible for the deaths of hundreds of thousands of human beings.

"What would be the point of that?" The General pressed Kahlil even as his attention was drawn over her shoulder. "I mean, don't people usually charge for drugs?"

"It is a sacrament, General," intoned Gethsemane, who had approached from behind and now stooped to greet enthusiastic Basil. "Like the blood and flesh ingested in your ceremonies."

"Sacrilegious," admonished Kahlil, spitting on the ground. "The both of you. I'm ashamed to even be here. *Astaghfirullah.*" After one scalding glance of disappointment for the General, the boy marched back to the temple with a disgusted shake of his head. "*Astaghfirullah, astaghfirullah...*"

"God has already forgiven you." Gethsemane's call merited a nasty look from the man, who doubled his pace. Smiling, the Bearer rose to explain to Dominia, "The earthly mind is bound by laws that will be violated tonight. Because Kahlil has not engaged in the sacrament, he must sit out; these laws cannot be violated in the presence of a closed mind, for that closed mind would be destroyed. Tonight, the veil of the physical world will be torn to shreds and remade, and the witnesses must have the veil parted in their mind if they are to survive. Not all the women here are initiated into the truth of the Ergosphere, either; and these more than any require the sacrament, so their minds may justify what they see."

The Bearer took Dominia's hand. "Will you come with me, General, before the ceremony starts?"

Reluctant to follow anybody anywhere after being drugged, she gruffly asked, "Come where?"

"Everywhere." The girl tilted her head to press that soft, silk mouth—softer than that of the nymph's, somehow—against Dominia's lips. Annoyance giving way to arousal, the General embraced the Bearer's slim body until the human turned her mouth away.

"I don't know." The martyr sighed and held the woman, whose heavily lidded eyes were the physical quality that most resembled the Ergosphere's naiad. "My wife—and then there's you. There's danger in messing around with a martyr."

"Only if you feed me your blood, General, or if I lose all self-control, as I was afraid I might yesterday...but I am clearheaded today. Bearers need nothing of the sacrament. That makes me the best person to attend to you. Won't you come along? We must make sure you're full of joy before the festivities begin."

Full of joy—full of something! These people were alternately in touch with the source of cosmic truth, or a jet stream of cosmic bullshit. But Dominia was forced to admit: it was hard to hold on to grief, fear, and resentment when in the hands of the Water Bearer and her friend, lysergic acid, once they retired to the baths. Far from being the terrible, downright demonic trip once feared, the General relaxed more than she had in weeks—months! Since Cassandra's death, or even before. Each time the caresses of Gethsemane crescendoed in what Dominia found to be a more enjoyable purification ceremony than the day's prior, the General had the surreal sensation of being so relaxed it was as though she had no body at all: as though it had been dismembered, burst, scattered in pieces among the stars of outer space. The Void of space. That nest for the real center of reality, that anti-space of the Ergosphere and the black hole around which it swirled. The cradle of all things: good and bad, life and death, Cassandra and Dominia. Her wife seemed so close, and so comforting, even as the General submitted to this near stranger. Each heartbeat pounding in her chest gave hope, seemed to say her existence was the only reason Cassandra lived in the first place, seemed to say nothing in this universe could exist without every other thing also existing.

But could a thing return? There would be opportunity for Cassandra, Dominia remembered while the Bearer anointed and dressed her. This time, the kimono was a woman's, and Dominia realized only belatedly (through a wandering mind that felt suspiciously as her Ergosphere *nous*) that the gown was that same Miki had worn the day before. Shimmering brass silk adorned with those long, midflight herons. As her consciousness mounted breathless heights, the General's body lifted her arms and showed the kimono's long sleeves to that hovering self. The patterned birds upon it appeared to move their wings. A still thing, given life. A single heartbeat, separating the dead from the living.

More heartbeats separated the dressing from the ceremony. Once both women had dressed and exited the baths, the Bearer led her by the lysergic-hot hand to the palace throne room: empty of the Lady, but overflowing with Her followers. Most crowded the edges of those pools flanking the path to the throne, but many more had been forced to fall back into the crowd. Still others were poised to contribute to the ceremony, each in her own special way. Overwhelmed by the suffusing fragrance of women, of lavender and frankincense and sweet plum, Dominia felt suspended upon the wavelike murmurs—the laughter, the weeping, the shrieks and moans of the crowd. The General squeezed Gethsemane's hand tighter and tried to laugh away the fright that crept in only because the drug left her, like a raw nerve, disposed to experience all passing sensations in triplicate. This was not always good.

Laughter, however, raised her up, and inspired more laughter. After a big, dimpled grin from the Bearer and a kiss that reminded her of Cassandra, Dominia forgot all her fear and became aware only of the intensity of the moment and its endless beauty. Basil bounded from the crowded women, anointed, the fur of his face having been washed only to be redecorated with the maroon lines of chalk or makeup. Guilt sprang as she leaned down to pet the dog and saw by his huge eyes that he, too, had been intoxicated by that evening's drug of choice—but, now more than ever, it was important to remember Basil was not just a dog: he was a man.

Yes. He was a man. Dominia's heart sank into a quicksand of grief when the nymph's counterpart pressed into her hands the playing cards along with Cassandra's diamond. She had never seen the Bearer acquire them. Dominia's hand tightened around the deck, its surface cool as that diamond whose pendulum swung against her wrist.

"Why have you come?" asked the Bearer of Dominia as the sound of the women diminished in a bobbing hush.

"For Cassandra." The General's words were weak: she knew it was not quite true even before the patient woman pressed her.

"Why have you really come?"

Lips parted, heart racing, Dominia lifted her eyes to see the red sky of night ("a sailor's delight," as her Father chimed) glowing through a glass ceiling she had ironically not noticed while having her sight restored. The question of why she had truly come barred from consciousness the beauty of that view. She felt on some mission for which she had been dispatched 331 years ago, which she had forgotten, or been made to forget. (Why—no! Thirty-two! Hadn't she passed her October Feast Night in the Ergosphere? Oh, spiteful Saturn and his ceaseless march.)

But wasn't that sense of mission the truth? The way it really was? Everybody in the room had a mission remembered to varying degrees: the not-so-simple task of living their lives. Last night, her destiny seemed unfair, but now, surrounded by these women waiting for Miki to surrender her body to the spirit of a pan-dimensional archetype with no static identity but for those it borrowed, many destinies felt worse than hers.

Of course, she had choices. Tobias had pointed that out. She could always turn and walk out. What was this silly cult business? It was her free will that was the valuable commodity, so why was she allowing herself to be railroaded? The thoughts swirled upon her as though from outside her: indeed, they felt so external, she imagined them in her Father's voice. Though normally the General might have struggled to free herself of the doubts he posed, the tangibility of the truth was self-evident while her mind was lubricated by the unfamiliar molecule. Thus, she could dismiss all his arguments against her selfishness, save one. That of how she missed Cassandra.

Yet Cassandra's life had ended in such suffering, and been one of such suffering even with its many moments of joy. To bring her back would be to force her to resume life from that most hateful apex of despair from which the only way forward seemed to be her own wife's gun. Was such a resurrection not the greatest of cruelties? Was it not possible that soothing oblivion, like sleep, served its purpose? That, to restore health and joy of living, the wounded spirit required ample rest before again enduring the material being in hopes of crafting a soul?

What did Dominia know of life and death? What was she doing, chasing this dream of happy resurrection—in logic's cold light, far less likely a success than the liberation of a dog and a man from superposition?

"Please." Her words for Basil were soft as a tear while the Bearer led them up the aisle to stand behind the throne. "Don't disappoint me."

Just once, the dog wagged his tail, then fell into solemn silence as the three took natural places with Dominia in the center and Basil to her right. To their flanks lay curtained wings, as though they were upon a theater stage. Dominia grew ill with a stage fright she had never experienced before. As if she had not, a thousand times, addressed centuries of men waiting to die at war! Her one consolation was that any eyes upon her were only upon her in passing. Most shifted uneasily from the throne to the doors, awaiting, as did Dominia, the glorious appearance of Miki Soto.

From her new vantage—still trembling, though less overwhelmed by her senses—the General studied crimson banners that had been unfurled down the columns. Man-height, thin iron braziers, like claws upon twisting staffs, were set nine on one side and nine on the other at even measure down the shallow pools. Their light prepared to support the room once night finished fading in. Those preparing women behind the columns were divided into band members, dancers, flower bearers, and still others who cared for covered boxes with contents Dominia could not divine.

The musicians were the ones who acted first, prompted by some secret sign or agreed-upon time to ring the room into silence with their cymbals. From the first iteration of their repetitive beat, they received perfect attention. Motion in the sweet, underappreciated periphery that she still expected to be a blind spot drew her attention right in time to see tiny, near-mummified Trisha carried upon an elaborate litter whose roof was a spiral of ornate gold and silver that spun high like the peaks of her Father's cathedrals. Four of the Bearers, Gethsemane aside, carried her. Behind this litter walked Lazarus, who moved with as much, or more, poise than the women.

Though the cymbals continued, joined by the eerie sound of wooden *suzu* bells, they did so with new, muted reverence. Women stood on tiptoes for better looks at the Lady: as a result, soon the whole crowd pressed forward with such desperation it seemed the front row would collapse into the pools. By some strength, they contained themselves well enough to watch Lazarus help the Lady from Her litter and sit, gently, upon the throne. The beat silenced.

Dearly beloved, began that strange symphony of voices, *you are gathered today to celebrate Our rebirth: but you know it is more than that. This is the rebirth of the Earth. For all appearances, it shall be the same; yet, We will find it new. We will know it to be new. We will be new. And what of that part of Us that does not survive the transition? This body? Where goes the Queen Bee with her finest drones when she feels it time to split her hive? She founds a new hive, which must seem to her absented kingdom a wholly different world. Let us pray.*

The mass kneeling was audible, an action that seemed impossible to Dominia, given how tightly the women were packed. As the General belatedly followed their lead, the Lady led the prayer. The chant, as ever, did not keep the martyr's attention (particularly not under the swell of a drug that increased the excitement of her blood, the pressure in her body, as if she was, at any second, to be swept back into the Ergosphere), but she perceived it was intended for the sanctity and protection of the old world and the new. *Let the light of the sun shine upon its face when it is young and full of hope*, the Lady prayed, which Dominia didn't understand. How could a sun fail to shine on the face of a world where life already thrived? It must have been a symbol. Like Amaterasu, Miki's sun goddess, looking in the mirror. Like being upon the Earth, yet knowing—no, feeling—one was also within the black hole at the end of time. That one was eternal and mighty. More than a frail body.

As the murmur that had hypnotized Dominia into contemplation met an end marked by the rising of the women, the Lady picked up where She'd left off.

The planet is a rocket for the species, and the species is a rocket for the soul, and let no Man, by God, rent asunder the soul from the flesh. In soul, the flesh lives forever; in flesh, the soul is born. What is lost that does not exist? What is undiscovered that cannot be found?

The sounds of drums gently picked up, and Dominia found herself breathless as the Lady pushed Herself from Her seat with Lazarus's guiding hand around Her left arm. *The differences between soul and flesh are mere illusion*, She insisted, taking Her first step in two thousand years. *All that exists is light working in harmony, propelled by conscious will.*

Paused at the foot of her stairs, the creaking goddess eased around to face delirious Dominia. The General flushed as the room followed suit.

General—the voices boomed in her heart like the timpani of the drums and some fragile strings taught to rise at her announcement—*it is your will that today directs the rocket of this world. You have a choice to make. Tonight is a night for miracles. Tonight is a night for the occluded to be revealed, for a being rendered mere concept to be given flesh. You could ask for money or power from me, but your Father could give you those. Only I can give life. Which life will you choose?*

A sharp breath clutched Dominia's lungs the way her hand clutched that diamond. That same cold diamond that beat against her breast with each running step away from San Valentino; that diamond that contained the physical memory of her wife but only implied the spiritual memory; that diamond that could have the spirit imbued, and bring the body back with it, bring back her wife, her wife, her wife, oh, Cassandra—she was sorry. Dominia was sorry, Cassandra: but that was just the way things were. The General had to be the person she'd always wished she was. The good and generous person forever struggling to be seen as such, and not that selfish, murderous martyr, party to genocide and anthropophagy. She had to be the person she wished she could be for Cassandra. After all: What was the point in having Cassandra back if nothing changed? What was the point in any of this, if all of it happened again?

"The dog." She shut her eyes while a light came to Basil's. The border collie, in his thrill, tapped his feet upon the marble floor. "Take the dog and make him—make him Valentinian. Bring the magician here, into this world."

The General's head buzzed too loudly to admit the ripples of relieved sighs—the one or two cries of delight—among many murmurs of confusion. Only Gethsemane appeared she had known this would be the General's choice—Gethsemane, and Lazarus, who met the General's watering eyes, and nodded. As the Bearer stepped forward, herding the dancing dog, the animal paused to kiss Dominia's hand.

Halfway down the length of the pools, the woman and the dog both stopped, and the animal looked around, so delighted that not one scrap of magical dignity remained detectable in the beast. But this charming hound was a powerful sight when the music rose into true melody. The Lady and Lazarus waited at the path's termination while Gethsemane stepped aside, into the water, and the dancers swirled into motion on either wing of the grand foyer at the hall's distant end. As, in a floral hurricane of veils and ribbons, they crossed one another's paths, the tremendous doors swung open to reveal, more doll-like and perfect than ever, Miki Soto.

Tears renewed themselves in Dominia's eyes to see her, surely as they sprang from all the women in the room; though perhaps that was attributable to those many bright, scarlet butterflies released from the cloth-covered boxes—cages, the General realized—at the opening of the doors. Upon a twin of the Lady's litter, one attained no sense of her beauty's scale; but, when the litter stopped at the path, opposite the holy couple, and the future avatar stepped out, the room beneath the music became a vacuum of sound. One dancer stumbled to see the chromatic train of the splendid bridal kimono, which was embroidered with an explosive array of jade and carnelian flowers, cool turquoise mountains and swirling, hypnotic dirt paths that repeated beneath panels of violet skies dotted by glittering suns—the same suns that gave the stained-glass fabric the yet-uniform impression of gold. Even the sash seemed woven in the Void, or the Kingdom, and transported to Earth. Considering the weight of the deck in Dominia's hand, this may have been so.

But could that gown compare to its bride? Miki wore no makeup, and the human's long hair poured down her shoulders in a perfect ebony waterfall. There was no one who could more resemble that statue Miki had admired the night before. Enchanted by the sublime appearance of her friend, Dominia failed to notice, until both figures were a quarter of the way up their respective sides of the aisle, that the Lady's old body mirrored Her new one step for step. Now the General's attention shifted, and in so doing, she caught the exact second a rueful metamorphosis overtook the old woman. A flicker of hesitation sparked in Miki's eyes as she, too, saw the way Trisha's feet blackened. That blackness rose higher toward her knees with every step: but the new avatar emboldened herself, and her face hardened as the encroaching old body dissolved into something not of this world. Whatever it was, it provoked, amid the many women, a series of gasps that ranged from awed to flatly terrified. There was no going back now, but Dominia struggled with her urge to sweep in and save Miki. Instinct fostered the wish that things could be different. Maybe there had been some hidden other path, and she had failed to find it.

But, was there? Were alternatives fatalistic wishful thinking?

Perhaps it was possible. Already, the impossible had been made possible to her, so perhaps the future would reveal some method of salvation. Hand on her heart, Dominia dared step to Lazarus's side to watch with him. Dared, for with every step the Lady took, the entire palace—perhaps all reality—jittered and echoed like a misfed film. Was this the changeover of the film reel, following Valentinian's metaphor? The space over the dog flexed in a way Dominia mistook for a trick of the light, of her eye, of mere dust or ash from the torches. But that quiver of darkness fomented itself, then shivered and grew until it wrenched a tear in the delicate brane of reality to reveal that same naked Void that consumed the Lady's old body. It was wrong, Dominia realized, to call such a thing "black"; it was the absence, even, of that much. The absence of negative space. Black was a shade of white, and negativity implied positivity—even absence implied presence. This could not even be said to be absence. What was it? What *really* was it? Dominia emitted a short cry to see this extra-dimensional blot (truly extra-dimensional, for she sensed it was but the three-dimensional appearance of a fourth- or higher-dimensional object, like a hypersphere, or a tesseract, but beyond the comprehension of any mortal model) expanded its navy border ever nearer the dog. Gradually, with each trembling pulse of its surface, the tear revealed the head, then the shoulders, then the sanguinary vest, of Valentinian.

She discovered she gripped Lazarus's hand; for how long, she couldn't tell. The improbable image grew along with the space around it, and all light in the room—all light pouring through the glass ceiling—streamed into its vacuous mouth along with any lingering sense of time, reality, or causality. The women farthest from the (proverbial and literal) event horizon were frozen in motion, while others stuttered in and out of existence, and those closest to the scene, paradoxically, appeared the most real. Gethsemane was at times replaced by the tiny nymph of the Ergosphere, yet was still the human Gethsemane, and in this transposition Dominia believed she saw what was, arguably, the only true Gethsemane, which had to be a combination of both, plus all the other bodies to which the nymph had previously bound herself on Earth. Time compacted: there was no time, therefore all bodies were present at once. The effect was possibly the most beautiful thing Dominia's material eyes had ever seen, a burning beauty that ached her head and made her avert her stinging retinas to the dark Lady as She reached that two-dimensional tear in space. From the other side, Miki had done the same, and when the image of the Ergopshere failed for those fractions of seconds, her friend's openly astonished face appeared as through a window. The archetypal expression of astonishment, close to the rift as she was. All who watched the scene trembled, the atoms of their bodies threatening to buckle under stress of the shift like a martyr's deformed proteins destroying themselves in starvation.

From a distance, Miki opened her mouth, and Dominia was amazed her friend's voice emanated from that same no-/everywhere as the Lady's choir.

Are You death, the young Lady asked as the old one reached to embrace her. Miki, though frightened, seemed compelled to do the same.

Yes, answered the voices of the Lady. *And because We are Death, We are Life.*

With the tilt of her head, Miki's eyes fell closed, and the darkness of the Ergosphere accepted her kiss, returned it, wrapped itself around her and began to dissolve—or began, perhaps, to dissolve into her. The oversize bow tied in back of Miki's kimono fluttered in the pressure of the tear like the wings of those butterflies fleeing through the open skylight panels. Blood red, their wings: red as the sky into which they fled, and red as the waistcoat of the magician who, a flickering light between the merging entities, lifted his head to admire the lingering insects. The dark figure of the old Lady had almost completely dissolved, and Miki, doubled over, stood between the General and the magician with her mouth open and her gaze miles away. When she looked up at Dominia, those unseeing eyes glowed white. The astonished General met her gaze and was, yes, dazzled—dazzled, like Amaterasu consulting her mirror. This clear white light swallowed Dominia's body along with all noise and sensation until existence vanished in submission to higher Truth.

This was not the Ergosphere. Not the event horizon. Possibly. She could not explain what this was, for she had not even a dream body here; yet she knew this space, empty and eternal, contained both Miki and Dominia. Moreover, she sensed in this place they were the same, and she talked to herself. Perhaps that was just the spirit of the Lady, which was in everything. Somehow, in a way beyond hearing, she heard Miki tell her, "I guess this is goodbye for me, huh? In that place, anyway."

"I can't believe you have to go."

"We all have to sometime, right? But, I know what you mean." Stillness. "I'll miss you."

"And I'll miss you. I never could have—oh, Miki."

"Don't cry!" Although there were no bodies, there was the sensation of touch, like a hand on a shoulder. "Big, tough General—don't cry! You'll make me cry, stupid."

"Sorry."

"It's important I do this."

"I know. But...thank you. I could never thank you enough, Miki."

"You can try when we meet again." Laughter rang in the fading voice of Miki Soto, whose body appeared, perfect and female and nude as the one into which Dominia dropped, and around which clothes appeared, and space re-formed, and the flying soul of her foul-mouthed friend called, "So cheer up, you silly bitch!"

These were the last words the ears of Dominia's body ever heard her friend speak, and they made her laugh, albeit tearfully. This meant she was forced to cover her mouth when the tears dissolved into a gasp to find, as she came to her senses, the Lady's new body had swooned beneath the intensity of the transition and had been caught: not in the arms of the Bearer, but—at long last!—those of Saint Valentinian. His head lifted to reveal a grin for the many flabbergasted women, who had, for the most part, seen a dog blink into the shape of a man. Even those nearest, for whom time's flow had been least interrupted, surely had not perceived the sleight-of-hand moment the exchange was made. A dog and an old woman in exchange for Valentinian. Impossible.

Yet, the impossible was inarguable. More so when, once the new Lady was passed to those Bearers who hurried up the path, he turned to wave at Dominia.

"Hey, buddy!" As he called out, she was stunned to realize his voice was real. *He* was real. Real! Clear, more static than the magician of the Void where all was dark and shifting. With him, hope became real, too. Driven to tears, she sprinted down the aisle to throw her arms around her patron saint, her dog, her friend. The laughing magician embraced her. "I don't know how I can ever thank you," he said into her scalp. The General's grip around him tightened with her sob.

"Just help me, please. Help me restore Cassandra's life."

"I will." He patted her, then released her to call, "But, first, why don't we party! My God, I have a body! Physical thumbs! I could dance!" Cheesily, he hopped into the air and clicked his heels while Lazarus arrived behind them.

"Don't hurt yourself. The last thing we need is a magician with a bad back."

"What will happen now?" asked the General of the mystic. "Will you stay here? Is this your marriage, too?"

He has made a union with Our body to allow it to receive Us, as We have made a union with Our body to maintain the world. In the arms of Gethsemane, Miki's frame straightened, and its eyes reopened to appear, for all the world, normal organs. The body's mouth, as Trisha's, did not move, and never would again. Yet, amid that vast choir of feminine speech, Miki's voice displaced the previous avatar's as the most prominent. *Lazarus's wanderings must be ended. Those final souls who would follow him only by knowing him will soon be initiated into the faith*—was She talking about Dominia?—*so it is vital he remains within Our reach. Elsewhere on Earth he would be too easily swept into the hands of your Father. Until now, Our actions—yours, and his—have had the capacity for variance. The choice you made tonight has limited the possibilities of the future. Of those limited possibilities, the safest for Lazarus is to remain by Our side.*

"Lazarus was Trisha's—boyfriend," said Dominia with a glance to the perpetually exhausted-looking man. "What does he have to do with the Lady? Why can't he retire to the Void in peace?" Even as she spoke, she caught Valentinian's glance and thought of his Mandelbrot lecture.

His blood, said the Lady, taking Her final, unsteady steps to the throne, *is Our body. With it, all worlds will have the keys to the Kingdom.*

"So you'll ship him to Mars when you're done here?" she asked wryly. Miki's body smiled as it eased into its seat.

Another like him will rise there, and his key will be of a different substance than mere blood. The same old story will continue again.

"What about me?" The General spared an anxious glance the way of the magician. All those weeks ago, she had been certain this moment would be how and where her story ended. She would hold Cassandra in her arms and—what? They would live happily ever after? What had she expected? What did she expect now? The gravity of the situation settled in. Having forsaken her country, her people, her Family and their Church, she had been labeled a terrorist, pursued across the globe, had eyes removed and replaced, killed many and been nearly killed—and all so Lazarus could get shacked up in a polygamous marriage with an avatar and her goddess? So Miki could lose her life? So a dog could be made into a man who scrutinized her from the corner of her tear-filled eye?

"What about everything I've done," she asked, "everything I've been through? Where will *I* go?"

We have much to discuss on that subject, General. The Lady folded Miki's hands in the colorful fabric of Her lap. *We shall require an army. When We have one, We wish you to lead it.*

Astonished by the flat implication that the Lady intended to initiate war, the General had time to ask, "Against my Father?" before the first, not-so-distant explosion rocked Cairo. As power failed outside the room, Dominia, along with the rest of the women, became abruptly aware of the thickness of night that had fallen above. In the distance, sirens rose. The light-poisoned sky relinquished its hidden stars only to see them dismissed by the next rocket, which, screaming past, destroyed in a violent spew of dust some part of the palace only visible from Dominia's position by the emitted debris. Amid the smoke, the sirens, and the screams, the General recognized the noble constellation of Orion.

XIII

Prisoner of War

Were it not for the thousand battles in which the General di Mephitoli had fought, there would have been no comprehending the horror underway. Between the sickly-sweet waves of the drug that opened the cleft between materiality and consciousness enough to render both distinguishable, all emotions were amplified, and those amplified emotions bled through the room so swiftly that fear, like toxic gas, raced between the bodies from the first scream. Shadows poured into the room. Some had guns, some had blades, but all shouted, and the General was never too disoriented or too peaceful to recognize a battle. As Cassandra's diamond fell into its place against her heart, Dominia snatched up the nearest brazier, and Valentinian, amid the madness, asked Lazarus, "Are we doing this already?"

"Do all the drugs you do in the Ergosphere impact your physical memory, too?" was the mystic's contribution as the Water Bearers, with ceremonial knives secreted somewhere upon their persons, fell into battle. The demons, named by the scream, "Al-Saalihin," were soon revealed as but men. Perfectly killable no matter how great their number as they poured, like ants through a beehive, into the temple's throne room. This recognition of reality elicited an inappropriate laugh from the General as half the women fled behind the throne, and half, ill-suited for any fight, charged to meet the men. She experienced an instant shift of priority, from defense of Miki—no, the Lady—to handling the threat. As she sprinted for the fray, Valentinian's distant laughter rang around the words, "Go get 'em, tiger."

Oh, did she. With animal grace surmounting that of the image into which the dreaming Void transformed her, the General covered the length of the marble aisle, pushed past women who arranged themselves to block the way, and began freeing space in which to fight by sweeping the brazier like a spear whose claws penetrated the breast of the first man she met. This action earned not just her first kill of the night but also a weapon: a vibroblade more eager than ever to cut down man after man. They forged a brief, unique relationship, the General and that blade, as the brazier fell out of her hands and the handle of the sword, in. Thereafter, the shimmering metal swept up, left, into another man's gut and through his comrade's hip bone like butter in such a slick, smooth, easy way that the martyr's drugged mind felt precious more than lurid fascination. The muted voice of her horrified conscience reminded her of the wish made to Gethsemane: but there was no time for hoping these men were willing to talk. In a free moment, she withdrew her gun from the sleeve of the kimono and emptied its rounds into the hearts and heads of three soldiers, and she wished she could apologize. Maybe that was just the acid talking.

Most of the women (indeed, most people) could not handle the mere concept of a sword fight on LSD, and certainly not amid a storm of gunfire. The General was not most people. Fighting had been her life for a longer period than memory served. On a mental front, she had spent three centuries fighting with her Father and Cicero. But it was the physical dance she always loved, and how well she knew those steps! By their nature, insurgents used unlocked guns; her own beloved weapon swiftly out of bullets, the General dropped it to snatch the first abandoned rifle she found. With it, she laid down a line of black-cloaked men, which allowed the Bearers to collect more guns from the wreckage. Gethsemane, trailing past, tugged her vulnerable consciousness briefly after and cost Dominia a nice scratch in the face. Even so, that same drug that distracted her produced a kind of tunnel vision, slowed time, and illuminated to her every intended movement of her opponent's paltry human muscles better than even the DIOX-I. Indeed, it felt not dissimilar from those times in the past, when prayers to the Lamb invited his spirit into hers to guide her victory. (The place she saw when he came into her—all that time, that must have been the Ergosphere! All her life, imagine! Yet never once had she known of that space, not in over three hundred years.) The flow felt more natural than running, more thrilling for the intensity of her connection to the sorrowful aspect of her duty.

After all—was it not that bleak, wandering Ergosphere to which she sent these men? Or were there those among the Hunters who had somehow, like Akachi, acquired Lazarus's blood, so their souls would fly at death to their eternal resting place? Would that be the Kingdom? Most of them thought it was Jerusalem or Mecca. Once upon a time, the fringe religious groups who were the forebears of the Hunters had placed symbolic emphasis on only the earthly city of Mecca, as had those more centrist followers of Muhammad who had drifted into the human conglomerate known as Abrahamianism. Most of these good Muslims still placed emphasis on Mecca, like their ancestors; but the Hunters, who also called themselves mujahideen, had shifted emphasis upon the movement of the Holy See of the Catholic Church from Mephitoli to Israel. This was not for a religious reason but a practical one: they recognized the Hierophant's specific interest in claiming Jerusalem and smiting the final tatters of what was once the most powerful faith in the world in hopes of absorbing the rest of its followers into his flock, and justifying his control of human souls. What he really wanted more than anything was what Jerusalem represented, and this Dominia knew better than anyone on the planet. What he really wanted, what he dreamed about at day (if he ever slept, which she doubted), was the night the Holy Martyr Church could finally claim it *was* the Roman Catholic Church, and nobody would bat an eye.

That night had not yet come, suffice to say. The word "mujahideen," which had once meant "jihadist," now meant something akin to its own brand of faith—one distinguished from the Abrahamians largely by the feverish psychopathy its members vented on martyr and human alike. They did not want Jerusalem for any particular religious reason. They wanted Jerusalem because her Father wanted Jerusalem. But perhaps they really craved the city for the other reason her Father desired it: all those souls, believers who took their faiths too literally and flew to the Ergosphere's interference pattern variants of Jerusalem or Mecca. Claiming either one of those would have disturbing implications for the Hierophant's spiritual power. Who knew what he would be able to do with, or to, all those souls? And who dared think he'd stop at Jerusalem, without going on to take Mecca? Then, one by one, all the Eastern countries, and their holy cities? The Hunters convinced themselves they did a service for mankind by keeping the Hierophant out of Jerusalem, and that was true to a certain extent, but the sad fact was that Hunter interference in and around the city was the cause of violence and turmoil. Was the suffering of the living worth the protection of the dead?

One of the Bearers screamed for her sisters to halt: all the women obeyed, which produced the uncanny effect of stilling the entire room—save for Dominia, who was midway through decapitating a man while deep in thought. Now, she returned to herself with some surprise for the carnage produced by the blade and her body while she ruminated on the nature of Hunters. With another glimpse of that elevator conversation, she regretted her lack of awareness, and turned with a surge of disdain to see Dr. Tobias Akachi standing behind the throne, one hand upon the Lady's shoulder.

"There." The dentist's teeth illuminated a room long-since dimmed by the crashing of its standing braziers and the disappearance of the sun. "You know, I do a bit of teaching now and then. When my pupils are unruly, I find the best way to attract their attention is to stand in perfect silence! They always look up, soon enough."

Dominia made a fast move forward until his pistol was against the Lady's head. As the martyr froze in place, the dentist carried on, "And when they continue disobeying, the second-best way to acquire attention is by threatening something they cherish. Put down your weapons, Miss Mephitoli."

"Do as he says." Lazarus's body was tense, but his words were so calm and gentle that one might not have expected the mystic to be surrounded by (merely incapacitated) bodies.

"How did he get up there?" asked the General, shutting off the vibroblade and lowering it to the floor. She was more reluctant to relinquish the gun when she had misplaced her precious antique somewhere amid the fray.

"I was given a private tour. This place has an elaborate series of escape tunnels, but they are not convenient routes by which to bring an army. Why, it is not even wise for all those fleeing women to use them now. A few men behind and a handful waiting at the end could cut them down like wheat!"

"Don't," demanded Dominia as the dentist laughed.

"It does not matter where they go today. We will see them again eventually, I am sure. Tonight's number of casualties is already high enough, don't you think? Why, I do not even wish to harm your false idol, but truth be told, I do not care one way or the other."

Now, the Lady's voices rose, Her lips unmoving as She said, *Let your finger be quick and your shot true, lest We open Our mouth and share Our true voice.*

"I suppose we *are* in something of a standoff! My death would be a worthy fee for killing you and sending your vile putrescence back into that unclean place from where it comes: besides, there would be someone to take my place, whereas I have read that if the Lady were to die before Her disease was passed on, there would no longer be a Lady on this Earth."

The goddess did not speak, did not move, and Tobias smiled in a vile way. The General, emotions tipping into panic with the drug in her blood, demanded of Lazarus, "Where's Valentinian?"

"The magician was here?" asked the dentist. The question made Dominia sick, but not as sick as when Lazarus looked on in pointed silence. After assessing the room, Tobias emitted another, lighter, laugh, perhaps of relief. "Well, if he was ever here, he does not seem to be now. He can never resist coming when called. Too great a lover of attention."

As the General's head whipped this way and that, no sign of the crimson waistcoat was found. The Bearer spoke of the drug as being necessary to ease a gap in reality. Had he ever been there, or was it all some hallucination at the peak of an acid trip? Or—worse, had his manifestation been dismissed by the presence of destructive interlopers? Whether or not this was the case, there should have been a dog—right? Where was Basil?

"There may be no magician to help you find the easy way out, General," continued Akachi, tightening his grip on the shoulder of the Lady. A low hiss rose from one of Her nearest Bearers. "But I am happy to offer a trade. These ladies up to their knees in bloody water may have their mistress—may abscond with Her far and away down that tunnel, if you and Lazarus come along without a fight."

"Come along to...?"

"Jerusalem," answered that ever-smiling leader of the Hunters, a man more openly jolly, and perhaps consequently less trustworthy, than even the Hierophant. "You and me and Lazarus and my men."

"For what?"

"Don't you, who have been forced by circumstance and love into flight from your oppressive country, wish to see your Father overthrown?"

"Not by the Hunters."

"That is a decision based on emotion, and not on logic. What does it matter to you who eliminates the Hierophant, so long as he is eliminated? I would think that, particularly to a martyr, it is all the same. Are we humans not insects to your kind? Or perhaps cows are the better analogy."

Though mere moments before, the General had thought of the scene as one between bees and ants, she could not help but find one insect preferable. The Lady and Her servants appeared concerned with eliminating the Hierophant because he and the martyrs presented a long-term threat to humanity, the planet, and, frankly, the universe at large. Her concern was with the balance of things, and the idea that consciousness should be given an opportunity to develop without oppression by its many enemies.

The motives of the Hunters were totally different. Although they spoke of religious liberty and piety, they were violent hate-mongers, and enslavers of women. To them, the Hierophant was an obstacle in the way of their own power. They were envious little men. He had wealth unending, whereas they had what they pillaged; he had stockpiles of weapons, as opposed to those secondhand guns Hunters acquired via back channels; he had the adoration of his people, crowds chasing his Void-black cars down the street and shoving their own family members out of the way for a chance to kiss his ring. The Hunters had been reviled since before the Hierophant had even come to power. They would have received much from her Father's death, and everything on that list was something no one wanted to see them touch.

Akachi's willingness to bargain for the life of the Lady (a valuable commodity, arguably a kind of superweapon, and, if nothing else, a bargaining chip for the Hierophant, who wished Her dead) was miraculous, though the General suspected this was motivated by the three most notorious Hunter disdains: women, religions not their own, and Red Market prostitutes. To be sure, there was some relief on the dentist's face when the General consented she would go, and he was no longer required to touch the goddess; but that might also have arisen from instinctual fear to lay hands upon the radioactive container of the Void. No matter how the blood of Lazarus altered the body's genes to make them less sensitive to its effects, even Dominia had hesitated: if nothing else, she had to give Akachi, a mere human, credit for his courage.

"Very good, Miss Mephitoli. I appreciate your level head. Most would have made a much stupider decision!" Chuckling, Tobias stepped back from the throne and allowed the Water Bearers to rush up. They slung their Lady in their arms with little more than a glance for Dominia on their way toward that back tunnel: Gethsemane, who led the way in this effort, let out a cry of surprise and the word, "Why?" to someone discovered in the shadows.

With reluctance, Kahlil edged into view. Dominia, her expression (and even her vision) darkening, understood how Tobias had managed his private tour. "Did you really think this was the right thing?" the General asked him, her tone as pitch as the world around. The boy evaded her gaze and tacked on an irritating shrug.

"Kahlil has been a Hunter since he was a child! He told me during our brief chat in Kabul that his father was one of us; isn't that right?" Laughing, Tobias meandered to the young man and clapped a hand upon his shoulder. "Though I imagine his father would have acted faster than he did... It took him such a long time to contact me. I was starting to get worried. But, one must trust the human soul in the end. He has a moral obligation to help the human race shake loose the blight of the Hierophant, and he knows it."

"Did you know about Miki?" Dominia demanded of the dentist. "Before you positioned yourself with Kahlil?"

"Hunters only use specific medical-care providers... It was not difficult to have the boy assigned to me. He is far from our only source of information about the goings-on of your Father's world, and the Red Market. Our intelligence indicates Miki has been groomed to sell her soul to these harpies for half a decade. Documentation regarding the search for the Lady's new avatar goes back further, almost a century. Your Father may claim to be psychic, or have his sacrilegious Lamb, or demonstrate immortality beyond the lifetime of even God's universe: but all I need is a cup of coffee and a morning to review some printouts, and I know the plans of all my enemies by the time the sun is up."

"And you?" Again, Dominia stared down Kahlil; now she got him to speak.

"I wanted to save Miki," the young man said, his tone miserable. "But they came too late."

"On the contrary. Just in time. But, you have always had a bad habit of putting women above the cause, eh? God's coincidence brought her in to me, rather than forcing me to do backflips to get her number out of you"—

Dominia's mind cycled through all the background coincidences that had occurred in Basil's presence and, perhaps due to his absence in her time of need, blamed the magician for the broken tooth that had brought Miki to this hateful dentist—"but I suspect you, Kahlil, were a pawn in the Red Market's game from the start! She began using you the second you met, in hopes of becoming the leader of a cult! That same cult assigned her to you long after the first time you engaged their services, didn't they? Because they learned your value."

At the boy's speechless expression, the man ranted on. "They intended to use you to get to me. They knew who I was and wanted to see me killed—wanted to use Miki Soto to gain intelligence on my security, or blackmail me. But they did not understand that I know their ways. They are not some innocent ring of prostitutes, whose morals are already of question. They are sacrilegious cultists—heretics, Kahlil, who wish me dead. In fact, seeing this carnage now, I suspect they meant to kill me this very night. But"—Tobias grinned—"they failed, because I had you."

"I just—" Humiliated to speak before the room on this strange web of conspiracy, Kahlil turned pleading eyes to the one person capable of understanding him: Dominia. "I tried to be her friend."

For once, Akachi's voice was solemn. "And now she is dead."

"Yes," said the boy, softer, his head turning in the direction of the escape tunnel through which the Lady was carried. "Now she's dead."

Tobias nodded sadly and, from his cloak, once more withdrew his gun. "I think it's kindest for me to send you with her."

Though, at the first flash of black metal, the General charged, a martyr was not faster than a bullet without entering the Void. Over the next year, hardly a twenty-four-hour cycle would pass in which, like the tragedy at McLintock Farm, Kahlil's death would not replay itself. In those moments, she would demand to know of herself why she had not learned enough by then to slip into the Void in a wink and cross that room in the second it might take to save his life. Why had she not already two thousand years, infinite years', experience of the sort had by her Father, which taught him to slip in and out of the Ergosphere like it was a coat? Somehow, it seemed her fault, that gap, though she knew this false every time she remembered the shock in the boy's exhausted eyes—as if death had woken him up, right before putting him out forever. Hail, Saint Valentinian. The shock on Kahlil's face would never leave it, much as that image would never leave her mind: it clicked into place next to Benedict's savaged body, where it lay with the McLintocks and sweet Cassandra in the section of her brain devoted to only its most haunting traumas. While the General froze with her hands in the air at the pointing of a hundred guns, Akachi shook his head.

"I despise traitors to the cause of humankind." The dentist holstered his gun. "And I cannot stand the thought of an organization of men who do not know what they want."

"You're a real bastard." Tears filled Dominia's eyes to see that same blood that coated her now oozed from Kahlil's dark curls. "He was a kid."

"The most dangerous kind of kid: one with information about us! As readily as he sold out the Lady, I do not think he can be trusted; at any rate, he has made it clear his loyalty is not with me, but with a dead woman."

"Miki lives. She lives in eternity. And Kahlil—" She had not seen him there, but, blinking rapidly, she insisted, "He's there, too. I don't care if he wasn't a Lazarene. I'm sure he had to be there. He was just some kid—oh, you *bastard*."

"Then perhaps you can come along with me, Miss Mephitoli, and tell me about it."

A pair of Hunters restrained her arms while a third attached one of the silver shock collars that were, in her native lands, a capital offense for humans to possess. The dentist made his way down the stairs to smile into Lazarus's face even as the mystic experienced the same treatment. "I think, more than any secret resentment or love, Kahlil came to me because he saw this was inevitable—because the good Lord chose to work through him, to give his soul a chance at redemption. The state of the world is not a sustainable one. Your kind have seen to that."

"Then why not join forces with the Lady?" asked the General. Behind them, men shouted for the women to clear away from the doors.

"Because the moral element is the only thing that elevates humans above martyrs." She had been taught similar things about martyrs, but did not respond as the windbag carried on. "The Whore's Market demands of its women a relinquishment of morals that is irreconcilable with the state of humanity. At best, they require reeducation. At worst, they are unsalvageable objects."

"What happened to all that garbage about the burden of sin being on the John, not on the prostitute?"

The cherry-picking dentist chuckled, his tone dark. "The sale of a body is one thing, but the worship of a golden calf is another. The Market would see this world turned into a global Sodom and Gomorrah; She speaks of balance, but we are those who wish to maintain the balance set in place by God."

"I've heard Hunters keep sex slaves." Her lip curled. "At least martyrs don't rape their property. Not in a way that's socially or legally acceptable, anyway—your kind seems to love it. Is that part of your balance?"

Infuriatingly, Tobias spread his hands. "It is the nature of the Abrahamian religions, and of God, to allow the keeping of slaves. We are all God's slaves, General. That is a point on which your people and I can agree."

"Then what distinguishes humans from martyrs?"

"God did not allow the existence of martyrs. That was a mistake made by man, for which we are rightly punished: but as we caused the problem, so, too, is it ours to solve."

She would have liked to argue all night, but the General was pulled down the hall to see, with a streak of pain, that men defaced with chisels those elaborate tableaux lining the halls. Where was the magician, for God's sake!

"Is this honestly necessary?" She related more to her Father every second, felt him bubble up inside her like tar as the slumping effects of the drug tightened her skin so her anger was quicker to rise. "Do you need to destroy beautiful things while taking innocent lives?"

"There is nothing beautiful here, General. Only sacrilegious icons of a false god that must, for the spiritual sake of humanity, be destroyed. Though, if you are going to react so strongly to mere carvings, it is a good thing we got your collar on before we reached the garden!"

Pale with indignity, the General turned helpless eyes toward Lazarus, who did not say a word. As they were dragged outside by their captors, bile rose in her throat. One at a methodical time, Hunters shattered the garden's statues to acquire the encrypted drives that, as Miki must have (stupidly, stupidly, oh-so stupidly) spilled to Kahlil, contained data on all of the Red Market women at a global scale. "In all fairness," the dentist said, "your teeth were beautiful works of art that were nothing to destroy. They were not even given a chance to do their jobs! But a blip on my radar and a few moments of chatter to mark your arrival to Cairo was all I needed. Good thing Miss Soto felt so comfortable with Kahlil. Or feels, rather—one had ought not encourage children to play pretend, so far as I'm concerned. 'The Lady.'" Tobias laughed, as did one of his men. It was this man who the General murdered by snapping his neck, a hollow kill to vent her fury for the annihilation of all this beauty that left her feeling worse. The dentist tightened his hand, and the switch secreted in his palm shocked not just Dominia but Lazarus.

"Behave yourself, please, General. Tranquilizers don't grow on trees, and it is not a short drive to Jerusalem."

If she clenched her jaw any harder, she might have bitten off her own tongue. After the statues were brutalized and the stocks of the palace pillaged with nary a police officer or military official in sight ("Because they understand we do them a service," the vile dentist explained), the martyrs were dragged through the front entrance and to the assortment of waiting T1-63 Rs. Dominia and Lazarus were pushed into the back of one along with three of their armed captors; Tobias remained outside with a mocking salute.

"How I would love to stay and chat, General—but that would be asking for trouble! Never fear. I'll be right behind you."

The vehicle's doors slammed shut, its engine roared to life, and, in a profusion of smoke and disappointment, the *tanque* set off on a course for Jerusalem. As good as alone for all the English the remaining three Hunters chose to speak, Dominia addressed the mystic.

"Why didn't you say something about this?"

"Are you going to ask me that when you stub your toe from now on, too?"

She managed a scoff to communicate but a molecule of her thundering astonishment at his attitude. "People *died*, Lazarus. I'd think that would bother you."

"And of all the people in that room, who killed the most? You, no question. If I had a problem with death, I'd have a problem with you."

Fair enough. Still, she couldn't take responsibility, lest her thoughts writhe into that sorrowful anxiety that, vibrating across her mind, almost paralyzed her now that her expertise in battle was restrained by the collar. Without that expertise available, the drug had nothing on which to focus her consciousness. Its effects were now free-floating and unpleasant. Far better to find someone else to blame. Far easier—and more relieving—to rail against the absent magician.

"Where is Valentinian? He was here, right?"

"Yes." An approving smile lifted the edge of Lazarus's mouth. "Yes, he was here. Thank you."

Though that settled her a bit, it didn't stop her. "Well—where the hell *is* he? You mean he just buzzed off when things got hot? What good is a magician if he disappears during battle?"

"What good is a magician if he's been stabbed to death?"

"Oh, he's not going to be stabbed to death; he's a martyr." With a wave of furious dismissal, Dominia crossed her arms and pushed herself farther into the corner to distance herself from their captors. "Not only that, but he's supposed to be a great magician! A bona fide Saint! Why couldn't he have stuck around and magicked us some armor, or a weapon, or—oh, no!"

The memory of her gun arose with that same bitter disappointment that always spawned on the recognition of a lost object. In it lay echoes of that horror, that shame, when she found it absent along with her wife. Now, Cassandra was with her, a cold crystal at rest upon her heart; and the gun, a priceless treasure many centuries older than its owner, and a tool on which the General relied for ages, was lost. But, it had been lost before. Anything was possible, some hopeful part of her reminded the rest.

That rest, bleak and annoyed, shouted the optimistic sliver down until it was no longer clear whether it existed. Despite the Lady's speech, things lost never seemed to return. Those who absented themselves tended to remain absent.

"Look"—the mystic rested against the black headrest of the vehicle—"I know it's a tough day for you."

"Excuse me?"

"An understatement, I know. But someday you'll feel about these memories the way I do about them now, so try to hang on to that. It's not as long of a drive as Akachi thinks, you'll come to agree. And, we're not actually having to drive it. Or walk. Again."

Speaking of walking. "The minute they let us into the sun, we'd ought to make ourselves scarce."

"Wouldn't that be nice? But these things auto-shock if they lose contact with the skin before they're shut down. That means when you start to disappear, it shocks you into staying. Even if that weren't true, there's no point to our vanishing, because Akachi will follow us. Hell, he's already there. Consider this. Subjective time here is best measured by steps taken in that other place; as we already discussed, different directions lead to different... fates, effectively. Like, imagine each fate's juncture point as an invisible peg. You trail a string behind you—"

"I fucking get it," snapped the General, sick of having things explained to her by the magician, let alone anyone who wasn't the magician.

"Sorry. I know, I just need to make sure you're with me, because it's important to understand that, as soon as our position is observed, there's no going back. Until then, you can alter the weaving by backtracking to your starting point, or returning to a previous juncture and taking a different route. When you get to reality again, it's like nothing happened—no time passed—or what happened was something different than what would have otherwise occurred—alternative time passed. This is even true if you travel in a group. But during this period of alternative time in reality, if another soul enters the Ergosphere with his own string attached to him from his own starting point, there is the possibility that he will meet another, or a group of others, along his journey. Then, the strings get tangled. Observation means that the positions of our...molecular souls, say, are now locked in. You know, like a waveform collapse... Sorry, I don't mean to overexplain." He saw the look on her face, though, in fairness, its tension arose largely from the simple act of trying to conceptualize this business in a firsthand way. The LSD helped her understand it in an emotional, visceral manner, but trying to intellectually recount and understand it felt like trying to retain a thought in the Ergosphere. It grew easier as Lazarus continued. "Anyway, from that point on, going backward in the Void to your apparent starting point will only take you back to your geographical starting point; it's all forward in linear time, unless you return to the initial point of observation."

"Assuming you don't get tangled up in anybody else's thread before then."

"Exactly," said Lazarus, as another nasty epiphany churned the General's stomach.

"Is that why my Father checks in on me every night? Because he's—solidifying time to make sure we can't go back?"

Perhaps it was the drug, and the way it cleft the Void, the darkness of the *tanque*, and the General's spirit; perhaps it was years of indoctrination. All the same, Dominia heard her Father's voice in her head; she seemed to sit in his dream-study while the disfigured *tulpa* thrashed in the shadows behind his chair.

"Certainty of an educated decision"—her Father spoke in words she had not heard him say during that moment, which made it seem more than mere memory—"is the hallmark of intellectual maturity. Certainty of a rash decision is the hallmark of stupidity. Uncertainty of any decision is the death of power. I try only to empower you, Dominia."

"That's basically what he's doing, yeah," Lazarus continued, oblivious to either a vivid figment of her imagination or a genuine connection to the Void. Perhaps due to the molecule, the latter seemed probable to the General. Indeed, she sought to feel herself in that chair, finding it preferable to the seat of the *tanque*, and tried to stoke her imagination like a sun into which she was tempted to step could she but find a way: yet it appeared for all the world that it stepped out of her. There was her Father in the empty seat beside Lazarus, hands folded between his knees as the mystic said, "But your Father has many motives besides that."

"Like what?" asked Dominia, focused on that figure who, in turn, set unmoving black eyes upon her. More than imagined, perhaps?

"Like luring you into his service. Getting you to betray me."

"How easily you could kill them all, Dominia," said the Hierophant, or his figment, or the General's own bitterness given by her mind a most appropriate shape. "They have no idea."

"How could he hope to do that? He can't give me anything I want."

"He can give you what you think you want, or what you think is good enough. What looks like what you want, what seems like what you want."

"Take the gun of the man to your left and shoot the one to my right, and by the time the fellow over there hits the button, you're upon him. You can fight through the pain long enough to see him dead."

"What do you think I want?"

Lazarus did not answer.

"Then, it's a simple matter of the driver. And if the mystic tries to stop you, kill him, too."

"What?" she asked sharply of the fancy. To cover herself, she turned her scrutiny upon Lazarus. "What—what do you think I want, please?"

"I think you want to be happy for once," said Lazarus.

Dominia's mouth opened in a jolt of emotional turmoil. Ashamed she had been angry enough to let him in and hear his ill thoughts of her friend, the General glanced to the place she imagined her Father.

The seat was empty.

XIV

O Vas Nobile

Though the figure vanished, and the LSD wore off six hours into the drive (following a miserable, sweaty, three-hour comedown), that was not the last Dominia was to hear of her Family over the next week. Quite the opposite: having been out of the news loop for what was technically over a month, much had happened beyond her awareness. This became apparent when, around the time the acid relinquished her state of mind but not the impossibly tight muscles of her neck, the driver flipped on the radio and tuned through the stations as if prompted by the rising of the sun. As the man said something in the (at the time, dying) language of Farsi, Lazarus snorted, and Dominia glanced at him out of—not curiosity, so much as obligation. The curiosity ship sailed with her last bit of energy.

"Tobias told him to make sure you hear the news," he explained. As the General rolled her eyes, the driver settled on a station whose distinguishing feature was its use of English. Specifically, a familiar, nasally form of English, spoken by her useless baby brother, Theodore del Medico.

"And just who are these people complaining about my administration, anyway?" he asked a boisterous crowd, having (apparently within days of his term as Governor of the United Front) dropped all pretense of being a professional in favor of off-the-cuff banter with his audience—flavored by a dash of fearmongering. "I'd say they were humans, but it's not just humans, is it, ladies and gentlemen? After all, there are humans here—the good sort, you know, who can see the bigger picture because they were raised in the Front and understand its culture. No: the problem comes from the west—or the Far East, if you'd rather—and brings with it habits, customs, needs that threaten to divide us as a people. And are we not one people, citizens? Are we not United? One nation, under God, indivisible!"

This was a violation of her rights as a sentient being. Theodore's voice was an audible war crime so piercing in its obnoxious emphasis that it was close to impossible to block him out. Last time, when she heard his voice in that holo-vision, she had managed the feat of tolerating it; but now, with her mental faculties burned out from nine hours of high-speed whirring, she couldn't find anything else to think about—certainly nothing preferable—and was forced to listen as the resounding applause of the audience reduced again to her baby brother's drone.

"There are those who have condemned my treatment of these illegal aliens as too harsh, but I say I am not harsh enough! They point to the news stories about kids in cages like I'm some monster, when the reality is these people come to our nation half the time specifically to destroy it, to rend us apart and foment dissatisfaction among you good and wholesome citizen. We are *protecting* their children, and we are controlling *them* by funneling them into registered neighborhoods—while still doing them the decency of allowing them to live here, mind! But that's never good enough for a group as entitled as that.

"They would have you think your nation, your government—your Holy Father!—doesn't care for you. They come to take food from our mouths and money from our wallets all so they'll be ready to rise against us on that fatal night. Some extremists, I have heard, even wish to"—his voice dropped—"euthanize the children of martyrs! Some of these immigrants might be good people"—this was added in such a half-assed way that Dominia and Lazarus made eye contact before the former rolled her eyes—"since China, India, and the Risen Sun are so tightly packed, along with the rest of Asia; but far more of them come farther, from the Middle States, or have been indoctrinated with the values of the Hunters' South American branch. We can take no risks. Our Adaptation Centers have already reduced crime and improved the living conditions of our true citizens beyond measure. It is our hope that by isolating those individuals who we believe to have come to sew dissent, we will sort out the good apples and set our future citizens on the path to right living."

Yes, having one's children taken away while one is made to labor on a fodder plantation will do that. Especially when said fodder is sent to the same concentration camps (sorry, "Adaptation Centers") where the children were staying. If they were (un)lucky, some compassionate martyrs were browsing the aisles right now, looking for a son or a daughter the way humans looked for puppies.

Once, when young, she had believed all that about dissenters, or lunatics planning to euthanize martyr children (though, in fairness, that was a genuine concern on occasions when Hunter cells found balls enough to attack a lesser town with a small martyr population). She had also once believed, quite wholeheartedly, that all humans were scum. Food at best, half-formed martyrs at worst, she had perceived them for the first 150 years of her life as filthy animals full of hate and resentment. But, over a long period of time, she found her opinion changing, and this was before her encounter with Benedict. Her nagging sense of wrongness about her lifestyle culminated in that moment with her Father's total disinterest in even paying lip service to his appreciation for her. He would say or do anything to get her to obey him, believe in him, kill for him—except respect her. She recognized with that simple brush-off—still recognized, every time she thought of it—that she was as much an object to him as every human he had ever killed, and he would kill her the way he had killed all his children. The way he had enacted so many deaths.

That's the kind of realization from which it takes twenty years of cold isolation to recover. By the time the General met Cassandra after a final, four-year spray of battles, she had been ready to eschew her speciesist perceptions forever.

Yet, it was so tempting—*easy*, too—to consider falling back into the trap of old, bigoted beliefs. Locked in a rumbling box with the same Hunters who, during a religious ceremony, invaded a palace, killed a score of unarmed women, and destroyed every work of beauty on the property, it was hard to remember there were good humans in the world. But—poor Kahlil's face emerged behind her eyes countless times. The issue of the Hunters was not an issue of humanity. The hacker had been human, and so were the women cut down in the throne room.

Was this the natural state of humanity, this struggle of mankind against mankind? Or was it perhaps the state of consciousness, which struggled between the species for fear of those foreign traits that rendered unrecognizable its own divided identity? Problems of race, gender, religion, and geographic location had plagued humanity since the dawn of time. Consciousness could make an argument of anything just for the sake of having an argument.

The radio prattled throughout the drive, occasionally relenting to Arabic and Farsi stations as the men checked the weather or took advantage of a break in the English broadcast to listen to a few songs. She hung on to those details because they made her think of the men as people, rather than things or animals, which was how her Father had conditioned her to think of them for the majority of her life. But, ah, was it not tempting—would it not have been easier—to cut their throats, as she had cut the throats of all those crude men in the temple?

No—that was the Hierophant. When she peeled her Father's conditioning from her honest opinions, the General uncovered, to her surprise, a wellspring of shame: as if she'd lifted a rock to allow the expulsion of some boiling geyser. Those men she'd killed may have been wretched—may have joined the Hunters knowing their lives would meet a bloody end at some martyr's hand—but Dominia could no longer shake the notion they had once been children, with hopes and dreams and mother and fathers. They were not always cruel and evil. No one was born a rapist, were they? But, if the world happened over and over again, was it not true that the seed of evil lay dormant in the growing mind, perhaps expanded backward to the newborn, the way the newborn expanded forward through time? Then there must lay seeds of good in equal measure. Why should Dominia, mere gardener, have blamed herself for turning over soil that decided to germinate asphyxiating weeds, rather than sunflowers?

How difficult to find consolation! Perhaps it was the acid. Perhaps, even more, it was the ceremony. The difficulty may also have rested in the notion that she once again had two eyes. Did she deserve them? And her teeth: By Elijah, what made her special? She had killed many more than those men had, and been crueler, too. She liked to look down on the Hunters for their misogyny, but Dominia had been, at times, a misogynist. Her soul was not clean of striking Cassandra any more than Cassandra's spirit was clean of striking her.

Was it the Hunters who were so repellent? The humans? Or was it all those undesirable traits of herself that the Hunters forced her to see by reflection? Their behavior was the logical conclusion of her own. A caricature. Was she not as bad as her Father, playing his game of Holier-Than-Thou?

"I wish you would tell me where that fucking magician is," she snapped at Lazarus somewhere during the fourth rebroadcast of Theodore's speech. This time it was with Arabic translations at which the Hunters jeered, nudged the General with their rifles, or, most appallingly, spat at her feet. "Not all humans," she reminded herself in silent ad nauseam until her irritation found outlet on Lazarus. The old man hardly opened his eyes, being exhausted as she and still just as sleepless due to the stimulant effects of the drug.

"I can't. Takes all the fun out of it when the rabbit pops out of the hat."

"But he's coming back?"

"I need you to have faith."

"And I need you to stop saying that."

"Well? It's true. I know, inquiring mind. You're desperate to know everything all the time. But the fact of the matter is that, sometimes, you can't."

"Is he in the Void?" she pressed, which elicited from Lazarus a groan.

"I don't know. Maybe."

"The Kingdom?" When he didn't respond, she kept going. "If he's in the Kingdom, I can find him. I'm sure that—"

His eyes opened, words as contorted by annoyance as his face. "Look, kid! I don't know where he is. Now that you've put him on Earth, he's got work to do. So do we. Having a shitty attitude isn't going to help. Jesus! How can somebody take acid and see something like that and just be so—pissy?"

"Oh, I'm *sorry*! Maybe I'm rattled after having had the whole thing interrupted by a bunch of fucking—" The humans were staring; the word she had almost used, "bits" (a reference to early asteroid mining), was a derogatory term understood across most languages despite its archaic origins. She closed her eyes to do some deep breathing before continuing in Mephitolian.

"I am having a challenging year. And this week has been, in particular, very hard. So please, Lazarus. I'm trying. I don't get the so-called benefit of having lived this before."

With an exhalation of his own, Lazarus squinted through the slit window. "I know. I'm sorry. I do have trouble remembering that sometimes. You have no idea how tired I am of all this."

"As tired as I am?"

A small smile touched the corner of his mouth as he looked back at her. "Maybe not." Blessedly, the *tanque* screeched to a halt. "Look, Dominia: I need you to keep this in mind for me. Valentinian has a lot to do, and not a lot of time to do it, which seems sort of weird, but it's true. If he spent his time here helping us, when you can help more adequately than he could—I mean, not only would that be a waste of resources, but certain things that need to happen might not be able to happen. I need you to believe in him, and I need you, whatever happens, to also believe in me."

"'Whatever happens,'" she repeated lamely, the words rolling over her tongue with distaste as the black doors of the *tanque* were thrown open. Light exploded in with such immense fury that she did, just for a second, feel it in her soul like the chilling dissolution of the acid. But Lazarus was right: she was hyperaware of her neck, of the tension of the collar around it and of her own furious desire to stay and throttle every man around; those things, like leaden weights, restrained the coming of the Void. Just as well. She didn't want to risk bumping into that useless magician, anyway. He needed to do what needed doing, she supposed—whatever the hell that was—but she was no less sore about the matter. It felt not unlike her parents' abandonment, and because of that, Dominia did not allow the hope that she could be saved by anybody but herself.

And then—then there was another small detail that, as she was yanked from the van, encouraged her to force awareness of the Earth beneath her feet and focus her consciousness on staying grounded despite the intensity of the vibrations in her body: as that darkness of the Void trembled in, so, too, had a strange series of terrible screams. In her periphery, there writhed gray shapes that could not assemble themselves into a form before her because she had not entered that bizarre, quasi-imaginary space. In those seconds in which she was exposed to the clamor, however, her mind tried to make sense of it. Amid the screams, she was able to discern, in languages her physical ear could not understand, a spray of agonized questions—"Where is Jerusalem?" "Where is God?" "What has happened to me?"—before her body was set before smiling Dr. Akachi.

"Hello again, Miss Mephitoli! And good Lazarus. I trust your journey was not too uncomfortable? It is not complete yet, I admit, but I expect—or hope—that you will find the last leg more bearable, being, as you are, with me."

"If only my Father were here! Then it'd be a real party."

"Be careful what you wish for, Miss Mephitoli! But that is unlikely. Our nation's defense is top of the line, and our base camp changes its many locations often, even in the course of one year, to evade his attention. Oh, every now and then he gets a valid piece of information, but I do not expect he will ever be able to find all of us. Certainly not at once. I suppose we are rather like cockroaches that way!"

"Your words, not mine." She squinted across the desert as her long-time dark-adjusted eyes adapted to the light. All around swelled the (oddly comforting) sensations of a ramshackle military encampment: trucks rumbling hither and thither, men practicing their shots in the clear morning air, boots on the ground, and the overall clank-and-clamor of energy. "It's a lucky thing I had you remove my DIOX-I, huh? For you, I mean."

"Oh, goodness, no! Lucky for you. After all, had you not volunteered, I planned to yank it out when next we met!"

The more merrily he laughed, the more Dominia wished to grind his face in the dirt with her uncuffed, perfectly free hands: but she knew that he—and one or two others with auxiliary remotes—hoped she would do exactly that. Instead, as was apparently in vogue, she spat upon the dirt. "I'll keep that in mind when I get you alone."

As the handful of nearby men who spoke English laughed along with the dentist, another pair pulled up in a light utility vehicle: unarmed and intended for reconnaissance or speedy transport, as opposed to the heavy-duty operations of a *tanque*. While the men climbed out, Akachi said, "Then you may be excited to know you are about to have an opportunity to do just that! There is something I would love to show you."

That was never a good thing. Time to find excuses. "And I'd love to come along, but this sunlight—I know the collar is keeping me here, but I feel like my body might fade off at any minute."

"Oh, Miss Mephitoli, of course! Never fret: we have a very advanced piece of technology to keep the blue light from your eyes and prevent you from being swept away to the end of time." Turning, the dentist said something in Arabic, and the man to whom he had spoken produced a pair of sunglasses. He handed these to Dominia with a shit-eating grin.

"You know"—she turned the glasses over before putting them on, as if in search of their anthrax coating—"if I didn't have this collar, I'd kill you with these." But, it was true. The sunglasses did stabilize her. Akachi was getting in the truck; with a helpless glance in the direction of Lazarus to find him silent, she asked, "What about him?"

"Lazarus will remain here at camp with my men."

At last, Lazarus spoke. "I can't do anything for your men."

"Now, that is simply not true! But, you need not fear. I know your blood is the most precious commodity this Earth has to offer. Gold, diamonds, coal, oil: all good as lead next to the blood of Lazarus. Killing you—as, say, desires the Hierophant—well, that is a shortsighted idea!"

"Not as shortsighted as giving my blood to people who shouldn't have it."

"Now, I think it is fair to say that if someone drinks your blood in this world, they have earned it! The good Lord would not have made the action capable of happening in the future if it were unacceptable to Him in the past and present. All things in the world of men are precisely as they need be at the given moment: all the damned are damned and all the righteous are righteous, and nothing can be done to deviate these game pieces from the colors God wills them to take."

Now it was the mystic's turn to be annoyed. "That's right. I forgot about your position on free will. How it's all an illusion. You think that because you don't have any, yourself."

"How fascinating it will be to talk to you, and learn what else you've forgotten about me!"

"Well"—the mystic stared down the dentist who was, in the end, little more than a human—"I remember how you die."

For but a second—a sweet, gratifying second Dominia drank like the Hierophant's wine—Tobias's mouth opened without a sound. The eyes behind his sunglasses even widened a hair. Bit by bit, he recovered and tried to laugh as though it did not bother him. He settled on an uncharacteristically tight smile. "Perhaps I will make you tell me about it so I can dodge this fate, eh?"

"How can you?" asked Lazarus, so dryly it was the General's turn to laugh. "You think free will is an illusion."

Again, that mouth opened; one of the English-speaking men glanced at the talkative dentist with his eyes narrowed until Akachi turned to him with an Arabic snap. As he and a few other men collected Lazarus, the dentist told him they would speak later. He leveled his gaze with Dominia's.

"Now, please, Miss Mephitoli, tell me you will accept my invitation of a drive. It is not long. Only a few hours. I think it important you see Jerusalem."

"Yes." She glanced at Lazarus as he was dragged away, her ears filling with the memory of screams. "I think it's important, too."

In mild relief, the dentist smiled again. "I am glad you agree. I am sorry—I did intend to remove your collar as a sign of respect, but I am afraid"—that laugh was yet a little warbling, a little unsteady—"your friend's commentary does rather have an effect on a man's mind!"

"Probably the smarter choice," agreed the General, tapping the metal device and fancying for the sensitivity of her cells that static built within them. Perhaps that was part of the reason for her foul mood. "But it is incredibly uncomfortable."

"Well, in the long-term we can discuss removing it. I suppose it depends on the changeability of your mind."

As the dentist patted the empty seat of the vehicle, the General evaded a man who intended to drag her over and made her way to the passenger's seat. With that ever-cheery mien set in place, Tobias resurrected the engine with the push of a button and advised her, "Be sure of your seat belt!"

How difficult it was to avoid saying anything to him! But, engaging him in conversation was a trap. The Hierophant had his way of goading people when in an outrageous mood, but it was Cicero who exhibited this quality on the regular: yet, even he, who had not so much as spared a teenage student from his taunting (the bitterness of youth's lost battles no doubt stoked the flames of future battles won, for whatever that was worth), failed to approach the soulless nature of Tobias's so-called cheer. Her relatives' laughter, even at the evilest of circumstances and the blackest of jokes, had seldom been anything but pure; and, in the case of the Hierophant, it had often been the gay laughter of a man who, one needed grudgingly admit, was of extraordinary intelligence and no meager stock of wisdom.

Tobias's laughter was patronizing. This was a man who believed the world was a pit of fools, and not in the harmless way Miki did. The Hierophant's laughter was the laughter of a man who waited for the world to teach him something new, and reveled in it, greeting each new piece of information with an excitement comparable to a child's. Akachi's laughter was the hollow sound of a man who waited to die, because he thought he already knew everything and scorned the notion that he didn't.

"So"—Dominia couldn't resist engaging him for the entire two-hour length of the drive—"how do you think you're going to die?"

"Trying to get into my head, are you, Miss Mephitoli? Good. That means I am already in yours. But, if you must know, I expect I will lose my life in a battle of some kind, like so many of my men. I can only hope by the grace of God that it will be a battle in His name, which glorifies Him and secures my place in the afterlife."

"You know what the afterlife is, though, right? Souls? The Ergosphere?" Burned out from the LSD, which had never quite elevated her drug experience from "vaguely uncomfortable" into "psychedelic trip," the General could not explain what had been so comprehensible when in the Void or influenced (however mildly) by the foreign molecule. Instead of trying to grope her way through an argument whose firsthand meaning she had lost, she settled on, "You're already saved, through Lazarus's blood."

"Blasphemy! That is pure and simple blasphemy. I forgive you for saying such a thing, but I must ask you to refrain from insisting on it in my presence. It is offensive to my spirit, Miss Mephitoli."

Was it possible for a person who had drunk of Lazarus's blood to be so corrupted their soul no longer sensed the truth? Or was he right, as he went on to insist, "The mysteries of God cannot be made known to us in this life. Once upon a time, the true Church kept the mysteries of Christ for Man, and by meditation on these mysteries and the acts of the sacraments, the soul could hope to transcend purgatory after death. Men of all stripes have meditated on this subject in all ways, and on achieving revelations from small to great, unique genetic markers are activated. The blood of Lazarus activates all these markers, along with many others whose uses we cannot yet explain. The Lord may allow the consumption of blood by the masses for now, General, but the cults that imbibe it are becoming as dangerous as the so-called Church of your Father. Soon God will see fit to smite them for their insolence. Then it will be a return to the old ways, when humbled human men and women understood that the mysteries of the divine should be kept for the afterlife. For mankind to insist that they are intelligible is not only blasphemous: it is dangerous!"

"Aren't you the guy in charge of the organization who says murdering martyrs is God's will? Aren't you talking to me about God's will and intentions right now?"

"There is *only* God's will, Miss Mephitoli, which is revealed over time. Not yours or mine. Even the will of your so-called magician friend is but a dream!" The General clenched her teeth at the thought of Valentinian but tried to find solace in the obvious anxiety he caused Akachi to provoke these semi-frequent mentions. "I find myself thus, and thus, it is God's will. Just as it is God's will you should be here with me; just as, I am sure, it is God's will you will come around to seeing things my way."

"Dubious" didn't begin to describe the General's attitude, or even her facial expression as, during the long, dusty drive to Jerusalem, Tobias proceeded to lecture her on everything from the inherently sinful nature of martyrs to the barbarous war crimes her kind had committed. "You, yourself," was a phrase which oft punctuated the monotonous drone, and it was, truth be told, the only thing that kept the General awake after the first hour. Now she was truly over the effects of the drug, worn from her battle, and growing famished. Not to mention drained by the unfamiliar heat of the sun, which, while no longer fatal, had already left her so sunburned she seemed to have laid her face on an iron.

The slightly worse part was the traffic as they approached the city. The highways snarled across one another to account for a populace whose size had grown completely out of bounds of the original, meager imaginings of its long-dead planners. In fact, the boundary of Jerusalem, she heard amid all his rambling, had technically been reached an hour into their drive. If they wished to hit the center of the city, it would, at this time of day, take three or even four hours. This was not an uncommon problem in that night and age: Dominia's long-missed San Valentino had, in the United Front's ancient nights, been a conglomerate of several cities that had merged together over time, proximity and environmental pressure—not to mention social laziness. It was easier to refer to the massive areas as one sprawling unit and the individual, former cities within as secondhand townships when one didn't know the area or didn't care. Had the General been driving Tobias on a courtesy tour of San Valentino before murdering him, for instance, she would not have bothered pointing out the boundaries of the counties within, like where San Francisco let out to San Jose or where that became Modesto; nor would she even touch the small boroughs within those. This was in part because he would not retain the knowledge posthumously, but mostly because he had no frame of reference for it. Maybe if he'd read Steinbeck. Doubtful.

However, Tobias did not show similar courtesy. He was too in love with the sound of his own voice to be stopped from naming every part of his city in agonizing detail, and explaining, until her slumping head was barely supported by her hand, how his cell was encamped in an area not far from what was once called Be'er Sheva. Once a jewel of its nation, it had been rechristened by the predominantly Arabic-speaking Hunters "Bi'ir as-Sab" and, from what Dominia could tell, had been trampled by the terrorist presence like the carpet of a Front farmer who wore his shoes indoors. As Tobias began to explain the city's name meant "Seven Wells" (or "Lion's Well," depending), Dominia groaned in frustration.

"I know! I know about Be'er Sheva. I've read the fucking Bible. Somebody swore some oath over water there, or something. Jacob had his vision of the ladder when he left it."

"That is good! Then you will understand God has been here since the dawn of time. Since long before the state of Israel, and the founding of Jerusalem! His design is such an intricate one that He understood someday

Jerusalem would explode to stretch as far as the Seven Wells, you see? That is why this country has always been holy, has always been contested."

"'The Promised Land,'" suggested the General dryly, unwilling to humor the hypocritical rantings of the most boring man on earth. "Yeah, I get it. But what about your spiritual promised land? Is this all there is to you? Earth, then death? And what's going on with death, then?" Somehow she'd not only gotten into a religious debate, she'd revealed to herself, by total accident, that she was developing beliefs of her own.

"Only at the true end of the world, upon the second coming of Christ, will the gates of Paradise open. For someone who claims to have read the Bible, I am surprised you do not know that! But that mistake you have just made, that dangerous mistake, is why I have brought you here.

"I am not an unfair man, Miss Mephitoli. Unlike your Father, I do not believe in punishing the ignorant for crimes they have not known themselves to commit. Quite the opposite. Minds can be changed, because they are only human, and God's truth is law! The highest law is not intelligible to Man."

"The poet William Blake once wrote it is impossible for the truth to be communicated in an intelligible way without being understood."

"I cannot say I have read his work"—of course not—"but he sounds like a heretic."

"Oh, by your standards, he was."

"My standards are God's standards, Miss Mephitoli. The only standards."

"And how do you know what standards are God's if nobody can know the highest truth?"

Tobias took an exit ramp, and they eased into the city in some long-neglected factory district—though, in fairness, what she had seen thus far looked much neglected already, war-torn by the Hunters' thousand-year, on-again-off-again occupation. "His law has been handed down from generation to generation in the form of His book."

"Yeah, thank God we've preserved all those rules about mixing fabrics and selling slaves."

"Indeed! Or else your Father might be at as great a loss as I. How do your people treat human beings who kowtow as 'Renfields' and other forms of servant but as slaves? And these consent, unlike the trafficked or encamped."

The most repugnant person on the planet, Akachi: lecturing her as if she didn't know. He turned the corner into a (fairly harrowing) area of town from which everything was obscured but the towering factories, defunct and appropriated, blotting out the sky to prevent a good look at the breadth of ravaged Jerusalem.

"Will you follow me?" He asked as though it were really a request when they stopped in the dusty parking lot of a seemingly abandoned building.

Grinding down her irritation somewhere far beneath her feet, Dominia obeyed only when, to her astonishment, he threw open the doors to reveal the testing facility of a superweapon.

Over the stomping of metallic feet sprinting in seven seconds from one end of the soccer-field-size building to the other, the proud dentist announced, "This is the world's first musculature-unifying suit: the ALIF-8."

"An exoskeleton." Against the northern wall stood an uncanny rack of empty suits that, at eight and a half feet with back legs poised to thunder across the ground with an almost-feline gait, recalled in some ways the articulating mode of the T1-63 R *tanque*; in others, the odious movement of the *tulpa*. As the in-testing device pummeled an already brutalized punching bag, she observed, "I'm surprised it took humans so long to produce something like this. Or surprised it was your kind who developed it, instead of a respectable government."

His eyes, visible as his lenses faded from their sun-exposed state to their indoor one, curled with glee. "Not for want of trying! I am told that, similar to the problems of space flight and the initial visions of the Light Rail, development on most such weapons halted as your Family rose to power."

"Same reason artificial intelligence capable of anything beyond brewing coffee is illegal in Europa and the Front. Can't have anything that might be used against him. Not unless he's developed it, himself, and can maintain control with the flip of a switch."

"Quite right. But now, the only thing preventing countries across the world from developing such technology—aside from the spies and lobbyist traitors he has slipped into the human populations—is slothful fatalism. We are all dying. The planet is poisoned by us; the species is held captive by martyrs. Why not submit to the idea and enjoy our debauched lives while we can? The average man is too busy enjoying himself to contribute to the human race, and those still motivated by the thrill of scientific discoveries are too afraid of provoking your Father to engineer any new military technology not meant for defense. But, you see, we Hunters have time on our hands, and there is no one to tell us to stop doing what was do. And we are certainly not afraid of your Father."

When, in a brotherly way, Akachi draped an arm around her shoulders, the tensed martyr allowed herself led on a stroll toward the exoskeletons. Closer, its structure was such a mass of wires, hydraulics, and metal bones that it resembled a skinned metal being, as though it were organs, flesh, and—well, a torso and head away from a living entity. "As a military woman, I knew you would respect what you are being shown. I can see you do, I can see it in your eyes! You know what devastation these things could wreak among your people."

Not untrue. The General leaned into the nearest suit and studied a graphene-encased battery pack tucked away within, its power source both surprisingly mobile and only accessible from the front, through the body of the human controlling it. The back was defended by osteoid plates of steel armor, and all pieces were designed in a way that, taken from the *tanque*, made it impact resistant: not even a fall would destroy them. "Martyrs may be swift and sometimes so gifted they seem capable of unholy magic—but, wearing one of these, I could break your hand with a twitch of my own!"

Across the room, a brick shattered in the hand of the testing unit, and the General tried not to roll her eyes or smirk at the image of Tobias choreographing with his men those actions he thought the most menacing. "So I'm supposed to be scared? I'm not leading his army anymore. It's not my problem."

"No, my dear, you are not leading his army. But what is a general without an army, eh? Not much more than the average man or woman!"

"Trying to appeal to my vanity to get me to fight for you?"

"Yes: and to acquire information! I do not expect you will disagree. Your Father took your life! Your life, and your wife."

"Let's not," said Dominia, words arranged through tight lips, "talk about my wife. All right?"

"Just as well: I have one more thing to show to you."

With his unpleasant smile still stupidly in place, Akachi crooked a finger to indicate Dominia should follow him to a door on the left. This door, in turn, led through a series of others, and the General was forced to stop many times to wait for the dentist or his men to unlock them. As she endured all this, he prattled on, and by the time they reached their destination, she was sickened: not by his words but by what she saw.

"Exo-suits are well and good, Miss Mephitoli, but there are still many problems with the logistics. For instance, one cannot easily smuggle these weapons into any old place! Your Father's favorite city, Elsinore, is a good example: it is enwalled and defended by land, sea, and air, to such an extent that there is perhaps no city more impenetrable upon the face of this Earth. How, then, is mankind to cure the infection of a source that cannot be reached? This problem has plagued me for many years, Miss Mephitoli. Ever since I rose to power. But I mentioned my solution before. When the body cannot send its white blood cells to fight a disease, an infected tooth, or any other trouble—when these white blood cells are simply not enough, what can be done? What must be done? One night, I awoke with a revelation! When the body cannot cure itself, the body goes to a doctor, a dentist such as myself—and what does that doctor usually do? He gives it an injection. He takes an external thing—in this case, the medicine—and injects it into the body. Or perhaps, as in my case, he comes to remove a thing, as if out of nowhere. Like that"—he snapped his thick fingers—"the body is able to once more fight its ailment. We are the medicine, General, but can you guess the doctor?"

As she refused to humor him, and he threw open a door to an external walkway whose bright glare made her grimace even behind her sunglasses, he answered, "Lazarus. His blood is the needle that transports us from one location to another: using that, I realized, it was possible for us to take our weapons into your Father's city."

"How is that? You can't even control how you appear in that place, let alone what objects are in your possession. I'll bet if I went there right now, I'd still have my gun, and that's somewhere on the floor back in Cairo. You can't seriously expect the ALIF-8"—she got the joke as she said it aloud and interrupted herself with a snort. "'Elephant'? What a stretch."

The gratified dentist laughed and annoyingly jostled her shoulders. "Too few people get it here! They just hear the Arabic letter—but, you were saying?"

"I just mean, you can't expect this to work."

"It is true that if I entered the Ergosphere with the suit on my back, it would not follow me. But that proved a solvable problem. Do you understand the chemical process occurring when you step into the sun and are hastened by the Ergosphere?" For a change, he was going overexplain something useful.

"I know some. The CRY gene has been activated and lets us see electromagnetic fields." The General forgot to hate Tobias while infected with scientific enthusiasm. "That's what allows flies and birds to perceive them regularly, right? Magnetic fields of some kind, at least."

"Very good, Miss Mephitoli, very good. Yes, you are seeing electromagnetic fields: others, and your own. I have heard it said that some old men who have traveled back and forth many times can even see them here, just like the birds and flies. And—"

"What I don't understand"—she interrupted him, eager to learn while in the presence of someone willing to explain anything—"is how this function is possible. This is a new sensory experience you're talking about, and in order for the brain to interpret a sense to the mind, it needs an organ—openings in the bone. What organ is it here?"

"That little bundle of nerves in your center, your solar plexus! Didn't they tell you?" They had, in fact. While she almost laughed, he led her to the final room, which consisted primarily of a metal detector. "Your entire body is the opening: your torso, your ribs, the gap between your rib cage and your pelvis. Your body has reinterpreted its relationship with itself, with your mind, and with light. When your newly sensitized CRY genes are exposed to sunlight, energy is carried through the nerves and increases the vibrational frequency of the body, which increases the vibrational frequency of that light. The more directly one looks at the sun, the more energy is transmitted, and the frequency heightens until the absorbed light wavelengths increase past those of x- or even gamma rays. At the peak of this self-generated radioactivity, molecules of the body effectively slip between the Plancks of reality and into the Ergosphere at the end of time, because such high physical vibration and perception is not compatible with material existence in the Lord's world. This is why the process is possible at night—moonlight is still sunlight—but disorienting. It is weak. Much like your half-formed martyr blood, which is an inferior poison beside that of Lazarus. Without Lazarene blood, your martyr molecules, also, are growing excited, but because your CRY gene has not been activated, the increased vibration serves to destroy your body from the inside out in a matter of minutes."

Due to her metal collar, Dominia was guided around the metal detector, although a number of scientists and research assistants stood in line for a routine morning inspection on their way to the office. "If an organ could manage such a thing for an organic body, why should it not be possible for an artificial object? We have machines that hear, and see, or substitute for the parts of us that do those things for our mind. Was it not possible that we could develop a device that excited the molecules of anything, everything, to that same extent? Was it not possible to use the blood of Lazarus to transport even basic matter from one location in space-time to another? After all, that is why it is possible for us to enter the Ergosphere at one location of space-time, and exit it a different location: at the end of time, the black hole envelops and contains all things as the throne of God, and therefore all things are in the same location. A hologram. It is all a matter of tricking the objects—and the hologram—into confusing two separate points in physical space for even a Planck."

As that aforementioned sickness settled upon her empty stomach, Akachi's men dragged open a heavy, lead-lined door to reveal another vast warehouse. Unlike the crowded lab of the ALIF-8s, this room's focus was singular as that of any church: beyond her breath condensing in the cold, her eyes were drawn, not to an altar, but to a gargantuan metal chandelier that, enrobed in wires and panels and glints of golden coil, hung above a similarly ornamented doorframe.

"Congratulations, Miss Mephitoli," said the smiling son of a bitch. "You are the only woman yet to lay eyes on humanity's first teleporter."

All the horrible implications thudded down as he drew her close to the object. The wires around the frame of the vast door twisted like sinews about a glass pipe that ran with auburn fluid she could only assume to be blood. Its color was echoed by that of the apple that sat innocuously upon the threshold. "It has been many centuries since it was difficult to recreate the cells of a specific individual from only a sample. I think your Father has not done this for the martyrs, not because Lazarenes with their blood vials are difficult to catch, but because he does not want to reveal the source of his power. But I have my own source." Tobias drew from beneath his cloak a chain upon which dangled a glass bottle, forever stained rust red. "And it only took a few flakes for us to create a mass supply of the most valuable resource this world has to offer. The travel is not at a superluminal pace: the one regret! This means, much like when we enter the Ergosphere, we lose time. But it still affords a kind of movement that is nonlinear, and far faster than transport by walking from the perspective of those on the journey—not to mention, far more discrete. When the device is fueled and its artificial CRY organs are stimulated by a burst of photons and the carefully measured decay of a radioactive isotope"—he waved a hand and, in the first demonstration by which Dominia was genuinely impressed (and secretly terrified), a doctor threw a switch that blasted the doorway full of flickering light that vanished faster than it appeared, along with the apple—"entrance to the Ergosphere is possible for even an inanimate object."

"But how does it know where to come out?" Her throat had dried at the sight of the emptied doorway, but that may have been the same brief radioactive exposure that stung her eyes. Hopefully the blood of Lazarus had rendered these humans resistant to the radioactivity. "A conscious being who enters the Ergosphere decides where to leave it and looks at the sun, but an object can't do that."

"No. But if one possesses a pair of finely tuned, ultra-accurate quantum computers"—so that was the chandelier—"and activates one, then activates the second at a time proportionate to the distance it takes to travel the Void from the first teleporter to the other, those two locations could be said to be physically the same when the calculations are made to the Planck. Both the same black hole. It was a matter of finding men cleverer than I to research all this, and to teach the doorway to match the coordinates of its photons to those of its specific partner, rather than any other doorway that might, by some happenstance, be active at that same Planck; the ratios of time and distance, I am told, are key in this. And we may thank your Father for the radioactive material the world has dumped on the fair continent of poor, abused Australia, because that was his donation to this project! In a way, you could say it is not the universe or the entity that is being tricked, but the doorway. It thinks its other side is far away! Were you and I to step through and join the apple, we would find ourselves several hours in the subjective future, in my favorite city in the world: Tunis."

"Carthage," she said, frowning. "We have a lot of intelligence about African Hunters assembling there, but the Hierophant's spent the last three hundred years politely avoiding the entire continent while warring with everybody else."

"Because he understands that, were he to go to war with a single country on the continent of Africa, China and most of Asia would leap into the fray. They cannot allow martyrs more land than they already possess; moreover, possession of Africa as well as Europa would allow him to slip a noose around the Middle States in a matter of decades. The right move is to head him off at the pass, as they say."

"You're planning an assault."

"Malta has been a sensitive city ever since your Father claimed it," he said, referring to an island that, like Venezia, had been retrieved from the greedy sea by her Father long after climate change deepened her waters. "Though it trades with human states, it is notoriously overfull of martyrs, and defensive when it comes to outsiders. It will not take much to begin a conflict there: one that will see us invited to Europa's proper shores."

"Then you'll ride your ALIF-8s through the Alps, playing Hannibal Barca."

"Hannibal made a few fatal mistakes: namely, being set against Scipio Africanus, rather than trying to reach him man-to-man. That is why I brought you here today, Dominia. I do not need to elaborate on the implications of this device. We have learned to set them up quickly, and a team of twenty engineers can now produce a working doorway, given the right prefab parts, in roughly twelve hours of assembly. The only problem is one of defense, and ensuring that the second teleporter is not interrupted in its future calculations: always a sticky wicket with teleportation, as science fiction taught us, but that is the nature of the beast! I think the risk is worth it. An endless army of men with guns, bombs, and ALIF-8s funneled through could destroy anything found upon its other side. And there is no reason for you to face them, so far as I can see."

"I don't intend to face them." Her voice was dark as her expression. "But I don't intend to lead them, either."

Irritation strained the dentist's mouth; for emphasis as he spoke, he slipped the glasses from his eyes, using them to gesture like a pointer. "So you will sit and do nothing against your Father? You cannot think this should be sustained!"

"You can't think the world is better off with your Hunters in control."

"You make my ends sound like some vain, cartoonish plan for world domination, my sister. Look at yourself!"

With childlike stomps, he stormed to a nearby table, removed from its cluttered surface a television remote, and flipped on the nearest of several two-dimensional televisions mounted to the walls of the room. The display arranged into a face Dominia knew too well, distinguished from that of the Hierophant's by age, its lack of composure—and its missing right eye, replaced by a custom DIOX-I making no efforts to disguise its nature. The implant, of crimson pupil and black sclera, whipped in all directions regardless of the position of its adopted brother.

"This was recorded yesterday." Tobias rewound the video of El Sacerdote standing at the pulpit of a cathedral in the heart of Mephitoli.

"Sacrilege," Cicero snarled, having abandoned the cultured, European priest of peacetime in favor of a preaching persona closer to the fire-and-brimstone brand on which humans and martyrs of the Front both thrived. "I have heard from the Lord and the Lamb both that there are those among the flock who have the temerity to question our teachings; those who have been, by their own, weak wills, swayed to such extent they now doubt that most evident truth that we martyrs hold so dear. We are God's chosen people, my faithless children, and let you all have no doubt—although I know so many of you, cowards that you are, surely will. Let not the actions of a pathetic terrorist, that coward of all cowards who ran from home to consort with enemy forces, dissuade you from your basic knowledge of the truth! That it is *you*, children, who are on the right side of God, of the Lord, of Christ, of history—you, and not the traitorous bitch who tore out the eye of your own hapless priest! Your own humble servant of the Lord! Will you, children, be so fearful and selfish, so base and animal—so human"—hisses arose—"that you will let the actions of one fool criminal decide the fate of an entire country? Or will you remain as one, a noble cause beneath the eye of God, so when He looks upon the Earth and sees His people standing together, He will know without fail that same truth those few, most virtuous souls among you have always known: that it is the martyrs who are righteous? For it is the martyrs who shall inherit the earth. It is the martyrs who are the true children of God!"

The General only realized she clenched her teeth when she caught Tobias studying her face. She shot him a withering glance that inspired him to correct his attention and redirect it to the rant of the near-foaming Eternal Son. "Who among you will be counted as the righteous in the coming nights? Who among you will be damned to an eternity of despair for your faltering hearts, your traitorous nature?" Voice lifting above the growing clamor of his parishioners, Cicero beat the edge of his pulpit with force that would bruise a human hand for several days, rather than the several minutes of his martyr's flesh. "There have been other generations of my Father's children, many before Dominia. I have seen them, and of them all, only I am left standing. Why? Because I alone have remained ever faithful to my Holy Father's will. Because I, his Eternal Son, lean not upon my own understanding, but trust in the Lord with all my heart."

"Filthy, unholy garbage," muttered the dentist under his breath, withdrawing from his pocket a rosary (a simple two-barred cross of the human sort, rather than a crucifix with a second crossbar dividing a horned circle as was the symbol of the martyr church). He toyed with its beads as Cicero, returning to Earth, smoothed his blond hair.

"There have been other whelps put down before Dominia. There will be many, I expect, in her wake. But let her be the first in the lifetimes of many martyrs I see here. My Father has authorized a bounty of five hundred million dollars for the life of Dominia di Mephitoli, whether her killer be human or martyr, foreigner or citizen." As the crowd's fervor scattered into a series of gasps, the General lowered beneath Tobias's watchful eye into the chilled metal of a folding chair. "Should she so much as show her face again, it will be the last time she shows it anywhere. Yet even if she does not return home (if hypocrites can be said to have a home), she will know no safety, for my Father waits ever vigilant for news of her resurgence. It will not be long, now; and when she does reemerge, we will be ready to destroy her. Let none disrupt this tenuous peace we have built with the human world and live to revel in it. Let none lead astray the souls of the Lord and ever find safety or comfort again. Let us pray, children: pray that the disgraced Governess is caught and killed for her crimes."

As a few cheered but more audibly knelt to pray, Akachi finally did Dominia the courtesy of pausing the recording.

"Do you see what I tried to tell you?" he asked her, in a way so gentle it was, from him, utterly patronizing. "I wish I could be more delicate, but I must be blunt, General. It should not matter to you who displaces your Father, because you are already a nonentity. As good as dead."

"Then I'd might as well throw my life away to kill you now, hadn't I?" She didn't move, whatever she said, too drained physically and too emotionally adrift to prove capable of violence. Tobias seemed to sense that, and made no move, himself.

"What a waste that would be! You cannot let this news sour you, General. I am doing you a favor. I am liberating you by pointing out the truth! Now, you are freer than you have ever been. All your previous self-definitions are lifted from your shoulders. That we should all be so free! But think of all you can do with that freedom. Think of the wrongs you can right, all the deaths and martyring you can prevent in the future."

Akachi touched Dominia's forehead, which startled her, as she had covered her eyes; but when she gripped his arm, it seemed in a black and terrible instant as though she had arrived again in the presence of the black sun. The factory fell away and all around them were the howling, writhing bodies of souls that tore at their hair, screaming and weeping and pulling at the sallow skin of their faces. Smearing their flesh with black ash and dirt, they were the only things in sight (waves of sorrow, a sea of sack-clothed screamers) as far as Dominia's one-eyed soul could bear to see.

Akachi shouted over the din, "This is what your Father has done! These are all those souls he's led astray, human and martyr. The Kingdom of God is unknowable in this life, Miss Mephitoli! Those who think it is will find themselves trapped forever."

"That's not true." Bolstered by thoughts of the Kingdom, she wheeled out of Tobias's clutch just as a wheezing figure at her feet made to grab a boot that was simultaneously the bloodstained hem of that regrettable kimono. As the circuit between their bodies was interrupted and the vision disappeared as it had come, the General insisted, "Surely those people are just lost. Trying to get into the Kingdom and not knowing how, regardless of their religion. They can't all be my Father's fault. Or—are those soulless beings?"

"Worse: they are beings with corrupted souls. Befouled souls. Your Father has forced them to misunderstand. How long they've suffered! And how many more will suffer. They cannot present themselves before God when mired in the lies of the Hierophant. And how many have you, yourself, put into that abominable place!"

Trying, somehow, to justify away her guilt, the General insisted, "Surely it's not so different from being lost in the Void," but she knew after she said it how wrong she was even before Tobias shook his head. The sub-radio frequencies mentioned by the magician and by Lazarus—that must have been what they meant, that altered, hellish zone of screaming souls.

"One does not have a self when lost in the darkness there, for there, one is part of the true mystery of God while also being separated from any notion of the divine. That is why one is anything there, and nothing; and it is also why there is no suffering there, because there is no knowledge by which one can suffer. But in that place in the Void that is called Jerusalem, an unholy trap, souls congregate: aware enough to never forget their suffering and what they have done to find themselves thus, but never aware enough to liberate themselves. That is true hell, Miss Mephitoli, and your Father is the Devil who puts them there."

She was tired of arguing about her Father's hand in it and opted to communicate her resentment telepathically. She imagined sending Tobias her hatred through their overlapping electromagnetic fields while she demanded, "And what do you expect me to do about it?"

"You know your Father's military better than anyone on Earth, except perhaps your brother. You know the plans of his cities and fortresses, the weaknesses he hides and the things he most cherishes. You know the ways of martyrs and can offer a beacon to those wise enough to repent before they die. The only question I have is: Will you repent, yourself?"

"I won't repent for being what I am," insisted the General, her eyes landing on the blonde female in the background of Cicero's speech. Innocent Lavinia, who was not by any stretch of the imagination there through choice of her own. "And I won't tell you that martyrs need to repent. You want to talk about repentance? What about you? What about all the people you've killed, sent to the Very Low Frequency perception of the Ergosphere? Because I get the feeling you've misled as many as my Father. You're as bad as him."

The humor had fallen from Akachi's face some time ago, but his expression grew particularly hard at that. "So you will roll over and accept you are dead, and your life is at its end? That there is nothing you can do to save yourself, nothing you can do to save anyone else? Martyrs really are less than human. They lack all the human spirit of hope and striving."

"Martyrs are more human than you. We kill for food. You're a bigot, a rapist, and a liar worse than my Father. He doesn't try to pretend he isn't evil when you get him alone in a room. He doesn't shoot a loyal man before an audience, then delude himself about his moral compass. The sad thing about you is that you think you're good."

In the face of her disdain, his words began to stumble, and all his blustering was revealed for what it was when he was reduced to petty schoolyard insults. "Well—well, we will see if you don't change your mind when we begin collecting Red Market whores for reeducation and repurposing. For all the time you spent with them, perhaps you are considering becoming one."

In lieu of comment, she spat in his eye, and was promptly given by her collar such a jaw-seizing, brain-frying shock that she immediately lost consciousness. Too bad: the General would have appreciated the horror on his face.

Though she regained consciousness halfway through the drive back, Akachi was, oddly, no longer in a talking mood. This, she gathered from her own gag and handcuffs, and from the way he spared her a repelled glance as she shifted in her seat. The silent treatment was immeasurably preferable to the dentist's so-called conversational skills, however, and the first scrap of rest she'd received in too long seemed almost regretful to leave behind.

"Every time we meet, Miss Mephitoli," he said as they reached the base camp, "you prove you and your kind are animals. A damn good thing your saliva is not a carrier for your disease like the rest of your fluids, eh? Camels and reptiles spit, General. Fish. Civilized beings do not. They possess self-control. With this, you cannot argue. I will prove it. Perhaps when you have humiliated yourself again, and proved me right, you will manage to rejoin civilization."

As Akachi parked the vehicle and threw open his door, Dominia was dragged from her side by a pair of burly men covered in the sweat and dust of their nomadic military life. Above the noise of the camp, the dentist shouted Arabic orders. This resulted in her being shoved the direction of a tent that was a cover for a bunker set deep in the dirt. The flimsy ladder down which she was forced to maneuver with wrists still cuffed gave way to a claustrophobic cellar, whose penal nature she divined not by its subterranean position but by the chains mounted in the bricks of its grudgingly added walls. A voice cried out, and one of the guards whipped off the cuffs while the other held the barrel of his gun against her head.

"Don't bother calling us unless you've killed him," said one man in thickly accented English.

"Killed who?"

Her captors retreated up the ladder, so the only one left to answer was the voice of her fellow prisoner: a voice absent long enough it momentarily registered as a stranger's.

"Dominia," it asked, "is that you? Oh my God! Oh, God, please forgive me! I didn't want to do what I did."

In the darkness of the corner, the General bent over the wincing shape. As her eyes adjusted to the dark, she recognized blinded René Ichigawa, who, arms over his head, wept and waited to die.

XV

A Rat in the Cellar

While far from a connoisseur of men, the General had aesthetic sense enough to know what an attractive one looked like. With his pointed, weasellike features and bony frame, the former English professor always appeared too untrustworthy to join that category, but now the poor fellow was genuinely repellent. The sharpness of his features was emphasized by his malnourished state and the dirt that had, over time, caked the corners of his grotesquely crusted eye sockets to seal them shut. Gagging, Dominia tried to redirect her gaze, but there was no better place to let it sit upon him, for his wristbones poked like daggers from his flesh and his belly protruded in a symptom of true starvation.

"My God, René, have they been feeding you?"

"The past few days. Mostly"—his voice dropped to a whisper—"I've been eating bugs. Oh, God!" His lips trembled into a tearless sob while he admitted, "I hear them scuttling around. That's how I find them. They get in through gaps in the bricks—these are only here for the chains. I don't even think the ceiling is supported, is it? It could collapse anytime!"

The five-foot, claustrophobic ceiling that forced its prisoners to sit upon the ground once they had descended the ladder was supported with one courtesy beam, but the General hardly blamed him for not knowing. His short chain kept him trapped in a foul-smelling corner arrayed with straw and newspaper. At least in Nogales she'd been given a toilet!

"René," began the General, but the man raised his voice in a series of terrible cries.

"Please, Dominia, please! You can't kill me, oh, God, I'm so young. Do you know how young I am? Forty-five! I still have another fifty years to live if I don't have any engineering done, and now I have to live them blind—but I still want to live them! Please, please! You have to forgive me for the train, and before. You have to forgive me, please! I didn't have a choice."

"Would you calm down? I'm not going to kill you." In fact, so many injustices, petty and profound, had occurred since René's betrayal on the train that she had almost been glad to see him until he'd reminded her of his crimes. Even so, she pushed her irritation aside, because Tobias no doubt hoped she'd ruminate on the betrayal to a breaking point. "That fucking dentist is trying to make me repent by proving some point."

"What point?"

The blood of all those men lying dead in the temple still stained the General's kimono: and the hot metal of Benedict's type O still filled her mouth, vivid enough to make her stomach ache with knowledge of its emptiness and its separation from the now-vital sun. "It doesn't matter, because it's not a point that's going to be made. We're going to find a way out."

"I don't think there is one." The blind man whined on while Dominia, severely stooped from her full height, felt the walls, the corners, and the dirt-embedded stones. "I don't even know how long I've been here! Two weeks? Three? It's so hard to tell."

Thin as he'd been to start, that meant the cells in his body were breaking down his proteins, or had been until the Hunters started feeding him again; funnily enough, he was now enduring a prolonged version of the experience had by sun-exposed martyrs. "How often do they bring you food?"

"I think it's once a day, but it was twice today. Oh, God." His voice quivered like a preteen's. "They're trying to fatten me up, aren't they?"

"Then they're doing a poor job of it." Grimacing, the General yanked a brick out of place from the wall and frowned at the dirt behind. "We could always tunnel out."

"*You* could," said René with a jerk of his chain. "I'm stuck here."

"I don't have time for your fatalism, René."

"That's easy for you to say! You're not chained to the wall like a dog. Oh, Christ, when I was little, we had a dog. I loved that dog! But my mother always kept him in the backyard and never let him inside. Is this karma? Is this what I get for letting her treat the dog that way?"

Though on the verge of saying the notion was ridiculous, Dominia found herself there again: abandoning Basil in the back of the *tanque* while she pursued René in effort to board the Light Rail. Valentinian had abandoned her, just like she'd abandoned him. Her incredulous mouth fell open. The real question was whether she was more appalled by her own actions than she was furious at the magician. In that fury, the martyr stormed to René's side, and while the man flung his cowering arms over his head, the General tore the chain from the shoddy brick in which it'd been anchored.

"Oh," said René, groping for, then picking up, the now-freed end of the chain. "Well—thank you."

"You know, Tobias tried to intimidate me by having one of his exoskeletons crush a brick, but I'm starting to think the Hunters just make shitty bricks."

"Maybe there *is* a chance," decided the mercurial professor, clasping his hands, then running the chain through them as he might a necktie. "But what will we do once we're out of here? You've seen the camp."

Her knee-jerk response was the same as in Nogales: murder the guard, then sweep through the camp as silent and bloody as the incarnation of Saint Valentinian. Well—poor turn of phrase, considering how sore she was at the moment with her patron saint, but one got the idea. "I don't know," began the General, with utmost caution. "Maybe, say...you distract the guard and I knock him out? If we find weapons on him, we kill him and take them."

"No! We can't hurt the guard!"

"He knows what he's getting into," said Dominia as, conveniently, the trapdoor was lifted and the minor glow of interior light showered in alongside a powerful flashlight beam.

"René!" The instantly recognizable, vaguely girly voice of Tenchi Ichigawa took the wind out of Dominia's scheming sails. "I brought you something extra today!"

"Oh, no," she groaned, while, his expression grim, René asked, "You see?"

"Who are you talking to down here?" asked the portly sailor. On turning at the bottom of the ladder, the beam of his miner's cap swung across René's unresponsive face and into the General's wincing one. With the delay of a second, Tenchi shrieked and lost the food on his tray as he pressed himself into the farthest corner.

"Oh! Oh, Mephitoli-san! Oh, *Kami-sama, tasukete kudasai*! Why didn't they warn me!"

"Because they're hoping I'll kill you, too. They saw how I let you go on the *Jun'yō*, and they're wondering if I'll do it again now that I'm starving and you're between me and freedom." Frankly, if either human was likely to whet her appetite, it was the porcine one, and not his skinny mustelid cousin. What a good opportunity this would be to test her self-control, along with her certainty about her need of direct sun! She tried not to dwell on the thought and found home in annoyance, demanding, "What are you doing here?"

"I—the same thing I was doing the last time you saw me." The trembling man held the plastic food tray like a shield over his heart. He seemed ready at a second's notice to spring back up the ladder to which he looked with increasing frequency. "You know—serving...the resistance..."

"Tenchi!" The chide provoked such a wince in the man that the martyr almost laughed and strained to drop her tone from a drill sergeant's bark. "You can't seriously think that the Hunters are in the right here. Don't you know about them? They go from human town to human town, conscripting the men and using their daughters and wives as sex slaves to recruit more men. Some cells even try to 'reform' women like me through rape. Any human who doesn't practice an Abrahamian faith is liable to be literally *stoned* to death in some of the crazier cells. *Stoned*."

"In the year 4042," added René. This elicited a dirty look from the General, who swiftly remembered he could not read it and told him, "What are you talking about? You were a part of the Hunters before my Father got to you! That's why they put you here."

"I was a free agent who was used and abused by both sides," insisted the sore man, crossing his arms and tsking at the jingle of the chain. The noise attracted Tenchi's attention.

"Your chain! What happened?"

"I happened," explained Dominia.

Full of terror, the chubby man remembered himself and drew back the step he'd just taken into the low room of the dungeon. "I'm going to get in trouble for this."

"Good! I hope you do." Her sleep-deprived, miserable irritation needed an outlet, and she unleashed it on the man who'd been hand-selected to taunt her through no fault of his own. "I can't believe you would be a part of this, Tenchi! You seem like a nice guy. You can't know everything these people do and accept it without examining the implications of what it says about you. You're supporting violence and theft from other humans, and you're directly aiding that human suffering by being here. And for—what, some stupid war you're going to lose? Have you ever even been in a *fist*fight, fisherman?"

"Did you see the suits?" asked Tenchi meekly.

The General snapped, "Yeah, and I'm not impressed. Your shitty dentist boss can take the suits and his teleporter and shove them up his—"

"I think they would give us a chance in a conflict..." As though remembering why he was here, Tenchi looked at the platter in his hands, collected the few scattered packages of food, and slid it across the floor toward René. The blind man leapt at the sound, groped across the dirt, and, with fumbling, desperate fingers, tore away the cellophane. As both Tenchi and Dominia grimaced at the sight of the starving man cramming his mouth full of ration-grade honey cakes, the General waved a hand.

"You've let them make you party to treating your cousin like this."

"Oh, no! If it weren't for me, they would have killed him outright. Everyone was upset when he showed up without you, and with those eyes. I'm so glad I was there! I begged the guys—I mean, begged, it was kind of embarrassing—"

"*Really* embarrassing," glutted René through a mouthful of nuts.

"—and Dr. Akachi said, 'All right. If he can survive until Dominia arrives, your cousin will be free.'"

"They just didn't tell you he was going to have to survive like this. Tenchi, why would you trust them? Honestly, I'm baffled. I'd think you knew better after staying in the magician's City."

The General realized she'd made a chronological gaff only after Tenchi's brow furrowed. "City," he repeated. "Magician?"

Vaguely, she remembered Gethsemane warning the sailor against revealing the future to Dominia. "Nothing. Never mind." Hopeful she would not slip up and kill him in the future, and that the portly man could be turned away from his so-called brothers-in-arms, the General pressed him. "But how can you accept being a part of this? How can you think what the Hunters do is an appropriate price to pay for overthrowing my Father?"

After a few seconds of thought, the sailor shrugged. "What other choice does a human man have in this world? Especially if he wants to help people in the Front, or do something to contribute to the dissolution of martyr dominance. I mean...it's sort of your fault."

She would have loved to argue, but, in a sense, he was right. The Battle for the Reclamation of Mexico had initially been won by the South American Resistance Army, but it was a costly victory that had shattered most of their best forces and caused other troops to be funneled from the Western Front. This had meant that, when Dominia freed herself and slaughtered the entire camp, then turned around to call in reinforcements before freeing what few captive martyr officers had been claimed from other victories, the two groups cut a bloody swathe across the remaining human militias and left them destroyed. When Cicero's unit met Dominia's in Tucson, he found her and her ramshackle group of six martyrs holding down a building that had once belonged to the Resistance and had been, long before that, a bank. In those sweet moments when first she saw her brother again, the martyrs were in the process of trying to break into a heavy-duty vault to acquire the humans within. How helpful Cicero had been at that moment! How good it had been to see him. They met outside the ruins of a nearby mosque whose crumbling façade was still emblazoned with the English block letter phrase, "HAPPINESS IS SUBMISSION TO GOD". In that reunion, he was more her brother than he'd ever been, or would ever be again. She's screamed with delight to see him! She longed for that moment, oddly, for although her nights at war were not good nights—that war more than any war she'd fought—they were nights when she had the illusion of Family. Love from her Family.

Her Family had been all that mattered to her then, even after the Hierophant's snub. Perhaps that was why the image of Benedict stuck so deep in her unconscious craw, though it had been too simple to murder him and every other man nearby. Perhaps that was why it bothered her so to see

Tenchi now, led by fear and ideal into the service of a cause so backward it was downright evil. She saw in the sailor too much of her old self, cutting into that bank vault and murdering a room of trapped soldiers with Cicero's help—and feeling it was fun. That was the last time she had fun killing anybody: even by that point, death had lost its glow.

And now, well, violence wasn't even an option. She could not bring herself to kill Tenchi, and for whatever sorry reason, after he collected René's tray, she allowed the tubby man to depart. She would need spend at least one night in this wretched place. But, ah, how quickly one night turned to two! Particularly as, to its credit, the cell served as a very fine, very dark place for a martyr—who had been given a psychedelic drug, forced to engage in a battle, dragged on a six-hour road trip, then made to spend another two hours driving in the sun before being electrocuted, and who was *still* not able to enjoy unconsciousness for more than an hour or so—to sleep, sleep, finally, sweetly, sleep. O sleep, O gentle sleep! Nature's soft nurse, as wrote the Bard. There was no energy left in Dominia for her mind to connect to the Ergosphere and provide her a dream—except, on waking, the memory of one: Cassandra, standing outside the City's marketplace, where the General had met Tenchi. She got so far as to touch her wife's hand, to kiss her orchid lips, before awareness of that dream faded off again.

When Dominia awoke so refreshed she felt like a whole new person, it was, by René's reckoning, some twelve hours later. "Not that I have a way to tell," he added miserably. "I base my guess on how hungry I am."

"I'll buy you a grandfather clock when we get out of here." Dominia sat with her back to the wall and her legs straight before her. As she bent forward to stretch before she exercised (much as one managed either in such a cramped space), she asked, "What did you think they were going to do to you when you showed up empty-handed, René? Say, 'Oh, that's okay?' Especially when you confessed the truth about your eyes, if that's how it happened."

"It is," he confirmed with a sigh. "I don't know. I was desperate! I was terrified the whole way to the Hunters, sure that any minute you would change your mind and come to kill me: or that Cicero or your Father would swoop me up again."

"Did they really send you to me, René? What was the Hierophant's plan with you?"

Apparently, René was supposed to spy on Dominia and stay with her to provide a consistent location to the Hierophant. Had things gone to plan, he explained, the Holy Family would have followed them all the way to the Hunters, and then to Lazarus. "He and Cicero came to me because he knew my cousin's connection to the Hunters, and threatened to kill me for it, saying I was probably a spy. But he thought we could make a deal, too."

"Why you, specifically? Surely there are plenty of humans he could have used."

"I don't know. A lot of my colleagues were busted before I was approached, which must be how they got my name. I think he spared me because of my education."

Entirely possible, or even probable. The Hierophant had a profound love for all art and music, but Western culture was his soulmate, and those involved in its preservation and transmission were, to him, salvageable. It was the same reason why Dominia had been introduced to the human from the start. When, three months after Cassandra's death, the Governess managed to look another person in the face without finding herself on the verge of tears, she forced her hollow body to attend a party hosted by one of Cassandra's artist friends. The whole thing had been twice as depressing as it sounded on recounting (exactly as depressing as she had expected at the time); but it seemed worthwhile to stretch herself, even as she, antisocial and avoidant, skeptically allowed the human to be introduced to her while she brooded about her exit in the corner of a black sofa.

"Dominia," the well-to-do friend had been saying, "Dominia, I have somebody here I think you *must* meet, and he's said he wants to meet you, too—pretty *bold* for a human, I thought, but, oh, what a *riot* he is! This is René Ichigawa. He's a professor at Berkeley and just *too* funny. You'd think he was a martyr if I didn't tell you!"

"I'm a poet, too," he'd been swift to add, as all poets are.

"It must be hard to be a human and an artist," Dominia remarked. René had laughed.

"I think it's harder to be a martyr and an artist. What struggles do you have to write about? Not even mortality oppresses you. A martyr will always have his home, but a human might be eaten tomorrow. That means I have to write like I'm about to die, all the time—and that means every new work I create is the best work of my life."

By that standard, Dominia was ready for her magnum opus. Tobias had a fair point when he said she was dead, thus liberated. This truth was comforting and depressing. Yes, she could go anywhere—in hiding. Yes, she was free—to live a lie and forever await violent death. She supposed she could just disappear, move to the City, but that required her to get outside, if only in moonlight, until she found better means. If only there were someone to help her. Say, a mystic, or a magician.

The magician, she almost understood. He had things to do, and was probably also passive-aggressively teaching her a lesson about abandonment. But that Lazarus had been in this camp, yet not tried to break her out, was a matter of mild concern. The idea of having come this far only to have something happen to her most valuable companion was an infuriating one, and she tried, to no avail, to get information out of the younger, rounder Ichigawa when he came the second day.

"You haven't seen a bearded man, have you? Martyr, older, maybe still stuck in a kimono?"

"I don't think I should talk to you about what goes on in camp," answered the dubious man, who sat just inside the squat dungeon to eat dinner with his cousin, ready to scramble back at a second's notice if the famished martyr got any ideas. "Nobody's gotten me in trouble over the chain because I don't think anybody's willing to come down here, but I know that if I say anything about anything, it will haunt me."

René brushed off his saliva-dampened hands, having finished a plastic tray of repulsive mashed potatoes, sad vegetables, and saltine crackers. "Here's a question for you, then! Why's the boss such a hypocrite? I heard him crying about the debauchery of Western culture when he was yanking out my DIOX-Is, but what should I hear while I'm being dragged to my new hole? Mozart!"

"I like Mozart," said the sailor defensively. René raised his hands in agitation.

"Don't we all! That's my point. These religious nuts try to condemn basic human qualities like a deep love of music, then fall into their own traps because they can't resist them! They just want an excuse to fuck up, the masochists."

The notion made Dominia laugh, recalling, for fleeting seconds, dear Miki. That first proper meeting in the dining car. As her smile faded with sudden longing for her friend—and pain at the knowledge they could not meet again on Earth—the General cleared her throat. "The Hierophant and Dr. Akachi could put aside their differences if we just got them together at a concert. My Father loves Mozart, too."

"See," insisted the blind professor. "Everybody loves Mozart."

There was something therapeutic about being able to talk to more than one person at once, but it was also relieving when Tenchi finally ascended the ladder. Tobias wasn't entirely wrong: the fat Ichigawa cousin was a tempting target for her appetite. With the bone-deep hunger of a martyr instilling itself back into her body on the denial of sunlight, the craving for human flesh was stronger than ever. Blood received from René could keep her alive, it was true, but nothing would offer the satisfaction of an actual meal quite like a shank of human flesh. The idea was almost impossible to ignore once she got it into her head. Everything in her sought to rationalize, say, borrowing one of Tenchi's fleshy arms. That wouldn't necessarily kill him, would it? Easy to replace, too. But, no. It wasn't right. Not knowing that he was in the City, and not knowing it was what Tobias wanted.

More than any problem with Tobias, Dominia could not stand to slip back into the roles of the old person she'd been; she could not relive Nogales, no matter how simple a way out violence formed.

"You look bad," Tenchi told her on the third night, sucking chocolate pudding out of a cup. How he acquired it in a camp where even basic rations were surely precious, she did not know.

"No shit." The General rubbed her forehead to work away its ever-growing throb. "I'm starving, Tenchi."

After a thoughtful moment, the fat man rolled her the apple that had formed a neglected splotch upon his tray. Dominia almost snorted, almost told him, 'That won't do any good,' but when her mind revived in a flash the image of Benedict, she bit her tongue and thanked him. It was the illusion of sustenance, she supposed, something to keep her stomach from dissolving its own lining. But it wouldn't help her shaking, and in the long run, it would increase the damage of starvation, because calories her body expended in digestion would be replaced, but the food wouldn't provide her body with the protein her dysfunctional cells required to maintain their own stability. She'd end up malnourished, like a duck fed bread instead of seed.

As, night by night, René filled out, being given more food than the scraps he'd received on his previous schedule, the General felt her muscles growing not only weaker but harder to control. Sit-ups had become a chore at an alarming pace in the dungeon, and push-ups grew out of the question as her hands lost the ability to manipulate objects. Part of the problem was her age. As a young woman, she could've gone without eating for a longer period of time; but around the age of three hundred, most martyrs experienced an increase in metabolism that was regularly attributed to the increasing instability of their cells. This was not a problem so long as one kept oneself surrounded with food or regularly attended Church for the blood of the Lamb, which was why martyrs had popularized cities to an extent surpassing even humans. It was also why, as the martyr population expanded to uncomfortable sizes, humans across the globe grew more nervous. Some even sought to donate their children to martyrdom (another popular cause of illegal immigration into the Front) as though to circumvent the problem altogether—or, in all likelihood, spare their own lives.

What a horrible thought that had always been to Dominia, who had been martyred not only without her consent, but without her knowledge. The way it happened was horrible, but also gentle. Morgan had been fortunate: too young to comprehend what it meant to be a martyr, or, say, know the symptoms of the disease that heralded its transformation. Thus, so far as she had been concerned, she was just a girl sick at home, like a hundred million other girls, future and past, sick at home. It had been scary, especially because her parents had been so upset yet so silent about what was going on. But, in retrospect, it was a kinder fate. Those last few days, her father sat with her and told her stories about the family genealogy so she wouldn't forget. Her parents were from the Front; her father was shrewd with investments despite his rural background, and they'd struck gold on stocks related to then-recent Martian terraforming developments. That same acuity with investments—and disdain for taxes—would someday attract the Hierophant to their door. Give him an excuse, anyway.

Dominia was from Mephitoli, but little Morgan had been named after an American ancestor who was herself the daughter of a North American and a South American. That North American line, further back in time, well—they really *had* been from Meph(Italy) if you picked the right set of ancestors. So, they'd moved there. But with every member of the Front at that point in time a mutt of lineage, they could have justified moving anywhere when Morgan was on the way. If only they'd picked the German ancestors, the Irish, even the Polish! But Poland, like every Slavic state, was martyr country in excess of even Mephitoli; Morgan and her family could have been murdered and eaten before she'd learned to walk.

Which was the worse fate? She had gone to sleep one day and died, like so many of those other girls sick at home. But, like a proportion far fewer than even that number, Morgan rose from the dead to find herself with a new Family, a new room, a new life, a new name. A new genealogy, to replace—or supplement, she preferred to think—the one her father had spent her last days teaching her. It was traumatic at the time, but naturally there wasn't much choice in the matter, and that made the trouble far easier than the struggle undergone by a martyred adult. Being powerless simplified the pain as much as being, in the way of children, unconscious to the horrible details of existence.

She shuddered to think what Cassandra had endured. In Dominia's current opinion, an adult's decision to become a martyr was sign of mental illness. Before Cassandra, she'd romanticized it. After the suicide, Dominia understood why her Father impressed upon his people the importance of martyring children, and enforced the taboo nature of human-martyr relations.

All this was why it was so disorienting when Dominia, awoken by pain in her ankle, looked down to see the metal plate of René's chain, its sharp corner darkened by rust. Or—no. That was blood, certainly blood. Certainly *her* blood. And its source, no doubt, was that to which René had alarmingly attached his lips. Ravaged by hunger and torn from dreamless sleep, the General hardly understood what these images indicated until the pitiful professor, caught in the act, scrambled away, wiped his bloodied lips, and cried for the umpteenth time, "I'm sorry!"

Perhaps it was all just a shock because, in the past three days, the General and the professor had exchanged surprisingly few words. What words they had exchanged had often been literary quotes. Between the two of them, they were able to remember a satisfying amount of *Macbeth*; and Dominia regaled him with her own recitation of "The Raven"—in her opinion, more soulful than Cicero's. This had been most of their relationship, to be frank. After the bootlicking would-be-Renfield had forced his calling card into Dominia's hands (at the time, she thought it the action of your typical martyr-chasing human who could nonetheless come in handy as a future slave/tool/meal; now she understood it as the action of an inept spy), the Governess found him soon trying to make an appointment with her office, ostensibly to petition for an artistic grant. In reality, once he had her ear, he passed her a book.

"What is this?" she had asked that hot July evening, bending to view the pages through which she flipped with one hand while unbuttoning, with the other, her stifling suit coat. "The focus of your grant? I expected it to be artistic, not scholarly."

Perfectly cool—no doubt trained in this, or vetted for this quality, by the Hierophant—smiling René stroked his trim goatee. "This, Governess, is something that could get me killed. But I don't think it will, because of what it means to you."

"And what does it mean to me?"

"Having your wife back."

She could have crushed the spine of the book like it was René's bony one. Indeed, she had been forced to set the volume down. "What would you know about my wife, human?" she asked him, her tone razor sharp.

The professor had not batted an eye. Instead, he proved the first to say what so many others along her journey had said in response to that same question.

"I know you loved her very much. Otherwise, you wouldn't..." He tapped his chest to indicate the diamond over Dominia's heart. "But I think you wear—her because you know there's hope."

She nearly laughed, but there was nothing funny about Cassandra's invocation by this know-nothing human. The Governess had thought seriously about killing him. Maybe she should have. In some universes, perhaps she did. Instead, in this one, she had flipped back through the book and found it to be a foreign holy text in an unknown language. There had been drawings that, at the time, had meant nothing to her, but had depicted a temple full of women, the arrival of a man, the sacred marriage of that man to one of the women, and that woman's ascension as a goddess. It had impressed her so little that she did not internalize any of the images well enough to remember them concretely: any, except for the image of the old goddess shedding her skin and fleeing, naked, upon the back of a tiger, ready to fly off the page and upon Dominia's desk.

"Why don't you try to explain," she had said, "and I'll try to decide whether to kill you."

Then, René told her the story of Lazarus. Not the Lazarus Dominia knew—the imaginary figurehead of a bunch of lunatic cult members. The real story had been so garbled by time and her Father that, even in its accurate tellings, it was Lazarus's blood that was capable of raising the dead; or perhaps it was something he did in a magical way. On that matter, René had never been clear. But as Dominia had pressed him to know why she should believe this was not a lie, he had said at the time, "Because I wouldn't mind drinking his blood if some of the things I've heard are true—and I would never drink a martyr's blood."

"I'm sorry," René screamed all of three months later, imprisoned with Dominia in the dungeon beneath the Hunters' camp. "I'm so sorry, Dominia, I never wanted this, but I can see you in my dreams—I see hunger in your eyes! I see the way you look at me when I sleep and I hear the way you breathe near me when I'm awake; it's only a matter of time before you can't help yourself anymore."

"René, what the *fuck*!" The level of violation was impossible to describe. Recoiling against the opposite wall, the General felt her skin crawl on a metaphorical level to join the physical sensation of the slow-leaking wound at the base of her ankle. "Why would you even think this was a good idea?"

"Because my flesh will be no good to you if I'm a martyr! No matter how hungry you are, you'll never think of eating me. Hey—maybe we can eat Tenchi together!"

"Oh, Lord love the Lamb, René, would you listen to yourself?"

"I didn't know what else to do," the man cried, looking for all the world like a bearded, blinded child. "I couldn't just sit here waiting for you to kill me."

"I wasn't going to kill you, but now you're definitely going to die. Frankly, I should put you out of your misery, but—shit." Furious, the General tore a rock from the dirt behind her and hurled it into the bricks not far from René's head. He winced. It was cruel, but satisfying, because it was the most cruelty she could afford to inflict upon a man whose death would mean a victory for the principles of a thoroughly unprincipled man.

"Please, Dominia, don't hurt me. Now I can help you get out!"

"You still won't be able to see, you know."

"But—but I'll be able to fight."

"You'll be able to blindly charge off into the night, trip over your chain, and get shot like any other idiot."

"But I'll be faster, right? And stronger?"

"You'll be incredibly fucked up and disoriented and probably won't be worth anything until you've had a meal—and I'm not letting you eat Tenchi. Fuck! What are we going to do?"

The choice had been stupid, burdensome, and now firmly set the responsibility of René's life on his nonconsensual creatrix's shoulders. Although she could easily kill him and avoid the whole issue (and get herself a meal before her proteins altered his), that wasn't an option. She would have to use the situation she'd been given. It wasn't all bad.

"Okay," she said. "Okay." Then, smoothing her hands over her face and back through hair cropped so short it resembled René's former professor cut and not his increasingly floppy, unkempt prisoner's mane, the poor General tried one more, "Okay," before laughing at herself. Her hand touched Cassandra's diamond.

Nobody had more than one chance to do anything in life. She had to remember that.

"Here's the deal, René." The General found some small satisfaction as he responded to her movement toward him by wincing against the brick wall. "Just relax. I won't hurt you, but it's important you know you are going to die."

As she sat beside him, he leaned away, but she caught his filthy hand and squeezed it until he squeaked her name. "It's going to hurt. You'll have a fever, and probably the shits, and those will mostly be blood. Your organs will feel like they're on fire—like somebody's just...reaching a hand into your body and squeezing"—she tightened her grip on his hand—"twisting your spine and tangling your intestines."

"Jesus, Dominia, do you have to tell me this?"

"You're going to die in this cell, floating in a pool of your own bloody sweat and bile vomit, because you chose to do this to yourself. And when you're dead"—her eyes burned like Valentinian's fire, so bright even the blind professor might have seen them—"I'm going to use your corpse to get us out of here."

XVI

The Price of Information

The positive aspect of René's adulthood: the protein's malformation spread faster through the body. The negative: it was much more violent than anything a child experienced. For the fortysomething English professor, the illness took three days. Dominia had been concerned more time would elapse; she would have been in dire straits herself, were that to happen. On the sixth day of her captivity and the third day of René's illness, as he shivered in the corner, covered in sweat while trying to maintain a conversation about Shakespeare's use of alchemical symbolism in his late romances, the General opened her mouth to point out how the use of alchemical metaphors stretched back to the cradle of civilization where lay the Middle States—

René was patting her cheek with a clammy hand and saying her name, as if he'd leapt across the room like the Hierophant. She barked out an irritable series of "What, what!" as she slapped his dirty palm away.

"I think you were having a seizure—you took a breath like you were about to speak and started choking. You were thrashing. Are you hurt?"

Yes, actually: her head throbbed, but she was still straight up against the wall and hadn't gnawed through her tongue. Best to accept the seizure had happened without making a production.

That same afternoon, René Ichigawa died without fanfare in Dominia's reluctant arms, and the General was concerned the martyring process that had killed him so hastily would complete his resurrection before Tenchi's next visit. Though the captives had gone to some lengths to hide René's state of obvious illness from the portly sailor, he had noticed his cousin's far sweatier condition on the second night. The third night, René had been too weak to stay awake for his cousin's visit, so Tenchi left the tray of food at the bottom of the ladder and hurried back up. He must have seen the intensity of hunger in the General's eyes, their blue tones reduced to mere shadows that matched the ones carved into her face by starvation-emphasized cheekbones.

The changes were subtle now, but she had already lost muscle mass, and this was a definite concern. She was not sure she'd be able to control herself well enough to maintain their charade. Once, on the ship, she felt a sense of pride about her self-control, and look how that ended! Even if it had been Cicero's fault, she had to admit she'd been well fed the rest of the voyage. Those last few days of sailing came upon her now with alarming fondness. It was possible that, when placed in front of more than one or two healthy, beating hearts, the General would prove Tobias right: snap as she had when given the chance to free herself from Nogales. And that was with courtesy bags of intranasal blood!

The worst part was that none of this would have been necessary if the magician hadn't vanished. If he was so powerful, he should have appeared in her cell to whisk her away at a moment's notice. Turn all the jihadists into statues, or transmute Dominia into a flea small enough to crawl through the crack where light trickled from the trapdoor. He could create a miracle—that son of a bitch could do it, no matter what anybody said—and he was nowhere to be found.

Yet—wasn't it a miracle that René had not woken to his second life the next time Tenchi whistled down the ladder? Who was she to distinguish between miracle and coincidence, fate and good timing, when she'd seen firsthand all space and time were one? With haste, the General gouged her hand on the edge of that same loose plate René had used to steal her blood: this, she smeared across her own mouth, then across René's throat and the front of a dirty shirt pre-stained with bloody vomit and bloodier sweat. The importance of gory freshness, however, was key. And it was more important still that Tenchi catch her in the act, so when the beam of light fell across them, she could look from where she hunched over René's corpse and absorb the sailor's girlish shriek in deliberate imitation of her Father's dignified calm. "René is dead. I'm sorry. Please get the other guards, and Tobias. I'd like to talk to him."

"Oh, René!" With a cry of terror, the fat man scurried up the ladder at a speed faster than the General would have expected him to even walk.

Now came the hard part. Now, she composed herself. Now more than ever, her Father's blood flowed through her veins, and she reviewed all the times he reacted with perfect ease to outward annoyances (those disruptions by boisterous children in Mass that so bothered fastidious Cicero, for instance—why, more often than not, the Holy Father was cajoling them into outlandish behavior to get his Eternal Son's goat). Wasn't this that certainty of an educated decision with which his specter claimed it sought to empower her?

"Specter." The word made her frown. Her deprived mind scrambled between subjects even as the trapdoor reopened. Was the root of "specter" not "spectrum"? Perhaps she had seen her Father after all, manifesting in her electromagnetic field: her own thoughts about him, summoning him, inviting him the way he invited her each night into his dream-study. One English voice amid several Arabic shouts told her to face the wall. Her mind was elsewhere. A thoughtform, or his true spectral presence non-temporally in her field, mistranslated into the visual cortex. Hallucination by definition, supernatural by speculation.

Whatever that image was, it had been right. Even as she faced the wall, she felt in perfect power. Perfect control of the situation. She controlled the most valuable asset of all. Not freedom but knowledge. Knowledge bought freedom. Tobias had plenty of freedom, but he lacked the knowledge that René would awaken. He did not realize he had been duped as he made a personal appearance in her prison, one man shoving a gun into the back of her head while the dentist checked the pulse of her dead cellmate.

"So he *is* dead. Now you understand what I was saying, General? You cannot help yourself. Moreover, you are so bound to instinct you cannot use reason! Every day I have sent you a fat, tasty pig of a man, and you chose to bleed this skinny rat."

"His death came out of more than hunger," the General explained, calmly studying the roots pricking out of the dirt wall's surface. "It was owed to René, for what he did to me, and for getting in my way. For getting in the way of our association, Akachi."

"Ah? Now, what would you mean by that?"

"I've thought about the ways I could say this: the problem is, I hate you, so I have a difficult time putting it politely. But you've forced me into a corner. Almost literally," she added, sparing a soft laugh for the wall against which her nose was pressed. "There's no animal so vicious or stupid that, given a long enough time to think and the words to think in, won't come around to doing what it can to save its own life. I don't agree with you, or your cause. But if René had done what he was supposed to—if he'd come here with me, become initiated by your group, and given me a chance to consider an agreement with the Hunters without duress—none of this would have been a problem."

"This all sounds convenient, Miss Mephitoli." Dominia was grateful her face could not be seen from this position. "How do I know you are not going to get aboveground and begin killing my men?"

"Besides the rifles, you mean? Because I would already be aboveground and killing them, if that were the case. Tenchi would be dead and so would these fu— fine fellows pointing guns at me."

"Look how you tremble." The dentist took up her hand so abruptly that she started away. "Your meal did not have much meat on him, eh?"

"That should tell you how serious I am about working with you," she said, every word more cautious than the last. "No matter how hungry I am—no matter how many men I could still eat—I refrain, for civility's sake."

Chuckling, Akachi patted her shoulder and said, "Perhaps there is something of a person left within the animal." In Arabic, the dentist delivered an order, and the man with the gun to the back of Dominia's head steered her toward the ladder.

"Where am I being taken?"

"For a meal, and new clothes! I would like to speak with you again, now that you are feeling reasonable. Perhaps we can forge an agreement! You, and Lazarus and I."

Her heart skipped a beat at the thought of seeing a friend who frequently evaded her mind during her duress. If she had thought of anyone, it had been Valentinian, and only in the most malicious way possible. But it was hard to think when one was starving and the cells in one's body (and brain) were losing the ability to keep themselves shaped. After six days' imprisonment in that wretched tomb, the General's brain screamed at sensory stimulus. The cardinal light of the setting sun so blistered her sensitive eyes that she tried to cover them and could not because of her captor's grip. She cried, instead, to think how weak she'd been made by her hunger, and how tight her skin was under the touch of her captors, and her body's urge to be free of her collar. How she wished to leap off into the remaining sunlight! The overwhelmed General lowered her head toward the dust as, in surprising numbers, men emerged from their small tents to view the passing martyr. Somewhere, Tenchi wept.

In the suffocating heat of the medical tent, which reeked of putrid wounds and sweet antiseptic even though it had been some time since the unit had seen combat, Dominia was handed a hot blood bag along with the promised change of clothes. After inhaling the ration (and snatching another from the nearby refrigerator when the guards were busy arranging René's body on a stretcher at the behest of the medic), the General loosed the stained brass kimono and redressed, ignoring the eyes that struggled to avoid her—and in this case had religious, medical, and prejudicial reasons to do so. They could get fucked, so far as she cared: she'd seen too many naked idiot men snapping towels at each other's repressed backsides to help but feel by the age of 331 (no, remember, 332, can't forget), that nudity in such a scenario was about as sexual as a mud puddle. That was her own opinion, at any rate. Some people no doubt found mud puddles sexy. She was getting damn tired of this world, Valentinian.

The clothes she had been given were not unlike the Hunters' own "casual" outfits—a shin-length gray kurta with a thick black bar running down its front and a pair of white pants for beneath. At the instance of the English-speaking guard, whose vocabulary on this subject was limited but who managed to cite "religious reasons," she donned the black kufi and wondered at the point of it since it was the same black as her hair. Better that than a hijab, she supposed, when it came for vision in battle, but greater head covering would have (perhaps falsely) reassured her she couldn't be whisked off into the Ergosphere due to her own inexperience. However, to her relief, they emerged from the medical tent to find the reddened sun had relented to plum night. She looked for the moon, and as she saw it remembered that trying to enter the Void in earthly night would only deposit her into that place's more terrible low ebb. A night in which the soul barely existed. It was not worth trying—not that way, anyway. If push came to shove and safety required a regroup in that other, more nebulous space, the General would need another way to enter the Void. Not to mention she'd have to find a way back out, if she were to do so before the sun rose. Her Father managed it. If only she had someone to ask. Oh, Valentinian! Where was that sorry bastard?

Not many steps from the medical tent, she detected the distant sound of music and realized with an uncanny shock of synchronicity that not only was René right—it was indeed Mozart that Tobias arrogantly played in the middle of a camp full of men ideologically opposed to most forms of art—but tonight it appeared to be that very Requiem that had lit her drunken soul so long ago. Then, as now, she had been separated from Valentinian. Those haunting voices, ah, how well she knew their notes! Lavinia performed the same in concert, with Cassandra and a choir of other, lesser, singers, after the latter revealed the beauty of her singing voice to more than just Dominia and rooms full of lucky schoolchildren. The Hierophant insisted on making a Christmas gift of lessons for as long as the Governess's wife desired, then enthusiastically organized the concert not more than a couple years later.

That had been a fine morning, and it had been good to see Cassandra so happy. So close to their sister. Perhaps that unconscious memory coaxed her into selecting the piece when visiting her Father's empty study. Ever after, all versions were inferior, but this variant was fine enough, and proved comfort when the quality crisped upon being pushed into Tobias's tent. No song, however, was comforting as the sight of Lazarus, who read, markedly collarless, beside a generator-powered lamp.

"Kiddo," he said as she hurried over to embrace him, the reality of a person friendly to her. Truly friendly, and not a user in the way of René. "You all right?"

"I wasn't sure what happened when I didn't hear from you after the first day, but—I was so stressed and hungry I hardly thought of you. I'm sorry."

"I'm fine; you never have to worry about me. Well. Not anytime soon, anyway." Weakly, the old man smiled, then frowned and tipped up her chin. "Same old story for the past four iterations...still got your collar on."

"Is it supposed to be gone by now?"

Tobias provided her answer as he entered the tent. "A funny question to ask. In point of fact, I toyed with the idea of having my men free Miss Mephitoli in the medical tent, but I decided it was better I do it myself. If she made it this far without changing her mind, I thought that a good sign. Before it was different, eh? You see"—he elbowed Lazarus in an obnoxious way before pushing the cylindrical key into Dominia's collar—"God inspired my choice, to teach you a lesson about how much you know!"

As the martyrs made withering eye contact over the dentist's head, the latch clicked free and the collar swung open. At the liberation of her throat for the first time in six days, Dominia enjoyed an inhalation so pure, so sudden, it elicited a head rush that bled the room of color. The General laughed at herself and touched her neck while the dentist said approvingly, "Isn't that much better! If you are willing to be a reasonable woman, I am willing to be a reasonable man."

"Does it require a lot of cognitive dissonance to believe the reasonable thing was killing René?" Dominia rubbed the impression left by the metal, wincing at the bruising that could now begin to fade.

"It is always reasonable to kill a traitor. Even Judas Iscariot agreed with that point, my friend; that is why he hanged himself in shame. René Ichigawa did not possess that level of self-insight, but you came around to it, yes?"

"I suppose that's one way to put it."

"Hunger was a motive, too, I'm sure." Tobias chuckled as he sat near the stereo. "My man outside the tent tells me you made short work of your ration. Are you still hungry? Shall I fetch the other Ichigawa cousin for you?"

"Why are you so eager to see me kill them? I thought Tenchi was one of you."

"Tenchi is one of those Hunters who is only a Hunter in the loose sense of the word. Think of him like Kahlil—that young man could have turned a toaster into a cell phone, and in fact I believe he did, to contact us with information about the Cairo ceremony! But that skill made him dangerous, as did his so-called moral stance. Tenchi is much the same. He is useful insofar as his sailing connections are concerned...that means he provides us with transport to the Front, and, for refugees funded by our cause, transport out of it; but there are many other men who are just as useful as he, for the same or similar reasons. And, of course, men of his use will grow defunct as we are able to establish teleporters. I am not eager to see you kill him, or anyone else. But I am eager to remind you that I, who need not kill to eat at all if I do not wish, am superior to you."

At the narrowing of the General's eyes, Lazarus said, "Tobias, please. We've discussed this."

"It is true we have made progress," the dentist agreed, "and more progress will yet be made. But I can see in your General's eyes, my brother, that she has not accepted my authority. And she will need to, if we are to defeat her Father."

"What about me?" She glanced at the entrance of the tent, then focused on the dentist. "I mean, Lazarus is integral to your plan and has uses even after the Hierophant is overthrown. But what's supposed to happen to me after this is over?"

"A wise woman, thinking long-term. You will be allowed to live." How gracious! "But you will need agree to live elsewhere, if you understand what I mean."

"I'm not entirely sure I do."

"There are options. Perhaps you would like to retire to your magician's sacrilegious Kingdom, eh? I do not think it will be a good idea come Judgment Day, but that is between you and God. Or, if you would continue this life, doing penance for what you have done, I suppose I could see to your deportation to the Mars colony. It is only Earth that belongs to mankind; we are to be her custodians, not those of Mars. Martyrs may do with it what you like. Indeed, it seems even suited to your names!" He was pleased with that, and missed the second withering glance Lazarus and Dominia exchanged while he chuckled to himself. "Martyrs from Mars. Better than 'Martians,' don't you suppose!"

"So my choices are 'get out,' or 'get out.'"

"Or die."

"Reassuring."

Brow furrowed, Tobias leaned forward. His body, pressing into the arm of his chair, outlined the gun hidden beneath his clothes. "Have I told you the full story, Miss Mephitoli, of how I, mere dentist, came to be leader of these violent men?"

Bracing herself for a windbag monologue, Dominia offered a tight, polite smile not unlike the one Lazarus presented. "No, in fact, you did not ever tell me that. You said you were going to be a...'slave.'" Rather a harsh notion, though not inaccurate if the martyr in her could admit it. All the same, Akachi continued without note of her reticence, pulling from beneath his shirt that hidden chain she had been shown in the warehouse. The stained vial glittered in the low light.

"We both keep something valuable around our necks." The dentist chuckled. "That is why I did not allow my men to take your wife from you. Did she keep you company in the cellar?"

In that cellar, Dominia had thought of Cassandra less than ever, perhaps because all hope of her return was dead and gone. Now, the General waited, stone-faced, and the dentist sensed his overstep but did not acknowledge it as he continued, "When I first came to the Hunters, I was barely more than a boy—barely better than your fat friend, Tenchi, eh? A bit thinner, but just as wide-eyed. I plied my services as best as I could among the men, but how hard it was to get respect! How hard it was to get them to see my ideas. They had so many resources, and what were they trying to build? More drones! More rockets! Stupid." Akachi waved his hand in disgust. "That is what your Father wanted from them, wasting time and energy on toys. The better plan was to create a more effective weapon. One that put mankind on the physical level of the martyrs, or higher.

"No one would listen to me. I was just some grunt, some child fresh from dental school who had never seen a battle and could hardly handle the sight of blood when it wasn't in a mouth. But then I was deployed to another unit, because, well!" He grinned. "A dentist always seems useless until the abscess, eh?

"The man on whom I had been brought to work was an important fellow. I did not realize how important until, under gas, he began talking before his procedure. Talking and talking, about how he had long ago acquired the blood of Lazarus from a man greater than him; he was not sure he deserved it anymore, which was why he rambled at the lightest touch of my drugs. When he was out enough for me to get to work, I noticed this." He lifted the red ampule. "I had heard the stories. I could not resist the promises of power. While my patient was unconscious, I stole a drop. Soon after, he was killed, and, because I was, at the time, learning how to navigate that unholy place, I went to the site of his battle by a shortcut through the Ergosphere and claimed the vial. But it was not the symbol they cherished on my return: it was the man. Why? Because the Hunters are a superstitious and changeable people, and all superstitious and changeable people are especially so when in the presence of the divine. By the grace of God, I appeared before them out of thin air, as had their prior leader. Their following me was more a question of my divine selection by the Lord than of respect for the blood of Lazarus. A question of my power, and their hatred for martyrs."

"And you expect them to listen to what I have to say, if I serve you?"

"*If* you serve me, yes. If you serve God. They will not listen to you if you are not a servant of God, Miss Mephitoli, but I see in your heart you possess the ability to turn your life around. All you need do is give me information."

"About?"

"About your sister, Lavinia." The request was so bizarre, so sudden, the General only laughed in bafflement, and Tobias did the same, though in a tone more mocking. "Now, General, do not think you can play games with me. I know Lavinia is invaluable to the Hierophant. I know he keeps her locked in his castle as though she were the most precious of gems. I would like to know why."

"She's an incredibly powerful woman with the temperament of a girl," responded the confused General. "He infantilizes her and keeps her helpless, because she's his favorite, and he's creepy."

"Please, Miss Mephitoli." The humor faded from his face. "Do not hide behind the charade of sibling rivalry. Your Father keeps no one closer than those who are most powerful."

"I told you, she is powerful. It's just—"

"If her memetic abilities were the only issue, would she not be ever by *your* side, provoking enemy forces to dance, or inspiring the women of besieged villages to drown their children? Had I a weapon powerful as your little sister, I would see her used. Instead, he keeps her on a shelf."

He had a point. Still, heels dug in, the General insisted, "Aside from what you're describing being a war crime, I don't know anything about that. He spoils her and keeps her isolated from the world for what he claims to be religious reasons. That's all I can say."

"You know something." Accusation, not speculation. He was an idiot if he thought she'd reveal anything she did or didn't know after three hundred years of intense practice at closely guarding Family secrets.

"All I knew was the black sun business. His promise that martyrs would walk in the day. I didn't know anything about Lavinia. Are you sure you're not jumping to conclusions?"

Fury twisted the dentist's face as he snapped, "Do not patronize me, General. I know when something is wrong and will not be persuaded otherwise. You know more than you are telling me."

Dominia was growing concerned this plan would take her down a longer route than anticipated—she might have to play the long con, until there cracked an opening by which she could escape into the Void or the desert. But, almost early as predicted, a terrible scream rose in the distance. Two more; a peal of bullets; silence, beneath the rising cries of "Dies Irae." As if from nowhere, the gun appeared in Akachi's hand, and he strode for the door with it aimed at the General while demanding, "Stay there."

"It's no use," said Lazarus. "René has been martyred. If he gets a gun he'll shoot up half the camp, eyes or no."

"Sounds like he's already got one." Dominia studied the untrained length of the next burst of gunfire. "You might want to tell your men to hurry."

"Lying, traitorous bitch." The snarling dentist looked as if he considered shooting the General but decided against it—wisely, from the way Lazarus was poised. Instead, baring his teeth and shouting in Arabic, Akachi dashed into the chaos of his rushing men to deliver orders and make them of one mind.

"We have little time." Lazarus hurried to bash open Akachi's weak desk and reclaim the flask containing the Ergosphere's waters. "Book it back to the medical tent and get a weapon before it's too late."

"Too late for what?" asked the General, distracted by another rush of footsteps outside the tent. No answer. Dominia, frowning, turned back, and said Lazarus's name only to discover she was completely alone. Again, she said his name, and again it only emphasized the point that there was no one to respond. These useless holy men!

She emerged from the tent in which Mozart's tubas blasted to find the camp had, in the space of seconds, been deserted. The astonished General hurried back along the route by which the Hunters had led her, finding the medical tent not by its size or her memory, but the body outside and the aroma of fresh death within. Her stomach snarled; she stepped inside to see René, assault rifle forgotten on the floor as he crammed hunks of meat from some soldier's torso into his blood-covered mouth.

His head lifted as she stepped inside. "Dominia?"

"Yeah, René, I'm here."

"My God, Dominia! I feel so good! I feel—" He laughed through his full mouth and swallowed its contents with a belch. "Would you believe I *smelled* you coming? I didn't even know I knew what you smelled like!"

"I'll try not to be haunted by that sentence." Dominia snatched the rifle. "Stay here. If things get hot and you hear it getting bad outside—just hide under a bed, or something."

"Roger, General," chirped the feasting martyr, who pulled out a slippery chunk of pancreas. "Oh, Dominia, this is great! All this time I thought it would be such a horrible thing, but...human really is delicious."

"We wouldn't eat it if it tasted like shit," she said, half laughing on her way from the tent before she fell into the camp's fog of silence. The tents themselves held their breaths, braced against the rising wind as Dominia was braced against whatever these humans could throw her way. They were, after all, just humans: but they did have tools.

The answer to Dominia's first question—where had everyone gone—came when she experimentally cleared, gun first, the square tent beside that of Tobias. Not unlike the tent covering the prison where she and René had spent the last week of his human life, this sheltered the entrance of a tunnel. Now the General understood, not only why her Father never bothered bombing Hunter encampments or otherwise engaging them militarily on their own turf, but how appropriate it was that her instincts likened them to ants. Beneath the ground rested an elaborate network of bunkers the Hunters had dug and outfitted as suited their needs—perhaps centuries old, at that. Small wonder the bricks had been so quick to turn to dust in that cellar. Perhaps it had once had four brick walls, and prisoners had, over time, destroyed the other three.

How many such Hunter colonies were hidden across the Middle States? There had to be enough to keep the various cells cycling between them, plus a few extra, "just in case." It was an astonishing thought on which she had no time to dwell. While gazing into the black pit of the tunnel, the ground pulsed in echo of her heartbeat. This was no fancy. This was something that moved. Something rattling the earth so violently that the General sprang into the open to put space between her and the four-armed, drill-outfitted ALIF-8 that spewed from the dirt like metallic pus out of an earthy wound. The two empty metal hands with which it pushed away clots loosed by its drills now lifted in fists to protect Tobias's fury-narrowed face.

"I cannot begin to express how disappointed I am to know it has come to this, Miss Mephitoli!"

An experimental squeeze of her trigger elicited no reaction in the suit, with a few projectiles of the spray coming close to its pilot but springing off a fist. When the thing crouched, as it now did, mere shards of flesh were revealed to an assailant; and when it moved, so, too, needed move its target. At the slightest hint of movement in that steel haunch, the martyr ran, arms pumping and gun bruising her chest. Cassandra's diamond crushed her skin, emphasizing the pounding of her pulse as the thing sprinted even faster than had the warehouse model. Above the impossible symphony of noise, Akachi's voice proved the most grating addition.

"You have made the choice to throw your life away when you could have been invaluable to the cause of the one true God. You could have saved your soul! But the Lord has seen fit to end your life. Others may think you are valuable—the Hierophant, the magician—but that is all the more reason why you should be killed. I only wish I had killed you a week ago, when first you fell into my hands! What a fool I am, trusting a martyr."

Between its broad strides—leaps—and the General's unfamiliarity with the area, the suit gained more ground with every step. As a drill impaled uncomfortably close to her back and was used by the thing to vault over her head, Dominia lifted the rifle, squeezed the trigger, and released a hail of gunfire that necessitated Tobias waste precious seconds protecting his face. In those seconds, the General skidded around a sharp right turn and made an immediate left around the next tent. Behind her thundered the suit.

"It is too late for me to spare your life, Miss Mephitoli, but it is not too late for you to enjoy a painless death. You have a gun—why not be like Judas Iscariot, eh? But, I suppose you are not capable of that degree of dignity—only of pretending you are."

With a tearing clamor, the suit charged through the tents around which the General was forced to navigate. In so doing, the ALIF-8 cleared a path like a goring bull flattening a fence for which it had never had respect from the start. It got so close behind her that her only choice was wheel around, drop, roll, and shoot blindly, then scramble back in the direction of the desolation to take advantage of the machine's one apparent weakness—the time it took to turn its unwieldy frame. What she did not account for, though, was the mobility of its arms, and one of those snatched the gun from her grip before she outpaced its reach. In the wreckage, she searched for something to replace it, and found, unsurprisingly, no weapons kept in the tents. The best she could find was one of the steel poles, which might serve as some semblance of spear.

"This is a tragic and humiliating death for a general such as you." One drill impaled the dirt near enough to Dominia's foot that she felt its oscillations. "Do you not wish to die with honor? Or can honor even matter to an animal?"

Something was wrong, amid all the whirring of drills. One ground at a louder, more rattling pitch, and as a steel hand caught her in an open-palmed slap that knocked her on her ass, she realized a tarp was tangled in the left drill. As her vision cleared of its black and red to reveal the mechanical man standing over her, the General showed her teeth.

"I don't know"—she slipped the pole beneath the collapsed cerulean tarp of the nearest tent—"why don't you tell me?"

Jerking the staff up didn't flip the tarp over the head of the dentist as she'd hoped, but it did drape the right drill, which had been so close to penetrating her guts that if she thought about the closeness of her call, it would ruin her ability to fight. Luckily, she survived. Even more luckily, Tobias required delay to wrench, with a metal hand, the ever-more-tangled pieces of fabric from a drill that only mucked itself up worse with each attempt to shred the tarp. By the time he'd extricated the piece giving him the biggest problem, the General was behind him with another, this tarp falling over his head and provoking a snarl of agitation. As, in the distance, Rex tremendae cried its opening chords like the heralding of an earthquake, the General used the pole: first to vault upon the covered back of the thrashing metal beast, then to impale it many times through the fabric of its prison. Now and then, the pole bounced off the plates of armor, but there were those sweet moments when it slipped between two metal joints to plunge through the oil-soft tangles of hydraulics that responded in hisses and pops too satisfying to believe. One last stab elicited a violent seizure in the left arms of the machine, which, frozen, proved so unbalanced that the blinded thing lost all equilibrium. It careened to the dark, dusty ground while the General sprang from its shoulders to land upon perfectly balanced feet.

"It's over, Tobias." With the tip of the pole, she nudged the still-whirring, twitching mound of metal and fabric. "This is why you don't use a prototype for battles."

No quip returned. For a hopeful moment, it seemed he was dead. She stepped nearer. "Listen to me: I don't want to kill you. I will if I have to, but I'd rather you let Lazarus and I go on our own. Where, I don't know. But we'll figure it out."

Again, no response. Now, with dread where once the General might have felt assured victory, Dominia removed her hat, then knelt to draw the tarp from the oil-oozing ALIF-8.

It was almost a surprise when Akachi's seat was empty. Almost, but not quite. Somehow, she had known: been unconsciously tipped off by the sag of the tarp, or the way the machine stopped moving, rather than continuing even a slight struggle. But, no. Without sunlight; without moonlight; without smoke, mirrors, or anything else Dominia had seen, the dentist had vanished into the Ergosphere.

Blood boiling with fury to find now even he felt justified in leaving her behind as it suited, the martyr snapped the metal pole over her knee and was about to use its point to stab the monstrous thing as though pinning a butterfly to a board. Yet, before penetration, her hand stayed. In the distance, after all, speakers played Mozart's Requiem. And, with a sudden, openmouthed shock, she understood what to do.

The attention of the General's soul mounted the vibrations of the music.

XVII

A Thousand Twangling Instruments

Perhaps, when using music instead of sunlight to manifest in the Ergosphere, she had expected to arrive in the doorway of her Father's study. Tobias was exactly hypocritical enough to use the Hierophant's thoughtforms as a nighttime entrance in (and maybe out) of the dangerous Void. But she had somehow forgotten she would appear in her old leather jacket, had not expected to find herself one-eyed. Even with her gun in its holster, to inspire that surge of love-hate!

And she had certainly not been prepared for the sight of herself engaged on the floor with the *tulpa*. Farther in the distance, the shrill screams of Jerusalem's writhing damned rose beneath the Mozart. She had not noticed it before, perhaps because her ears had not been tuned to hear it. Not been prepared, as she had been prepared to see her Father.

"Why, Dominia"—the Hierophant glanced from where he read in his seat, back to the obvious proceedings—"what an unexpected pleasure!"

Brow furrowing, the General opened her mouth. Confused as she was, she spoke only with struggle. "Haven't I already been here?"

"Part of you has, in a sense. That is the trouble with overindulgence." Wearing that innocent look, he sipped his own waiting glass of red wine. "Very difficult to become drunk and maintain a firm sense of linear time. The most common mistake of the conscious mind is the delusion that it observes all it does within the expected chronology. One assumes minute to minute we experience just the present. But in dreams, my dear, the past and future are as present as now; even in reality, time is only a suggestion. A mere condition of conscious existence."

Perhaps it was that muddying of distinctions in time that so distracted her. Whatever the reason, she lost track of why she'd come. Indeed, to be once more immersed in that boundless space of the Void was treacherous in ways she'd just begun to understand. Separation between then and now—that self on the floor and this self that sat in the empty chair—was impossible. Pleasure yet throbbed, lust yet boiled high in her blood; but no sorrow burned for Cassandra, because she was sure that thing was not Cassandra. Barely, she clung to the sound of the music: to the spinning record she drunkenly pulled off the floor-level shelf.

"I came here through the music...I didn't know I could."

"You are always welcome in my study, dear girl."

"No, I mean—I didn't know I could travel through music."

"There are a thousand secret ways into this place scattered across the world, but none so fine as music. Art lifts the soul as wind, the wings of birds, that we may climb to heights unknown by the paltry body." With hand adorned by his gold piscatory ring, the Hierophant caressed the record player's wooden edge. "Mozart, Bach, Rossini, Wagner, Sullivan, Homer, Shakespeare, Waterhouse...do you know what you and Mozart have in common, Dominia?"

"An early death," she almost answered; but the question was rhetorical and, given the way he smiled, he might have heard her, anyway. "You are both fine artists." He answered himself with a joshing wag of his finger. "The art of war is fine as any other: the martial arts that rule the body write poetry in physics. Every fatal battle is a sensual dance between souls who have agreed, without their body's conscious consent, which one of them shall die."

A battle. Yes! That was it—why she'd come. The battle with Tobias. The General's mouth opened in a frown of distress. To think she could forget! She locked eyes with her own, panting self on the floor beneath the odious thing. "Which one of us agreed to die tonight?"

"Between yourself, and the Hunter?" The Hierophant's eyes sparkled like onyx gems set in the pale olive of his face. "I think you both know the answer to that."

Outside, the night of the Void had almost completely fallen. In reality, not much time had passed because she had not moved save for the steps it took to reach the empty chair—although even if she walked back to the doorway, the fact that she had come to the Ergosphere for a Planck was now indelible. The Hierophant had seen her. But he also must have observed Tobias, so she asked him straight, "Have you seen him? The dentist? Tonight—my tonight, if you can tell one from the other."

"I can, because I pay careful attention. Yes, I have seen the dentist flee into the dark tonight. I have known him to use my study coming and going ever since he stumbled upon it in the daytime and recognized I came and went, for the most part, by way of artworks. I believe he finds the process easier than traveling by sunlight or actually educating himself on higher, spiritual matters, for the man has a poisoned and petty soul, and cannot make himself confront it in the bright eye of day. But, God will force the confrontation at his death. Can you see, my one-eyed child, how he sealed his own fate by condemning others to it? By spreading superficial and incorrect faith among his men? Say what you will of our Church; *I* practice what I preach. For the most part." Behind his lifted glass, he winked.

Too true. Granted, she believed her Father because she wanted to—but the Hierophant had a point that alleviated the last of her doubts about the VLF manifestations of Jerusalem, Mecca, et al. Tobias and the Hunters were just as responsible for those trapped souls as her Father. Every false leader of every false spirituality from the beginning of time was responsible for those souls: any superficial cult that did not provide sufficient frame of reference for its followers to navigate the afterlife. From that perspective, Tobias and the Hierophant were both just as evil—and she knew which manifestation of evil she preferred to deal with long-term. "Will you tell me what I need to do to kill him? How I catch him? What happens if he leaves the Void before I do?"

With the twitch of a lip longing in palpable way to reveal the answers she sought, the Hierophant seemed bound to refrain. Instead, he allowed his eagerness to be betrayed in the way he leaned forward, hands folded between his knees. "What you and the rest of your fine artist brethren all have in common, my girl—what you and Mozart have in common—is the ability to absorb those universal elements that make your particular art form grand. In all his journeying across the face of Europa, Amadeus consumed every scrap of music he found, and analyzed that spark within that made each piece transcendent. Through those sparks, he built a mighty flame."

Above the distant screams of the lost souls, the General heard the rippling trumpet of an enormous beast. An elephant. She lifted her head in the direction of the sound as the Hierophant continued, "The great artist lets nothing come between him and his work, and uses every smallest stimulus as fuel for the fire. Even sexual fantasies are, to the artist, fuel for inspiration, rather than the millstone they present around the necks of the uninitiated."

With a shock of recognition, Dominia's attention returned to her Father's mouth, whose remembered words she emulated with her own, with the same timing, cadence—everything—as him. "Sexual fantasies," the Hierophant and the General spoke together, in proper context, "are a misapplication of the creative libido down into the sexual drive, rather than upward, toward God."

At her wonder, her Father smiled, and continued as he had before: though now, his motions were different, and it was she who rose, slowly, from her seat. "The average man is incapable of salvation because he is so wrapped up in the material world that he cannot see his own lust for flesh is truly a lust for a higher power. The average martyr, even, cannot be saved, and the best he can hope for is a close connection with his community in the form of the living Church."

Her boot steps echoed across the chessboard floor, a beat to the Hierophant's words as she crossed to stand over herself and the horrific doppelgänger. Every second, it looked less like a person. "When we find our lover manifested in the flesh, we derive from them a surge of inspiration because the soul is liberated from the surly bonds of lust. Our fantasies are revealed as the poisonous wastes of time they have always been. Idle hands are the Devil's playthings." He lifted his own, suddenly full, glass in toast to her.

"That's why we need art," agreed Dominia. The distant instrument of that animal spurred her first step off the lighted island of the study, into the black abyss.

"Yes. Yes, my girl. That is why we need art. That is why we need you."

Drawing her gun, the General glanced over her shoulder one last time. Her watching Father rose to see her off to the hunt. "Was it you in the *tanque*?" she asked him, studying the face that so studied her. "Really you, I mean."

Thinly, he smiled. "'*Wenn du lange in einen Abgrund blickst, blickt der Abgrund auch in dich hinein.*'"

As expected. Gun in hand, the General plunged into the inky dark, muscles coiled for her kill. If at any time in the future she had even the slightest probability of crossing paths with that which she sought—that beast, Tobias, who led her so astray she stumbled by accident into the Kingdom—then it was already impossible for the dentist to escape alive. And this place was all about probability, right? That he was at all audible seemed evidence of her victory, which pumped her dream-fast muscles into an altogether more uncanny pace. The rush of such running—nearly flying—filled her with delight, and the darkness whipped through and around her, over and under her. She nearly leapt for joy, heart racing, body light as it had been when first she'd learned to love the art of battle. Yes, yes—it was an art, was a joy to her. This, she could never deny. As a girl initiated into the Church, she had disliked the killing of even criminal humans for the Noctisdomin Mass, but had always loved a good boxing match, always thrilled at the satisfaction of a well-implemented strategy. She had been reluctant to free herself from the Hunter's prison by means of violence, but violence was the oil paint with which she had coated the world's canvas to produce the painting of her life. Tobias thought a human's ability to survive without violence set it as a superior species, but, in the dark, the General did not see it that way. Was it not said, after all, that the tiger was superior to the elephant when it came to the food chain?

When Dominia skidded to a halt and listened above the dreamy silence of her thought-body for the sound of the beast, she feared she was lost. What she wouldn't have given for her compass! Or for more warning as, with a terrible bellow, the freight train–animal thundered from the darkness to run her down or gore her with tusks not so different from the dentist's drills. As she had when fighting the exoskeleton with the assault rifle, the General aimed, but realized before the second charge it could do no good against an opponent such as this. In the Void, death meant waking up to reality. Once she killed him here, she'd have to catch him on Earth; and he could just as easily slip right back into the dark night of the Ergosphere. An endless struggle.

After holstering the gun, the General braced herself to meet the animal head-on, hands against goring tusks, because no matter what that putrid dentist loved to say, an animal was no match for a martyr. A martyr, though not an animal, had an animal within: as the elephant in her grip transformed with an alien shriek and a twisting explosion of particles into an eagle, and her hands were crushed by the piercing grip of the raptor's golden talons, the General found within herself the claws of that great tiger. Snarling with hunger, the predator leapt to latch fangs in the throat of the screaming prey. This feathery mane soon became a furred one, and the molten blood of a lion filled her mouth, swam up into her brain, became therein the poison of a thrashing serpent that she resisted—that was simplicity itself to resist. Her own knowledge of the Ergosphere far surpassed Tobias's, if only because she so humbled herself before the experience that she acknowledged she knew nothing. It was the tiger within her that beat back feather-wingéd lizards and lion-headed serpents until Tobias, who had tried to be so many things he had forgotten what he was, crawled across the ground, laughing, mad: half man, half writhing, bloodied beast.

"Will you kill me, General?" asked the dentist, his bright teeth glowing. "Will you kill me, and send me back where I started? Have you not learned what it is to die here! Nothing, nothing at all—it makes what we have felt here a dream, barely remembered."

Being addressed by her title brought her back to herself more clearly than the sensory stimulus of seeing her target as a partial man. The gun had somehow found its way back into her hand, and now, free to have the conscious experiences of a humanoid, Dominia realized there must have been some source of light for his teeth to glow. She turned, and in the distance, there it was: the fountain.

"Of course," she said, her focus caught completely. "Be'er Sheva."

Before she basked in the glory of the implications, the beast behind her sprang and knocked her face-first upon the dirt. With clenched teeth, the General suffered her face to be slammed into the ground: ground scattered with life from that holy fountain, whose waters Lazarus used to reproduce her eye and teeth. That water—the same water, as all water—that was the

Lady. That same water tended by the Bearers, through which one accessed the magician's Kingdom.

As Dominia's head was slammed back down into the ground, something snapped behind her eyebrow and she tried to remember it was only a dream. Still, she felt terrible, and the blood obscured her uncovered eye so that, when he turned her over, she was almost completely blind. His hands were around her neck, and they were attached to human arms, but what was beneath his waist seemed half a lion's haunch and part of a snake's long tail, with one eagle's claw that struggled to find uncanny purchase on the ground. "Maybe I send you back, eh, and am right there waiting when you arrive, ready to crush your skull! Then I get the satisfaction of killing the greatest martyr General twice in one night."

"Nice fantasy," she would have said, but it was hard to speak when choked by hands strong as a martyr's in the dream-space where so many things were equal it was hard to tell one object from another. But, better than saying it, she thought it. In a snap, the word "fantasy" recalled her Father's words: "The great artist lets nothing come between him and his work, and uses every smallest stimulus as fuel for the fire. Even sexual fantasies are, to the artist, fuel for inspiration."

Of all the tools at her disposal, one had been available since the start of her journey in the Void, but was single-mindedly eschewed. Now it possessed a higher purpose. The General's eye closed. Cut off from the perception of blood as well as the Ergosphere's aether, the Higgs field, or whatever it was her brain believed she was breathing, her mind began to fog over just as she reached out for the *tulpa*. Oh, sweet duplicate of fair Cassandra, so cruelly maligned. Did not the doppelgänger want her love? Could she give it if she were dead?

Could she give it, *still*, if the *tulpa* shared her body? Was it not better for the nebulous shape-thief to have a body separate from her own? A gateway into the real world, where it could receive all the love Dominia might offer?

The General must have been seconds from death when the deformed, burned, defenestrated, and bleeding future of the monstrosity erupted from the fountain with a terrible scream. Its ability to hold Cassandra's shape after its ordeal in the Kingdom had reduced to a horrific series of mouths: each opened to reveal her lover's face within, mouth after mouth, an infinity attached to arms that stretched forward, all screaming Dominia's name. This attracted the attention of the dentist just before it leapt on him with such force that both were knocked clear of gasping Dominia by several meters. Scrambling up, the General retrieved her gun, then limped to watch as the unwatchable thing swallowed Dr. Tobias Akachi, starting from the feet.

"God, help me," he cried. The mood she was in, the General found no humor in the plea.

"You said you became a Hunter to escape being a slave to the martyrs, Akachi. But you said it yourself. You're still a slave; and your master doesn't give a damn about you."

As the doppelgänger reached his neck, his eyes rolled up into his head, and by the time its teeth crunched apart his skull, not only did the thing bear a closer resemblance to Cassandra: it had put the leader of the Hunters out of his misery. The *tulpa* lurched to its feet, hand wiping its mouth, and smiled warily at the General.

"Dominia," it said.

Amazed her gambit had worked, the General did not speak. She extended her arm. Its face lit in so real a mimicry of Cassandra's, it elicited the same physical elation in Dominia. As the thing fell into her embrace, near crying for joy, she cradled it, her cheek against the top of its head.

"Thank you for coming to me."

"Love you, Dominia." It turned its whispering face toward hers and tried to hide the hollow nature of its eyes with a deceptive smile, lips parted to betray a glimpse of satin tongue. "Love you, love you."

"So you'll be able to come back to Earth, now, in place of him?" The General tipped the thing's chin up.

"Uh-huh, Dominia. Love you forever, Dominia." How dotingly it smiled up at her. The counterfeit's hot body ground against hers with the promise of mindless, eternal devotion.

"Good." She lowered her head to meet the thing's kiss while lifting her gun to the back of its head. "Thank you."

The sensation of the dream suicide was impossible to describe, perhaps because it was all such a terrible implosion that it snapped her back in time and space like a rubber band. In an infinitely small parcel of experience—a Planck, she supposed—she whirled back through all her interactions in the Void to the point in reality where she entered it: poised, with her makeshift stake, to impale the battery of the ALIF-8.

The *tulpa*, which had consumed Akachi's thought-body and, due to the binding of Lazarus's blood, his real one along with it, emitted a terrible shriek beneath the searing light of the full moon. The repulsive parasite, revealed for what it was, thrashed within the prison of the lifeless exo-suit on exposure to imperfect darkness. As it clawed at itself and its surroundings and her, the General was so disoriented to find them thus that she was nearly swept by its gray hand. The freak twitch of a dying metallic arm offered protection enough for her to spring away in pursuit of an assault rifle that would now prove far more useful. By the time the thing extricated itself from the ALIF-8, the

General was ready to unload a satisfying magazine into the twisting thought-form. When that was empty, she was upon it with the pole; and by the time the pole broke in her hands, the thing was dead.

Panting, covered in the black blood of that entity that dissolved at her feet into a substance not unlike the oil of the exoskeleton, Dominia looked up to find the encampment of distant Hunters, having ascended from below-ground, watched from the negligible safety of their tents. As they began to reveal themselves from their labyrinth, most in superstitious horror but some in what appeared to be genuine awe, the General threw down the remains of her makeshift spear. Amid the slick of the leftover demon floated the dentist's false teeth, his glasses, and the ampule that once was private trophy of his rule. This, the General secreted before addressing the crowd.

"Those of you who do not like what has happened here, leave. Tell your like-minded brothers in other cells to do the same. The rest of you belong to me."

Absolutely no one moved, save for what it took to translate her words. A few men laughed. Several adjusted their grips on their guns. She didn't blink.

"Bring me my traitorous whelp, René."

A murmur rose amid some of the men. When she did not move, the murmur gathered to a clamor and movement rippled through the crowd. René's shocked cry pierced the night, along with the sounds of violence. The discharge of a gun concerned her until, thirty seconds later, the thrashing martyr, too new to be truly dangerous (or even competent), was dragged through the crowd and tossed at her feet by a party of several soldiers.

He began, as usual, with, "Please," but, exhausted of hearing him beg, she snatched him upright and covered his mouth. With the blind and temporarily mute martyr under her arm, Dominia scanned the crowd again, and lifted her voice in command to the man who watched.

"Lazarus. Come out."

The crowd hushed. Again, the only sounds that rose from them were the necessary ones—the ones required for the men to part so Lazarus, having been who-knew-where, could meet Dominia with the placid calm of a person who knew precisely what was about to happen. She presented René's filthy, whining face, one hand still over his mouth and the other now resting on his forehead to drag open empty eyelids. Lazarus splashed the water so abruptly that René could only scream, as had Dominia.

Around them, Hunters murmured, and the General lowered René to the ground while he screamed about the alleged pain and burning; all the while, he clawed and kicked. Lazarus stepped away, replacing the flask on his person, to watch with a barely suppressed smile. Abruptly, René's sobbing relented to the hilarious gasps of a small child who realized they had not, after all, hurt themselves.

"I forgive you, René," Dominia said, as gently as she had ever said anything to the professor. "For everything. Open your eyes."

To the wild astonishment of the Hunters, he did.

"I can see? I can see—I can *see*!" René sprang up, screaming the words, clutching his face, his eyes wild. From the depths of the crowd, Tenchi emerged, looking just as amazed to cry at his cousin, "René?"

"Tenchi! Oh my God, I can see you! My own eyes, my real eyes—Tenchi!" Giddy, the former professor ran for his cousin and, in a move that surprised them both, swept the man in his new martyr's arms as if his portly cousin were a tiny girl. "I've never been so happy to see you!"

"Others among you who suffer from ailments, come to us and we will cure them." Dominia looked from face to face in a crowd that dropped to its knees, and she experienced that thrill her Father felt while grocery shopping. Too bad she had to ignore the pleasure of pride in favor of the right thing. She kept waiting.

"Who among you needs to be healed," she repeated, and Lazarus translated in Arabic, Farsi, and one or two other languages she didn't recognize offhand. Now the first man, perhaps not much older than René but limping as though he were twice that, made his unsure way to the martyrs. He paused some meters away, began his sentence with "I—" and then, after reluctant consideration for the General, spoke to Lazarus in Arabic.

"This man says he has killed many of our kind, and pleasurably."

"And I have killed many of your kind, and pleasurably. You need healing."

Lazarus repeated this in Arabic, while, with hesitation, the man drew closer. "We forgive you," she told him while Lazarus blessed him. For this man, the change was less pained, but no less wonderful to behold: in seconds, his leg remembered how once it walked, and ran, and danced, as now it did so before his brothers-in-arms.

The line of men that grew proved three hours long. When all was finished, and the night found it still had room for rest, the General had her army.

XVIII

Shvu'a

Not as many men left in the night as Dominia had expected. In the aftermath, most deserters crawled off not because she was a martyr, but because she was a woman, and a lesbian. The unit was better off without them; she hoped the rest of the Hunter cells would follow suit, though she had the feeling this one, which had observed the miracles of her battle and Lazarus's many healings, might splinter off from the rest of the terrorist group, and perhaps manage to maintain ties to one or two small units. Fine by her. She wanted nothing to do with the Hunters, except for those who respected the notion of change.

Although she had been invited down into the tunnels and thus, the true encampment, Dominia refused that night, seeing them as too close to that prison that she'd shared with René. She slept in bliss, better than she had in many weeks—her whole adult life—beneath the open sky. Without fear of the rising sun! Glory. The next morning, she and Lazarus instructed the formerly crippled, selectively English-speaking pilot, a man whose nom de guerre was Farhad, to introduce them to those who remained. She thought all the while of Valentinian: particularly when one man, too young to have run off to such awful war games as indicated by his enthusiasm for Dominia's exploits, burst out in the delighted Arabic of an excited boy.

"He says you are like, ah, a 'magician,' Mahdi," explained Farhad, smiling a little, himself. "Making Tobias disappear."

After a few such interactions, it became apparent that Tobias had not been well liked in camp, but his leadership had been accepted. The dead dentist had been right on one count: they were an exceedingly superstitious group of people, men desperate for a faith to fill the empty, violent hole inside. The dentist's fundamentalist Christianity had not mattered to most of the camp, which leaned more toward the Islamic branch of Abrahamianism. That they had seen him appear out of thin air had been enough, much as simple observation of the General's bloody victory had set them straight again. This became clear when she recognized Farhad had called her "Mahdi" as a title. The word rang a bell with the Arabic- and Islam-illiterate General, though she could not remember its context.

"Is that 'General'?" she asked Lazarus as they rounded a corner in the mine-shaft-like tunnel system to the hand-carved rooms where "acquired" women slept or cried or kept their children quiet.

"No—it's an Islamic thing, or it used to be before the Hunters stole it. The Twelfth Imam, who will dispense justice and battle al-Masih ad-Dajjal during the apocalypse."

Trying not to roll her eyes, the General said, "They were calling me 'al-Masih ad-Dajjal' until last night."

Farhad, overhearing them, explained, "That was the fault of Dr. Akachi. The true al-Masih ad-Dajjal and Iblis misled him, as he misled our people. The world. If what you told us last night is true, about the ship and the hospital, then Iblis has gone to enormous lengths to ensure all societies view you as we are viewed. A terrorist."

Though she may have inherited an army of them, the title blanched her face with irritation. "I'm not a terrorist. I've never bombed a marathon because the Hierophant was there."

"If you wish different means"—the man gave a shrug—"that is up to you. We will follow. But the tools we have used on our jihad until now have been useful."

"Against your own kind," the General snapped, having seen plenty enough of the kidnapped, abused women. "Your guerrilla methods mean nothing to the Hierophant, to any martyr. It would be like humans fearing the collusion of cows. Collect the women and bring them to the surface with whatever things they've been allowed to keep. They're leaving."

Looking as though he had been slapped in the face, Farhad turned helpless eyes toward Lazarus, then back to Dominia. "Mahdi, please. These *sabaya* are fair property, granted us by Allah: men of all faiths, Abrahamian or not, keep women in this camp. Not even Akachi meant to separate us."

That was where she'd heard that title before. Her brain presented her with the fact at as inappropriate a moment as ever: there was a science-fiction novel, about a man who was Mahdi of a bunch of space people—it was one of her favorites as a kid, after she got out of dystopian fiction and into straight sci-fi stuff. Turned out a huge series about a guy—a displaced duke—who had named himself after a space mouse contained a bunch of deep, metaphysical stuff. Proof that sometimes even beneath her Father's tight censorship, foreign notions had slipped through the cracks, protected by the veil of literature. Every story she had ever read had prepared her for this journey, in a way. How funny; how frightening. How reassuring. The nature of her mission was amplified by the fiction as she gazed into the face of tragic reality.

"That's because it wasn't Akachi's duty to dispense justice." She spared a glance into one of the chambers and met the thoroughly tired eyes of the woman within it, who grew slightly more awake in the face of her confusion to see a free female staring back. "Send all the women up. If any are left behind, I will know, and there will be consequences."

Farhad, gritting his teeth, watched the martyrs turn the way they'd come, then snapped in Arabic for the listening women to do as they were bid. On the surface, Dominia waited beneath the sun. Soon, confused, displeased rabble drifted from the many entrances to the tunnels below. Beneath the ground, a loudspeaker emanated through the halls. One by one, the women emerged, thrusting their hands over their eyes and squinting in the light, huddling together in a mass of covered heads and ankle-length gowns. Pain clutched the heart of the General, particularly to see the children, but she kept her breathing level right along with her head.

"This encampment has changed its allegiance." Lazarus translated her words in curt Arabic. "The process of this change will be long and painful for the men, but for you, the change will be sudden and joyous. You are all free, now."

As a murmur arose, half excited and half frightened, one woman on the end spoke up. "To go where?"

A fair question. Jerusalem, even from Dominia's short drive to an industrial suburb nowhere near the tremendous city's center, sat in sorry tatters. Beyond all the traffic and crumbling cement sound walls, her drive with Tobias had revealed innate war-inspired poverty, with many empty and unkempt businesses tended by none but impoverished citizens. Unable to work due to injuries or lack of status, the extremely poor could not even lease and herd genetically engineered goats as those in rural regions. When the Hunters had fallen upon the city, the city model had become unsustainable, and in the face of a staggering death toll alongside crumbling infrastructure, the whole state of Israel was no longer exactly prime real estate.

"Well," began the General, "the Hunters own buildings in Jerusalem." She based this assumption on the single factory she'd visited, but this was true in less a legal sense and more a territorial sense when it came to the city. Indeed, it was just beginning to settle on her that, although other groups would murmur, technically it was not her group that was the splinter faction. Those who refused to follow would be splintering from *her*. In sweeping Akachi from his place, she had become the leader of the Hunters, inheriting their property along with their war and reputation. Not all bad, she supposed. "It is not desirable to go back to a place of painful memories, I know—for most of you, Jerusalem was not even your home to begin with. But that is a place to start, if you wish, or if you wish, I will gather the resources to send you to your homes."

Another English-speaking, now-former *sabiyya* spoke up with disdain. "Look at the big Western heroes, fixing slavery. Some liberating army! Half of these women have not even been to school. Their homes are destroyed! The ones here longest think al-Mawta have displaced the martyrs and now rule the world. They are mad, ill!" The girl's eyes filled with tears. "If I had stayed any longer, maybe I would have been. They killed my father, my brothers—what is there for me now? What is there for any of us?"

Distant footsteps reverberated through the Earth; the General mistook them for those of her belowground men amid a mind which sought a means to soothe such pain. "Maybe I can't help you. But this is Lazarus," began Dominia, until the old man caught her gesturing hand.

"They won't know who I am, most of them. Women around the Hunters aren't allowed to study their doctrine. Not beyond the basic Abrahamian parts of it."

"Why is that?"

She felt the Lady's voice seconds before she heard it, rattling deep in the center of her own diaphragm, and the diaphragms of all those many around. *They know it takes few steps, upon learning of Lazarus, to learn of Us; and once a woman learns of Us, the world of men has lost her forever.*

Dominia, startled by the clarity of the voice, turned to see the litter, still in the distance, borne by the four older Water Bearers who had whisked away the Lady. Where the others had vanished to, or where the rest of the many women of the temple had gone, the General could not be sure. Nevertheless, it was with an admixture of relief and pleasure she saw, walking in procession before the litter with a parasol that shaded her ornately decorated dreadlocks, fair Gethsemane.

These women are Ours, the Lady declared. *We told you, Dominia, you would lead Our army. This is that army; so are the men belowground, though they do not yet know.*

Smirking, and forgetting, perhaps, that the distant face was only Miki's in theory, the General arched a brow. "I did the killing, but it's your army?"

All armies are Our armies, borrowed or stolen. We've stolen this one back. Or would you, General, reject the gift We offer in exchange? You'll command an army thrice the size of this, if only you would battle in Our name.

Here, the General was reluctant. Now divine and inter-dimensional politics were muddied into an already filthy matter that looked ever more like war. She could not believe in her heart the things known by followers of the Lady, no matter what miracle she had seen or what festival she'd attended. Perhaps this was related to her bitterness over Valentinian's abandonment.

Yet, she somehow could not shake the idea that her reluctance to tout the banner of any one self-proclaimed deity was borne, in part, from knowledge of what Valentinian would want of her. He would not want to see her kowtow blindly to any one faith. But did that mean she kowtowed to him? She wasn't sure. They hadn't discussed it. Was she being a child about this, like a girl who thought if she were good enough, her parents would reclaim her from martyrdom? Was she, deep down, acting out of hope that right behavior would draw the magician back into her sphere?

"I can teach my men to battle in your name," the General allotted, "because they cannot do battle without a name to do it in, and my name isn't enough. That is why I must do battle in my own name: nobody will do it for me, since everybody's so busy fighting for you."

You do battle in your name, and the name of the magician, mused the goddess as Her litter paused at respectable distance. The parasol-holding Bearer lowered her sunglasses to wink at Dominia. The latter flushed, but did not move, and did not deny the increasingly apparent position of her neglected fealty. *Very well. This is fair. You will come to Us in time, as do all women. And all Our women will come here. You have the drives?*

Farhad, graciously, had shown these to the General and the mystic during their tour of the tunnels. Dominia assured Her of this until the goddess bobbed Miki's silent head in pleasure. *Very good. We shall summon Our scattered women to the city of Jerusalem; the time is long overdue.*

Perhaps the city's name on divinity's dream-breath was what stirred memory of the wailing souls looking for God in the Void. "I was shown a vision of Jerusalem in—Your waters, I guess. The Ergosphere. Is it true? Are all those people lost souls?"

There are many who seek Jerusalem and cannot find it, because they have been misled in life, or have misled others. Jerusalem, herself, is a pure and holy place. She is not responsible for misdirecting signposts. Those souls you see suffering are martyr and Hunter, murderers who repent in public but do not come to God in their hearts, those who are false of faith or lack the emotional faculty to experience it internally in its truest sense. They are half-formed souls swathed in robes of guilt and shame. It is better to spend an entire life unconscious than to dally with religion and swear half-true oaths.

This bothered Dominia as much or more than the thought of soulless spirits wandering without identity in the Void. What a tahgmahr religion could be! After running her hand over her forehead, the General waved toward the tent that had once belonged to Tobias. "Why don't You go ahead and take that tent until we find someplace decent in the city?"

No: We will remain with the women for now. Speak with Gethsemane.

Hesitant even as the named human closed her parasol, Dominia pressed, "There's nothing I can do for You?"

Your most important duty is to listen. Go, General. Dominia relented to the gentle tugs of the Bearer upon her arm. *You were right. There are many changes to be made. The ones within yourself are no exception.*

In the cool shelter of the tent, the General sank into the chair once inhabited by Tobias to find Lazarus had not followed but remained outside with his divine ménage. Grateful to be alone with the woman who poured wine from the bar cart set against the far side of the tent, Dominia said, "You didn't warn me about everything that was going to happen, and I get the feeling you knew some of it."

"Such a warning would have only made my work harder." So she had known. All the Bearers must have. "I think it was difficult enough to relieve you of the burden you felt toward poor Cassandra, who would, I know, not wish to see you suffer."

That was quite true. Yet in all the tumult of the past week, Dominia had not had the luxury of guilt. She had become so swept up in the wildness of events, she had not even felt guilt for her lack of guilt: the true sign of...well, some sort of progress. As the earthly body of the nymph neared, wineglass in hand, Dominia extended an arm. The woman responsively filled her lap. "I haven't given up hope that I'll see her again," said the General, determined, the faint impression of the recent dream still fresh in her mind. "But I don't think Cassandra is my priority right now."

"There is too much to be done." After pushing the cup to the General's lips and forcing her to take it in her hand, the Bearer drew from her boot a small black phone that activated at the touch of a delicate finger. "I have been asked to show you this. It was an encrypted broadcast, transmitted to the upper echelons of your Father's military personnel."

The recording that played was more subdued than those featuring Cicero and Theodore; yet, for its gentleness, the message was grave. At a plain desk before a stained-glass window of himself blocked almost entirely by the high wingback of his chair, the Hierophant sat with mournful expression. To his left elbow stood the Lamb, whose face inspired a pang of sorrow for the theoretically gentler of her two parents but who, nonetheless, was her enemy.

"Oh, children." The Hierophant heaved a piteous sigh. "It is with such pain we find ourselves thus. But, I am sorry to say extreme measures must be taken when faced with insurrection and terrorism such as that committed by my daughter, Dominia di Mephitoli. You are already aware of the bounty on her misguided life; but I do not wish for you, my men and women of the military, to think there is nothing you can do to help your country but remove the increasingly apparent head of a dangerous and, frankly, evil regime.

"This world of ours demands a certain order. Much as animals in the wild possess a predatory hierarchy, the same can be said of conscious beings.

What are men and martyrs both but animals, ensouled—souls, embodied? The predators and prey together form an elaborate web whose spinner we dare not hope to know. Each thread, delicately balanced against its neighbors, comes together by nature's plan and animal's instinct. That which eats functions with that which is eaten in careful harmony. Yet, it is always in the instinct of those predators imbued with consciousness to rise above the natural order and inspire full submission in their prey—even knowing the damage this may cause the structural integrity of the web as a whole.

"This dilemma—the choice between symbiosis and conquest—is one that has haunted me for over two thousand years. When I must see my martyrs die, my children lose their lives in the sun and good people meet the horrific end of starvation, I wonder if symbiosis is the just choice. These past weeks, since the betrayal of my daughter and the bombing in Kabul, I have begun to determine it is most assuredly not.

"The time for symbiosis has ended, sorry though I am to say it. The time of the martyrs to begin seriously considering global dominance is now. To that end, I wish to give you a gift. My beloved Lamb has informed me that the time for us to reveal our plan has come. Over the next several years, military and engineering capacities will all be directed toward one particular goal: the sustainable blackening of the sun. This is no fancy, no comic book plot. This is the true inheritance of the martyrs. This is what I give to you, children. Your Father has eternally walked in the sun. Soon, all of you will join me."

The clip ended. Gethsemane, studying Dominia's tense face, slipped the phone away. "Do you understand what he's saying?"

"It's practically a declaration of war. Yes—I understand what he's saying."

There was no one, save perhaps Cicero, who knew as clearly what the Hierophant said when he spoke. This time, however, the translation was easy for anyone. As soon as he felt comfortable, the martyr army would be coming, and it would not be coming for her. It would be coming for Lazarus.

"We will have many forces, General," cautioned the Bearer, still studying the martyr's stoic face. "But we will need more than that."

"We'll need, among other things, a preemptive strike." With the edge of the glass pressing into her lower lip, Dominia marveled at how her Father could be so cordial in his hostility. For her part, she was full to the brim with only the latter; she wished, was tempted indeed, to sweep into the Ergosphere to confront him, though that would do no good. Dominia did understand, however, what drew Valentinian to spend time with the Hierophant: for she, even with Gethsemane in her lap, felt quite alone in the middle of that camp.

"You disappeared after the ceremony."

"I intended to meet you here, General."

"And the rest of the Bearers?"

"They are attending to the women who escaped the temple, and organizing the rest."

"But what of the magician? You must know where he's gone."

"Must I?" At the martyr's stern expression, the human offered a thin smile. "He is in the Void, General. The Ergosphere. I have seen him in dreams. He meets me there to educate me."

"On what?"

"On doing better service to you. I have been committed to your cause. I am afraid, however, that I am good at this juncture for little more than company."

"I get the feeling you're good for more than that." The martyr contemplated the evasive girl and slipped Cassandra's diamond from over her own head. After a moment, she hung it around the neck of the Bearer. "Can you keep her safe for me?"

"As though she were my soul."

"Thank you." With a sideways smile for the gem that glittered in the low golden light of the tent, the General felt for an instant the graze of Cassandra's fingertips down her cheek. "Would you leave me for a time?" she asked the woman, who nodded, but faltered before standing.

"I was also asked to give you this." Gethsemane withdrew from her other boot that familiar deck of playing cards, dropped in the throne room of the Lady and left far behind with her revolver. "When I dreamed of him after the temple, I found this on my person. I am not sure"—she admitted with a shifty look away—"it was entirely a dream."

"Did he say anything about my gun?"

The laughing nymph ducked from the tent. "That you'd ask about it, anyway."

Just as well. For now, she was surrounded by guns. Not having it here inspired the hope that she would have it back when she needed it. The comfort provided her by the deck of cards was more reassuring than any antique weapon, anyway.

Less comforting was that message from her Father. How strange to think, a mere six months before, the General would have been on the receiving end of that video—would have been filled with patriotic vigor. Well...not quite so much as she would have been as a youth. Still, she had not expected her life to change in the severe ways it had: certainly not at this rate. She had never expected, not once in her life, to be called a terrorist. Yet, here she was. The head of a cell of them, and the leader of an army—arguably greater in size, for all the Red Market women, than units she'd led for the Hierophant. And with intentions she respected, if under the guidance of the Lady. There was a kind of self-respect in that: perhaps that was what she was learning. She wasn't clear. She only knew that she had changed, and very much. But the most profound change of all was her instinct to genuflect before those cards.

Alone in her tent amid her growing army, Dominia di Mephitoli prayed for victory against the Hierophant. She was not sure to whom the prayer was addressed; but, if God wasn't listening, the magician certainly was, and he would help her prayers be heard. That, somehow, proved more reassuring. But somebody else also listened—somebody who thought or wished or dreamed he was God, though he coyly danced around the subject whenever asked outright. Somebody who seemed next to her in a sandalwood haze, whose specter knelt beside her. Somebody she so loathed to see here, in this place, in the midst of victory, that she kept her eyes shut and prayed: raised her voice: all but shouted her supplications for the divine against the smugly spoken words of the Hierophant's unwelcome phantasm. A being so real her own ears heard him say:

"You'll have to let me know if you get a response."

Had to get the last word, didn't he?

[ed.: The following is a copy of the Rosary of the Holy Martyr Church as it is practiced in the time of Dominia di Mephitoli. It is the English version of a prayer most popularly said in Modern Mephitolian, which appears to have its structural root in Latin while containing many words of Germanic influence. As the General has high familiarity with many works of English literature and her companions use it regularly, it seems probable English is used as a lingua franca.]

THE ROSARY OF THE HOLY MARTYR CHURCH

Make the Sign of the Cross

In the name of the Father, and of the Lamb, and of the Eternal Children.
Amen.

Recite the Creed

I believe in God, the Father Almighty,
Creator of heaven and earth,
And in the Holy Lamb, his Second Son, our Savior.
He was preceded by his Brother,
And borne of the Hierophant's blood.
He suffered under humanity's reign,
Was martyred, died and was buried.
He descended into hell.
On the third day, He rose again.
He was shown Acetia,
Returned to Earth,
And is seated at the right hand of the Holy Father.
He has come again to judge the living and the dead.
I believe in the Eternal Children,
The Holy Martyr Church,
The communion of saints,
The forgiveness of sins,
The resurrection of the body,
And life everlasting.
Amen.

One "Our Father"

Our Father,
Good servant of God,
Hallowed be Thy Name.
Acetia come,
Thy Will be done,
On earth as it is in heaven.
Give us this day our daily flesh,
And forgive us our weaknesses,
As we forgive those who fail us by their weakness.
And lead us not into heresy,
But shepherd us from ignorance.
Amen.

Three "Hail Lavinias" in the Names of Faith, Hope, and Charity

Hail Lavinia,
Full of Grace,
The Lord is with thee.
Blessed art thou among women,
And blessed is the miracle you represent,
The Protein.
Holy Lavinia, Daughter of God,
Pray for us sinners now, and at the hour of our death.
Amen.

One "Glory Be"

Glory Be
To the Father,
And to the Lamb,
And to the Eternal Children.
As it was in the beginning,
Is now,
And ever shall be,
World without end.
Amen.

The Mysteries
(Repeated Five Times)

1 "Our Father"
10 "Hail Lavinias"
1 "Glory Be"
1 Elijah's Prayer

Elijah's Prayer

O my Elijah, forgive us our sins, save us from the fire of hell, lead all souls to heaven, especially those Lazarenes who are in most need of Thy mercy.

Hail Holy Hierophant
(Said After Five Mysteries)

Hail Holy Hierophant
Father of mercy, our life, our sweetness, and our hope. To thee do we cry, poor banished children of Acetia. To thee do we send up our sighs mourning and weeping in this valley of tears. Turn then, most gracious advocate, thine eyes of mercy toward us, and after this our exile show us the blessed fruit of thy blood, Elijah. O clement, O loving, O sweet Holy Father.

Pray for us, O Sacred Servant of God,
That we may be made worthy of the promises of the Lamb.
In the Name of the Father, and of the Lamb and of the Eternal Children.

Amen.

THE LADY'S CHAMPION

Come to me once more, and abate my torment;
Take the bitter care from my mind, and give me
All I long for; Lady, in all my battles
Fight as my comrade.

—Sappho, "Ode to Aphrodite"

I

The Flight of the Governor

Would Governor Theodore del Medico go down fighting? Probably not. Look at him there, his chestnut head sometimes bobbing with shrill laughter above the crowd. Oblivious to eyes on him outside of those he paid, befriended, or paid to befriend. Teddy had no more chance of escaping fate than he did of noticing that teashaded individual who studied him from across the bustling restaurant of eight hundred customers.

Also oblivious to this predatory focus, though it came from a member of his own table, the Franco-Japanese professor of English whose name was René Ichigawa overexplained to a dreadlocked woman called Gethsemane, "You can hardly find good dim sum in the United Front anymore. It's only going to get rarer if the military keeps rounding up humans on the West Coast! Lucky thing New Elsinore has a strong base of hardworking, hard-eating immigrants who've been here too long to throw out. That's true of the whole nation, though. We can thank all those second-generation migrants. Especially after the war with Mexico! The coastal regions lost a lot of families when the militias were called to account in the aftermath, and most of them had already sent their healthy young men south to die in the war against—" He coughed a little and cracked his neck in the direction of their silent friend, who spared him a resentful glance even as René carried on.

"What the Midwest doesn't understand is it's *all* immigrants now. West Coast, and East. They don't understand that when they let their government act this way, it's their neighbors being taken. And they always seem to forget that their families were immigrants, too!" The pedantic Berkley professor, caught up in his own rant, turned to the disguised individual—the only other UF expat at the table. "When was the last time you met an *actual* Native American?"

"Why doesn't the Hierophant have his men shut these places down, or use them to trap big quantities of humans? Especially if they're focused on Asian populations." This was asked by René's cousin Tenchi, who sat another small plate atop his growing pile. "Seems like an irresistible lure to me!"

Their disguised member studied the portly man, mustache quivering into a frown. The place was packed, and loud, and Governor Theodore, along with anybody who cared, was far across the ballroom-size restaurant—but did they need to reference the Holy Father? Any mention perked ears in a martyr hangout. In a human establishment? Bad idea.

Gethsemane sensed this displeasure and refilled the teacup of that most important, silent member as René explained, "I'm sure he does use a few of them as traps, but he has to leave *some* for the legitimate populace. People would be incensed if he just started shutting down Asian businesses. Overnight change hasn't been tried since the Black Night. There's a complicated licensing procedure— *Xièxiè*." Sweet relief! The professor paused to show off another of his many languages by addressing the businesslike, hairnetted woman who swept up their plates. Her partner in crime, stopping her cart, interjected, "Pork *schaomai*? Chicken *schaomai*? Shrimp dumpling? Chicken feet?"

"Ooh," sang Tenchi, pointing at the cart, "chicken feet, please!"

"Can we hurry this up," the mustached member said with a sharp glance over the shades. Tenchi turned guilty doe eyes on their leader as the waitress, uncaring for any inter-table conflict, further stamped the well-marked card and thrust a small basket of fried chicken parts before her fellow human. Organic chicken, too—none of the lab-grown stuff. This place could have been raided on that ground alone if they didn't have all the proper licenses.

"There's no reason to rush," said René, reaching over for one of the greasy feet. This, he stuck into his mouth to suck tiny bones free of flesh even as he spoke. Gethsemane did not bother hiding her disgust as the professor continued through smacking lips, "Our— appointment's having a good time, so we'd ought to, too. I mean, look at him over there!"

Too true. Theodore's piercing laughter was audible beyond almost a thousand patrons chatting and laughing in a wider variety of languages than one could learn in a single human lifetime. Every time he laughed, so did his party of twelve, and so did a few of the guards hovering around him. Guards, hah. What kind of martyr needed a security detail?

One who had been warned what might happen to him. The mustached infiltrator sipped tea filled by Gethsemane and watched the Governor of the United Front yuck along with his cronies. Tenchi insisted, "See, dim sum is great because everyone can have fun! Chicken foot?" He offered the basket to their quietest member, for whom Gethsemane took on the burden of shaking her head.

"No: we're"—she waved a finger between herself and the mustached individual—"trying to be ready for action."

"We'll be ready to act, *Mom*," said René with a sigh and a roll of his eyes. "Anyway, we're serving good purpose. How weird would it be if it was just a couple of intense-looking *gweilos*, not eating and not having fun, staring at the Governor from across the room? Alarm bells."

"That's a racist thing to say, René," chided Tenchi.

"Oh, so you know that one! I was going to say 'a couple of intense-looking *gaijin*,' but you'd obviously know and complain about that one."

Gethsemane shared a withering glance with her shaded friend at the cousins' instant argument. She seemed just about to ask something of her martyr companion when Theodore, with a hand upon the shoulder of a friend, pushed himself up from his table. The disguised member of their party stood in the same instant, unnoticed in a packed room where people perpetually stood up and sat down while jabbering waitresses pushed fragrant carts to and fro. This near-invisible figure cut a calm, smooth path in the direction of the bathrooms where Theodore had gone with a guard.

René sucked a tooth. "Guess we'd ought to settle up."

The dimly lit men's room already seemed something out of a horror movie, with limitless stalls and too few people coming in and out to jive with the size of the restaurant. The guard who had accompanied Theodore like a parent taking his child to go potty stood daydreaming as five men urinated and left without washing their hands. More filtered in one by one. Teddy, naturally, had shut himself in the stall to pee, and yammered to his guard even as he did.

"Don't you just love how they know me here," the Governor prattled over the sound of his urine. Having tarried a second too long and drawn a glance from the guard, their observer hurried into a stall near Theodore's. The preening martyr continued. "The best thing we did this year was move my offices from San Valentino to New Elsinore. It's nice to be appreciated by the citizens—nice when people, even humans, can see reason. Those San Valentino people, it's just too close to home for them! I had a waitress actually thank me tonight for the work we've done in getting the riffraff out of our country. Would you believe that? Scrap the bit about 'this last year'—it was the best decision I've *ever* made, moving the capital from San Valentino to New Elsinore. And the people agree. The West Coast has gotten all the attention since Trimalchio had his paranoid little power trip before Dominia's control, while out East it's nothing but neglect! No more, I say."

With his toilet's flush, Theodore zipped his trousers. The hidden observer, pulse raising, prepared to be known. A second flush followed the Governor's and their doors swung open in time. "It's sort of like being a celebrity. *Really* a celebrity, instead of just being part of a famous Family. Like I've finally done something that I can be proud—"

This pair of flushes covered the sound of the electrodart gun's safety being released, but the guard was still quick to see the pistol and shout, "Sir," over the sound of Theodore's mindless blather. Sad to say, it didn't muffle Teddy's feminine shriek to see the drug-laced electric dart crumple his bull of a security man upon the bathroom floor. Always too bad to leave a fellow martyr in that condition, but it would be bloody chaos whatever happened. The General needed get the drop on the violence now, before the violence got the drop on her.

"Frederico," the Governor shrieked. The two unlucky humans in the bathroom reacted with shrill cries and swift departures while the single most useless member of the Holy Family reeled toward his assailant and recognized her with prompt horror.

"You! Oh, no—oh, no, no!"

"Just shut up, Teddy." Dominia jammed the pistol into his back and, with every shift of the toy in her hand, missed her relic .44 Magnum. Lost for over a year! Poor old friend. It would send a sterner message than the non-lethal weapon she held. "We're not going to hurt you, but I would appreciate it if you were compliant."

"You just shot a man in front of me, you're sticking a gun in my back, and you say you're not going to hurt me?" As voices rose outside the bathroom, tears formed in the corners of the Governor's eyes. "And I've told you a thousand times, my name is 'Theo'!"

She was going to throw up. "Will you please come along with me, 'Theo,' so I don't have to pistol-whip you unconscious and carry your sorry ass all the way to Jerusalem?"

"*Jerusalem!* I can't—" Eyes darting to the door, Teddy laughed in an unsteady pitch and said, "I can't go to *Jerusalem*, Dominia, please! It's a *war* zone! Father's been bombing it looking for *you*! Haven't his forces been actively clearing neighborhoods? I can't go there—not with you! He'll think I'm—*with* you, you know. What do you want from me? What good could I possibly be to you?"

"Are you in there, sir?" called a guard outside the door. "Are you alive?"

"Yes," the sweaty Governor responded, prompted by the jut of Dominia's gun in his back. "Yes, yes, I'm here! I'm alive, I'm fine. Frederico—"

"I am the General Dominia di Mephitoli, and I have incapacitated your man. If you do not relieve yourselves of your weapons and make way for me to exit with the Governor, I will kill him, and you will all be similarly disposed of." After a second of thought, she added some old-fashioned Bitch of Europa menace. "I don't wish to do that to your families."

The men outside were silent. Theodore gave a soppy exhalation, his hands held high on either side of his head. "She really means it. She means it, please, I can't die! Or—God, she could shoot me in the spine. I could be paralyzed! Please, believe her!"

For God's sake! The idiot didn't know the difference between a regular gun and an electrodart gun. It was as if he weren't a martyr—couldn't be healed from even a real shot in the spine with a little surgery and a month of physical therapy! Were these not dire circumstances, she might have given him a clout of annoyance, both for Theodore's nature (could one even damage the spine of a spineless man?) and his belief that Dominia would hurt him. Almost seventy years they'd known each other, and still he bought this. Perhaps that was her issue: why the world had listed her public enemy number one for a year. Her acting was just too good.

If not hers, certainly the Hierophant's, whom she was braced to see at any second. When would he appear, chiding and clucking like the old hen he was? She had to get this show on the road.

"I need my brother for a chat," Dominia said through the door. "Let us leave and no further harm will come to anyone."

Silence resounded until another scream rose from the dining room, and Dominia tried to stifle her annoyance. "What is it?" asked Theodore. Outside, shots were fired. "What's going on?"

"Just wait." She closed her eyes and tried to remember how many times this plan was discussed with her so-called assistants. How many times was René told to leave the building as soon as she got up? How many times had he said, "Sure, I'll take Tenchi right out"? How many times did she stress a minimal body count to Gethsemane? She didn't want any conflict, let alone bodies, whether dead or incapacitated.

Dominia glanced at Frederico. Not that she was one to criticize on that account.

After a few seconds' squabbling and more silence filled by the whimpering of Teddy, the bathroom door opened. She relaxed to see blood-spattered Gethsemane, calmer than the Dominia. "I apologize. Things did not go according to plan."

"So I heard." The General caught Theodore by the collar of his sports coat to drag him out of the bathroom. "The police will be here any minute, along with the military and special investigators."

The difference in the room was a startling one, because those eight hundred people had flooded for the exits and still pushed through. Fewer were left than one might anticipate. This ease of escape was largely due to the kind waitresses, who had parked their carts along the perimeter of the massive room before fishing weapons from their aprons. Only a handful of customers yet hovered near the escapee-crowded doors to film the proceedings from their phones, watches, or DIOX-Is. At this stage in her "career", Dominia felt the recordings were a good thing, and allowed them to proceed.

There was a lot to be shown. It was impossible to know who had made the first move—René, or one of the Red Market girls masquerading as waitresses, or maybe Gethsemane—but the end result was that the security detail hired to protect Theodore now amounted to a pile of corpses. The Lady's women did not abide by the General's new nonlethal preference. Theodore's personal friends had fled at the first sign of trouble, judging by the bodies, but the Governor still uttered a womanly shriek on seeing the remains of his staff.

"Please shut up." The picture of barely repressed impatience, the General thrust her little brother toward her human lieutenant as though holding a kitten. "The collar, now, quickly."

Before Theodore could ask, "What collar?" Gethsemane slapped the device around his neck. As Dominia tugged the fabric of his shirt to obscure the silver choker of the brand that once she'd worn, herself, her human companion bowed toward the nearest waitress.

"You've done good work tonight," said Gethsemane, and the General nodded her superficial agreement as the waitress put her gun back into her apron, then fixed the plastic of her gloves.

"Anything for the Lady," answered the woman, who waved her colleagues into the removal of the bodies. "And anything to get rid of that boneheaded bigot of a Governor."

"Weren't you the one who thanked me?" asked pathetic Theodore. He'd barely finished his question before the General and the earthbound nymph were dragging him through the vacated kitchen still so cluttered with utensils, in-progress dumplings, hanging ducks, and half-carved chickens that it was no less of a tahgmahr to navigate than were it full of chefs. Dominia filtered out her brother's whining tone of voice with a well-practiced ear and turned her attention toward Gethsemane.

"What's the ETA to the tarmac?"

"Twenty minutes."

"Followed by an easy, breezy three-hour flight into the middle of the Atlantic. Why aren't we just making the whole trip that way, again?"

"Flying?" asked queasy Theodore as the women continued speaking.

"It's true that the E4 is risky, but if we can make it to the extraction point, our journey will be cut in half."

"And if we can't, or if it fails, we might crash into the sea instead of flying straight across, which would have been the easiest and safest." The wonders of prototype technology developed by the labs of terrorist organizations! "It's not so much that we're hitting a moving target as it is that our target is an incredibly small and specific region of space-time. There's too much opportunity to be shot down between takeoff and extraction. I appreciate that they couldn't smuggle the components for a whole new teleporter into the Front, and that the jet is ultimately faster than walking the Void the whole way, but I still don't like using the E4 to maybe, possibly, show up in Tangiers just to take the teleporter to Jerusalem."

No talk of teleporters and interdimensional jets could transmute Teddy's terror to curiosity. "I can't go on a plane, Dominia, please."

"You have voiced this opinion many times, General, but it is nonetheless the option we have taken. Strictly speaking, your Father could dispatch drones anywhere across the globe to strike our plane. No flight route is truly safe."

"But some are safer than others. And some would keep us from risking you." She studied the beautiful human, who kept her gentle features turned ever forward, and resembled only in her boldness that nymph with which the Lady's servant was linked. "If the E4 doesn't fail, and doesn't crash, it could end up stuck in the Ergosphere."

"Then I will fight to remain myself, while knowing my sacrifice was a worthy one."

The Governor hadn't finished. "I understand you want to take me to Jerusalem, but can't we—take a ship, maybe, like a respectable—"

Theodore shrieked as the General zapped him into silence with the collar. A mild jolt, more effective than a slap in the head. Not as satisfying, though. "I want you to make sure," she continued to Gethsemane as they hauled the somewhat-subdued Governor up several flights of stairs, "that you have everything ready for an emergency situation. The last disaster I need is to lose you, René, Tenchi, or Farhad for a reason as stupid as Teddy."

"Now you're hurting my feelings."

Dominia at last addressed her brother as she hauled him out to the roof of the building, where Farhad landed their helicopter in the available space: a mere lifeboat to the greater E4-GL3 unit that would sweep them to a safer mass of land than the Americas. "I just mean to say that it's not like we're going to kill you, so losing my—friend's life in exchange for yours is out of the question." Even now, even here, she was hesitant to refer to Gethsemane as her "girlfriend," and this earned one long blink from the stoic woman who otherwise continued her visual sweep of the area.

"Aren't my men's lives worth as much as your friends'? Is that a helicopter? Oh, Father! Father, where are you! You said you'd always protect me."

Now he was crying. Dominia tried not to roll her eyes as the grown man (over a hundred years old, combining human and martyr years!) hyperventilated when the simple flying machine touched the ground with the delicate bounce of a ballerina. "Just give him the pill now," she urged.

As Gethsemane rooted through the handbag in her elbow, the red-eyed Governor gulped out the words, "What pill?"

"It's not a hard-core tranquilizer," Dominia insisted. Gethsemane lifted the little pink speck and said in her placid tone, "This will help you, Governor, to relax on the trip."

Even before his sister clarified, "Just one of DIOX's stupid benzos," Theodore had already snatched the pill from her fingers with a hilariously birdlike movement of his lips. He now swallowed it dry, eyes leaping between the faces of the two women and the open flanks of the helicopter to which he was again pulled.

"Please, let me sit between you."

"That is perhaps a good idea," agreed Gethsemane. Dominia watched from the corner of her expressionless eyes as the woman climbed into the helicopter, her kaleidoscopic dress shifting against her mocha thighs, and Theodore drew from both the General's line of sight and the human's tone all he needed to know.

"Oh, no, you two aren't— *Dominia*, didn't you learn your lesson last time? Humans and martyrs mingling only leads to trouble!"

"You were a human who mingled with martyrs," Dominia reminded him, climbing into the helicopter and shouting among the din of the propeller and distant scream of sirens, "*Asre'*," as though Farhad did not know to hurry up perfectly well, himself. As the women strapped themselves in and helped the fumbling Governor, the General continued, "Anyway, it's none of your business with whom I'm doing what."

"It's simply wrong," insisted the stuffy man. "I mean, meeting a girl in a club for a night is one thing! But somebody you *know*? Long-term? A human!" Dominia tried to stifle another eye roll and succeeded only because Gethsemane leaned forward as though to kiss her. The General presented her face as such, expecting an opportunity to horrify her younger brother, when in fact Gethsemane's aim was to whip the (surprisingly well-adhered) mustache from its place upon Dominia's upper lip. While the General first swore, then sneezed, both Theodore and Farhad laughed, and Gethsemane settled, smirking, back into her seat. With a resentful glance for her brother, the General drew the gun that was not, strictly speaking, hers, and swapped it for a more fatal model in the back of the pilot's seat.

"I didn't mean to laugh," the Governor whined, but Dominia glanced at the ceiling of the helicopter.

"It's not for you, dingus." From the breast pocket of her suit coat, the General removed the pocket scope and screwed it on; Gethsemane did the same, and Dominia tried to find some sanity in the girl now that she'd worked out her feelings. "Tenchi and René left as planned?"

"The second they could—they were the first ones out."

"What happened in the restaurant, then?"

"I did not see how it was possible for the engagement to end without you swarmed, General. I made a call."

Annoyed for her defiance as much as for the rapid-pace Spanish prayers uttered by her brother, Dominia gave in to her urge to clout Theodore. "Stop doing that. You'll draw the Lamb's attention, assuming it isn't here already."

"That's what I'm *hoping* for! Oh, God, don't let me die!"

"You've already died once," remarked Gethsemane.

"That was terrifying, too, but not like this. And I don't want to die again, forever! Dominia, please."

He clutched her sleeve at more or less the same instant Farhad said, "Drones," so yet again, his plea was ignored. Both women leaned from the helicopter, guns steadied upon their forearms and heads lowered to their scopes to fire into the well-illuminated night of the United Front's new capital. The police and military reaction had been quicker than Dominia had hoped, but the incessant glow of New Elsinore—Longacre Square, an exposed, neon heart—illuminated her targets better than even her abandoned DIOX-I could have. With but two natural eyes, her shot was phenomenal. Gethsemane, not so trained as her companion, still made quick work of a pair of drones while Theodore sobbed, "I barely even know what's going on."

There wasn't much to know. Wasn't it all self-evident? He was being kidnapped. The police and the military were trying to rescue him. The General might have explained it to him had they more time, but she was just as happy—or happier—to wait for the benzo to loosen him up. Until then, her focus was on meeting the automatic fire of the nearing drones with patient shots that sent them reeling into the miasma of lights. Every glance she took after them made Dominia sick—not for heights, but for memories of living in the Front. She had another home, now. Her own city. She had to remind herself.

Of course, what was that self she reminded? She had felt herself less and less over the past year. This would not have been so alarming had it not produced a physiological effect: a kind of numbness in her cheeks and hands, as though she was literally not feeling herself. It was hard, most nights, to admit the source of this oppression, but seeing New Elsinore with its black Hudson river and glittering lights reminded her of San Valentino, reminded her of happier times she dare not imagine, and dredged the feeling again.

This numb sensation reached its apex when the Lady suggested it was time to respond to the Hierophant's year-long campaign of bombing and pussyfooting troops into territories around the perimeter of Jerusalem by less cowardly, more direct action: the acquisition of Theodore, who, deserving of the position or not, was one of the most prominent martyrs in the world.

A few weeks back, in the center of war-torn Israel, the General had accepted an invitation to come to the Lady's chambers, to watch Her recline upon a chaise lounge and speak without moving Her lips in a sound that was the voice of each woman who had hosted the Lady. Each woman, including the present avatar, Miki Soto. The chambers rested within Jerusalem's library, ever growing to keep out the Hierophant in the tradition of the ill-fated statues from the Cairo gardens. He could not bear to bomb a collection of rare and beautiful books; therefore, the corner of Jerusalem with that vast library was the safest spot in town. The immediate increasing of the library's size had been Dominia's idea, and had become an overarching background task across the first several months of her leadership. The following year, as UF and Europa troops pressed into Jerusalem and began, block by block, building by building, to clear the city of Hunters, Dominia worked harder for the Lady than she ever had for the Hierophant. Yet when called to that silken, windowless palace room in the center of the library, it was not for praise of her efforts.

You have not been doing your work lately, the Lady observed when she arrived.

The boggling General tried to laugh, but the noise caught in her throat. "I built you a palace in one month and filled it with books to keep my Father away. I've disciplined the men who once abused your women and whipped both groups into a genuine army. My Father's troops have pressed into the city using my presence as an excuse but that same presence keeps our men and women fighting ferociously to push him back. We've begun to experiment with the Ergosphere teleporters, and I've trained men in the navigation of the Void—Farhad and three of his pilots, and Gethsemane, although she's a little…unstable."

That is not the work We mean.

It was only in intuition that she took the Lady's meaning. "You want me to drop the defense and move against my Father."

The time is coming that an aggressive move shall need to be made—and sooner, rather than later. Do you know, Dominia, what happens in the Front even now? Do you think those humans can withstand his tyranny any longer than Jerusalem can brace itself against his bombs?

Yes, she knew what was happening in the Front. A mass culling. Concentration camps. Deportation, and not back to the respective home countries of those immigrants detained: deportation to city centers across the UF and Europa, for fuss-free food. Not that Europa was any less inclined to violence than usual. Since Dominia had risen to control of the Hunters, Israel had voted to exit the union of the Middle States in a double-edged sword of a move that gave the General and the Lady control of the holy country, but that also left that same state without any official political allies. The Hierophant immediately massed troops in Turkey, increased military presence in Cyprus, and received permission from the Middle States to rid their region of his terrorist daughter. The rest of the world, terrified of being accused of terrorist collusion, strove to mind its own business. Therefore, outside of cells in Tangiers and Tunis, Jerusalem was alone, and so were the Front's immigrant humans.

Your Father must be shown that what is happening in the Front is not acceptable. The Lady sat up, feet tucked beneath Her body as Her Bearer hurried forward with a tea tray of fruits. As she fed the obligingly parting lips of the physical avatar and the Lady's voice carried on, Dominia thought of a ventriloquist routine she'd once been forced to endure for Lavinia's feast night. *A disruption must occur if we are to catch his attention without declaring outright war, and the largest and most vocal disruption would be the deposition of Theodore.*

Though at first she laughed to think of her idiot brother and the useless figurehead he was, her laughter faded, for the Lady hadn't sense of humor enough to make a joke. And besides, the General could see the reason in it.

There was, after all, something Dominia wanted to ask him.

You wish to ask why your Father really keeps Lavinia locked in her high tower? Always probing where She wasn't welcome. Dominia narrowed her eyes in the then familiar displeasure of having one's thoughts read without permission. *As if you do not know already.*

"The best reason to get Theodore is for his own good. He's a simp. There so a member of the Family can be present on the continent until the Hierophant finds a replacement child for me."

Or he wins you back.

"He's not going to win me back."

Are you so sure? What if he were to offer you Cassandra. Would you believe him?

Oh! The dashed hopes! The broken promises. The wound was not as fresh as it once was, but its grasping by the cruel hands of sadistic outsiders enflamed her pain worse than ever. "We've been through this," said the General. "He can't give her to me. You can't. Nobody can."

You can. When all of this is over, and you have crushed your Father—when martyrs are under control, and given the grace of God's forgiveness—then you will have Cassandra again.

After the travesty of the Lady's ascension ceremony, Dominia wasn't interested in raising her hopes. Time to focus on a more relevant topic. "I don't think this is a good idea. The liability here is extremely high."

But, as you said, you are doing Theodore a kindness. Extricating him from an evil life. He could serve much purpose in this place, were he to find the glamour in compassion that he finds in your Father's way. But there is something important you wish to know from him, as you have only just thought.

"Something you and Lazarus know," said Dominia darkly. The Lady's chewing lips smiled.

Something you already know, deep down inside. Deeper down than that secret you keep from even yourself.

The General listened to the antique clock upon the nearby writing desk, counting its ticks in time with her breath. At ten, she unclenched the jaw she had not realized to be clenched, and asked, "Are we finished here?"

You will call to order a meeting and suggest as We have. Lazarus is more inclined to agree with ideas from your mouth.

"Why is that?"

Because—the Lady had chuckled on Dominia's way out the door—*he knows it is not worth the trouble of arguing with you.*

Perhaps not. One could go so far as to say that the General was the sort of person to make up her mind before she'd gotten all the facts, but that was because it was a wandering mind that fell easily into the flow of her work—a flow only shattered by Gethsemane's high cry above Theodore's smug, "Serves you right," and Dominia's matching, "Are you all right?"

"My arm." The human grit her teeth, looking over the side of the helicopter. "And my gun."

"Stay back, Gethsemane. Theodore, shut up. I'm still thinking about shooting you."

Blessedly, he obeyed, and in the relative silence, Farhad was as slick a pilot as Dominia was a shot. Between those two factors, by the time the police copters were in reasonable pursuit, the path was almost entirely clear of drones. Good thing, too. With one foot wedged beneath her seat and the other crammed beneath that of the pilot, the General released her seat belt to clamber into the empty passenger's position in the cockpit. Theodore scoffed. "Are you insane?"

"Why don't you get useful by making your tie into a tourniquet." Dominia shifted the massive, emergency-only weapon Farhad had been forced to jam between the console and the headrest. As her hands wrapped around the cold metal of its grips, she frowned. Would it always come to this? Would she never be able to escape this awful cycle of blood? Once, she'd hoped to make the late dentist, Tobias Akachi, her final human kill.

With the Hierophant's troops pressing upon her city and opening conflict with her soldiers, she had not taken long to dash her own hopes, like a former smoker who slipped back into the habit after a bad day at work. All smokers knew it was a whole lot harder to quit than it was to just keep lighting cigarettes.

As the weapon lifted into the Governor's view, he shrieked. "Is that a rocket launcher?"

"I thought it was a ridiculous suggestion, too." After checking the sights of the weapon, Dominia looped one arm through a strap mounted in the chopper's ceiling and leaned into the open air. "But after I thought about it for a while, well...it was sort of inevitable that this kind of scenario would emerge."

"But a *rocket* launcher?"

"Technically"—Gethsemane raised her voice over the aiming system's occasional beeps—"it is a rocket-propelled grenade launcher."

"Oh, *pardonnez-moi*. Sorry I don't know the difference." He seemed set to go on until a burst of laughter rose from him. He had noticed the necklace swinging around Gethsemane's neck and said while tying off the gunshot wound, "I know that diamond."

Dominia took her shot at that announcement, as a loudspeaker-augmented voice called, "Terrorist Dominia di Mephitoli, deliver the Governor to safety and stand down." This unfortunate timing made it seem like the police chopper's explosion into thunder and smoke and death was causal—a direct result of its attempts at hostage negotiation, rather than of her idiot brother's decision to bring up her dead wife at that very second. Good luck trying to get the government to empathize with family problems at a time like this.

Gethsemane repeated her only response. "It is my duty to bear Cassandra for the General."

Theodore looked between them, now sufficiently drugged to be more aghast at Dominia's relationship choices than at being in a helicopter—or the center of a very serious shoot-out. With a smug wave of hands before his arrogantly shut eyes, Teddy said, "Dominia, I hate to say it, but you've reached a new low. I mean, not just climbing right back into bed with humans, but making her wear your dead wife? Like a necklace! You weirdo. Was that an anniversary gift?"

"It is my duty," repeated the Bearer, who reached under her seat with her good arm to pass Dominia another grenade. Irritated, Theodore leaned forward to address the pilot.

"Do you speak?" he asked, and Gethsemane answered for him, "To you, Arabic." This elicited an eye roll from the Governor while the General, still half outside the chopper, ducked within to evade a spray of gunfire from a dedicated drone. This straggler was caught in the explosion that claimed the second police chopper, whose propellers burst in a brilliant marigold blaze before the machine wheeled into the sprawling park below.

"Do you speak Arabic?" the Governor deigned to ask the human beside him. When she nodded, he asked, "I don't suppose you'd tell him I'm rich, and that I'll give him a lot of money and immunity if he lands this thing and lets me out?"

"And why would I tell him that?"

"Because I'll give you money, too?"

"What good is money?" As the remaining police helicopters stood down, Gethsemane made no move to tear her eyes away. A wise choice. The General, like a dog guarding the lambs, remained stone-faced outside the helicopter until they were well away from the island and able to pull north: the shortest route out of the city's jurisdiction on the way to the landing strip. The Water Bearer continued to speak over the eerie whip of the copter through the wind. "What good is money to anyone? The world is ending soon. This one, anyway. It will be very different. Money as it is will not matter anymore. Not to your people. Not to me."

Poor Teddy looked as if he didn't quite know just what to make of that one, but of course, there was no one with time to explain it to him. For her part, the General was preoccupied. It wasn't the relative ease with which they had accomplished their goal that made Dominia suspicious. It was that they'd accomplished it at all. The Ichigawas would be checking in at the government's airport using false Halcyon accounts just a mere twenty minutes after she'd fed her younger brother that pill—only lightly tainted with Lazarus's blood, in case of emergency.

Because Dominia was almost certain that there would be an emergency.

So be it. She could handle it. Given danger came in the ideal circumstances, anyway—but it would have been nice to have a little foreknowledge. Then she really could have handled anything. That was the rub, wasn't it? Especially when all your enemies, and even some of your less helpful (read: absent) friends, had been through this great, sordid game before. Sure, Lazarus was on her side, but he was so old and dry about it, and so withdrawn about what information he actually knew, that it was impossible to count him as wholly trustworthy.

For instance: at no point in the past year had he once acknowledged the alarming frequency with which Dominia heard the voice of the Hierophant in her head. Worse, he had never addressed the external visitations. Like now, as her Father spoke unseen from the periphery of her restored right eye, approximately he would sit were he in the passenger's position beside Farhad:

"It is woefully difficult to know who to trust in a world such as this."

"Such as yours," she muttered, taking advantage of her position outside the vehicle, amid the relentless beating of the rotor, to address her pursuer aloud. It was an alarming habit in which she engaged with increasing frequency since the traumatic *hieros gamos* of the Lady and Lazarus, so far away in Cairo. A bad habit, talking to him out loud, but she couldn't shake it.

"At least you know to whom this world belongs." His innocent retort led her to look sharply into the seat and find it empty but for the assault rifle. Good. That couldn't always be said of the apparition that haunted her, almost nightly, since its first appearance in the *tanque* from Cairo to Jerusalem. Sometimes her Father's specter remained when she looked at it, staring her down in defiant mockery of her impotence to accomplish its dismissal.

Gethsemane, noting Dominia's eyes narrowed for something unseen, leaned past fretful Theodore. "Are you all right, General?"

"Fine," she lied, reaching into the helicopter for the sniper rifle as, from below, similar fire shattered the air. "Stay back, stay small, and keep the Governor from getting shot. You think what I did to your man in that bathroom was bad, Teddy?" With a glance for her terrified baby brother, Dominia leaned out once again and flicked on the high-powered scope. "Just imagine what Cicero would do to these guys for accidentally killing you."

II

In the Event of a Water Landing

After their escape from New Elsinore airspace, Dominia was almost looking forward to their second flight. How sad, what passed for pleasure these nights! It was only natural, though, that she would be grateful for even two or three hours of smooth sailing. For one agonizing year, the General had no rest.

Just over a year, truth be told. If she was counting the months, it was something in the order of fifteen. Maybe eighteen. It was certainly that if one counted Cassandra's death as the starting gun of her bloody, tiring race. And race she had, from San Valentino to the isle of Japan, and then aboard a train to Kabul, to Cairo—and finally, against her will, to the Israeli desert. She'd remained there since, her race contained to a constant cycle around Jerusalem's vast cityscape. Here to build goodwill among Abrahamian humans by making public appearances in Catholic Mass and allowing the global broadcast of her hasty confirmation as a nice big "fuck you" to the Holy Martyr Church; there to investigate the ruins of a drone bombing or to join a unit in pushing back UF troops; off to her labs for a chat with the researchers about her needs from them; and somehow in the course of that same day, she'd find time to throw on a suit and scrape and bow before the Knesset, the legislative body of the state of Israel, to beg that what meager legitimate funds the isolated nation had left be given to her army.

Yeah. She had her army. Her homophobic, misogynistic, trash heap of a terrorist cell had straightened out somewhat when forced by honor or religious principle to follow a lesbian and work with a cabal of prostitutes—but only somewhat. Some still forgot their rank when (in)convenient, and the seven-something-foot martyr had more than once resorted to screaming in their human faces until grown men wept like children at her feet or, in the harder examples, deserted the unit.

Such improvements gave no satisfaction. Praise the saints there were people like Farhad, reasonable men who assembled around her within a fortnight of her control. In a technical way, this de facto jurisdiction extended to Hunter-plagued Israeli cities such as Tel Aviv, which had clung to its glamorous atmosphere in the face of its country's violence so that it resembled a kind of coastal Vegas. So she'd heard, anyway. She hadn't seen it, herself. No time. If not for the doings of her few loyal men, she would have been awake day and night, falling ever more behind. Israel—yes, even Tel Aviv—had been bombed no fewer than thirty times since November of 1997 AL, with Jerusalem in particular facing a brutal thirteen drone strikes. And amid it all, there was the Lady, pouring money into the ad campaign that had encouraged Israeli voters to separate from their union and leave themselves undefended.

Dominia could understand why She'd done this. It made Israel really theirs—gave them license to do with it, its funds, and its military as was needed, once she discerned the depths of Tobias's tendrils through the Hunter network. The scientists were her best friends in this endeavor of sorting out the power structure, and the scientists revealed to her that even Tobias had suppressed certain avenues of research which the General was more than happy to encourage. The former leader's reasoning had been that plenty of research on transport, medicine, and other constructive avenues was done elsewhere. He wanted to focus on what he believed to be "military technology."

This was the problem when you let a dentist into a military profession. It took a soldier to understand that all technology was military technology. Take, for instance, a secret project stowed from even the dentist's prying eyes: the E4-GL3, or the Electromagnetic Glider. Why everything had to resolve to an animal name with these people, Dominia was never sure, but by God she loved those eagles. Filled a woman with real patriotic vigor just to see its oblong shape beneath the tarp as their helicopter set upon the dirt of the abandoned Vermont farm they'd enlisted for the job. There had been a lot of trepidation about whether the thing would be able to make it into the Front at all, but the trans-dimensional vehicle was designed for discretion while flying above Earth. It was, first and foremost, a stealth plane. It just so happened that this stealth plane could, upon entering a safe range, rip through space-time to the point in the future where it would find itself on its associated landing pad, safe and sound. And a stealth plane that allowed its passengers to skip half their journey, well—that was military technology if ever she'd heard of it. It might not have been able to carry a hundred of Tobias's anti-martyr exoskeleton ALIF-8s, but it would get their asses out of Dodge, and that was all she wanted. Even Teddy, still clamoring on about this horror and that indignity, was silenced into a few seconds of astonishment when Farhad whipped the tarp from the cigar-shaped object.

"Is that a—is that a *UFO*, Dominia?"

"It can't be unidentified if it's ours," she said, masterfully refraining from tacking on an unnecessary (but deserved) "dipshit."

"But I mean—it *looks* like a spaceship, like something out of a video game or a—"

"Because it's a new model. It's just a plane like any other at the end of the day."

Easier to let him think as much, anyway. It was, in a way, just a plane; but it was a plane designed to navigate inner space, rather than outer space. The graphene-coated surface of the E4 was, strictly speaking, a series of two-dimensional objects stacked to resemble a three-dimensional object; this trans-dimensional quality of graphene was the only thing that helped Dominia grasp why the substance was so conductive to the teleporter technology developed from the blood of Lazarus, because the deeper she stumbled into the scientific explanations of what was happening when electrons and their little friends were introduced to the material, the thicker the dictionary she needed to grab. At certain moments, she wished she'd gone into engineering or medicine rather than the military, but the medical field wasn't exactly thriving with geniuses. Look at Teddy. Everybody had their own specialized knowledge, she supposed. She couldn't tell you just how it was the damn plane functioned; but she could tell you how to use that same device to annihilate a nation, or entertain her brother into passivity. Once in his cushy seat with another pill, a collar-free neck, and a book to ignore, his tune changed so much he didn't even notice Farhad's smooth takeoff.

"Well this isn't so *bad*," Teddy said—repeatedly said, because the drug dampened one's ability to form memories. "I don't know why I was in such a fuss over flying before. I mean, it's perfectly *normal* to most people. Isn't it, Dominia?"

Lifting her cheek from her hand and her gaze from the window, the General said, "I used to commute via plane almost every week during the height of our military involvement in the 3900s, going from war theater to the proper Front to Father's castle and then off again. Even later in the special forces, and then again during the South American Conflict, it seemed like I was always flying. I was glad when I was promoted to Governess—some time to rest. If you can find it, anyway."

"Tell me about it! I've never been busier in all my life. No wonder you ran off!" The lazy man waved his hands with his flippant mischaracterization of Dominia's motivations, distracted while she made sly eye contact with Gethsemane. "I admit, some days I've thought about doing…well, not the *same* thing, obviously, but—I just don't understand what's happened with you, Dominia." His stream of consciousness having become less a train than a car driven by a drunk weaving in and out traffic, Teddy crossed his arms and settled back into one of six seats in the tiny cabin. "Even if you can't take the pressure, that's no reason to run off and join terrorists."

"I'm leading the terrorist organization now. Or its splinter, anyway." Offense over his half-baked aspersions would be laughable as experiencing hurt feelings on the pitiless observations of a toddler. She squinted to study the night through her reflection against the window. "Terrorism, like terror, is a state of mind."

And it was one that sought, increasingly, to envelop her. As a sad result of her control and Israel's exit from their union, the Middle States were more chaotic than ever—and the same could be said not just of its official governing body but its unofficial one. With the former crux of the Hunters now led by one of the organization's avowed enemies, those many satellites and associate terrorist cells had refused to acknowledge her fealty and insisted on splitting off. As expected. There were now such groups as the New Hunters, the True Hunters, the Old Hunters...the list went on, and those were only the English tags the news channels gave them. If she got into the Arabic, Turkish, and even the Farsi variations, there seemed little point in even calling them a unified organization. The General had not given a name to her units, but she supposed it was no more proper to call them Hunters than it was for the world to call her a terrorist.

That was what she preferred to tell herself, at any rate. As the cabin lights stubbornly cast her ghostly reflection against the dark glass, she avoided eye contact with that phantom double as though in shame. She refused the title of "terrorist" and struggled to maintain her old identity, but the truth was that the person ready for Saint Valentinian in the McLintock farmhouse just over a year before was a very different woman from the one sitting in a plane flown by a Hunter with the kidnapped Governor beside her. That difference was clearer all the time, but there were plenty of similarities, too: there she was again in the restaurant bathroom, blistered to hear sounds of violence outside a mere fifteen minutes before she would blow up a helicopter with an RPG; the gunpowder smell of rotten eggs in her nose, and the abrupt end of thousands of screams in those thousand battles of hers; the abrupt end to the scream of Benedict, Cassandra's beloved husband, when he was just some kid sent to war. It was not a death like a military death, not even a death like the slaughtering of a human for food—although it had been in defense, in a way. Her mind could never escape it, never justify it. Could never justify its own care, either, since she knew she only cared because of his relation to Cassandra. This deepened the shame.

Nothing in her life was meant to be this way. To feel this way. Dominia could not help but think that she'd never been meant to experience that feeling of grief or guilt. A martyr should have been stronger. The General was supposed to be stronger than this—supposed to be a cold, dark child of the Lord with no pity in her heart for human cattle. She was supposed to be successful, clever, and well-liked by her people. She was supposed to be happy. Supposed to, supposed to… Dominia was increasingly far from the self she once expected to find within her body. Increasingly far from the person she had thought herself to be, who she now realized never existed. It was that self that she expected others to see, and that self that inspired constant surprise in its owner by its perpetual absence.

Should it have surprised her? She had given up everything she wanted. Everything. Her eyes skipped across to Gethsemane—more specifically, the diamond lying in the dark notch of the woman's clavicle—then away as she found the matter-bound naiad studied her with great eyes painted in colors like seawater that recalled those crashing waves, the cerulean sky, the taste of salt on sweet Cassandra's impossibly plush lips.

Sorrow! Yes, there was that pang of sorrow, that ache of shame, that terrific tragedy of the question that kept Dominia self-occupying night and day—working until she was so exhausted she could not but collapse into a sleep where she was still not wholly safe. For some reason, when the blood of Lazarus altered her body such that mere human food and a bit of sunshine left her healthier than the false protein ever had, she'd expected the swap she forced in her sleeping schedule to alter her dreams. If that couldn't cure her tahgmahrs—*nightmares*, she had to remember to call them now—nothing could.

And clearly, nothing could. Still, she once a week awoke with the crinkle of her wife's eye plastered across her mind. Then she would be forced to ask that question she so carefully avoided in waking: *Have I given you up?* In such moments, she was shamed by her own reluctance to think on her wife. Was that the real way in which Dominia gave her up—neglect of thought? Was it wrong to avoid thoughts of Cassandra? Was it wrong to *hate* thinking of her? Was it wrong to nonetheless pray every morning and every night that she would someday hold this world's, that world's, any world's, most beautiful soul again in her own arms?

Dosed though he was, Theodore must have noticed the brief direction of Dominia's melancholy gaze. "Why are you *wearing* that?" he pressed of Gethsemane again. "And don't give me this nonsense about some duty."

"But that is the reason, Governor." With her left hand primly in her lap and her wounded right arm elevated with a makeshift sling provided by Theo's torn coat, the human insisted, "I fear a matter like this is beyond your understanding."

Teddy laughed, too doped for offense. Dominia shrugged. "She's right. I don't pretend to understand it, either."

"Yes," agreed the girl, her tone still matter-of-fact. "Such issues are also beyond the General's understanding. At least, at this point in linear time."

"Why do you speak like a robot? 'At this point in linear time.'" He pronounced the words like an early text-to-speech computer program, stilted and artificial. "If you hadn't bled right in front of me, I'd have thought you were some kind of android."

"Sometimes," admitted the Gethsemane with a sad chuckle, "I feel like one. Perhaps it is all the time I've spent working in the Red Market." She glanced at Dominia, who had heard her story just once, in the dark, after the human thought the martyr wouldn't remember. A miserable story, about human trafficking, and how cruel people could be to kids. The General respected how hard it had been to talk about it by not talking about it, herself, and the human obviously appreciated it. For the sake of the present audience and her desire to leave her early history unspoken, Gethsemane summed it up in simple terms. "One does not require rescue from the Lady and Her formal organization of working women as early as I did, then go on to maintain much desire to experience emotion."

"Running around with prostitutes, terrorists, murderers, and thieves." The sighing Governor shook his holier-than-thou head in a habit learned from the Hierophant. "What kind of person does that?"

Unbuckling her seat belt, Gethsemane said, "In all fairness, sir, I have not worked in that capacity since I was twenty-one, when the Bearer awoke within me and I was promoted from the fold into my true role. However, this is another matter I would not expect you to understand. Forgive me, General." The tall woman stooped to move forward, but her dreads still brushed the weapon-stuffed overhead compartment. "I believe Farhad will require company to ensure he is fully awake."

"Now that's a horrible thought." Teddy giggled. As Gethsemane disappeared up the aisle of the plane and shut herself up with the pilot, the kidnapped Governor returned his attention to both his present sister, and his absent one. "Doesn't she remind you of Lavinia? I mean, not in looks, obviously. Maybe it's her devotion to you, her loyalty. I can't put my finger on it."

"I hadn't thought of it," lied Dominia, having noted the comparison on more than one occasion—interestingly, not to Gethsemane's earthly form, but to her nymph counterpart. Leave it to Teddy to see through the dreadlocks. "You should know better than anyone."

Not even drugs could keep the sour note from his voice. "What's that supposed to mean?"

Innocently, Dominia said, "Only that you've spent so much time with her," as though not referring to a notoriously un-secret romantic crush widely regarded as—for lack of a more exact term—kind of creepy, considering Theodore, as a human, had been the doctor assigned to monitor the welfare of the comatose Lavinia when she was roughly twelve. Nothing untoward had happened, of course. At the time, his feelings for her had been strictly those of a caregiver. But since Lavinia awoke into the spotlight, and Theodore was rewarded for his efforts with that oft-cherished "gift" of a late-life martyring, it had been impossible for the public to miss the puppyish mannerisms Teddy adopted in his closest sister's presence. Certainly, they had been impossible for Dominia to miss. But the crush was such a harmless and pathetic thing, and Lavinia was so oblivious to it, well—sad to say poor Theodore's unrequited love was more of an international running gag than the great romantic saga he envisioned.

"Of course I've spent time with her." His tone was as defensive as the hunch of his shoulders. "More time than you, anyway. Always too busy off in the Front to come home and visit your Family. We went four—no, five, years without seeing you that one time." Yes, a fine couple of years. Not as fine as the Canadian vacation, and not motivated by anger so much as apathy, but still very fine, very fine. She tuned back into his rant. "Poor Lavinia misses you, she looks up to you! Do you know how disappointed she's been?"

"When was the last time you visited Europa since taking the ship to America?"

"Don't try to make this about me." His voice mounted that womanly pitch that inspired, as always, Dominia's smirk. "I don't deserve any criticism. You're the one doing the kidnapping here!"

"That's right. And you're giving me a lot of lip for somebody who's been kidnapped."

"Well, I just don't see the point! You'll only succeed in getting Father all riled up. Cicero, at least. He cares more—well, not about *me*, but about normalcy."

"That's what I'm hoping. And I'm also hoping you're more valuable than you let on."

"Of course I'm *valuable*. But what's helped you see the light?"

"Other than the fact that our Father martyred you instead of killing you when Lavinia woke up, call it…the inspiration of a friend."

As much as Tobias Akachi could be called a friend. Of course, Teddy tried to point out, "You know everything that I do. More. This job is the first time Father's trusted me to so much as take out the garbage."

Gritting her teeth at the horrendous euphemism for genocide that she herself had been guilty of using many times over (then wondering if she overthought it and he really meant "take out the garbage," which was possible), Dominia inhaled. "But I think you *do* know something, Te—Theo. Something you're not telling. Why did he martyr you? Why not just kill you?"

"Well *that's* very kind of you, Dominia."

"That's how *he* thinks, not me. I'm trying to think like him. If I were him, and knew all the things he knew, I would only martyr you if you were of use to me. I would only martyr anyone if they were of use to me."

As she herself had been martyred for a strange and abstract destiny: for purposes of ending the modern world, and granting victory to one side or the other. She studied her brother and tried with caution to evoke the spirit of her Father without literally invoking it, as she had in Akachi's van when the Ergosphere was still so close and her mind, translucent with psychedelic drugs. She imagined the Hierophant's being, could smell in the center of her mind the distant edge of sandalwood and frankincense—a walking Mass, that man, their Father, who disguised pragmatism with joviality and could make anyone in the world feel as if he loved them most of all not seconds before seeing them put to death. Or, more rarely and always more brutally, killing them by his own hand. He did not martyr Theodore out of affection. Not out of generosity or kindness. If the man had secrets that the Holy Father did not want Dominia to someday learn, the most expedient thing would have been to kill him.

Instead, knowing through his admitted dry run of reality that this moment would come, the Hierophant had martyred Theodore and made him part of the most powerful, spiritually decadent *Famiglia* in the world. And if Dominia were the Hierophant, she would only do a thing like that if Theodore possessed information the Hierophant wanted her to have—if the kidnapping of the Governor served no use but to turn her around in circles. Then why had the Lady given her the task? Surely the divinity knew all her Father did, and more.

She was tired of being a pawn. Blindly wandering at the behest of those who knew the many histories of the many realities happening for eternity. Who was to say it was a matter of chronology? Perhaps Lazarus was placed arbitrarily in any one of an infinity of random, concurrent probabilities, and was therefore present in all his lives at once, as she had felt herself so physically in another world. That world of the Kingdom. The magician's world.

That son of a bitch, Valentinian. There was still not a trace of him: not after all this time. True, she hadn't looked hard for him. Her work in the world had kept her from finding time to try and visit the Kingdom within the event horizon of the black hole at the end of Earth's linear time. Many flesh-and-blood, living people needed her help, because they still experienced matter and time as normal people.

Dominia experienced it, too, of course. But, having been in that strange other place, that Void, that dark essence of the black hole, the General was numbed to the sordid reality that her Father considered his. She saw the strings. The whole social charade reminded her of the concerts in which her Father would employ Cassandra, who had by the end of her life moved from Noctisdomin school into a career as the music teacher in a very fine Holy School (one of roughly four hundred across the United Front, all exceptional academies where exceptional human children learned that they would, nonetheless, always be inferior to martyrs). Those concerts were but a handful of extensive interactions American Cassandra had with European Lavinia, who did everything with tooth-gritting perfection because pleasing their Father was the girl's sole reason to live.

For the first—oh, almost two hundred and fifty years she was alive, Dominia was able to enjoy concerts and theater as sheer entertainment. But when the Hierophant wanted Lavinia to be a star for his entertainment and felt he needed to drag Cassandra into it, the then Governess was exposed to all the dramatic minutiae that came with her wife's preparation for the show. Voices of background choristers going out, Lavinia being a spoiled drama queen about some costume…it was all such a tahgmahr. And it was all Cassandra would talk about for a while, there, too. The concert, her nerves, how grating Lavinia could be when given license to exercise her undeserved political powers—or, worse, her protein-given ones.

Yet, for all the stress and angst and nonsense those scattered nights of buildup brought to the General's life, she would gladly live them again if that was what it took to be with Cassandra. It was a heretical, human belief among the women of the Red Market that the universe unfolded in oscillations, existing again and again in alternating amplitudes of existence and nonexistence. Dominia had come to believe that, and not because Valentinian had told her so or Lazarus had proven it with many lifetimes' worth of foreknowledge. She had come to believe it because, with what was left of Cassandra relegated in this world to a shiny little stone around Gethsemane's neck, the hope that her miserable life would happen over again was all the hope Dominia managed.

She had to tell herself that this effort was worth something. This time wouldn't be like those last times that she couldn't remember, but that were implied by fairly convincing arguments for a cyclical timeline (or timesphere, perhaps). An infinity of failures, which demanded to know: What, precisely, had she failed? What were the incorrect variables in those iterations abandoned by Lazarus, the magician, and her (un)Holy Father? What was out there, out of her control, ready to get her—and what was within her control, only to serve as the means by which she might destroy herself? A year's worth of unanswered prayers and tahgmahrs and unceasing work had left the General more hardened than ever before, and more ready for anything to go wrong.

"Anything" happened sooner than she'd hoped, but it made her glad for their plane's speed: they were practically within extraction zone by the time the jets came into screaming distance. Through a window clarified by reduced cabin light, she caught the abrupt appearance of a trio of monstrous hypersonic planes that tore through the sound barrier at Mach 12, or about 2,747 kilometers per hour faster than most missiles developed by humanity early in the Hierophant's rise to power—a difference of about 1,707 miles per hour to those stubborn rural folk of the Front. Any chance they had of completing their journey to the landing pad in Tangiers dropped to zero as soon as those enemy aircrafts were on Farhad's radar screen. It was already too late to avoid projectiles that were comparably faster than the hyper-fast jets, and surely informed by exact knowledge of their location—probably from the Lamb, as much as any battle fought with his help in her once-lived life. Teddy, well hypnotized by his two sedatives, had begun dozing off around the time of the first impact. He awoke with a squeal while Farhad's tinny voice clicked over the cabin speakers.

"Mahdi, we are being targeted."

"No kidding," was her response, as Theodore cried, "But I'm *on* here, you idiots!"

"They know." Head low, Dominia ducked from her seat to the cockpit.

"So why are they shooting at us, then?"

"Because they're trying to shoot us out of the sky, of course." She smirked, feeling a responsibility to find humor in the situation while avoiding the obvious fact that the Hierophant didn't care if Theodore lived or died. As she reached the door, it slid open to leave Dominia face-to-face with Gethsemane.

"There are more missiles coming, and the fighters will wheel back around, but it will take some time. We have countermeasures available at our disposal, General."

"Not enough countermeasures to handle all they're going to throw at us," Farhad said without so much as blinking, lest the precious microseconds mean the difference between another direct impact and a near miss. "Already, that one strike— We are looking at very serious damage and will not be able to fly much farther."

"I thought you couldn't speak English," said Theodore sourly from behind Dominia's shoulder, rendered brave enough by the drug to leave his seat in the chaos of an emerging dogfight—the exact time he ought to have stayed sitting.

"As we tried to tell you the first time, he just doesn't want to speak it with you. Not that anyone does." Dominia turned her attention back to Gethsemane. "All right, listen. We're going to—"

"General." Gethsemane's expression was tight as another screaming missile rocked the plane. An alarm had begun to go off, and the martyr grit her teeth while her closest adviser took her hand. "We must evacuate reality early."

"This is why I told you that you shouldn't have come."

The naiad offered a thin smile. "Then I would have lost my life in some Jerusalem bombing while you were out of town. This is how misfortune likes to play its cruelest games. I'd rather risk staying in the Ergosphere forever than failing you, General."

"It's dangerous for you," Dominia repeated.

"I do think I come out a little less myself, and replaced by nothing…but I do not think anyone—even you—can safely do this forever." The General could already smell her Father's cologne, the pressure of his presence creeping through the plane as the human gently said, "I see in your eyes you agree. Well: you are very strong. Frighteningly strong! And you have only one woman to be. I am two women; that makes me as strong as you." A playful edge danced along the woman's tired smile. "Perhaps stronger, if I could but dream as much."

No kidding. Certainly stronger. Gethsemane made a selfless decision with such knee-jerk ease that it was almost implicit she had thought of it before the moment. Dominia always struggled with such things, herself. She'd lost Miki and Kahlil within fifteen minutes; she was pained at the thought of losing another friend, if not to death, then to a kind of subsumption of the soul. Was that the true nature of madness? A frightening notion.

But would the General rather lose her friend, or see her entire party blown to smithereens? To parachute to their arrests? A thousand paintings whose violence was illustrated to an outlandish, sometimes lurid degree flickered through her memory like a series of martyr trading cards. She could not speak. There was never any good in speaking of the tortures, the war crimes, her Father had committed. Never any good in inspiring fear. Hope was the way, and the generous sacrifice of her human friend was the source of a sliver of optimism. She squeezed Gethsemane's hand, then released it. "We have to go soon, before the electronics go down, or before the battery blows and we lose the BLP."

"A blip," said Theodore, pale, now, no matter how many pills he'd taken. He glanced up to the lights as he repeated the common nickname of the Blue Light Projector, then asked, "This jet is equipped with a blip? What do we need that for? Dominia? You know blue light will *kill* us, don't you? That much blue light? That's why it was *invented*, you understand, it's the same technology as those damn fences, those thresholds!"

Yes, she understood why the idea made him upset. The BLP was a device humans commonly installed in all sorts of solar-powered vehicles, personal and public. In fact, the Light Rail was only lacking a BLP in every car because its construction had been partially sponsored by the DIOX corporation, which Dominia now understood to be controlled by the Hierophant. The use of Blue Light Projectors was simple, though highly illegal in the United Front and other martyr-controlled territories if not in the form of a DIOX-approved threshold kit. Otherwise, if one found oneself trapped in one's home with a martyr as one's uninvited guest, and negotiations (for lack of a better word) took a southern turn, one could flip a switch to flood the room with sunlight-approximating beams. These, hyper-concentrated, were far more brutal than actual rays. BLP units vomited a room so full of light that even humans could only bear exposure for a few seconds without welder's goggles. Though true that, in the case of a unit such as the one on the plane, extended use would drain the associated battery to nothing with alarming efficiency, even a twenty-second exposure would blind and wound a martyr long enough for a human to find means of escape.

And, in the case of the unit on the plane, it was only intended for a single use before requiring recharge. The threshold technology employed on the E4 was not intended as a defense against martyrs but as the means by which the aircraft could raise its electromagnetic frequency and pierce into the Ergosphere. Like Akachi's teleporter, the whole plane was an artificial solar plexus in that the entire craft was able to exit physical spacetime. But it had to be tied to a future/present destination point by way of entry at any one of several carefully decided past/present positions in space-time, calculated to a narrow window of extraction space for any given potential exit. In ideal settings, the E4 had made it to the landing pad but once. The other three wasted planes now qualified as cosmic junk sitting where they'd crashed in the Ergosphere, because nobody could figure how to get them out. At the start of the experimental project, she'd been presented with four inter-dimensional jets, and three had predictable failures of timing for one reason or another, usually due to imprecision of location. Planes weren't sentient, so they couldn't look up at the "black sun," aka Earth at the edge of time; the BLP and all other electromagnetic devices of the crashed jets were rendered nonfunctional; and most people were uncomfortable about spending a lot of time in the Void, so very little follow-up had been engaged, and there was precious time to ruminate on failure, anyway. Better to focus on the one success and see if it could repeat itself in the field—that had been the aim. The reality was success had no chance of repeating itself, and they would have to crash the plane into the Ergosphere's interpretation of the Atlantic Ocean.

Good thing those pills she'd given Theodore were laced with Lazarus's blood, containing the real sacred protein. The proudly worn vial of old Lazarene blood she'd obtained from Akachi had successfully traveled in and out of the Ergosphere a great many times along with her, but that didn't mean it would have an effect on a soul who hadn't imbibed it on Earth if they were trapped in a device such as an E4 during a malfunction. Who knew how hard it would be to get a non-Lazarene out of that place, assuming they arrived at all?

But, maybe it was for the best that such a spirit stay there. After all, the purpose of the old mystic's blood seemed to be escape. That was just how fucked up her Father's world was, Dominia supposed, how corrupt and base—a granule of blood like those in the pills could save a person eternally, even when taken in ignorance.

"Try not to freak out too much, Teddy," urged the General, grabbing him by the arm like a teacher grabbing an unruly pupil. "Gethsemane, Farhad? Ready?"

"We have to be," the pilot observed as their pursuers again howled past. "Activating the BLP, Mahdi."

Amid the sirens of enemy jets and the pleas of Governor Theodore, Farhad filled the cabin with mock sunlight, and the real world dissolved into a figment of imagination.

The amount of time required for Theodore to notice he was not burning to death, and the related amount of time required for him to stop screaming was—well, impressive. While inky black bloomed about the smoking, rattling, beeping E4, the electronics systems failed, and Dominia gave a sigh of relief as all alarms stopped along with the BLP. That same darkness of the Void plunged unnervingly into the cabin of the ship, smiting all vision and leaving the crashed object as nonexistent as the rest of the landscape in the Ergosphere's bleak nighttime presentation. This was why she'd hoped to skip over it: this, and Teddy's ceaseless screaming, now turning into weeping even as Farhad groaned, "Please, Mahdi, will you turn on a light!"

"Just wanted to see if he'd stop screaming, first." With a chuckle, Dominia lowered her head and did the one interesting thing she'd learned over the last year—she spoke the True Word for "light."

If a person asked her in the waking world what that True Word was, she couldn't have told them. Not because she didn't want to but because it was physically impossible. As she had learned before the Lady's union with Her new avatar, True Words in the Void stood beyond language. Rather, they *were* the objects they represented. The magician had once impressed her with his parlor tricks of making fire out of thin air, and when new to this place, she'd regarded his talents with a childlike glee. Now, she understood what he'd done, and understood why what he did was purer than her Father's manipulation of thoughtforms from the dark atmosphere. Valentinian, that saint who was once a dog, was not creating or manifesting anything. He was speaking True Words, which bore so little resemblance to terrestrial speech that, when they were spoken, the mouth did not move. The object but appeared, as light blazed forth across the cabin's interior in a pure golden halo that emanated from the speaker. True Words could not be communicated. They needed be divined, as the Lady had taught Dominia in a series of unrecallable dreams over the previous summer.

"No wonder I understand every word spoken, and all written words," she'd once said to the Lady, after the weight of the ceremony had been given time to settle upon her. The oh-so-generous goddess found regular occasion to greet Dominia in Her chambers for reasons other than bad news, and the General used these meetings for spiritual guidance. Well she understood the magician's pain. Without the Lady, Dominia would have had no one with whom to discuss these matters. Gethsemane had no practical experience, and Farhad, though imbued with an incredibly deep well of religious knowledge, was exclusively devoted to the Islamic faith. Despite her spiteful, PR-related conversion to the Catholic variation over the previous summer, Dominia was interested not in faith but in truth. She knew the Lady would understand her when she said, "The only real words there are the highest ones. Everything else is just ideas."

The entity, kneeling upon a satin pillow across from her, seemed stiller than one of those unfortunate Cairo statues. Nonetheless, Her words rang clear, always seeming to use Dominia's brain stem as Her antenna. *There is no name for the language of the Ergosphere, though many have heard it and tried to put a name to it; but in naming it, it is no longer itself. A named thing is not a wholly true thing. When a thing has a name, it is objectified. It is drawn down into the Earth and into a mere symbol in the mind. That is why, when the truest, highest words are spoken, they will create the object that they evoke, because they* are *the object. Do you understand? All other words, all human words, are metaphors. The words We speak are the only real ones.*

Her lips parted, Dominia shifted upon the tatami mats of the avatar's room. She thought of the magician, making fire and playing cards and electricity from thin air. "Will you teach me these words?"

You will learn a few in your life. We will teach them to you in dreams. Only in dreams. In waking, We will take them from you. The True Words are not for the pleasure of the living but for those who have burst from the Void into the physical Earth. Were we to speak these words, it would mean the end of reality. Only during such times of flux as on the eve of Our wedding can these words be spoken safely, to any effect. Only during such times can they even be remembered upon Earth.

Dominia was so used to people refusing to give information that she was not even surprised. "Don't you think it will come in handy for me?" she bothered to ask, and the deity's avatar smiled.

They will serve you greater purpose after death than before, child; and after death, it will be the only tongue you speak.

Well, the General had always been the type of kid who wanted to grow up fast. To the Lady's credit, She kept Her promise, and Dominia had a series of weird dreams beneath the peak of the Dog Star and the festivals venerating it. Interestingly, such festivals were common amid the Red Market women and the martyrs back home. Everybody could agree on a few things: to her Father's people, bright Sirius and its nearby companion, Procyon A—the star that hosted the promised land of martyrs, the not-yet-formed planet Acetia—was a symbol of the distant future from which the Hierophant hailed to bring them the protein's good news. To the Red Market, the Dog Star was the symbol of about forty esoteric things that Dominia hadn't fully grasped, mostly because she didn't care. She was more concerned (as had been Akachi before her) with building up her armaments, and rebuilding a body that had suffered a great deal of malnutrition, physical trauma, and battle without rest. Her vision, tunneled by hatred, saw only those moves that would best organize her and her people against her Father.

She was so devoted to her one task that she could not even remember the extent of the dreams that had taught her the Words—but, as the Lady said, that was also by design. Dominia remembered nothing of her dreams but awoke the next morning with the feeling of important information slipping from her grasp. At first proper sunlight, she would hurry into the Ergosphere, and discover to her astonishment that she now knew with a click the True Word for a basic concept like "light" or "pebble." How did she learn them? The aggravating part was she had no idea. Instead, she had the sense she'd always known them, and had forgotten them until the Lady had shifted something in her memory.

By a stretch, the most important word she had learned was the word for "reality," which allowed her to wink home from even the Void no matter where she looked or what the status of Earth's morbid silhouette. She could even take a friend or two home with her—maybe more, they hadn't tried. Such small abilities made the scientists' research in the Ergosphere's nighttime Void somewhat safer, and it had even inspired a few of them to pick up meditation and spiritual devotion to the Lady in hopes that they, also, might be able to divine the True Words and carry on such work without Dominia. More religious sorts might have found such material intent a profane thing, but the General approved of their habits wholeheartedly. The sacred Words were little more than another set of tools to her, and she swiftly trained herself to use them on entering the Ergosphere, where dream and reality were one in the same, and where the raw information of matter's hologram was present in the strange interference pattern legible only with the laser of consciousness.

But was the metaphor (the damned metaphor) a perfect one? Did the laser engaging the playback need to be identical to the laser doing the recording? What did that mean for her consciousness? What was the recording laser? It made the poor General's military head spin; she had spent three centuries religiously avoiding questions of spirituality, and now she'd gotten herself obsessed with holograms, and begun to wonder about the magician and his relationship to not just True Words but *the* Word. The old spiritual symbol of the Logos, for which, Gethsemane had once said, the Dog Star was one of many attached images.

What did any of this mean? The General was getting obsessed with the idea of perfect Words and holograms and blah-dee-blah, as René mocked when she drunkenly confessed this sort of thing to him. But, of course she was obsessed. Maybe some of it would help Cassandra return. Maybe she could divine Cassandra's highest name and speak it, and there she'd be—or somehow a computer could step in where the sacred and the psychedelic could not, to derive her wife's actual consciousness with a sad combination of algorithms and silicone. Maybe, maybe. All she could do anymore was say, "Maybe," even when her little brother's fear turned to wonder at the great blaze of light, and his eyes sought purchase in a place where there was none but the faces around and hints of the cabin implied on the edges of the glow.

Theodore, touching his own face and then releasing the other hand, which had clutched his sister's arm, calmed enough to speak. "What is this? Are we dead?"

"Maybe," she admitted. The first time she had come to this place, after all, she'd stepped into the certain death of the sun. It was a kind of death, she supposed. She glanced down at herself with her single, unpatched eye, at the leather jacket she had not worn in real life since well before the tragedy of Kabul. "I mean, who's to tell the difference between 'dead' and 'alive'? We already died once, after all. Technically."

"But what's happened?" pressed the Governor. "We were about to be shot down just now—right? And then the BLP, and now...why do you look—like you used to? Even your hair, it's so long again! I feel strange." His hand fluttered against his forehead while his seeking eyes darted between Gethsemane and Farhad. The pilot appeared much himself, albeit older, which bolstered Dominia's sense that perhaps things might work out all right. Even Teddy, now that she focused through the Void-muted glow, seemed dressed and groomed beyond his current station.

But—Gethsemane. They had experimented once with taking her into the Ergopshere, and Dominia had halted the experiment soon after it began to whisk her friend right back out. Now, "right back out" meant "back out into the nighttime waters of the Atlantic Ocean," but it sounded almost preferable to standing there and watching her skip like a corrupted video between shards of the earthly woman she was, few sparkling features of the nymph, and—recalling the *tulpa* as much as her wife—expressions and mannerisms resembling those of Cassandra. That was perhaps due to the diamond around Gethsemane's neck, still hanging even in this space where the human's dress had changed and was sometimes a priestess's garb—sometimes nude or protected by wooden armor, as had been the nymph. Elements of Dominia's dead wife were the only visual constants. A lynchpin, or a yoke. Hard to say.

"There's nothing to be alarmed about," the General assured Teddy, and herself, and Gethsemane. Nonetheless, her brother's eyes remained wide with obvious fear. "We've got to get to shore now. Just a little walking to do."

"Walking?" Teddy's eyes boggled, and Dominia nodded.

"The plane's out of commission. They all lose power once they hit the Ergosphere without making it to their landing pad. Electromagnetic devices don't work here. Not by any means we've been able to find, anyway—so we're going to have to cross on foot. But don't worry! I mean, really, don't worry. It's bad for your health here. And for mine."

Of course, such a thing was hard for even Dominia to remember during the next instant, when that spectral face appeared in the window of the cockpit's door.

III

A Sailor Out of Time

What a funny thing, fear! A familiar face when we least expect it is worse to us than a stranger's, as was the face of former *Jun'yō* first mate, Tenchi Ichigawa, whose smiling features appeared half illuminated by the circumference of Domina's glow. At the scream of everybody in the cabin, the sailor screamed, too, and dropped from the window with an unnerving lack of thud upon the Void's un-ground below. Delay induced by the shock sweeping aside, the General dashed to the door, threw it open, and leapt down beside the groaning man before the stairs could lower.

"Tenchi! What are you doing here? *How* are you here?"

They'd discussed this many times over the last year. Tenchi was the reason his cousin knew as much as he did about Lazarus; why wasn't the sailor a confirmed Lazarene? "I don't understand it all enough, yet," he would say. Or: "*Eto*...I'm afraid it will change me, I guess." But here he was, rubbing his head as he sat uneasily up on the implied ground, saying, "Well...I can't explain that."

"Can't, or won't? Have you lied to me, Tenchi?"

"I wouldn't!" Pulled to his feet as the other passengers of the plane leaned out into the glow, the rounder Ichigawa smoothed his sailing uniform and said, "I had to—to take the blood, and to come here, to this spot." After a glance of reluctance back to the watching faces, he fessed up to Dominia: "The magician told me to."

The magician! Valentinian? That former dog of a deadbeat friend? "You saw him?"

Tenchi nodded. "He brought me here. He met me when I came into the Ergosphere and told me I had to help fix your boat."

"This isn't a boat," Farhad told him. "It's an experimental plane."

"Really? I think she looks kind of like a submarine..."

"Forget all that." Hands on his shoulders, Dominia attempted to contain Tenchi's interest because anything less could be downright dangerous. "When did you come into the Ergosphere, Tenchi?"

An anxious expression twisting his mouth, Tenchi tried to glance away at Farhad until Dominia tightened her grip. "I'm not supposed to say yet… He said it will distract you. You'll try to do something— Well. I'm just supposed to fix the ship."

"Plane," Farhad corrected again, stepping down, then helping Gethsemane do the same. The sailor looked at him, aggrieved.

"The magician told *me* she's a ship. Maybe she's both. But anyway, I'm supposed to take care of her."

"How do you expect to take care of a plane you think is a ship?" The pilot stepped aside to let the first mate climb aboard, and all the while, the Governor worried the cuff links of his posh suit jacket the way his lip worried against his teeth.

Teddy asked, "Can the ship get us home once you've fixed it?"

Ichigawa, followed by Dominia, stooped to investigate the instrument panel of the cockpit. "I guess so… To be honest, I'm not sure what the magician expects me to do."

"Had you ever met him before?" the General asked while the sailor settled into Farhad's vacant seat. As Tenchi bent forward to better read the labels of the panel, the martyr rested her hand a few centimeters above it to illuminate the text. "In real life, before the Ergosphere?"

"*Iie*…he met me here, as soon as I came. I followed your—" The little man winced before continuing with a sigh. "I just did what I was supposed to do, to come here. When Earth disappeared, there he was with his red waistcoat."

That was Valentinian, all right. "But what about your cousin? What about the airport, Tenchi? Didn't you catch a flight like we discussed?"

"Well…I really think you should talk to the magician."

Before she could press him further, Farhad called from outside the craft, "There is no damage to the hull, Mahdi. I cannot see well, but I've touched where the damage should be—nothing." The plane's surface reverberated with the knock of his fist. "Hear? Solid."

"That's because it's the soul of the plane," she answered, which made Tenchi look up in some surprise.

"Soul…"

"Didn't the magician explain anything about this place to you?" she asked him, which elicited the shocking reply, "Oh, of course! We've had three whole days to talk."

This wasn't her Tenchi. Not the Tenchi at the dim sum restaurant. This was the Tenchi of the future. Three days in the Ergosphere was closer to three weeks on Earth. Something happened between the restaurant and the sailor's entry into that other space: something that had caused him to become a Lazarene, brave the Void, and meet the martyr saint of death.

Dominia didn't like that one single bit. But she had to pretend she hadn't copped to anything as the cheerful little man clarified, "It was just strange, that's all. I wasn't sure what he expected of me… I can do some basic mechanical things, but to fix a whole ship by myself? In a place like this? But he just kept telling me, 'Don't worry, you'll get it when the time comes! You've got a vivid imagination. That's all you need to speak to the soul of a ship.'"

Hands sliding over the instrument panel, Tenchi said, "I still don't understand what he meant. But if this is the ship's soul…why won't she work?"

"We can't figure it out. This is the fourth craft we've lost to the Ergosphere. Have you seen one of these before?"

He shook his head. "I never got to see the things we engineered…not my department. But it bothers me! Why make a plane, a jet, that looks like a submarine?"

"Well, we did technically crash into the Atlantic Ocean, or come close to it before entering the Void. And, as the Lady says, Her darkness and Her waters are all one in the same." Dominia watched nervous Teddy ease down the stairs and gingerly lower the toe of his shoe to the dark ground. "Not that it matters here. Anyway, the E4 is built like that for reasons of stealth and speed; it's like its own entry point teleporter, and designed to whip to its end point."

"So it's *meant* to travel into this place."

"Not really…more to pass through it, like a tunnel. The ones that enter this place stay here, because we can't figure out how to get them out. An electromagnetic failure." She frowned, arms folding, and thought of her own electromagnetic field, which was not absent, but so barely visible in the glow from her speech that one couldn't possibly see it unless one looked for it. "Valentinian and Lazarus taught me that souls in this place *are* electromagnetic energies, essentially… Maybe that's why the craft doesn't have the ability to function. Because it has no consciousness, therefore, it has no soul."

"What? No consciousness?" The sailor almost laughed at her, but he caught himself and said, "You Westerners! I always forget…what a stagnant world you inhabit."

Everybody knew more about spirituality than she did—even Tenchi! As he went on to say, "Shinto reveals that everything has consciousness. I guess it's not fair to say Easterners only believe that…after all, that's what alchemy is, right? Crazy old guys talking to the spirits of molten metals. But that's not so crazy. We call them 'kami' in Japan, these spirits, these energies…"

"Thoughtforms," Dominia almost said; but as she opened her mouth, the body of the craft rumbled and groaned, then fell silent once again. The sailor laughed in surprise. "See? She's a living thing like any other spirit in this world…all made by the same deity. Maybe that's why I've been so afraid to come here! I knew I wouldn't be able to see the world the same way. Not ever again."

After reflecting on the notion that the magician would not have set her friend to a task that might endanger her life, the General nonetheless felt obliged to warn the human of the perils of thoughtforms. "Sometimes, imagining things in this place can be dangerous."

"That's only if the thing you're imagining is bad! Or if you don't know what you're imagining. The magician told me that much…but he doesn't have to tell me that the souls of ships are always good." The craft gave another rumble, and to Dominia's surprise, the needle of some dial twitched to life. Tenchi, beaming brighter than the martyr's light, said, "This must be how he wants me to fix the ship! By paying attention to her. Of course, it's so simple… How could she work if nobody knows she's living?"

Interesting question. What was the sound of one hand clapping? If a tree fell in the forest without somebody to hear it, *did* it make a sound? She got those old Zen koans now. Miki would be proud. "I guess that's a good point… Still, I don't understand."

"The ship needs electricity to function on Earth, but here, things function by thought, so I guess…call it a thought-powered ship?"

"Plane," said Farhad, leaning into the doorway. "I do not wish to alarm or interrupt you, Mahdi."

"Carry on."

"There are lights, Mahdi."

"Maybe it's an *airship*," Tenchi muttered, while Dominia patted his shoulder and continued, to Farhad, "What do you mean, lights?"

"Blue torches," the pilot said, to the drop of the General's stomach.

"Those aren't for us." Leaning past Farhad, she glanced out of the E4 and tried to maintain a neutral expression for the path of torches unfurling, as ever, north according to the ethereal guide of her just-hinted compass. She had no desire to follow them, and tried to turn back to Tenchi.

Undaunted, the pilot went on—his tone cautious and respectful, but all the more aggravating for it. "If I may say, Mahdi—" She whirled on him with a dark look that squeezed out of the human man a nervous laugh, even in a place where there was no such thing as death.

"It is just—how do I say—the night in this place is very long, Mahdi, and—"

"And we will make our own fire to rest, away from these. *Real* fire."

"Ah, but it is just that—perhaps these are gifts from Allah, yes? In place for weary travelers…"

After a helpless assessment of Dominia's stony expression, Farhad turned toward Gethsemane, whose glittering features in this place apparently resembled Cassandra's more than ever when she wanted something. (Purposeful? Hard to say.) These sweet eyes reflected from the diamond said with Gethsemane's voice, "We are all very tired, I think, General. Do you know these lights? Know them to be foul? Perhaps they are of the magician."

This, for whatever reason, lit the hot fire of nauseous offense in Dominia's cheeks and gut, and she snapped despite herself. "The magician's lights are real fire. Fire spoken with words like mine. Not lights like...these."

"Whose lights are these, Mahdi," tried Farhad, delicately. The General cursed herself for having hidden this issue from her friends rather than warning them ahead of time.

For one long year, she had been training select men and women in the use of the Ergosphere, and at no point in time had she either revealed or admitted any knowledge of the fairy fire torches that were said to appear in her presence during the nighttime Void-state. All the more reason she preferred the daytime manifestation. Then her Father was only likely to appear when she was alone. In this place, he liked to lure her to him. Her method of avoiding the lure had been a refusal to acknowledge its existence, but that clearly wouldn't work now. Not with all her friends (and Teddy) right here. Gethsemane, who had given up encouraging Dominia to share her worries, watched her now. The martyr tried to indicate with her eye that they were better off not discussing this in front of Theodore, but, of course, all parties only waited for her to speak. Irritated, she cleared her throat and stepped down past Farhad to make a grab for her brother. When Teddy ducked out of her grip, she admitted in a half mutter, "The lights are my— Father's."

"What!" The Governor all but shrieked the word before he was off at a sprint in the direction of the torches, giving Dominia only a second to turn her accusatory look on the humans and tell Tenchi, "Stay here and fix the plane," before she needed bolt after pathetic Theodore.

"Father," he cried, "Father! Oh, *Daddy*"—she could have vomited and actually stumbled a step, giving him slightly more headway and further annoying her—"you've come for me! Even in this place, you came for me, O Heavenly Father—"

"He didn't send those torches for you, you twerp." Dominia's limbs pumped at double time, but the General was amazed to find how fast Theodore was in this place. Perhaps out of terror. "He wants you to follow the torches, but not so he can save you."

In the distance, she could see it. Now more than a door and a disembodied office, her Father's thoughtform study resembled a box. A whole room, as if torn out of a building. The exterior, artfully covered in floral wallpaper, still appeared to float in space. But for that path cleaved through the thick darkness by those wretched torches, it would appear unnervingly unanchored. "Why else would he send them if not to *save* me?" On shrieking this, Theodore slowed sufficiently for the General to snatch the back of his rumpled coat.

"So he can attract *me* here," she told her brother, giving him an irritated mother-cat shake.

"It's all about you, isn't it?" he began—but with his next breath to speak, his nose wrinkled, and his words succumbed to a cough. "What is that *stench*?"

It had trickled into her nose in like time and zipped her back through her journey across the world, and earlier. To the military, to parties as a teenager, to the cloying scent of her human father's clothing. Most of all, it brought her to this place, the Ergosphere. To her Father's study and its most regular unwelcome guest, the prospect of whom made Dominia release Theodore's collar and sprint for that door, herself.

"Tobacco smoke."

As she drew closer, the air grew denser—not just with the scent of cigarettes but the sound of music, wholly unfamiliar and not her Father's classical preference. Perhaps that was why this night, for the first time, she entered the study without knocking and without thought for the fact that she had managed to stay away one year straight. Inside, she found beside the pool table not just her Father but also that bastard, chain-smoking magician, Valentinian.

"Hell," he said in time with the Hierophant, a second before he was pinned to the bookshelves by his jacket's lapels while capping on the belated, "O!"

"Give me a reason I shouldn't shatter your imaginary skull with my fist and send you back in time so far that you're stuck as a dog again."

"Missed you, too, buddy," wheezed Valentinian, almost laughing, while the Hierophant smiled with those inappropriately blithesome fuligin eyes.

"There is my little tiger, at last! A bit late for most of the holidays, but we still have New Year's. I knew if I kept extending invitations, you would eventually come."

"Where have you been?" Dominia continued, oblivious, to the magician. "I gave up Cassandra for you, and now I find you here? With him? And dragging Tenchi into this?"

"Strictly speaking, you *delayed* Cassandra for me." Valentinian continued speaking in a casual tone, either unwilling or unable to disappear with the General's fists clutching the cherry velvet of a jacket she slowly recognized to be new. "We're just taking the long way. The right way."

Dominia jerked her head toward His Holiness. "How am I supposed to trust you, finding you with him?"

Beyond her shoulder, Theodore stood in the doorway and cried with cartoonish relief, "Father!"

"Tut, tut, Theodore." The Hierophant's guileless expression brimmed with self-aware amusement. "I am disappointed in you, lad."

Dominia turned to regard both her Family members, specifically Theodore, and the way his face fell as he asked, "Disappointed in me?"

The Hierophant offered precious more gesture than a solemn shake of his head. "You and all my other children have been warned, time and again, of the horrors wrought by the consumption of the blood of Lazarus. No martyr who has tasted it may be saved."

"But—"

"You have committed the one unforgivable sin, my boy. I'm afraid you are damned for eternity."

Horror filled Theodore's face, and his slightly aged hands clasped one another before tightening like a noose around his embroidered silk collar. "What? What do you mean? Surely you can't be serious."

"I'm afraid I am most serious," said the Hierophant, offering an earnest lift of his brows toward the hairline that, in this place, so resembled Cicero's they might have passed for twins. The cover story of the holy man from Acetia who adopted the appearance of the first human he martyred was the only thing that prevented the General's rampant speculation, because with all the things she'd been exposed to since her flight from the city of San Valentino, she was more open to the idea of her Father's extraterrestrial heritage. As to whether Valentinian's story that he was, in the first iteration of the universe, one of the original discoverers of the sacred protein...Dominia still wasn't sure it passed the sniff test, and somehow that made her Father's story seem dubious, too. Never mind that nobody had explained to her just how it was the fictional saint had gotten himself stuck as a dog, or any animal. It was all so baffling, even after a year in which to absorb it.

Imagine trying to explain all of that to Teddy in any way he'd believe or understand! Now she understood why they veiled so much knowledge from her. She also saw why it was so easy for her Father to manipulate two whole continents of people. His power meant it wasn't some small deal to Theodore when the Holy Father sincerely said, "There is no saving you now. Your soul shall be damned to hell."

The UF Governor took a step forward, his wide eyes watering. "No! No, that can't be."

Dominia said, "He's full of shit," but Theodore didn't seem poised to believe her.

Valentinian told her with an aggravated wave of his hand, "You want proof you can trust me? Let me go, and I can save him."

"Save him from what?" the General asked, but he waved again. She found the change when she followed his hand: the shimmering, wobbling panic that overcame poor Theodore's form. It was as though the ground had quite literally dropped from beneath his feet. He had become a one-man earthquake for as much as he trembled, and as Farhad arrived on the scene along with Gethsemane, it was in time to see the Governor, his mouth a superposition of four dozen different pleas, beginning to disappear.

As the Hierophant continued droning to Dominia (or himself), he leaned upon his pool cue like a cane. "The incredible thing about a damned soul"—his eyes followed Valentinian's dash to Theodore—"is that one must ask oneself whether the person in question could be said to have ever existed once their spiritual substrate is diminished back to its quintessence. When unfired clay is remolded, what happens to the old figure? Does it still exist within the new object, the cup or the bowl?"

"I exist," insisted Theodore at high pitch while the magician grabbed what seemed to be only one of (or part of) a series of shifting fragments that came together to form an impression of a man called Teddy. If Gethsemane was a collage of three women, Governor Theodore was a single man shattered into a cubist portrait.

"Yeah, buddy!" As he would a child waking from a tahgmahr, Valentinian soothed the victim of the Hierophant's mind games. "You exist! Just pull yourself together and keep existing. You don't need his permission to exist."

"Strictly speaking, as I created him in this martyred form—"

Too annoyed with her Father's lectures to suffer another word, Dominia snatched the pool cue from his hand and shattered it over the edge of the table. The Hierophant made a hennish noise of displeasure while the magician continued talking Theodore back to sustainable shape.

"Is that any way to treat your Father after not calling for a year?"

The General's lip curled. "I'd do worse if I could do it in confidence that your whole study wouldn't disappear with you and leave us floating in the night." Now centimeters from his face, she considered the splintered stake of a cue that she'd unconsciously waved under his nose. Had she developed a temper problem? Her Father's pale eyebrows lifted, along with the smirking corner of his lips, as if to ask her what she thought.

Meanwhile, Theodore continued to miserably whine above the tearing vacuum sound of his own soul's struggle to maintain its integrity. "How can I be sure that I exist?"

"I'm talking to you. I—care that you exist." This, from Valentinian, was not convincing. Braced, the magician reached into the holographic form of the Governor as though to hold him in place. "Come on, look, I can touch you. We're in this together."

"That doesn't mean anything," argued Theodore, always poised to shoot down comfort in a time of distress. "You might not exist either, for all I know."

The magician rolled his eyes toward Dominia. "Trust me, pal, things would be a lot easier for me if I didn't. I'd be the first to tell you if I didn't exist. You, though! You're clearly existent. Come on, Teddy, stick with me."

"How do you know my name?"

"Oh, so it's 'your' name? Who's 'you' if you don't exist? Who's Teddy? Cogito, ergo sum, brother!"

"I—don't—" Blinking eyes that came together into but one pair, his body solidifying again, Theodore jerked out of the grip of the magician and said, "Don't condescend to me, please! I'm not a *child*. I know who I am but I—I can't really be *damned*, can I? How can I? I didn't do anything."

"You're not damned," began the magician. As the Hierophant opened his mouth to interrupt, Dominia pushed the cue into his chin until he shut it again. "Nobody's damned, for Christ's sake…you religious types, I swear. You're too gullible, and gullibility is terrible for the soul! Souls need assurance. Confidence! They need substance." Shaking his head, Valentinian removed his pocket watch and handed it to the more-or-less singular Theodore. "Take this."

"What good is a watch going to do when I'm eternally lost?" That said, no matter how miserable he was, Theodore was never too miserable to accept something free. He allowed the magician to clip the watch to his belt loop and said once it was done, "Wait, is this thing broken?"

"It doesn't matter that it's broken. It's something from outside you. It'll keep you grounded, even if you're not thinking about it, because I couldn't have given you that if you didn't exist."

"But what's the point of existing if I'm to be damned?"

Even he had his limits. The magician looked behind Theodore, to the humans who watched in quiet astonishment. "Will somebody please tell me if *I* exist, or if you can hear me? Because he can't seem to. Good Lord… listen, buddy, Theo—the Hierophant's not in charge of deciding whether you're damned."

"He's not?"

"No! Of course not. Who'd let him be in charge? He bullied his way to the top worse than Dominia bullies you." While the General made a noise of displeasure, the magician went on. "You're in charge of your own affairs. Nobody can tell you that you're damned but you. Okay?"

"But he—"

"Is a guy with enough money to run an earthly organization that claims to serve God. But what evidence does he have, outside of money and a bunch of followers, that he's God's servant? Dominia and I and anybody with the blood of Lazarus can disappear, reappear, do all the things he does. You can now, too."

Although he was taken aback, her baby brother was still in the mood to argue. "Well, he has the Lamb, of course." Teddy looked over at Dominia and the Hierophant as though the magician were an idiot and they were in on it. "The miracle-working savior of the martyr race, one of the first two transformed by the blood of the Hierophant! The intercession between Man and God, Earth and heaven!"

"And where do you think the Lamb's miracles come from?" Valentinian gestured around. "Right here. You're standing in the same place where the Lamb does his supposedly holy work. Your Father just wants you to think you'll be damned if you come here because if his secret gets out, everybody will be fighting for a way in."

"What?" Theodore laughed, again looking over at his Family. "No, he—"

The Governor's laughing face fell when he saw Dominia's stone-serious expression and the Hierophant's almost-smiling one, the latter's just barely managing to contain its mirth and thus looking rather strained with or without the pool cue almost up his nose. "Father," tried Theodore, tone delicate as possible, "that's not true, is it?"

"It would be most inconvenient for me to have the whole society of martyrs running in and out of this Void," replied the Hierophant, his expression as innocent as the night he was martyred. "Strictly speaking, from the perspective of my earthly Church, you *are* damned, whether you accept it or not."

"Yeah." The scoffing magician bent his head to light another cigarette. "And from the perspective of objective reality, nobody cares."

"How can you say that? You heard him, didn't you?" Teddy began once more to fall apart until Gethsemane strode up from behind to cuff him in the back of the head. He was more himself after that than he had been once the (now laughing) magician had dealt with him, and seemed more willing to listen as the human waved her arm around.

"How can *you* say that, having seen this place? What is this space, this infinite potential, and what is your so-called Protomartyr beside it? The Hierophant of *what*? My goodness! Do you think anything of Earth matters here? It's the other way around."

Dominia, smiling to hear how Cassandra's emotional mannerisms seemed to infect the normally stoic Gethsemane, relaxed the cue beneath the Hierophant's nose and tucked the wooden shard into his breast pocket with a pat. "Here I was, upset to see you, when it turns out you're able to handle Teddy's deprogramming yourself."

"Is that so," said the Hierophant, behind the glittering of those just-crinkled black eyes. "Silly me."

"So." She whirled toward Valentinian, who loped to collect the abandoned half of the cue and, by his touch and an unheard word, restore it whole—or, more aptly, grow a second half for it, as the original other half still sat in the Hierophant's pocket. "What in the hell are you doing here, with him? Do you mean to tell me that all this time, if I had followed his lights, I would have found you here, too?"

"Not necessarily," said the magician, bending to line up his shot of the blazing three ball. "I do have a life."

"Yeah." The General laughed in a way so sharp that Valentinian scratched and swore to see the lightly bounced cue whirl off, nudge the three, and promptly pocket itself. "Doing what? Because it's not helping me."

"Excuse me," said meek Theodore, "I've had kind of a shock? Can we talk for a minute about—"

"Shut up, Teddy," demanded the General in time with the magician, who then went on to drop his voice and say, "But can *I* talk to *you* a little while?"

"About what? How disappointing you are? Or do you want to try to convince me to make another mistake?"

With a look somewhere between irritation and mild hurt, Valentinian extended the repaired cue to the Hierophant, who traded it for the shard in his pocket. As the magician rendered the cue a panther-headed walking stick—strictly ornamental, she suspected, as he was once a martyr, and wore the face of a late thirtysomething man despite his hyper-advanced age—he fell into stride for the western of the four doors Dominia had only now noticed. Too caught up in fury for Valentinian and concern for Theodore's condition to take in the many new details of the room. This concern became more of a regret as the whiny Governor, over the sound of a knock on the ornate door opposite the one opened by the magician, demanded, "Why won't anyone tell me anything? My Lamb, I've been kidnapped! Drugged and forced onto an *airplane*! An extra-dimensional airplane! Not only that, but a helicopter, one without doors or anything! And threatened! A man was shot in front of me! My soul, condemned unjustly! And now I'm being kept in ignorance!"

The Hierophant, who had hastened to respond to the knock, cracked open the door and made a sound of delight. He threw the portal wide as, in increasing pitch, Theodore carried on, "After all that I've been through, the least—the very *least* you 'people' could do for me is *tell me what is going on*!"

"We can't," answered the guest, who Dominia recognized with a surreal lurch to be herself, exactly as she was, studying her with a kind of calm that indicated she would be prepared for this moment when it next arrived. "We don't understand it all, ourselves."

Pleased as punch, as he himself would put it, the Hierophant looked between his duplicate daughters, then considered the cue in his hand. "Care to close out our dear friend's game, my girl?"

"With pleasure," said that other Dominia, that future Dominia, that impossible-to-explain shadow (or more real) self of herself, who watched the Hierophant turn back to study the best position to place the white ball. Theodore looked the way Dominia felt: confused and nauseous. Though no doubt he couldn't comprehend the awful feedback loop of making unbroken eye contact with oneself. That feeling of being a camera filming a screen of its own output until—

"Are you coming?" Valentinian's words snapped her back to the present and out of the single-eyed gaze of her inscrutable other self. The magician stood at the start of a new path that blazed with healthy red torches, and she hurried to his side.

"She wasn't kidding," muttered Dominia at last, shaking her head. "I don't understand this place."

"You understand it more than you're willing to admit. Hell of a lot of implications to the truth, after all."

The farther they walked from that strange centrifuge of the Hierophant's study, the less dizzy she felt. "What implications are those?"

"I don't know. Religious ones? You tell me."

The General crossed her arms and found she had to consciously slow her step lest she overtake the magician, who was inclined to stroll with leisure rather than hustle as far as possible from her Father. "I'm starting to sympathize with Theodore, scary as that is. I think everybody around here just gets off on denying information, and nobody wants to say what side they're on. I've spent the past year trying to convince myself you didn't use me to get a body."

"Look," said the magician with a belabored sigh, "I can see that you're pissed."

"You left me when I needed your *help*. We were captured!"

"And? You worked it out. Now you run an army."

"For somebody else."

"So? That's what you did before, for the Hierophant. Why's it stuck in your craw now?"

"Because—because I was *done* with this! I was done with the military life, remember? I was the Governess before—"

"Before Cassandra killed herself." The magician studied the General's hard face. "Before you decided her life was worth more than anything in yours."

"And what happened? Everybody made me believe it would be worth it to pick you over her. When will I see her? When will I—when will I be anything but alone?"

Her hand lifted to hide her straining mouth. As the magician said, "Oh, kiddo," she snapped, "Don't patronize me! This fucking place, it makes me so emotional."

"You're always emotional, Dominia. You just can't hide it here."

"Please shut up." Her fingers pinched a triangle over the bridge of her nose. "I could have used your help so many times this year. I've prayed for your help, every night, every morning, like some…stupid girl."

She laughed sharply as he said, "Yeah, I know, and I appreciate it."

"So, why didn't you *help* me!"

"Because you did a fine job helping yourself! You haven't needed my help at all. Look how far you've come in this past year! Do you know how much most people accomplish in the average twelve-month cycle? Practically nothing. If they're lucky, they get a raise at work, maybe they lose some weight, maybe they have a kid, maybe, maybe…but at most, the average person gets one or two big things. You, kiddo, are having a red-letter year. Obtaining an army, instantly doubling its size by working with the Red Market and establishing further ties with the Lady—you run a *city,* for Christ's sake, a whole state from the district of Tel Aviv and east for miles, with satellites in Tunisia, South America, and even a couple in the UF. You keep looking at these things as burdens, but ultimately you have more control than ever. You've got a bright, bright future, and you haven't needed me to ensure that. Yet."

"When I do, will you be there?"

"Haven't I always been since we met?"

The whines of the dog that had led the General to rescue Miki Soto from traitorous René, the defiant sapphire eyes of Basil while he stopped the train. Her eye teared up but she couldn't relent. "You disappeared during the nastiest battle I've had in a long time, and haven't been around since."

"But I'm here now. Not for too long—things to do—but I want to be here for you, morally."

"You just don't want me to be alone with the Hierophant," she said, sniffing. He laughed as he offered her a handkerchief.

"True."

"Thanks for that. I don't think I have it in me to listen to him drone about…Lamb, I don't know, dreams or history or something."

"He's a walking sleeping pill sometimes, for sure." Chuckling, the magician resumed guiding Dominia west. "Will you trust me, kiddo? I know you're pissed: you go to all that trouble of replacing my dog-body, and both the dog and my body vanish…but I promise it's for a good reason. There's a lot of catching up to do after all that time wasted on four legs."

"Can't you at least tell me why you've spent so much time away?"

"I can tell you that it concerns a lot of people you love, including your little sister." That gave Dominia's attention new vibrancy.

"What about Lavinia? Can you tell me what I want to know?"

"All things in their time. Theodore knows more about her...and you know what Theo doesn't." The magician met Dominia's eye in a way so significant it pushed her heart down to regions neglected, to thoughts abandoned and cut out from the rest of her being. Thankfully, she could not linger there, for in the distance she saw what she first took as a statue of black and silver. Its shape, however, she knew with all the mixed thrill and sorrow of an estranged child for their parent. There, in the distance, stood the Lamb with his silver ram's horns—so still that if she had not known him for his patience, she might have thought him frozen in time. His black cloak did not even stir at his breath.

At her wonder, Valentinian reminded her, "The Lamb is always here. Even when he's on Earth. Always in two places at once. You can't imagine the stress. He can't get very far from his body, but he was able to come far enough tonight to visit you."

Lazarus had discussed this with her once, she recalled. This was what made him so effective when it came to altering probability and sometimes delivering external information in the form of epiphanies. While his body was on Earth, here stood his soul, contemplative as a man staring into a pool of water, his horns reflecting a muted echo of Valentinian's red flames back at the torches that cast them. Surely it was simple for a spirit who saw so much to arrange things—or nudge things—on Earth, much as Valentinian created things from the Ergosphere with the ease of speech.

"The last time we met, it didn't go so well." The General was hesitant to approach her preferred parent when she realized Valentinian would proceed no farther down the path. Gently, the magician smiled.

"Maybe from your perspective. He doesn't care what happened before. There's something he needs to show you. You need to understand that what you're doing really is the right thing, and you need to— Well. Just see."

"And you? When will I see you again?"

"When you need me," said the magician, a twinkle in his eye. The General shook her head.

"You know"—she glanced at Lamb, then back up to the magician—"you people love to talk—

"In useless riddles," she told the open air where once the magician stood. Allegedly stood, at any rate. She could never be completely sure of anything anymore. The General turned back to find with a start that the Lamb now stood a hair's breadth from her face.

"Dominia." He extended his hand. "We haven't much time. Things here move quickly. My body was far from here when my spirit departed to come to you, and it still is, but I will be drawn back when it is forced to move."

There were so many things she wanted to ask. To say. She wanted to reject the hand he offered and argue with him about why he'd felt the need to alter probability so her Father lived on to ruin the world. Why he didn't alter it to stop the blast in Kabul that had killed all those human runners. If the Lamb could inspire feelings, why couldn't he inspire compassion in his followers—in the Hierophant—instead of this intense hatred? The hatred buzzed alive in her ear when at last, saying nothing, she took his hand and saw through the eyes of his body to experience what a head-splitting, soul-wrenching hurricane it was to be the Lamb—especially the Lamb standing at the head of a church, with all the people begging:

Please God

Please, please God

Please! Please please-please! Please God, please o God please God won't you HEAR me GOD why aren't you LISTENING to me God PLEASE LISTEN TO ME no not HIM ME BECAUSE PLEASE GOD I NEED YOU MORE THAN ANYONE IN THE WORLD RIGHT NOW, RIGHT NOW, RIGHT NOW, I BEG YOU, GOD.

The Lamb was not God. But the Hierophant had done a very good job of making martyrs think he might be God, or part of God. Just like the Hierophant, himself. The Lamb. The Son of God. Christ's message was *all* children were children of God, but who would listen to the message in a world like this? Who had listened to Christ, and who would listen now to this sad fellow with the ram's horns—implants that, meant to filter out some of the bombardment of radio-wave thoughts broadcast through the semi-constant low-frequency chatter of infinite minds praying all the time, only served as a funnel for those beggars front and center? In exchange for the loss of fidelity of those wild parishioners on the sidelines of the gathering, the implants amplified those early-to-arrive worshippers whose thoughts were ceaseless prayers for miracles without understanding a miracle's cost—without understanding that the smaller the probability of the thing they asked, the harder it was to enact. Not for the Lamb but for reality, which was always for the Lamb a strange word to describe the trembling of atoms in his fingers. No—this trembling of atoms. There were no fingers. There was the illusion of fingers reaching out to grasp the pulpit, and that illusion made the wood real by way of touch. Merciful touch! It was all the Lamb had to remember where he was.

Swaying behind Cicero, he reflected that it would mean nothing were he to collapse then and there. His brother would carry on using him. Strictly speaking, the Lamb always felt this fluish way because of excessive amounts of both dopamine and serotonin, and altered forms of dopamine and serotonin—created, of course, by the protein, which took an almost-sentient pleasure in warping his psychic abilities beyond the point of any recorded living martyr's. Not considered a problem, then, these spells of weakness, and they never prevented Cicero from hauling him country to country, plastered to his obsessive side as if the Lamb were a child given to wandering off in shopping malls. Mustn't let him wander off. Must parade him around in front of these desperate, empty, sad people who just wanted to meet God, to know their doings were permissible and that their lives were worth something. They just wanted to be terrible people while still deserving love.

Of course they deserved love, even these—but that was not the Lamb's responsibility. It never had been, but, oh! They had certainly striven to make it that way! Somehow they had convinced themselves that it was all God's fault—not anything in particular, mind, but "it," "everything," "anything." To a martyr, the Lamb was God on Earth: the winked and nodded Second Coming of Christ. They could not understand what the real Second Coming was meant to be, could not fathom that it was not a paltry and sorrowful man of flesh and pained spirit who watched the worshipers leap like dogs at Cicero's command: Sit! Stand! Kneel! Sit! Kneel! Kneel! Kneel! He would have told them to *crawl* if there were enough space between the pews, and they would have eaten it up. Cicero would have, too, for that was the kind of man he was. Mad with power and somehow bitter that he had not even more—just as he was still bitter that the General had torn out his eye. So bitter, in fact, that El Sacerdote had made it his mission to make everyone he met see what she had done. He wanted to make everyone uncomfortable with that big, black, neon-pupiled eye that roved at random, filling up Cicero's brain with useless Halcyon information as though it might see Dominia out there, praying, in the audience of his vulgar show.

"In the Churches of Europa," sneering Cicero admonished the crowd, "they are silent when I speak, and allow the Spirit of the Lord to wash over their hearts. Is it so important that your neighbors know how spiritual you are, you who bark and yelp your prayers in response to mine? Shut your mouths."

This was typical for a United Front church and typical for how Cicero dealt with it, for there were always so many new churches each time they swept through the nation that each needed to be taught El Sacerdote expected a certain degree of passivity among his parishioners. People of the Front were often much louder and more boisterous—happy—than their European counterparts, in part because the martyr population was smaller and they were not forced to live with the reality of their situation as much as the Europeans in capital cities who walked down a street and saw through the windows of any local butcher's shop the slaughter and dismemberment of humans. That was how the Hierophant had willed it. He had seen fit to render the human a base animal. To strip all dignity from the race rather than repressing the protein and covering up its existence as Elijah begged of Cicero that fateful night the Hierophant knocked on the brothers' door. He brought with him the false protein they themselves were so close to developing with Lazarus, whose name in those days was no more "Lazarus" than was Elijah's "Elijah" or Cicero's "Cicero." Elijah hadn't believed it a just gift—or just a gift—and was far more frightened to see a man, so towering, appear as his brother's perfect, though slightly aged, duplicate. But Cicero!

Elijah had never seen Cicero so excited as the moment he threw open the apartment door to find himself in the hall. The reformed geneticist turned scornful priest had been so keen to explore his Hierophant-given abilities that he hadn't anticipated the horrors of the martyr appetite—hadn't anticipated that appetite's effect on society, nor that all efforts to cultivate an artificial meat would fail.

Or maybe he had anticipated all that. The Lamb had. He had seen it clear as day and could still see it now, without even turning his head (though that was what it felt like, looking into various probabilities: turning a head that didn't exist). When his beloved brother held him down so the Hierophant could force the change upon him, Elijah awoke from his first death and found he could see all dimensions, everywhere, extending in all directions. Impossible directions. He could see with overwhelming terror that this was the future, this was the future, this was the future—and the future could only lead back to the past until all this could be undone like a knot tangled in the fabric of time. He had seen in that same instant what it was the martyrs truly devoured when they devoured the flesh and blood of man, because it was not a simple matter of the demands of misfolded proteins, or overexcited molecules that craved union with the sun. The protein part of the meat they ate, after all, was easy enough to solve with a bit of stuff from a petri dish! It worked for humans. Why didn't it work for martyrs? What was it that martyrs truly devoured? What was that awful truth in the background of hunts, meals, Noctisdomin Mass?

There was more to man than his flesh.

The Lamb could not explain it, but could show Dominia what he saw when, as usual, humans were put to weekly slaughter at the altar, dragged screaming and pleading in handcuffs and those very same electric collars devised to keep martyrs under control. The General saw through the Lamb's eyes the quivering overlap of an energy, hot and rosy. What was it? Fear? Sorrow? Souls? All of the above: emotion-despoiled electromagnetic energy. Those same fields that bonded the self to thoughtforms and guided the way in the Void—that was what martyrs truly devoured.

As always, the Lamb submitted his own throat to be cut by El Sacerdote, his blood added to the dish as the holiest and most significant portion of the sacrament. That blood was the reason for the Lamb's perpetual travel from church to church and back again, for that blood kept the martyrs who consumed it from requiring human flesh for another week. In this blood, Dominia could see and feel (for she was in the blood, part of the blood, a droplet now trickling out of the Lamb and into the great trough of herself) a substance that rendered martyrs submissive, that altered their brain and addicted them to the Church and burdened their bodies with guilt and shame and sorrow so they could not imagine anything beyond the material world. Heaven, to them, was but a shallow pair of pearly gates sitting on a bunch of stagnant clouds. God was a meaningless word, a faceless old man who kept them manacled like the blood of the false Lamb.

Was it that wretched stuff, not just hatred and shame, that kept thoughts of martyrs bound to flesh—focused on petty things like money and faith, rather than liberation into Truth? That was the nature of the Ergosphere, after all. Dominia had nearly forgotten! The Truth. The Truth, into which she dissolved as all the blood evaporated and there, in the distance, sat the Hierophant's study. Of course, the Truth seemed so impossible to verify she could not trust she existed within it even with perception of herself relative to another object! She shivered as she set out on her own dream-feet toward that distant box that glowed like the two trails of lights leading from it.

What had she and her men spent the last year trying to do but prove all this—yet how could even the greatest researcher prove anything when his instruments did not reliably enter the Void with him? What did technology mean when electric crafts on Earth were powered by imagination in this place? Measuring all this in any meaningful way seemed a process that would take years, if not centuries, from the material perspective. It was stunning the Hunters had cobbled together a formula to figure out how far in the future the exit teleporter needed to be activated for anything to go from point A to point B. Amazing they'd figured out how to make a mobile variant of that technology function even 25 percent of the time. In the time frame with which the Hunters had been working under Dominia, there had been no way to make meaningful progress in this strange new science of dreamtime travel. Asking for some sense of self so soon after seeing through the Lamb's eyes...that was just too much.

The door of the Hierophant's office stood before her, the automation of her feet through the dark leaving her to question whether she had existed until this moment. As if under remote control, her hand extended in a fist that rapped against the office's eastern door. Teddy could be heard shrieking,

"A man was shot in front of me! My soul, condemned unjustly! And now I'm being kept in ignorance!"

The Hierophant, who had hastened to respond to the knock, cracked open the door (which she now saw was carved with an elaborate rendering of the birth of Adonis, bursting forth from the arrow impaled in his incestuous myrrh-tree mother) and made a sound of delight. He threw the portal wide as, in increasing pitch, Theodore carried on, "After all that I've been through, the least—the very *least* you 'people' could do for me is *tell me what is going on*!"

"We can't," answered Dominia, studying her own self with that one eye wide as hers had been. "We don't understand it all, ourselves."

Pleased as punch, as he himself would put it, the Hierophant looked between his duplicate daughters, then considered the cue in his hand. "Care to close out our dear friend's game, my girl?"

"With pleasure," said the real Dominia, that present Dominia, that most-real-yet self of herself, who watched the Hierophant turn back to study the best position to place the white ball. Theodore looked the way the past shade of Dominia felt: confused and nauseous. Though no doubt he couldn't comprehend the fascinating feedback loop of making unbroken eye contact with oneself, the feeling of being the output of a camera that filmed its own output. But on what screen?

"Are you coming?" Valentinian's words snapped her back to her own present and out of the single-eyed gaze of that less whole other self who wheeled around, saw the magician at the start of a new path blazing with healthy red torches, and hurried to meet him. As the door (this the tragic hunting Death of Adonis) swung shut, its slam caused the Hierophant to miss his own stubborn fourteen ball. This left the white cue glowing with a shot made just for Dominia to take out Valentinian's missed three.

"Please, somebody"—Teddy sank into one of the seats by the fire—"is there any more of that drug you gave me before the flights?"

"Not here," said Dominia. The crimson ball, a spinning comet, cracked beneath her hand into the gold-striped nine and sent them into respective side and corner pockets. "But we can talk about it back in reality."

To her credit, the General realized she'd abandoned Tenchi in the darkness of the still-deactivated airship sometime before she'd closed out the game of pool. Her human friends assured her that the torches had left the craft in visible condition, therefore protecting the Ichigawa cousin from dissipation. But after her own experiences wandering the nighttime Void in the form of a tiger, she finished that game in three shots (one of which seemed physically impossible even as she watched it) and thrust the cue into the hand of her Father. Even he, to his credit, appeared impressed, and tucked the stick into the crook of his elbow for a golf clap.

"Brava, my girl. Another round? A glass of wine?"

"Wine," Theodore began, even as his sister dropped a hand upon his shoulder.

"We'll pass." She nodded in the direction of Gethsemane and Farhad. "They don't imbibe."

"Such a shame. Spiritual reasons?" As the humans stood, frigid and silent except for the occasional sound of Cassandra's laughter or humming as it jittered from the area of Gethsemane's heart, the Holy Father waggled the cue along with his brow. "Convert to the Holy Martyr Church, my children, and you may imbibe all you please."

"Leave them alone," said the General. "You've done enough damage to Teddy. Speaking of—are you ready to go?"

"But I have questions," the shrill little man said, trying (and failing) to twist out of his sister's grip. "Why would you do that to me?"

"Have to keep Dominia on her toes somehow, don't I?"

"What the— I'm a *person*. Father, I—" With a pained furrow of his brow, Teddy scowled between the two martyrs, then asked the Hierophant the same question Dominia had asked an infinite number of times over the course of not just her journey but her life. "Why did you martyr me at all if you're just going to try to disappear me? If you're not going to rescue me from *them*? Why did you martyr me just to put me through all this?"

"Oh, Theo. Your beloved Father wishes you no harm! No death can come here. I'm only playing a game with a few people who don't concern you, and sadly you're in the middle of it. Don't worry. Since you've made it this far, I'll swoop in and rescue you soon enough."

"Okay," said Dominia, repressing a gag, "we're leaving now."

"No! I want to know!" Now, Theodore was successful in jerking out of her grip, and he stormed up to the Hierophant in a terrific imitation of a more menacing man's rage. "Why are you letting this happen to me? Why bring me this far, then try to kill me?"

How the Hierophant's face changed in a moment like this, when it was time for the truth to come out! She'd seen that ice-cold expression at the same party that had sent her packing to Canada for two sweet decades of no contact with her evil, dysfunctional Family, but there was no memory that could recreate it nor no description that could do justice to that flip of a switch within his offended mind. "Because you're just not that *important*, Theodore," was his razor-blade answer, which left the man visibly shocked, hands spread as if defending a physical assault. "To Lavinia, you are. But not to me. Do you realize, lad, that if I killed you at this very instant, you would awaken back on Earth, floating in the ice-cold waters of the Atlantic Ocean? Do you know how terrible it is for a martyr to drown?"

"What's wrong with you?" Teddy fell back one step, then several when the Holy Father remained immobile. "Are you—are you feeling okay, Father? Don't you know it's me?"

"Don't patronize me, Theodore. Of course I know it's you. Your ability to whine is impossible to imitate. You asked; I but answer. You speak as if all I have ever done was an act of cruelty when you *asked* for this life. *Begged* me for it. I generously rewarded you with the Family bloodline and the platonic company of my most beautiful, purehearted daughter, and you act as if it has all been some burden. I am 'allowing' this to happen to you because you are not as important as the events in which you are involved—and I tried to 'disappear you' just now, as you put it, because Dominia is at this moment responsible for your life. Your death while in her custody would cause her tremendous pain—pain to such extent it might annihilate the remains of her spirit." Now those eyes, obsidian daggers, flicked in the General's direction. She watched with her own blue orb shadowed in hatred. "Never fear, though, Teddy." His attention returned to his shell-shocked youngest child, and his tone of voice lightened just enough to emphasize how black it had been but seconds before. "Soon enough, you'll be returned to safety. And once you're in *my* custody, you will be safe again."

The look on Teddy's face as he glanced toward Dominia indicated he wasn't so sure.

IV

Assume the Port of Mars

An encounter with the Holy Father's true persona had a way of changing his children, as Dominia could have told Theodore. But any warning to such effect would have been lost on a Family member still enthralled by that perfect mask of the jolly old trickster—Lavinia would be crushed by exposure to those treacherous turns of mood, taken with him as she'd always been. Teddy was a close second place for the intensity of his delusions when it came to the Hierophant, and the frightful experience's effect on his mind showed in the hunch of his shoulders and the twist of his silent mouth on the way back to the airship.

For some strange reason, the black sun hadn't risen in the sky. Knowing what she did of time in that place, she suspected some event had yet to unfold. The notion would make no sense to her waking brain, but there it seemed somehow natural that anyone or anything that wanted to interact with her could hold time's march through its day/night cycles. Especially if that thing was the Lady.

Slowing her pace to match Gethsemane's, the martyr investigated her scattered human friend and carefully took her hand. This action seemed, however briefly, to solidify the woman into the state she was on Earth—that beautiful, dreadlocked creature whose heritage was such a combination of countries and cultures that she seemed alien enough without the added aspects of the naiad. "We'll get you home," said Dominia. This was the wrong thing to say; the girl didn't speak, but her throat made a noise like Cassandra's nastiest laughter. "You don't think so? If I can't protect you, surely your Lady will, and She's all this space."

"My Lady will use me as She sees fit," the Bearer answered in a resigned tone. "After your Father's words in the study, I am concerned that you feel responsible for my condition as much as you do for Theodore's."

"Of course I feel responsible. I let you—"

"It is not up to you to 'let' me come or go anywhere," the human said, not unkindly. "I came with you because such a thing was demanded of me—and because I could not have rested with the thought of our last meeting being a sorrowful one where one or both was lost to war."

After a glance over his shoulder for the women, Farhad hurried his pace to increase their privacy while the General said, "I don't see why you have to think about our last meeting at all."

"Our paths are about to diverge, Dominia." The human used the martyr's name so seldom that the latter listened all the harder to her friend's words. "I have thought on the matter some since we came ashore with the Ichigawas last week... You remember the Lady, and how She insisted to you that I come?"

Who could forget? That had been at that meeting in the library basement after Jerusalem's twelfth drone bombing. Sixty-three civilians had been wounded and twenty-two were already among the dead. Teddy's kidnapping, suggested by the Lady a mere two nights before this incident, sounded better to Dominia all the time.

Lazarus, however, had disagreed. In their makeshift war room, the old mystic had sat across from her and defied the Lady's anticipation that he would agree with whatever the General proposed. "We don't need Theo," he said. "There are safer ways to start a war if that's what you want—and if it's really information you're after on a personal level, well...we know everything we need to know about Lavinia. What we don't know can be extrapolated."

"Maybe *you* know about Lavinia." The General stared him down across a veritable ocean of charts, atlases, time tables, flight paths, and one or two example electrodart guns. "Have something you'd like to share with me? With the rest of the group?"

"I don't know." Lazarus returned her stare as coldly as she delivered it. "Do you?"

It wasn't that the General and Lazarus hadn't gotten along over the past year. However, it was undeniable that, as time went on, tensions rose, and Dominia had begun to sense that, day by day, they reached a point for which the many-lived man spent each life waiting.

In service to those tensions, she was careful with her words. Then again, Dominia was always careful when discussing her younger sister. "I know more about Lavinia than the public, but I don't know as much about her as Theodore, and I don't know with any degree of certainty why my Father has kept her locked up. All this time he could have been teaching her how to control her emotions and use her powers responsibly. Akachi was right. It's more than obsession. My Father doesn't do anything without good reason, and he doesn't get attached to anyone on a personal level. That indicates he's keeping her locked up for some purpose, but what?"

"Maybe to lure you back home now," Lazarus posited. The General scoffed and waved the thought away before looking at the Lady, who studied the room with Her unmoving face. The still body, kneeling upon a slightly raised platform against the northern wall, reverberated with the same symphony as Dominia's skeleton.

There are worse things than that the General should face her fear.

"Yeah," Lazarus came back, his expression tight. "Worse things, like what we'll have to do to get her back after she's trapped. We can't risk it. You know better than anybody here all the resources required if we allow her capture."

The same number of resources as will be utilized, anyway. We are already at war.

"And you think kidnapping the Governor of the United Front is going to soothe that war?"

It was a fight nobody wanted to get in the middle of. As the room hovered in uneasy silence, the goddess calmly responded, *Theodore is a weak-willed and sycophantic individual. To rally him to Our cause shall be next to nothing, with rich long-term rewards.*

"Yeah, but he's made out of paper. It's just as easy for him to blow back his Father's way the second we let him. The second—"

This all assumes the plan will go wrong, and the General will be captured. Is that what you anticipate?

The annoyed old man studied Dominia's face (for its own part, arranged in displeasure) and concluded, "I suppose we don't have any better ideas."

With the gates of Elsinore tightly barred and traffic in and out of the city controlled, consider how low the odds of anyone slipping in and out to deliver information, establish a teleporter—or, in a dream, free Lavinia with any measure of success.

"I've already agreed to it, haven't I?"

Looking satisfied for as little emotion as the unmoving face that had once belonged to Miki Soto now expressed, the Lady turned her attention to Dominia. *To soothe the fears of Lazarus, bring Gethsemane with you.*

"She doesn't need to come," Dominia said while the Bearer stood at attention and showed no signs of opinion. "She'd be risking her life for nothing—I've already expressed tonight how wary I am about your suggestion of letting First Mate Ichigawa be responsible for our physical passage to the Front."

Perhaps you would prefer to walk through the Ergosphere?

"That's what I'm saying. Gethsemane *can't*. I've seen her." The General had bristled, nearing the point of dropping the last pretense of respect. "If something goes wrong with the E4 and Gethsemane is there—"

Then it must be Our will that this is so. Would you, mortal, contest Our will? The will of Our Void? We, who gave you sight? Who taught you to speak? Who crafted the world in which you live?

Oh, Dominina hated this. Hated the impotence, hated the genuflecting, hated the service. She was absolutely through with this life of submission to those in power. And it wasn't so much that Dominia wanted power, herself. It was just that she didn't want to watch people in power hurt those she loved anymore. Gethsemane had done much for her in the past year in terms of showing her that she could still bond, at least in a guilty way, with another being. The human *had*, despite Theodore's judgement, relieved the burden of Cassandra in a tangible way. Dominia knew that Cassandra's remains were cared for, adored, polished, and worn in a way that honored them—a silly thing, perhaps, but it was important to her. It made her feel like her wife was alive and...maybe on vacation, somewhere. They had tried that once, about fourteen years in, when Dominia was afraid it wasn't working out. Her wife had gone off somewhere for a year, just to see what it was like to be alone. The Governess had been miserable, sick as a dog. Oh, Cassandra...what a beautiful thing it was, coming home after work one morning and seeing her bags in the foyer. Smelling the edges of her perfume in the air. Dominia still couldn't even remember climbing the stairs.

Somehow, the diamond around Gethsemane's neck made it seem like that moment of reunion was still a possibility. Her human friend even went so far as to accept the burden here, in this place where it added to the shifting of her body (and, no doubt) the shifting of her mind. As that loyal friend called her back to the present with a gently chided, "You have fallen silent, General—take care not to be lost in thought, as you tell me," the martyr stopped her.

"I think it's too much, asking you to carry my wife for me here. I know your strength, but you're dealing with enough with the nymph—I don't know, leaking into you—"

"Revealing herself in me."

"Sure," said the General, trying to chuckle and coming up short. Instead, frowning, she took the Bearer's hands. "Did the Lady tell you something, anything, that we—you—can expect on this journey? Did She send you here to die with me, or for me?"

The human's eyes lowered from Dominia's to study the ground as illuminated by the torches. Ocean waves, frozen in time, felt flat beneath their feet though they visibly rippled across the illuminated portions of the path. "After all that you have seen, do you really still believe in death?"

That old surge of panic, of loss to discover her tears washed Cassandra's blood from her hands—wasted upon the carpet like her brain matter. "If death isn't real," said the one-eyed General, "it does a good job of pretending it is."

"Yes, it does. But you have met him, yes? Death. So have I." As Dominia gathered her meaning, Gethsemane confessed, "In the escape tunnels of the Lady's temple, when we fled with Her—"

Son of a bitch. That was where he'd gone! Of course Akachi would have a handful of of men waiting for the women. Even if he felt the odds weren't in his favor, it would have been worth a shot. Mentioning it to Dominia would have been humiliating for him when his plan fell through, but as Gethsemane described how the half-baked Hunter assault on the escaping women had been foiled by the appearance of the magician, all the martyr could think to ask was, "Why didn't you tell me?"

"Because, I—" Now the woman looked supremely uncomfortable and seemed to struggle for an explanation; it was the most discomforted Dominia had ever seen the stoic human appear. "He turned their guns to birds that pecked and chased them back to the tunnel's exit, and I watched and laughed with everyone, but then—something happened. He did not ask me to keep it to myself, but I…I am a woman of faith, General, and know my spirit is bonded to a fae, a nymph beyond all space and time, but I have no firsthand experience of a thing like this."

Time stopped, she said. The birds in the distance froze midair around the heads of the men they harassed; the women froze midlaughter, midapplause. Even the Lady was still. Only Gethsemane and the magician had remained mobile, and he had turned around and spoken strange things to her. "You are the daughter of the Word," he'd said. "All Bearers are daughters of the Word, and you above all its daughters are cherished, Gethsemane, for it is you most cherished by Dominia. Many times you have died—it is the duty of all Bearers to live many lives and die in miniature as the universe dies in grand, unseeable scale. But no more will you perish, and just as it seems the eve of your death has come, there I will be for you, instead, with one more task for you to commit upon your father's behalf."

When time restarted, it did not simply restart: rather, Gethsemane came to in the Lady's safe house, many miles away, with no memory of what had occurred in between. None of her sisters remembered even the Hunter assault in the tunnels; and the Lady, while not denying the event had happened, had Herself encouraged Gethsemane to keep the event quiet. *Your sisters are not so advanced as you in ways of the spirit—they would be jealous to hear such a thing, not understanding what it means, that you are favored by your father.*

"I have seen the magician in dreams before that time," the woman explained, "but that night was the first and only time I have seen him in person. This past year I grew convinced it was a dream, but…"

"But now you think your time has come."

"It is not time as you mean it. Not death as you know it."

Trying to contain her bitter anger at the forces around her and their penchant for giving friends just to strip them away, Dominia instead tried to focus on practical aspects. "If he says he'll take care of you…I guess that's all I can ask."

"I believe him, General. But I am…reluctant to leave this behind."

"From what I can tell, the other side is just more of the same. But better." With a squeeze of her hands, Dominia released her. The human bowed her head to remove Cassandra's diamond. As the little gem lowered into her palm, it was with the relief of an anxiety the General had not known she'd felt. There was the feeling in her face again. She lifted the gem to her lips to kiss its cold facets, and only on lowering her hand noticed the shocked gaze of Gethsemane trained somewhere behind her. The General turned, and against the distant dark, illuminated without need for her Father's profane torches, stood the Lady.

There is no difference between death and life. Death is an external illusion, as Our Bearer has tried to communicate to you. Walk with me, General.

As the goddess turned away, the martyr hesitated until her human companion cried, "You must go!" and physically pushed her off the path. Dominia, laughing slightly, turned to chide her, but was stunned. Empty space stood before her, the path back to the airship—and her friend upon it—vanished.

Wisdom keeps you from arguing too long with Gethsemane, for you know she has a duty. You know despite your trepidation that you take the right course of action. Irritation bubbled up in the General, who, after putting on Cassandra's diamond, stalked to the Lady's side. *In liberating him from the Front, you will do Theodore—and others—a great kindness, and receive information in exchange. And information is the truly fundamental element of this universe.*

"Where are we going?" As the deity continued apace, each step was accompanied by the eerie rattle of an invisible *suzu* bell, and Dominia felt faint anxiety to see the Lady walk, real event or no. That many-womaned entity smiled but a hair, Her lips unmoving even in the Void.

Have you not yet learned the futility of questions? We are here to show you something.

"But my friends—"

You will meet them again. This is not for their eyes.

A light grew in the distance toward which they marched, far greater than the lights pouring from the women. It seemed at first as though a true sunrise grew over the horizon of the world, but as she remembered they walked through the Ergosphere of a black hole that was little more than the encoded version of the planet Earth, she recognized by sound a black-and-silver block of sea that, animated unlike water for miles around in that frozen camera obscura of a half-world, foamed wildly within its confines.

"Is this some kind of dream?

All things are dream here: especially at night, when all the landscape is submerged in the darkness of Our waters. Even the Earth's waters are no match for them, and Earth's waters are a hungry, violent force. The Lady lifted a hand rendered invisible by the trailing sleeve of Her robe to gesture toward that ungenerous sea. From this distance—if distance could be said to exist in a place where waters roiled in the light of an invisible moon—the wrath with which that ocean thrashed was evident, its waves leaping high and collapsing upon their siblings like overexcited dogs presented with dinner. The closer she drew, the more its color changed—or gained, as its black waters bloomed crimson. The Lady, unhesitating, made her way to its very edge to watch the waves lap Her feet.

What do you do when you have done all you can, General?

Following the Lady's suit, Dominia gazed into the waters and saw, reflected like a broken mirror by its foaming surface, a face that she first mistook as hers. She was just trying to discern what was wrong with it, this face that sat where she should have seen nothing or her own—until, as his hand burst forth to grab her ankle, she recognized Kahlil.

"You put me here," proclaimed a voice that she did not hear so much as feel. As though it reverberated not through air but through the hand that was joined by another to pull her into the reddened waves. *"I wasn't prepared to die, but you let me die. You knew what he would do. You could have saved me. But you didn't even move."*

Though she drew her gun to extricate herself from the grip, the General was awash with shame. "He would have killed you if I moved."

"You're the expert on killing."

Dominia pulled back the hammer of the gun.

"I guess so."

She had hoped the effect would be something akin to what one saw in old zombie movies—the two-dimensional sort she favored as a little girl, before the reality of being a monster wore away the charm of fiction. In all those stories, there would be moments where something happened like a half-rotted arm was blown to bits by a single, dramatic shot. This was not that. The bullet made contact with the arm that gripped her. At the second of impact, she was back in the Lady's temple, burying sheets of lead in the waves of men who came, body after body, to throw themselves at her like wheat begging to be threshed. All these bodies with families, these spirits with mothers and fathers and no souls, no hope—where had Dominia sent them? Where had they gone when they died?

Her mind flew back to the present conflict. She could not fire again. Could do no more than look helplessly over her shoulder. She hoped to find help from the Lady and instead discovered, in one piece, Tobias.

"Will you kill me again, General?"

As Dominia's mouth gaped in shock, the revenant forced her into the waves.

Time—if time could be said to exist in that place—halted the instant the General broke the strangling surface of the garnet waters. These were not like those waters that had transported her, miraculously, to the Kingdom. A raging tsunami of angry atoms comprised this ocean, a sea whose depth knew no more limit than did the vast collection of beleaguered souls assembling it. As Dominia drowned among them, she sensed their numbers to be very nearly limitless, and marveled: Had she killed so many in her life?

"Yes," was the resounding cry that seemed to come from her own mouth, forced open by the terrible pressure of the waters and filled with their bitterness. *"Yes, you have done this to us."*

A thousand battles, the Bitch of Europa. She had stopped reading about monsters because she had been one—yes, been worse, more pitiful, more contemptible, than one of the Lamb's dogs. Dogs had no sense of morality or consciousness, and dogs loved and cared for not just other dogs but other animals. But Dominia had turned off her ability to love. To care. She had rendered herself as deeply unconscious as possible so there could never be any question of what she did. Never any hard thinking. Any possibility of failure.

But, oh, on the other side of that! How love and caring had rushed into her at the proper time, like the horrors of reality on waking from a happy dream. Cassandra had been the medicant for her ills. A chance to be kind and gentle. An excuse to be a Governess, and stay her killing hand. Yet, she had kept that gun. A badge of who she had been. Of who she would, deep down inside, always be. The General.

"You've already ended the world for thousands of people," accused Akachi's death-paled voice, rattling her brain as her insides screamed for help. *"Why shouldn't you flee to your Father's side and end it for the rest of them?"*

She wished to have the voice to defend herself: to tell them she only did as she'd been ordered and that now—now, too, she was only doing the Lady's will. But there was no way for her to speak, to fight the current that dragged her ever deeper to the abyss.

"Just full of excuses," was Kahlil's response to her struggling thoughts. *"You're a user of people as bad or worse than Iblis, himself. You didn't care enough about Miki to save her. She was just a tool to you."*

Dominia couldn't bear it. She hadn't used anyone—hadn't wanted to, hadn't meant to. But hadn't she done it anyway?

"You have," answered a waver of a voice, softer and more tragic than any she had heard. Horror filled her to recognize Tenchi, of all good people, in that mass of unwashed spirits and corrupted souls. Hadn't he just been by the ship, and before (or after) that, in the Kingdom? It was impossible for him to be here, wasn't it?

"If you proceed along this path, I will never make it to the Kingdom."

But he wasn't more than a mile away, off fixing their airship!

"If you proceed along this path, I will never make it to the Kingdom."

The voice could only echo its one statement over and over, and the General's mind so burned she could only think in patterns—the words "Lady" and "help" over and over until the clamor of accusing, dead voices were hushed by the choir of the goddess.

We have brought you here for a reason. All of this happens for a reason. These spirits that assail you, these waters—what are they?

Her crimes? Her guilt? Her sorrow?

They are the same as anything else. Information.

At last, Dominia's sinking halted, and the waters burst around her. As they cleared to leave her floating in the Ergosphere without even ground, she discovered not only the Lady but, far as the eye could see, characters of various alphabets. It was as if she still possessed that DIOX-I that collected every passing Halcyon account and cluttered her vision with augmented features—but now, the world to be augmented had melted away, and she only saw its data.

"What is this?" The General marveled across this new sea of names, statistics, numbers, and letters arranged in no order or pattern she could discern except most of them were stuck in a single failed process, and many seemed to be nouns that were verbing in one way or another. Akachi swinging (she assumed his arm, up to defend his face from the *tulpa*), Kahlil springing (away from Akachi), Tenchi (tragically) begging for his life. Hundreds, thousands, more she did not recognize, names and functions she did not understand. Most were frozen in permanent stutter.

The conductive nature of salt water permits the transmission of subtle radio frequencies over short distances; it is a carrier for information, and the oceans here in the Void are overfull. As the Lady spoke, the General found her eye could stay on one fact no longer than a second before leaping to the next. *That same dark water of Our ocean is found everywhere in this place. Once a dreamer has been submerged in its substance, the encoded information of reality is everywhere one could look. This brand of perception is where the magician does his grandest work to intercede with the normal functions of reality. This is where you shall do yours.*

"Mine?" asked the General, seeing Tenchi's name again. "But what about him? Tenchi, he's here with us. I just saw him. What is this ocean? How can he be in it and without it?"

Because the Tenchi you see is the Tenchi you have already saved in the future.

The Lady turned to brush a fingertip across some piece of data floating past. A screen could not have been said to appear, though that was how Dominia perceived it, in a way: first one news broadcast, then another, until a great symphony floated across the back of her mind while the Lady activated data point on data point.

"—national tragedy as Governor Theodore del Medico—"

"—kidnapping at the hands of the terrorist organization now controlled by Dominia di—"

"—suspect in custody, thanks to an anonymous tip. Terrorist Tenchi Ichigawa—"

"—detained at the airport—"

"—no word yet on the location of the Governor—"

"—though the stolen jet crashed, no bodies were discovered—"

"—execution to be broadcast live—"

"—suspected to have escaped by boat, leaving Ichigawa behind."

Dominia, on the verge of tears, demanded, "But that's not true! We didn't leave him behind— René was—" Paled, the General looked into the face of the Lady. "René. He betrayed us again?"

René is a martyr now, and not one of your sort. He is not a man with a vision of a higher order, or a better world. He sees only this one, and sees his future in this one as being short-lived if he does not make good use of his new genetics.

"But what about Tenchi?"

If you were to proceed to Jerusalem with Theodore, Ichigawa would not make it to the Kingdom, for he has not yet consumed the blood of Lazarus on Earth from where you stand. He is a religious man, but has been too frightened to gain full initiation into the faith. Perhaps—the Lady's lip twitched—*you would do well to save all souls by tricking them, as you did Theodore. It is the easier way.*

The easier way, to be certain. It was always easier to trick somebody into something, rather than preparing them for what they'd actually have to do. That was why she found herself here.

You cannot prevent Tenchi's capture. By the time of your E4's crash, it has already occurred, and your Father has solidified your presence in this place. But there is time enough for you to reach the location of Tenchi's execution.

With a thought for the vial of old Lazarene blood, around her neck along with Cassandra's diamond even in this place, listless Dominia began to understand her fate. "I'm not saving him. I'm trading myself for him. I'll show up, have enough time to save Tenchi, and then they'll ship me off."

To Kronborg, in Denmark: yes.

The Hierophant possessed many castles, but it was Kronborg Castle in the European city of Old Elsinore he most favored for captives, for raising new family members, and for generally enjoying his "downtime." The climate was favorable to martyrs, and its distance from any (sensible) human-habitable nation was vast. Having grown up around the warm and coastal Mephitolian landscape, with its sweet nights and its dreamlike cities, she had no special love for that dreary place. But, ah, now that she thought on it, how she missed her home! Particularly that real-life Atlantis, Venezia, that drowned city raised from the dead by the Hierophant's passionate love of restoring that which had been beautiful so long ago that people had forgotten it ever existed.

Grimacing, Dominia tore her thoughts from nostalgia and leveled her gaze with the Lady. "You're trying to make me want to go back to Europa."

You want to go back, Dominia. Of course you do: it is your home. Do we not, all of us, long for the past?

"Do you?"

We are the past, and the future. But most of all, We are the present. All things are present in that which We are: therefore, We feel no particular longing for any one thing. But you have the dubious fortune of fully experiencing the present. Of experiencing desire, loss, and all emotions. Therefore, you are more powerful, and more whole, than We are.

Laughing, Dominia asked, "How am I supposed to be more powerful than you?"

Because it is not Our job, or the job of Lazarus, to create the world. It is your job, as much as its destruction also lies in your hands.

"But *really*, why me? Why, why? I don't understand why I'm whipped up in all of this."

Because you are the daughter of the Hierophant. And not any daughter. You are one who commiserates with the Lady and her children. You are a hero who shall bridge both worlds. And the strength and purity of your wish, not only to be someone different, but to rectify what you have wronged…this is something that cannot be matched.

"All I want is Cassandra back. I didn't wrong her. I didn't wrong anyone. I was only ever doing my job."

The silent Lady studied Dominia's face, names and numbers floating between the two of them as though to demonstrate how incorrect she was. At the thick silence of the deity, the General scoffed.

"I suppose you're right…it's my duty."

You have always known it to be your duty. You have denied the weight of responsibility—have run from it. But will you now take it on? There is more at stake than the life of the human named Tenchi Ichigawa. The goddess plucked the name from the air and held it between Her thumb and forefinger. *He is but data.*

As She released the name to fly away, the silent General watched it go, then watched the Lady's unmoving face as She approached in the company of those grave bells. *Now begins the most dangerous phase of your duties. I urge you, no matter what happens, do not forget your loyalty to Us; and do not forget this place. Have you Akachi's necklace?*

The General nodded, and the goddess touched her forehead. *Then make good with your friends when you awake. They will understand.*

"Lady"—Dominia's body dissolved, but she still had a litany of questions before she proceeded forward in this great task. All of them, she knew, would go unanswered if not asked in these seconds—"tell me, please: How is it that Cassandra's diamond comes to this place so reliably—Lazarus's blood, even, or the plane with the blood running through it—when other objects we try to bring within might or might not be with us when we arrive?"

Because the diamond is Cassandra, of course. And the blood of Lazarus—that is like asking why you can carry a key to the other side of its door.

As her forehead burst into a trillion golden molecules, the General started awake to find herself by a fire she had made to crackle comfortably beside the dozing airship. Gethsemane lay in her arms and Farhad snored on the other side of the blaze, with Teddy and Tenchi tucked safe into seats of the E4. Around them, darkness relented to the gray of morning.

Understanding as she did, she wished it hadn't come.

V

Ten Thousand Leagues Across the Sea

Theodore was second to wake that morning. Stirred, perhaps, by the General's soft footfalls as she leaned into the E4 to ensure the well-being of the sleeping men. While she dismissed the fire, her brother crept out to greet her, and whispered in the soft light of dawn, "Get inside!"

"It doesn't burn," she said, hearing Valentinian's soft reprimand of her bullying ways and therefore avoiding tacking on some unnecessary cruel nickname—though a couple did spring to mind. "It's not really a sun that's about to rise. People just call it that because…it's easier. But it looks black."

"Black Sun— Is *this* Father's project?"

With a glance for her sleeping companions, Dominia jerked her head in the direction of the plane's other side. As she rounded the craft with her relative and got some meters away, she asked, "Do you remember what happened last night?"

"Do you not? I went to sleep praying all this would turn out to be some dream…considering the way last night went, I guess it's stupid to ask God for help! What *is* this place? Are we in hell?"

All the old familiar questions. How was she to explain any of this to somebody like Teddy? "Well, it's like—like we're asleep. Do you know how light is a particle and a wave? Consciousness is like that, too. And when a brain is asleep, or dead, the ego enters a low-frequency wave state that can take our consciousnesses here, too—but a high frequency also allows the state, in a more desirable and controllable…"

Oh, the look on his face! She drifted off on seeing her own failure to engage him. Now she understood the dilemma of the holy man and his magical son when confronted by her military mind. Theodore had spent a whole life worshiping money and had sought membership in the Holy Family not out of spiritual devotion but financial gain. There was no celebrity on Earth like a Holy Family member, reviled by some but adored by too many—and literally worshipped by an interesting cross section of both camps. Any car in which the Hierophant rode was bound to be the cause of traffic jams and, from time to time, complete closure of whole towns as people suspended business and camped along his travel routes just to fling themselves against the surface of his car, begging for a handkerchief or a ring or a kiss. Such trifles (the kisses especially) he delivered in abundance, but the devotees he loved best were those humans with mental illness severe enough to buy the martyr lie that the fastest, most guaranteed route to heaven for a human being was to be devoured by the Hierophant. If women screamed to sleep with Dominia, men and women alike emerged in morbid handfuls to beg to be eaten, even in part, by His Holiness.

Failing him, any Holy Family member would do, and the closer they were to the Hierophant, the better. That meant that a martyr on the level of Theodore would never be at risk of starvation. He was a simpering, whining dolt amid his peers, but because he was a famous martyr, he could walk into any club on Earth and attract abundant attention from that most unpleasant subset of Renfielding losers who would settle for a quick fuck and the donation of some blood in exchange for the dubious honor of having been with one of the Family. The General had never been interested in obtaining food from such a source (not to mention the risks of accidentally martyring some stupid fan), but Teddy loved the ease, and although he only had real eyes for Lavinia, he wasn't hard up for company. Earth held for Dominia's stupid younger brother everything he ever could have wanted; and, like most individuals martyred in adulthood, his life revolved around a semisecret terror of death. He'd walked the planet for a hundred years, and nowhere in there had he taken the time for any kind of spiritual or moral insight.

Yet—hadn't Dominia been that way? Lamb! Who was she to judge her brother's ignorance when she had spent over three hundred years doing just the same? Her own wife had taught Noctisdomin school every week for decades before moving on to specialize in music, and never in that time had the General—the Governess—considered such matters, herself. She hadn't wanted to. They frightened her. In that moment, standing before Theodore and called to answer his questions, Dominia wondered for the first time if a lack of spiritual interest was not rooted in fear. The same fear she saw in Theodore's eyes and heard on the edges of his questions. The General knew that fear very well. She, too, was afraid—afraid of what God would think of her many atrocities.

Or was she just afraid of her own opinion? She wasn't sure. She hadn't checked in on herself for years. Too busy taking care of other people. After answering a few basic questions about the substance of the place (and the electromagnetic fields that, with the increase of dawn during their conversation, began to appear in those brilliant alien colors to spur only further queries), she asked her brother, "How are you doing, Theo?"

"Oh, God." He waved both hands in the disgusted fashion of an old woman waiting for Saint Valentinian because she found life too exhausting. "Who knows? Who cares? I feel like I've had my whole concept of existence upended—my whole life! Everybody here is acting like this stuff is no big deal. You know…when I was a kid, I wanted more than *anything* to be adopted by some martyrs."

Here, the General did not smirk, because that was a fairly common dream among a certain brand of human. Nor had she been blind to the way Theodore preened about for his first twenty or so years as a quasi-immortal being. "If only we had traded places."

"If only! Some nights I would pray—really *pray*, Dominia, feverish prayer for hours after I should have been asleep—that my parents would be killed, and all my potential could be seen."

"Prayer doesn't work like that, buddy." With an awkward glance over her shoulder for the jet shielding them from their human companions, Dominia tried to give him an out. "Were they…abusive to you?"

"Oh, no," he said, crushing the last possibility of empathy for his personality. "They would just send me to bed without supper for things like back talk, or what-have-you…but that's a *sin*, you know, denying children food!"

"Is it? That's what Father says. Maybe it's a cruel act to withhold food from a martyr child, knowing what starvation does to us, but is it a sin?"

Teddy wore the answer on his haggard expression. "That's just the thing. I was *sure* it was days—has it been days? I can't tell here, I know we just got here, but for some reason—anyway, I was *sure* of that days ago. And now… he tried to *disappear* me, Dominia. Like I was somebody he didn't even know. First he damned my soul without any recourse; then he tried to make me think I didn't exist!"

"That's the Holy Father for you."

"But he's not supposed to be like that to *me*. I'm a martyr! His child!"

"Welcome to my world. He's culled his children in the past." Before them, extending across the landscape like the kings of Macbeth's vision, Dominia saw the generations of historical Holy Family members who had been martyred and had their martyring completed long before her human birth. She did not ask if her vision was as sensible to feeling as to sight, nor if the vision was only of her mind. There was no difference here, and no real answer. Not even Theodore's lack of response for the image marked it as true hallucination—perhaps it was but a reality only she saw. She tore her eye from those many bleeding and eviscerated Family members whose memorial paintings were forever seared into her brain, and continued her warning to Theodore. They would vanish if she ignored them. "Father's children get too powerful, or get their own ideas, or discover something about him and his society. Then they have to be taken out." There: already gone.

"But not me! Let's face it, Dominia—I'm a gross little sycophant!" While his sister laughed in shock, Teddy offered a small, self-deprecating grin. "I mean, for most of my adult life, I've made it my job description to do whatever he wants me to do. He should know I'm not going to hurt anybody, let alone him! I'm not a threat, not on anybody's side in—whatever *this* is! I don't even want to be involved with all that stuff in the Front. You think I want to be all the way out there, with all those human hicks, dealing with their half-person problems?"

Prickly, Dominia said, "I love the people of the Front. They're good, kind, hardworking people. Hopeful people. Martyrs have been living in their territory for almost two thousand years, and openly ruling it for centuries—but they still believe it's a worthwhile place to live. That being near their friends and family and neighbors is worth the risks."

"Of course you love the Front, Cassandra was there for you! But me? Once I've slept with a woman once or twice, she won't give me the time of night! I have to settle for humans... I guess I shouldn't judge you."

"Maybe your problem is that women aren't into sycophants."

"I *know* that." He sighed pathetically and stared out into the graying Ergosphere, at the peaks of solid ocean water that drew themselves, crystalized, from the darkness. "It's not like I haven't tried to make a name for myself. I'll have you know I graduated—*very* high in my class in my medical program. I had so much *promise*. I knew so much!"

"That's why the Hierophant tried to get rid of you. He knows how much you know, and he doesn't want you telling me." Yet allowed him to come this far—why, she now understood with sickening clarity. Her brother protested on.

"But you *know* everything I do. More!"

"We know different things. And I think there's at least one thing he's sworn you to total secrecy about...I know what it is, but there's something I think you can help me confirm." The edges of an admission ached a jaw she shifted in silence before she continued. "I think it's sort of true, what he was getting at yesterday. I don't think it mattered much to him that we were able to acquire you. In fact...I think he even prefers it. He knows this is the most expedient method of getting his hands on me. Trading you for me."

As he took her meaning, Theodore hacked out a high laugh. "You're going *back* to him? After you went to all the trouble of getting me?"

"I have to. Our man, Tenchi— I have to."

"That sailor? What *about* him? He's sleeping in the plane!"

"Time is very complicated here. I can't get into it now, but"—she thought of brave Gethsemane once more, accepting entry into the Void and taking Valentinian's word that he would come for her—"this is bigger than me. The Lady guided me here, insisted certain people be here with me—She set all this up so that I would have to turn around." With a surge of bitter laughter, the General covered her face in her hands. "Oh, you bitch. It was the only way to make me return to Europa."

"You can't just kidnap me, then leave me with these strangers while *you* get to go home!"

Her hands dropped. "You really want to go home to the guy who tried to annihilate your soul because it would ruin my mental state?" At Teddy's immediate silence, she continued, "Ultimately, I'm going back to save Lavinia, so you should be grateful. At least, so far as *I'm* concerned, that's why I'm going back."

"Save Lavinia! Save Lavinia from what? Herself? Not Father— She's the only person in the world he wouldn't hurt."

No time like the present. Even so, that present seemed long, and her forehead burned with unspoken thoughts. Focused off on the dusty dawn as seen through the warping bands of her field, she wished for but a moment she could be anywhere but the body whose mouth formed the words, "I'm going to ask you a question, Theo. It's something I'd like confirmed before I make this rash move. I just need you to remember that I probably know the answer, so it's okay to tell me. And, anyway—you have nothing to lose after what happened last night."

Visibly dubious at the idea of releasing sensitive information, even cut off from reality and the Family, Theodore asked, "What is it?"

How to say it? How to ask? More importantly, how to ask it in a way that would elicit the truth? She hadn't thought on it much, hoping the words would come in the moment. Thankfully, they did when she opened her mouth. It gathered its sound after but a second of hesitation.

"Does Lavinia understand that she's fertile, or has he somehow hidden it from *her*, too?"

The look on Theodore's face, from the brief, gobsmacked part of his lips to the bloom of his pupils, told Dominia all she ever needed to know from him. For just under sixty-eight years, Lavinia had been in the public eye. Throughout that time, the General feigned ignorance of her condition with the kind of acting that deserved not award but prosecution.

Perhaps because he had nothing left to lose, or because of the way she chose to ask the question, his response was: "No—she has no idea."

She found sweet catharsis embedded in those words. So Dominia was not a fool to do this, this going home. Not a complete fool, anyway. There was a reason for her return. A far more foolish thing would be leaving the world's only fertile martyr at home with the Holy Father until he decided the time was right to start experimenting.

"But how did you know that?" asked Teddy, whose bafflement never faded.

Maybe she did know more than the Governor had ever known. Maybe the problem was Dominia's, for being unable to admit those facts she held. "He keeps her locked away, doesn't he?"

"Well, yes, but she's also *dangerous*. That's plenty of reason to control her movement, it's no reason to think…really, though, how did you know she's fertile?"

With one more look at the edges of her sleeping companions, Dominia waved her brother close. When he bent his head, she cupped her hand and whispered for a time in his ear. Just two short sentences. Two small facts, which Theodore hadn't known, and which so shocked him that he pulled away from Dominia with a new, perhaps visible, appreciation for her evil. Or maybe she was just projecting.

"Please." She glanced at her companions. "Don't tell them. I don't think they'd respect me anymore."

"Dominia…I had no idea you had it in you."

She managed her grimmest smile, which left her eye untouched. "Neither did I, until it was all over."

"No wonder…no wonder." Frowning, Theodore shook his head, and looked at Dominia without a hint of his usual clownishness. She'd never seen him so serious, in fact, and it almost worried her as he stood in contemplative silence for an uncountable time.

"You know," he decided at last, "I don't think I've ever had what it takes to be a martyr."

"Very few people do."

"But you do."

"Yes. I wish I could say I 'did,' and that the person I was then was a totally different person from who I am now, but…I have to bear responsibility for my own sins." With a glance toward the E4, then up to the black sun illuminating the darkness, Dominia realized that sun also illuminated something new *in* that darkness. Beyond and through and within her compass glowed neon threads: thin jet-stream lasers that, thinner than strands of silk, were suspended in the air and seemed, at certain points, gathered in clusters. As she noted these and became amazed, new ones appeared, and others faded. Violet was the color of these new threads, rather than the gentle cerulean of the ones prior. The astonished General looked all around herself, and as Teddy asked, "What is it?" she grew sure he could not see them.

"I don't know." With a delicate touch, she stroked a lavender thread that inspired a fascinating flash of understanding. Namely, that the threads represented digital data. All the information one might retrieve about an electronic device—from its location based on its IP address to its purpose to its user's name—could be divined at the tap of a thread. How *easy* such a thing might make navigating one's way across the Ergosphere! Retrieving information! *This*, or some variation of it, was surely how Lazarus and Valentinian found their ways across this space more precisely than by their warping compasses. Some artifact of her dream-epiphany—if it had been a dream at all. Perhaps if she had dreamed of the True Words while staying in the Void, she might have retained the memories of those dreams, too. She regretted she hadn't.

She was more uncertain of dreams all the time. That moment more than any seemed to indicate dreams may well have been closer to reality than she'd have cared to think, as Tenchi's sudden cry pierced the air. Both martyrs leapt to immediate defense, Dominia out of instinct and her brother out of terror, but both soon recognized the sound as excitement.

"*Yatta! Wakarimasu*, oh—oh, I *get* it, okay—"

Then the air rumbled with the life of the aircraft: no more the stuttering on and off of yesterday's brief efforts, but the prolonged rumble of a plane ready for takeoff. Floored, the General darted to the jet's other side, past her stirring companions, and called to the wide-eyed first mate. "Tenchi! How did you get it working again?"

"I—I don't— I had a *dream*. And I learned the name of the ship, it's—" His words abruptly ended in the manner of someone trying to work a True Word into a sentence, and the lights of the cabin blasted so bright it appeared the BLP might have come back online. As Dominia comprehended in a click, the sailor frowned. "I just said it, but no sound came out."

"Because, you genius, it's not just a name. It *is* the ship." In wonder, Dominia said, "Say it again," and watched Tenchi's face. No hint of movement crossed his mouth, just as no movement might have emerged from Dominia's while she called up light or fire; yet there was another burst of power in the ship, another groan as if from a living thing. The General laughed and slapped the human on the back.

"Look at you, Tenchi! This is incredible. I understand, now. Any ship coming in or out of the Ergosphere has to be—amphibious, you could call it."

"Like me, General," Gethsemane said, sitting up and rubbing her eyes amid all the excitement.

"Yes," agreed Dominia. "Like you…a physical, earthly thing, imbued with the spirit of a Word…or a Word's daughter. Bound to the blood of Lazarus, somehow. But how?"

Farhad, who was not as on edge as the veteran martyr but still a high-strung man of war, had determined the commotion that awoke him was not a threat, and now shifted about, consulting the broad bands of an electromagnetic field that quadrupled in size as the airship—or amphibiship—came online. "If it could give a man like Tobias Akachi a soul, why could the blood not impart a spirit to a plane? Allah would not permit a righteous man who loved his ship to be eternally without her, or a pilot who loved his plane, or a rider who loved his camel. The spirit of your gun is here, Mahdi. Perhaps Tenchi was brought here because it was known he would connect to the plane in an…emotional way."

"Emotional valence," said the thoughtful General, crossing her arms and regarding both the sailor and the craft. "Personality has to be given to the thing…someone has to think well enough of it long enough to produce its real name. You're saying its name, Tenchi, though it doesn't sound like it. You know a True Word, now. Did the Lady come to you in your dream?"

"No," said the sailor, looking and sounding surprised. "You did." At Dominia's start, the sailor continued, "It was so vivid—I thought I was awake! You told me you wanted to talk to me before bed, after everybody settled down. After you started the fire for the night." An event of which she had no memory, but go on. "We walked off a ways with your light, and then you… started showing me these pictures in my head."

Frowning, Tenchi touched his forehead and laughed. "It's funny. It's not that I'm remembering the name so much as…I have to remember the sequence of pictures you showed me leading up to the name, and then I remember it's—"

The plane's radio cranked on, and the disembodied voice of none other than Valentinian carried throughout the amphibiship's cabin. "—for the weather. Looks like another calm day over the Atlantic Ocean, folks, but 'calm' doesn't mean 'short,' so if you have someplace to be and a craft of some kind to travel there in, I'd get along as soon as possible. Never know when conditions will change out there, and especially never know when conditions will change in reality. You'll know you've gone far enough east when your friendly neighborhood magician stops you for the night. And if you're planning to walk"—Dominia's ears perked up, her expression remaining neutral even as the eyes of her companions turned to scrutinize her—"then just be glad your Father shot you folks down well before your intended extraction point, or else you'd be in for an even longer march. Thanks for listening: now back to the music."

Said "music" was just a hissing wave of static. With a frown, Dominia stepped aboard to shut the radio off, then turned to see her friends crowded at the door.

"Are you separating from us, Mahdi?" Farhad stroked his beard before offering, "The men will suppose you a traitor if we return without you. If you are going where I suspect you are."

"I have to help somebody." She glanced at Tenchi. The sailor, flushing, lowered his gaze until she looked back at her other friends. "Several somebodies. Lavinia, my sister in Elsinore—she needs me more than you do. I've been plagued by that this year, and I need to face it."

"I wish you wouldn't go," Teddy whined while she hopped down from the craft.

"I wish I didn't have to. But I do." With brief acknowledgment of the woman who stuttered between, say, half the hair or one of the eyes of the nymph before jolting back to her own features, the General said, "Nobody here needs me much longer, anyhow."

"No," said Gethsemane. "But we want you."

Tender words that took some strength to be spoken from a woman who would put the will of her deity over her own life. It was the will of that deity that had sent Dominia thus—but also the weight of her own guilt. With that in mind, she glanced at Theodore, and asked, "Still want to return to the Family after everything that happened last night?"

"Oh, of course not! Get me as far away from him as possible. But…" He studied the humans before saying to his sister, "After what you said to me back there, you're doing the right thing by going back for her. Somebody needs to."

"Thank you. Travel safe, everybody. I have to—" Her heart sagged in her chest and the General turned to avoid revealing her sorrow. "I should get going. Don't want to drag this out."

Definitely not. She was tired of parting ways with her friends. Once, Miki and Kahlil had left her by way of that cherry-colored rental car. Now both of them were dead, strictly speaking, though she had seen both—Miki's body, and Kahlil's spirit—last night, in her dream. "Dream." What was a dream in this place?

Maybe just a conversation hidden in a private pocket of the universe within the self. Without looking back at the vanishing point of her friends as the humming amphibiship rose under the hands of Farhad and his spiritual copilot (first mate), Dominia set out east and received help from those threads that had overflowed from a recent pocket of hers. The data collapsed, reformed, recolored based on her intention. Each step, she followed not her imprecise compass but the ethereal veins that guided her directly to Tenchi's execution in America. Three weeks from his capture: this date, implied by the sailor's testament to walking three days, was confirmed by the threads that contained enormous assortments of information conveniently arranged by humans. How incredible it was! How convenient the mortal development of the Internet made navigating this formless space, which was dark even in daylight!

"It is most convenient," agreed the voice of her Father, who startled her only slightly as he appeared to her blinded right.

"Where did you come from?"

"I thought I would accompany you, since it seemed to me you could use a friend in a moment like this."

"A friend, yes. Not you."

"What better friend have you than I, my daughter?"

She tried not to roll her eyes. "Can't you just wait for me to come to you? Do you always have to show up to bother me?"

"Then you would be alone with your own thoughts. Far worse than listening to me drone on." Still smiling, he plucked a metaphysical thread that Dominia could not herself see at that moment, her mind being focused on other matters. "Isn't it funny how all it takes for us to gain a new power in this place is to *notice* something? To apply a bit of attention—of consciousness. So much is revealed when we wake up to what has been around us all this time! At any rate, as you were thinking—yes, my dear, the Internet is convenient for mortals. More convenient, still, for those entities that thrive in multiple dimensions. It's far easier for thoughtforms to enter the human mind when they have the gateway of digital data. All the stuff on your computer is but a physically intelligible form of pure information. To attract a so-called demon once upon a time, one either had to be very sick, or very curious. Now all that attachment requires is the Internet. If I can find any person in the world by studying this stuff long enough, imagine what effects could be had by a thoughtform attracted to some vapid vessel emptied out by a panoply of funny cat pictures and permutations of cartoon frogs."

Ridiculous. "Are you trying to tell me the Internet is a cause of spiritual or demonic possession?"

"It can be. There are a few other ways for one to be possessed. Think about it—that old classic horror-movie method of reading the wrong grimoire isn't a far cry from visiting a nefarious website or adopting the nasty predilections of a terroristic chat room. Anytime one gives up control of one's mind to a concept, that is, strictly speaking, a form of possession: extremist politic groups possess fragile human minds all the time, hence the Hunters and the very UF militias you've put down. However, in a place such as this, one is tempted to symbologize the concept—"

"Please!" The General sighed in exasperation. "Please, I just got up and I had a long night."

"So sorry to hear that, princess. Rest assured, your suffering is soon at its end. With these threads, you can even navigate in the dark, albeit at your own peril. I only mean to say that, even through a digital interface, the mind of the individual is a powerful portal into this place and back. Into the future, and eternity."

"Did you come here just to pontificate?"

"No, my dear. As I said, I came to keep you from being alone with your treacherous thoughts. Would not want you feeling bad about all this, would we?"

"'All this'? What's 'this'?"

"Why, this business of your running away. Of Cassandra. *I* think you did the right thing, darling. Doesn't that matter for anything?"

"Of course you think I did the right thing." Laying her hand across her forehead as though to physically shield her brain from the onslaught of the Hierophant's words, she said, "You corrupted me."

His tone was infinitely calm and inappropriately teasing. "It's always my fault, isn't it, Dominia?"

"It *is*, damn it! It's your fault that I was martyred! That I turned out this way. I didn't ask to be martyred. Fuck—I never asked to be born as a *human*!"

"Didn't you?"

The General's mouth opened to silence, then shut in like fashion, and she realized only then that she had, at some point, stopped walking to focus on arguing with her Father. Nonetheless, the black sun continued its dark journey against its indigo backdrop, as though the contents of their conversation (or perhaps the distant journey of her companions) was enough to move that great dot toward its destination, and the end of Tenchi's life. As she carried on at double pace, she said, "Maybe a past me, my last self, set me up so I could be here, sure. I freely admit that if you ask me right now if I'd do all this again just to be with Cassandra—if that was the only way to be with Cassandra again, I'd do it. But *I*—the 'me' I am right now, with *my* memories and *my* choices and *my* future still open before me—I never asked for any of this. You never had to show up at my parents' house. You never had to martyr me. Theodore has every right to be pissed at you. Why did you do any of that, if you knew what would happen?"

"Because, my dear girl! I love you."

"Oh, shut up."

"Now you're only hurting my feelings. It's true."

"Okay," she said, trying not to roll her eye as he carried on, "Who could *but* love such a scrappy cub falling into their arms, ready to fight them to the death! My good, bold girl with such big opinions. I knew your fate and wanted to save you. I wished to give you the immortality of martyrdom because I think it is still possible for you to make the right choice."

"It's a false immortality! Martyrs die all the time."

"You would know." That ugly little smile! She tried not to bite off her own tongue, particularly as the Lady's voice emanated from her left periphery.

Waste less time tormenting your daughter. You are the murderer of races, of planets, and of a greater number of humans than even the General.

"Yes," he said, with that look of cartoonish innocence, "but all those deaths were necessary, if you ask me. Dominia cannot say the same. Therein lies her problem."

"Are you both real?" she asked sharply, while the two walking behind her carried on with only the Hierophant's unhelpful, "I imagine I'm as real as she is."

You, Dominia, are a distinct entity within the Ergosphere, the Lady more helpfully explained. *Easy to find. A landmark of your own. It is the energy you exhibit. Space bends around you.*

"Me?" she asked, but the Hierophant already carried on. "Since you are so eager to join in on conversations to which you were not invited, O Lady, let me give you context: we were just discussing my concerns that Dominia cannot accept responsibility for her actions and wants, more than anything, to blame the woes of her life upon me."

"I take responsibility for what I've done, but I don't take responsibility for what you've done, or what you've made me do."

"What I've made you do is, strictly speaking, most of what you've done, for most of your life."

No wonder she was such a violent person, as much as she was forced to repress around him! With a twitch of her hand, the General turned her attention toward the Lady. Under the light of so-called day, Her image seemed infinitely more unstable than had Gethsemane's: it consisted of not just Miki Soto but her red-haired predecessor, and hers, and, and, and, until Dominia looked so deeply into the Lady under the black sun that she saw the first, hefty avatar, whose melanin-dark skin was baked further by the sun and whose body seemed immobile (and who, in retrospect, probably began the tradition of the Lady's permanent carriage from place to place in the mortal world). Despite her size, this manifestation glided with feminine ease across the frozen waves of the Ergosphere.

Not shown among all the visions was that black entity that had appeared briefly during Miki's ascension. Dominia realized with an uncanny chill that this was because the being was the substance around them: the black waters of the Lady that contained all forms of data, including the dead, and potentially dead.

"Yes, Dominia," said the Hierophant, again annoying her with his observation of her thoughts. "All the dead dwell here, though I have never discovered the means by which to contact them. Have you?"

"Why don't you just dig through my head and find out?"

"I understand that you saw the dead, yet I do not understand the mechanism. But what potential if one *could*! Why, even bodily resurrection would be possible."

"Please," she begged, but he went on.

"I mean it, my girl, I mean it from love for you! Would it not be glorious to bring your Cassandra back into the world? Even after the crime your cruelty forced her to commit against herself?"

"I didn't force her to do anything. And I wasn't cruel, either."

"I'm not certain your wife would agree."

"Look!" The word was expressed as a hiss while she wheeled on him, having barely fought the impulse to clutch the lapels of his jacket and crack his nose with her skull. "You want to have this fight with me right now? No problem. I loved Cassandra. I did everything I did *because* I loved Cassandra. What she did to herself was a calculated decision to hurt me. If anybody was cruel, it was *her*. Right?" On turning to the Lady, Dominia was deflated by the multi-woman's cold appraisal.

There is no conscious being without fault in the world of the Hierophant. The Lady was polite enough to refrain from offending the General, who deserved to be offended. *The difficulty is not in having faults, or even in their improvement, but in their admission.*

There was the old motherfucker with his Shakespeare: "'The fault, dear Brutus, is not in our stars, but in ourselves.'"

"I can admit my faults," the General insisted, pained, drowning in her own arguments and sorry self-denial. "I can admit everything I did while in my Father's service. I orchestrated genocide. I didn't even do it, myself. I stood like a coward in the shadows, where I helped suggest and design a calculated effort to eliminate undesirables in the human race while trying to attract new, other undesirables for future food. But I only did this because of the values *he* instilled in me."

What else have you done as a result of what you were taught was acceptable?

The General's throat closed as if in allergic reaction to the truth. She turned her blinking eye to the light-bled sky, avoided her Father's gaze, hurried her pace. "I did what I had to do. I did what I had to do for my family, and for my species, and for my own sanity. I did what I had to do for my wife."

"You did it, also, to hurt her," suggested her Father. "Even if only slightly."

That did it. She couldn't stand it anymore. "And I'm sorry," she blurted, eye squeezing shut at a sudden flicker of Cassandra's face across her imagination. Flushed with the pleasure of love, stained with the tears of loss, lifting from the toilet bowl that fateful night after their marriage. That night when it was too late to do anything about the reality of the situation. Too late for

Dominia to change her mind. "Yes," the General admitted in the thick silence of the Ergosphere, despite her stinging throat, "I'm sorry. Yes, I did."

She did. She put her wife to bed and left her, ostensibly to go out for some wine. Instead, she chartered her private jet to take her home to Europa, and went directly to Venezia's small but beautiful palazzo. The refuge's lease was awarded to her after her some long-forgotten victory when she was about Theodore's age, and would almost never be visited after the following nine months. After that, it was forever tied to the discovery of Cassandra's pregnancy.

A car waited for her at the airport, having been alerted to her arrival. Would she be staying long? She didn't know. She wasn't even sure what she was doing there. She had nothing to say to the driver. She had nothing to say to anyone. The car took Dominia directly to that old property where she discovered who else but her Father. She didn't mind. It was, ultimately, his domicile.

"What a pleasant surprise." He looked up from where he sat reading in the parlor of her master apartment, his voice so full of pleasure it could only be described as a crow. "Is Cassandra awake, a martyr at last? Have you and she decided to honeymoon here? I shall be out by midnight, my girl."

Just listen to him talk. She slipped her keys into her suit pocket and sat across from him, in the high-backed chair by the empty Renaissance-era fireplace she studied for a long time—such a long time—before saying anything at all. Then, perhaps because of some particularly empty set of cherub eyes gazing out at her, the General scorned the barren stone mantle and said to the Hierophant, "Cassandra was pregnant."

He did not speak. Did not even move, the book still resting upon his knee with his hand upon its cover. She had a need to fill the silence, much as she wished she could fill that vile hollow that opened in her chest to comprehend this betrayal. "I'm not sure what to do."

"We will do everything we can to support her, of course," had been the Father's answer. Dominia studied him, expression bleak.

"She's very sick."

"She will survive."

"Will the baby?"

"Yes."

"You're positive?"

"Do you wish it were otherwise?"

Her lips pressed thin, the General said at a dark octave, "I wish this wasn't a problem."

"New life is never a 'problem.' My girl"—his tone took a dangerous turn of its own as he rose, the book in his massive hand revealing itself as a copy of *Divina Commedia* as he meandered around the coffee table—"I hope you are not suggesting what I think you are suggesting. Termination is one thing for a mere human—but for a martyr?"

"I don't know what I'm suggesting." Though unruffled by his approach or the danger in his tone, which seemed in that instant an almost welcome threat, she remained still as black marble Juno, gazing with empty eyes up at the book he rested on the mantle. "I just wish this hadn't happened. If I had known—"

"If you had known, you would have waited to martyr her, and martyred the child when it was old enough, yes? A happy family."

"I don't know. I don't want children. I've never wanted children—never wanted to do that to a child. Force it to be in this world."

Shaking his head, the Hierophant said, "Yet, how I wish it were otherwise! I so long to be a grandfather again. You've denied me for too many centuries."

"Would you settle for being a Father again?"

She had meant it as a joke, maybe. At least, that was what she told herself over and over through the years. Joke or not, the second the suggestion left her lips, it was too late. All that mirth in his eyes. He had waited for this moment—had known before Dominia presented him with Cassandra that this was how things ended up. How Dominia hated him for letting it get this far! Her love was a ploy to him. A means to acquire the new child he wanted. And not just a new child. A child born a martyr, rather than martyred in life.

After finding his quiet daughter sufficiently deferent to his soft-spoken threats, the Hierophant strolled to the bar to pour them both drinks. "Do you know, my girl, the true joy of parenting? It is the shaping of not just an individual but of a new generation: the future of a species. The trouble with being a martyr is that parenting is difficult—often traumatic for the child. But what a wonderful world it would be if our race could propagate the same as any other! How much suffering could be saved if the protein did not wreak havoc on the reproductive cells of the body, and we could produce live children."

With two glasses of burgundy wine, he returned to pass her one. "Most pregnant women would never knowingly be martyred. Those in a position to be martyred are not often in a position to be pregnant or are not interested in such things. My own legal restriction on the martyring of pregnant women is one of—well, it does rather pose me a problem, does it not? I am used to reviewing the martyring of children, or I was before our effort at population expansion these past few decades. We are a highly selective breed. And, frankly, the majority of martyr pregnancies will certainly end in the death of both mother and baby. The amount of nutrition required to maintain both is untenable. Trust me, I have studied this subject. But it *is* possible to maintain the child to birth. And what is possible, to even a narrow degree, our good

Lamb can make reality. He could turn the odds in favor of mother and baby; and being given as they would round-the-clock medical care with attention and techniques far in advance of public technologies available at present… imagine the possibilities."

"Why is this so important to you?"

"She must be no more than five or six months into her pregnancy—you met her in July, and we're in September now, so she must have conceived long enough before your meeting for her to have known."

"She told me she's five months."

"Ah…so just before your trouble at Nogales, give or take a few weeks. Very interesting." Acting like he didn't know, as always. She hated him twice as much in memory! But in that moment, what he proposed next was so extraordinary that she simply couldn't feel anything, let alone hatred. "If the infant is a girl, her ovaries will be developed by now, but her eggs may not be complete. Lamb be willing…"

"You think the baby would be born fertile."

"I'm certain of it. The transition sterilizes a martyr because of the death process the body undergoes between their human and martyr existence; normal functions of puberty in a prepubescent are aborted and replicated by the protein, which cannot replicate healthy reproductive cells and cannot, therefore, generate novel life. But when the protein is introduced in the womb, it presents a unique opportunity in the appropriate circumstances, with the right medical care and a mother who can survive to term. In such a theoretical case, the protein is like a third parent. The sperm, the egg, and the protein make equal, early contributions to the fetus, the shock of the death is lessened, and prepubescent functions are uninterrupted. Was Cassandra deceased long?" At the shake of Dominia's head, he continued his thought. "With a child in the womb, there is a longer, enforced incubation period in which the protein can make improvements, and more resources to improve *with*—Cassandra's resources."

Staring out into space, the wine staining her lips more opaque with each sip, the General said, "She lied to me."

"She did not know what else to do," was her Father's gentle assurance.

"Will you help me, really? She can't ever know about this. Can't know that you're responsible for this."

"*You* are responsible for this, my girl. But she will not know. At the opportune time, we will make it all seem very believable that her baby has died. This will not be difficult to mimic. The protein will take advantage of the baby's state of un-life and alter much, causing many physical problems until she is completely developed. But however difficult it is, when the moment of delivery comes, the infant will be out of your hands before poor Cassandra has even had a chance to think about what happened. Why, I'm even feeling inclined to offer you a promotion for bringing all this to me up front. I so value your honesty, Dominia."

"And how will you keep her from figuring out your new kid is hers?"

"Oh, we'll concoct something. Will she have time to think of such things as the new Sponsa Prima of the United Front? As I said, there will be complications in the process, and the child will need be hidden from the public eye for some time. By the time our people become aware of the new Family member, Cassandra will have long convinced herself that her child died. She won't connect the two."

"Do you think she's stupid?"

"Of course not—but do you realize how paranoid she would have to be to believe the truth?"

After finishing her wine, Dominia took a second bottle and returned by the same jet on which she'd left. Maybe on her departure she'd intended to leave Cassandra for good, but now she returned with a better alternative and gentler face, her fury having been purged by the time her wife awoke after a long, dense, coma-like slumber.

"We'll get through this," Dominia swore, smoothing her wife's golden waves. "I promise. We'll get through this together, Cassandra."

By the time the General was freed from the shameful memory that she had ignored and denied for almost a hundred years, it seemed that the Hierophant and Lady had both left her. Both, surely, had business to attend to in reality; and both, surely, knew that she drew near New Elsinore. She had traveled days while plunged in those awful thoughts. Somehow, it didn't alarm her; perhaps because she had no emotional energy left after reviewing that terrible meeting.

Above her, the black sun had vanished from sight. The tangles of red thread were far more numerous, and she wondered if this was not a result of the livestream of the execution. Vultures tuning in to watch poor Tenchi die.

Good. She wanted an audience.

The strings she followed converged at the reflection in the Void of that physical point in space-time that concerned the psyches and phones of so many across the globe. With a chill, Dominia plucked the heart of the threads, and saw uncountable news broadcasts all discussing the same thing: Cicero's demand that the Governor of the United Front be returned, with Tenchi's life at stake. First Mate Tenchi Ichigawa, the terrorist.

More like Tenchi, the good-natured sailor who had never done anything wrong—who had encountered Dominia at the start of her journey and been a friendly, generous, albeit cowardly little fellow. A purehearted and sweet enough man that he could even bond with an inanimate ship, and render it animate. This was a man who did not deserve to die for any so-called cause.

Closing her eyes, Dominia focused on the strings beneath her hands, and spoke that True Word for "reality."

This method was never any less disorienting than her trip through space had been. Particularly not this time, as the black Void submitted to the image of reality that she had half seen replicated in the news broadcasts reflected by the threads. A New Elsinore court building, full to the brim with reporters: with Cicero and the Lamb, and, most of all, Tenchi, who let out a tearful cry of absolute joy as the General tore the vial of Lazarus's blood from her throat, shattered it against the desk where the prisoner awaited his fate, then sprang across to wipe her bloodstained fingers over Tenchi's mouth.

"Drink the blood, Tenchi," she urged amid Cicero's shouts that the guards, already moving in, needed control of Dominia before she hurt one of the screaming reporters. "Drink the blood, and when you end up in the Ergosphere, walk east until you meet the magician!"

"What are you talking about?" he said, instinctively licking his lips at the moment massive hands claimed the General's arms and gun barrels were pushed against her head. She laughed all the same to know that Tenchi was saved, and lifted her gaze to find one intrepid reporter whose cameraman still filmed from where they cowered in the corner. Too devoted to the story of a lifetime to worry how long that lifetime would be, it seemed.

"I am the terrorist Dominia di Mephitoli," she said, grinning in defiance as her face was forced to the table and her wrists, cloistered by the tight snap of electrified cuffs, "and I've come here tonight to surrender."

VI

Jiggety-Jig

On waking in her old Kronborg bedchambers, the first thought to cross Dominia's mind was one of suicide—but the window had been left unlocked, so she supposed her Father hoped for the possibility. Not an option. After sitting up, she absorbed her second conscious element of the room: the bar, fresh-stocked with a panoply of spirits all artfully topped with a cheerful plum ribbon whose attached tag read "Welcome Home."

The third action of the homecome General was the defenestration of most bottles out the unbarred window and into the snowy gardens below, followed by the emptying of another—with a regretful whiff of wasted whiskey—into the roots of some hapless shrub too far beneath to be seen. A brusque knock upon the door attracted her attention as she turned for another. On her call of admission (in Mephitolian, the dominant language of her speech for the rest of that life on Earth), the Lamb stepped inside, a thin smile beneath his close-clipped beard.

"Making yourself at home, I see."

"Good night to you, too, Rabbi. I've come to the conclusion I have sort of a drinking problem." She hefted the nearest vessel of rum. "Want some?"

"This early in the evening? Please, as big a glass as you have." The General permitted herself the luxury of laughter and turned to pour her gentler parent a glass. He, arms folded, asked, "How was the...uh, flight over? Devolving from New Elsinore to Old..."

"Fine. The men Cicero assigned to accompany me only smelled a little nervous, from what I could tell through the muzzle. At least they were polite. How was *yours*?"

"Cushy." Accepting the drink, the Lamb lowered his ram-horned head to sniff the glass's contents. "Suppose you want to know about your friend."

"He's still alive, right?" Not that it mattered, him having had the blood, and her having seen his future spirit. One way or another, he was in the Ergosphere, and that would be true even if he'd been killed on Earth. That said, the thought of Tenchi's bodily death devastated her. Luckily, the Lamb nodded.

"Yeah—Cicero kept his word. You came back. Didn't bring Teddy with you, but execution's still off. Although—I'm sure you know this—it's mostly your Father's doing that stayed his hand. Cicero would love to slaughter everybody who's ever called themselves your friend after that whole marathon thing."

"I was stressed at the time." She jutted her chin in the direction of the door. "So, what's the deal? Am I under house arrest, or..."

"What do you think?"

"Of course not. Free to come and go as I please."

"I'm pretty sure he's having a car delivered for you today. Maybe tomorrow."

The snorting General studied the bedroom in which she'd finally parted ways with those cagey guards following about twenty-four hours' worth of check-in, transportation, and checkout. Had she not administered such hasty captures and deliveries, herself, she would have been disoriented, but to be fair, the bedrooms in Kronborg were disorienting enough on their own. She had always disliked the castle's style of placing its beds so they floated in the center of the floor, rather than standing with the support of a sensible wall. This was a problem with most of their estates, which, aside from a few modifications and the odd added balcony or torture chamber, were fussily maintained in their "proper" condition. Kronborg was the exception in its architecture—whole wings had been added to the castle with the Hierophant's cautious oversight—but the added rooms could have passed for original parts of the building, so carefully they had been furnished. She didn't see why it mattered where the damn bed went, or how the furniture looked. With a palace like Versailles, she could understand, but Kronberg's design had always been more forgiving. Surely the bed could be put in a more comfortable position.

Lord love the Lamb, but she was already thinking about the place like she'd moved in to stay. Time to get Lavinia and get the fuck out.

"I'm glad to see you," the Lamb said, snapping her from thoughts he knew like his own. "But do you think it was the right thing to come back now?"

This room was no doubt as bugged as any other in the castle, with the Lamb two parts concerned Family member and one part sorry pawn. He may well have come to visit her of his own volition, but more likely he'd been sent to butter her up. That was the way things had been ever since she was a kid. Good cop/bad cop didn't even begin to cover dealing with the Lamb and Cicero. No matter how friendly the Lamb may have been to her cause, she could say nothing incriminating of herself, the Lady, or her intention to assist Lavinia. But even if she shared no information, interactions with her Family members could be perilous to her resolve.

In the many histories of infinite universes, the General must have defected a litany of times for a laundry list of reasons, none of which she knew. This meant the Hierophant also knew of the possibilities and may even have known a few of the concrete ways she defected before—which meant she could pretend she was open to the possibility of returning home for good, as long as she didn't come on too strong.

The best solution was, as usual, a concoction of lie and reality. "I couldn't imagine what else to do," she said with a shrug. "I looked at myself and said, 'What am I doing?'" This was true. "I couldn't keep treading water out there. Just waiting for…something. I haven't felt myself at all lately. Then when I heard about Tenchi…it seemed like it was time to come back."

"Tired of waiting for the sky to collapse." The Lamb observed the open window through the murky glass of his drink. "Why sit around when you can collapse it, yourself?"

Best not to answer loaded questions, even from semi-sympathetic mouths. After two millennia of being beaten down by Cicero and the Hierophant, the Lamb was ultimately worth about as much as one of his own dogs. Speaking of: "Add any new animals to the collection since last year?"

"Oh, always a couple…you know how it is."

Yes, she did. The Lamb had a sensitive heart. He couldn't bear to leave abandoned the pets of those humans unlucky enough to attend a martyrs' Mass. Most relocated pets adjusted to their new homes with little problem. Dogs, and especially cats, forgave even homicide given sufficient food and affection. Could the same be said of God?

"Your Father would like to see you, when you get a moment." With one last bob of his throat, the Lamb drained the glass, set it at the edge of the emptied bar, and retraced his steps to the door. "I wouldn't have bothered you if he hadn't asked me to tell you that…not that I don't want to see you, but I'm sure you want some time alone."

The General offered a wan smile. "It's not that I don't want to see you, either."

She caught the barest edge of his upturned mouth as he shut the door. Alone, the General consulted her reflection in the vanity across from that oddly centered bed. No matter how often she studied it in reality, the vision of her body never aligned with what she pictured in her head, or how she appeared when wandering around in the Void—the Ergosphere. (Cogito, ergo…) Yes, she could shower in a downright glorious bathroom of which Hamlet never dreamed, could dress in one of the crisp white shirts and black suit pants stocked in the closet, could smooth back her hair and comb pomade through its dark strands until she looked like the bureaucrat she'd become after the army; but she felt forever her leather jacket, her flowing black hair, the phantom cup of a patch against her shut right eye. This person who she truly was felt like a great secret within her. Some source of power from which she could never be separated. The only consistency between these two selves was Cassandra's diamond. Her little wife who was with her in the Ergosphere and remained with her outside it—even if that wife could not be said to know.

It was that diamond that put her friends on her mind as she strode down the great checkerboard halls (not unlike her Father's dream study), past courtiers, servants, and a few human slaves. All of them marveled and whispered to see Dominia again. Now that she considered it, it had been some months since she'd spent any prolonged time in Kronborg. When she visited it in the wake of Cassandra's death, she'd hardly been of mind to take in her surroundings. Now alert, it was revealed to her that in the time she'd spent living and working in the United Front, the fashion of the castle women had grown stuffier than ever. An elaboration of petticoats and bustiers rendered most female specimen more akin to walking umbrellas in the midst of a windstorm than the sleek beings Dominia so loved. Meanwhile, men's fashion had remained the same over the past hundred years—save the number of breasts given a suit, or whether items such as hats and capes were "in." Seemed like "in" for short capes, "out" for hats. Easy. Was it any wonder the General preferred a more masculine fashion sense, even with long hair? Life was less complicated in a button-up shirt.

Of course, the explosion of suffocating fabrics for women was due in large part to the influence of one particular fashion maven, who was only a maven because no one dared tell her no. This same unqualified influencer dashed around a distant corner with such a furious *tap-tap-tap* of slippers—of both herself and her bevy of attendants—that Dominia fancied a small army of gazelles charged down the hall. It was only Lavinia, who, on seeing her older sister from across the distant moonlit path, let her great black skirts fall swishing around her feet so as to clasp her hands over her heart and cry, "Oh, *Ninny*!"

"Lavinia," said the General, bracing herself much as she would while in the presence of the Lamb's dogs. Lavinia hurtled down the hall and threw herself, weeping, into Dominia's arms with such force that the slim girl might have bowled her over amid the added weight of all those petticoats.

"Ninny! Ninny, I've been so *worried* about you! Oh, I'm so happy you're *home*! Where are you going? We have to talk! Were you scared?"

Hard to answer twenty questions at once. She settled for two. "Father wants to see me. I was never in any real danger." Simpler to lie on that last bit than to point out that Lavinia's beloved "Daddy" was responsible for most—or all—of the danger in which Dominia had been put. Bad personal choices aside.

Granted, were her choices all that bad? Looking at Lavinia's tearful face, the General couldn't help but think there was no possibility for her sister's life to have gone another way. Would the Hierophant have *allowed* Cassandra to keep the child, had Dominia not donated her to him? Would that have been all the more traumatic for her little wife? Hadn't this been the better choice?

"Ninny," said Lavinia, "you're frowning! You've got that little line you get in your forehead. What's the matter?"

"Nothing's the matter, Lavinia. I've just been more worried about you than you've been about me, that's all. And I'm still worried about you."

"Worried about *me*, silly!" As the Princess of Europa tittered, so did the coterie hired to shield her from loneliness—and perhaps, Dominia now realized, shield her from knowledge of her own fertile body. Two of the gutless harpies hid behind their fans while a third, attractive one, made brazen eye contact with the General. "Why would anyone worry about *me*! I'm the most spoiled girl on Earth."

At least she was sort of in touch with reality. Dominia forced a smile. "I guess I was worried about you, worrying for me."

"Oh, that's silly." With a sudden fox-sly look about and a dropping of her voice, Lavinia leaned in to ask, "Do you have to go see Daddy right *now*?"

"I better get it over with, don't you think?"

In an adorable moue of concern that resembled a dilution of Cassandra's soft features, the girl nibbled the edge of her lip, then replaced her lip with the pink tip of her gloved thumb as she gazed through the hall-length windows. Rather than acknowledge what may come of the meeting with her Father, Dominia would have opted to continue contemplating dreamy Elsinore's old world—frosted with snow like this, the town looked to the General like a movie set. She'd been here in summer many times, but she only ever pictured it in winter. Happy and peaceful times, winter. Reality insisted on intruding, much as Lavinia insisted on disrupting her thoughts with the urgent whisper, "Won't he be very angry with you, Ninny?"

She laughed. "That's your second understatement after assuming you're the most spoiled girl on Earth and not the most spoiled girl in this universe—and every other."

"I suppose I'm more spoiled than anyone on Mars. But you're trying to distract me! Don't you think you should come and spend time with me before you see Daddy?"

With a brief spell of nausea, the General eyed her adopted sister. "Do you know something I don't, Lavinia? He's not planning to execute me or anything, is he?"

"Oh, of course not! I hope not— Ninny, Daddy would *never* do that. At least, not since you came home." With her silk-enclosed hands fidgeting anxiously before her, Lavinia glanced once more out the window. "Can't I at least walk you to his office," she insisted.

It came to the General then. This was the worry of a little girl for her older sister's emotions. She was afraid that Dominia was secretly afraid, and trying to be brave. In all fairness...for Lavinia's sake, the General manufactured a smile and squeezed her gloved hand.

"Sure. You can walk with me."

The Princess of Europa's expression flipped in an instant, and she turned to her followers. "Why don't you girls run along and, oh, I don't know... amuse each other somehow!" While Dominia coughed at Lavinia's innocent choice of words and tried to keep her mind from inappropriate territory, the princess waved away her pretty friends as if shooing birds from window boxes. "I haven't time for you now, please! I must be alone with my sister."

"Is it *safe* for you to be alone with her, Your Majesty?" asked that girl who had eyed the General for reasons Dominia's ego mistook as attraction. Lavinia wheeled on this servant with a sharply narrowed gaze.

"Does my Daddy pay you to second-guess my decisions, or does he pay you to be my friend?" (*Slave*, Dominia mentally corrected.) "Run along now! I'll fetch you somehow when you're wanted."

Or put up a big, bratty fuss when they weren't telepathically where she expected them at the exact second she arbitrarily wanted their company again. Though aware of this fact as Dominia was, the girls obediently hurried away in a bustle of whispers—and one furtive glance from that scrutinizing one. Outside the occasional passing courtier going for an evening constitutional around the castle, the women were now alone, and Lavinia became a chatterbox. Oh, she had missed Dominia! She had cried for nights after that awful business in Kabul, but the General didn't need to worry because Lavinia had already forgiven her. Although Cicero—well, Cicero was another matter. He was *very* cross. But that was just like him, wasn't it? Not that he had ever been cross with Lavinia all that much, but, why, she had *seen* how he could be, and she had *certainly* seen how he was after all that business with his eye. Now, just why did Dominia *do* that, at any rate? Didn't she know the Golden Rule? Daddy's testament? "Do unto martyrs as you would have them do unto you"? Remember, Ninny? Ninny? Remember that?

"You know," said Dominia through a strained smile, "for some reason, I've always been bad at that one."

T(he)i(r) talking paused outside the door of the Hierophant's office, outrageously oversize and set at the end of the most strategically imposing hallway in any of his properties. Of significant length, its walls were decorated by tapestries that, one per century, detailed the Hierophant's various conquests and cultural developments. From his early years on Earth dancing between the Russian Federation and the North American Empire of the United States, through the persecution and emergence of the martyr people, past the colonization of Mars, and to the present day. The most recent three contributions prominently featured Dominia's many bloody victories with increasing prominence, until the Battle for the Reclamation of Mexico formed the centerpiece of the latest. It had been commissioned and produced to be ready for the turn of the century, and was revealed on New Year's Day of 1997 AL, two years earlier than its standard due. When asked at the time, her Father had cheerfully responded he'd "wanted to get a hop on things." Now, the General understood he had wanted it here for this moment. To remind her all she'd done in his name. His psychological cruelty never lacked in detail.

From within the office drifted the eerie sound of music—what else but Mozart's Requiem. With a nervous look for the General, Lavinia pressed again: "You're sure you really *have* to see him now?"

"It's now or later… I'd rather get it over with."

"Will you come see me after, Ninny, and tell me what happened? I'm afraid. Daddy's so frightful when he's cross!"

"Surely he hasn't had many reasons to be cross with you," said Dominia, who now studied her sister's expression in search of some truth she knew not what. Lavinia's eyes dropped from the General's face, and the girl turned back the way they'd come.

"I can't be good *all* the time, Ninny. Goodness! I'm a saint, not God. But, oh, Ninny—" The girl frowned and fussed a moment, then darted back to plant a kiss on Dominia's cheek before she once more hurried down the hall. "I've missed you, I want you to be *here*! Please don't give him a reason to lock you up, or—oh, just don't."

"I'll try not to." The General squeezed out one last laugh, watching her sister go, before turning her attention back to the towering door. With a deep breath that came in time with the voice of *Tuba mirum*'s tenor, Dominia knocked its ivory-inlaid surface.

"*Entrez*," rang his pretentious reply. Steadying herself, she pushed open that great portal with both hands to find the Hierophant writing at his gilded desk with the fire crackling soft (and normal) in its marble place. Cicero, in one of two leather seats across from him, turned both his good eye and the rolling black one against this intruder to his appeal, then froze. His organic pupil dilated while the red one bloomed eerily within his DIOX-I.

"Dominia," acknowledged her curt brother, implied uncle, and least favorite Family member. She shut the door behind her and the Hierophant, in tone far more joyous, also called, "Ah, my Dominia!" and sprang from his seat to embrace her whether she wanted it or not. "My girl, my girl, my poor prodigal daughter"—she thought of the Lady, grimacing in his embrace, and hoped he couldn't read her thoughts here while he stood in the flesh—"mere words are not sufficient to relay my true relief. You're home! My dearest daughter is home, at last. I have spent every second of this year pining for your return."

"Good to see you, too," the General said, glancing but once at Cicero. She, for one, was glad to pretend she hadn't seen the Holy Father since last September's marathon. His immediate uptake of the charade was tacit reinforcement of his prior reassurance that El Sacerdote knew nothing of the Ergosphere, or the true nature of Lazarene blood. As he released her from his hug and she suffered his kiss upon her cheek, she marveled to see he'd even worked up a watery eye. Bravo. "I'm sort of surprised I'm allowed to wander around here, after all that's happened."

"As am I," muttered Cicero, turning his attention to the window behind the Hierophant's deserted wingback chair. "I hope the bruises from your acquisition last night have disappeared, sister."

"More or less," she assured him, glancing at her wrists, then studying that same empty seat. "Hope you're getting used to your cyborgan, 'brother.'"

Said eye whirled in her direction as the Hierophant, tutting, hid his smile on the way to reclaim his chair. Dominia remained in place by the door. "Now, children—this is why I brought you both here for this conversation. I'm sure after all the sordid business of the past year, there's nothing you would both like better than to ignore one another completely!"

Cicero, passive-aggressive as a cat, folded his hands and turned his face toward a bookshelf. "'Ignoring' is not on the list of things I would do to my sister, Father, if I had my way."

"So we're talking about each other like the other one's not in the room?" Cicero deigned to shoot her a dirty look while she continued, "Because if so, 'Dad,' I know a real douchebag with an over-waxed moustache, and—"

The Hierophant snapped his fingers until she stopped. "The same as it ever was, I see. My goodness—how long it takes carbon lifeforms to grow up! I am still engaged in the process, myself." With that twinkle about his eye, the Hierophant straightened the pages before him and set them neatly aside. "With dear Dominia, the odd immature moment is more understandable, at least from my perspective—although you are well over three hundred, my dear. Far too old for these shocking displays of immaturity. We will discuss that in time. But so far as you are concerned, dear Cicero—"

With his brows lifted in a way that mirrored the shocked arch of Cicero's, the Hierophant wagged his finger. "You are the most powerful priest in all my Church, aside, of course, from myself. Old as your brother, the Lamb, at two thousand! Yet, how easily you submit to the very *human* flaw of wrath! Too long you've held this grudge, this loss of your eye. How very many classic passages could either of us quote on this very topic? Each more on the nose than the last! 'Turn the other cheek,' 'an eye for an eye'"—he glanced at Dominia—"although that second is better advice for *you*. Won't you sit?"

Once Cicero scooted his chair as far left as the unsubtle squeaks of its stubby legs allowed, Dominia filled the vacant seat. The Hierophant folded his hands after favoring his children with an approving smile.

"There. It's so nice to have the Family back together again, don't you think?"

"I just saw Lavinia," said the General, licking her dry lips. "I've missed her. It was good to see her again. It's good to be welcomed back by somebody who cared that I was gone."

Worked like a charm every time. Tension could almost always be defused by shifting attention from the conflict at hand to the subject of Lavinia, for she seemed to inspire as intense an adoration in Cicero as she did in the Hierophant and Theodore—perhaps more, and in a way Dominia suspected was far more prurient than El Sacerdote was willing to admit. Mere mention of the girl could bring a bit of light to his beady black eyes. Doubtless moved by the spirit that the Duchess of Florence inspired, he landed a frosty pat upon the back of Dominia's hand. "We all cared that you were gone, my sister."

"You cannot begin to imagine," enthused the heartily approving Hierophant on his son's obvious lie. "How you've *worried* me! Not a night goes by that I do not think of you or what you have been doing. Not to mention the people you've been running around with! Hunters, Dominia? I cannot understand."

"I've been in a very dark place."

"To react to your wife's suicide by taking sensitive information to the enemy—sensitive information about which you knew, at the time, truly nothing!—in pursuit of an obvious dream…my poor daughter, yes. A dark place, indeed." Plucking up the hand that Cicero had touched, the Hierophant pulled her arm across the desk to kiss her unwilling knuckles, to pat them and say, "I am sorry you were so lost, and that I did not see. That I did not think to help you. We failed you, my girl. Poor, troubled Dominia. You have lived a harder life than I ever intended for you."

Though taken aback at the almost genuine tone of his apology, the General reminded herself that no matter how good it felt to hear these things, they were almost verifiably false. Her weakness for his empty repentance was never so much because she believed he loved her, or maintained a single kernel of goodness. Rather, this vulnerability to his gestures emerged because, for centuries, she had paid deliberate overattention to his panache for flattery and placation. How else was she to cope with her circumstances? As a child, she had been a captive, given no choice but to favor his good qualities while blinding herself to his bad ones. But there were plenty of times in those young days when—as she did when he turned to Cicero and said, "Now that I've broken the ice between you, my boy, if you would leave us...I would like a word with Dominia alone"—she was acutely aware of the Holy Father's more frightening capabilities. Blood drained to the bottoms of her feet. When she tried to slip her hand back, the Holy Father maintained his grip with a clamp of his hands effortlessly disguised as an affectionate pat.

"I suppose I must trust Father's judgment," crooned Cicero, who crossed himself and kissed his knuckles in the Hierophant's direction. "If His Holiness sees fit that you should come and go as you please, who am I to second-guess? Good to see you home, Dominia." He threw open the door and, with one arm, yanked the heavy thing shut behind him. "We're just all glad you're in one piece."

Alone with the Hierophant—and not in the dream of the Void, where he either could not hurt her or could only do so negligibly—Dominia willed her pulse to stay slow and calm, because she could tell he took it with that great grip around her left hand. This, she studied before glancing into his bleak eyes as he said of Cicero's comment, "Yes we are. The human world—the Hunter world—is of exceptional danger for a martyr. You know that, Dominia."

"I didn't know what choice I had," she said, unwilling to move even to shrug. "I didn't see a future if I stayed."

"For yourself, or for the planet?"

As her Father released her hand, having no doubt decided that she was sufficiently anxious, she studied the pale teal vein of her wrist. It was true. Cassandra had not been the only motivation in Dominia's abandonment of the Front, the Family. Only the final nail in the coffin. When, after her wife's death the General had grown queasy about an idea that her Father had announced at a secret military conference—that was the lowering of that coffin into the ground. Project Black Sun, which she had not understood at the time, had seemed ridiculous but terrifying, and sent Dominia on a one-woman campaign to flee the martyrs' oppressive religious state.

Now, the plan was only terrifying. She'd no idea back then how it could be possible for martyrs to survive in sunlight, as her Father claimed it would be once the project was fully initiated—but she'd felt deep concern that the attainment of such a goal would mean the destruction of the planet in addition to the human race. The idea of unhampered martyrs seemed unsustainable then, when she knew nothing of other dimensions, the value of virtual data, and her Father's possession of all of it. Did a martyr want to come and kill you? They just had to pop into your living room. No need for threshold technology, what was the use? Just be a good little sheep, don't say anything controversial on the Internet—Lamb, don't even *have* the Internet—be quiet, polite, obedient, ignorant, hardworking. Then maybe—just *maybe*, if you're very lucky—you or the people you love won't be turned into meat. The situation of Dominia's time, magnified to a point of absolute, unspeakable conclusion. Giving the entire race of martyrs the blood of Lazarus with the Hierophant's claws still in their minds would jeopardize reality, the Ergosphere, maybe even the Kingdom.

"You want to get your hands on Lazarus." She settled as far back in her seat as she could, her now-free hand folded over her ribs. "I understand, but I think what I thought when you asked for my help in Kabul."

"Very disappointing, if true. I have concealed the secrets of Lazarus from our people to protect martyrs from themselves until this race possessed sufficient foothold on the planet—and until we had possession of you." While she snorted, he continued. "This is truth. You are key in managing our people and their relationship with that sacred dream-space. Before the crises of your time, our population would not have been prepared to take it with the seriousness and respect required. After this comes to a head, and you are once more at my side, they will comprehend the gravity of the Void within the context of the Holy Martyr Church."

"So you haven't shown them yet because they lack a frame of reference? That's ridiculous. Let them build their own. Why do they have to experience it through the Church?"

He smiled thinly. "Without a frame of reference to apply to my Church, they will not continue to listen to me. I have told you this already—the problem with Regulus, and so many others in generations before yours. My advice is critical if the species is to survive; and if the species remains obedient to our cause, why do martyrs not deserve the blood of Lazarus?"

"It's a cultural problem, mostly. What would they do with themselves, these people—"

"*Our* people, Dominia, *your* people."

"—what would martyrs do," she corrected in irritation, "if given unlimited access to that place? To thoughtforms?" She lifted her eyebrows at the mere implication of that odious Memory Bride that had cleaved to her thoughts and produced a corrupted, ignorant duplicate of Cassandra, then succeeded in transitioning to the physical world, even if only to die at the General's hands. "Do you really want a planet—a universe—full of thoughtform demons and martyrs not limited by the sun, or even physical space-time? How will humans survive? Uninitiated martyrs will run out of food, and initiated ones who can metabolize sunlight—"

"Oh, such martyrs will still be encouraged to follow the same diet they always have. It keeps us bonded to the Church and assists in the attraction and creation of thoughtforms, though such things are possible to accomplish without the aid of anthropophagy. However, it is undeniable that the traditional martyr diet increases the efficiency and simplicity of the creation of thoughtforms."

She bit her tongue, refrained from stating how thoughtforms weren't necessary for a Lazarene who knew a True Word, but she also supposed such a fact was beside the point for him. It wasn't about True Words, or thoughtforms. It was about keeping his species morally and psychologically crippled—keeping them trapped in a cycle of shame, which, in turn, kept them crawling back to the Church. Back to Earth. "You're going to cause the destruction of the human race. All sentient life."

"My dear, small-thinking daughter, that will never be an issue. I have gone out of my way to see to it! Come here, my girl, look with me."

The risen Hierophant pushed in his chair and strode to the window, where he waited patiently for Dominia to catch up to him beside the frosty glass. His breath condensing upon it, he first doubled over his massive frame and angled up his head; once satisfied, he drew Dominia down by the shoulders to point at one of the brightest visible cosmic bodies, its twinkle bright despite the city below. "Do you see that? Mars, my girl. As we speak, thousands—tens of thousands, by now—are working to transform its soil from barren rock to wholesome earth. All to sustain human life! The time of suicide or android missions launched from our lunar base is long over. The negligent ancestor of Carol McLintock"—the General grimaced to hear the name—"has, by now, died and left behind her Martian farm to Carol's optimistic aunts, or perhaps, already, her cousins. They live and thrive and receive monthly shipments that I do not even have to provide anymore! China, that blessed hermit nation, sends them, thinking they are helping humanity. All those happy colonists, fleeing martyrs for greener pastures...what do you suppose they are doing? They are multiplying—multiplying so that, by the time we martyrs require the services of their planet, they will be ready to generously accept the burdens of their betters—and perhaps even begin another colony elsewhere."

"You're breeding a planet of slaves," marveled Dominia, not astonished by the fact so much as his flat admission. "You're *prepared* to ruin this planet because you've got a backup."

"And many others, though much farther away and in the distant future aside from a few Luna-related plans we're drawing up—but how simple a thing it might be, reaching another planet from the fabric of the Void, rather than through negotiating physical space-time! Imagine." She turned to see that the manic sparkle of his eyes had kindled a fire that burned like the sizzling fireplace nestled between his bookshelves. "A true master race: multidimensional planet-walkers, who, as fertile and sun-loving as any other species, could colonize a planet with little more effort than that required for a healthy hike—even a drive, with toys of the sort you and your friends rode in on. And if you are very good, very dutiful, and prove you've changed your stripes, I see no reason why the former Governess of the United Front might not one night be the Stewardess of Planet Earth, once I have taken off to oversee Mars."

She didn't register that temptation until seconds later, too hung up on a phrase of his that had elicited a snort. "'Planet-walkers'? You mean planet-eaters…it would be one thing if mankind were capable of such a thing; there's a chance they'll go someplace and help the people they find, rather than out-and-out annihilating them. There's goodness in humans, or the possibility of goodness, anyway. But martyrs who believe in your teachings are too far gone. They'll show up and ruin it all. Devour and terrorize the populace."

"Such a thing takes time; and perhaps, in a few planets' worth of experiments, we will come to a more sustainable solution. If only you would pay attention in Church! We provide an important service in God's universe, my girl. We are not mere devourers of flesh and blood—these things are only symbols. We alleviate from the world the pain of mortal sin and take it on ourselves. It is the will of the Lord that we clean the conscious universe everywhere we go."

Frustration tightened her throat, especially as he looped a big arm around her shoulders just before she was able to get out of his reach. "You really think God approves of killing?"

"My daughter, it is God's will! God's gift to us is this universe, and in exchange we keep it pure. We are its custodians, yes, but what ingrates would we be were we to leave such vast swaths of this greatest gift unused?"

"Maybe the rest of it isn't a gift for you."

"True, it is not necessarily a gift for me. But it is a gift for the winner of the game, and I intend to win."

"Whatever bullshit is being played out between you and the magician, you mean."

"Myself, the magician, the Lady, Lazarus, and, of course, you."

"The pawn."

With a gasp of displeasure, the Hierophant cried, "Why, my girl, not at all—not at all!"

She spared him what was intended as a dry glance but found herself reeled in by the earnest arrangement of his expression. "You, my girl"—he jostled her—"are the queen, if you are any chess piece at all. That is not a matter of gender: that is a matter of power. Long before martyrs, the queen was the vizier, you know. He who stands behind the king and overshadows him. But if you insist on feeling like a lowly pawn, never forget that a pawn upon the opposite side of its board *becomes* a queen. Choose a direction, my dear, and move as you please."

"As long as it's back to your side."

"I would be nothing without my finest General. That's why Cicero is so jealous of you, you know! Before you came along, he was my best warrior. After, well, I admit I always appreciate his abilities, but your prowess in battle, and your mind for strategy, is most admirable. How many victories have you delivered our nation?"

"Not enough for you to care about me." Maybe it was stupid to say, but she was on edge, and felt like laying into him as much as she was allowed. "Not enough for you to have stopped me from doing something so cruel to my wife when I was out of my mind with betrayal and grief; not enough for you to have given me an ounce of recognition when I needed it. When I asked for it. Any relationship with you is only ever on your terms."

"I see you're still just as jealous of Cicero as he is of you...ah, my silly children. Would it fix your feelings if I called you my favorite child? Then would you return to my service, and bring me Lazarus?"

Part of her wanted to laugh—bitterly—at his idea that this was a reasonable request. She could just give up the man who had helped her, had given her back her eye and her teeth, had given her his truth-revealing blood! A simple trade. No effort at all.

Feeling helpless and stupid for ever having listened to the Lady—wondering if that Ergosphere apparition of the goddess was not some thoughtform sent by her Father, or something else altogether—the General searched her mind for alternatives, delaying tactics, and misdirections. In the end, she could only come up with the pathetic insistence that, "Lazarus is my friend."

"Oh, my poor girl! I know he is. I'm sure you left quite a few friends behind! But, if they are still alive when we have completed the operation, I will be more than happy to pardon them."

"Operation?" she asked, weakly. He lifted his brows.

"A preemptive strike of Tunis and Tangiers, and a surge of troops in Jerusalem. In fact, it's been on for a fortnight— I suppose you were in the Ergosphere for a couple of weeks during your stroll across the ocean, weren't you? We're already ten nights to New Year's. Lavinia's Feast Night is but a few cycles away! You came home just in time."

The Lady had not warned her about this. No wonder the landing pad of the plane didn't work: it had as much to do with being too far from a reliable distance as it did with the fact that, by the time they were supposed to appear at the landing pad, the city of Tangiers would have been under assault and all prearranged plans to take its teleporter to Jerusalem would have been cratered. Dominia sickened while he carried on: "After you gave us such a good reason to attack by sweeping away Theodore, why—we would be fools not to take advantage of the opportunity."

So Jerusalem had been falling since before she'd arrived at Kronborg. Hard to keep her mind on the present, suddenly. "And you expect me to give you all the information I can to help you cinch the conquests."

"You have returned to the Family, haven't you?" He arched a brow and tightened his grip of her shoulders. Dominia, for her part, studied the city and tried not to feel the slightest emotion. "It would be a pity to see you defect again after we've gone to such pains to welcome you back with open arms and no questions. Such as, why you have suddenly decided to return"—the phantasmal reflections of his eyes bored into the reflections of hers like black drills—"or why I should believe you won't betray me again."

He shouldn't believe it. She could lie flat in his face without a hint of guilt. Indeed, she felt a certain righteousness: that she might say or do anything in the carrying out of this task, because she was champion of the truth. Her heart was pure, and now forever a captive of humanity, if it had ever truly been otherwise. Thus, so long as she knew in her heart that it was a lie when she said, "If you must know, it was a disappointing experience," she could speak what was needed with impunity.

"My poor girl," said the Hierophant, releasing her with a pat so he could return to his seat. "You will have to tell me all about it sometime. I see from the diamond around your neck that I was right in warning you. The Lady is not what she seems, and Lazarus has no real power."

"What about the magician?" She idled past his bookshelf upon seeing a copy of the *Odyssey*. The characters of its title remained as static as one would anticipate while her Father smiled at her question.

"What the magician can do is amazing, it's true: Valentinian is a fellow of talent. But you, my girl, are infinitely more talented than that."

In this, she was tired of pressing him. There was knowledge there with which he teased her, with which everyone had teased her. The only way she knew to deal with it now was to take her Father's own patented sour grapes approach, which she did by changing the subject. "I appreciate your generosity in…accepting me back."

"My child"—his tone held genuine warmth as he reclaimed his pen and returned to work—"there is nothing you could do to me that could not be forgiven. Even if some gesture is required to prove your sincerity, your Father's unconditional love is always with you. I will see to it that Cicero forgives you as I do. I'm sure, once you have been punished, he will come around."

Ah, yes. There it was! She was wondering. That familiar sweating of her palms, the needle sensation down her neck, the unconscious edging of her body toward the door. It had been centuries. "'Punished,'" she repeated, almost laughing, her faltering smile falling entirely when the Hierophant looked up from his writing with a stern, illegible face.

"Of course. We can't have you running about all over the human world without consequence. People died because of you. Don't you see to it your officers and soldiers are well disciplined for infractions against the rules of your service?"

She had never been so aware of the tick of a clock in her life. Trying to maintain her usual sense of confidence, she arched a brow and dryly asked, "Going to have me whipped? Partially flayed?"

"No, no, of course not. You know as well as I do that corporal punishment is useless. It only serves to titillate those who employ and observe it, while doing nothing to prevent future infractions: far better such activities should be left as the bedroom play they are. As for flaying, well...that is rather dramatic, but somewhat more on target. I have always been in favor of long-lasting reminders—nothing obvious or socially humiliating, of course. Just a small secret between yourself and your Lord. A means by which you can forever remember to be a humble and good servant, rather than a rebellious apostate. Flaying is rather much for that purpose." Returning his attention to whatever he wrote, he suggested, "I think one leg will suffice."

All efforts to keep her pulse calm buckled under the weight of a single second. A scream—her own, or maybe Cassandra's—rose up in her head. "What?"

"Cicero insisted I take both, but I said—"

"No." She felt she stood next to her own body and had to grip the bookshelf nearby. "No, I— You're going to take my *leg*."

"Only one, my dear. A symbolic gesture. I'm sure you can understand it. Why, in the end, it will be beneficial to you! I have already ordered a replacement. Some engineers will be by to measure you for it in a few nights. You will find it a vast improvement over your original, and identical in every way."

Her fingers tangling through the chain of Cassandra's diamond, Dominia glanced between the door and the Hierophant and wished she could die on the spot through some merciful intercession of Saint Valentinian's. "But—but I came back of my own will, I—I thought you forgave me. You weren't going to ask any questions."

"Have I?"

"This isn't forgiveness."

"Forgiveness is not free. It requires some effort on the part of those who are forgiven: and there are times when willful penance is not enough. I assure you, princess, I am not taking your leg out of spite. Far from it! It is because I love you, and so intensely wish to forgive you, that I am doing this. How else could I forgive all you've done without some gesture? Some assurance that you will put your best foot forward"—he tried so hard not to smirk that the effort strained his mouth—"and that you will always be with our Family, no matter what happens."

She was too numb to be angry. This was why she had never had trouble on the battlefield, why she had never feared death. Her Father was so much worse than war could ever be.

As cautious as anyone tiptoeing over broken glass, the General wet her lips and pronounced the words, "Surely there's an alternative. If I could say, your forgiveness seems to me"—he lowered his pen and she feared she might vomit—"sort of…conditional. I thought that God's love was…"

"Oh, but I am not God, of course. Though you *do* flatter me…I am but a man of flesh and blood like any other." He rose from his seat and she began mentally searching the room for a weapon, trying to remember whether there had been a letter opener on his desk at the start of the conversation, regretting the lack of a poker in this particular fireplace, wondering about the density of that paperweight, having a difficult time listening to what he said, something something something "—true forgiveness is therefore, ultimately, in the hands of God. The forgiveness of men is a luxury."

"The forgiveness of men comes at a very high cost," she observed, trapped without any defense as he came around the desk and stood before a woman who towered over most men, but who had to crane her neck to see the holy Father's face. "You already took something from me because I left. You took my eye. I only got it back because of my friends."

"Oh, my child"—he gripped her chin with fingers so swift she relived, with post-traumatic horror, the awful feeling of her eyeball being plucked from its socket—"don't you understand? I didn't take your eye because you ran away! That had nothing to do with any of this."

Her eyes, at the visceral memory, at the epiphany, at his presence, filled with a fine gloss of tears. As calmly as she could, through the staggered breath and half smile of terror, she asked, "Then why did you do it?"

"I took your eye because you took mine, first."

Of course.

Of course.

There was no Acetia. He was no alien. The martyr planet from which her Father heralded was Earth in her terrible future: her dark future, where things all went horribly wrong. The General's lips parted. The Hierophant smiled at her understanding and released her chin with a paternal pat upon her shocked cheek.

For a time, she didn't speak. She only marveled at him, at herself, at the whole world and the insanity of reality. A whole globe of people, blinded by logic. The same man could never be two places at once. Time travel wasn't possible. Etcetera.

"How?" She tried asking, just once. He chuckled.

"What fun would it be if I told you that now?" Squinting, she tried to discern a difference between his eyes—any hint of DIOX-brand artificiality—and found none. As she verified both were organic, he continued, "You understand that I must take something from you for what you have done to the Family now, as opposed to what you did to me then, during a marathon, a whole lifetime and persona ago. Yes? At any rate...don't you feel *silly*, now, for flouncing off to Canada! How could I favor any child *but* Cicero? I used to be him. I can understand his anger. Therefore, I require your leg."

There was no way to argue him out of his sense of justice. No begging. No escape. Shocked as she was, the General could not move her legs; for that matter, she no longer saw the room in which she stood. What was she doing? Why had she returned? To face her guilt for—what? Had she really done anything to merit this? Maybe. The Lady must have thought so. The Lady had sent her back here because—why? Because war was inevitable? Because an inside man was necessary for the scheme to work? Because, because, because—but then she remembered she had chosen to come back, not just because of Lavinia but because of Tenchi. The swirling horror of her mind ceased long enough that, finding herself near the door and her Father back at his desk, she managed to ask, "Would you tell me one thing? Where are you keeping Tenchi?"

"Mm? Oh!" The Hierophant glanced up from his work, pen wiggling in recognition. "Yes, yes, your sailor friend—well, it just so happens we stayed his execution and ordered his transport to the nearest consignment camp, but some funny business happened on the bus ride over...I just received an e-mail"—he turned away to awaken the desk-integrated holo-display computer with a wave of his hand and swiped past a few floating windows in that same limp-wristed motion—"something about his disappearance... I've not bothered to respond yet, but I don't expect we'll make his hunt a priority."

"Thank you."

With a tap of his pen against the temple of his forehead in a mocking salute, the Holy Father said, "Close the door on your way out, dear. So glad to see you back."

VII

The Girl with Silver Hands

By her late fifties, Cassandra could no longer stand her urgent pangs of conscience. While she continued to cook for the Governess nearly every morning, and Dominia often returned from work to any number of scrumptious porcine fragrances—her wife a permanent nightdream with that lacy pink apron—Cassandra began to refuse meat. Only at Mass would she consume flesh and blood, she said. That was what the services were there for: why the Lamb gave his blood and why the Churches kept it on hand to be replenished at his next stop. Other than an alleged connection with God and a nontemporal connection to the Last Supper—which was, to put it lightly, reinterpreted in the hands of martyr scholars—the purpose of the Lamb's blood was to give martyrs an option to cannibalism. The rest of the week, well—some martyrs thought it sinful (or at least antisocial) to fast, but Cassandra knew God approved.

Dominia, alarmed, did not approve. For weeks, she pestered her wife about drinking blood, if nothing else. To her present shame, she once went so far as to slip a bit of type A into Cassie's wine one morning. This had only resulted in an astronomical argument and a broken glass, so she didn't try again. She just watched in silence while her wife—a martyr in every sense of the word—fasted, week after week, suppressing superficial pangs of appetite with malnutritional salads, the occasional side of lab-grown beef, or a bowl of vegetable soup.

Each week would begin with optimism and good spirits. Most workers loathed Noctislunae, but it was Cassandra's best night. Each night after, her condition degraded into tremors, insomnia, and, once or twice, a Noctisfrey seizure that necessitated attendance of the Noctisaturnon service as well as the usual Noctisdomin one the following night. This was discouraged. The blood of the Lamb was a commodity, because with so many churches and fifty-two service slots in any given year, he and Cicero could only visit each church so often. So for all her trouble to follow her conscience, Cassandra would sometimes be subject to a sideways comment from the priests and priestesses of their local parish—those same who happened to be her colleagues. The shaming got to be so bad that she had to leave the Bible school business behind. That was when she started to focus on music.

But through all the physical and mental turmoil, Cassandra was in higher spirits than ever. The General's heart broke even now, in Kronborg, to think her wife could only be happy while starving! Dominia wished they had known the truth of Lazarus's blood during her life. Like so many other truths, her Father had hidden that from her. Yes: her Father hid that which could have saved her wife, morally, spiritually, bodily, eternally. Oh! That bastard! How Dominia hated him. How she hated him, and hated that he now wanted to lead the martyr race on a multidimensional march of evil.

Lazarus had explained to her once that she was responsible for ending the present state of the world for martyrs. Things had to change, and change was painful. The right change, Dominia could see, was a complete upheaval of current social values, structure, and even physical presence. There was much to be said for the idea of the martyr race migrating into the Ergosphere once enough research could be done into the subject. But before that issue could even be approached, a complete psychological rewrite of all martyrs was required. The Church, if not in need of destruction, certainly needed a new leader.

And so long as he lived, her Father would never relinquish his position.

Yes—she had thought before how, in the end, her goal was the death of her Father. But now she was confronted with the notion more strongly than ever before. More than that, she was confronted with the notion that it was his death or her death. The issue with her death was not so much any lingering fear of it. She fully trusted that when her body died, her spirit would remain in the Ergosphere. Even if she had to collect herself in the Void, she was prepared for it.

No. Her concern was that if she died, she could do nothing more to stop him. A planet full of martyrs was one thing. A planet full of martyrs who didn't need to fear the sun and who could conquer, world by world, the vast seas of the universe while bringing thoughtforms into earthly existence—now that was a tahgmahr beyond all reckoning. But perhaps it had happened elsewhere. Perhaps it had happened for her Father to find himself with such power and such long memory. When he said he came from Acetia, he meant that he came from an Earth where he was victorious and martyrs had spread their tendrils through reality.

Dominia's head swam as she made her ghostlike way through the halls of Kronborg, thinking through the many General di Mephitolis who'd come before her. What had been different of them? Why had they failed? Though she knew she would persist after, what was the moment of death like? Had she ever sold Lazarus, the Lady, the Kingdom for a leg?

Maybe her standard litany of questions was the wrong thing. Perhaps the best strategy was to imagine the worst possible iteration of herself and strive to be that iteration's exact opposite. It was with great pain that the image came upon her, the trashy cover of a proverbial pulp novel about space piracy or some such business: the one-eyed, one-legged General with the odious Memory Bride draped around her hip as she ruled a hollow world from the depressing city of Old Elsinore. Appalling. Dominia paused against a corner near the primary garden doors to rub the bridge of her nose, and when she looked up, she recognized one of the courtiers gossiping beneath the nearby marble statue of the Lamb. René Ichigawa, who recognized her the same instant and tore off like a rabbit without explanation to his companions. The poor pair looked all the more shocked when the General sprinted past in pursuit.

"René! René, you bastard, there's nowhere to run!"

That wouldn't stop him from trying. After blazing through the vast French doors and down a path more thickly lined with snow than trees this time of year, he recognized the proximity of the General's pursuit and thought he'd get smart by taking a right turn across the pond—the pond that, while frozen this time of year—

"René," she cried, "don't, you idiot!"

Too late. He'd already stumbled though the tree line and now skidded across the ice, trying to take a shortcut in the direction of the hedges until he made his inevitable plunge through a weak spot into the frozen water.

Then, naturally, it was a lot of, "Dominia, help," and, "Please! I haven't been swimming since I was ten!" Sighing, the General took the time to remove her jacket before easing her cautious way across the ice. She reached into the breach, and René, despite his splashing, still had wherewithal enough to try to use her as a ladder rather than accept her help as savior. After at least one kick in his face and a few treacherous warning snaps of the ice beneath her, she managed to extricate René and toss him, wet and shivering, onto the snowbank of the shore. Her own lips slate, Dominia turned him over to the sound of his profuse thanks only to slap him once, sharply, right in the freezing face.

"Listen to me, you little shit. The only reason"—she slapped him again because he marveled too much at the pain of the first slap to pay attention to her words—"the *only* reason why you're still alive right now is because your *cousin* is alive. Okay? Consider yourself lucky—very lucky."

"Dominia—"

"Because if he *weren't* alive, you know what I'd be doing right now?"

"Dominia, please—"

"I'd be yanking out your fucking *leg*, because that's what the Hierophant's going to do to me!"

"I—Jesus Christ, what? No, Dominia, please, I'm telling you! This wasn't my idea—what a stupid plan, I kept telling them!"

"Telling whom?" The General hissed the words with a glance for the lights of the palace. Nosy faces pressed to the glass panels of the doors and a couple of windows down the hall. "Keep your voice down."

"The Lady! Lazarus! Everybody! You think I want to be here? Last time I was around these people, I lost both my eyes!"

Mouth open in shock, she slapped him once more and demanded, "Stop lying."

"I'm not! I swear to you, I'm not!"

"You mean to say that not only did the Lady and Lazarus know I'd end up here, but *everybody* knew I'd end up here? I mean, I've started to feel like the Lady put me here on purpose, but...Lazarus? *You*? Even Tenchi? Oh my God!" No wonder he hadn't wanted to say anything in the Ergosphere. It had as much to do with chronology as it did with his bosses telling him to shut up in advance. Below her series of mortified realizations, René babbled on.

"*I* didn't want to do it. Please! I'm sorry. I didn't want any part in this. You think I wanted to hand Tenchi over to these people? He *volunteered*! You could ask him! You know, if they haven't just killed him anyway. What a stupid idea all this is!"

Dominia pulled away as the English professor's rant continued. "It's this—fucking cult! I can't believe he got involved in that Lazarene stuff. He grew up with Shinto tradition! Freedom fighting, I get, but these religious ceremonies, and then agreeing to drink some old dude's blood...I mean, it's crazy."

"You literally stole my blood."

"Well, *yes*, but that was for *survival*. This is for religion. It's different."

Seeing how he shivered and the peacock tint of his lips, the General retrieved her jacket to drape around his shoulders. "So everybody knows, huh? How many bodies is 'every' body?"

"There was a meeting. Tenchi, Farhad, Gethsemane, the Lady, Lazarus, and I were all there, and a lot—a lot of soldiers, Dominia. Tons."

"Did you count them?"

"Oh, I don't know. One hundred? Two? I'm not a math professor, I'm an English professor."

"Your attention to detail is incredibly helpful." She was about to give up on him when he added, "How am I supposed to keep track? There were people from all over the world, tons I've never seen before. I talked about it with some white guy who lent me a lighter outside the venue."

Lighter, huh. "Tall guy? Thin, dark hair, blue eyes, sort of a shabby red waistcoat?"

"I thought his suit seemed pretty nice, with a jacket, but—how did you *know* that?"

That good-for-nothing mutt. "We've met," she said. Was it worth telling René that the guy who'd lit his cigarette was really the border collie—or had been stored in the border collie, or reflected in the border collie, or bonded with the border collie—that had journeyed with him for thousands of miles? Not when the secular professor wasn't even willing to sit through a Lazarene ceremony. The General busied herself by rolling up the wet sleeves of her white shirt and returned the subject to her irritation. "So everybody knew, huh…"

"Mostly. Bits and pieces, at least. The meeting I went to was an informational one more than anything; everybody else, including me, got some need-to-know stuff in private. My need-to-know was that I had to turn in my own cousin and act like I wanted in with the Hierophant now that I'm a martyr. They won't tell me why I'm here, or what I'm supposed to do now that I'm here. I think I'm supposed to figure it out when the time comes, but I'm freaking out. It's pretty serious, Dominia. And they said the more you know, the more danger you're in."

No wonder they didn't tell René a thing, considering how he'd spewed his guts in a snap. "Everybody around these parts loves withholding." Feeling all the more aware of her right leg, she added, "I'm already in danger, regardless of how little or how much I know."

"Yeah, nobody mentioned anything about you losing a *leg*. I might have cast a no vote after you saved me in Bi'ir as-Sab. I thought I was signing up to *help* you!"

"I'm sure you did sign up to help me, which is why I need to make it look like we're still pissed off at each other."

"Wha—"

The crack as she kicked his jaw was significant, but not as significant as it would have been were she wearing boots instead of oxfords. Even so, René went down like a big sack of satisfying bricks, which she dragged inside by the collar. Not fully unconscious, the new martyr continued babbling through a dislocated jaw that softened his *r*'s to *h*'s and made the word "party" sound rather hilariously like "potty": "Oh, God, will this heal? There's supposed to be a *party*, Dominia! I can't go to a party like this."

"A party?" She paused several meters from doors vacated by the courtiers. "For what?"

"The Hie—you—"

This was getting old. With the thick snap of ligaments and bone, Dominia fixed her undeserving progeny's jaw so he could, after yelping and working it back and forth once or twice, explain, "Your Father's insisting I stay for a New Year's party. I'm worried he's already on to us."

"Of course he's already on to us. That's why I'm not supposed to know anything, and why he's starting to tell me everything. When is the party supposed to be?"

"New Year's Eve."

"Must be my deadline."

"He's going to take your leg at the party?"

"That, or just before. 'Party' is sure to be a euphemism, knowing him. Or it isn't. Sort of a coin flip with these people…I suppose we'll find out." That said, she resumed dragging the yet-dizzied man into the hall. He curled into a wet and bruised ball on the cold tile floor, one hand upon the aching hinge of his jaw.

"How long have you been waiting to do that to me?"

With a stifled grin, she stepped past him, in the direction of Lavinia's apartments. "Don't make me hurt your feelings, too."

Those courtiers, nervous as they were curious, emerged from the nearby lounge to assess the scene, then darted back when the General laid eyes on them. Suddenly, her grin was easy to suppress. All humor dropped from her and she was the General once more, colder than the icy waters from which she'd pulled René.

"Traitors and I don't get along well," was her only explanation. The two glanced at each other before she gave an irritated wave toward René, just the sort Lavinia might have when demanding her "friends" pick up some trash she'd littered in the garden. "Could you take him to his guest room, please?"

Even if she couldn't fully manage her tone, she curtailed her language with courtesy. That counted for something, right?

Jacket lost to René, the General made her damp way to Lavinia's quarters, a set of living spaces and several bathrooms that felt rather like a sorority despite the classical aesthetic and the high, rich wainscoting of the walls. Maybe it was the television in the artful salon that made it seem that way, or the couches, or the proliferation of women's magazines and trashy romance novels left behind when Lavinia tossed her brigade out into the castle. Kronborg bore little resemblance to what it was in Hamlet's day—hell, little resemblance to what it was in Dominia's night! There was a *kitchen* in here, now. Come to think of it, that was why it felt like a sorority. The smell of baked goods emanated from the cramped kitchenette and nobody had bothered to wash the dishes, but neither were there any cookies to be found. Speaking of a bunch of girls who could use some titillating corporal punishment!

Too bad they didn't have a haven of cute women when Dominia was forced to stay in Kronborg. She might have liked the castle's drafty halls a bit better with a few extra skirts swishing around. (She turned her head too sharply at Lavinia's footsteps, and the chain of Cassandra's diamond twisted to choke her; she laughed to think of her jealous wife.)

"Ninny!" Lavinia's voice twinkled with excitement as she emerged from her bedroom at the end of the hall, but her expression soon gave way to a wrinkled nose. "Oh, my, Ninny, you're all—what *happened*?"

"Can I borrow your hair dryer?" asked Dominia, lifting damp arms. "I'm freezing."

After a few minutes—ten, to be exact—spent talking Lavinia out of her "wonderful" idea that Dominia borrow some of *her* clothes, the stubborn princess admitted the hair dryer that had run amid her begging *had* done a fine job, she *supposed*, if the General was fine with looking like a boy.

"This is just how I feel comfortable," said Dominia, shrugging as she might when talking to any unworldly child. "I don't look like a boy; I look like Dominia. But just so you know, a lot of ladies like the way I look. One of your girlfriends seemed to, anyway."

"They're not—*girlfriends*," sputtered Lavinia, so flush that the General laughed. "They're girl *friends*, it's a different thing. I am above such unwholesome activities." Her eyes closed in a stuffy way that nonetheless registered to Dominia as very dear, because she saw so much of Cassandra's sleep in it. The girl turned away before her eyes opened, so she didn't see how sad the General had grown in those two seconds. "Not that it's wrong for somebody else to get up to…*business*, but I'm a saint, Ninny. I can't do a thing like that!"

"And I'm technically a saint, too. Or I was."

"But you're a saint of *war*. Nobody says you can't fall in love with anybody."

"And you can't?"

"Well, of course I could fall in *love*, but it must be *pure* love. Not trivial, fleshly love. No offense."

"None taken." Frankly, she'd been busy feeling astonished by the variety and size of the makeup collection littering the vanity where she sat. Bigger, even, than Miki Soto's before her bridal ceremony. "You're awfully into makeup for somebody who doesn't have a boyfriend."

"*Now* who doesn't know anything? I don't do makeup for boys, I do it for fun. Cicero helps me with it each evening! I can do it myself, of course, but we like to talk. He's such a good brother!"

Good, creepy…a fine line with all martyrs, but especially with the Holy Family, and exceptionally with Cicero. There had always been something indefinably weird about him. Some mixture of incestuous idolatry and profound resentment toward the Hierophant that plagued every room El Sacerdote entered. Now Dominia understood that, and all his fawning over Lavinia, too. And she understood her Father much better. Was that the fate of Cicero? To move on to another reality and make his own? If so, was that because he left to spread his proverbial wings—or was that because he was forced out? The salvation of this world didn't mean the destruction of another, did it?

"Did you have a bad meeting, Ninny? You're frowning again."

"I don't know if I should discuss it with you, kiddo."

"I'm not a *kid*, Nin—Dominia." The General managed to keep a straight face as the girl went on, "I'm absolutely grown up. I know all kinds of things!"

She wasn't in the mood to have an argument with somebody who was so wrong they didn't even have the frame of reference to comprehend their incorrectness. Instead, investigating a bottle of perfume, Dominia said, "I was given a very ugly penance. I just wish there was some alternative."

Her frowning sister leaned forward. "What penance?"

"Lavinia," chided the General, but the girl, literally on the edge of the bed, insisted with her hands upon her chest, "But I'm an *adult*. Really, I am! I've been awake for almost seventy years! When *you* were seventy, you'd already been high in Daddy's army for four decades!"

"That's because that's what I trained for. He bred me for that purpose." And others, she knew now, deeper and more inexplicable. He was a scheming, untrustworthy bastard, the Hierophant, but Lavinia had stars in her eyes for him—loved her Father more intensely than any other child, adult or not. Everything he did was right, so far as the girl was concerned.

But, Lavinia also carried a deep love for Dominia. There had been instant attachment on the little girl's part when she awoke in that young woman's body. So much so that Cassandra had been jealous at times, and Dominia suspected this was because, deep down, her wife always knew the truth. Even before that feast night where the Hierophant's mocking had not slipped past Cassandra's drink-lubricated consciousness. December finished out with an eerie quality and Mrs. di Mephitoli did an impeccable job of hiding her suspicions for a while. But Dominia soon discerned that something was afoot: her wife scrounged through the Governess's old documents one night when the much-demanded politician had been called away on weekend business that ended unexpectedly and allowed her home a few hours earlier than thought.

The General hadn't been that bothered by the awkward return, because the letters she "caught" Cassandra in were correspondences with Lavinia. Despite her sometimes weird bouts of jealousy over how adored by Lavinia

Dominia was, the Governess's wife had never taken much interest in the Merciful Miracle of the Holy Father—frankly, the girl was a tremendous amount of trouble when she awoke. At least she awoke with *any* sense of language at all, for understanding if not for speaking: that was a miracle capping even that miracle of miracles, more than twenty years of clinical death spent in a period of growth that ended in crystalized life. Lavinia awoke in a state of physical perfection, that peak at which most martyrs stopped aging. She had never lived at all, let alone lived outside the Holy Family.

And she was immensely lonely. Even living across the ocean in the Front, Dominia saw that. The poor Princess of Europa with her paid-for friends didn't even have those until she was about thirty or forty physical years old, when the Hierophant deemed her socially competent. That meant Lavinia was awake for *twenty years* before she was "allowed" to have a friend, even one subsidized by her Father. Talking to her before that point had been dangerous, especially if the person doing the talking was a young man. Other than the Lamb and the Ciceros, Teddy was the only man Dominia could name who was allowed within arm's length of the Eternal Virgin. It was all a bunch of bullshit as far as the then Governess was concerned, and she showed her protest by drifting away from the Family. This was also an effort to keep Cassandra as far away from Lavinia as possible. But to quell her guilt for this, and for leaving Lavinia alone, she began to write her sister letters. The Hierophant had read them to her, at first, then written back childish correspondences the struggling savant had "dictated"—prompted, edited, and surely augmented by him, of course, but it was a start. Then, as her grasp of language and reason improved, and her rampant emotional problems (along with their resulting memetic contagions) began to wind down, letters had come from her own shaky hand. The confidence in these lines grew over the years to true calligraphy, fine as their Father's—sometimes Dominia still suspected he slipped his own letter into the mix, as talented as he was at everything, forgery included. Even if that was the case, she was glad to know Lavinia got those letters. They were all very boring, and she never talked much about Cassandra in them beyond what her wife's job was like at the time. Nothing of their fights or troubles.

So there wasn't anything wrong with Cassandra reading those letters, per se. The Governess wasn't thinking about Lavinia's strange Feast Night party anymore. She hadn't even connected the events until too late, when she realized in bloody hindsight that her wife had been searching wildly, desperately, for any scrap of information about whether her suspicion about her daughter was true. And—perhaps more importantly—whether Dominia had known.

What Cassandra never could have understood was that Dominia was just too careful. Even with herself, she was too careful. She had worked hard to avoid thinking of any of this since the baby was passed off over ninety years ago. Now, after seventy years of Lavinia's conscious life, Dominia had the opportunity to stop being so careful—and the painful irony lay in the caution that was required when relieving herself of these cares. It would be easiest, the General decided, if she not dive right into the subject of Cassandra's parentage. Better to start with what the Hierophant planned to do to Lavinia's beloved older sister. Perhaps once she understood the gravity of that, the girl would be more conducive to understanding what had happened to her—why Dominia had done as she'd done, and why, in the end, it wouldn't have mattered whether she'd gone to him about the baby, or he'd come to her.

After suffering her nagging thoughts, a reluctant groan, and Lavinia's pleading expression, the General relented. "I can tell you some of what was said at my meeting with him tonight." The girl's eyes, blue as Benedict's, lit like great lamps in the low light of her room. "But you have to promise me you won't tell anyone."

"I won't! Oh, I promise, Ninny, I won't."

"Not a soul. Not your friends, and definitely not Father."

"Never! Please, what did he say? Are you okay?"

Still reluctant, the General sat at her sister's side, voice as low as her head. "I don't want to tell you this because I don't want you to think I'm trying to turn you against Father."

"Nothing could do *that*, Ninny! You don't have to worry." A delicate hand landed upon Dominia's shoulder with that birdlike touch. "I know you know how much I love Daddy! But I also know how scary he can be sometimes."

"He told me he wants to—" Just say it. Say it out loud. Make it real to someone more important than René. "He's going to take my *leg*, Lavinia."

The series of emotions through which Lavinia's face cycled was so unnatural as to be unreadable in the circumstances. The mere sight burned the worst brand of cognitive dissonance across the General's skull. Her little sister's features widened, grew overjoyed, then caved into laughter.

"Why, *Ninny*, but that's wonderful! Don't you see?"

"No." She was numb, more alone than she'd been while lying in the ruins of the McLintocks' china. "I don't see."

"That just means he *loves* you, silly." As the Princess went on, the General paled. Not at the unwinnable battle before her but at something much worse edging into consciousness. "He really has forgiven you! If it were otherwise, why, he'd have you killed and wasted."

The nauseous General regarded the daughter sacrificed on her wife's behalf, and said nothing. Lavinia frowned in the face of that silence, struggling for something to say. Given an epiphany, she sprang to lock her bedroom door, and as she did, Dominia's mind began to scream.

"You know what, Ninny? I know you're scared."

Please, no.

"But since you shared a secret with me, I'll share one with you."

Oh, please, please, no.

"And then you'll understand why this is something you should be happy about!"

Oh, God, Lady, Lamb, please, God, Saint Valentinian, no.

All smiles, Lavinia hiked her many skirts high above her pale leg. After perching upon the edge of her vanity seat, she detached the DIOX limb from the stump of her amputated thigh with the practiced hand of a woman removing a garter.

"See," chirped the girl, all sunshine. Dominia's mouth hung wider than her horror-ringed eyes as the oblivious child continued, "It's nothing bad at all! Daddy loves *me* more than anything in the world. That's why he took my arms, *and* my legs. We're the *luckiest*, to be eaten by him while still alive on Earth! It's an honor, Ninny! Don't you understand?"

The General could think of nothing to say. Nothing.

Nothing.

Didn't she understand?

Didn't she understand!

Her mind, a whirlwind, wouldn't operate. She left her body for a period of indeterminate length and was drawn back by the girl's nervous voice.

"Ninny, why—you're laughing but you look so—"

All of six seconds later, Dominia was stooped over the edge of the toilet bowl in her sister's bathroom, once again plagued by that nausea from the Hierophant's office; nausea which she had not, in the first place, fully escaped. Maybe she would never escape this sickness again. Certainly not as she remembered in a horrible flash of hindsight the very party in which Cassandra came to understand the truth. In her mind's eye hovered once more its glorious centerpiece, of which all the guests, Dominia included, had partaken.

That delicate woman's arm. That—in retrospect—familiar woman's arm.

"That was your arm at your feast night two years ago," she said, lifting her head to slump against the enormous bubble jet bathtub. Lavinia stood, mortified by her sister's illness, at the edge of the bathroom to which she'd hopped. "The one before Cassandra killed herself…that was you we ate for dinner."

"Of course! It was my last limb, so Daddy wanted to share it, and, why—I thought that was just so special and beautiful! Why are you sick, Ninny? Did you eat someone rancid?"

"I…no. I'm sorry, Lavinia." Eyes filling with tears, Dominia lifted her hand to wipe her cheeks and then her mouth and sob, "I'm so—oh, sweet Lamb, I'm so sorry."

"What on earth *for*?" asked Lavinia while her sister bolted up and slipped past her, through the doorway. "Ninny, wait—"

"I can't stay here right now, Lavinia, please. I have to think."

"But, Ninny, don't you see? I'm trying to show you it's a *nice* thing."

There was simply no way for the General to respond. Still nauseous, and now with the taste of bile burning her throat, Dominia stumbled back in the direction of the gardens. The only place for her now was the most clamorous room the entire castle had to offer, and one of its best attended: the kennels.

It was no secret that the Lamb loved his dogs, and the love of dogs—indeed, all animals—had become one of the most popular pastimes of martyr life, right behind alcohol abuse and sadomasochistic sex. Dominia, during peacetimes, spent as many seconds as possible in the presence of the animals, because they did not care what or whom she ate so long as she shared some with them. Nor did they care if she did not eat anything at all. The Hierophant frequently had when she was a little girl named Morgan who, like Cassandra twenty years before her death, could not be persuaded to eat flesh without a great amount of doing. She had been criticized by everybody, and even the Lamb had tried to persuade her to eat normally rather than going by his blood alone. The dogs didn't try to pressure her about anything, though.

This particular group of dogs didn't even care that they hadn't met her before, not once in their entire lives: they simply bounded forth en masse to dance with big dog grins around her feet and spring up, paws bracing against her hips and stomach as they tried to bowl her over in impressive demand for affection. Normally, she would have responded to this behavior with laughter. Given the circumstances, and, seeing that she was completely alone with them, the General di Mephitoli allowed herself to dissolve into nearly hysterical tears.

Being alone with animals had a way of releasing emotion. Even with Cassandra, she restrained herself, forced herself to be the strong one for a woman who needed more support than the Governess. But certainly as a troubled little girl and a supremely surly teen, Dominia had found the company of dogs provided her with unconditional permission to feel. Then, as now, she could let go, crouched in the corner like a real sad sack while a few particularly enthusiastic mutts attempted to love-bomb her out of a sadness whose expression was universal.

"Oh, God." She hugged one at random and covered her eyes with her free hand. "What am I going to do? What have I done? You can't imagine—of course you can't"—she almost laughed—"but, oh, God, I never...I never stopped to ask myself what I was doing. I'm such a horrible person. I—I just wanted Cassandra. I didn't know how to handle her baby. I didn't think...I didn't want this.

"What am I doing? How did I expect this to end? I can't lose my *leg*, but my friends— Lavinia—oh, my heart. I only ever wanted Cassandra."

It was so hard to cry. Humiliating, even alone, as if she betrayed her own self-definition by experiencing an emotion unrelated to a calculated expression of violence. How often she had wept along this journey! This idiotic series of battles like none she'd ever fought. Yet, never had she wept like this. On the floor, every last ignored burden crashed back to her. How she'd changed! How she'd changed and how she'd suffered, and for what? She asked herself what she was getting out of a certain action, not about the nature or consequence of the action. She had wanted Cassandra out of all this mess, but the lengths to which she was willing to go for her wife now seemed foolhardy. She had tossed her life away for a woman who'd killed herself. A woman who could not return to this life, despite all the General had been told. A woman who could only return in the flesh when the universe was born again, and Dominia herself was born again. Would she have no memory of everything she'd suffered to attain? Would she be better off without those memories?

Even if Cassandra could come back, what reason would she have to forgive the General?

With another self-pitying sob, Dominia opened her eyes, about to reach for another dog, and froze in an astonishment that caused her to second-guess her own sanity. The animal before her, which of all its peers listened most astutely to her lamentations (and with none of the concerned supplications of its cohorts), was a most recognizable border collie. Through wet hiccups and soft gasps to stabilize her breath, the General wiped her face to better see.

"Basil?"

Head low, the still, gentle dog leaned forward to sniff her hand and give one affectionate lick. Then, all business, Basil turned on his heels and trotted away, past the lesser animals and around the corner to the next row of kennels. Holding her breath, the General clambered to her feet and straightened out her clothes, then stumbled forward with a cadre of dogs at her heels. As they rounded the corner, Dominia's breath released, and more than half her followers bounded to greet, with barking delight, Valentinian. The Saint of Death stooped to pet the wise-looking border collie before him, a grin already on his stubbled face.

"Aren't dogs the best," the magician said, his sigh one of sheer admiration. "They always know just what to say."

VIII

Dimethyltryptamine

Had anyone ever been so angry at the answer of their prayers? And not "answer" in a monkey's-paw, vengeful-djinni way, but a real, true answer—was it normal to feel, amid the kaleidoscope of relief and surety and sanity and hope, that iron-brand singe of rage? The General could not say. Certainly not in that moment when her anguish transmuted into fury for the magician before her, whose expression, down to the very angle of his eyebrows, remained smug as ever. "Looking a little red there, buddy."

"I am...*surprised*," she managed to calmly articulate, realizing her left hand was bound in a trembling fist. She forced it open to pat the nearest mutt. "Just...surprised to...find you...here."

"And I am *proud* to see *you* are working on your anger management," said the insufferable man, but in such a tone that the General couldn't help but crack the tiniest smirk. With one of his own, he waded through the dogs to offer Dominia his right hand. She shook it while trying to decide how humiliated she needed to be for all he'd overheard, then studied that most patient border collie.

"I thought—"

"What, that Basil would just disappear forever when I replaced him? No, no. I just got a body. He's as much a Void-walking, soul-having good boy as any sapient being I've ever known. Isn't he? Isn't he!" With a few well-placed words and a bend of the magician to ruffle his coat, the noble animal's stoic demeanor melted into playful puppitude that, inspiring like in its playmates, sent the whole crowd rollicking around the rows of kennels like a great canine sand devil. "He belongs in this world, has always had a body here. That can't be taken away by the Ergosphere, although time makes it seem so."

"What happened to your first body?"

"Well, we have an error in reality. Imagine what the first Cicero did when he crossed the boundaries between universes the first time."

"Hence, your deletion?"

"But now I've been given a new body—*thank* you," he added, pressing his hands together in a gracious aside that surprised her. "It means so much to me, I can't tell you. With this, I'm able to alter the closed system. There also happens to be a lot of traffic in the Ergosphere right now, anyway, which can provoke minor reality fluxes. Like with an electric current running through copper wire—electrostatic force pops one valence electron from a copper atom, and that liberated electron finds another atom, in which case the electron's negative charge boots out another electron. These days—ever since the time of my liberation, in fact—people have been a lot more in touch with the Ergosphere. That's our current. People coming, people going; and there's one electron I don't need to worry about. Guess who popped out of existence?" Valentinian drew a circle with his index fingers and Dominia smiled in relief.

"Tenchi!"

"Yeah, buddy, you did good work."

"What about Gethsemane?"

To her annoyance, he smiled and said, "We're talking about Tenchi right now—anyway, he was right to be nervous about taking the blood of Lazarus. Tenchi's the kind of guy who, once he stumbles into the Kingdom, well… good luck getting him back out. He's not dead—I see that look on your face. He's just moved. A living refugee."

"If he intended to leave and come back," Dominia added, "he would have looked a lot older, right?"

"Generally speaking, but not necessarily. Most people have an inner vision of themselves that isn't aligned with their external presentation, and that frequently includes age, whether they picture themselves younger, or older… but creatures without strong inner representation and an excess of emotional desires—an animal, or a primeval or traumatized individual—can be subject to this form of possession. Consider it more like spiritual radio. Of course, try it with somebody who can talk, and they freak out."

"So you intercede through animals—unless the goal is to provoke madness." She needed not think on her Father now. "Is Basil in danger here?"

"He'll feel it if he is, and react accordingly. He's his own man now, for the first time maybe ever. I've always been inside of him, dormant, waiting for you. More…sitting with his data in the Ergosphere and watching it, manipulating it. But it's all the same in the end. Now, after being separated from me and exposed to the Ergosphere on his own, he's a genius dog, in touch with the ebb and flow of information, and knows when he needs to make himself scarce—and when his favorite person needs some comforting."

The General lowered her misting eyes to blink them clear. When at last she could bear the magician's face, she found it strange to see in physical reality. She had waited for his arrival with great impatience over the past year yet been so busy that she had practically forgotten his appearance, if she could be said to have seen it at all in that in that dreamlike Void. For some unnerving reason, she found as much resemblance to her own blue-eyed, black-haired features as those of Lazarus's. "I suppose you won't stay long?" she asked, her tone cool.

"Yes and no. I mean, again, I'm a busy man. But I can't leave you hanging when you're suffering so much, Dominia."

She turned away to study the romping dogs. Valentinian went on, "I want to help you."

"Do I deserve help, after what I've done? What I've caused? God—what I've *done*." She remembered Lavinia's stump with a shudder and covered her eyes as if to banish the memory from their sight, where it would nonetheless endlessly cycle until its horror was reduced to mere fact. Such a process could take weeks, months, maybe years for something so heavy. Certainly a gross amount of tahgmahrs. A shallow gasp wheezed from Dominia's lungs. "Don't I deserve to lose my leg, too? I was responsible for—"

"Not for that," said the magician, his tone more gentle than she'd ever heard. "You did some bad things, Dominia, it's true. So has everybody. But you're not beyond help; and you're not beyond change, or goodness. You're not responsible for what your Father chose to do to Lavinia, or what Cassandra chose to do to herself."

"Cassandra—"

"Was a very troubled woman, no matter what you think you did. Hey." He leaned into her watering field of vision. She forced herself to look at him, forced her expression to remain as stoic as possible. "Listen to me, okay? Everything you've done, everything that's happened— you can make it right."

"And you'll help me?"

"Of course. That's why I'm here. I know you feel lost and lonely and probably more afraid than you ever have in your life, and I'm sorry. Nobody's telling you anything, and when we do tell you something, it's almost always bad news. But I've got some good news for you. Something to show you."

"Everybody's got something to show me tonight."

"But this is a good thing. A really good thing. I'm going to show you why humanity is worth protecting, why staying on the right side of this thing is worth it in the end."

"Why I need to lose my leg."

"Why it's all going to work out okay."

Lips tight, the General glanced to the window and the bright night outside, which lit Kronborg's garden via reflection from the bejeweled blanket of snow. "Trust you, huh…well, I don't know how you expect us to be able to get out of here unnoticed. Can *you* navigate the Void at night? Even you have to stop and rest."

"Well, sure, because it's creepy as shit. But we don't need to go through the Void. That's the wonderful thing about the Kingdom—fairy-land rules." Dominia was awash with mild surprise as the grinning saint elaborated: "When you've eaten food from the Kingdom, you can forever reach the Kingdom directly."

"What? How?"

"Oh, you can reach it any way! It's not dissimilar to the blood of Lazarus. The truth is that a sufficiently practiced person could enter the Kingdom by contemplating a bottle of water." From the breast pocket of that new velvet jacket, the magician withdrew his cigarettes (in a snazzy gold case, no less). "I've noticed you've been returning to Earth using the Word, for instance."

"I can't enter the Ergosphere with it, though. The only reliable method I've found for night travel is artificial light, BLP. I can travel by some music, but not much. I think my Father might go by paintings—his dream study's floor reminds me of Vermeer—but I can't figure out the method and I don't have time."

"Ah, he knows about forty different ways. That's the benefit of fooling around for two thousand years! I'd have to write a guidebook to describe them all…everybody's got their favorite. And you're right, the Word can only be pronounced by an earthly tongue at a time like the Lady's transference, which means it's *no bueno* for getting to the Void from reality. Anything a mind bound to the three-dimensional brain manages to 'remember' is a lesser approximation. That's why I favor this." The smiling fellow offered her a cigarette, which she accepted reluctantly.

"Why do I get the feeling this isn't even a normal cannabis cigarette?"

"Oh, buddy." The magician laughed so that he might have rubbed his hands together, were they not full. "You remember those little cobalt flowers from the Kingdom?" At her visible surprise to find he was able to get them through, he wiggled his eyebrows. "Just because flowers don't have mouths doesn't mean they aren't as much an individual as you, or Cassandra's diamond. Ableist," he teased, which got him a much-deserved elbow in the gut.

"Fella can't make a joke…anyway, those flowers grow around the Kingdom's water sources, but they prefer salt water, and tend to die just as soon as you bring them into the real world. Even dead, they know where they came from—it's stored in the dried cells of their petals. Moreover, they are symbolic here. Another way of thinking of the lost souls of the Void."

There was Gethsemane's ethereal nymph, declaring blandly how many of their pond's visitors were drowned. So the dead were poured into these flowers; they would be traveling to eternity by the contributions of the lost deceased. Better than traditional cannibalism, she supposed. The magician summed up, "When that energy is released with a little bit of fire or a spark of electricity and inhaled by a Lazarene with the substance of the Kingdom in his body, it points out the nearest door to the Kingdom."

"No kidding. And what happens when a non-Lazarene smokes it?"

Inhaling amid the crackling of the cigarette, which he'd tipped his head to light, the magician laughed. "They get good and fucked up!"

While Dominia allowed him to light her cigarette, she glanced at Basil. "What about him?"

"Oh, like I tried to say, animals come and go as they please. I have no idea how it works with them if I'm not pulling them in or out. I've never asked. I assume they're one with the Ergosphere already anyway, and contact with it—such as when a spirit like myself bonds with them—slips them free of time. What am I, an encyclopedia?"

"Sort of."

The taste of the cigarette was a far cry from the standard sourness of nicotine, though some tobacco had been sprinkled in to cut the offensive flavor of the flower. Its smoke, too, burned like nothing she'd inhaled, and she choked as Valentinian said, "You want to try to hold it in as long as possible… won't take much."

On and on she puffed, feeling anxious as a high schooler toking behind the bleachers. She glanced once, twice, in the direction of the door, and all around for cameras, holo or otherwise. Thank the Lamb, there was no one imminently coming for her. No one who would arrive, anyway, before Valentinian's attention was drawn toward one of the kennels. "Oh! There it is."

Yes, like a magic-eye puzzle. She saw nothing at first, but after one long drag, and after he put his hand into it, she saw that not just one but two kennels became from her perception a door into that marble hotel lobby. Reality around her warped, and she leaned forward into an intense gravity that twisted even the colors of the world, yet her vision's position remained upright. As if her senses had separated from her physical body. Within the door, the new front desk clerk of the City's hotel typed at her invisible keyboard with the receiver of a perfectly visible rotary phone jammed between her cheek and shoulder. Dear Miki Soto!

Dominia was so excited to see her friend, and so altered by the cigarette she'd smoked, that she didn't even remember running through the doorway. But, ah, what colors! It all seemed brighter on the other side, with the moment of transition on the threshold the brightest of all—even if she only held it in her memory secondhand. As if the explosion of light and vibrancy had been too much for her immediate observation. Behind her, the doorway had vanished as it came, but the General paid it no mind. The bored clerk looked up, did a double take, and promptly dropped her phone.

"Dominia! Holy shit!"

Completely forgetting her work, Miki vaulted the desk and greeted her friend with puppyish enthusiasm while Dominia responded in like manner. "Miki," she cried, "oh, I can't believe it! You're really here!"

"Hell yeah I am! I—hey, you can't smoke in here!" With a tongue-dampened pair of fingers, Miki pinched the cigarette out before allowing another squeal. "Man, I didn't know you'd be showing up! Not so soon, anyway. You'll never *believe* how great this place is! They gave me a cushy job at the front desk a couple of days a week, and the rest of the time it's just, like…so *chill*."

It was at this moment that the General realized her friend spoke, as had Tenchi, in perfectly intelligible Japanese. Dominia hadn't remembered more than five sentences of the language since her wartime assault. Interesting how the Ergosphere made all languages resemble one, while the Kingdom rendered all separate but intelligible. Dominia observed that aloud, leaving out the bit about the Ergosphere.

"Oh, yeah," said Miki, clearly "over" that particular feature of living in the Kingdom, "that's a thing here. I can't even tell what language the locals speak. It's this totally different thing like maybe from the future or whatever; I just know I can understand it. But guess *what*!" Looking ready to burst with excitement, Miki waited, and the General realized belatedly that she was actually expected to guess. It wasn't hard.

"You're a biological woman."

"Yes! Dude! Oh my God! You can't imagine— Here, look—" She was starting to lift her skirt, and Dominia laughed, staying her exhibitionistic hands.

"That's fine, it's fine, I'm sure it's even better than your very realistic last one…" She squeezed those hands that she still held. "I'm so happy for you, Miki."

"Thanks, man, me, too! Oh, Dominia, look at you!" The laughing porter slapped her in the bicep. "You look like a seriously bad bitch in this place, *senpai*."

"Just in this place?" asked the General wryly. The grinning clerk straightened her scarlet cap.

"Yeah! It's the eye patch and the hair. Once you cut your hair on Earth and lost your badass leather uniform, you started looking like a divorce attorney."

"Thanks," commented Dominia, while Miki went on giddily saying, "I can't believe you're here! How did you get here? How long are you staying?"

Now the General glanced over her shoulder and found, to her annoyance, that the door was not the only thing missing. Surprise: the magician was nowhere to be found. Looking back at her friend, Dominia shrugged. "I'm not sure. I guess I'm supposed to see something here? Or do something?"

"Don't you know why you came?"

"Strictly speaking, I was brought here...hey." The martyr followed her friend back to her post and leaned against the counter, trying (and failing) to see the computer at which Miki re-stationed herself. "All the people from Earth who have been stored—or, brought to this place as refugees—they come through this hotel, right?"

"Oh, sure."

"Do you know Tenchi Ichigawa?"

"Why." Miki adopted a theatrical glower. "Are all humans supposed to know each other? Racist. We probably just look like a couple of talking bento boxes to you."

"That's not—"

"I'm kidding, you martyr bitch." Miki tipped her cackling head toward the infinite ceiling, which echoed like a coven of hidden witches. "You should see your face... Hell yeah, I know Tenchi! He's our courier."

Relief! Sweet relief. The General ran her hand over her face with a gratified sigh as the clerk glanced reflexively at her outbox. "As a matter of fact, he just— Tch! That bastard." Miki whipped a letter from the otherwise empty box and brandished it at Dominia. "He missed one! We don't have Internet or e-mail here, he needs to take his job more seriously."

"But you're on an invisible computer," said Dominia. Miki rolled her eyes.

"One computer does not a network make, smart-ass. We're trying to get it up and running... Hey, do you know your way around here?" Turning off her acerbic *tsundere* routine in favor of big *moe* eyes, Miki wibbled her lower lip. "Will you please take this letter to the market plaza and deliver it for me?"

And Dominia, though initially reluctant to wander the City without a guide, understood she needed to do it when she read the name beneath Miki's fingers: "McLintock."

"Sure," said the General, trying not to betray the complex admixture of anxiety and hope growing beneath the breast pocket into which she tucked her cigarette. "Won't you get in trouble with your boss for this?"

"Who—the last Lady? Trisha? No, Tish won't care. Her shift doesn't even start until...well, later. Time is sort of weird here, I can't explain it. Anyway, just run that to Mrs. McLintock for me. And don't lose it!"

"What is it?"

"It's her stipend. The refugees need money to stay in the City, just like the citizens, and so this guy—you wouldn't know him—"

"Valentinian?"

"Okay, I guess you *do* know him—anyway, he funds the refugees' presence in the City through the hotel, and they in turn pay the hotel for their rooms."

"So it's just a big circle, sponsored by the martyr Saint of Death."

"Seems sort of silly, but it works."

"Why can't they just stay in the City for free?"

"What is this, communism? Hell no! If they want to live somewhere for free, I guess there's another City in the desert, way farther West, and it's different? They aren't down with money, so commies can go there. I don't know the deets, I'm a refugee like anybody else. Anyway, I don't think it matters. Definitely not as much as taking Mrs. McLintock's wages to her before the end of the day, so she can pay her way back into her family's room at the end of the night!" With a shooing motion, Miki waved Dominia off. "Gee whiz, the minute you ask somebody to deliver a letter, they want to talk for hours… Some of us have to work, you know."

After a sly wink, Miki resumed her typing, or tried. She realized with a few keystrokes and a sharp gasp that she had left the phone off the hook. After yelping into it, "Hello? Hello?" for a few seconds and receiving only dead air, the girl hung the thing up as if it were guilty of some great injustice.

"Damn…that was the telephone company, too. I'd already held forty minutes!"

"What did you hold them with?" asked the General, who ducked a hurled clipboard on her laughing way to the street.

Above the Kingdom shined a sun more beautiful than Earth's, but just as harmless. Funny: she had been able to move in its rays for a year, yet still she lifted her hand in instinctive shield, wincing back, then, after a few seconds' remembrance, edging out of shade with her good eye still protected from the blaze. Vaguely, she recalled the route she'd taken with Gethsemane and began to head left, its opposite direction. She had no compass here, but if Dominia's bearings were correct and the sun still set in the west, the market lay east.

The City was a sight to behold, with its flowing hills centuries ago covered in masonry so exquisite that the white stone crested like sea-waves. Set decoration to artfully accent the queer-yet-natural variety of costumes that, elsewhere, might seem anachronistic. Here the mishmash was only a natural sign that men's souls had fled to the Kingdom, however it was perceived, in infinite masses and by infinite means since the dawn of existence. The blood of Lazarus must not have been the only means in. Didn't that peplos-draped woman who passed with a sensual smile resemble illustrations of Sappho? Dominia turned her head but could not tarry to see, carried along with the pace of busy walkers all around as they surged, a river, to their destinations: she settled for remembering that meaning-laden final stanza of the poet's "Ode to Aphrodite."

What a miracle to behold a woman of such genius! This place was of a very uncommon sort, to be certain—yet not uncommon at all, for it seemed in that time and space perfectly normal. Each second spent there felt more natural than the last: Not only that, but freer! Godlier! Look at all those good people! Look at all that joy!

What had the Lamb shown her in the Void when she saw through his eyes and watched the martyrs devour the blood and substance of the sacrificial humans? Was it not the sin her Father proclaimed, but that part of the self that, bound by the electromagnetic field of the brain, could for whatever reason not escape when it was devoured by a martyr? That meant martyrs were even worse than they superficially seemed, for each one was a walking prison who contained at least part of the self of each person they'd eaten. Was anyone devoured by a martyr doomed to the fate of those souls her mind had conglomerated into the bloody ocean of her dream? Were martyrs that unsalvageable? The General could not accept that possibility. She could not afford to believe anyone was beyond salvation. If they were, she was surely unworthy of it, herself.

At last, on instinct, the General looked up and found herself at that corner where she'd first seen Tenchi calling her name and running, breathless, through the crowd. Though now she had expected—hoped—to see him, he was nowhere to be seen, and she glanced, with another soft thud of anxiety, at the envelope for Mrs. McLintock.

What would she say? What *could* she say? It was miraculous that such interface with eternity was possible, even for vision—but how could speech cope with the enormity of interaction with the living dead? Especially when that living dead had all the reason in the world for hatred. And who was to say this was even the right McLintock? Carol? Perhaps it was her mother, or her mother's mother, or whatever woman who before her had fled to the Mars colony when it was more than a wild and dangerous frontier. For her part, Dominia could see the appeal of escaping to space long before she boldly entered the gate of the busy market, passed a few stalls in search of the McLintocks' fruit stand, and was struck in place by the incredible sight of none other than young Murph McLintock shouting for their buyers. Forever the eight years at which Dominia had shot him in the head, rather than allow his martyrdom.

Her hands numb with shame, the astonished General was nonetheless more shocked when the boy responded to his own recognition of her not by freezing in terror or running away or screaming for help. Rather, his face brightened, and he called her name.

Every head in that marketplace turned.

It took Dominia a few seconds to register this. By then, silence spread like yet another wave throughout the crowd. A few people shuffled, smilingly, from out of her way. She could not help but think some looked familiar, but became preoccupied by the boy who dashed to hug her, tightly, around the waist.

"I don't understand," she said, her eye wet and batting as people, looking pleased, arranged themselves to murmur softly and watch the unfolding scene. "How did you get here?"

The grinning boy studied her, and said, "Well don't *cry*, please! It's nice!"

"She's crying *because* it's nice, Murphy," said Mrs. McLintock. His very tired mother looked here a little less tired. After wiping her hands on her apron, she emerged from the crowd to accept the envelope from Dominia's amazement-loosed grasp. "Thank you, General."

"You're— I'm so sorry." Her lips strained in a way that made Carol exhale and fan her eyes with the envelope.

"Well, goodness, don't make *me* cry, now. It's— Don't think of it, please."

"But I *do*."

"I know." With momentary reticence touching the eyes above her straining lips, the dead woman patted her hand. "But don't. At least, not as much, or as sadly as you do."

Stunned, the General tried to speak, and failed. It was as she had guessed. What use were words before the dead? Before, worse yet, the forgiveness of the dead? What forgiveness—what at all—did she deserve in life? Her mind was a spinning Ferris wheel, but not so spinning as it was when the boy released her. Then she looked up through the crowd, through its many faces, and, in a crescendo of beautiful glory, focused beyond the shoppers and salespeople and couriers. Rendered that much more beautiful through the stained-glass filter of tears, she recognized the people around had edged wide to reveal, as or more astonished than Dominia, that vision that had driven her each step of her long journey.

Oh, her absent heart! There was its beat again.

IX

Cassandra

Life does not always afford catharsis. All too often, unresolved pain remains an open wound forever, or seems to while we live. But perhaps that is only so those catharses that do arrive—those moments of relief that signal the annihilation of lifelong tension—mean that much more to us as we lie awake, counting each soft breath from the parted lips of a lover we thought we'd never see again.

A lie? A dream? Nothing that felt this way could be either. Dominia and her deceased wife embraced by the overflowing fountain of the plaza, and, weeping, Cassandra succumbed to kiss after kiss. Between each sob and each press of lips rang their words in duet: "I'm sorry, I'm so sorry, forgive me, I'm sorry."

"You have no reason to apologize." Dominia touched that warm cheek. The damp beads of Cassandra's tears burst under fingers that had missed, missed, missed this sensation. "Oh, Cassie, Cassandra—oh, I've missed you. After all I did to you, you don't need to apologize."

"But I do. *I* did that to myself. Nobody did it to me, least of all you. I was just so…angry and shocked and hurt and I—I did the thing that would hurt you the most." Those perfect eyes, big glass marbles of the world, wrapped themselves in a new sheen of tears. "I thought I'd had enough of living, but I was in so much pain! And the depression made me so shortsighted. Death wasn't even real to me until I was already dead."

"Oh, Cassandra…but what are you *doing* here?" Dominia turned her own trembling lips skyward, then back to her wife, whose honey curls were then plastered with laughing kisses. "I thought you were *lost*. That was what they said. The dead wander in the dark night of the Ergosphere forever, get trapped in low-frequency vibrations or…Lamb, whatever, when they have no soul. When they kill themselves."

The hitch of Cassandra's breath made her tighten her grip. "I *was* lost. I was lost eternally. I'm here because you saved me, Dominia, just like you saved everybody else."

Lips parted, the General looked up and saw through her tears the faces of the surrounding crowd. Their faces revealed themselves to her struggling memory now that the first dominoes of recognition were tipped. There was the man who must have been Mr. McLintock, slipping through the shoppers to hold his wife; Sakaki Kurosawa, the cutest of the Japanese nurses killed by Cicero in the hospital massacre, was there with her coworkers; a couple of soldiers she herself had destroyed on the same occasion were there with their wives and Kahlil, whom Dominia almost didn't recognize without glasses. All the people she had ever killed, failed to save, watched die—every single one of them was there. Even that son of a bitch Tobias Akachi, who smiled along with the rest of the watchers. Even Cassandra's first spouse, Benedict, had a misty eye and a gentle smile as Dominia savored her long-awaited reunion. Long-awaited, long-wished, hardly-dared-to-dream! Oh, Cassandra!

"I've hurt all of these people. I hurt you. And Lavinia. She's still being hurt because of what I did. I don't know if I can help her."

"You can. You will." Fire burned beneath the shimmer of Cassandra's eyes, beneath her trembling voice. "I believe in you."

To hold her! Dominia clutched her fair wife to her heart, feeling once again that body as, for over a year, she had only in memory, dreams, sorrow. But this! Oh, this. The General endeavored, somehow, to abate her own tears, and kissed the sweet-smelling head that tucked so perfectly into the crook of her neck. Like home, that feeling. "I don't deserve your belief after what I did."

"Don't say that. We *all* believe in you."

"But I made you so miserable. And I've hurt so many people. I hurt you."

"Dominia..." Cassandra lifted her head, and the irreplaceably soft touch of her fingertips nearly foiled the General's efforts to stave off tears. "I hurt myself. You never hurt me the way I did. You never made me miserable. Is that all you think— that we were miserable?"

"Of course not. We got along. I thought we were happy most of the time."

"We were. You gave me so much. Don't you remember? You made mistakes, and I was in pain, but even so...we were happy. You remember how you used to come home from work, and we'd curl up by the fire and I'd read to you, or we'd turn on the holo-center and the whole room would be our movie, or you'd draw me until I fell asleep? And how you bought me pets, and took me to the zoo, and helped me to start going back to Mass...to start teaching Noctisdomin school. I teach it here, too. Only"—Cassandra's eyes and mouth crinkled with the weight of her smile, and Dominia battled the urge to kiss those delicate webs until they bruised—"I get to teach the truth, here, and it's just Sunday school."

"Less annoying to say in English, not that it matters here...I bet you're even better at it in this place. Those children loved you so much. You were the gentlest, most compassionate person in their whole lives. I know you were in mine."

Her jaw deforming in that sweet way it did when she tried not to cry, Cassandra patted the General's cheek and then, as if not knowing where to lay that hand, her yet-living wife's heart. "If that were true, I would have talked to you more, instead of doing what I did. I just didn't understand. But being here, I learned—the way it was is the only way it could have been."

"But that's not true. I had free will. I made an evil, selfish decision to give away your daughter so I wouldn't have to share you with the memories of the person who loved you before."

"You took care of Cassandra." Benedict approached from the edges of the crowd to shake Dominia's hand. "For a longer time—and in better ways—than I could have. And Lavinia...she's not really mine, now, is she?"

"What do you mean?" Even before her question, the General felt the magician's presence behind her—or smelled his aromatic drugs, more like.

"She's the protein's. And not the true sacred protein...the false, deformed protein held sacred by the HMC. When Lavinia was in poor Cassandra's womb, and Cassandra was martyred rather than receiving the proper genetic treatments—because the Front decided long ago that health care is only a 'right' for martyrs, if rights even exist anymore—the protein went to work on the developing fetus." As the people of the Kingdom resumed their business, Dominia turned, Cassandra still in her arm, to watch the magician. "Your courtship was incredibly fast."

The General averted her eye. "I've criticized myself, but if it weren't for that, I don't think we would have had all those years together."

"Yeah, that's probably true. But I'm not bringing it up to throw stones. Trust me, I know how it goes! You meet an amazing woman—your dream woman—and move right in with her because, hey, you're waking up together all the time, anyway, so you'd might as well! Then some crazy shit happens and it's too late to turn back because your books are mixed on the shelves and you can't sneak all that out while she's sleeping, now can you?" As the women laughed, Valentinian summarized, "Emotions are never a perfect science."

Cassandra leaned that long-lost head against Dominia's shoulder, and the General struggled to focus as the magician went on, "But, like I was saying, Lavinia's DNA was edited even as her body and brain and tiny organs put the finishing touches on something resembling a fetal form. About twenty weeks in…that's why pregnant women and their fetus never survived this before you. Too early and the protein would just edit the fetus out of existence like it was an error. Too late and the changes would be minimal, but brutal enough to cause any infant's death. Between those two extremes, there's a sweet spot that nobody's been lucky enough to hit; and if they did hit it, they didn't have the medical care to maintain the condition. But in that sweet spot? The protein can alter not just a child's genetic and physical structure, but the genetic and physical structure of her descendants. The eggs in her ovaries are the world's only viable eggs containing martyr DNA. She may have technically died in the womb just like everybody else died in life, but she died twice—the first time, the baby died because her mother died. The second time the baby died, she died because that was when the protein began to truly afflict her. It picked a certain point—after it finished stripping out her father's DNA for its own, no doubt—to take her offline until she reached her full development. 'Full development' also includes puberty, and all the finishing cognitive touches of a young adult. Her situation was so prolonged because it was a two-step process of complete transformation. If Lavinia can be said to have a father—or any parents, at this point—it's the malformed protein."

Chilled, the General asked, "Then how can she be saved?" Or, better question: How could the world be saved from her? The magician, looking earnest, stared into her face.

"Lavinia is a deeply troubled girl, but she has a pure heart. Superficially, she is corrupted, because she has no way to comprehend the truth. But if she were to know the truth—if she were on the right side—can you imagine how powerful she would be? Can you fathom what would happen if you were able to convert her to the Lazarene faith, as pious a girl as she is for your evil Father's teachings? Most importantly, the true sacred protein is a hop, a skip, and a jump away from the malformed protein, and she is that malformed protein walking upon Earth. If her body and blood could be set right—healed by a great miracle such as that which gave me a body—consumption of her substance would have the same effect as that of Lazarus."

"How could such a miracle be possible again? No, forget that—the real miracle is getting her on our side. You think she can be turned against him, after what he's convinced her to do? After I betrayed her from the start, before she was even born?"

"Lavinia just wants to be treated like an adult. She wants people to tell her the truth, and she wants to be alive. However badly she's hurt by the reality of the situation, sometimes a little hurt is necessary to wake the fuck up." At the slight scowl of the Noctisdomin school teacher, the magician waved his hand. "Pardon my French. Here: you can't heal from an illness you don't even know you have. Better?"

With a steadying exhalation, Dominia glanced between Cassandra and Benedict. "I think being in this place and having the perspective you do is giving you all an overly optimistic perception of what's possible. But...I'll try."

"You'll succeed," said Cassandra, leaning up to kiss her wife. "I know you will."

"And after I succeed," asked Dominia of that beautiful face, "where will I find you?"

Valentinian, from somewhere in the distance, said, "I'll take care of it," but that wasn't enough. It would never be enough. Nothing was worth this moment, this slight weight of her body, this perfume of her flesh. It was real: so real!

"Couldn't I just stay here? I mean, since in eternity, she's already been saved by the best version of me." She asked it only half joking, and Cassandra smiled at her jest while, irritated, the magician said, "There are universes where you've done that, and it absolutely—*pardonnez-moi*—fucks *me*. That means I have to spend another two thousand Earth years tooling around, waiting for the next 'you' who will hopefully be less of a lazy deadbeat. And a reset isn't a party for you, either."

"I wish you could stay." Cassandra squeezed her hand. "But you *are* the best version of you."

"That's a horrible thing to say!" The General laughed, and her wife smiled.

"You're so much better than you know. Stronger. And someday, you'll be happy, too. But you have to keep fighting. Keep fighting for me. Keep fighting for Lavinia. I know you can save her. You can save us. Somebody has to do it, after all, since we're here."

With a glance for Benedict, Dominia brushed the hair from her wife's face. "I guess you were never really mine. Not my version of you...not the one meant for me, if I'm the Dominia to survive this."

"But how I love you, even so." As Cassandra turned her closed eyes against the General's palm and those soft lips brushed its heel, Dominia strove to maintain her composure. "Even if I'm only the Cassandra you save—only the Cassandra who sets you up for the Cassandra who gets to be yours—everything you did for me...everything we endured and enjoyed together...I'll treasure it forever."

Tearfully, but not painedly, the nodding General bent her head to kiss, one last time, the wife she'd loved and wronged so much that the thought of it had been enough to drive her around the world. To destroy that world. To remake that world. With tears of her own, a hand that patted Dominia's lips, and a mouth that strove to say anything but came up mute before relenting into that familiar smile of resignation, Cassandra took Benedict's hand. After one last look over her shoulder for that particular General, she disappeared into the crowd as if she had never been there at all. But she had. Oh, she *had*.

"Was it everything you'd hoped it would be?" asked the magician while Dominia covered her watering eye.

"I hoped I'd get to keep her when I finally saw her again. That I wouldn't have to watch her go, ever."

"Someday, you won't anymore." His hand landed upon her shoulder, and she turned to look at him as he swore, "I promise you."

"Why are you so intent on helping me, Valentinian? Why have you come here, if you're a wanderer through the universes? The bodiless man isn't obligated to be anywhere. You're liberated. You told me before that you were born into this world as the son of the man now called Lazarus, and his wife, Trisha—that your family, along with Cicero and Elijah, discovered the protein together, but that they stole the credit and power in that first universe. Usually people want to get back at somebody like that because of money, or a sense of obligation of setting things right, but you're the most slothfully amoral saint I've ever met." While he laughed, she emphasized, "I just don't understand why you're helping me. You even have your body, and you're still helping me."

"I'm *especially* helping you because I have my body! Christ, you're so used to constant betrayal that you just don't even understand what loyalty is anymore…poor dude. We'll get you fixed up when this is all over." As he began to navigate through the crowd and back to the hotel, she followed only because she had no choice. "If it would satisfy you to know I have other motives than helping you, then rest assured. You're right when you call me a universal wanderer. I go everywhere, and, unbounded by time as I am in this condition, I see my many future conditions in other universes—see those other universes, and what lies above and below them. When you're like me, you realize how big the big picture is: and the irony is that it's bigger than you could ever possibly realize."

"What was that about 'future conditions' in 'other universes'? You mean, outside of this cycle of the universe where I live?"

"I'm telling you, buddy…this thing is huge. And what I mean about 'future conditions,' well, that's a little complex. To be honest, I stopped worrying about it, though future conditions of myself, as I nudge into the businesses of other universes, might."

"Are you talking about reincarnation?"

"Getting hung up about your own identity is a key mistake most people make, especially when they start talking about the concept of reincarnation. Mostly because they forget that they made a choice to be a part of all this while in eternity. Of course, that's by design. Ultimately, we're all just the

Void, imitating people. All thoughtforms, yet all truth. In the service of that truth, I am seriously committed to helping you solve the problem of this world. And, of course, when I do solve the problem of this world, it liberates me from being a part of this particular cycle of existence, thereby freeing me up to be part of a new cycle of existence. A new rung of the ladder."

"So reincarnation isn't being a bunch of sea monkeys before being a smart dog and then finally turning into a man?"

"No, no, that's reincarnation, you're right. I'm talking about transmigration. Different dimensional axis of soul movement, *y* instead of *x*."

Lamb, this shit made her head spin. As the saint stopped in an alcove to light his cigarette, the General said, "So long as I'm not responsible for sticking you as a dog."

"Told you, that's your old man. You understand why, now, too."

"No kidding! Having two of the same person in one reality can't be healthy."

He nodded. "Reality itself knows what he's done, and doesn't like it. Every time he shows up, it's around the same time in 1974 CE—the year Cicero was born, years before the creation of the protein. I think I've told you this before—he tries to kill my parents before I'm born, standard timeline interference mistake. Instead, he finds the Lady and her cult, established from the dawn of time in preparation for his coming. This was not anticipated by the first Cicero, because nothing like this existed in the original function of reality. But the next version of him is always more prepared than the last—the output of one iteration forms the input of the next—and his presence inherently disrupts Lazarus's whole ability to form a relationship with my mother. She gets put on a different path, instead of continuing in academia and getting into proper genetic research or dying by the Hierophant's hand. From the first iteration and throughout each thereafter, my mother gets made into the Lady instead of being my mother. Therefore, I'm never born, and my linear-ish stream of consciousness continues working on the system from outside, intervening in small ways such as through dogs and other animals."

With a slightly wrinkled nose to recall the flirtatious behavior of Valentinian toward the (admittedly attractive) redheaded Lady who worked at the hotel's front desk before Miki, Dominia asked, "Why didn't he just turn around and kill Lazarus when he showed up to martyr the brothers?"

"Several reasons. The most important reason, of course, is that, without Lazarus, the martyr race has absolutely zero hope of ever achieving complete universal dominance, and your old man does not dream small. Lazarus and his assistants, the brothers, discover both the sacred and malformed proteins with or without the help of Trisha; but because of the eternal nature of the sacred protein, as soon as he experimentally infects himself, he remembers everything that's ever happened with all of this before and knows to destroy the sacred protein sample before going into hiding. The same night he did this in the first universe, Cicero was creeping around the lab, and stole the only protein which was present: the malformed one. In every iteration thereafter, he never gets that far…the Hierophant gets to him, first. They don't even have to worry about the samples anymore, and Lazarus doesn't worry about destroying them. He just books it into the Ergosphere. Poor old man! In these iterations, he only lives to discover the sacred protein because the Red Market was formally organized for the sole purpose of defending his totally oblivious life. Imagine…stalked by a secret conspiracy of gorgeous women without knowing!"

Dominia sighed. "What a waste."

"Yeah, he was a real dork before he was infected with the protein…now he's still a dork, he's just too angry all the time to seem like one." Chuckling, the magician nodded to a passing individual and stepped from the alcove to resume their stroll. "Anyway, ignorance has its fringe benefits…he also spends his whole human life being stalked by your Father, who, for a solid thirty-ish years, kept tabs on Lazarus—from 1974 until the discovery of the protein—waiting for the RM to slip up. Lucky for us, those women might be more insane than even His Holiness."

"You're not kidding," muttered the General, glancing down, and thinking of the Lady who sent her to her doom. "I don't have to lose my leg in all this, do I?"

"If you did, it would eventually be restored."

"*I don't have to lose my leg,*" she repeated with expectant emphasis, "*do I?*"

"If you do as I say," said the magician, with seriousness enough to raise alarm. "If you follow the plan."

"The plan I don't know about?"

"The plan that you *will* know about, as long as you follow the plan."

Amazing. Not a trace of humorous self-awareness in him. At least, not for this.

In the lobby of the hotel (too soon to leave, it seemed to the General, the powder fragrance of her wife still clinging to her clothes), the magician said, "I've got something for you, but you're going to want to find a place for it as soon as you're back home."

"Does she have to go *now*?" Miki called from behind the desk. Dominia's throat tightened while Valentinian heaved a sigh.

"Yeah, didn't think about that…you ladies should say goodbye."

Dominia, stricken, looked at her friend to see her sorrow shared. "I'm not going to see her?" asked Miki.

"Oh, *you'll* see *her* in no time from your perspective, Miki. This is eternity we're talking about. But from her perspective, she won't see you but in passing, and maybe sometimes in dreams. Not for a long time."

"Man." Miki put aside the phone and rounded the counter. "You're eating up my whole day with this phone thing...oh, Dominia! Dude"—she squeezed the General around the waist with such an iron grip that the martyr grimaced—"I miss you so much! I can't wait until you're here to stay for good. But you have to get your shit right before you can, okay?"

"I'm working on it." She laughed and inhaled once, deeply, calming herself and catching that lavender aura that followed her friend—that very same that followed a great many Red Market women all about the world. "I'll miss you, Miki. But I'm so glad you're happy."

"Thanks, man, me too! I don't know what I'll start doing with myself once I adjust to being here, or where I'll go—where any of us will go—after this place, but I'm looking forward to making my time worthwhile."

"I'll try to do the same with mine on Earth." The General patted Miki one last time before extricating herself from the girl's grip. "Be good, now."

"Maybe," said Miki, waggling her hips as she made her way back to her post. Through years of in-the-moment acting practice, the human did a good job hiding her misty eyes from all concerned. Valentinian, guiding Dominia back to that center sitting area, patted her hand.

"General, General...you're the bravest person I know. Just hold on a little longer: keep pushing forward. When this is all over, however it's turned out—the situation has to be better than the one we're in now, right?"

"I can't afford to stumble into a worse one," she said with a laugh, feeling freer than she had in at least a year and a half. As the magician lifted his lighter and she retrieved her now slightly crooked cigarette to lean into the sizzling blue arc, she asked, "But what about you?"

"What about me?"

"Will I see you again before this is all over?"

"Before this is all over...yeah. Once before this is over—and once, at the exact moment it is *finally* over, because I will have one more thing to ask of you. Which reminds me: I need to borrow something, if you wouldn't mind."

Without stopping to clarify her consent or tell her what he borrowed, the magician reached behind her ear as though to make a coin appear. Instead, he produced a small iridescent coil that, thinner than a hair, curled upon itself into a tiny sphere. This vanished between his fingers as he said, "I've got a project going on in the background here. Science fair stuff compared to my more theoretical business. Still necessary, though!"

"Going to tell me what it is?"

"Later. If I tell you now, your knee-jerk reaction will be 'no.'" While she rolled her eye and puffed away at the joint, the magician took her hand. "But before you go back, I just want to thank you for all you've done. For all you keep doing. I know it's not easy…but we're almost there. Just keep fighting."

"I will," she said. As his gaze fell from hers, she followed his focus, and her breath hitched.

Between the rows of ferns enclosing them, that gold-and-cerulean doorway opened into the Kronborg kennel. The disorienting thing was she did not even become conscious of the intention to walk forward. She simply noticed the doorway, then found herself upon its other side. Yes—back to Earth. Basil at her feet, joint pinched between her fingers, and the magician's hand replaced with none other than a relieving (if shocking) sight for her sore eyes: her lost gun. Still too in the afterglow of dreaming to register the full oddity of the find, she shifted the joint to the corner of her mouth and reflexively checked its chamber.

One bullet.

"There you are, Ninny!" Lavinia's sigh of relief bounced from the corner of the kennels, startling the General out of her reverie (or, possibly, out of the Kingdom, for who was to say that the happenings in the Kingdom were not mere symbols for the happenings of reality). With a surge of adrenaline and hyper-trained reflexes, she stowed the weapon under the back of her shirt before she could savor the reunion. Her sister carried on without notice. "I was worried when you went off like that. Are you all—euch!" The girl's sound was a crossbreed of disgust and indignation. "You can't *smoke* in here, Ninny. Think of the doggies!"

In one swift motion, Dominia pinched the cigarette out and crammed it away, not worried if it broke. The General felt more liberated than she ever had, whatever happened. By the Lamb, she was downright high! (Or by Valentinian's drugs? Hard to say.) The blessed truth whispered to her by the universe that night—that one encouragement she had ever needed—played out in phantom kisses relived by her giddy mind. Cassandra was not lost! Anything else Dominia had learned that night—any threat or horror hanging over her head—was nothing compared to the thought that she had, just moments ago, held Cassandra in her arms. Ah! She could weep had she the time, but she had none, and could not excuse her weeping in front of Lavinia except to misappropriate its source.

"I'm sorry I ran, Livvy. I guess I didn't know…how to react."

With an anxious glance for the door, the Princess edged through the dogs and tangled her fingers sheepishly amid the sumptuous folds of her dress. "Her" fingers—ugh. One wretched remembrance proved more evil than Cassandra's presence proved good, and brought the General's mood down a few notches. Lavinia, innocent to these thoughts, said in anxious hush, "I didn't know how you'd react, but I guess I didn't expect *that.* I've never shown anyone before."

"Livvy..."

"Daddy *told* me people wouldn't understand—even other martyrs. They don't understand anything about me. But I guess I thought you would understand, and that it might help you. You being so scared and all, maybe it would make you feel better to know I'd been through the same thing."

"But *why*, Lavinia?" The General tried to stifle from her voice those notes of natural horror in favor of warm and open concern. "Why did he take your limbs?" She knew his internal reasons, of course. She just wanted to know his excuses, and Lavinia seemed eager to supply them after decades of keeping the issue to herself.

"Well, the first time—you can't tell *anybody* this, Ninny, you hear me? Anyway, the first time I was about...forty, and I was sad that I couldn't marry anyone. I just wanted to be a part of that deep, deep love that a man and a woman share! That you had for your wife. Even Cicero and the Lamb seem happy together, though poor Lambie is always so tired from his work...but his plight just reminds me that being a saint is too important. I can't throw away everything I represent to the Church and to God! Worse, if I had to look outside the Family for a man, and he swooped me away, why, whatever would Daddy do?"

Yuck. Focus, Dominia. Her little sister continued, still in her own, purer world. "He would be so sad without me. But the temptation to have a boyfriend was just so *strong*! I had all these sinful thoughts and couldn't focus—couldn't do *anything* but lay around and sigh. Finally, I asked Cicero for his advice during confession, and he talked to Daddy for me. He's so helpful! They both were, and so understanding...Daddy came to talk to me right that very morning as I went to bed, and said he had a good idea that would solve all of our problems!"

"You gave him your leg because you felt sinful for wanting to be in love? To be an adult?"

"No, Ninny! I gave him my leg—well, you can't tell anybody *this*, either, but I told Cicero what I did in confession because I tried to run away once, too, and after I was foiled by my girl friends...they didn't tell on me, but I felt so guilty. I knew I had to confess to God." At Dominia's visible surprise to hear all this—that the devoted girl ever had one iota of desire to get out of Dodge, as they said in an ancient Western show—Lavinia crossed her arms. "I told you earlier, Ninny, I'm not perfect! And, my goodness...you think it's a fun time sitting around in these castles while you and everybody else in the whole Family gets to run around all over the planet, wherever you want?"

Poor Lavinia. No one in that world could have ever known the sorrow the General felt for this girl, who should have been her daughter as much as Cassandra's. In that rejection, the child had lost not only her psychological self but the greater part of her bodily self. What kind of life would she had lived if Dominia had not sold off the unborn infant to her Father? Would it have been possible, by any stretch of the imagination, for the mothers to make their way to safety anywhere in the world? Could they have ever had any modicum of happiness here? She would only plague herself with the questions she'd neglected for a century if she continued down that track.

"Trust me," the General tried at last, "running all over the world isn't the privilege you'd expect."

"But I want to decide that for myself! I'm sure it's scary sometimes, and that the world is very harsh, especially to traveling martyrs—but, Ninny, don't you love coming and going as you please? Don't you feel so strong and brave? I think you must. You're the strongest person I've ever known." Her voice dropped and she edged in, conspiratorial. "I was very worried about you, Ninny, but I was also very happy for you when you left. I thought—I hoped that you would find peace somewhere, maybe. You've always been so troubled. There are so many books about you, you know? I've read a few, but I don't have a head for military biographies, so they take me a long time to finish... but you've done such hard things. In your letters, you would only ever talk about governing work and the happy things you and Cassandra did, and I always thought...I guess I got the sense after a few decades that you did that on purpose, you know. Being optimistic in front of me. That you were trying to support me, so I wouldn't worry about you."

Aching with the weight of long-suppressed guilt, the General tried to assure herself there was no time like the present. "There's a reason for that." The pure sweetness of her sister's earnest face forced her gaze away; she was no more able to stare into its glow than was a non-Lazarene into the heart of the sun. "Lavinia—"

"—must be in here," interrupted Cicero, as the door pushed open and the cadre of dogs charged to greet him—save for Basil, who, while theoretically no longer possessed by the magician, seemed no less displeased by the prospect of Cicero's presence. Though, admittedly, it was odd for the dogs to be so thrilled by El Sacerdote. They preferred the Lamb, which was why it did not surprise Dominia when both brothers rounded the corner. If anybody was surprised, it was Cicero, who seemed shocked, then displeased, to discover the General along with Lavinia. Any hint of levity scalded straight off his face and left his expression tight beneath his devilish goatee.

"Ah. And our other dear sister is also here. I do hope we are not interrupting you girls."

Although Dominia was about to forge some cover story, Lavinia leapt in so immediately that the General was once more shocked by her younger sister's "naughty" streak: she had a heretofore unknown ability and willingness to lie, which was just more proof she was a natural member of the Holy Family. "Oh, I was just showing Ninny some of the new dogs from this year, and talking about the after-party! I'm so *excited*, Cicero, aren't you?"

"Yes, my dear, it should be very fine time...did you tell Dominia about the play?"

It must have been a special occasion. The Hierophant and Cicero (or Cicero Prime and Diet Cicero, as she strove to think of them) loved having concerts at the drop of a hat—as or more frequent than their parties, though the two were often paired. Theater productions required much more time and effort than the standard gala, meaning that the Ciceros, depending on venue size and location, could only force their actors and crewmembers to pull off about ten to twenty shows a year while working their thespians in repertory. That was to say, ten to twenty separate shows, of which there were sometimes nightly performances, over the course of that year-long season.

A human who had never visited the European theatere might not imagine the size, grandiosity, and variety of shows available in the town of Elsinore, but they frequently did not need to imagine: the Elsinore Theater Festival's shows, like most forms of theater whether human or martyr, were broadcast globally across a variety of monetized streaming services generously open to human countries so they, too, could line the Hierophant's digital wallets with the imaginary bits of encrypted data everyone had agreed somewhere along the line to be a measure of wealth. Every human who considered themselves high-class endured a love/hate relationship with martyr culture due purely to the quality of their theater. As they stood, at present, in Kronborg, and it was the Elsinore Theater Festival, she guessed, "A bit of Willy Shakes, I suppose," to be rebuffed by Cicero, "No, in fact. It is Father's original."

While the General made long-trained eye contact with the Lamb—a sort of brief, exasperated mutual stare used in place of an eye roll when present company made sarcasm unsafe—she maintained a pleasant smile. "That will be great," she said, while the Lamb said, "Pity about the double-booking, though."

"Yes," agreed Cicero, shaking his head. "I should have very much enjoyed an opportunity to see the opening night—but, duty calls."

"I wish you were going to be there, Cicero." Lavinia worried the black lace frills of her overskirt with gloved hands at which the General could hardly bare to look—particularly not when Cicero took one up to kiss.

"You know I shall be with you in spirit, my girl. At future performances. But the Lord does not wait."

The General maintained her smile, thinking happy thoughts of the place she'd been instead of all they discussed now. "You're going to be in the show, Lavinia?"

"Oh, she shall be the star, of course."

"Of course," echoed the Lamb. He stood from where he'd crouched, having mussed sufficiently the ears of the border collie that trotted back around the corner, invisible to the DIOX-I's scrutiny and Cicero's arrogant inability to recognize the animal that had stopped the train. "And the Holy Father had to be sure he had his part, too."

"Naturally, naturally," said Cicero, all happy agreement as he studied Dominia's face like he tried to read her mind. "I'm sorry to say, sister, neither will you be able to attend the premiere performance of Lavinia's play. Though I'm sure we could find a way to access the stream, if you and I wrap up our ceremony soon enough."

"And is this all going to be before the party?" asked the General, to which the priest agreeably said, "Consider it preparation," with that dark, expectant look in his eye. He knew, of course, what she divined. This ceremony was when Dominia would lose her leg, which would probably then be prepared and served for the New Year's party once the Hierophant's show wrapped up.

That was assuming, of course, any of these events were allowed to get as far as that.

"Where is this ceremony?" she asked. Cicero, pleased to tell her, waved a hand in the direction before dropping it upon Dominia's shoulder to guide her along. There she was again, ten years old—human and martyr years combined, mind—and on her way to a beating because she'd snickered in church at some rare verbal gaff of El Sacerdote while the Holy Father was elsewhere on business, where he couldn't make pretentious suppositions about the Freudian roots of corporal punishment. Interesting how the younger Cicero hadn't raised a hand to her in the Hierophant's presence—once she got big enough to hit him back. The first time she broke his collarbone was the last time they'd had a physical altercation until the one on the train. Now those early respites of Cicero's to treat the "bratty" (read: normal) girl as he thought her behavior merited seemed coordinated efforts on the part of the Family to mold Dominia's behavior and establish the Holy Father as a savior force. He was a doting, generous, compassionate protector, His Holiness, until he wasn't anymore.

No wonder the Hierophant was such a jolly old fucker all the time. He got his bad temper out while living the life of that same hateful priest who gripped her now, and said with a sneer-edged smile, "Shall we take a look? Arrangements are being made in the chapel. It shall be a rather more intimate affair than the show, but still quite pleasant. Always a joy to welcome a lost lamb back into the fold."

That hand was so much like her Father's as to be identical. Amazing they'd gotten away with the con for so long! But reality was just so absurd in this case, anything was easier to believe. Why, Cicero and the Hierophant had similar ways of speaking? It was only because Cicero had his nose stuffed so far up the Holy Father's ass—because of two thousand years of cohabitation and co-working. They looked near completely alike, save for the distance of two thousand years or more, which, on a martyr's face, rested like sixty or so without the upkeep of occasional genetic engineering? That was because the Hierophant was an alien, bequeathed with alien technology, and had taken the form of the first man he'd met on Earth.

Incredible, the fairy tales people let themselves believe.

"Do we have to see the chapel now?" asked Lavinia, with a glance for her sister and a clear desperation for someone to tell her something true. "Ninny and I were just catching up."

"I know you wish to chat with Dominia all night—you'll doubtless chew her ear off soon enough—but Father does have a need for you. You've lines to practice, queen mother Bathsheba." At Lavinia's pout askance, Cicero clicked his tongue. "Now, my dear, don't fret. You shall see the chapel before the ceremony, I'm sure."

The Lamb brushed his hands free of dog fur while studying the General. "You can always talk to Dominia after your rehearsal." This meant, "Be careful what you discuss with Lavinia after her rehearsal." She could see it in his face even as he dropped back to let Cicero lead them from the kennels and into the greater building. With a smile for the Princess, Dominia said, "Don't worry. I'll see you soon enough; and if I don't, you can always come to see me."

Anxiously, the girl nodded, then was out of sight.

Kronborg's chapel was certainly intimate by the standards of some of the Hierophant's most ostentatious and thus most favored basilicas. But, to Dominia's eye, it was no less flamboyant, and floored with that same ominous checkerboard tiling she'd begun to assess with particular wariness. Worship had been suspended so workers could prepare for the ceremony of Dominia's alleged contrition. As a few buffed to golden shine Christ and his thieves on prominent display, several human carpenters below slaved over the construction of some wood structure, which, in pieces, went unrecognized by the General.

"I do hate to allow the house of the Lord to be disrupted by such clamor," said Cicero with a distasteful glance for those indentured to the task of construction. "But the dimensions of the crucifix shall be such that constructing it outside our modest chapel is simply not an option. Did you know, my dear, that the Romans may have popularized the act of crucifixion, but they did not invent it? They only learned it from the Phoenicians around the time of the Punic Wars, in the third century BC. It is thought to have originated with the Assyrians and the Babylonians, but the Persians perfected it...and, of course, your savage Hunter friends still do it to our people all across the globe. Many have had their martyrdom completed in the pattern of the Greatest, much to the Lord's sorrow. Christ died upon the cross, after all, so none of us would have to. And you do not have to die upon it, either: but you do have to take some time to think about what you've done."

The General observed the construction with a new and sicker eye. "I thought that I was just going to be losing a leg."

"That, too, my girl: but all things in their time. It is a *punishment*, after all. Not some simple operation. It is vitally important that you be aware you are about to lose your leg, and even more important that you remain aware the moment you do."

"And how is crucifixion related to the loss of my leg?"

"Upside down," explained the Lamb, looking particularly dead inside as he studied the crucifix, then the face of his daughter. "For a long, long time."

With far greater pleasure, Cicero expounded to the very anatomy-conscious General that, "The upper half of the body lacks in valves to retard the flow of blood, as man was not made to spend his time hanging inverted without a break. After, oh, ten or so hours in such a position, the average person's head will burst from the intensity of the pressure. But we can't have that, can we?"

Tightly, humorlessly, the General bared her teeth.

"We will suspend you by your right leg," explained El Sacerdote, continuing on with perfectly mild expression. "It will soon fall asleep, and quickly thereafter—in the grand scheme of your torture—be dead, for the protein cannot heal your tissues without circulation! Just think of what a clean and easy job the amputation will be when all of this is over. No blood to heal the atrophied fibers of those muscles. But we will take measures to ensure such a thing does not happen to the rest of you, so long as you truly have returned to the Family."

On noticing the depth of her silence, the Lamb said something that she assumed was some dry form of comfort. Dominia couldn't hear his words above the pounding of hammers.

X

The Fourth Empire

Never in her wanderings had the General felt so tired. Though she'd slept when dropped off at Kronborg, the series of brutal revelations—punctuated by that one joyful moment of promise—left her in sore need of unconsciousness to process all she'd learned. Sleep knew, and it eluded her with a sadism resembling that of her so-called Family. Rather than rest while the Hierophant and Lavinia were across town in Elsinore's sprawling Elizabethan theater, she paced her room.

This was beyond the burden of Odysseus's homecoming to suitors plaguing his wife. This time, Odysseus returned to discover the suitors had *always* been there, skittering in the dark corners of his home as cockroaches might inhabit the dwellings of lesser men. The cockroaches here were deceptive, articulate, and alarmingly omniscient. They were also consummate schemers. The air buzzed with the vibrations of their treachery: an only semi-imagined quality palpable to her after her time in the Ergosphere and its nighttime Void.

The Void. She could slip into that Void with such ease. She needed an extra hour or so of rest to think and feel sentient, but she didn't need it to slip into that other place. She didn't even need to smoke the magician's bent cigarette to skip into the Kingdom, if she could tolerate wandering through the dark. A formless Void was almost preferable to staying, especially now that the information around her had resolved for her eye into those digital threads. Failing those, she could just light a fire and be patient. Then, in daylight, navigate her way—

Where?

Nowhere.

There was nowhere to go. Not really. In theory, she could wink back to Jerusalem and join the battle there. Then? She'd be once more up to her elbows in killing—human and martyr alike. More than ever, violence did not seem the worthy way. If evil could have been said to exist, martyrs qualified, but they were only evil because the Hierophant had carefully groomed them to worship the worst in man. It was like breeding dogs backward into wolves, which he had also more or less done, although in the case of canines, he kept the killer hounds in separate kennels, far away from the gentle family dogs who only wanted to love and be loved. Nothing of the bloody business of their cousins.

Remarkable how similar animals always were in the end, though. When they were afraid, or ashamed. Even animals could be penitent. After a beloved cat had died and Cassandra had mourned it (Dominia secretly mourned it, busy being strong for her wife), the General had talked her into a dog. They had to compromise somewhat, as Cassandra was partial to small dogs, whereas Dominia felt if one was inclined to get a small dog, they'd might as well get another cat. In the end, they'd settled on a miniature shepherd breed originating from the climate-ravaged prison colony of Australia. The dog in question was not so small as to annoy the General, nor so large as to annoy Cassandra. He instead managed to routinely annoy them both by getting into trash, digging up the garden, and engaging in other excusable dog faux pas. Each time he was caught, he exhibited humiliated facial expressions and sulky mannerisms such as leaning his face sadly against the nearest cabinet: inevitably, the women would relent into petting and consoling the petulant pooch until his mood improved.

Even the decidedly not sapient dog had felt shame. The Hierophant somehow lacked that quality. He may not have been an alien in body, but in heart and soul and mind, he was one just as much as any little green man. Perhaps living so long had wrung the decency out of him—but, considering Cicero, it was more likely he'd never possessed a sense of it to begin with. Rather than developing decency, he'd grown a sense of humor. The younger version of the man was more inclined to bouts of rage and intense physical sadism; the older version had gotten all his rage out and just lived for seeing the moment his victim understood what was about to happen. In that light, she was surprised the Hierophant had not been there to see her reaction to news of the impending inverted crucifixion: then again, she supposed he had seen it before.

Yet she struggled to believe for an instant that the Hierophant remembered all he did from the top of his head, however he touted the supposedly lost Roman rhetorical art of memory. It was undeniable that the protein enhanced his faculties in that regard—beyond the point of even the average martyr, it was evident—but there was more to all this than had already been revealed.

It would help if she knew what was going on the night of the so-called party. It would help more if she knew what was happening in Jerusalem. He had given her no television, but if his surge was at all successful in enclosing the Lady's library, supply lines were cut and Dominia's soldiers were trapped. Allegedly. The Hunter tunnel system extended an astonishing length and often incorporated existing tunnels beneath buildings and sewer systems. Even if her Father's militaries closed off the city at the same time as the teleporter in Tunis and the landing pad in Tangiers, many fighters and civilians alike had reasonable odds of evading their death. Many neighborhoods had been evacuated of citizens by her prior efforts, and now by the UF and European armies, but more civilians remained.

And as for Dominia's own inner circle—had the Lady fled, or did She remain? And what of Farhad and Gethsemane? She hadn't gotten back on track to press the magician, she realized now.

It didn't matter, truth be told. Their fate was in Valentinian's hands, and of course their own. For her own part, Dominia's fate began to settle upon her with a distinct sense of nihilism. That unreliable saint had gotten shifty when she'd pressured him about her leg. Seemed like she would have to come to terms with that—and since he hadn't even mentioned the crucifixion to her, well, she was going to have to accept that, too.

All the more reason to do anything other than mope in her room. She was now working on a limited timeline to determine the nature of the New Year's events, outside of removing her leg. Figuring out who would be at each event and what each event was would be key to developing some—any—contingency plan.

Good thing the Holy Father was out practicing his lines. No time like the present to go rifling through his stuff, especially since there was no telling when she'd get strung up on that cross. The trick would be getting to his office without attracting attention.

The castle was thick with spies, whether mollycoddled martyr children or brainwashed human slaves who believed their masters deserved all they took. That was to say nothing of the martyr courtiers themselves, the many painters and poets and sculptors and lords and ladies and distant Holy Family relatives and hired friends and *their* friends and often the lovers of all of the above, each circulating through the many halls to see and be seen gossiping, admiring the great many pieces of plundered art displayed upon the walls, listening to the finest music, or occasionally engaging in a jolly bit of torture—though never without *reason*! Martyrs were not cruel, as the Hierophant assured them. Torture was justified with certain breeds of evil criminals, and, of course, traitors. Given the opportunity, martyrs the world over would tell the General she was lucky the Hierophant planned to leave her with her life.

In a way, they were right. The Lady was also right. So was Dominia's own conscience. Returning home to face this horrific punishment—or, at least, to be faced with the prospect of it—was necessary. There were no better options. After two hundred years of genocide, she had imperiled an entire world by giving her Father access to a fertile martyr. Sold her daughter to the Devil. And for that, he'd made her Governess of the United Front. At the time, she had been too depressed and too corrupt to care. There was no fixing the past from the present. But there was changing the present so the future could be better. There was repentance—not for the world's sake, or Cassandra's sake, or even her own. No: for Lavinia's.

So, for Lavinia's sake, she emerged from her room with that long-missed gun still down her back. The Hierophant and his favorite daughter and whatever "lucky" actors selected for the occasion would be tied up in rehearsal for hours. As to Cicero and the Lamb, she was not so sure. They had parted ways twenty minutes before, after showing her the crucifix and walking her to her door.

She needed to be careful. Kronborg was not the Holy Father's largest demesne, but it was grand nonetheless, and overfull of threats to her security. She needed creep from the hall containing her bedroom and through the church wing without looking like she crept. Then she'd have to pass a series of tearooms—long since converted to more bedrooms and offices, but a great deal more salons, studios, and reading rooms. Those would be better attended, but, like the diners in the train car that first time speaking to Miki, perhaps they would be too caught up in their amusements to pay her attention. Perhaps. Although she would like very much to handle all of this by not handling any of it—that was, by slipping into the Void—the first and foremost thing she needed do was dispose of her weapon.

The sad fact was, the good old gun gifted to her after her campaign in the Pacific (by the Holy Father, of course) now caused her more trouble than benefit. That single bullet meant one of two things: suicide or a lucky shot. And if she kept it on her person, well—perhaps it was her metaphysically one-eyed nature, but the General (not with two earthly eyes *and* her spiritual one all squinting in unison) could see no realistic opportunity for its use against anyone but herself before the undisclosed time of her ordeal. Therefore, if the gun was to be of use against anyone external, it had to be somebody's else's problem.

Though she had not been made privy to "the plan," Dominia had gotten to know the Lady, Lazarus, and Valentinian pretty well. René Ichigawa's useless ass had to have been positioned at Kronborg for a reason. If Tenchi had been willing to stake his life on the bet that Dominia would make the correct decision, it would have been easy for him to get himself caught: but

René had been enlisted into the scheme despite his cowardice and skepticism, and had, when one thought it all through, no reason to have been involved in the plan in the first place. That was worth consideration. She did not by any means trust him, but in this situation, she had no choice. It had crossed her mind to give the weapon to Lavinia, but the girl would find the burden unbearable with her heart not fully won and Dominia was not certain the girl's heart could ever be fully won. Even if they won it enough to win the night (and somehow purify her corrupted blood, as Valentinian had suggested a miracle might), would her leadership be enough to ensure the safety of the future? Was there a way to show her truth enough to prevent backpedaling into a grim extension of this violent path?

That feeling of Cassandra in her arms. *You can do it.*

Yes. She could. Dominia's truth could liberate Lavinia—but it would need to be delivered soon. The more truth delivered at once, the better: and the General was keen to deliver it before the Hierophant had her swinging by her ankle. A thought inspired by the distant sounds of carpenters sealing her fate, nail by nail.

Concern for the location of Cicero's position started to nag at the General when she passed beyond the ominous clatter of the church wing. That concern magnified until she swept through the tiltyard rather than risking the tearooms. Long since converted to an overflowing greenhouse that burst with exotic herbs, South American flowers and vines even in the midst of winter, the altered jousting arena was a good place for somebody who wanted privacy: or somebodies. As she ducked through rows of sumptuous plant life, she spotted the Family's beloathed priest submitting, among a peacock's tail of orchids, to the embrace of his partner. She thanked her stars the Lamb was sympathetic to her interests and passed down a different row, of exotic jungle mimosa trees wrapped with garlands of flowers whose aromas rendered the General unsmelled as the kiss rendered her unseen and Cicero's flurried thoughts (had he emotion enough left to relent to love) rendered her unheard. Praise the Lamb, praise the Lamb: even after her disgrace and reluctant return, the Rabbi remained sympathetic to his daughter.

In fact, as she emerged from the tiltyard and resumed her perfectly casual way to the Hierophant's office, she could not help but consider the Lamb must have been *very* sympathetic to her ends. There was no doubt that he knew the magician had given her the gun. Yet he had said nothing of the matter to Cicero—had he, her weapon would already be gone and she would be confined to her quarters. She had the distinct feeling that, however the bullet was spent, the Lamb approved.

Was this a good sign, or a bad one?

At last she reached the former storerooms converted to a series of guest bedrooms upon the Hierophant's acquisition of the property and his considerable alterations to its size. It was now a matter of locating that particular cell in which Ichigawa stayed—and a cell it would be. While the suites were reasonably furnished and quite elegant in and of themselves, this set of bedrooms and laughably tiny bathrooms were as sizable as the allotment of a favored prisoner: a purpose for which they were frequently engaged. Locating her implied prisoner of choice was not difficult, because even without a martyr's senses, she could have picked his whimpering through any door.

"René." She knocked, courteously warning him as she began to turn the knob. "It's me. I'm coming in, okay?"

"What," he called as she carried through the motion, "not *you*!" The professor sat up from bed and cracked his skull on the bookshelf above with such ferocity that even Dominia saw stars.

"Lamb, René, are you all right?"

"No! Who puts a bookshelf so low over a bed?"

"A sadist," observed Dominia, studying the collection of books with which the Hierophant had decorated René's shelf. Such gems as *The History of Torture*, and a play by the ancient European prisoner-poet Genet. *Deathwatch*. Through these, she thumbed in cursory search of a bug. "Nice of him to provide you with reading material."

"He's very subtle." Rubbing the top of his head with a grimace, the man sat up in bed and searched for trousers to shield his skinny legs. "Do you just come barging in on everyone like that? What if I had been naked?"

"Like I care. Welcome to war, Private." As Dominia recognized her yet-damp jacket had been hung over the head of the casket-size shower, she slipped into the bathroom to reclaim it, then thought better. Instead, she called him inside with faux irritation while looking hither and thither for holo-cameras. Scanners built into the walls, most likely. Plus the showerhead? No: too indiscrete. "What's this hole, René," she said in mock irritation, fingering the yet-damp fabric of the drying jacket. "It didn't have this when I gave it to you."

"What do you mean, hole?" Irritated, the now fully dressed professor marched into the tight space with her, and she yanked the coat down from where it stood drying to brusquely cram it in his hands.

"See?"

"No, I don't."

"Well, never mind. It's not mine, anyway." Still feigning annoyance, she moved as though to put it on and, in a sleight of hand that would have pleased the magician but remained hidden from the perception of even a full-room hologram, slipped the gun from her waistband to the equally black fabric of the jacket while it still hung near the level of her hips. A look of disgust crossed her face. "Ugh, still wet. Keep it." She thrust the jacket and gun back into his hands.

"Of course it's still wet! Did you—" His true annoyance melted into an expression of shock once he shifted his grip on the jacket and felt its contents. "Is—"

Trained by three centuries of battle, her reflexes kept the next three equally loud words from escaping by virtue of a hand that slapped down across his mouth. "Don't argue. Okay?"

Slightly, he nodded, and as she drew back her hand, she asked, "Did the Hierophant tell you what you'll be doing before the party?"

"I don't know..." With an uneasy glance at the damp and dangerous parcel he cradled like a North American football, René stepped back out of the bathroom. "He asked if I'm a religious man."

So the professor's "pre-party" obligation was to attend Dominia's ceremony of repentance. "Aren't you excited! You get to watch me lose my leg. Does that even us out for earlier?"

"What—no! I already told you how freaked out I am about that! And not just for your health, but—I want to be a martyr so I can live forever, not so I can watch amputations. Maybe that's what *some* people are into."

"Like the Hierophant, and Cicero, and a whole lot of other religious nuts who are going to be very torn between a place as an observer of the ceremony or a seat in the Hierophant's play. Speaking of"—the General glanced at the digital clock glowing crimson in the upper-left-hand corner of the room's one smartwall, displayed with a summation of the weather and local traffic conditions—"I have to run. But I need you—"

Faltering, reluctant to speak out loud, she lifted a finger to silence him. From the drawer of the tiny scribe's desk crammed into the corner, she withdrew a pad of paper and a courtesy pen. Anxiously contorting her arm and back to shield the pad from anything suspect in the room (cupholders, lampshades, certainly the aforementioned smartwall along with any stupid ones), the General scribbled a note while René leaned over her shoulder to watch.

This thing has one bullet. If you are for sure going to the ceremony, try to sit where you'll get a clear shot.

"Of whom?" he asked. She flashed him a grim little smile as she wrote: *If you can't get Cicero, then I guess me.*

"You want me to—" Lips sealing in agitation, René snatched the pen from her to scribble in elegant-yet-illegible scholar's cursive: *You want me to shoot Cicero?*

I like that you're more concerned about him.

With an annoyed look for Dominia's lame attempts at humor, René jotted: *I'm concerned about me.* Several underlines, and a very emphatic wave of his hand on slamming down the pen.

Starting to feel annoyed, herself, Dominia tore the top three pages from the pad, folded them, and tore them apart while she flat out asked, "Do you think he's going to let you live in his world if he gets his way in any of this?"

Mouth open but soundless, brows knit in deep irritation, the professor relented with a sharp sigh of disgust. "*C'est naze*," he muttered. Awash with relief, Dominia clapped him on the shoulder, then strolled into the bathroom to flush the scraps of note.

"Thank you," she told him on her emergence.

"Yeah, yeah…get out of here. Now I have to figure out…" He waved his free hand and shook his head with a stifled Japanese curse. "What a liability… Dominia…"

The smiling General slipped through the door and left him to his muttering. Too bad, in retrospect, she hadn't been able to bring the jacket: it would have been a fine alibi, the laundries being relatively close to her Father's office. But there was no time to look for a better solution. The thing to do was to look like she had every right to be walking where she was—and that was true. She was allowed anywhere in the castle. Only her intentions were suspect, and who knew? She might very well change her mind at the last second. Unlikely, but such a line of internal nonsense helped her look less sinister.

Only once—one time—was she noted with any scrutiny by anyone she saw. Near a depiction of *The Breaking of Saint Severian*, wherein Valentinian gleefully bashed the limbs of a man upon the wheel, the General rounded a corner and ran almost face-first into Lavinia's sharpest little friend. Their martyr reflexes prevented collision. Nonetheless, the scrutinizing girl, wig askew, recoiled as if they actually had impacted and regained her composure with a narrow-eyed, "Oh." As in: "*Oh, it's* you."

"Sorry," said the General, continuing apace toward the chancery, gritting her teeth to feel the girl's gaze boring into her back. She forced herself to amble all the way to *The Interrogation of Saint Titania*, seven paintings down, before looking back. There, she found the courtier gone and took a breath that echoed beneath the soft music filling the chancery wing.

Paranoia wasn't bad in Kronborg, but even there it had its excesses. Within grasping distance of her Father's office, this was the ideal time to slip into the night-blackened Void and steal her way behind his lock. She just had to convince herself it was the right thing to do. What good was that place, after all, if not to allow her passage through solid walls? She needed caution—a single step in that place meant a variable number in reality—but she now possessed means of navigation. Information. Regardless of whether the Hierophant had left a computer running in his absence (unlikely), that room was full of information. His sleeping computer, yes, but more analog information: books. Was it not possible that information kept in books could be seen in the Void with perhaps greater ease than information encoded as ones and zeroes?

Confident she was alone, the General let her body slip through the atmospheric religious music of the chanceries and into the formless, unlit nighttime of that other space. Working with the Ergosphere, whether day or night, was not so much about learning how to create anything as it was about carving the rules of its workings from its own strange substance—and the more that was revealed to one, the more could one reveal to oneself by way of reason. Much as thoughtforms could be fished from the darkness by the magnetism of thought, so, too, could Dominia's consciousness sculpt from the Void's black innards a new perception of the data around her.

As she contemplated this in the darkness, the information adjusted to her thoughts. No longer did it appear as threads demonstrating the connectivity of electronic devices. Rather, information pulsed all around, massed together in great golden clots of foam. Bookshelves. Though each office held an abundance, the General needed only find the brightest assortment of lights. No room in that castle contained more books—and a greater wealth of information—than her Father's study. In the center of these bright clusters, she spoke the True Word of "reality," and dropped back into her body.

Yes: like disorienting magic, there she was. Standing on her Father's desk instead of the floor, perhaps, but all the same, she'd appeared within a locked room without so much as touching the knob, and laughed at herself in astonishment.

Then, she was back to business. Careful to keep her shoes from touching another centimeter of furniture, the General dismounted the desk and looked for clues of her Father's foul intent. The (literal) desktop computer—a hologram PC built into the Hierophant's otherwise untouched antique desk, a device that amounted to a projector lens set responsible for projecting both images and keyboard—had no doubt been locked, and if it wasn't locked, then it was a bigger trap than his whole office. If there was a single room in the castle not being constantly recorded, it was this, but she wouldn't have been amazed if he'd made an exception for her imminent presence and gotten scanners installed the week before.

In other words, Dominia knew she would get caught. It was a matter of gathering as much information as possible before in the hopes that, somehow, in a dream or the actual Void (maybe even after her death if that was what it came to) she could transmit the knowledge to her friends. Even help herself. If there was any evidence of past efforts or future plans, it was worth the risk.

Perhaps unsurprisingly, she needed only look far as that desk on which she'd manifested. Papers sat, still arranged as they'd been during the earlier meeting. Those papers front and center were none other than *The Curse of Bathsheba*, the final treatment of the Hierophant's play. He'd been working on it while she spoke with him, and the scene in question was troubling: drawn not from the human Bible's story of queen mother Bathsheba, but the martyr variation. In the Old Testament, Bathsheba was mostly an unfortunate married woman who was lusted after by King David when he saw her bathing. Whether or not she was raped as so many mythological women was unclear, but she and David were nonetheless punished unilaterally by the death of their first child. May have had something to do with David angling her husband to the front lines where the man died, thus allowing the king to marry Bathsheba—but that was a matter of debate. Whatever the reason, after the first kid, many others followed: including the future king, Solomon. A magician, Dominia noted wryly. In the human version of the story, this child claimed the throne by peaceful means, through his mother's influence on the still-living David.

All that was in the Old Testament, though. The Post Testament revisited the queen's story, and many other stories, with purportedly true versions handed down from the priests of Acetia. Hogwash: from the Hierophant's degenerate imagination. Beneath his pen, everybody in the Bible had their bad qualities ramped beyond reason, and there was quite a lot more amputation, cannibalism, slavery, and black magic than in even the Old and New Testaments. One had to admit this was almost impressive. When it came to the story of Bathsheba, the focus was on her rise to power as queen mother, assisted by the prophet Nathan. David died more or less at the start of the story, and a few—one might say, "liberties" had been taken with the essential natures of the characters in the story. Not to mention the means by which Bathsheba and her son attained power! Mostly, as one might have expected, this was through the mass slaughter of their enemies.

The play evidently meandered for some time before it got to that point, because it looked like it was Act III or IV before King David was confirmed dead. In the scene Dominia's Father had been touching up, Bathsheba was responding to news of her husband's intended heir—Adonijah, the son of another of David's wives—with an anger most humans might have considered extreme. In her rage, martyrs said she wished the children of mankind to die before being talked down to simpler solutions by Nathan; but before his intercession, her wish was not for death by simple means like flood or plague.

ACT IV
SCENE III

(Queen Bathsheba's chambers. She paces in agitation while the prophet Nathan watches. Smoke rises outside: Adonijah sacrifices cattle in a public demonstration of his claim to King David's empty throne.)

BATHSHEBA
The constancy of od'rous meat poisons
A scent meant to call us to the table,
Emulating instead death's fecund stench
And rend'ring that which was once called "sweet," foul.

NATHAN
The sacrifices of Adonijah.
Fatted calves and oxen for the Lord,
To celebrate—and thus cement—his rule.
Haggith's son always thought himself the king.

BATHSHEBA
Let no one think this impudence will stand.
To dream! My son, his royal seat displaced,
Standing at odds with uncertain future—
How can the Lord allow me such a slight?

NATHAN
His retribution comes in subtler ways:
Namely, within the actions of His men,
Acting without knowing themselves actors.

BATHSHEBA
And doth the Lord not possess women, too?

NATHAN
Aye.

BATHSHEBA
Then find his retribution in me.
Find justly rage within this breast, Prophet,
For I burst with it, as Death's bloodied air
Marks a battle lurking on dawn's rose cusp.

NATHAN
You would do violence in your good son's name?

BATHSHEBA
Why should I not do violence? After all,
'Tis what my husband imparted on me
When, by his violent passions, he conceived
To lure me from my poor Uriah's home
And first, to trick the man—then see him die.

NATHAN
Of these acts, Queen, our Lord did not approve,
Nor now does He approve of this ascent.
Monarchy is given divine consent,
Which Adonijah hath not in this case.

BATHSHEBA
Yet he burns oxen at my son's altar!
Those wretched sacrifices rot the air
So Valentinian's perfumes plague my mind.
All I can think now is of sweet Death
For those who are the source of my cruel grief.
After all, the Lord hath punished me, too,
Taking my first child by David's loins
And killing him, unnamed, soon after birth.
Even now, God grants me no recompense!

NATHAN
Being the king's best wife, no recompense?

BATHSHEBA
Not when my real power is a fraud
And I'm belittled by that very might
That, in hollow victory, comes with crowns—
And costs the lives of my husband and babe,
Firstborn through no fault it could name
To death that keeps me awake counting stars.
The Lord hath let so much slip from my grasp—
I will not lay down and let this go, too!
I will not long suffer this rancid stench!
Ah, how my breast burns with fury, Nathan!

That's the flame that boils my blood to venom
And fills me with a wish I'd dare not speak
Were David not in Death's red velvet hand
While remnants of my power ebb away.
Canst thou not see it in my very eyes,
This foulest wish of which I am not proud?
Look! Look into my eyes. Look deep in them.
Lookst thou in my eyes and see my pure wish:
That every human know firsthand my pain
And by their own hands murder their children—
As David, by his treachery and lust
Marked our first child for death by the Lord
In a cruel retribution for his sins.
Let no firstborn escape their parent's clutch
Until the heart, once started by love's hands
Is culled to silence by the very same.
May second, third, and fourth, and so on thrive.
My Solomon, wisest of my litter
Was fifth from my womb, yet he is the best:
While first born of me soon thereaft' withered.
There were no such problems with all the rest!
Much as Adonijah is Hagitth's boy,
A harlot David met while off in war:
And how much trouble he causes me now!
You see? Those firstborns robbed us first of joy,
And to an altered life they formed our lure.
Therefore, cave in their skulls! Make sure they're dead!
Slay all God's firstborn children in their beds.

NATHAN
Surely you don't mean that, Your Majesty.
"Do you like it?"

Her Father's voice, unexpected at such an intense moment of the reading, startled her into dropping the page. His movement across the study was so quick that he not only caught the paper before it fell but also caught her hand before she sprang away. Holding it there and staring into her frozen face, his own bearing the smug expression of a cobra, the Hierophant spared the briefest of glances to the text. "The atmospheric alteration rockets are ready for the climactic storm sequence, the orchestra has practiced until their hands malfunctioned, and every seat in the house is sold out. Yet, with the premiere right around the corner and rehearsals nearly wrapped, I can't keep from making the odd change here or there. The language must be perfect! This word, that dash—Shakespeare would understand."

"I wouldn't call this Shakespeare." She assessed the hand whose bones he could snap by tightening his fingers a quarter pound of pressure more. "Webster or Ford, maybe. Very dark."

"Perhaps, but who could blame poor Bathsheba? She did suffer a lifetime at David's hands, and by Act IV we find her on the cusp of seeing her lineage denied its glory. After all she endured, it is only right the throne go to her favored son. Her reaction may be rather extreme, I admit, but the Bible can't be corrected, can it?"

"No more than can its author's brain."

With a banal grin, he said, "At any rate, Nathan goes on to talk her down into a subtler scheme. She is only mortal! All mortals say things that they mean with only fleeting emphasis. I don't think Bathsheba's reaction is all that irrational. We all know what it is to suffer a broken heart, don't we, Dominia."

"I didn't know you had such an organ." As she studied his hand and her own within it, her twisting mind formed a blender of terror. "Lavinia is playing Queen Bathsheba."

"And all those people—hundreds of thousands of human families from all across the globe—will be paying to watch."

The General mentally catalogued the room in search of an actual, physical exit, and was as relieved as she was disappointed she had already gotten rid of her gun. This play, this scene. He had left it out to mock her. Left it out because he knew she would come looking. Because he wanted her to know that, buried within the text of his play, was an order designed to come out of the mouth of a girl capable of controlling the minds of watchers who made eye contact with even her recording. Some weaker willed wouldn't even need visuals. The words would suffice. Lavinia was being taught to give an order of genocide.

And the Hierophant wanted Dominia to think there was nothing she could do about it.

Her lips were dry as they parted to form hushed words. "Don't you understand this is a war crime?"

"Of the highest order! In fact, if I get the prose to a fine enough quality, I am not sure the condition will be curable. You know how it takes fine art to overcome Lavinia's mental viruses; but when the virus itself is embedded in fine art, well..."

"Why?"

He released her hand to study the page in the lamplight. "I have been waiting for an opportunity like this for quite some time. It was important that tensions already be high before I made my move, that war already be underway. No sense in ruining a perfectly good world! Better, in my opinion, to let you stir everyone up first. Give them a reason to get curious again about the martyr world and give them a night when, burning with curiosity to know the fate of the surrendered General, they tune into the paid livestreams and end up with their own family's blood on their hands."

"You think it will be good for the martyr population if their food source dies out?"

"Now, my dear, try to be less dramatic. It is only the *first*born that parents are being urged to euthanize. The second, third, and so forth, these will all be safe, and many deaths will be inconsequential ones—of older generations who turn on their adult children and suffer. Although I do wonder what shall happen in the case of stepchildren..."

"You're an animal," said the General, not even thinking of Tobias as she spoke.

The Hierophant smiled. "Aren't we all, in the end? Animals capable of crafting consciousness, and consciousnesses capable of crafting reality—nonetheless, housed in animals. But think of what this will *do*, Dominia, aside from imparting a sense of seriousness in the humans and sparking interest where political isolation has been the rule for centuries—China and India, in particular. All the other Asiatic countries have overflowed into ours, and the South American ones. Think how this will ease the burden of mankind upon the Earth!"

"Not all martyrs are as strong willed as Holy Family members. What if they kill *their* children?"

His hands spread in a mild shrug. "Then they hadn't will enough to be martyrs in the first place, and will be arrested or turn themselves into their local police in the aftermath. I fail to see the dilemma."

She didn't know how to argue with someone so completely insane. She could only remain quiet and calm as he lifted his brows. "You think me some super villain, but rest assured, I did not come lightly to this decision. The most important point imparted by this method of extermination is clear: the evil resting within martyrs is that same evil resting within humans."

"Of course it is," said Dominia. "Because martyrs are just humans."

"Yes, well, you know I prefer to discourage that line of thought. We are so much better than that! This has always been a matter of dissent between us. It was from the start of all this—from the moment you began to pout about my Project Black Sun. Do you not understand what it is of which you are a part? This is the Fourth Roman Empire, my girl! I dare not speak such a thing aloud, dare not announce it to the world—the last man who did was a racist, petty methamphetamine addict. Although I have more claim to the

Empire's lineage than he, to speak such a thing before the geopolitical stage would be as conducive to diplomacy as Lavinia striding into a party while announcing she's the prettiest girl would be to her making friends. We all know what this is. The humans know this is beyond them—this destiny of the Empire to revive eternally—and that is why the Caliphate hunts our kind. Not out of a humanist ideology but an envy for our power. Even these wretches, my child, these murderers and terrorists with whom you've run for a year—even they believe martyrs and humans are different creatures." At the obvious tension of her whole face to be captive of another lecture, he lowered the page.

"But there is no reason why the differences between martyrs and humans need remain a controversial topic for you, or the few like you who insist on belaboring the point. You have changed, of course, after seeing the world. And I know the tender part of you that has always struggled with its empathy for humans may well never be the same after these changes. But the humans have emotionally manipulated you and beaten you, badgered you off the righteous path I and Cicero and the Lamb placed you upon all those years ago. How we wish for you to be willingly guided back! Because, you see"—his attention was caught by something outside the window—"I cannot help you if you insist on remaining with the losing side."

Pushed to her edge, the General lost her respectful tone along with any hesitance. "You can never win. As long as the magician exists, you'll never win, ever. Hell, Valentinian doesn't even need to be real. As long as a new world somehow appears, that's all it takes. And people keep telling me I'm the one who makes this new world happen, so—"

"If you refuse to remove your thoughtbody's eye patch in life, the world is recreated by default when you die." That was a disturbing bit of information hitherto unshared with the General. Enough to deflate her sense of power. "If I martyr you and you are wise, a world is created. If I martyr you and complete your martyring, a world is created. You understand now why I cannot afford to leave you unmartyred, no matter the trouble you cause me. With you, I always have an exit strategy when things become troublesome."

Fine, fine. All well and fine. "But you're still failing in some way. Still failing to sustain the lives of martyrs. The life of the planet. Your own life." His black eyes glimmered without moving from the window while she fished through his psyche, looking for that key. "You haven't won an iteration yet, or you—some version of you—would have stopped this game when you had. Some Cicero always moves forward. In a perfect world, wouldn't your whole Family—duplicate of you included—stay together? But you don't. Something is wrong. You're still trying to find your perfect solution, the way the magician looks for the best version of me."

"Just like you look for the best possible reality. Just like all the rest of the players, of course, search for theirs. But I am in a unique position, for there is no reason Cicero or I need go to another world yet. Things have not become so bad as to require abandonment. You could remain perfectly alive, all of us happy in this world, living life the way it was before. You, my General. My daughter."

She did not speak, studying with narrowed eyes the blurred text of his play. Now, he deigned to glance at her. "Do you suppose you are the only woman in the world who has lost a wife?"

"Shut up, please."

"If I were you, I would not address me like that at this moment in time." Her blood turned to refrigerant gas as he continued in perfectly casual tone, "I mean it for your sake, Dominia. Do you think this is a healthy mode of dealing with grief? Running away from it? I will be the first and most wholehearted in telling you that trying to find joy in a new world ends in more crushing disappointment than the initial loss."

"It wasn't the grief I was running from. I was running from you."

With that perfect, blasé smile, the Hierophant waved her over. The reluctant General stood beside him to see what had caught his attention through the window. Her stomach lurched: its frame enclosed the slithering lights of a *tanque* caravan. She could sense what had happened even before the Hierophant told her.

"Though you likely think I returned just to catch you in the act of snooping through my office, try to be less self-centered. I admit I received a message that one of Lavinia's friends thought you up to no good, but I had already been forced to leave rehearsal early after getting a phone call of actual importance. Jerusalem has fallen, Theodore has been rescued, and some of your most important friends have been captured alive. We didn't need your help when I asked you before, about turning in Lazarus. I just wanted to see if you would volunteer. As usual, you stooped to my expectations. How tragic! You could have saved your leg at the cost of nothing not already lost."

While she pressed her forehead against the cold glass to watch the procession through his taunting reflection, he said, "You know, I have always found the name 'Israel' to be a fascinating one. Jacob's name, after that angel ruined his hip in their wrestling match. The name of the promised land—this iteration of the political state was founded with primarily Jewish intentions, you know, before it began accepting religious refugees amid the Holy Martyr Church's success. Yet its etymology is controversial. Though some Hebrew scholars argue it means 'God strives,' 'Israel' really means 'He who struggles against God.' A more appropriate name for a man who tricked his brother out of his birthright and grappled an angel!

"It is in the nature of the chosen to struggle with their destiny of service to the divine. Perhaps that is why the religion of Islam—'submission'—had so many historical arguments with their Hebrew brothers before I came along. Perhaps that is why you were drawn to that rebellious house. My chosen daughter, my dissatisfied Israel. If you would but learn to submit! Then, you would find peace."

The block letters of that old Tucson mosque upon her liberation from Nogales: "HAPPINESS IS SUBMISSION TO GOD." Her Father patted her shoulder, then turned to answer the knock of prearranged guards upon the door. "Seeing how restless you are," he told her on the way, "I'll make sure your crucifix is prepared by sunup. Nine nights may seem like a lot, but we can't have you getting into even more trouble, now, can we?"

XI

The Plight of the General

Within her first hours hanging from that cross, Dominia's thoughts turned so often to her human childhood that she began to think this was that famed pre-death flash of life before the eyes. Perhaps it was not the rapid-clip flashback she had always pictured. Perhaps, rather than the snapping back of the mind to the beginning of the next iteration, it was only the stultifying cycle of treacherous memories churned by the sorrowing ego near the grave.

Once, many years ago (oh, so many years!) when the General had been a human girl named "Morgan," she was a morbid thing. To a child still so close to the fresh side of the Void that the realities of existence seemed more dreamlike and unreal than the concept of nothingness, death and its uncountable manifestations held profound intrigue. There were so many, seemingly *benign* ways in which one could die, or find oneself mutilated, or endure some other sudden shock of tragedy in this brave new world.

She had also, like many children around the age of five, been fascinated by those few forms of consciousness alteration available to small minds, namely: spinning in rapid circles until the house twisted upside down and she crashed in the middle of the living room to the sound of her mother's criticism; or standing too quickly and stretching with too much vigor so as to produce that dizzying starburst behind her eyes; or hanging upside down over the arm of the couch until all the blood collected in her head and the room began to vibrate.

"Don't do that too long, now," her father (the real, lost one, not the capital-F fucker who stole the title) said to her one afternoon, not long after she had mentally applauded herself for beating her own "record" time.

"Why," she had asked, before leaping to, "will I *die*?"

"You'd want to sit up before you were likely to die," was the response from behind the slim glass tablet on which he perused the news with a slowly scrolling finger. "But, yes—if you stay like that too long, it's possible to die."

Young Morgan's mind had turned in eager fascination to the question of how a person might look after dying in such a way. Would they bloat up like a big grape? That was what she had pictured at the time. A child's cartoon. Not this.

Dominia had already pinpointed the places in her forehead where blood might eventually shoot out in little jets: mostly around her temple and cheekbones, but certainly from her eyes, which felt after only four hours as if they would burst. Electrified manacles binding back her arms notwithstanding, the inversion had not been a totally unpleasant experience for the first twenty minutes. It wasn't so bad, she told herself. She had one leg free—her left—and by means of this she was able to brace herself against the fifteen-foot-tall crucifix and do something like a sit-up. Held for a time, this relieved a bit of the pressure of her eyes, and gave her an opportunity to think of something to do. Of course—it also exhausted her, so she needed do so sparingly.

To be honest, if not for the electrified manacles, she'd be slipping into the Void. A small current would have been beneficial in this regard, but threshold technology could produce one with a voltage and respective current high enough to stop a human heart. The physical pain therefore prevented the escape of a Lazarene into the Void, as attention was fundamental in their flight. But there wasn't much to be done about this collar of hers, any more than there was much to be done about escape, or about—well, anything.

Because the reality was that the infamous General Dominia di Mephitoli was going to die.

There was no going back. She understood that with new clarity when strung up by her leg, which she already could no longer feel but for the occasional needle-buzz when it jostled with her efforts to sit up. One leg free or not, this movement was no easy feat: she had been given a stiff leather bodice to protect her modesty, and a one-legged pair of like trousers. This allowed her—along with any visitors—to monitor the intensifying purple tone of flesh visible through the straps of the harness that clamped her thigh, supported her knee, and extended up the length of her shin, where it was attached by the ankle piece to its swinging tether. Its black coloration served as the frame of a vile window to the status of the doomed limb.

Yet, it was not just her limb that was doomed. Her heart was as fixed as the molecules of the diamond she had been allowed to keep, draped around her wrist rather than her neck so that it would not fall but be forever there, with her, while she endured. (And promote a healthy current in case of electrocution!) There was nothing the Hierophant could offer to tempt her to his side: nothing he could say to enlist her in putting down the Market or squelching the Hunters before tying Earth up for him in a big silk bow. Not after seeing Cassandra, and not after seeing what he had done to Lavinia. He knew that, which was why she was here.

There were other reasons, too. Given nine days to work on the softhearted princess, the General may well have accomplished her goals of liberating the most brainwashed girl in the world. The Holy Father knew that as well as he knew Dominia had no intention of helping him take Jerusalem, or Lazarus, or any damn thing ever again.

The situation, which had been entropic from the start, could only hasten its degradation from this point. Somewhere in the castle—in the rest of those cell-like guest rooms, further cementing René's position as honorary prisoner—her friends awaited their fates. So did Theodore, that useless asshole, although she supposed she couldn't be mad about it. Letting himself get captured again—he wanted to go home. It was her fault for thinking he could change. Disappointing he couldn't, of course, but it wasn't like he'd made any promises, or anything.

Who had been delivered to the Hierophant? Which friends sat in the castle? She had gotten to know so many people in the human world while on active duty for the first time in almost a hundred years: Which of these had died, and which yet lived?

It was not very long, to her surprise, before she was given partial answer. After she had begun to understand her sit-ups did more harm than good by not only exhausting her, but bruising her ribs against the cage of the stiff bodice, she succumbed to her hanging condition. At least she could savor the odd wiggle of her free leg. How long did they seriously intend for her (or her eyes) to last in this state? Lamb, she wasn't going to lose her sight, was she? Not again! As though he knew her thoughts, the Hierophant picked that moment to enter, midconversation, with none other than René Ichigawa, whose restored eyes widened as they rested on the chapel's ceremonial centerpiece.

"Dominia," he automatically said, while the Hierophant assured him, "Oh, yes: which is why I brought you here."

Ever given to inappropriate cheer, her Father waggled his hand at Dominia in a finger-wave on his way to collect the tall ladder against the matroneum. "You see, René, poor Dominia has gotten herself into a bit of trouble—nothing good ever comes of snooping around, you know—and, being her friend, I thought you might like to help her out."

"Help her how?" The professor warily assessed the General, who was not interested in wasting words before the Hierophant.

"Crucifixion and suspension are useful tortures, you see—not because of the convenience offered when bleeding a corpse or preparing to amputate.

The true cruelty of crucifixion comes from its asphyxiation. Not breathing very comfortably by now, are you, Dominia?"

When she did not respond, he paused to lay a broad smile on her. Then, he directed his attention back to his guest. "In upright crucifixion, prisoners exhaust themselves by having to push their chest up in order to catch their breath. Hard enough as it is! The eventual cause of death is almost always asphyxiation. In this case, however, additional pressure is being put on our good General's lungs as a result of gravity's involvement in her predicament. She knows Peter's pain now, in part. But we need her to last nine days, or she'll miss the New Year's celebration! And martyrdom, miracle that it is, can only battle gravity so long. So, I've come up with an idea. Every twelve or so hours, I shall send someone in—or come by, myself—to help her breathe. Yes, that's right, Dominia. Your friends, who love you so dearly, will be given an opportunity to prove their love for up to an hour at a time by getting on the ladder and holding you upright. As far as they can, anyway. You'll get a chance to breathe easily and get a bit of blood flowing back into that right leg, since we can't have it rotting off before Cicero claims his prize—and your friends will get to see you one last time before their deaths. Isn't that generous of me?"

Her dry lips, swollen with blood, at last suffered themselves to part. "Hoping we'll crack? Talk about something vital in front of you?"

Shrugging, he said, "Your operation has no vitality left. What does it matter if you do or don't discuss your hopeless dreams? The result will be the same. Enjoy your hour, Ichigawa-sensei." With a self-satisfied little bow and an eyebrow wiggle for Dominia, the Hierophant whisked off through the nave and out the chapel doors.

Alone with the General (more or less), Ichigawa asked, "How did you stand that guy for three hundred years?"

"You know how it is with family." Dominia left it at that, using her free leg to swing herself aside and give René a chance to place the ladder against her cross. "You don't seem like much of a heights man to me."

"I'm not afraid of heights. I'm just not sure about ladders." Easing his way up a few rungs, René got level with her head and then, after some consideration, looped an arm around her shoulders and said, "Sorry if this is awkward to you."

"Don't worry," she assured him while he folded her up toward her leg, much as she had been doing with her sit-ups. Each careful rung higher, he pushed her uncomfortably up the length of the crucifix before him while she continued, "I'm completely past the point of caring about a concept like dignity. I just appreciate your help."

"Any—time." Huffing, René scaled the ladder to its height until, in the most painful relief she'd ever experienced, Dominia's body folded up past her legs. Blood—cherished blood!—crashed into her right leg with such a vivid, physical drop that the General cried out.

René asked, "Are you all right?"

Through a pair of stinging tears, she laughed.

After a few minutes' shifting and one occasion of almost dropping her, René determined that, by gripping the crossbar of the crucifix with that arm that cradled Dominia, he could support both himself and her with relative surety. "An hour, huh," he said, and she snorted.

"Poor you. Try twelve. Try nine *days*."

"Look, I'm sorry. But I'm trying to help you."

Agitated, the General studied the leg that, shade by shade, faded to a grayer variant of its usual tone. A step up from the raisin color into which it had settled. "Sorry to be short. I just feel…helpless."

"I can imagine."

"Did you hear about anybody from our side being brought in?"

"Oh, yeah." Dominia turned her head enough to see René's bafflement. "But I don't—well, I don't know."

"Don't know what?"

"They're reporting weird things about the Battle for Jerusalem. I caught something on the news yesternight—actually, right after you left my room—about some kind of unidentified object plummeting over the Lady's library and taking out a bunch of Hierophant soldiers…" While Dominia struggled to avoid any external expression of relief, love, joy at the mere thought of the E4 returning from the Ergosphere, René sweetened it by adding, "And then something about people coming out—like a saint the martyrs are superstitious about? I don't know. No offense, but war makes people crazy, and I think they were seeing things. But whatever it was that came out of the… crashed plane, I guess they've started to call it, it caused the martyr forces to retreat and regroup."

Bless Valentinian! She was close to praising him out loud by sheer accident when the professor ruined it all again. "I guess by the time the martyr forces returned, their confidence was back because they'd turned the omen into something in their favor. They even closed in on the Lady."

"No!"

"No, no, it's— She got away or something, I think. The news is playing it off like it was misreporting, but they were damn certain when I saw the broadcast that Her capture would be any minute. She must have shaken free from their clutches."

Thank the Lamb—for the Lady's sake, and for the world's. If there was any truth at all to the Lady's footfalls upon the Earth being the indicator of imminent apocalypse—whether causal or correlative—she could only imagine what a disaster it would be when her Father's troops tried to force the goddess's avatar to walk.

Trying to turn her thoughts to more pleasant issues, she asked, "Did you happen to see or hear who *was* brought in?"

"I think I did, but I'm not sure whether I saw everybody. It didn't seem like many prisoners were brought here: I only saw Farhad and Lazarus."

"And Tenchi? Gethsemane?"

"Nowhere I saw."

That filled Dominia with relief as much as trepidation. Hopefully that meant they were alive and in the Ergosphere—Saint Valentinian, walk with them. She was sick enough as it was that the True Protomartyr had been brought in. "You're sure it was Lazarus."

"Definitely. He was placed in the room four doors down from mine. I don't know what happened at the battle to land him here, but I know he didn't look happy."

"He never looks happy." Under normal circumstances, she might have smiled while she said such a thing. Now she had no energy. Drained physically and emotionally, Dominia could only try to keep her mind from her condition by asking René the first thing she thought. "Have you ever been happy, do you think?"

"Always asking the hard questions, Mephitoli-sama..." The professor glanced away, to the gilded pulpit that seemed to float above the room. "What is happiness? I don't think I know what it is...I don't think it's real. I don't think it's possible to be happy. It's not—" His arm, straining, required that he shift her, like Atlas, upon his other shoulder. "It's not a condition you attain. It's like...a field."

Smirking, Dominia asked, "The happiness field," and he reacted with a defensive tone, not understanding she only smirked because his supposition was so apropos after all she had lately experienced.

"Yeah, a field. Like an electromagnetic field, or something... You know how when you run electricity through a coil, you get a magnetic effect—but in this case, the electricity we're talking about can be anything that engenders happiness, and that magnetic effect attracts more positive things. So, when you ask me if I've ever been happy, the answer is no. I guess I haven't been happy, because I don't think it's possible for anything or anyone to actually meet the human ideal of happiness. Nobody can 'be' happy. We can't even 'be' ourselves, for God's sake."

"Why weren't you a philosophy professor, instead of an English professor?"

"Because I don't have the patience to waste my time with anything that can't be proved...if I'm going to be spouting improvable nonsense, I'd rather write fiction. Philosophy, it's all a bunch of talking in circles."

"But sometimes we experience things that can't be proved. Things unique to our own existence, or beyond the capacity for description."

"There's always an intelligible explanation for any mysterious phenomenon."

Thinking of the gun that she had passed to him, she asked, "Is there?"

How she wished in a way beyond wishing that she could know he'd kept the weapon safe! That she could know for certain that he was on her side. But one could never be too careful. She would have to suffer in agonized curiosity and turn her attention elsewhere: for the remainder of their hour, the two discussed literature.

Too soon—much too soon—that hour was up, and the Hierophant made his reappearance to wave Ichigawa down the ladder. His Holiness jeered to Dominia as her body sagged back into the hanging position. "I hope you enjoyed your break, my dear. I shall see you again in another twelve-ish hours, yes?"

Twelvish hours. She could do that. She had passed many hours in total silence, in the military and as a prisoner of war. This was the same. She was a prisoner of life—her Father's life. Would death not come as liberator? That was how Saint Valentinian was depicted. Why he was the patron saint of slaves and prisoners, as well as death and artists. Was she not freer than she had ever been, hanging by her once-more purpling leg, knowing that no matter what happened, the end drew near? Indeed, the longer she remained in her inverted position, the more correct such a notion of freedom felt. It seemed to her as if her Father's world had always been upside down. Perhaps her death by this means, trickling back through time to the beginning of her life, was why.

If her death produced a new world by default, did the creation of a new world mean her death? She was fine with that. How tired she had grown of this life! Of this place! Look at this garish chapel, begging to be seen. The source of such strife, such incomparable heartache! It was one of the most beautiful rooms this life had to offer her, and it was built of human bones and plundered gold. There was a higher, truer world than this. She had known its substance. She had held Cassandra.

She had held Cassandra.

Nothing could undo that notion. Nothing could convince her it was only a dream, or a fantasy, as the Hierophant tried to when he ascended the ladder at the end of those twelvish hours and offered her blood-throbbing brain a momentary respite. As he held his daughter upright as easily as most men held a baseball, his attention turned to the Kingdom. She endeavored to avoid so much as the slightest reaction when he indicated knowledge of its existence by asking, "Has the magician bothered to teach you how to come and go from the Kingdom this time? You know—if you taught me, I'd set you free this instant."

Faced with her resolute silence, he filled the air with preposterous theorizing. Oh. That was René's problem with philosophy. She got it, now.

"I personally suspect the Kingdom is a hallucination instilled in subjects by the magician, which is why I cannot seem to find a way into it."

"I believe you will be there," she opened her mouth to generously say. The Hierophant appeared almost surprised by that.

"Oh? Because you will show me how to get there?"

"No. Maybe. I don't know." But, by the Lamb, she had seen Tobias Akachi there. A human to rival her Father for the evils he had committed—yet he, too, had been in the Kingdom. Wry humor quirked her lips even in a time like this, and she turned her aching head to lift her eyebrows at him. "You keep trying to get any piece of information you can out of me to get me back to your side—Lazarus, the Kingdom, anything—but I should be the one trying to appeal to you."

"To my better nature?"

"You have no better nature."

"Ah!" He chuckled and patted her back. "You took the words from my mouth. To what would you appeal, then?"

"Your soul." The statement elicited a patronizing coo as though it had charmed him, but she had thought much on this over the past twenty-four hours. "Your soul can always be saved."

The Hierophant's jolly humor faltered not one iota. If anything, he seemed moved to sheer delight. "You would preach to me while hanging from the cross I put you on!"

"I would save you."

"Wouldn't you rather save yourself?"

"That's not possible. I've thought this through, Father—and, remarkably, I'm not so sure you have. What good are your thoughtforms when you have no body? They wish to work through the soul to manifest on Earth. What good is a soul with a dead body? Your study, your books—hell, even your torches and your fires will abandon you. And you know that. That's why, when whatever apocalypse I bring destroyed the culture your forebear built in the last iteration, you fled to this new world. Cicero." His black eyes sparkled in merriment to be addressed by his secret name, as close to a real name as anyone could hope to know of him in this life. "But you could change all that. Make the choice to change yourself, before Saint Valentinian decides it's time to force the change."

He was unflappable. The head games her Father routinely turned on others broke against his frontal lobe like waves shattering against rocks. "I must say—I have always found it interesting that the magician is capable of using you to suit his needs when he feels. Yet here you are, allowed to hang from a cross.

Allowed to lose your leg! A fine way to repay you for all your hard work. Not unlike Bathsheba, no? Perhaps I'd ought to have given the role to you."

He wanted to get her into an argument. Wanted to get her passionate about his immortal soul, or the Kingdom's reality, or the magician's righteousness. As if it were the magician's fault that she swayed back and forth like a tetherball, starving, trembling, thinking with increasing fondness of the moment when all this would graciously end.

Seeing his cursory efforts to seduce her into his service were for naught, the Hierophant lowered her at the end of the hour with a few solemn *tuts*. "How much trouble you would save yourself, if only you would be reasonable. You are afraid to betray a dream, as if it were more real than reality. As if it were worth more than your Family!"

"Cassandra is my family," said Dominia, defiant to the end. "More my family than anyone. And I will never betray her again. I've let her down enough."

"I suppose you have."

If she weren't upside down, she might have spat to watch him walk away. Instead, she tried to breathe and focus on that memory of her wife's gentlest smiles. Oh! Cassandra. She had to believe they would meet again at the end of this. That it would be in the flesh, in reality. Not, as her Father had said, in some dream.

Because he did have a small point in that. Whatever the Kingdom was, wherever it was, it was a conception of eternity, but it was not linear reality. Its time and the feeling of its time functioned like a dream, and Dominia could not help but feel that if she lived there, she would never accomplish anything again. Nor would she be able to leave after a certain point. The world would need to end for that, and in that case, she wouldn't remember anything. So, she might theoretically have Cassandra, but she would be forced to lose her once more even if Dominia would again have the pleasure of reliving (in ignorance) that beautiful moment of their meeting.

The General couldn't stand the thought. This had to be the last time. If it meant this was the last time, then she could withstand this. She could withstand anything. She would have Cassandra, and there was no alternative.

After twelve more hours, Dominia was startled from a dreamless sleep into which she had not meant to wander, nor known she could wander in her current position. Farhad was brought to her, and struggled more to support her weight upon the ladder than would any martyr.

"You are deceptively heavy," the pilot exclaimed, his laughter nervous as the ladder rocked back, then forward against the crucifix, while he used both hands to support the General. "You do not look as if you should weigh much more than my sister."

"It's muscle mass, and the fact that I'm dead weight right now. But thank you for doing this, Farhad."

"*Afwan*," came the grunted response. "I am sorry to see you in such a situation as this. Iblis is a coward who would eliminate you by easy means, rather than honorable ones."

"There are no honorable deaths. Just stupid ones, and expected ones."

"Which is this?"

"No reason it can't be both, right?"

The slightest smile lit Farhad's voice. "Even in a time like this, you are a very funny person, Mahdi."

"I like to make people laugh. When I do, I almost feel something that's not…awful."

"Have faith, please." To hear him say it with such insistence gave her pause, and the General glanced over, her blurred vision etching out Farhad's bearded features like a camera's slow-to-focus lens. "You will survive this, Mahdi—this trial on the cross like the prophet Isa, who is alive in heaven and waiting for you to heighten the war against Iblis and ad-Dajjal. He will come, then, and unify the world."

"He doesn't need to wait on my account," said Dominia, much too tired to argue and never having been interested in doing it when it came to religious matters. She had never had particular belief or disbelief in Christ, and now that she understood the workings of the Ergosphere, the fact that Jesus of Nazareth had been possessed—sorry, "descended upon"—by a pan-dimensional archetype now seemed as self-evident as the color of the sky. This simple detail of the nature of reality could trash even the most devoted martyr's belief in the HMC for just the reason that the Hierophant had carefully limited their understanding of the Bible to a violent brand of semi-literalism. The martyr position on the matter of Jesus as the Son of God was that he was, most certainly, that; and, especially since the Roman Catholic Church had fled Italy (for, sadly, Israel), the Holy Martyr Church had claimed it *was* the Catholic Church. It was merely an extension of that most revered and historic institution. The real, human Catholic disagreed with this notion, because the Post Testament added a whole new set of blatantly sacrilegious beliefs. Namely, that the Second Coming of Christ had occurred in the earthly form of the Lamb, who was the martyred son of the Hierophant—himself, merely God's highest servant ever in pursuit of the clearest light of divinity.

When she mingled among religious humans, particularly Farhad, she learned that the popular human conception was quite the opposite. Oh, sure, she'd heard people call her Father "the Devil," because he called himself that for a giggle and cherished the title. But what had surprised her was the depth of the demonology that had been applied to the Holy Family, and the almost universal understanding of these theological positions across Christian, Muslim, and Hebrew faiths. (The Catholic Church, treating the Bible—especially Revelations—on a symbolic level, was one of the few ironic holdouts who denied the Hierophant was anything of supernatural power, infernal or divine.) In the eyes of most human faithful, the Lamb was not the Second Coming, but the anti-Christ, and the slave of a foul demon who called himself the God of this world. This had been Kahlil's belief, but it was all pretty far-out stuff to her, especially when she started asking Abrahamians about their particular stances on Jesus Christ. With perspectives differing so vastly on the subject, it didn't seem possible to the General any one religion should be more correct than another. Nor was she thrilled at the notion of waiting around for the Second Coming of a Messiah, alive in heaven or not.

Though she had to admit, the Islamic notion that Jesus never died on the cross was pretty comforting in the given circumstances.

"Have you considered, Mahdi, that the tether might be undone?"

"A deficit of free hands aside, they'd be all over me before I made it to the doors."

With a reluctant glance over his shoulder, Farhad studied the restraint around her ankle as she had herself studied it closely over the past cycle. Its substance was flexible, with a bounce not dissimilar to bungie cord. Given her position and the fact that one leg was free, it would be easy for her or anyone dropping her to dislocate her leg before it was even amputated. Any effort to free her required guaranteed success. Further, the tether was secured at the top of the cross, strung through the metal loop of a weighted cap that had been slipped over top the two-barred crucifix to render it the horned variant preferred by the HMC. The whole thing resembled a bisected version of the old astrological symbol for Mercury. Maybe she could pull her way up and chew through the tether, but she was increasingly weak from the effects of starvation, and she suspected the tensile substance was as durable as it was conductive. This last thought was posited to Farhad, who looked shocked when she mentioned her hunger.

"I did not know. All this time, I thought you shook from fear. I should have known better than to think you afraid." Looking around his person with irritation, he said, "They have taken all my weapons, of course, my knives and guns, but I might withstand the pain of your teeth if they are sharp enough—"

"No, Farhad." She tried to smile for him and just couldn't physically manage it. "But thank you. It's just better. Trust me, being in this position for this long..."

"I see."

"Only about a week more," the General observed. "I can do it."

"You can, Mahdi, and will. I believe in you." Cassandra's voice echoing with Farhad's managed to elicit the corners of Dominia's smile while the pilot went on, "Please: believe, also, in us."

"I do...after you were able to get back from the Ergosphere, especially. I hope I get to hear that story some night." Hesitant to discuss it with all the monitoring resources the castle had to offer no doubt focused on them, Dominia nonetheless felt obliged to ask, "Did Gethsemane return to Earth with you?"

Pending a soft exhalation, Farhad shook his head. "The magician you've told us about—the man from the study of Iblis—he flagged us down once we had flown for a day, as he promised on the radio. This man...perhaps you do not know this story. He reminds me of the servant of Allah, Khidr, who met and challenged Moses. I do not know why he does the things he does, Valentinian. But I believe he does them in the service of Allah."

"What did he do to Gethsemane?"

"He took her out of the plane with him, and when Tenchi and I emerged, the magician was alone."

"How was she looking when he took her away?"

The man's expression grew hesitant; he glanced up at Dominia's leg, perhaps deciding whether it was worth burdening her with the truth in her current circumstances. "When I was a small boy in the state of Syria, my uncle was an imam; he could answer any question about the Quran and tell many of its stories from the top of his head. The one I remember best is the one everyone remembers best. The story of the Seven Sleepers. These men, Mahdi, these Christian shepherds, they enter a cave near Ephesus to hide from Roman persecution, and by the grace of Allah, they are allowed to sleep for three hundred years. Their dog lays across the cave's entrance"—she recalled Kahlil's aggravation over dogs, and wondered what he would think of that story—"and even he survives for that phenomenal length of time. When they leave the cave, they return to the city and find it changed—now Christian—and their story is proven true because the coins with which they try to buy food have not been in circulation for three hundred years. After they realize what has happened to them, they die on the spot, praising Allah."

"I love a happy ending."

Farhad chuckled. "That was always my problem! As a boy, I thought, 'Why didn't they just stay in the cave! They had to face death anyway. If they had stayed in that cave forever, they never would have died.'"

Dominia saw where he went with this even as he cleared his throat to say, "I think—perhaps the best thing for your lieutenant is that she remain in that sacred cave. I did not recognize her by the time the magician led her from the E4."

That was surely so, but it did not make Gethsemane's earthly loss any less difficult. In a way, it would have been easier if the human had lost her life in a battle. Instead, Dominia had lost Gethsemane to the magician's machinations. What was intended for the nymph's vessel? The General might never know. She had accepted that already, but it stung her to think such a thing when she considered she might have protested.

All this horrible groping in the dark. She was used to depending on herself; to getting herself and her men out of anything. Lying down—upside down, to be precise—and allowing all these losses to accrue was challenging in and of itself. She couldn't be sure, but she suspected she'd had at least one seizure while hanging, sometime after Farhad was forced to return to his cell. She had been unconscious and had only realized it when she'd faded back in with an awful headache and the taste of blood in her mouth. Food deprivation seizures didn't usually start so early into the martyr's starvation process, but she had a suspicion the stress position worsened it. She'd have to take drastic measures to keep track of her consciousness. The General had begun to fill the time with singing. This humiliated her, so she kept it soft. At least in Nogales she had been able to walk around her cell, or rest. She could talk to Benedict through her cell door during his shift. There was a similarity here, her jailers and friends taking shifts with one another as they were. Her Father came alone at the fourth respite of her ordeal.

"I was quite impressed by your decision to spend all this time fasting, Dominia. Are you hoping to purify your soul in this process, as you made your last-ditch effort to save mine? Religions worldwide have a proud history of sacrificing food in exchange for higher wisdom."

"I want no part in leeching human spirits to feed my own. Willingly given, or no."

"You are going to spend the rest of your life refusing to eat when you cannot spend time in the sun? Some things never change."

She did not voice her suspicion that the rest of her life was worth, by that point, all of six days. That would encourage him to drop the number to five. Instead, she sternly said, "I've seen what it is we really eat."

"Sin and fear and doubt."

"*We* fill these people up with fear and doubt. Martyrs do."

"Had we nothing to frighten, we could not exist—and fear is not an objectively ugly thing. Fear's only object is to end its own existence, for when we fear, we are repelled from the object that instills the feeling in us. Fear is a beast that lives only to die, and when it possesses a human being to a point said human conflates themselves with their fear, the result is the kind of fatalism that keeps martyrs well fed."

The Hierophant considered the sallow face resting in the crook of his arm, his own features arranged in an expression that was, for once, convincingly genuine. "You look at your life and see only my greatest cruelties. Creating you, and this exhausting sprint on which you've forced yourself. These two alleged crimes of mine bookend your existence as if to drain that existence of all meaning—but your life, the life I gave you, has contained much more than this. And it is a life that can go on from this point, if you let it."

"And then what? More of this someday, in some other form?" She laughed bitterly—a noise that in this case was more like a low, wheezed "ah-ha"—and was then overcome by a wave of convulsions. Clicking his tongue, the Hierophant cradled her to his shoulder and patted her back. Doting as any parent presented with an ill child.

"It does not have to be like this. Nothing ever had to be like this, my girl. You chose this."

Her eyes shut. "Please, go fuck yourself. That must be why you spend your time with another Cicero, anyway."

"I know it upsets you to hear, but you must face the truth."

She did not respond. When he was certain she would speak no more that night without his provocation, the Hierophant patiently said, "Now more than ever, I see you are jealous of your brother. But remember: knowing all this trouble would come about, I martyred you just the same. Because I can use you, yes—but wouldn't it have been a simpler task to martyr and slaughter you right off? I have allowed you to outlive many of your forebears. Only Cicero and the Lamb are older. All the pitiful whelps who preceded you, whose martyring I completed years before your human infancy—they were too base and unworthy in the end to meet my needs. Going on evidence from past iterations, it seems no matter what assortment I select, the results are more or less the same. I, like Goldilocks, am caught between children: this one, too vain; that one, too indolent; the next, too unpredictable. The list of flaws goes on. But you, Dominia—what a good girl you were, *always* were, for centuries! Your problem has only ever been, in my opinion, Cassandra. Oh, you liked to fuss with me as a small child, loved to argue and debate and scowl and stomp your foot when nothing you could do managed to infuriate me. That was why I frightened you so much, I think. Why I still frighten you now. Because I am calm. Because I know what is going to happen."

"How do you know? How do you remember? Did the last Hierophant tell you?"

"Aside from the protein, and methods of Roman orators lost on a world that prizes smartphones and personal assistants, I find the best means of securing memory is by writing things down while they are fresh. When I reach a new world, the first thing I do is begin a new notebook listing my crucial points—points on which the Lamb's predictions are, for one reason or another, obscure."

"But why go to a new world at all? If this keeps happening again and again, why this consistency of a Cicero moving across the boundaries each time?"

Merrily, that hateful bastard laughed. "Why, because I have outgrown the old world. You know how tight a leash I keep on you and your sister. Imagine how carefully I confine myself!"

XII

La Pittura Infamante

Oh, for a glimpse into her Father's mind! Perhaps he *had* shared with Dominia some hint of that specter that pursued him world to world. If so, she struggled to divine it. To say that Cicero had left the last iteration only because he wanted his own sandbox in which to toddle, well—that was not all there was to it, surely, but good luck getting anything more. It wasn't worth fighting through his layers of obfuscation. Her energy was better spent elsewhere.

Things were only bound to get worse from here on out, and that was a horrible thought, because she was already having seizures. Her right foot, bound within the iron manacle in which the leg brace terminated, was now permanently discolored to the shade of cement. The limb had begun to follow suit. And, oh, how tired she was! When she included the time before the dim sum restaurant and her restless half doze upon returning to Kronborg, she had gone something like four, almost five, days without real sleep. Well—she was able to recount one period of sleep she'd grabbed, because when she awoke from it, she found her vision had spontaneously inverted itself. The dizzying effect of perceiving the world as right-side up while the body hung suspended was so overwhelming that she cried out upon perceiving it. Aside from that instance of waking, there was no way to know when she was asleep, or what night it was. She had lost track of even her own consciousness.

And she had lost track of all time, but she did have to admit the hours, of late, felt shorter than her 333 years already made them. Sixty-minute blocks of time dilated into seconds. Perhaps she slept and was just not aware of it, but it certainly did not feel as such because, ah, how her muscles ached, how her teeth itched, how her body trembled and her stomach seemed it might rupture from its own acids as they ate into its tissues. A few times in that third day (she tracked any semblance of space-time by chanting in a dreadful mantra the pattern of her visitors, an act that occupied an unpleasant amount of her mind and was also, at times, alarmingly hard to recall), she tried to tamper with the binds about her wrists and received a nasty, high-voltage shock. After she had recovered from that, and her body moved reasonably again, she set about suffering herself (literally, suffering herself) to tangle her bind around her sleeping ankle. By wrapping the tether, again and again, around her leg—an act that caused the dead limb terrible pain and caused Dominia to gnaw on her already bitten tongue—she could draw herself up that loathsome frame custom-built for her torture. At the top of the cross, she found the flexible tether was one solid piece that had been looped through the great metal circle and had been attached somehow inside her ankle's metal gauntlet; in fact, as she looked, it seemed the tether had been attached at the time of welding. She'd hoped there was something to tear or unhook, or perhaps that in their haste the carpenters had not securely attached the horned cap to the top of the crucifix. Alas, their craftsmanship was sublime, for it had meant their lives. There was no easy way out of this. She was in the careful process of lowering herself back when the doors opened and the General, gritting her teeth, slipped. The nasty fall of the final four feet did not dislocate her leg, but did wrench it and leave her more physically out of sorts than she'd even been before.

"Didn't mean to surprise you," said Lazarus, looking over his shoulder at the shutting doors, then the ladder he almost unconsciously retrieved. "I'd save my strength if I were you…there's not a lot of good to be done. Not from your position, and certainly not now."

In spite of her pain, the endorphins released by her brain at the sight of her friend were on the level of any street drug. "It's good to see you. And good to see you in one piece."

"For now, anyway." With a wan smile, the tired old man edged the ladder beneath Dominia at a slightly sharper angle than used by the others and, cautiously, backed his way up it, informed by experience that the best way to support Dominia's body was back to back. She saw what he was going for and urged her weakened muscles to sit up, her burden relieved when she felt the old martyr's brace. For the first time in days, her body could relax as he continued up in a backward, crab-like fashion. The act left her in the fetal position but at least more upright than before, and like this, she could endure the hot agony of blood rushing through abused ventricles. "You look tired already," he said.

"I feel tired already. I've been here for nights, after I was busted trying to get a glimpse of the Hierophant's script."

"He'll do that…writers are so sensitive about showing their work around. You know the truth about Cicero and the Hierophant by now, right?"

"Top contender in the category of 'things I wish you would have told me any time over the last year.'"

"What good would it have done if I had?" He shrugged against her back, his shoulders pushing hers and provoking a sting. "Knowledge is only so much power. Sometimes it's a catastrophic burden. You can't fix the past that's happened, so you can only change the future; and you have to trust you'll know what you need to know in order to make that change at the right time. Just like everybody else in the world—except your old man, anyway. The Hierophant's always lived through this before, so he's always one step ahead."

That would mean, in the proverbial Mandelbrot equation of reality, that the Hierophant was the variable under iteration.

But if Dominia was not a variable, what was she?

Her mind could not trail after the thought. Eyes closing and brow furrowing in sorrow to lose its thread, the General asked, "Then what are we supposed to do?"

"Rely on you. Like I said a couple of seconds ago, sweetheart." He talked to her now as he never had—a gentle grandparent—and it made her body tremble with inexpressible tears because she knew and he knew she was dying. "You'll know what to do when the time comes."

"When I'm dead."

He said nothing. She regained her composure and exhaled, inhaled, tried to enjoy breathing while she could. Tried to learn what she could while she could still learn. "I saw Farhad. Did anyone else come with you?"

"Other than Ted? No. They thought they had the Lady, until the men who had Her realized their terrible mistake. She's elsewhere now."

"Why did they bring Farhad?"

"He was one of the four beings that emerged from the E4 when it crashed into the Lady's library in the middle of a very intense standoff." This aspect matched the report René had mentioned, with the story that had started off as a UFO, then turned into a downed plane. "You can guess who the four were, I'm sure"—Farhad, Theodore, Tenchi, and Saint Valentinian—"and also guess why only two were obtainable."

"Because Farhad would have leapt into the fight, Teddy was meant to be caught, Tenchi has other interdimensional fish to fry, and Saint Valentinian's never around when you need him."

Lazarus laughed, lowering his head so as not to bump hers. "You know well as I do that's not true, but it does feel that way sometimes."

Yes, it did. But, he was right. She had needed him more while weeping in that kennel than she had in the entire year spent praying for him. More than she needed him now. Frankly, she didn't want to see him now. Because the next time she saw him, she suspected he would be acting in that most grim capacity for which the saint was responsible.

Funny to think of him now in that role. Funny to think she had ever regarded him as fictional. But had he ever been a man? She sensed he was more than man or fiction and probed the sage on this point. "Do you have any memory at all of the magician being your child? Even a dream?"

"No. Either the magician has stolen those memories on purpose, or he's lying, or the sacred protein failed to retain its own memories of the initial world because it wasn't expecting it would have to. Do you have any inkling, any static memory, of what happened in the last iterations? It's not written in your brain, but for me, it's backed up in my blood, and my blood rewrites my goddamned memories every time after that first time. Christ, oh, Dominia! Do you know—something like ninety percent of martyrs return to life without anything special about them at all. Of those who do, maybe half of those powers are more impressive than basic parlor tricks. I think Cicero does have a gift—memory—but it pales beside his brother's abilities."

"And they really were brothers in life?"

"Yes! That's my *point.* Their starting genetic codes were just—*that* close"—she could imagine him holding his fingers a hair apart—"yet the Lamb inherited all he did and Cicero got the ability to remember everybody's birthday. If my own genetic code was just microscopically different, I always think maybe—"

"There'd be no saving the world, or a single life. Because there would be no way for us to enter the Ergosphere."

Lazarus sighed. "Yeah. Yeah, I know. I guess I just look forward to someday being able to relax, and enjoy a life, or something. Or enjoy being dead! You know, I've never been to the Kingdom?" At the General's shocked noise, the man said, "I'd become a citizen, for sure...but I guess I just never have time. I'm needed here. But someday, Dominia—I'm going to get a sweet slice of eternity. Maybe Trisha and I...well." He chuckled. "I don't know what she'd think of me now, with the beard and all, but I'd hope that in eternity I'd have a bit of youthful charm returned to me. It's the blood, you know. Memory ages you."

"That's why the Hierophant looks so much older than Cicero, but why is he so much larger?"

"You'll laugh."

"Try me."

"Okay. Every iteration is a little smaller than the last." She did laugh. "It's true. Ask the magician. He'll explain it."

She might have teased him more, but then she thought about fractals, and how, to find the Mandelbrot set hidden within the edge of the Mandelbrot set when viewing the function as a colored image, one had to zoom into the fractal for an unnerving eternity before finding the miniature duplicate. It only pushed to mind that trail of thought she hadn't the wherewithal to follow before. "If the magician stole your memories of that first time, Lazarus—"

"I don't know that he did."

"But if he did, why would he do such a thing? And if it's not true, why lie about being your son?"

"Maybe because the weight of the actual truth is too much for us to bear. I don't know that he's lying, necessarily. Valentinian does look a lot like me… anyway, I'm pretty sure he's not evil, per se, but I am pretty sure by now that it's his fault all of this happens on repeat."

"Yeah?"

"Oh, yeah. I don't think the universe was always caught in a loop like this. I don't think martyrs were always a problem, and I don't think they will be if we can set the universe in order again."

"And you think it's Valentinian's fault?"

"Usually, when a thing like this starts, it's because somewhere along the line, somebody screwed up, and screwed up bad. You may be responsible for remaking the universe, but where did you get the power for remaking the universe? *How* do you remake the universe? I'm sure you've asked yourself that enough already, so I won't. But I just mean…I think it's a bunch of bullshit that the responsibility is on you. If anybody's responsible, it's the magician."

"I've missed you, Lazarus."

"Well, I'm here now, kiddo," said the old man. "For a little while."

Little, indeed. Too soon he was gone and there she was again. Alone with her thoughts, her trembling, the ceaseless calendar of her memories, and the awful anticipation of her fate. Three days hanging, longer without food. Far longer, still, since she had felt safe or comfortable for anything more than a handful of seconds at a time. Dominia could not feel her face, which was good, because if it was anything like the rest of her, it would be in agony. Her flesh was tight against degrading muscles devoured by her hungry body. By the proteins that could barely maintain a functional, noncancerous shape. She tried to focus on one thing Lazarus had told her during his visit: what had come when she'd asked him if he expected her to die. If the instant of death would be worse—more painful—than this.

"You know where you're going after death. Most don't. You can endure this, Dominia. If I can endure living over and over, you can endure suffering this way just once."

"Just once I can remember."

"Isn't that as good as experiencing it just once?"

She supposed. Still—what a depressing thought! To be yet another in a long line of failed Dominias. How far she had traveled! Across the very globe, in pursuit of a dream that she had known to be ill-fated from the moment René appeared in her office. Yet, she could not help but dream it, pursue it, for nothing else bound her to the world after so many years of sordid living. Nothing but Cassandra, who weighted her to reality. Who she fancied she could, with increasing clarity, feel. As if she were with Dominia, there, in the chapel.

If only. If only she were really there. All this would have been unnecessary. If only this were the more dreamlike of the worlds the General inhabited! Alas, this was not the case. Her world had become suffering, marked by throbbing skull and cheeks not felt for quite some time. It was endless, nagging pain, and a parade of friends and relatives sent to mock her with their brief relief, their sudden absence.

To her surprise, the fourth day saw Theodore sent into the chapel, looking fretful. Even he proved relief to see, though until she knew for certain he hadn't contributed to her friends' capture, she couldn't help but feel a bit standoffish. Hence, rather than joyful greeting, she asked, "What are you doing here?"

"Father sent me in— I have to climb up there to do this? There's no other way?"

"Are you really asking me that?"

Sighing, Theodore took his turn on the ladder, and at Dominia's question of why the Hierophant had seen fit to torture her with Teddy, of all people, the Governor exclaimed, "Because he doesn't *trust* me! Because it's a load of— He thinks I want to help your little human friends! Frankly, he owes me an apology after the way things went down in that— *wretched* place, that Void— and Jerusalem! Hah. I'll tell you about it sometime. The explosions! I was almost shot. Frankly, I think I was in more danger from Father's own men than I ever was from you and your cronies! But you know how it is, hoping for an apology from him… Anyway, he did get me out alive, so I guess I have to be grateful. Thank goodness he saved me from your band of criminals! I was worried. Not for me, of course. For Lavinia."

This clumsy lie, told at a rapid clip and nervous pitch and packed with unnecessary, meandering details all in response to her simple question about why the Hierophant had sent Teddy in to prop her up, reassured her that her friends—and Theodore—had come intentionally. That the Lamb was not confirming these notions to the Hierophant was a very curious point that emerged again on day five, when the ram-headed man in question was the next to mount the ladder and give her support.

"You've been awfully quiet since I returned," tired Dominia observed, head rolling back against the shoulder of the Lamb's black cloak. In her sleep-deprived state, even this fabric felt too rough. He considered her statement—and its true sentiment—a few seconds before responding.

"I guess I just hate getting in the middle of all of these things. I'm sorry to see you up here, but things will work out the way they'll work out. There's nothing anybody can do. Certainly nothing I can do."

"But that's wrong. You manipulate probability."

"Sometimes, in little ways. I can't make a big change for anybody. Not out of nothing. And the changes I initiate are only…entropic. I can't turn water into wine, or straw into gold. I can't heal a person, but I can increase the odds of them becoming well."

"Still—you see so much. And hear so much. Surely you can do more than you've ever let on."

"I've done enough. I helped your Father gain power."

"But why? You've never been like him. You were always kind to me. A better parent than he was, no matter what he'd like to think."

His eyes trailing from the General, the Lamb said, "I've been by Cicero's side since I was born the first time. The human time, if you can say Cicero was ever really human. He was always a little like a robot, I guess. But the protein changed him as much as it changed me. Power changed him. And—well." His lips turned up in a dark smile at some taboo reality. Some act that changed the Hierophant into the free-spirited tyrant he was, which could not be spoken without consequence. The man once known as Elijah settled on saying, "I can't explain it any more than I can explain to you why I've let him do the things he's done. We're brothers. We've always been brothers, but since we were martyred, we've been closer than brothers. We can't help it, you understand. We're each the only person the other can trust and—he helped me. When I was first martyred, hearing all the voices and seeing things from the Ergosphere that weren't present in reality, he took care of me. Evil as he is. And so I help him—because I love him. I know you can understand that. I love him because I have to believe that, somewhere, something inside him is redeemable."

Her attempt to save the Hierophant's soul fluttered back to her with genuine sorrow. "I guess I know what you mean." Glancing over at the Lamb's dark curls as she tilted her forehead against the cool metal of his right horn, she asked him, "If there are two of Cicero, why aren't there two of you? If only one person can slip into a new universe, how could he stand to leave without you?"

With a macabre smile, the Lamb repeated what he had said at the start of her questioning. "I guess I just hate getting in the middle of all these things."

She understood why.

Her next tormentor, after the nightly visit from her Father, was none other than Cicero—but she was so tired, so beyond function, that the best she could manage was to focus on the rhythm of her breathing while the brother who was but the seed of their Father gloated, "How right it is to find you thus, Dominia, after all the trouble you've given us. And all the difficulty you've given me, personally, over the years!"

Baffling. "I never did a damn thing to you."

"Aside from spurning my authority, and that of the Church, at every turn? Why you've so stubbornly resisted attending my sermons and accepting Father's grace, I shall never understand—You are a *martyr*, woman, better than anything on Earth and deserving of glory. Yet you would scrape about in the mud with the humans! As if their lives could ever amount to anything."

"Humanity did just fine before us. Better."

"They destroyed the very planet. Before Father raised it from the waters of the Mediterranean, Venezia was drowned by rising seas thanks to the negligence of men. Rising seas that saw the deaths of many fish, replaced by his own well-funded programs. Why, the very waters of the sound around Kronborg would have ruined this fine castle had His Holiness not seen to its restoration and protection."

The place had survived a fire before him; she would rather Kronborg had seen a flood than fallen into her Father's hands, but this was like wishing the sky were yellow, or that Cicero would shut up. "Humans abuse the world," her brother continued. "So we have taken it from them, as you rightly took Lavinia from Cassandra's irresponsible hands."

"Is now the time for this?"

"When else are we to bring it up? You and I both know you are destined to lose more than your leg. A time like this is worth some self-reflection from the both of us." After consideration, El Sacerdote said, "You know, Dominia, I never hated you."

"Oh, please."

"I suppose if I was a bit strict with you, it was because I was trying to save you from this. Prevent it."

"Father told you this was coming?"

"Of course. He told me everything." At his sister's snort, the Holy Martyr Church's most notorious priest adjusted his grip on her to demonstrate a shrug. "What else would you expect of him?"

"Nothing less. It's just sort of funny I don't even have temporal privacy. You remember that summer we stayed in France, and he took down all the doors in my apartment in Versailles?"

"You were doing an awful lot of drugs that summer, my sister."

"I was nineteen! An adult. And I still found ways."

"Yes, well, you have always had trouble with connecting consequence to action. That's why you insist on blaming Father for what happened to Cassandra! Why, he wasn't even the one who talked to her on Walpurgisnacht."

How amazing. Even in a situation like this, even battered by a chain of horrific revelations, her faltering heart still managed to drop. Yes, that strange and uncomfortable feast night—normally one of the best of the year—wherein Cassandra exited the annual "Raven" recitation to have a crippling panic attack in the nearest bathroom. They had caught a silent jet home, had a bizarre fight, made up (so Dominia had thought), fallen asleep on the couch—

She could not finish her thought. Could barely open her lips to ask, "What happened on Walpurgisnacht?"

"I'm shocked you hadn't heard. She confronted me, Cassandra. A fine time to do it, too, in the middle of my favorite holy night!" As Dominia's practically disembodied spirit was nonetheless struck by bolts of pain, the priest explained, "Amazing she'd been able to compose herself the whole night until that point, planning to say all she was."

"Let you have it, did she?"

"As I've never experienced!"

"Good."

While the priest chuckled, he said, "As my ego recovered from her dressing-down of my every quality, she bashed me with the fact that she knew Lavinia was her baby, and that we had conspired to take the infant from her, and that we had wanted her to think she was crazy…"

Oh, no.

"And, why, she was off on such a screed, I had to bring her down somehow."

Poor Cassandra.

"So I just told her, 'You should be having this conversation with your wife,' and left her on the balcony where she'd dragged me. And then…"

And then, the recitation. And then, the silent jet home. And then, that bizarre fight the second they hit the front door. Dominia asking over and over, "Why won't you tell me what's wrong? Why won't you talk to me? Cassandra, honey, please."

"It doesn't matter," had been her wife's only response, over and over, for thirty dysfunctional minutes before her broken tone changed. Her watering eyes locked on those of the Governess like a pair of lasers, she asked, "Would you ever lie to me?"

Would

You

Ever

Lie
To
Me?

The words rang through the chapel even now, bringing Dominia that same surge of alarm such a question always brought a liar. "Never," she had lied. "I would never lie to you. Never, about anything. Why would you ask me something like that?"

Cassandra clammed right up again. Saying only little things like, "I guess I made a mistake," or, "There was a misunderstanding," when pressed as to what had caused her change of mood or the sudden silence through which Dominia could not break.

Only now, the General realized she could have. She could have broken through that silence and maybe even saved the life of her wife. All she had needed to do was tell the truth when it mattered.

And she hadn't.

"Please leave," Dominia said, so softly that Cicero didn't hear it over the sound of his drone. She raised her voice, repeating, "Please leave," and adding, "I need you to go, right now, go, please," adding the same words in all the languages she knew: English, Mephitolian, Spanish, that smattering of half-remembered Japanese and her year's worth of shitty Arabic. "Get out, get out, get the fuck away from me, Cicero!"

In time with her words, she had begun to thrash so violently—at best, a half-deliberate set of movements—that before Cicero could react, she'd succeeded in knocking the ladder, along with its occupant, sideways across the chapel. While the priest, his foot tangled in the rung upon which he'd been perched, crashed to the floor with a terrible cry, the dryly sobbing General felt the joint of her hip slip with the full-length fall and suspected her leg had finally dislocated.

Oh, Cassandra. If only Dominia had been a better person! While the priest, bruised and cursing, limped out of the chapel with only the briefest of sneers for his sister, the General thumped her head against the crucifix, but soon lost strength for even self-abuse. Such a thing would do nothing but harm, anyway.

Lazarus was right. Nothing could be done to fix the past. But the future could always be made better. Dominia was determined to make it so, and her heart sped with that determination when the door opened but a few unscheduled hours after Cicero's departure. The hinges' squeak punctuated the pain of a familiar voice.

"Oh, Ninny."

She couldn't believe it. The Hierophant had brought Lavinia? While the General blinked stars from her sleep-deprived eyes and tried to lift her head, the girl hurried up the chapel—accompanied by, of all God's good creatures, Basil, who already crept near the base of the cross. Her back aching as she spared energy to see him, Dominia uttered the words, "You shouldn't be here."

"I know, Ninny, but I couldn't *stand* it. I had to see you. You know this doggie, don't you? Isn't he the one from the train? He's been with us for weeks, but I only recognized him when he was next to you. I won't tell, I promise."

Dominia believed her, but the holo-cameras tucked in the chapel ceiling wouldn't stay so mum. "I'm sure our Father would be unhappy for you to see me like this. Especially without his permission."

"Daddy can pound salt," said the sassy girl, eliciting a real smile from the General. "Look at you up there! Oh, that's not *right*. I didn't have to do this when I tried to run away."

"Well, you also weren't successful in running away. You didn't help the enemy. You're too valuable."

Frowning, Lavinia glanced around and, spying the ladder, sheepishly said, "If *I* were the one who took you down, Daddy wouldn't be able to do anything about it."

"He would find something to do about it, all right. Just, please, Lavinia, go back. I can't stand to see him do anything more terrible to you."

Frowning down at the dog she stooped to pet, the Princess, up well past her dawn bedtime, studied her own pale hands. The hands she used, anyway. The same subject must have rested heavy on the girl's mind, for she soon said, "You know, Theodore is safe! I'm so happy. I was worried, but I…after you and I talked the other night…" She faltered, and frowned. "He doesn't know. At least, I don't think he knows. I haven't told him, and you know—these darn things are so realistic…I can feel with them just the way I could feel things before, so it's all the same. This fellow doesn't know the difference, does he?"

Basil did not wag his tail, because he knew the difference very well, but continued allowing the girl to fawn over him with her mechanical hands while he assessed, as reverently as an animal could, the woman suspended above. Dominia held the dog's eye contact in perfect understanding of his respect for her plight while Lavinia went on. "People will know the difference, though, when I tell them. They'll suddenly see it the way I do…little differences. Sometimes I move too fast, or I'm too strong, even for our people. And if you reacted the way you did, as close as you are to me and as long as you've known me, why…I suppose I can't expect somebody like Theodore to react differently, can I?"

"You love Theodore back, don't you?"

It had been the silly source of a lot of teasing over the years, but the way Lavinia glowed with the innocence of true love just to have the question asked told the General all. "He's so gallant, Ninny. Of course I love him. You know—he probably doesn't care, or think it's a big deal—but he was the first person I ever remember seeing, even before Daddy. Can you believe that?"

"Oh," said Dominia, "I think he cares."

"Really?" Hope sparked bright in Lavinia's eyes before she smothered it with a wave of those delicate hands. "Not that it matters. Our love must remain the pure, courtly kind. What I symbolize to everyone—it's all too important. I can't let it be thrown away because of some silly crush, can I?"

The General had the feeling those words were not Lavinia's but Cicero's, drilled deep into her head. Yes, Theodore was absolutely silly: one of the silliest people Dominia had ever met by any definition of the word. But, Lavinia was right. He could also be sort of kind, even if he was a selfish idiot who let himself be a tool of the state. The flaw in his compassion was that his moments of kindness were not rooted in hidden goodness but naïveté. In fact, that was his problem. Theodore was too naïve to be evil.

In that respect, he and Lavinia were the perfect pair. Dominia's cheeks hurt with her effort at smiling, so she stopped. "I think you should live your life, and make yourself happy."

"I don't think I'd know how to live my life if I could." Still in fair humor, Lavinia laughed the words while she stood to brush her hands free of dog fur. "I don't know anything about the world—anything at all. Do you know how excited I was to ride the Light Rail? Oh, Ninny, it was so fun! That must be what you feel like all the time. Well…not right now, but you know what I mean."

Dominia did not respond—could not, until she was pushed by Lavinia's regret that: "Everybody treats me like I'm made of spun sugar because I didn't wake until I was grown up—but I know things. I'm not stupid, Ninny."

"No, Lavinia. You're not. That's not why our Father keeps you confined."

"Oh, I know why he does *that*. It's because he wants me to be safe, but—"

"No, Lavinia, please. Please listen to me." The girl quieted while Dominia, struggling for breath from her position, arched her ruined shoulders to fill her lungs. "I don't know what you're going to think of me after this, but I don't think I'm going to be around much longer. I'd might as well tell you now, and make it fast, since he'll be here any minute. Probably watching us right now…I'm sorry, Livvy. I haven't told you the truth. No one has ever told you the truth. Not about yourself, and not about your life. You're fertile. Our Father doesn't want you to be out on your own because you'd discover that, or—far worse, in his opinion—you might find a nice, human man and make a child without his knowledge."

Though the stained-glass windows of the room had been shuttered against the light of day, Lavinia's eyes seemed to glow as they widened with her sputtering mouth. "How...but—that's not right, Ninny, he wouldn't do that. Daddy wouldn't— I'm not a *dog*, Ninny. He wouldn't *breed* me. Not even if I could get pregnant. But that's silly. That's silly, Dominia, and you know that it's silly. Martyrs can't get pregnant."

"He keeps you at home because you bleed every month, right? Other martyrs would know."

Humiliation, along with horror, lined the girl's face. "Why would he tell you about my—my illness—"

"It's not an illness! It's menstruation, Lavinia."

"What is—" The girl frowned, her perfect brow furrowing with bafflement. "I know an awful lot of words, Ninny, but I don't know that one. 'Month'?"

Sweet Lamb, but the Holy Father had managed to shield her from *that*. Dominia shouldn't have been so shocked—the girl never lived a human life, never had a female parent, never read anything that wasn't in her approved Biblioteca reading list and never spoke to anybody who wasn't paid by the Hierophant to keep their mouths shut. Yet, for the girl to have been kept in the dark for almost seventy years about a basic fact of her own body—it was so abhorrent it was almost impressive.

"That bleeding means you can have a baby." At the girl's visible skepticism, Dominia pressed, "You *can*, Lavinia. You can, because you weren't ever a human. You were born a martyr. You're Cassandra's daughter."

The ninety-year-old tumor of the General's lie dropped from her mouth, and in that instant revealed to her how burdensome its weight had become. She had never realized it—never once felt its creeping mass build until now, free of its pressure, she was confronted with the faded image of Lavinia's eyes growing big, bigger, her brow furrowing and her mouth uttering, "But I don't understand," in a voice so soft the General barely heard it. Not over the thud of blood bearing down on her ears.

Gently, as if trying to talk an eggshell out of breaking, Dominia tried to explain. First, about Benedict. Then, about Dominia's loneliness. Finally, about Cassandra. She thought about trying to make some excuse, like that the General thought they couldn't give the baby a good life—but that would have been another lie. Cassandra was a natural mother. Dominia was always the problem, Dominia and her fear and her lying, and so Dominia said, "My heart was broken, and I wanted to break hers, but I couldn't bear to give her up, or reject her child to her face. Not when she was so lonely and afraid. So desperate for my help. Those vulnerabilities that brought her to me in the first place, those were the reasons I loved her. They were why I wanted to protect her. Yet, I punished her for them. I told our Father about you, and I thought, until recently, that I had made the right decision. But last year, everything fell apart. That was why Cassandra killed herself, you see. She knew. She realized what had been sitting in front of her face for almost a century, and she was destroyed by it. The weight of my lie...what I did...I killed Cassandra, Lavinia. I killed your mother. I took your arms and your legs."

Tears falling upon the tile floor and the fur of the watching collie, the General shut her eyes. "I am so sorry."

For a time—too long, by Dominia's reckoning—there was no answer. She was too frightened to behold the girl's expression. But when that soft voice did reach her to reveal itself full of astonishment, she forced herself to behold its stunned speaker. "Then you would have been my mother, too, wouldn't you?"

"Yes," admitted the General, whose despair paid no heed to the light of Lavinia's face, or the way she stepped forward with hope in her smile. "But I failed you."

"Oh—*Ninny*. I wish—I wish I could hold you, Ninny, I—" Lips trembling, the girl glanced down at the dog, then gasped as conversation rose from the hall outside the chapel doors. "I think you're right, Ninny. I shouldn't be here."

"No," Dominia agreed. "But I'm glad you came."

"Oh—oh." The fretful girl took another step toward the General, tugging her cloak around her. "I can't leave you *now*. I can't let this happen."

"You have no choice. You'll be busy acting in a play that will kill half a planet's worth of human children."

"I—it's only a little cull," Lavinia defended, almost admitting she was a willing participant in the proposed murder of the firstborn. "Daddy says... Daddy..."

The furrow in the girl's brow said it all, and Dominia managed to raise both her own.

"The Holy Father says a lot of things, doesn't he?"

Looking stricken by the notion of their Father's fallibility, Lavinia glanced around the room and, at last, turned to follow Basil's loping route to the door. "I don't understand why he never told me any of this before," the girl murmured. "Doesn't he love me? I thought—"

"The Hierophant does love you, I'm sure, in his way. He most loves what gives him power: and you are the most powerful person he has ever known."

That was certainly the first time Lavinia had heard a thing like that. If any notion of self-empowerment had ever come upon her, nobody on Earth had paid it any heed. The girl cast another reluctant glance for her hanging sister before hurrying away, and it was with an awful lurch as the Princess and the dog slipped through the door that the General caught a glimpse of her

Father's massive frame. But the truth had been disseminated, and he could do nothing.

"I think we will make that your last visitor," declared her Father, leaning into the chapel. "You do have a way of violating those few privileges you are given, my girl."

"Don't you hurt her," shouted the General. Her Father only chuckled at her outrage.

"Why should I have to, when you have done such a fine job? I'll see you at your next break, my dear."

The slam of the shutting door echoed through the chapel but could not compare to the sweet opening of Dominia's soul. Crucified or not: she had waited too long for this moment. The truth had fermented within her, and now drunkened her to private tears that she, dehydrated, could not afford to weep.

XIII

Suspension of Disbelief

Eight days. Eight nights. A human being, as Cicero had pointed out, seldom made it one day in such a state. Even with respites such as hers, a human being by now would have expired. At the very least, their leg's necrotic condition would have spread farther up their thigh. No, no. Dominia's dark flesh ended just above her knee (or below, spatially speaking—she'd lost track of up and down long ago). How much longer could she have lasted beyond even her torturous nine days? Without blood, the protein inhabiting her muscles and skin could not long maintain its resistance of tissue death. Every drop of blood was localized in her head, and had been there for a while. That leg looked long, long gone.

It was safe to say the General felt unwell.

She had gone this long without eating or having the blood of the Lamb before, she thought, maybe. She couldn't remember. Numbers had become meaningless. How long had she been stuck in the dungeon with René? Maybe not this long. Or maybe longer. Her life was an uncanny blur. Each passing second contributed to the disintegration of her neurons as they self-consumed, dissolved, or were reedited into cancer cells. This alteration of her physical brain reduced her inner life to little more than an uncontrollable chain of abstract images that blossomed without meaning or warning, sometimes grating on her nerves in a physical way and occurring again-again-again-again-again. Those cogent thoughts retained were the same thoughts over and over. Her mind was trapped by itself and cycling into a horrible whirlpool that would not, could not, end so long as she was trapped in this body: this hanging body: this suspended body for which everything was oblivion yet eternal: this prison of form where each minute, each second, peeled off far into the distance of infinity. Each time her fading consciousness found, within the substance of her atrophying muscles, joules enough to control her thoughts, she willed the second of her death that much closer, begging for its shadow as a pastor begged the miracles of the Lamb.

Perhaps God despised her for the crimes she had committed against mankind, her wife, herself. But she had no lingering fear of hell. Hell was not the Void. Not being nothing for all eternity. *This* was hell. This material compilation of the abstract data of the black hole at the end of being, this place of her Father's, was a waking tahgmahr. But that may have been a self-possessed notion. Material chauvinism, perhaps. She had to remind herself that she had seen the suffering of the souls hovering in the Very Low Frequency variation of the Void around Jerusalem—all those many unfortunates who had conflated that which was heavenly with that which was substantial and could not, even in death, shake themselves of their delusions. They would rather have felt themselves betrayed by a negligent God than dare connect with the entity on a personal level.

Understandable. Dominia, personally, was terrified of God. The experience of God. The idea of plunging into that highest, unspeakable godhead with her naked soul made the top of her head tingle even now—maybe more than ever—in a kind of spiritual inkling accessible even in these physical chains. To contemplate what the Jewish Abrahamians called "Keter" while in the Void—surely that was to invite a kind of annihilation, for better or for worse. What soul, especially those bound to the VLFs, could bear to realize this mating of the godspark to its source?

This was why the religions of the world employed clerics. Much as martyrs, whether knowingly or not, craved to know that dark aspect of God through the evil works of the Hierophant, so did humans seek God through the intermediaries of priests, imams, and rabbis. The Red Market women who served the Lady likewise could not have been said to seek God directly, for they pursued only the feminine aspect of the divine, and only through the vehicle of the Lady's avatar. Dominia felt safe with the Lady for that reason. One could argue She was God…ish. Maybe that was the origin of "goddess." Had she energy, the General might have laughed at that thought, then been spat upon by a hoard of angry feminist historians and etymologists. But what did she care of history, of gender, of politics, of language? She stood on the edge of death and her only thoughts were of God.

There was only one person she knew who had, so far as she could discern, sought with true tenacity that which one might call God. Not her Father's perverse idea of it. Not society's, either. The term was often condescendingly accompanied by stereotypical images (man with beard, clouds, harps, angels, snore), yet remained so deep in true meaning that its casual use curdled the blood of those most militant atheists. But somebody she knew had wandered the universe—proven fundamental in rerunning the universe again and again—and in the process had, she suspected, come to intimately know the divine essence propelling the movement of everything. That same seeker was the only entity she had known to intercede in the world. Wretched as she felt, with her hands having been forcefully folded by her bindings for eight days, the General did what most hopeless people do, and prayed.

"Saint Valentinian"—she exhaled and inhaled and laughed in a hollow, hacking sound that caused real agony at the base of her ribs because her lungs were compressed to shapes like little prunes—"I need help."

The church was so perfectly silent that she heard the distant footsteps of a guard charged to watch the hall since Lavinia's audacious visit. Somehow bolstered by the quiet, Dominia lifted her head and batted the watering eyes that bulged with the pressure of her skull. When she spoke, her swollen lips felt they might crack, or, to her absurdly working mind, fall off. "I know you're busy, like you keep saying every time I see you...and I don't even know what you can do. What the limits of your intercession are. But I—I wish I were dead."

She allowed her head to drop back against the wood of the cross and gritted her teeth. Her eyes shut to a phosphene mandala of pain. "I wish I never have to live again. If it has to be like this...if this is what life is—why was I ever born? Why am I worth nothing more to you, or my Father, or anyone else, than any other tool? I'm as much a person to you sons of bitches as the hammers that made this cross. Is this *nothing* to you? Is this suffering nothing to you? I understand what I've done—all that I've done. I know I'm a horrible person who deserves to suffer, but please, please, let it end!"

You would accept eternal failure to save the pains of one last day?

Astonished to hear any voice not her own—let alone this choir reverberating from within her degraded auditory cortex and broken Broca's area—the General allowed her blurring eyes to open. Nearly blind as she was with the pressure of the blood in her skull, the Lady was as clear as ever. Perhaps clearer. More real and substantial than reality—though there was a wrongness to Her that the General only recognized as She began to make Her way down the aisle. Halfway, Dominia twigged to the problem. The Lady walked, though this was, ostensibly, reality. With each step, the goddess gained an inch of height, until, before the General, She towered the twelve feet necessary to stand above the head of the hanging woman.

"I heard if you walked it meant the end of the world."

It does. You seem surprised that your prayers were answered.

Before the goddess, the General needn't struggle to organize her thoughts. Her mind was sharper than ever, as if she'd eaten and slept and bathed and engaged in about a decade of cognitive behavioral therapy. Happiest of all, she could speak without pain. "Surprised to have them answered by you, maybe."

The magician and We are closely allied. You and the magician are closely allied. You are closely allied with Us. We have come to help you, as you asked. If you truly wish to put an end to all of this, We can take you now: but this will all occur again, and this iteration will be rendered obsolete.

And another iteration would take its place. She felt all the sicker at the thought. "I can't go through all this again, knowing it or not."

Then We will give you a far more valuable gift.

With Miki Soto's head, the Lady bent to place a kiss upon Dominia's aching lips. In what could only be described as a miracle, she felt not her death, but the death of all pain, as if agony was a skin that shed on the Lady's contact. The General's actual physical condition had not improved. Her leg was still dead—so dead that it *required* amputation at this point—and her body was still bound, but she had no sense of it. This was not a matter of numbness, or endorphins. It was as though the General observed herself from outside her own body; and as she copped to that sensation, she sat upon the nearest pew. Watching her own swinging body, meeting the gaze of her own helpless, blood-filled eyes.

"Are you sure I'm not already dead?" asked Dominia of the Lady. The entity sat, in normal scale, directly to her left. Did they speak in words, or Words? What was the difference?

You are no more dead than any martyr whose martyring is not yet complete. Look: here comes your Father.

As the Lady said. The doors opened and, per usual, in strolled the Hierophant for his anticipated mocking session. He said something unintelligible. Only as she focused in on him did his words clear themselves. Presently, he dragged over the ladder with the assurance that, "I suppose you'll want to know Lavinia is in good order. Be relieved, she is."

"Is this my soul I'm in?" Dominia's nose was a sharp closed parenthesis that abruptly ended the world: the hallmark of her missing eye.

It is always your soul that you are "in." Reality is the hologram cast by the projector of the black hole, said the Lady, eyes never leaving the crucifix. *The travel of the soul through this space is less akin to the movement of ghosts through physical space, and more akin to the result of a physical entity navigating a holographic field. This experience of bilocation is more likely to happen when one is asleep than at any other time, due to the wave flight of consciousness from the low-activity, low-frequency electromagnetic field state of the brain before rapid eye movement begins. But such a phenomenon is also likely to happen in meditation, as well as instances of great physical trauma or duress. There are many who follow Us who use the term "astral projection" to refer to such a phenomenon, but that term more appropriately describes reality, yes? It is all a series of projections produced by the mind.*

The General could not think to respond, fascinated as she was by the experience of being outside her body in so distinct and lucid a way. While the Lady spoke, Dominia rose and walked straight up to her climbing Father. Remarkably, she was poised just below him, yet he noticed nothing. She asked of the Lady, *"Can I go anywhere this way?"*

Yes. But beware, General. To enter even the daytime Ergosphere without one's body is a treacherous proposition. Without physical root, as without consciousness, the soul is as good as drunk or drugged, or worse. A flailing ego, run rampant without its guards.

"So a black-out drunk is a total suppression of consciousness in favor of rampant egoism," observed the General, turning away from the crucifix. *"Explains a lot of my own drunk behavior. Did he mean what he said? Is Lavinia really okay?"*

You may see for yourself, as it pleases you.

The nodding General intended to step toward the doors and instead found herself propelled forward. It was as if she floated in the womb of outer space. Astonished, she rose to the high ceiling and then, truly ghostlike, wafted through the wall of the chapel—to the office, where Cicero's right-hand man busily arranged El Sacerdote's vestments for the ceremony. Farther down the hall, in the gallery, humans decorated for the party to follow on New Year's Eve that Noctisthor. If Dominia had her way, that party would never happen. The year 4044 CE/1999 AL would ring in with the death of the Hierophant, or the death of Dominia, or the deaths of both: but there would be no cause for celebration on a day bound to mark the beginning of a culture's destruction. The question was, would the destruction be of martyrs, or of mankind?

It was not an easy decision to make. While flying through the castle in pursuit of Lavinia's chambers, the phantom General saw so many martyrs along the way. Plenty she knew, in passing if not as friends. For the most part, these were just regular people. Stuffy rich people, but still people. The average martyr had no hand in the hunt and slaughter of humans, had no part in the genocide orchestrated by the Hierophant. That genocide Dominia had supported and helped him envision. Globally speaking, the average martyr was much like those in the town of Elsinore, and less like Dominia: and though she wished to write off the desires of adult humans to be martyred, she recognized now that these were but people with passion such for life that they were willing to trade every scrap of their humanity for a chance to enjoy it just a little longer. They were artists and friends and lovers and siblings, children and parents.

But the humans were all of that, too. And long as the Hierophant was in charge of European and UF society, there could be no chance for humans to live in peace. Not without their rights and lives infringed upon by the mere existence of their predatory counterparts. There was hope, the General believed, that martyrs could change, and the world would improve—but this cancerous growth in the brain of the global organism needed to be removed as soon as possible, or the whole creature was liable to die.

At last, in lonely Lavinia's chambers, the General found the girl, while better treated, in no small amount of trouble for her decision to visit Dominia. Who knew what the truth had provoked the princess into doing or saying? At the peaks of her tantrums, Lavinia was capable of frightening behavior. But now, like most girls who'd worn themselves out with a tantrum, she cried in her bedroom. Alarmingly, Basil was not with her; nor was the girl in the mood to rail to herself in convenient Shakespearean monologue about the injustices that had befallen her, so as to give the General some easy insight into what had happened before—or what would happen next. The watching shade could only take solace in this vision of the girl alive and well, unhurt in anything but spirit. That ghostly hand of the General lay upon Lavinia's golden curls, and, as though feeling it, the princess's tears ebbed to a few indignant hiccups.

"I know you feel betrayed," said Dominia—sure, if nothing else, Livvy's soul heard. *"But it's because you see you have a chance to do the truly right thing after such a long time of being told you were already doing the right thing. And you will do the truly right thing. I know."*

She had to.

As the General was about to leave, she noted through the wall a most curious thing—aside from the notion that she could...well, not see *through* walls, for she also saw the walls. But her senses were beyond their usual limits, and strange effects were undeniable. Plain as if her consciousness mimicked the omniscient, camera-style sight of a dream, she watched merry Teddy stroll through the emptied suite to knock upon the door. The girl, anxious and not knowing her Father visited Dominia's uninhabited form, called, "Who is it?"

"Someone who wants to brighten up your night," sang Theodore. While Dominia restrained a spectral eye roll, this announcement elicited a gasp of joy in her sister, who sprang from bed to throw open the door and dive into del Medico's arms.

"Oh, *Theo*! I'm so glad you're home. Just knowing you're back in this castle makes me feel secure. If it wasn't for knowing you were safe, I—oh, what a state I'd be in!"

"I wasn't ever in *that* much danger..." Nice to hear him admit it now! "Once we were out of the plane, anyway. What's the matter, though? I can't remember the last time I heard your rooms so empty."

With an anxious nibble of her lip, the girl studied the reading nook where the General's spirit happened to hover. "I sent my friends away for the evening. I just can't bear it... You saw Dominia, didn't you?"

Theodore nodded, his face full of uncharacteristic tension. "A few days ago, but I saw her."

"I wasn't supposed to, but I did... I thought Daddy would be mad, but we got to talking, instead. Theo—Theo, did you know Cassandra was my mother?"

Shock, pure and clear as the ringing of any bell, reverberated through Theodore's features before it faded to anxiety based on the weight of his conversation with the General. "No. Dominia told me only after—the kidnapping."

"So you didn't know..." Relief visible in her blue eyes, Lavinia caught Theodore's hands in hers and frowned in contemplation. "I don't think anybody knew except Daddy and Lambie and Ninny. It was Ninny, she...she was sore at Cassandra for lying to her. But now she—" Her lips trembled, a look that shot the General through the heart. "You don't think Daddy means to kill her, does he?"

"I won't let him! He's been out of *hand* lately, that man."

"You can't say that about Daddy." Even now, Lavinia's voice hushed with concern. Theodore, glancing around, guided her to sit upon the edge of the bed. There, he held her delicate artificial hands in his doting, oblivious ones. It was only beside Lavinia in this way that the General recognized the slight dishevelment of his otherwise vainly kept hair and clothes; and she certainly had never seen him defy, or imply he intended to defy, the Hierophant's will. Yet, this he did when he leaned in.

"He's *just a martyr*, Lavinia. Just like you and me. Not some alien sent by God! I can't even begin to tell you all the things that have happened to me, all the things I've learned. But..." He lifted his hands out of hers to move them at a rapid clip, and the General recognized the sign language in an instant; it was that same she and Lazarus had used on their first meeting. Elsinore alone was home to quite a few deaf human slaves punished for gossip, theft, or eavesdropping. Some martyrs even had all their slaves mutilated from the start. Dominia never thought that was right: privacy was the price you paid when your commodity could speak and hear. But the price was compounded, because Lavinia had learned the silent language of these unlucky slaves, and Theodore, if he had not learned it in school, would have no doubt learned it just to speak to her in private. Assuming she didn't pressure him into it, desperate for a friend who wasn't a paid servant liable to run off to her real boss at the first whiff of thought crime.

I've seen some things you wouldn't believe, bunny. Dominia tried not to gag at the private choice of sign to avoid the cumbersome spelling of "Lavinia." She focused on his words. *And I've experienced crazy things, but the long and short of it is that Father tried to* kill *me!*

Once the shock wore from her face, the girl signed, *If that's true, why are you still alive?* A fair enough question, especially of Theodore, who audibly stammered in annoyance before going on in silence.

It's—complicated. It seemed like it was a half-hearted attempt. He also "playfully" excommunicated me, but I haven't heard him mention it since we got back here. I think he's just hoping I'll think I was crazy.

But when was this, Lavinia continued to press. *Before you got kidnapped?*

After, he let slip, and he and Dominia winced in time. *Like I signed, it's complicated.*

That's not possible, though. After you were kidnapped, Daddy was already here at home. Matter of fact, he hasn't been away in months! How could he have threatened you?

I don't think it's safe to explain, Theodore signed, much to Lavinia's exasperation. In that moment, the General sympathized with her more fully than ever. Dominia had, herself, been confounded left and right by constant refusals to enlighten her. Even Miki Soto seemed to have known more than she. Now, she could not help but think her enforced ignorance was a kind of karmic retribution orchestrated for her behavior toward Lavinia. And, of course, Cassandra.

Pained, the General looked away—and her keen senses, unhampered by material walls, detected the figure of Cicero looming down the distant hall.

What to do? She could not interrupt them, not as Lavinia signed, *If it's unsafe, if he's planning something against you, you should flee!*

For once in his life finding some bravery, the (former) Governor of the United Front expressed, *But I came back for you. I couldn't leave you alone here, because I—I love you, Lavinia.*

Awe passed over the girl's face in a tender crimson wave, and the General felt terrible guilt. As if it wasn't bad enough being voyeuristic party to a private moment the princess had so long awaited! Dominia had to find a way to break it up before—Lamb forbid—Cicero did. Now they embraced, and it was as sweet as it was ill-timed. Violent panic rose over the specter. She tried to sweep a vase of white tulips from a nearby table like some horror movie ghost only to find her powers to interact with the material world were limited. Perhaps nonexistent. What could she do? How could she alert them?

Another knock answered her prayers and startled even her, for she had not seen this body move through space toward Lavinia's chamber. Both would-be lovers tensed in cunicular anxiety before the princess stood to straighten her dress. Amid the rustle of fabric, Theodore tiptoed in the direction of her bathroom. "Come in," she called when he was well out of sight, and the door opened to reveal—praise him!—none other than the

Lamb. The ram-horned man assessed his daughter with the sort of bland expression he'd worn while remonstrating a far younger Dominia for things about which he had no personal concern, but which he knew were hot buttons for the Ciceros.

"Hello, Livvy." His eyes trailed not in the direction of the bathroom but in the very deliberate direction of Dominia's spiritual body. As his head turned back toward that bathroom to say, "Hello, Theodore," the General saw, as if in double exposure, a second jaw and mouth upon the Lamb that ran in sluggish time with the first. A spectral jaw that said, *"Hello, Dominia,"* before catching up to merge again with its partner.

While Theodore leaned into sight from the bathroom, the Lamb told Lavinia, "Just thought I'd come chat with you before Cicero fetches you for dress rehearsal...your Father will meet you there."

The General drew the Lamb's split attention toward her spirit once more. *"Was it the horns that kept me from seeing you through the wall?"*

"No end to their utility," said his second mouth.

Meanwhile, Theodore shared an anxious glance with Lavinia. "Is Cicero already here?"

The Lamb said, "In about ninety seconds."

Face rapt with horror, Lavinia looked at the Governor and, then, at her closet. "Get in there," she said, not just leading him into the walk-in space—more like a hallway used to store clothes—but cramming him, with those too-powerful arms, into a mess of chiffon and silk and lace hanging from the left set of shelves. "Stay quiet, Theo. Oh! I'm sorry. Leave when they're gone. I'll see you at the performance, at least, won't I?"

"Of course! I wouldn't miss it."

The girl's face glowed. Had Dominia ever known young love like that? She feared hers was a jaded brand before she'd even been kissed. Acute gratitude infused her body to know Lavinia was not so scarred. *"Will you keep her safe?"* The disembodied General asked this of the Lamb, whose physical eyes again traced over her spectral form before focusing on Lavinia's bookshelves.

"Nobody is safe until you've killed your Father."

"Why are you helping me," she pressed. His gaze glazed off into infinity.

"I hate to see you upset, Lavinia," said the Lamb aloud. "Your Father can be obsessive to the point of destruction...and so can Cicero. I know because he's been that way with me my whole life. We're special, you and I—in different ways. And if he can't use what's special, then he doesn't want to know it exists."

"I thought you loved Daddy," said the sheepish girl. The Lamb smiled.

"Of course I do. But that's the hard part of loving an evil person."

"What's that?"

"Figuring out what to do when you realize that all along, you've been good."

Cicero knocked upon the door and, much as Dominia had with René, did not tarry for answer from within. Rather, he opened it immediately, chiming, "Time for the theater, my pet! Are you ready for the final dress rehearsal? I simply cannot wait."

With the tensest smile the General had ever seen her wear, Lavinia offered her hand. "At last, my servant has arrived with my royal litter. Let us hence!" With a wave of her free hand, the girl seemed as though to laugh, but the sound rang hollow. Cicero, too self-absorbed to note his little doll had feelings, simply smiled at the Lamb and played along with her.

Was Lavinia won? It was difficult to know, but Theodore's position seemed certain. Dominia watched with relief as he crept into the vacated room, mopped his brow, and exited once he was sure the trio had left. Her friends had indeed come here of their free will, and Theodore had been a convenient means and reason by which to do that. She thought of the *tanques* that had brought them in and could not help but wonder how deep the operation went. Had they thrown the Battle for Jerusalem? No wonder they didn't tell her what they planned, if that was the case. She never would have agreed to it, ever. Call it stupid pride.

Still—what a relief to know the General still had an army behind her. A small one, and described as "ragtag" by only the kindest, gentlest critics…but, an army. She had to consider—had to hope—they had something planned for this occasion.

In the castle tearooms, the General traveled cell to cell and confirmed the presence of her friends. She confirmed, too, that Basil had been given his own cell. This meant it was possible her Father did not realize the dog and the magician were bodily separated. (She tried not to distract herself with visions of the Hierophant mistakenly lecturing a border collie as though it were his nemesis, but she did need to laugh at *something*.) Lazarus and Farhad were still well and alive, and truly, Gethsemane was nowhere to be found.

Perhaps Dominia was better off investigating elsewhere—like the stage meant for the ill-fated play, with its storm-bringing rockets and its vast orchestra pit. The Elizabethan open theater, off on the southern side of Elsinore, rested upon the artificial isthmus of a glorious, darkly wooded boardwalk thrusting out amid the cold Baltic Sea. The stage itself was separated from the audience by a trough of water allowed to lap through for a bit of scenic interest; but aside from that, once one entered the confines of the reception area, the open-air theater's only relationship with the ocean was the view through its lobby windows. How she longed to see it from above! But it was as she contemplated flying off to admire it that she finally felt something, anything: her Father's brisk pats against her earthly cheek as he said, "Dominia? Dominia, my girl, have you even been listening to me at all? Are you there, Dominia?"

"Not really." Her response was automatic. In the nauseating blink of an eye, she found herself held "upright." Blood flowed into her legs and, praise the Lady, she remained unable to feel anything of substance. "I guess my thoughts have been elsewhere."

"I would encourage mindfulness, given your circumstances. These are the final hours you will have this leg. You ought to cherish them."

"Not like I can do anything with it, can I? It's already dead."

"I suppose, if that's the way you insist on looking at things. But a more optimistic mind-set would go a long way. What is death but the opportunity for rebirth? You know that as well as all martyrs. When this is done, and you are unburdened by your guilt, you will have a new, pure life stretching ahead. Won't it be a relief!"

Nothing he gave her would ever be relief. She would accept no gifts from him if they both somehow survived. All he gave was evil—poisonous. He had existed at least four thousand years and in that time managed to, with varying degrees of control, undo two iterations of Earth. There had to be some way to stop him or his duplicate from destroying another.

Muddled though her thoughts were, it seemed to the General that the best way to stop him was to stop Cicero's transmigration. But how? From her position, how?

Her friends. She would have to rely on them. Had to hope against hope that somehow, improbably, something would go so right that it didn't matter how wrong everything else was. But how difficult it was to be so helpless! Helplessness was a plague on the senses, the psyche. Its cloak whipped her back to that awful instant of Cassandra's death; it made her feel as she had when, a little girl, she awoke to find her family on the verge of ending. There was nothing worse than helplessness. If it was true that the best ending to all of this would leave her alive with her wife, then, by the Lady, the General would never let either one of them feel helpless again. She would do anything in her power—everything!—to stop that from happening. For three centuries, she had been beholden to her Father's every whim. She had been his slave. Literally, his Bitch.

She would never let that happen again. No matter what it took.

More uncountable hours passed, lurching ever closer to that fatal one. The ceremony of her alleged penitence might have been smaller than the *hieros gamos* of Miki's ascendance, but it still managed to be, in every way, infinitely more pretentious. That was the way the Hierophant's ceremonies were. Some people found martyr religious ceremonies to be of exceeding beauty, as much as any Catholic Mass from which they derived nine tenths of their symbolism and habits. Dominia, however, never found them anything but stuffy. If God was anywhere, it was as far away from this bunch of pricks as possible.

Although, in all fairness, the General was so desperate for a change of state that her heart was consumed by joy when Cicero and his priests, accompanied by the silent Lamb, entered the chapel in such flurry of movement that the doors seemed to have burst. The gaggle of godly men spoke loudly about their preparations, as if she were just another decoration.

"Let's have a dry run, if you all will indulge me." El Sacerdote strode past Dominia without sparing her so much as a glance. He deposited his sacramentary upon the altar and called, "Positions, lads, our imaginary *Introitus* is ending."

Struggling as she was to see through her own eyes, the General had to squint and do some creative reconstruction of the scene to recognize the objects held by the priests. They were not merely censers and books: one was a small dagger made of, or plated with, gold, and one was a bastard sword whose hilt had been encrusted with jewels.

"Now, after our *Introitus*, I intend for us to open with the *Confiteor*; then, Deacon Greholda, if you would read from the Gospel of the Lamb…"

But she, thinking of these weapons—in particular that largest weapon, which consumed her attention now as it would later her leg—she could not focus on Cicero's words. Not until the priest holding the sword got out of her way and allowed her to make eye contact with the Lamb; not until she was able to make out, amid all the underwater audio effects of her near-bursting eardrums, the word "Lazarus."

At that, the Lamb stepped up to accept the dagger from the priest. There was Cicero in her vision again, miming the space on the floor before the Lamb as if Lazarus knelt for the slaughter. Cicero, still senselessly, ceaselessly talking, strode to take the sword from his compatriot, then turned to demonstrate (in slow motion, with no physical contact) how he would hack off the General's leg, right there, above (below) her knee. There were distant words to the effect that it would take several blows, so, in the case of excessive thrashing, her bindings would need to remain until the ceremony was over—but it would be in poor taste if the penitent was also electrocuted as consequence of her natural struggles, not to mention of no small consequence to the sword's bearer. Therefore, the electrical component of her bindings would be deactivated before the ceremony.

"I hope you will not let us down, dear sister," said Cicero, at last condescending to address her.

She did not condescend to respond. She just made hard eye contact with the Lamb, and chose to pray to him by means of his favorite form of prayer:

not thinking at all. Instead, she took it on faith that he was as supportive of her as he had pretended to be all these years.

The Lamb did not look away, nor did he make any move to comfort her, nor give any indication she should expect comfort. All the same, she took strange comfort in his gaze, and allowed this comfort to carry her through to the start of the ceremony. The priests returned in their vestments to open the doors and welcome those few lucky, noble parishioners given the honor of seeing firsthand Dominia's act of penance. Anywhere from one to five at a time, martyrs made their slow ways in, openly gawking at the nine-day-rank and tortured General. After they averted their eyes from the inevitable glance at her face, they'd cross themselves and genuflect before their entrance into a pew from which they strove to stare at the victim without further eye contact.

Let them look. She didn't want them to be completely disappointed. Not after all the good money they paid and time they'd wasted and asses they'd kissed to get them to this moment, invited here. At least they would have the pleasure of seeing her strung up, if they weren't going to witness an amputation.

Hopefully. Hopefully. God, willing. Magician, kind. It was already an encouraging development to hear that her bindings would be grounded. She nursed that sign the way she nursed images of Cassandra. When it was time for the long, drawn-out ceremony to begin, and perfumes of frankincense announced the procession of priests and prisoners—Lazarus, Farhad, and, amusingly, Basil—she was emboldened to see them. Shackles and doom be damned. Her friends were there with her, before these insufferable bastards. Alongside them, she was invulnerable.

And then, to bolster that hope—here came René, looking as shifty as he ever had. Late—disrespectfully and embarrassingly late—wearing Dominia's jacket, scurrying in after the procession. The doors closed as he snatched a seat in the back with a genuflection so half-assed that the laughter of the General interrupted the *Introitus* and led to a lot of uncomfortable coughing and shuffling among the parishioners. This was visibly echoed by the aggravated thrash of Cicero's black eye on his otherwise stoic march to the altar. The cyborgan whipped to Dominia, then to the back of its owner's head in search of the disruption's source, before El Sacerdote got it under control.

She wasn't sure what her alleged brother had expected from her. True penitence? Perhaps the prior Dominia had shown such, and the Hierophant had assured Cicero that this would be the case—but this Dominia was through with every bit of the sorry institution that was the Holy Martyr Church. How annoying that the final hour of her life should involve her in a religious ceremony!

Annoyed as she was at the tail of the pompous introduction, the General felt her teeth might snap in her skull at the force of her grimace. In the hands of one of the priests was not the aspergillum usually used to contain holy water but the globus flask used by Lazarus to collect and transport the waters of the Ergosphere. This, they wasted in sprinkling upon perfectly healthy martyrs, taking it up and down the aisles as was generally done during Easter Mass with so-called holy water. You could get that shit out of wells so long as you had a priest around. To get the Lady's water, you had to go to a specific well—or a geyser, she supposed it was now—and bring the stuff back to Earth. Pouring it on these tools! It made her chest hurt even with the deity's blessed pain removal.

Cicero, meanwhile, opened with that rambling confessional prayer he had threatened to use for the occasion, delivered while standing before Dominia so as to stare at her while he rattled off the long list of sins called by name in the longer and more Hierophant-favored variant of the Latin prayer. The worst, most tedious one, in which parishioners agreed with the priest that thrice, through their faults, they had "*peccavi per superbiam in multa mea mala iniqua et pessima cogitatione, locutione, pollutione, sugestione, delectatione, consensu, verbo et opere, in periurio, in adulterio, in sacrilegio, omicidio, furtu, falso testimonio, peccavi visu, auditu, gustu, odoratu et tactu, et moribus, vitiis meis malis.*"

Blahdiam blahdione blahdoio blahdavis. Modern Mephitolian was identical to Latin in many respects save for a lot of German roots and loanwords, yet in this context the stuff was somehow still dry enough to put her to sleep.

"Sin rots the relationship between the soul and the Lord," Cicero surmised, the prayer having been completed once the priest carrying the stolen waters halted outside the General's periphery. "One need look no further than my eye—the eye of your own humble servant of God—to see its effects upon the world. Its effects upon the self, and the selves of one's fellow man! Dominia's sin was what took my eye from me, children: but the Lord, in seeing her penance and my suffering, saw fit to provide us with the circumstances for a miracle."

Now she understood why the Holy Father's DIOX-I, from his time as Cicero, was undetectable. It was because he had no DIOX-I. Both his eyes were perfectly real. She understood so well—and was, for her part, so fatigued by horrible tortures and emotional revelations—that she was not the least bit shocked or surprised (as were those many screaming parishioners) when the black DIOX-I of the priest faded into a deactivated state and was, by his own hand, yanked out of its cavern with a scream of victorious agony. After hurling away the bloodied cyborgan, the half-blind priest wrenched the waters from the hands of his lesser assistant. Before the worshipers, Cicero tilted back his head to waste the remainder of the Lady's water on the restoration of his own eye, rather than the healing of the lame or the curing of disease.

What a surprise. Even less surprising was how, after demonstrating his new, healthy eye to the roaring martyrs who abandoned horror and shouted their praise for the Lord, he resumed his pedantic sermon on the subject of sin as if he had not just committed the most egregious one Dominia could name.

She had sinned against no one this past year, save those people she had been forced to kill in righting her Father's wrongs. Her sinning—her conscious, intentional sinning, at least—had ended with Cassandra's death. Though Cicero and her Father loved to pretend they were arbiters of sin, Dominia had learned only she could tell herself what was a sin and what was not. A sin was a crime one committed, ultimately, against oneself. It was not one's neighbor one truly hurt. Not the families of the murdered or the victims of rape. Not even God was hurt by one's sin. Rather—each sin, no matter how ignoble the soul, piled against the spirit of the sinner until it boiled out of the body and took the form of physical recompense. Because that was what it took for the truly depraved sinners to cease their sin. It took arrest, or execution, or, in Dominia's case, the loss of the one thing that ever gave them any scrap of joy.

René's face appeared intermittently as he leaned from time to time around the oversize hat of the woman before him. Dominia thought of his summation that happiness was a field—and then, she was forced to wonder whether Cassandra had ever really given her any joy. Was joy but a chemical reaction? A state temporary as any other? Was the entropic world too cruel a place to sustain the feeling long-term?

She didn't believe it. Couldn't believe it. Happiness was possible. Cassandra was possible. The end to all of this was possible. Across Elsinore, Lavinia recited lines that drew them ever-closer to the boring play's surreptitiously deadly climax—yet such a thought arose with relief in the General. The end to all this lingered so close as to be surreal. Once more, she fell out of the body that she had not felt since the Lady's visit one day prior. Once more, she observed herself from outside. She stood just within the shut chapel doors while, across the room, the chanting priests arranged their prisoners. Here was Cicero, accepting the sword. There was Lazarus, forced to kneel before the Lamb as El Sacerdote called to his worshipers, "This moment is the moment for which all our ceremonies have been mere preparation. The blood of the Lamb, mere metaphor for the forgiveness of the Lord, is the means by which we wash away the sins of this world—but with the Holy Father's guidance, the blood of Lazarus is the way we higher men will open ourselves to the next." Here was the Lamb, being handed the knife. That was Cicero, brandishing the sword. The bite of its metal edge should have chilled Dominia's physical thigh.

"Sin is a dead limb that weighs us down," summarized the maggot to her Father's botfly.

Unwilling to wait a second longer, cagey René Ichigawa stumbled up from his aisle seat with Dominia's gun in his hand. How funny. Poet, professor, political dissident: ultimately, history would mark René as an assassin. Too soon for anyone to notice and too far from anyone who could stop him, he tripped to the exact spot where stood the General's phantom and clumsily fired her old weapon at the second Cicero said, "Luckily for you, my sister: belief is a sword."

In their analysis of what happened that night in Kronborg's chapel, those brooding historians would be forced to come to one conclusion: the murder of the Lamb and the freeing of the General Dominia di Mephitoli (therefore all the events of the night that led to her permanent disappearance, the death of the Hierophant, and the final destruction of the Holy Family's vile institution), was initiated by one highly improbable bullet trajectory, and one very coincidental power outage. The rest was a mess of conspiracy, paranoia, and implications that were downright magical.

Certain basic facts were agreed upon. The Lamb, who had noted sway over probabilistic outcomes, saw the shot being fired—and, more importantly, had seen it was fired at Cicero. He, along with two other priests, moved to cover his brother; only he was fast enough to get between El Sacerdote and the would-be assassin. Not that he needed to, or should have. René's bullet—the single bullet remaining in the gun returned to the General by means the textbooks could not comprehend—ricocheted off one of the metal horns of the Lamb, snapped the tether hanging the General from her crucifix, then ricocheted once more—this time, off the metal cap of the crucifix, which altered the trajectory enough to allow the projectile to bury itself in the Lamb's brain.

It was also a fact—mere coincidence, most impressed—that Kronborg Castle's power died along with the Lamb. Elsewhere in those frigid walls, security PCs lost their connection to the prisoner's cuffs, and the remote-controlled devices, already grounded, sagged open around the wrists of the prisoner, Dominia di Mepitholi.

The speed with which all those events occurred could not be communicated by any historian, no matter their effort. Women screamed; the General fell; Cicero uttered for the first time in two thousand years a noise that Dominia's spirit interpreted as a cry of horror the instant before impact with the cold tile floor returned her to her flesh.

"My brother," El Sacerdote screamed as worshipers poured through the doors. "My brother, oh, Elijah! No, no, oh—that lying bastard!"

Her leg was beyond saving; though, perhaps thanks to the Lady's water across the floor, or her first chance to be upright in over a week, the General felt better than she had in days—even if her heart ached to see the death of a Family member who had treated her with a decency not found in any iteration of Cicero.

There was no time to mourn. The rattle of chains muted the sounds of chaos as Lazarus bent over her, hastily seeking to keep her awake and slip her hands from the parted cuffs.

"You'll be okay," swore the mystic, not able to move his hands within a particularly wide range, but able to touch her face well enough. "You've got it from here, kiddo."

There was no time to ask. Not even time to cry out. Her friend's face changed; his body slumped. Cicero withdrew the sword he'd plunged into Lazarus's back and fluid streamed after it. Not blood. Not that good, sacred blood that saved so many souls, human and martyr alike. No: in a strange miracle she could not then explain, her friend's fatal wound wept water.

Without giving in to amazement or redemption or the urge to make some gloating speech, Cicero nudged the mystic aside. The priest plunged the blade between Dominia's ribs.

Steel pierced her heart.

XIV

Anamnesis

For several seconds, the General could not place the nature of the silence where she stood. It was not the silence of the Ergosphere, nor of any other thing she recognized. Why, she could not even well remember where she had just been. She only knew that, like a sleepwalker on waking, she found herself upright, on two good legs, with darkness all around—except a disembodied row of ghostly faces that floated before her.

She could not recognize the silence until a white moth flitted past her eye. With its help, she pieced together where her spirit stood: visible in this moment of her death in what was, truly, a miracle. Upon the Elizabethan stage, the manifestation of Dominia turned to see Lavinia. Too astonished to pretend she gave a fig for the show she was in, the princess stumbled forward a step.

"Ninny," she whispered, while the Hierophant pressed, "Say your line."

As quickly as she had appeared in the spotlight, the General disappeared into the more familiar silence of the Void and left in her place the seventh avatar of the Lady, who raked Her steely gaze across the crowd. This information did not come to Dominia by any brand of firsthand sensory experience, for she was not there to see the Lady's body flicker into her empty place. Rather, she felt the abstract knowledge as if by some organ she could not place. She could hardly place herself! Again, again, again, she was consumed by the piecing of the sword through her flesh and against the muscle of her heart. Again, again, again. As if that was all she'd ever been: pain, burning pain. And failure. The darkness around her replayed it with detail so cruel that the nothing that was once Dominia was forced to remember that moment again, the way memory cycled through the tail end of a terrifying tahgmahr even when one was clearly awake, safe, in bed. Lazarus's face, then Cicero's. Then, the point of the blade. As bad a dream as any.

Dominia had suffered many tahgmahrs as a girl, waking often to the sound of her own screams. While she remained a child, on the instances the Lamb was home for these terrors he would arrive to comfort her almost before she was awake—but as a teenager, or during his many transcontinental trips with Cicero, she had been forced to learn how to rationalize, on waking in a cold sweat, why the images that caused her to shake were false, and now absent. Then, as now, she felt deeply alone; but then, as now, that feeling resolved itself into her own sense of space and bodily security. Dreams of being kidnapped from her parents and murdered by the Hierophant resolved into the truer, parallel reality; dreams of her own failure and murder by Cicero resolved into much the same. To have died, she needed to have been alive. And to observe her own death after the fact, she had to have some basis from which to do it. Therefore, she could not be dead in an eternal sense. Therefore, even after death, her soul was swiftly derived from the darkness of the Void and the trembling of her trauma.

There was now a certain comfort in the Ergosphere's dark night. The absence that it marked was not the absence of Dominia. Thanks to experience during her life using the blood of Lazarus, any postmortem confusion about her Self had been brief as she'd been promised. She perceived her thoughtbody as she always had—and, though she stood in the dark with no so-called black sun of Earth's stolen light hanging above to illuminate her path, she did not feel at any more risk of disappearance than she might have in reality. Yet there were still risks. Still traps. And the simplest trap of all was walking anywhere.

If she did not move, time would not pass. This, she knew as well as she knew that, on Earth, she was dying. Should she return to it, that body, she could not imagine what would happen. Her high-frequency consciousness floating around in wave form now would collapse into particle form on entering the vicinity of her brain's fading electromagnetic field, and then, what? How would she perceive it? Was it possible to perceive at all if one's eventual fate was simply to fade into the dirt like the rest of matter? Better, was a return to such a dying body even physically possible? Was the brain's electromagnetic field what kept her consciousness in place?

Was her awareness—particularly her continued awareness now, in this place, in this moment—not, in and of itself, evidence of her permanent security?

"There is no such thing as death," answered Saint Valentinian, behind her. Yet if she looked, she knew she would not see him. On he spoke. "Not from an eternal perspective. There is only the illusion of death. If you are aware enough to see that death is an illusion, you can never really die; and if you were never aware enough to see that death was an illusion, you were never really alive. Those unconscious individuals who have not crafted souls, whether by blood of Lazarus or any other means, cannot experience death in a way that matters."

"That doesn't make it right." Dominia closed her eye as if to shut out the notion. "Every death matters. I've caused more deaths firsthand than anyone I've known or read about. That matters."

"Death is more a dream than this dream-space."

"Then something—someone—needs to wake those people from the tahgmahrs of their deaths."

"Will you?"

Dominia opened her good eye, and the dark night of the Ergosphere lit with crisscrossing beams of information. To her death-opened mind, they represented every possible arrangement of physical information—in every color, too. Even colors the General had never seen before. As she touched a cerulean thread, the information represented once more changed. Now, to a vast collection of lights. She found she could, in a delirious way that she could not retain and yet did in a way beyond knowing, reach into these lights and absorb their content: books, albums, films, private journals, tattoos, blueprints, legal documents. The entire creative capacity of Earth represented in a swarm of potentiality. So many lights filled the darkness that they appeared less a collection of individual orbs and more a vast mist of will-o-wisps stretching through the Void.

"There is an infinite variety of ways to view the information of eternity," the magician told her. The lights refolded themselves (for that was the only verb Dominia could use to describe a process so beyond description) and became a series of objects resembling crystals, all of them in some way interlocked with their neighbors. These revealed tangible data about every physical object, imparted to the General's consciousness in a brush. For example, she laid her hand on Kronborg, and knew then not just the history of the building represented, but the history of all the pieces of wood and stone that built the building, and the history of their trees and quarries, and the genetic lineage of the seeds and sediment they once were, stretching far, far back into the dawn of time. All the builders who were involved in its making, all the coins that financed it and whence they came—

"This is incredible." Dominia marveled, pulling her hand away, feeling herself falling too deeply into a well of information she sensed was of limitless length. Traveling far enough into any one single jewel could reveal the entire array. "Valentinian…is this God?"

"I don't know how to answer that, other than to say, 'If you can describe it with words—even True Words—it's probably not God.' People are always looking for God outside themselves. But 'God' is a word invented by Man, to distinguish a phenomenon Man needed distinguishing. Everybody has a different vision of what it means. Is consciousness God?"

The crystals around her collapsed into dust, and she saw fewer lights scattered about, but still a great many: each of infinite brightness, arranged in the dark like blinding stars. As she turned her head to find the one that she thought to glow the brightest, the General marveled to find it emanated from within her.

"I don't think the question is one of God's substance," said Valentinian. "Even from this height, God is an unknowable force of nature by definition. At least, by my definition. What's your definition of God, Dominia?"

Hearing her own name in that place sent a palpable ripple through whatever substance could be said to form her body; the external reminder firmed her spirit as once it had when she was lost. She closed her eye and said, "I don't know. Somebody like you, I guess."

"Woah. Thanks, buddy, but I have to worry about your standards."

Chuckling, Dominia said, "I mean, you're versed in all of this. You maybe even are responsible for this, on some level. It's hard to tell with you."

When she opened her eye and found him standing there, she expected it, and was not the least bothered. "*Are* you responsible for this, Valentinian?"

"Sort of. Does it matter?"

"I guess not." Exhaling in a breath that was only theoretically necessary, the General asked, "Is this it, then?" She met Valentinian's eyes. "Is it over? Am I dead?"

"With that attitude."

"What can I do?"

"Anything other than 'nothing' is a good start. One advantage you've given yourself is taking zero steps. You remain suspended at the instant when death is imminent—when Cicero's sword pierced your heart. Consciousness always leaves the body when the brain knows death is a foregone conclusion, and it perceives its flight in different ways depending on the persona's level of awareness for these matters. For some people who aren't going to experience their own death, or can't, it engages in a sleight of hand to tuck them off to bed in a way they won't mind so as to use the light of their consciousness again next time around. But for most, the veil tears in one way or another, and we experience the truth."

"What about those people who don't have a conscious light?" She thought, as she asked, of Cassandra. "Those who don't even have souls to be bound to the Very Low Frequencies? Do they just disappear?" She imagined a confused soul taking a step beyond the moment of their death and leaving themselves irrevocably stranded in the mists of the Void, but then realized these soulless individuals had not even vessels with which to step.

The magician, unconcerned, emphasized, "You can perceive this information *any way* you want."

Frowning, Dominia contemplated death. Throughout the course of her life, the General had carefully venerated the dead. The dead she made, and the dead she knew. She lost soldiers to the battlefield, friends to depression, and, as her human family aged, all artifacts of her humanity to Chronos. She had not been a praying woman until her final year, but she had been a respectful woman, and had kept in her mind a long list of names that the DIOX-I had offered to digitize for her while in her possession. This, perhaps, was what she expected to see when the information of the black hole resolved itself into a form representing the dead: some list, or the wide variety of floating names awash in the ocean of her dream about the Lady.

But that had been a nebulous pool of information that included potential deaths. It was more abstract than that which she sought now. The organization of the black hole's information into the dead of *her* world, from *her* iteration of *her* reality, was a different and more specific request that yielded a different, far more startling result. Nothing but the Void, and the magician, standing before her as he had.

"Where did the information go?" she asked, even as she began to understand.

"Did you ever ask yourself what dark energy is? That force that hastens the expansion of the universe; that energy with a proposed scalar field called 'quintessence'—it changes over time and is attractive or repulsive, depending on the ratio of its potential energy to its kinetic energy."

Reaching into the darkness of that place's night, the General marveled as he said, "The information stored in the black hole is only an abstraction of what we would consider physical objects. Unsouled people, for purposes of the Ergosphere's categorization, are the same. The information and energy of these unilluminated beings cannot be physically destroyed any more than it can be *abstractly* destroyed. It only seems to be destroyed. In reality, it has been stored."

"In the cloud," observed the General wryly, which made the magician laugh. "Dark energy is really..."

"There are a lot of beings with psychic substance in the universe, and a lot of things that seem to die or get destroyed—including inorganic and non-sentient beings or objects. One of the reasons quintessence changes over time."

"'This quintessence of dust'?"

"Science, Shakespeare, and metaphysics have been involved in a torrid love triangle since long before Willie picked up *The Triumphal Chariot of Antimony* in 1604 CE and started going even heavier on the alchemy references."

"But how can anybody distinguish one member of the dead from the other in a format like this?"

With the giggle of a goofy teenager, the magician shrugged. "I know, right? It's not only like finding a needle in a haystack: it's like finding a needle in a haystack that's been covered in tar, and the needles and the haystack are also tar, and you might become tar if you spend too much time monkeying in it."

"Okay—so what do I *do*?"

"Try praying," said the man, winking again into nonexistence to leave the General, as usual, annoyed and alone. Of course, it was when the magician was at his most annoying that he was usually imparting a very important truth. This somehow made it all the more annoying.

But, it did make sense. When she was lost in the Void, her form exchanged for that of a tiger, the prayers of Miki led her back to herself. They reached her and she heard them—and, just now, when Valentinian used her name, the General felt a great many degrees more substantial. Was it not the desire of the dead, surely, to be remembered? Honored? Called out and spoken to? No wonder so many cultures practiced careful ancestor veneration. Even if, in the course of the physical universe, the expanding collection of unsouled personas separated from Earth were unable to hear the prayers of the living, in the black hole they would know.

What strange complications were inspired by eternity; in what strange circles it forced the mind to turn! But it made perfect sense to her now. Still in place, the General knelt, and bowed her head until it touched whatever could be said to form the ground. She had asked Farhad to teach her the proper posture for the prostration that Muslims called *sujud* one night when she could not sleep. After observing it in the quarter of the encampment's men who practiced the faith, she found the position to be the only way for her to approach the godhead.

Now, in the hour of her death, she was glad she learned it. Here she was, less than nothing, asking for the world. Upon sorting her disordered head for prayers, she selected her long since memorized one for the dead on behalf of Saint Valentinian. There were several other she knew, actually, including one adapted from an old Catholic prayer for souls in purgatory, but they were too short.

Though the words to that Catholic one finally made sense to her! Purgatory made sense to her, now that she found herself here. And how *many* souls there were in purgatory—how many souls there *must* have been in purgatory! She remembered Dante's travel through it guided by Virgil. Did the writer imagine the scale of the place? A place that, by definition, had to encompass the righteous pagans of tens of thousands of years' worth of good people who, through lack of opportunity or lack of interest, did not cultivate their soul while on Earth? And what of hell, the VLF bands of the Void? There had been *so many souls*, such a great many. Who would pray for them all? Which of them, the lost, had hope to find themselves in this world where consciousness forever waxed and waned, where humanity eternally suppressed itself in the form of martyrdom or something—anything—else?

This notion struck Dominia so severely that she found she could not complete her third simple prayer, which had been generically said for all the souls of the dead. But now...well, now. After considering the vastness of the operation before her, and her position frozen on the cusp of death, the General said to herself: It's a good thing I tried to memorize all those names.

She also said to herself: If I don't have names, I have faces, and occasions.

And she also said to herself: I think I'm going to feel like I've been here forever.

But she also said to herself: All things can be accomplished by doing one portion at a time.

So, one portion at a time, one prayer at a time, one name at a time, the General Dominia di Mephitoli, former Governess of the United Front and the notorious Bitch of Europa, began to beg the forgiveness and freedom of the dead.

There were so many names. If she had given the DIOX-I permission to catalog them for her, its software would have crashed. The General had fought a thousand battles (okay, more like eight hundred, seven hundred and ninety-five...she'd rounded up) and usually killed no fewer than fifty men, herself. That was a staggering number of dead, and a staggering number of names; and she wasn't sure that, forced to recount the list on Earth, she would have been able to remember them all. Indeed, as she herself had just considered, many names had been irretrievable on Earth due to time or severe destruction of dog tags and facial features—or, in some very awful cases, the mass destructions of cities and/or encamped individuals. But, in the Void, as she repeated the same short prayer with each iteration single-mindedly devoted to one person (often more than once per person, for she could never pray enough), the names blossomed without the least effort on memory's part.

It was the other way around. Effort was required not to produce but to endure the memories arising with each name. Though on Earth thoughts of killing haunted her with increasing concern until her conversion to decency, here, memories of each death came upon her like an accusation made by the dead—or made by her against herself on their mute behalf. The more innocent the person, the more painful the memory. Working back from the officers killed on their escape from New Elsinore and the martyrs she'd allowed to die in the dim sum restaurant, she wasn't off to a great start. By the time she got back to Tobias Akachi, she heard his chiding.

"Now you feel bad about killing me, eh? You did not seem to feel bad about it at the time. Nor did you feel bad about it at all during the last year of your life. Not until now, this very moment. You expect me to forgive you?"

Feeling obligated to respond as though he were really there before she continued on to her next prayer, she licked her lips and allotted, "Well, no."

"Then what do you expect, General?"

What did she expect. What did she expect? "I expect you'd want to be some place better than this." In the immediacy of that place, she re-experienced the surprise of seeing Akachi's big smile in the crowded market square. "Someplace that's not just miserable death, floating around in the vacuum of space with only your memories of the end."

"What do you actually want from me, General," asked the spirit, or Dominia's memory of Akachi, or something that borrowed his voice. "If it is not forgiveness that you want, why bother to feel guilt over all these deaths?"

That was a good question, in a way, although it oversimplified the emotion of guilt into an option. In the General's opinion, it was the furthest thing from. Guilt was like pain; it was not a bad thing in and of itself, but it was a sign of something wrong. Both guilt and pain seemed to thrill the masochist and antagonize the sadist. She did not dwell in guilt because she wanted to, or because she expected forgiveness. After all, what would she do with it if she had it? What would the forgiveness of her victims matter if she had yet to forgive herself?

"I guess I need help," she decided. "I'm appealing to you, Tobias, because I need help, and I know that you do, too. Neither of us liked the other in life, but it doesn't have to be that way here. Nothing matters anymore."

The spirit gave no answer. She went on, emboldened by his silence. "I don't want you to forgive me—but if you would help me pray, maybe that could help us both. You're a Christian man, right? You can help me call out the dead. People I don't know. Since you're here, you have your own guilt, too. Might make you feel better, right?"

"And you think my dead will want to hear from me any more than your dead want to hear from you?" Tobias's voice was now so clear and direct that he must have stood before her. She did not lift her head to look.

"Of course they won't want to hear from you. You did something to them that you need to pray about."

After a few seconds' silence, the dead dentist scoffed, and his footsteps echoed around the General until he found a place to kneel behind her. "If there is one thing I do not like, it is a martyr who is closer to God than I am."

The softly smiling General restrained her desire to tease him for the wording of his comment and resumed her prayers by throwing out one for the dead *tulpa*. (Not too many, though.) Name by name, falling out of the rough chronology and instead allowing them to emerge as they would in her mind, the General prayed for the souls of the dead. The lost dead, the historical dead, the influential dead. All those many martyr saints depicted in paintings, real and false. All those who had died by her Father's hand before she was ever born. But, most of all, she prayed for her dead. In the distance, their lights bloomed awake in acknowledgment. How was it she could even know so many names? They were incredible to her, these prayers pouring out at a rapid clip. The most recent ones felt just as raw as the oldest ones: those first kills on battlefields long since rendered simple farms and normal cities, as safe and happy as any others.

"It shouldn't surprise you," suggested the Lamb as she realized she'd forgotten to pray for him, although she had been responsible for his death in incidental fashion. His horns were gone—she had never seen him without that false silver halo. "It's always given me headaches, the way you worry things over in your head, again and again, even when you tell yourself you don't care about them. Of course those old wounds seem fresh, Dominia."

"Sorry," she said, not without a trace of humor. "And I'm sorry about—I'm sorry you had to die."

"I'm not," he assured her. "'Long-suffering' doesn't begin to cover my experience, being Cicero's brother. And the Hierophant's... If it mattered to me, and I wanted to live, the bullet would have missed. Actually, I had to nudge it toward me a little. Your friend is a terrible shot."

He was trying to be funny, but the good Rabbi's downright desire to die broke her heart. Who could have blamed him? Paraded around from town to town to have his throat slit every Noctisdomin...she'd want to die, too. "I'm sorry that living is such misery for you."

"'Was'—in this state, anyway. But it's all right. The next state will be better. Probably. It can't be worse. Do you want me to help you pray?"

"Could you, please? I've got a lot of ground to cover."

"Then it's a good thing," said the Lamb, kneeling beside Akachi, "that we have so much time."

He wasn't kidding. Dominia was grateful they had all eternity to shuffle through the masses of the dead. The list unfurled in all intangible directions while her mind leapt across time from one battle to another. Once, she looked over her shoulder and found more people—many more—than had announced their presence to her. Some, unrecognized, had perhaps been summoned by the ruminations of the Lamb or Akachi. These spirits also prayed for those they had known or wronged; and of those spirits, a few came forth to add to the effort. Their number grew before her eye, and the General, chilled, returned to her fervent prayers with renewed vigor. When she could not remember or did not know a name, she pictured a face, and evoked a battle, and remembered the impact of her weapon or the sound of her gun's discharge.

The way she figured, at least one hundred thousand people had been put the slaughter, directly or indirectly, by the General's hand. This did not touch the many destroyed en masse in the Black Night. Yet, this was not a fraction—not a seed!—beside that multitude of souls forming the quintessence from the beginning of linear time. Still, she needed continue; still, she prayed, though her heart despaired that the task before her was impossible. As this despair reached its peak, a hand touched her head. She looked up, and found Kahlil.

"Jeez, will you relax." He said that, perhaps, as much to himself as to her, for in this space, no spirit was yet purified of their anxious death memories. Emboldened by the sorrow in her face, the young spirit knelt beside her. "Try to look at it like this. If you save everyone in the future, then they're already saved in the past—so they're praying for you, too, forever and ever. What is that? 'Teleological' thinking?"

"Every moment," she murmured. "Every prayer, shaped to a purpose."

Yes: that notion was, somehow, very encouraging. Prayer did little perceptible good other than serving as a kind of spiritual cell phone, but it did have a way of bolstering the speaker in a time like this. In an eternal time like this, where the information making up reality went unmoved, yet the veritable army of souls behind the General grew to limitless expanse. It was a good thing that time did not exist in that place, however, and that issues of thirst and hunger did not matter: based on the time it took an individual in reality to recite the prayer on behalf of Saint Valentinian, it would have taken the General 3,472 earthly day/night cycles to complete her penance.

If she did not eat.

And did not sleep.

And did not excrete, or move, or think a thing that was not a plea that the souls of the dead be granted the eternal rest of paradise and comfort of Valentinian rather than this state of nothing. This state of suspension. Perhaps it was those great many unheard prayers of eternity that had helped the General so quickly find her soul after death, rather than her year of training in the Ergosphere. She could not be sure.

Just over nine years of prayer and penance, densely packed into a single instant. A single instant of death. The only movement the General made—which, while hypnotic, also kept her aware of her thoughtbody and maintained its integrity apart from the Void—was the movement of her waist, up and down, as she bent to the floor for each new prayer, then up again to cross herself. Then, again, back down. On Earth, even the martyr General would have collapsed from exhaustion, but there was no exhausting her now. Not here. Her legs, quite literally, became one with the base of the Void, but she did not cease for an instant her meditations save for those brief splits in which she grew aware of the overwhelming noise of the crowd, the murmur having long since grown to a persistent buzz, clamor, roar. She prayed; they prayed; in the Kingdom, their eternal selves surely also prayed.

And, as Dominia neared the beginning of her career—those long-lost nights of Lieutenant di Mephitoli, Private di Mephitoli, and all her many variations—a change overtook the Void that was, in and of itself, miraculous. Without any spatial movement on the part of the General or the passage of a single second in reality, the black circle of Earth at the edge of the Ergosphere rose as though they sat at dawn.

Or perhaps—perhaps it was not so much that, as it was that the quintessence around them evaporated. A vast army of souls chanted their prayers behind her, drops of water condensed from that bleak mist of indistinctness and fear.

Around her neck, the diamond of her wife beat back and forth: a pendulum whose sways marked another soul, another soul, another soul. Reminding Dominia each time, *I'm here, too.*

I'm always here with you.

All this continued until, so suddenly it surprised her, the General looked up, and saw all the darkness had cleared from the sky. She understood why the Void's darkness was said to be unclean even beyond its radioactive signatures, for it was filthy with the psychological toxins of all these unpurified souls. But as the place grew cleaner, so, too, did its cleanliness hasten, the prayers multiplying exponentially until a whole world of people, past, present, and future, had been derived by the connections and good wishes of those lost spirits whom the General pursued—of those *nous* who saw the labors of Dominia and were moved by her anguish for the person she had been. Those individuals had distinguished themselves from the quintessence, and the quintessence was no more, and the beauty of clear space revealed to Dominia a glorious truth. Even the darkness of the black sun had disappeared, as if the black hole returned the light it had stolen from the planet's face. There was the glory of Earth, the radiantly mossy soul of itself resting upon the edge of the Ergosphere.

"The black sun of your Father's is a fiction." She tore her eye from that great swirl of blue and green only when her periphery noted Valentinian's form. "Just like death. Here we are, suspended at the end of the planet's history: eternally frozen in this moment of destruction, when that which was once Sol of Earth ravages, in an eyeblink, its already dead infant. Then this black hole will be devoured, and that one; in other galaxy clusters, other black holes will devour other black holes. Yet I say again, the black sun is a fiction. There is no such thing as death."

"The Earth looks so new, and alive." The General's eye filled with tears to see the glory of the planetary atom hanging above her head. "Like it was just born."

Kneeling at the side unoccupied by Kahlil, the magician crossed himself and prostrated as had Dominia. "Because the moment of destruction is also the moment of creation, and it is also an eternity. Can you imagine what eternity is? What it really is? What maintains it?"

"God," she supposed.

"But what is God?"

Even now, annoyance for him crossed her face. "I asked you that."

"If you'd stop asking other people that and think about the question for a while, you might astonish yourself with the real answer."

The General dared not interrupt his prayers to press him further, and intended to resume her own: yet she realized with an uncanny feeling of relief she had but one more prayer to utter. When she tried to remove the necklace from her neck, it was with an urgent chill of panic that she found it gone. Had it fallen off, somewhere into the Void? Her head lifted to see where it dropped, and then—there.

Ah, there.

There!

"How can I deserve your prayers?" Cassandra, wan from her time in the Void, stood before her—not yet brightened by the peace of the Kingdom. "How can I deserve to live at all? To have lived, and thrown my life away... oh, I didn't understand until I saw your face. Until it was already too late. I didn't understand until that second that, as long as I was alive, I could recover from anything. That I could adapt. I didn't realize until the second it was too late that I could have hated you, and you still would have loved me, and stayed with me, and taken care of me, until I didn't hate you anymore. Or even if I hated you forever."

"That's the way it always is," said the magician sadly, "in that last second. All our errors become so clear."

"It's why I can't—I can't possibly deserve better than this." Cassandra wept, the back of her hand against her lips.

For the first time in the equivalent of nine years, the General rose. Behind her the prayers had hushed, but she'd stopped hearing them, anyway. Step by step, Dominia closed the distance between herself and the spirit of her wife.

On Earth, Basil licked her face.

"You did what you did because you wanted to hurt yourself—and me—worse than I hurt you. I'm so sorry, Cassandra."

While the body of the General di Mephitoli eased open its half-blind eyes to study the dog above it, the muted sounds of Cicero's weeping filled its ears.

"In those seconds you first appeared to me, I thought you were perfect. Your body, your face, the way you smiled, the way you held yourself—the way you looked at me. Everything about you in that second was so perfect. It's how I always think of you."

Beneath the hand of Lazarus's sprawled body lay the dagger intended for him.

"But nobody's perfect, Cassandra. I should have known that, and accepted it, instead of reacting to your imperfection like it was a crime."

The earthly body of the General relied on what was left of its muscle memory to claim the dagger. With this ceremonial weapon, it slumped toward Cicero's back.

The true body of Dominia touched Cassandra's face, so cool and soft that it was like touching the meniscus of a glass of milk. "I hurt you, then spent a lifetime trying to make up for it with the force of my love. But instead I made you the prisoner of my lies. And I have to—" Dominia fought a hiccup of tears to no avail, and her facade crumbled to trembling lips in an expression that, as ever, was mirrored in her empathetic wife. Especially as the General forced herself to say, "I have to let you go."

Dominia turned to see Benedict stood in the spot where she had prayed. She took one step to the side.

As Cicero sobbed over the body of the Lamb, the General plunged the dagger into his ribs.

"Benedict." Weeping Cassandra covered her face. "I can't be seen by you this way."

"What way?" He hurried to his lover's side and took up those hands Dominia longed to take, herself.

"At my worst. My cruelest, my stupidest."

"Honey," said Dominia, at the same time and in the same cadence as Benedict. This elicited a wry smile out of both before the man allowed the martyr to go on, "I don't think there's anybody here who hasn't been cruel or stupid at some point."

"We're all just people," said Benedict. Cassandra's lips trembled in that rapid, familiar way that ached Dominia's jaw with the urge to kiss her calm.

"But I don't deserve people," protested the woman. Dominia wiped tears from her cheek, at last drawing back her attention.

"You feel that way because I made you feel that way. And I'm so sorry, Cassandra. You deserve people. You deserve happiness. You deserve a family. All the things that I couldn't give you here."

"Maybe," Cassandra continued lamenting. "But I took from myself any chance I had to live a happy life."

"Happiness is still possible," insisted Benedict.

"Eternity is a long time," said Dominia.

Although, for a glimmer, hope lay in those doe eyes, Cassandra squeezed them shut. "How can I be happy, thinking of my daughter? What a fool I was. She was right in front of me all those years and I never saw it. Of course not. I didn't want to see it. The things he's *done* to her, Benny, oh! To our daughter." The woman emitted a sob that broke the General's heart.

"Dominia will make it right," said Benedict, but Cassandra wailed, "How? How can anything that's happened to Lavinia ever be put right?"

"Tonight is a night for earthly miracles." The magician rose to his feet. "Tonight is a night where anything is possible."

"If that were true—if all this about eternity were true—then where is my daughter now?" Lifting her head, briskly wiping her eyes to reveal their defiance, Cassandra demanded, "She should be here, if this is eternity."

"This is more a holding cell," Valentinian said. "For you immovable individuals with too little soul and too much grief keeping you from transcending someplace higher. Your daughter isn't here because she doesn't need to be."

At last! A spark caught the dampened tinder of her spirits. Cassandra stepped past Benedict, toward the magician. "Where is she?"

"You'll see her. But Dominia won't see any hint of you for quite a while—and this you, the you that remembers everything she does for the world, she won't see for a long, long time. So...you know."

Her hand a fist at her breast, Cassandra turned to see the stoic General, who tried with every fiber of her being to remain stoic. "You've done so much for me," Cassandra said, coming to hold Dominia's hands.

"I would do so much more for you, if I could. If I could change the past."

"You don't have to. Even though I hurt you so badly—even though I killed myself—you still looked for me. You traversed a whole planet just to find me again, and died, and came here. You spent an eternity in this place, just to remind me that I used to exist. That I used to be a person. That you used to love me."

"I still do love you," Dominia swore. "I will love you forever. I'll never love another beside you."

"But I wish you would." Color returning to her being degree by degree, Cassandra blinked her wet eyes and touched her wife's face. "I wish you would let yourself forget me. Then you might be able to be happy."

"There's no such thing as happiness without you," said the General, who bent to kiss those perfect satin lips, which pressed back; parted into a breath of air like Dominia's name; dissolved into atoms of light that embraced her, then filled her. In the space of a second, her senses were overwhelmed with the infinity of her wife's existence, of her kisses—of, not that sad death, but a long life joyful in the face of many sorrows. The warmth that filled the General was indescribable, as was the force that punched her chest as she was penetrated by this…what, if not soul? Spirit, she supposed. She could not fathom what it was in truth, in its highest form, this essence of Cassandra: nor could she imagine why it flew into her as if to settle there.

But, as the personas—those consciousness-less or consciousness-tainted egos—of Benedict, Akachi, Kahlil, and all those others began to dissolve into light and do the same, the General understood. This was how a soulless spirit might be bolstered for eternity, might be given a soul. She had more than enough consciousness to go around. Her lungs winced while her mind was barraged by more entities than she had known to exist. With each spirit came each one's reality. Before the feeling of one existence could pass, another burst through her like a gunshot, and another, and another: a great chain of people all plunging into her, and all of them, spirit after spirit, reminding her that there was one dead spirit outside of herself for whom she'd yet to pray. Barely enduring those glowing bolts, Dominia eased to her knees and spoke one last prayer for Lazarus.

"Do you think I need it?" asked the old man's spirit.

She laughed, moaned in pain, closed her eye against the cold tears of divine ecstasy. Before her, the True Protomartyr knelt. "Praying," he said with a chuckle. "Salvation. I just want to rest! The way I see it, I'm already saved. Same way you are."

"The protein?"

"'By you,' I was going to say—but the protein, too. Maybe you're right, though. Without the sacred protein, after all, you wouldn't be able to save anybody."

As that soul dissolved and entered her, she found that he was right. The true sacred protein was a greater hero than she was. An eternal connection to this place, to the divine. Was there any point in praying for a set of friendly cells? She thought of the E4, which had a name, a True Word—and dear Tenchi, who believed all things in the world possessed some form of spirit. So, as those effervescent spirits plunged into her, the General rationalized that she owed it to the protein to pray for it. Perhaps she might ask it for its help.

Perhaps it, too, had a true name that might reveal some avenue of assistance.

Her forehead against the cool un-ground as she submitted to the ceaseless flow of intrusions, she plunged into the depths of herself and prayed for that very same protein that had led her this far—prayed it might continue to lead her, and that it might spread itself beyond the reaches of its malformed cousin. That it might teach her to do the works of the Lord. That it might act to her as a friend and companion. That it might see her Father's regime collapsed into the dust from which it had been built.

And then, as the True Word for that which was known to men as the sacred protein bubbled to the surface of her opened mind, Dominia's memories of the past rose with it.

More than any, it brought the memories of the first function. The same as this iteration, or nearly. Without the organization of the Red Market, without the Hierophant, without the foreknowledge of her hateful Father. The Family: it had been Cicero and Elijah, Dominia and Cassandra, Lavinia and Theodore. And what a terrible, violent mess all of it had been! What an endless sea of sorrows worse even than this world. Then, as now, Dominia had died after seeing to the death of the Lamb. Then, as now, she had found herself praying endlessly for all those she wronged. But the prayers in that place had been different, the Catholic prayers, for then Valentinian did not exist in even the fictional sense. Again and again, she pled for the eternal rest of the damned and lost and lonely beings of purgatory; then, as now, she had prayed for the sacred protein, and determined once it revealed its True Word that it, too, had a soul.

Valentinian, the martyr saint of death and the incarnated form of the sacred protein, genuflected down before his mother at the instant she sat up. He asked, "Do you get it now?"

"You are the sacred protein. Its spirit."

"You didn't create me. But I was born of you, Dominia. Your Word." The surge of white energy blazed into her with such force that she was rendered speechless, and could not even comprehend the irony of discussing the Word at such a time. "You derived me from the sacred protein's bond to your soul. Gave me life here. And now you've given me flesh. Because you've given me flesh, I can help you trap your Father.

"Do you know how much information you can store in a hard drive while respecting the structural integrity of the universe? You don't have to answer that." He smiled doggishly into her eye, unseeing above her pain-opened mouth. "The answer is ten to the sixty-ninth power bits per square meter. The standard Earthling brain—martyr or human, for those keeping track at home—has one hundred trillion neurons, which is an incredible amount of storage space. The brain is the only storage device that must run a twenty-four-seven program simulating an entire world. Almost, anyway. Without sleep, we'd be in trouble! Have to dump that RAM somehow. Do you know how much your brain is doing for you during your waking hours? You look at an apple, and you don't see the real apple. Your eye is interpreting it, coloring it, flipping it right-side up, then you go, 'Oh, that's an apple.' Every day, you walk down the street, and you see a thousand apples: a thousand things, a million things, that your brain is perpetually constructing and interpreting, then selectively presenting faster than I can snap my fingers. Not just that, but all it remembers! All those once-glanced faces that come to you in dreams, or those fragments of chatter invented just for them. Every mind contains infinity, but the infinite contains every mind; and that which contains every mind *becomes* infinite, you understand."

She fancied her limbs dissolved, overwhelmed by the force of the souls plunging into her with their flowers, their straw hats, their fishing boats, their starry nights and beautiful mornings and all the things they once had and wished to have again. She felt it all; and what was "it"? The world, she supposed, swiftly passing the point of supposition. The General had been forced to her knees and needed to be held upright by the magician, whose arm she gripped with such a viselike hand she was surprised he did not wince.

"Every person you know, everything you've ever experienced—it's all part of the black hole, Dominia. It's all a part of you. If I am the soul of the first True Word, you are the soul of that vast, encompassing spirit: the Lady. You create new iterations of the universe, new models, to trap your Father there. Instead of moving into the afterlife or transmigrating to a higher state of being, the old wretch is so broken up about the death of his brother—and, now, so addicted to power—he'd rather flee to our simulations of the original universe and delude himself they're real, tangible iterations. Ever since your first death, I've helped you do this. Helped you physicalize it all for him, to give you another chance to end his life and set right what you've done.

"You asked me once what you were in the metaphor about movie theaters. I let you think you were the projectionist, but you're not. I am. You're the screen, kiddo. And we're about to run this film one final time."

The vibrations of her rib cage made her feel as if her very internal structure sought to drill through her flesh. "It hurts," she said. He embraced her, her friend, her son, her personal manifestation of the Holy Spirit within the sacred protein as projected through her genetic code. Still the spirits flowed. "Why me?"

"Because that first time you died you didn't do what everybody else does and start praying for yourself. You started praying for everybody else. You, that first time, realized the formula of consciousness plus ego equals a soul. You, that first time, invited them into you and became infinite in the process. You realize you could have moved on to the Kingdom by now and seen Cassandra? She's already there. It's eternity. But that idea never even crossed your mind. It was worth more to you to trap your Father and liberate all those spirits than it was for you to be happy. In the infinite probabilities of infinite people, it's infinitely easy to take the lazy way out. You refuse to allow that—maybe because I keep coming back and pushing you," he added, chuckling. "But that's one of the reasons you derived me. It doesn't have to hurt."

At last, the river of souls ceased. The impact of the final spirit was so thunderous that the disoriented General returned to her senses to find the magician disappeared. His voice from all around her—from within her—said, "Take off your eye patch."

After all she had endured for the sake of keeping it on, and all she had been warned of its removal, the moment arrived to a very reluctant Dominia; but neither could she stand the pressure, for her intuition cried that if she did not find some relief, even her powerful thoughtbody would be lost among the screaming masses within her. The weeping masses within her. All those souls of the world who wished, in the purest way of wishing, only that they could live again. It didn't matter whether they did it a little better, a little worse, or just the same as last time. And if she could make their dreams come true—if she could give them a chance at redemption—it was worth her own suffering through the same.

The General of the old world removed her eye patch and the Lady's eye opened. The hyper-density of the spirits within Her collapsed Her form, that old self bursting beneath the pressure of the knowledge contained: bursting, yet, reforming with the dark substance of the Ergosphere that very material world. An eye opened in Her that was not an eye at all—it saw beyond all information, all structure, all time. Above the howl of the geyser that streamed from Her un-eye's socket, the magician said, "I prefer to derive reality through a mathematical model, because it's so streamlined. But what I find works best for you is true sight."

The darkness of the Void that had returned on its emergence from Her skull now swirled back upon Her to crush Her body in a wave: as that darkness inhabited the very substance of Her flesh, She saw it for what it was. Ink, or phosphors untouched by electrons. But, more often, ink. She looked beyond this ink, into the shapes they formed around her, with her, beneath her, and read their words in a way that was not the absorption of new information but the remembering of old. Or, better than remembering, the revealing of what she had always known. Broken through, she read the Words upon the pages of her life and found she spoke them aloud, True Words forming reality from her invisible mouth in the Void while the vanished magician said, "Once you have words, you're going to need numbers. That's easy, because they're implied right in front of us. Anytime there's one, there's an infinity. Though frankly, you don't even need one—.999 repeating will do, since it equals 1, but we're lucky we don't need to concern ourselves with that. Since I already know I'm a given, we have to distinguish enough other numbers to fill a number system. And since we—or I, anyway—have ten fingers..."

In the vastness of space, the magician reappeared. "One," he counted. Then: "Two." A beam of light pierced the darkness, then another, then another. Nine he counted them, before the Lady repeated their names. From these lights emerged the souls of the Bearers, the first beings of the Kingdom, which, in turn, revealed the existence of the Kingdom. As the Lady's opened eye transmuted into the waters of that crystal pool, the magician drew through it those souls desperate for refuge from the bleak landscape of Ergosphere. Within that same desolate plane, that pool was envisioned not as a perfect mirror of water but as another world. That world spoken, eternally, by the voice of the Lady.

Now, She understood how long—and how infinitely short—Her journey was to be.

XV

Anno Domini 1974

Trisha Robbins was twenty years old when a then unknown cabal of prostitutes began seducing her from academia to fulfill her destiny. Of all seven avatars before the Lady herself manifested upon the Earth in that distant, fatal future, one could easily argue Trisha was the most significant—and most visible. Yet she was not affiliated with a spirituality, as had been Her previous embodiments. Nor was she of a distinct race or cultural affiliation, which was a trait particular to the people of her place and time. She was a modern woman living in the United States of America, a nation of immigrants founded upon the backs of genocidal religious separatists. Therefore, religion was in her DNA, but far be it from the geneticist-in-training to acknowledge such a thing! Not before she began to understand her role in the world.

Ironically, though she studied biochemistry and would, in another place and time, have been responsible alongside her husband for discovering what martyrs called "the sacred protein" ("Our only child," she would have joked at the sundry cocktail parties upon its discovery, before her worthless lab assistants stole a malformed variation and took it in secret by terrible mistake), Trisha had never been as interested in her genetic background as in her mental lineage. She venerated no more ancestors than she did deities. The spirits she praised were Newton, Darwin, and the wise words of then living sage, Dr. Carl Sagan. His book, *The Cosmic Connection*, had spoken to her from a bookstore's new-release section just the year before. This man wrote in a way that made her believe science fiction was possible. Imagine, terraforming a planet! Imagine, a race of people who never died, but might voyage out into the far reaches of outer space like an infinite collection of dandelion seeds! It was not an American that Trisha foremost considered herself; it was an Earthling first, a human second, and a scientist third.

Budding scientist, at least. In her Pomona College dorm room, she dreamed every night of a future that seemed as if it would never come—not with so many years of study between it and her. Her roommate majored in French in a way that mostly involved drinking at parties, missing her classes, and occasionally remembering to show up for exams, but Trisha worked so hard through her first year of study that it took a month into year two to realize a fellow was making eyes at her. That crossroads of time, October 1974: her roommate, while unwrapping a vinyl album sent to her by her mother, said, "So are you going to *do* anything about that guy?"

"What guy?" had been the redhead's oblivious response. Her boggling roommate lowered the cardboard sleeve, allowing a glance of the cover—the band Styx had released an album lazily titled *Styx II*, and Trisha had been blissfully unaware of its existence until her roommate started humming some song she'd heard playing in her home radio station in Chicago. Tish had a feeling she'd like it even less played twenty times a day from the poor students' turntable in the corner of their room. She had zoned out into thoughts of the device's cost when her roommate told her the name of the man she'd noticed admiring the pensive, analytical Robbins girl.

Oh—him. Yes, she did know him. A very fine-looking fellow, with dark hair and piercing blue eyes, who (nervously, she would realize on future pondering) inserted himself into her campus library study group. She hadn't realized it was because of her. Her roommate's annoyance on hearing this gave Trisha the sinking feeling that something would "be done" about it. Sure enough, a day later, the quiet young man asked her out to ice cream. Like it was the 1950s! So wholesome. And, well, he was too good-looking to pass by. Trisha was very good-looking, herself, but it was a confidence issue with her. She had never expected to have the pick of the litter, so she usually didn't; her focus was so plastered to her books that there was no time for something as frivolous as boys.

Almost.

They tend to say opposites attract, but this same cliché-prone "they" also tells us that birds of a feather flock together. With him, Trisha felt what she could only explain as, well—a cosmic connection. Sure, sure, they both had very similar dreams for their futures. Both came from similar socioeconomic backgrounds, both had similar political ideals in that period of sweet, post-Nixon relief. But nothing felt quite the way it did when she found his paperback copy of Sagan's 1973 book in the bedroom of his off-campus apartment. Then, she *knew* it was love. She'd never believed in love, or fate, but here were both, and neither would be denied. Of course, it made perfect sense she should meet another budding biochemist in college courses that led down that career route, but the similarity of their dreams—to heal the sick, to perpetuate the human race through the stars, to believe beyond all doubt that death was defeatable—before the presence of that book felt, for lack of a better description, like a sign.

They talked for hours. Only talked, the way people did in movies. Then, like a gentleman, he offered to walk her back to her dorm in the still-warm darkness of the Claremont night.

Claremont. What could be said of the place where she spent so little time? It was *safe*. She had never felt threatened there—not once—so it was a great shock when, from the darkness of a storefront along their meandering route, two figures stepped into the sidewalk on their passing. Trisha's body tensed, although she told herself she was a fool; but, before she dispelled her fear by turning to ask the shadows if they wanted to pass, her would-be lover made the mistake for her. He had enough time to utter a cry before the blackjack fell upon his head and his body crumpled from Trisha's arm. A scream began to peel past her lips as she turned to see the assailants for herself, but she was so shocked when she found them to be a pair of stylish women in military coats that the noise tapered off like the expiration of a leaking balloon.

"He'll be fine," said the woman with the afro. Her Latina sister whisked a few strands of hair from her tanned face, then stooped to drag Tish's boyfriend into the building from which they'd come. While Trisha, senses somewhat regained after the start, began again to cry out, the black woman sucked a tooth and closed the distance between herself and the redhead.

"Please quit it with that racket or we'll have to do the same to you, Miss Robbins. Then you won't feel there was any choice in the matter."

Confusion after confusion! It felt as though confusion were the wave, panic the medium, and Trisha the shore upon which it all broke. "How do you know my name?"

"We were told to watch you, and to be ready for the moment to move. The time is now; we are changing history tonight."

"'We'? Changing—what *is* this? What are you doing with J—"

"If you go back to your dorm room in the next fifteen minutes, you will die. You and your boyfriend, both. This is his only opportunity to do it. When he misses, it's over for him. To rise to power, he has to get started yesterday—metaphorically, I mean—and that means he can't afford to botch it up by killing you late in the game. He shows up in 1974 and tries to kill you sometime in the course of that year. Tonight's the night this time. It's now or never."

What did these words even *mean*? "He," who? What sort of stranger just walked up to somebody on the street, incapacitated a man, and started *saying* things like this? While a limousine whipped around the corner, the dark woman turned to greet the reemerging comrade, who dusted her hands to indicate she'd relieved herself of their burden. Trisha managed to grasp hold of her thoughts enough to ask, "Who? Who wants to do this to me?"

"A man not yet called the Hierophant," answered the black woman. As the limo slid to a halt and fluttered open the women's military coats to reveal the shimmer of bright fabric beneath, she popped open its back door. "Will you come with us?"

Trisha, with an anxious glance over her shoulder for the building where her suitor had been dragged, wrapped her arms around herself. "What about him?"

"He's being taken care of. In a few hours, we'll drop him off down the street from his apartment. Make it all look like a mugging."

"What am I supposed to say to him?"

"Please." The dark woman pulled the door wider while her compatriot stooped to get in. "Just a ride around the town. Half an hour. Let us show you something."

"What?"

"The truth."

Her skin crawled. She'd rather have been anywhere other than there. To do anything other than get in! But she sensed there was no alternative. With a reluctant step toward the car, she asked, "Will you at least tell me your name?"

For the first time that night, the black woman smiled. "I'm Gethsemane."

Tish had seen vehicles like this in movies, but even so, it was hard to believe the little minibar rattling behind the three other women already in the car. Hard to believe the shag carpet, the smell of pot, the disco ball, the specialty cocaine mirrors lying out on a couple of knees, anything—anything about it. Especially not the women themselves, who seemed an arrangement of not so much models from a runway in Milan as tropical birds from a mysterious jungle moon light-years away. Absolutely stunning and…not particularly shy in their choice of wardrobe, to put it politely. While Trisha cleared her throat against improper thoughts, Gethsemane and her friend removed their coats to reveal equally elaborate (and slightly less suggestive) dresses beneath. The black-and-white sequins of Gethsemane's illuminated the cabin as though it were a light of its own.

"What *is* this?" asked Trisha of the three new women. They looked between themselves, then studied her.

"It's a conspiracy," suggested the one with hair so pale blonde it was nearly white.

"Like a cult," said the third, whose curly black hair, arranged in an immaculate bun, received the occasional pat from a fussing, jewel-covered hand.

"No," said the woman in the middle, a Native with her long hair in simple, elegant plaits, "it's just some criminal organization of—"

"Hookers."

"Whores."

The one in the middle looked annoyed at her sisters. "—Prostitutes."

"Independent working girls," clarified Gethsemane patiently. "On our way to a convention, of sorts. You are not invited."

"I wouldn't want to be," insisted blushing Trisha, hands upon her chest, while a few of the other women smiled. Gethsemane, their apparent spokeswoman, went on.

"Not tonight. But another night, perhaps. Our sisters are all correct; the women in the service of the Lady are all of those things. A cabal, a cult, and a conspiracy. But the truth is the *real* conspiracy, sister, you dig? It embodies everything around us. It is the oxygen we breathe and the food we eat, and is in itself embodied by those things. The Lady is nothing more than the sentient embodiment of the truth, and She has appeared throughout time in an infinite number of ways."

"'The Lady'?"

"She is that which the Hierophant wishes to suppress and kill. She has been hidden since the dawn of time, asleep within all of us: man, woman, and child. But only some can contact Her, and fewer still dare Host her. She lives upon the Earth in the form of an earthly woman and guides us from the shadows. Not all women who worship the Lady are ladies of the evening as we are; and not all women who worship the Lady worship Her in Her highest form; and not all women who worship the Lady in any of Her many forms believe that the avatar is the Lady; but I have seen that She is the Lady, and know it, and urge you to believe it. We, all of us, are Her keepers; Her Bearers."

It was all so very laughable. She might have, nearly, were it not for the circumstances at hand. "You gave my date a concussion and told me somebody plans to kill me so you could try to recruit me for your cult?"

"No," said Gethsemane. "We did those things to save you, so you will be our next Lady."

When silent, the vehicle was a whole new car. While Trisha's brain churned into fifth gear, she asked, "Excuse me?"

"We believe there are certain requirements to be the next avatar of a Lady at a given period," said the Latina woman. "You fit the requirements of the era, but you are an unusual case because you were not chosen by the Lady or Her followers. You were chosen by the Hierophant. Because he wants to kill you, we wish to save you. And what will happen tonight—"

"What *will* happen tonight?"

At Trisha's pressure, the five women exchanged a web of glances.

"Tonight," said Gethsemane, "when you return to your dorm room, you will have proof that what we say is true."

Her stomach sank into a foul pit of quicksand. "My roommate," Trisha said. Gethsemane placed a hand upon hers.

"I urge you not to think of her now. The Lady—"

"This is ridiculous," snapped the student, emotions exploding with every furious word that peeled through her lips. "I believe in science. I was never even a *Christian* growing up! I've never believed in anything I can't see, and now you're trying to tell me to believe in this? This is *crazy*. You're all crazy, let me out of this—this crazy car!"

It was the only adjective with which she could articulate her thoughts. It *was* crazy. It was one thing to have cultists try to recruit you. This was the seventies, the heyday of cults and inexplicable murder. The practice of hitch-hiking had disappeared that year, along with a bunch of girls up in the state of Washington. America's cultural landscape was such a fucked-up death trap most places that it was better to avoid all eye contact and hope the scrub you passed at night wasn't the next Charles Manson. But this was *Claremont*. And these women weren't recruiting her to join their cult; they were recruiting her to be its leader. To make it stranger, these weren't cult members of the weird, gross kind you read about in the news—neither did they fit the pervaded cultural image of prostitutes. The Latina woman all but confirmed that when she said, "I used to feel the way you do. I'm a trained anthropologist, and when I was young, I believed in only what I could see in physical human history. But then, I saw the pattern in many cultural artifacts and mythologies across the world, and saw who I was inside. Then the Lady showed me the way to Her, and to the truth."

"What is the truth," pressed Trisha. The women smiled as the limo pulled to a stop.

"Like I said." While the door opened from the outside, Gethsemane pressed against Trisha so all those women could pile out into the populated night. The open door allowed their chatter to mix with the clamorous sound of tens or hundreds of other women making their excited way into the grand hotel and its surely packed ballroom. "Tonight, you're not invited. You're not ready, sister."

"Then what in God's name makes you think I should be your next Lady?"

"You don't believe in God, yet you protest in His name; you see what power society has given men? Even language is a tool of subjugation in this world." The door shut and left them, now just Trisha and Gethsemane. The car once more began to move. "Language was once made to elevate mankind, men and women both. It is said by our faith that a woman was pivotal in forming the first spoken words more intricate than simple sounds, and that the Lady first came to this woman, in whom She longest dwelt, and through whom She first revealed assurances of the spirit and eternity.

"But language since then has been perverted. Rather than revealing the truth, it veils. We speak the truth in every word we say and every gesture we make. We see it everywhere, in such a proliferation of symbols that we could never begin to collect, experience, or understand them all in a single human lifetime. But you will, because you are the Lady. You thirst for knowledge, for the solutions to life and death. You will have them."

Trisha was still concerned about feeling like a hostage, though the car was gentler (at least quieter) when absent the other women. "I'm not trying to be rude, but I just feel like, if your organization has been watching me, then you should know—"

"That you're going to be a hard sell? Oh, yes." Gethsemane smiled. "We know. But we also know that you will come around."

"And how do you know that?"

"Because, it is written."

"Okay." Trisha laughed, glancing out the window. Sweet relief! They'd turned around the block to reorient themselves toward campus. "And that's supposed to convince—"

Glass shattered across the cabin of the flipping limo, which, with an explosive metal cry, rolled, then skidded out of its lane amid the honking of cars and the sound of someone else's scream. At the crash of the stretch vehicle into the corner of the nearby building, all noise was obliterated. That would be what Trisha gathered later, from the news. At the moment it happened to her, the crash was but a crescendo of animal terror: Wondering, hoping, begging, please, not tonight. Not here. Not like this.

She'd hit her head on something. What, it wasn't clear; nor was it clear for how many seconds she'd lost consciousness. It must not have been long—Gethsemane had just begun to push herself up from where she'd collapsed within the upended vehicle when a foreign hand, huge by the standards of any person of the day, slithered in to pluck the Bearer by the neck as though she were a kitten. Out of the limo, that splendid woman was pulled screaming, and there that beautiful embodiment of Gethsemane met her end amid the torrid snaps of bones. Trisha was too tired and too blank with shock to react. She lifted her head an inch and let it fall again.

A face peered into the vehicle: a man's face, so pale and androgynous from that angle that it seemed to bleed into the face of a woman. A Lady, who stood before Tish in a strange, dark place that had no sound yet was sound, itself. The eye could not take the Lady in, stunning as She was. Sometimes it seemed to Trisha that She had four arms, sometimes three eyes, sometimes a halo or a crown shaped like the moon, or a warrior's helmet, or a wingéd sun that blazed in glory a few inches above Her head. Those uncountable eyes glowed like the light from Her mouth, which spoke words Trisha knew at once to be beyond anything terrestrial.

You will bring the truth into the world to lay the path for me, She announced to Trisha. *And when this has been accomplished, I will leave my present body to take on yours—and you will live forever.*

"I must be dreaming," insisted the stubborn student, who in this place did not wear glasses, and did not realize it until she reached up to adjust them. Laughing sharply, she looked down at herself and found herself buxom in a way she had always been but now for the first time experienced. She had never felt confidence before, but here, her lovely nature was a simple fact and exuded from her being as glory from the Lady's. *"I don't believe in ghosts, or a god or the devil, or witches, or magic. I don't believe in you."*

My existence does not hinge on your belief, human, or your lack thereof. You will believe soon. Awaken now. Return to your room. You will be protected.

"Why is all this happening?"

The world where all this did not happen proved this one's genesis. Therefore, all this must occur infinitely to create a world where it does not happen, where it cannot be caused. We all must sacrifice ourselves to protect all other universes from our reality.

"I don't understand."

You are a woman of science, and yet you do not understand the oscillations of the universe, or the implications of relativity, or the secrets hidden within the human's genetic code. I do not fault you; no woman or man of science will fully understand the latter for a very long time. But the secret of a repetitive universe—the secret of my existence—has been encoded in the products of the human mind since that first day's dawn. Every story ever written contains My same substance. You will see, but not with your eyes.

"How?"

The Lady did not speak. She only turned and, with a wave of her arm, revealed to Trisha that which six other avatars had seen before her, and in as many guises; but she saw it not as a palm tree, or a beehive, or a column, or a ladder, or a twisting serpent, or a spiral staircase. She saw the double helix chemical rungs of a towering strand of DNA, which coiled into the infinity of space and tugged at Trisha's very bones.

"What is *this?"*

This, said the gently smiling Lady, *is that thin wall through which God speaks to mankind.*

A series of gunshots interrupted the Communion with the Lady so suddenly that, though the conversation may have continued in eternity, Trisha snapped back to her body. The androgynous face from the window was nowhere to be seen. As women called out and someone uttered a distant cry, footsteps clattered down the street, and a siren yet many blocks away began its mournful howl. The twisted door was forced open after a few seconds of grinding and struggle. Trisha covered her face with her forearm as a few more glass shards twinkled down like falling stars. "He's gone," said the woman, whose face resolved into that of the anthropologist. Trisha struggled to maintain even this level of focus. "Come on; we need to get you out of here before the cops show up."

"But Gethsemane," she began. The woman looked pained and reached into the vehicle.

"Please, not now. We need to go."

The accident must have happened on the other side of the block from the hotel. Surely, he knew about the meeting. Knew where to come after he found Trisha's roommate alone in the dorm room. That was what Trisha would eventually decide, anyway, when she realized there was credence to all these strange tales. For now, as she was helped out of the crumpled limo, the twisted neck of morbidly still Gethsemane was sufficient evidence that life could never be the same. Not after tonight. While Tish held back tears, another smaller car squealed up to the scene. The Native woman didn't wait for the doors to shut after her passengers before she peeled off. Shaken in every sense of the word, Trisha tried to hold on to the pure feeling the vision had left within her breast. Tried not to lose it amid all the horrors of reality. "That crash—"

"That was the Hierophant. He is not of this world—this iteration of the world. Were it not for him, the Lady would not exist, and the man with whom you spent tonight would be the husband with whom you discovered a reality-altering pair of substances. But you would also be responsible for many terrible things."

"How do you know all of this?"

"The Lady has made it very clear. We are on the cusp of a silent war. In truth, we have fought this war for many years already, and laid much groundwork for it. The truth is all around you, Trisha. You will start to see it when you look closely."

"What about Gethsemane? My roommate?"

"Life is temporary in this flawed place," said the Native woman. "In truth, it is eternal."

"So you're saying you don't care that people are dying tonight?"

"People die every night, everywhere. We are sorrier to lose Gethsemane now than you could ever know; but someday, we will see her again, and later still, she will be born again, here again, in this iteration of the world. This is the way with Bearers."

Trisha was in such a daze she hardly realized it when they pulled in front of her dorm. From her clutch purse, the anthropologist withdrew a business card. "There is a library here. A very small one. There you will find many books on these subjects. Please study. When you are ready, and you understand what you must undertake, we will be here for you."

"Where will I find you?"

"You will know when you are ready," said the woman again.

Trisha glanced anxiously in the direction of the dorm.

"You will be safe," said the plaited woman. "We will watch over you in the coming months to ensure your safety while you embark on your true studies, and while you come to us. As it has been said—if he does not get you tonight, then you will never die."

The cloud of horror that had settled across the dorm building was evident from the moment she stepped foot within. Her body, already burned out from adrenaline, yet endured another pulse of the stuff. She doubled the pace of her steps to reach the third floor when she found people murmuring in hallways, doorways, common rooms, and every corner of the building like a cluster of terrified cockroaches. Worst, all regarded her in a way that stopped their conversation and hastened her steps. She knew what she would find, but she would never believe it until she arrived at the peak of proof she would receive about the reality of the night. She jogged through the hall of that destination floor while crying her roommate's name. The crowd of attendants, police, campus security, and nurses all tried to keep her out. They failed.

The matchbox-size studio was thick with the scent of death, which seemed impossible to her, as the death had only just occurred. Perhaps it was the smell of organ meat? She couldn't think when every thought in that awful scene was had to the beat of a skipping record: that very same her roommate's mother had sent just a few days before. "Lady—" cried the record, an uncanny chant while Trisha wept over the bloodied body of her dead surrogate. "Lady— Lady— Lady— Lady—"

Her roommate's mother gave her that record while tearfully sweeping off with the final box of her daughter's things. Seeing Trisha's wary eyes lingering on the album, the older woman said, "She would have wanted you to have it," thinking in the good-natured way of a grieving parent that her little girl might live on in her friend. She did not know the significance of the album, whose particular skipping song was overlooked as evidence by the police in favor of the fact that it *was* skipping, mere effect of the obvious struggle.

Only Trisha understood it was a message to her—only Trisha *could* understand. And even though she understood, she felt mad in thinking it. Yet such a coincidence was beyond mere happenstance. Her roommate's killer had selected the point in the song down to the very second.

She was almost glad he had. The objective taunt bolstered her resolve that the events of that night had happened. Otherwise she would have been adrift in a sea of questions. Not that knowing was better! Such tangible confirmation of the Lady's presence haunted the student. Trisha was expected to ease back into classes with the help of a great deal of counseling and the sorry reassurance that her dorm was watched (and she was sure that it was, by agents a great deal more competent than campus cops).

But night after night, she lay awake analyzing the contents of that vision. That woman (Was it right to call such an entity a mere woman? Of course. Trisha was a scientist, not a cultist.) and that great spiral of DNA, and the place—and the *feeling* of that place! She could not understand it, nor could she understand why she so longed to experience it again. Why she had felt so whole in those seconds of interaction with something in which she did not fully believe.

It was a few weeks before she went to the metaphysical library. Mostly, she was embarrassed to be seen someplace so goofy. At the time, she remained naively firm in her skepticism and could not see it had become her personal brand of fundamentalist thought. A true scientist understood critical thinking did not involve the automatic rejection of a challenging belief; and Trisha was, at that time, only a scientist-in-training. Some training, anyway. She had become so preoccupied by the nightly memories of her vision that she'd started missing classes. It was around that time, just before winter break, that she decided to take the plunge and visit the weird strip mall "library."

The first day she was there, the librarian behind that counter—though a stranger to her—seemed to recognize her. Instead of paranoia, Trisha felt a relief that came from so deep within her she could not be sure it was from her own nervous system. The books populating shelves in that rented storefront were not of the sort Trisha usually read, and she turned up her nose at titles by figures such as Aleister Crowley to such an extent that she began to edge her way back to the library's entrance. How was she to leave without offending the librarian, who tried not to stare at her only visitor? But it was then Trisha noticed it again: *The Cosmic Connection*, sitting on a display labeled "Staff Picks." Beneath this book sat four others: *Synchronicity*, by psychiatrist Carl Jung, another book published just the year before; Robert Anton Wilson's (again, brand-new) book on goddess worship, *The Book of the Breast*; the cumbersomely titled but intriguing work of a Dr. John C Lilly, *Programming and Metaprogramming in the Human Biocomputer*; and—much to her displeasure, for she had already resolved to check out all the books on that display before she laid eyes on it—Aleister's *Book 4*. His guidebook on magic with a *k*. Screw it. As she collected the books, she told herself that she did not enjoy every book her university professors crammed into their curriculums, either.

When she dropped the tomes on the front counter and asked, "How much to join the library? It's private, right," the librarian perked.

"For one week only, it happens to be free. You picked a lucky day to come in!"

The penniless student strongly suspected luck had nothing to do with it, and the contents of those four books would confirm it—not just their printed contents, but their actual, physical contents. The great irony of it all was she would, in some months, come to hold Crowley in high regard; the entity that he called the Scarlet Woman would then seem the Lady to her in all but name. But at the end of 1974, with those first four books fresh in her dorm, what should slide out of the Lilly volume? Not a proper bookmark, or the usual haphazard replacements for one such as the standard receipt or old grocery list or expired movie ticket. Nothing usual by any means when the baggie containing six cartoon-printed tabs of LSD dropped into her lap. Extremely considerate on the part of the last reader (or that librarian), since Mr. Lilly's techniques utilized the chemical. Such a thing could have been dangerous, but Trisha was (almost) a scientist. Though she had not so much as smoked a cigarette, she felt, in the wake of her vision, that she already had experience in the neighborhood of psychedelics.

Alone, she took two tabs of the acid; two weeks later, she ceased her classes in favor of more important studies. Four years later, while intermittently working a few menial part-time office jobs, Tish volunteered a handful of hours at a battered women's shelter—a new inspiration that had come to her the morning after a later acid trip. All the workers, she sensed, knew the Lady. They put on a very good act of pretending they didn't know her when she first started coming by; but there was a deliberateness about all the things they said and did that Trisha's senses declared to be somehow false. The shelter, like her new apartment, was in Claremont, but whether out of his embarrassment, her shift of interests, or the manipulations of the Lady, she never bumped into her would-be suitor after the event he surely remembered as a mugging. Just as well; he would have monopolized her valuable time, which she increasingly sensed to be short.

Then, one day, she saw him on the news. The Hierophant. Not being interviewed, featured, or anything like that. A blink-and-miss-it glimpse of his familiar face looming in the background of joyous Catholics celebrating the election of Pope John Paul II. Just there, smiling, filling some space in the news broadcast's B-roll. Maybe wondering if Trisha saw him.

The next day, she began to write a book that would be published in secret by a company suggested by that librarian, who had become Trisha's best friend since the tragedy of 1974. Every month, Tish came in to return her books, and lo! There would be a new display, with new, auspicious texts to elicit in her frontal lobe a kind of urgent itch. Any guilt for abandoning her academic path was tempered by the notion that she had replaced it with another—one more in need of an objective, scientific mind than any discipline she had seen.

At the same time, she began to understand why so many occult books descended into rambling, or why its practitioners seemed crazed fools. It was impossible to describe the experience in a linear way. It was impossible to recognize what the anthropologist had called "the pattern," this great chain of symbolic similarities spread across culture, medium, and intention (or lack thereof). Cultures that had never known one another bore profound similarities. Historical figures superficially unrelated became linked in subtle ways that often related to magical practices or drug use. She at last understood what Christianity was secretly speaking about, and recognized it was identical to the thing everybody else spoke about. Her reflexive anti-religious stance began to relax. Trisha at last saw spirituality for what it was: a model. A model for reality, like a mathematical model, or any other.

Finally, five years to the evening of the incident, she returned to the hotel on the off chance that the worshipers of the Lady communed again that night. Behind the counter, why— who should be there but that little librarian. Five years of chatting, and Trisha had never realized she had a night job. As she had the first time they met, the girl perked, and Tish could only think to ask, "I'm inquiring about the convention."

"Yes, Miss Robbins. An invitation for this Saturday's event has been left for you." Smiling, the librarian-slash-concierge placed a red envelope upon the counter between them. "I was told to say they look forward to seeing you."

"'They'?"

"The convention members, of course."

"And what is the name of the convention?"

"Our hotel's administrative staff is not permitted to divulge such information," said the chipper young woman. "They look forward to seeing you there."

Was the hotel in on it, too? They must have been. Who *wasn't* in on it? The day came and she glitzed herself up as much as possible while still maintaining modesty, more anxious every second. Suppose it did just turn out to be a bunch of prostitutes? Some weird trap? Human trafficking? Yet as she parked her car down the street and trotted up to the growing influx in her awkward heels, a few women turned to greet her. In that instant they recognized her, and she, also, recognized them: the Bearers, they had called themselves. The Native woman, who this year sported the most elaborate of all her sisters' updos, extended her hand.

"Well," said that woman, whose name was unknown, but who could not be called a stranger. "Are you coming?"

XVI

Enthousiasmos

If somebody told young Miki Soto that, as an adult, she (or her body) would lead a battle that would end the world as man and martyr knew it—well, suffice to say she'd have been pretty dubious. She had never believed she would be in a battle, period! Tell her to march, and she'd have laughed in your face between bites of a burger that never seemed to affect her delicate weight. Secretly, she worked hard to keep off the excess pounds. Her mother had always told her if she made exercise part of her routine, she would never have to think of it; and that had been a necessary advisement, since she'd been a pretty chubby kid! But, then, she'd also been a very depressed kid, and food had been her most comforting and nonjudgmental friend. A sandwich neither recognized nor cared what gender she was, so a sandwich didn't obliviously remind her, sentence after sentence, reference after reference, conversation after conversation, for the first seven years of life, that the whole world—even her own mother—thought she was a boy.

Oh, she never *blamed* them. It was a natural, though flawed, assumption to think that something with a penis wanted to have that penis, or felt like that penis belonged to it. But Miki had hated, hated, hated the thing from the instant she was conscious of the difference. Potty training, a time of trauma for all children, had been a horrible revelation for her; and as her interest in dolls or her mother's elaborate wardrobe was spurned as "weird" and "effeminate," she could not but feel a constant sting of pain, which turned into bitterness against God, which was easy to transmute into self-loathing. Maybe this was because she felt her mother would have loved her from the start if only she'd been born into the right body. Then Miki wouldn't have had to deal with seven years of displaced misandry and deep resentment for which Yoriko would spend the rest of her daughter's life repenting once the truth was fully communicated.

To Yoriko's credit, Miki had given up trying to communicate her gender around the age of five, so for the two years in which the child most grappled the issue, there was nothing Yoriko *could* have done. But the ultra-popular geisha—who spent vast amounts of time busy in e-zine hologram shoots and meetings to approve overpriced galactomyces-based beauty serums for her growing brand—might have had a chance to correct the problem had she picked up on the five years of clues exhibited by an increasingly emotional child. She had reacted to Miki's mischief involving her clothing with fury for a boy who had no respect for his mother's things, rather than with the relative impatience she would have shown a girl who only wanted to imagine she would someday be as beautiful as her very splendid mother.

But no matter how cruel and blind that mother was, Miki did not blame her; Miki blamed the divine, and herself. Only the cruelest of deities would put her into this body, this wrong body, so that the whole world would mock her without even knowing it. She decided perhaps she had done something wrong in a past life to merit such an existence—a tragic thing for a child to think, but natural given her culture's teachings about reincarnation. She wept every night for how hard an otherwise easy existence became when one was told every day they were someone they weren't. Amid her weeping, she sought an explanation. There had to be some reason, damn it. She couldn't accept that the universe was so unjust as to do this to her for no reason—to take from her the thing she felt would make her existence the smooth ride she deserved.

It would take Miki many years to understand that the life of a woman was hard. As a child in the wrong body, biological females seemed to have it so easy. The issues were all so simple then. If they wanted to look pretty, no one would stop them; if they played with dolls, that was fine; if they lived in the culture Miki did and fantasized about being a beautiful, famous geisha like Yoriko, people thought it fairly normal (though not necessarily ideal). Of course, there was something deeper to Miki's envy of biological females; something that she could not articulate at such a young age. They were allowed to be themselves. That was all she saw of women, and it slayed her with jealousy. She did not understand then that the life of a woman was still, even in 4012 CE, rife with danger. Issues like rape and sexism were not time-specific problems, or even human problems; they were *mortal* problems. They were problems with existence, and would always be there so long as conscious beings had free will enough to make the wrong choices.

When Miki was seven, Yoriko was raped by a client. The geisha decided to retire from her career to focus on her skin-care line, whose profits she now partially dedicated to a foundation responsible for investigations that Kyoto police did not prioritize. That was to say, sex crimes against sex workers.

Yoriko did not approve of the "lifestyle" of women who sold their bodies, she explained to Miki once, long after she had learned her daughter's identity. The geisha thought the higher ideal was to make oneself into an untouchable piece of art, like a painting behind glass. The rape, therefore, had not just been a repugnant invasion of the temple of her body. In Yoriko's mind, the rape was some strange slight to her vanity—and Miki could tell you that vanity was Yoriko's foremost trait. The assault "reduced" her to the level of "mere" sex worker, which was perhaps why the old bat began to deal more compassionately with them. It was certainly why her anger problems exploded.

Miki did not understand all that at the time, of course. She only understood her mother was home much more often, sleeping much more often, and angrier than ever when she was awake. A bad grade or a missed chore (keeping in mind Miki was barely seven years old) could now elicit a slap once reserved for back-talking or outlandish displays of disobedience. Those few activities they enjoyed together disappeared. Very benign things, like visiting Kyoto's elaborate rooftop gardens, or taking the train to Osaka's amusement park, or going up to Hokkaido for some fresh crab (oh! Natural flesh from the sea was better than anything fake modeled off land mammals)—no more. Miki was more alone than ever in their big, empty, Western-style house, and struggling with more self-loathing, too. Day on day, she told herself none of this would be happening if she had only been born in the right body. Then, her mother would be warm—friendly to her the way she was to women, not cold and businesslike the way she was with every non-client man Miki had ever observed. Clients got the warm treatment from Yoriko until her retirement—but even while she worked, she would come home at night, swipe off her makeup, and complain to her child, "Men! They're all such bullying, tedious wastes of space. Thank goodness for artificial insemination! Don't you ever grow up to be like that, Minoru-kun. Listen to a woman now and then, instead of yammering all the time. Ugh! I thought if I had to listen to him for another minute I was going to vomit all over the tatami. Finally I fed him so much sake he fell asleep, the idiot. His wife will have to come drag him home…her problem now!"

These things would have been cruel to say to a child who was really a boy; but to say it to a child who was secretly a girl was the height of spitefulness. Every night, Miki learned with increasing clarity that her mother could never, ever love her for as long as the child was called "Minoru." At least, this was what Miki convinced herself—and it was not far from the truth, but it was still a mistake on the child's part to allow these negative feelings, seven months after Yoriko's retirement, to drive a suicide attempt.

Of course: Was it a total mistake? Without that night of despair, elicited by a slight so small in the grand scheme of life that Miki couldn't even recall it as an adult, she might never have had her vision of the Lady. She might never have gone on to become Her avatar. One second, the girl was hanging from the handle of her closet door, and the next minute she fell through her floor, slipping between Plancks into another space. Into a Lady's arms.

Oh, Miki, said that glowing kami upon whom the child trembled to look, and upon whose face was written a compassion surmounting that of any living being. *I didn't know.*

Miki? How strange. If she was startled to hear herself addressed by a name she had never heard, she was all the more startled to find she *knew* the name was her real one. It was in her surprise that Miki looked down at her body and hiccupped into tears. She was not a child at all, and certainly not trapped in the body of a chubby boy. She was a beautiful woman, dressed in a kimono more elaborate than even those in which designers begged to dress her mother. As her watering eyes disrupted the vision of the herons upon the gossamer fabric, she cried, *"I'm a woman!"*

Of course you are. This is your real body. The kami released Miki, for it knew she wished to hold herself. *The body you will have in the future.*

"The future...my future." Lifting a sleeve to hide her tears, the girl said, *"But I don't have a future. I can't live like this, hidden away. I can't live with her. I'd rather die!"*

You are a butterfly, Miki, as is every caterpillar. Time has yet to unveil it, and you have many more years before you will make your cocoon. But caterpillars can be very beautiful; they can be themselves.

"I can't," she lamented. *"My mother hates me."*

She doesn't understand, and is an unfair woman. Would she but loved you no matter who you were! But she does not see that she abuses that which she most treasures. It is the caterpillar's mother, sweet Nature, who grants her beautiful colors before she even has wings. Show your mother that you will someday be a butterfly, and she will color you. At the girl's fearful silence, the entity urged, *She will understand if you tell her in the moment she finds you.*

"Who are you?"

You don't know me yet. Someday...but that is not me. It is a version of me. I am more than that, now; and I never will be that again.

"Then, what are you now?*"*

The kami did not speak. It merely wiped a tear from Miki's cheek, then cast that tear into the black abyss around them. There, the droplet expanded into a form that Miki would never find concrete words to describe. A tesseract, perhaps, or the E8 lattice—both were the close concepts upon which she would someday come, but even these did not describe the visual experience of the object. This lotus of intense beauty that possessed an infinity of shimmering, shifting petals, each containing an infinity of its own. To look upon it, Miki felt the weight of all of time, and could feel for an instant her own future understanding of this, this experience, which at that time was simply alarming and hypnotic. Someday she would understand that this object was the same that Trisha perceived in the form of the DNA double helix; but she would still not fully, personally, manage to articulate what it was, even when living in the Kingdom with Kahlil.

Nonetheless, looking upon it in that place, she could sense her life was but a pinpoint in the timeline of existence. Smaller than a pinpoint—smaller still. She sensed that the length of time between herself and her true body was not so great as it felt to a mind that had lived not quite eight years. Indeed, Miki was practically nothing at all. But it was inarguable that she was something, for there, in a facet within a facet within a facet, behold!

The worried face of her mother, shaking her awake.

There were many other things she saw, too, in little half-had glimpses: another life as a maid, the motion of hands and a clatter like keys; but all these she forgot as the face of her mother gained in clarity. The many lotus petals of that multidimensional fractal folded the rest of the universes away and left her with the one called, to her, "reality."

"Minoru! Minoru!" She had never seen her mother cry. In that moment when she became conscious of Yoriko's warm arms and the splashes of her tears, the girl felt *this* was the true miracle vision. Forget the tesseract! She was so dazed she nearly forgot the Lady's words, until hers bubbled up of their own accord.

"Will you call me 'Miki'?"

Her mother, half laughing for a brief second of relief through her tears, managed, "What?"

"It's just—if I have to be a boy here, can't I have a name that's more like a girl's?"

"Oh!" The motions of Yoriko's hand, which had been mechanically rubbing away the impression of the belt in her child's tiny neck, froze in a comprehension that was also quite possibly the grown woman's very first experience of shame. "Oh," she said again, new tears springing up in those beautiful eyes, "*oh*, I didn't know!"

While her weeping mother clutched her (weeping, surely, out of joy as much as embarrassment to have missed every one of a thousand signs), Miki also heard the lamentation of the kami. It had come in the same tone, with the same depth of sorrow. The words had even sounded Japanese, in a way, but she knew they weren't. They hadn't even been the English her mother insisted they speak around the house. She sensed they weren't a human language. At some point, she tuned back in on her mother, who had been repeating variations of, "Forgive me! I've been an idiot—a total idiot! When you were littler and would argue that you were a girl, I thought—I thought you were just too young to understand. I didn't realize you were really…forgive me, oh, forgive me!"

Miki had just been saved from suicide *and* had come out as transgender—and here she was, patting her mother! Comforting *Yoriko* through *her* tears! The life of a narcissist's child: small wonder she should someday get on quite famously with the infamous eldest (living) daughter of the Hierophant. But, narcissist or no, Yoriko was the best possible parent for Miki, especially from that point on—though her maternal value may have peaked in those moments after her apologizing, when, collecting herself with a birdlike laugh, the former geisha sat up and daubed away her tears with the edge of a designer handkerchief.

"'Miki' is a very pretty name. Have you wanted me to call you that for long?"

Miki shook her head. "I've always wanted you to see who I really am…" She frowned, and could not think of a cautious way to say it. "The name…a kami told me that name, before I woke back up with you."

"Kami *desu*," repeated the woman in wonder. "You visited Yomi but didn't eat the food there. You're a smart girl." Being called a girl by Yoriko in such a casual way was so flabbergasting—so validating!—that a sheen of tears brightened Miki's bloodshot eyes and made it hard to focus on her mother's questions. "What was the kami you saw?"

"A beautiful woman. She—" The thought of having had and lost that marvelous body drove Miki out of her post-death daze and into a profusion of childish weeping. "She showed me my body. The body I'll have someday. I'll be so beautiful, like you."

"What woman," pressed her mother. "Izanami?"

"Maybe," agreed the girl, before her intuition gave an unpleasant twist, and she decisively shook her head. "No. Or maybe, this goddess and Izanami are sometimes the same, but she wasn't Izanami now. She couldn't have been, because I wasn't afraid. Even if I met Izanami at her most pure and beautiful, I think I'd be very afraid. This Lady, she was so perfect—bright—"

"Amaterasu," breathed Yoriko, and this elicited a more agreeable chill.

"Yes," the little girl hummed, removing from the unstable shelf of childish memory her culture's fables, which she remembered better at that time than her mother's Halcyon contact number. "Definitely, Amaterasu—but, in her cave. Before all the gods throw a big dance party to bring her out." The girl could not help her grin. Of all the stories she had by then been told of the ancient Shinto gods, that one most filled her with joy. Yoriko smiled, too, and mopped away her daughter's tears with that same fancy handkerchief.

"And how do you know that?"

"She was in a dark place, trapped—and sad. Susanoo should apologize for breaking her loom, and hurting her friend."

"Yes, he should—but he never will." Rocking back upon the heels of her stylish slippers, Yoriko said, "She'll need help coming out, won't she?"

"I want to help her," said the girl, holding back bold tears. "I want to be like Uzume, and dance so well that I make everyone happy. To call her out again."

"Then," agreed her mother, "we'll need to make you a pretty bronze mirror."

Few children experienced such an overnight change for the better. The very next day, Yoriko took Miki out of a school where she didn't get along with anyone and began to work on her transfer to an all-girl's school, where she could transition superficially without much fuss. It was far easier, and more sensible, than trying to get children to accept their current classmate's change. Even in that day and age, the subject of what to do about transgender children caused fierce debate in the Empire of the Risen Sun. Like opinions about women, homosexuality and other issues of human rights, these things waxed and waned with the centuries. It took a martyr's perspective to understand how little any of that mattered in the long run, which was often why such identities were considered inappropriate; but those same small-minded people usually eschewed genetic engineering and croaked, turning the tide back and forth every fifty or so years.

Socially speaking, things looked up for the Japanese transgender and homosexual communities around that time, but the subject was still iffy, so Miki had to be cautious yet adamant about the true nature of her identity. She was tired of being misgendered by well-meaning peers, teachers, and strangers, and she wasn't about to let those same individuals turn around and tell her she'd grow out of her own soul. Even Yoriko, after all, had mistaken Miki's initial protestations as some kind of phase or misunderstanding on the part of a toddler not equipped to comprehend gender. But when, in those weeks off of school, Miki's haircut appointment was canceled, and her wardrobe was completely changed over, and even her bed was replaced without warning to one with frills and curtains like a Western princess (maybe even *the* Western Princess—you know the one she meant), it was like a whole planet fell from Miki's shoulders.

Oh, her mother was still incredibly—sometimes shockingly—passive-aggressive ("No wonder she was such a *homely* boy," Yoriko once chortled in Japanese to a friend during tea time, right in front of Miki. "Her really being a girl and all! Isn't she pretty now?"), but that was just the way Yoriko was. It was all bearable when Miki could play the little-girl games from which she'd been ejected, or consigned to male roles. Now in "House" she could be the mother, and be a downright bitch just like Yoriko. Ah, childhood! Many pretend husbands, daughters, and dogs were slapped across the face with fans, slippers, and rolled-up paperbacks. In retrospect, it did explain her adult specializations in sadomasochism.

Somehow, in spite of how quickly Miki took after Yoriko when allowed to be herself, the girl made scores of friends in her new school. Friends! She'd never had any before. Slowly but surely, she started to have places to go that were not her own (still slightly oppressive) home. Meanwhile, Yoriko assuaged the girl's body image frustrations with mountains of gifts and more validations than the selfish old (okay, middle-aged) witch had ever given anybody. But it wasn't the stuff, the support, or the friends that kept Miki going as she blossomed, through the help of hormones, very mild genetic therapies, and—at the long-awaited age of eighteen—surgery, into a beautiful young woman.

The Lady was always there with her, after her suicide attempt. She couldn't explain how she knew it. She never *saw* Her, after all. Never even in dreams, though these did become more vivid after the experience. There was one time, though, that rocked her world and made her question her whole interaction with the entity.

It happened a couple of years after her vision. For some reason, the news always reported tabloid gossip about the martyrs and what they called their Holy Family. Ostensibly this was done to give people a glimpse into the existence of the enemy, but there were plenty of Japanese women who kept their eyes on Lavinia's current wardrobe. Yoriko was one.

Miki hadn't ever given a shit about the enemy, to be honest, for better or for worse. Japan was a safe place these days. Martyrs weren't welcome after the Pacific Conflict, and Miki lived in a happy snow globe of assumption that she would never, ever meet one of those predatory fiends. Hell! Even if she left the island nation, the odds of encountering a martyr were fairly low. Something around getting attacked by a shark or being struck by lightning. Okay...not that low, but *still*. No way was she going to have to worry about something like that! Consequently, she would laugh and roll her eyes when her mother, like all Japanese mothers, would use the boogie(wo)man that was Dominia di Mephitoli in early, ill-fated attempts to get her child to behave. She was still out there, the Governess of the United Front, always waiting to appear on the island with her Father and snatch up disobedient children when the supply of immigrants ran thin.

W-H-A-T-E-V-E-R. Especially once Miki was allowed to be a girl, there was no getting her to behave. Not even the infamous General/Governess/etc. could threaten her. Nobody!

Except—with a bored glimpse up at her mother's program playing in their holo-corner one afternoon, Miki dropped her portable video game in shock.

There, with Roman nose pale beneath her stern lapis eyes, floated a clear vision of the Lady.

How? It was more static and mortal than that vision, yet—Miki knew. The shape of the face, of the non-glowing eyes…it was all the same. "Who is that?" the girl asked her mother, who admonished her in surprise.

"Miki! Don't you pay any attention to the news, or social studies? That is the Governess of the United Front, that devil, Dominia di Mephitoli. I can't even stand to look at her damn face! Ugh." While the hologram's muted lips moved, Miki stared into the floating face with wonder before her mother plucked up the remote to fast-forward with a sigh.

"Just get to the Florentine…blah, blah, blah…"

Miki hid in her bedroom for a while after that. Now there was an experience to keep her up at night! The Lady was a martyr? Not just a martyr but one of the worst, most evil martyrs in all history?

She couldn't understand it. In that other place the Lady's image had been beyond comprehension or explanation. Yet when Miki thought of it now, there stood Dominia. That kami, awash with light, had the same face. She confirmed it with research that impressed her mother and earned her a couple of valuable history books that she wouldn't crack open until the Red Market expanded her interest in self-education. Even if she'd been into reading such heavy shit at the time of receiving those tomes, it would have been too much. It was already too much to sweep through her hand-me-down e-reader after doing an image search for "Governess of the United Front" and seeing image after image of the goddess from her suicide attempt.

There was no telling anybody about this. Ever. She had to keep this to herself. This was insane. She might have been seriously unhinged. And at such a young age! What was wrong with Miki? Had she just seen the Governess in the background of news broadcasts, and been presented that image by her brain? Why? Why would her brain choose this evil martyr to represent Amaterasu? Why would Amaterasu take this form before her? The idea was a source of great spiritual consternation.

Yet, she knew she was not wrong. The Lady was real, and had chosen her. Had saved her. Why, she didn't know. She didn't know that any more than she knew why or how the martyr was tied to the Lady. Why she could not unconvince herself—why she eventually came to accept—that the two entities, no matter how evil one seemed, were one in the same. Maybe there was something to her mother's suggestion of Izanami, after all.

But it could not be Izanami. Could not be something evil, this kami, this Lady. No matter whose face She used, She was good. And She did not directly communicate with Her human charge, but She did seem to send some messages, somehow. Sometimes, going about her daily routine, Miki would get a flash of inspiration to do something drastic—eat fewer sweets, start working out, start wholeheartedly venerating Amaterasu—and Miki felt compelled to follow the action through. Good thing she wasn't being told to, like, stab somebody, or something, right? Though, admittedly, one of those impulses did lead to a pretty vicious falling out between herself and her mother. See, what had happened was, Miki was about fourteen when she started expressing real interest in following in the footsteps of her mother's work. After her experiences, Yoriko was reluctant but knew her daughter was smart and driven enough to make it in the ancient business of Japan's most fetishized class of women. Therefore, after school, Miki's schedule was crammed with music lessons, dancing lessons, elocution, etiquette, calligraphy, flower arranging, foreign language lessons, posture—for the Lady's sake, she had to relearn how to *walk*! It was about two years before Miki realized being a geisha absolutely, unequivocally sucked, no matter how romances written by Westerners tried to make it seem. Why did her mother do it? Miki asked her once, and, outside of the fact that her mother began training her around the age of seven, Yoriko had insisted that the career of the geisha was a living art that was to be kept alive.

Miki wasn't so sure about all that anymore. It was the opposite of her personality to be quiet, demure, and obedient—to sit and pluck her shamisen like a boring doll. Was this what she wanted to do all her life? Snore, snore, snore! No, thanks. About the time Miki was supposed to be promoted from *maiko* to actual geisha, which might have been a little more interesting, one of her fellow *maiko* mysteriously quit. That was all the incentive the admittedly lazy girl required to leave, herself, and put her skills of being an amusing beauty queen to work in hostess clubs. Yoriko wasn't happy, but what could she do? Her daughter, who had adopted the last name Soto while apprenticing as a geisha, was free to do what she wanted with her career, and working in hostess clubs wasn't so different from that most ancient of doll-like women's arts. So, her mother put up with her change in career until the day Miki was at the market picking up a shoulder of lab pork. That day, her abruptly missing former coworker bumped into her—or, more appropriately, came running for her while screaming, "Soto-chan, Soto-chan," across the crowded stalls. Always got a couple of hilarious stares from the Japanese, that name. Miki grinned at the strangers who returned to their business, then at her approaching friend. While nursing the stitch in her side, the tanned young woman stopped to kiss and hug Miki, and tell her (in the semiprivacy of fluent English) what she'd been up to: prostitution.

"You're Red Market," whispered Miki, trying not to be visibly disgusted but letting her shock remain. "Isn't that dangerous?"

"No, it's great! The women all take care of each other... Actually, I know a couple of girls who know your mother—from the foundation, isn't that funny?"

"You didn't tell them about me, I hope!"

"Of course not, of course—but, *Miki*—" The girl's voice dropped even lower, and the hostess was forced to lean in. "You have to come meet some of them. This industry, I'm telling you, it's much better than being a geisha. More fun. When you're a geisha, every man thinks he owns you. It's like he's renting you out for party decoration or something! But when I'm working for the Red Market, I'm so free. The Market and I are the ones in control."

"Sounds like some kind of weird, sexual pyramid scheme. But I guess a weird, sexual pyramid scheme is just a cult, huh?"

Though the girl's made-up and childish sticker-accented face flashed with annoyance, her expression regained its sly quality perhaps too soon. "Actually... you might call it a cult. A lot of the women involved, they do their work for religious reasons, to reach out to men and connect them with the divine."

"What do they worship?"

"I don't know. They're really obscure about it! They won't tell me its name, they just call it 'the Lady.'" The title, which was the same she had privately applied to that kami, shot a chill straight up Miki's spine while the girl went on. "I think it's Amaterasu, or something... I don't know, I don't care. I'm in it for that *money*, girl!"

"Good money?" asked Miki, as if she needed convincing now that the compelling nag of intuition built an electric tingle in the front of her brain.

"*Girl*," emphasized her friend, waggling her bleached eyebrows in a way that Miki's natural-colored ones echoed. "You don't even know."

She sure didn't! Hot damn. Yoriko threw Miki out as soon as she discovered her daughter had reacted to two nights spent shadowing a pair of experienced Red Market recruiters by quitting her stupid hostess gig, which was a-okay. It was time for Miki to spread her little wings and fly. And did she ever. She moved in with her *ganguro* friend and started turning tricks, which was weird at first but quickly became a total blast—especially when she discovered that most masochists didn't even expect or want the gratification of getting laid. Then she talked to her manager (aka, the woman who took a "small finder's fee" on behalf of the Market until Miki was a formal member, which wouldn't be until she was vetted for an interest in the Lady and trained as a priestess) about becoming an exclusive dominatrix.

Then, much to Miki's delight, she spent ten solid years embarrassing her mother at every turn. The young woman took particular joy in slipping work anecdotes into speeches given for the women's foundation, which she was often expected to do "[...]so some good [could] come out of [Miki's] [expletive] stupid career choices," as Yoriko put it one very drunken New Year's.

But, even if she didn't approve of Miki's lifestyle, Yoriko did seem proud of her daughter. She was proud of Miki because she knew Miki would do whatever Miki wanted to do, and there was nobody on Earth who could stop her.

What Yoriko didn't know was that Miki's actions were a compromise. Oh, yes, Miki did whatever she wanted to do; but she did whatever she wanted to do with respect to the wishes of the Lady. She worked hard—very hard—and, after receiving basic training as a lowly assistant priestess, became recognized as one of most valued (and valuable) members of the Red Market Kyoto branch when she was—well, an age older than twenty-six. Do we have to use numbers? Such *constraining* things...genetic engineering and martyrs in general meant that age only got relevant when it was advanced, anyway.

As her demand increased, another Market privilege revealed itself: travel. Meanwhile, her bank account grew as men literally paid her to take vacations outside of her claustrophobic island. Yoriko, of course, didn't approve, and was nervous her daughter would get swooped up and devoured by a martyr as soon as she set foot on foreign soil. But Miki knew she had nothing to worry about—the Lady was a martyr! How could a martyr be allowed to hurt her? Her fate was sealed. She knew she would be okay. Too bad Yoriko hadn't traveled some, herself! It might have done her good. But, no. The old crow believed she'd heard enough about the world from her clientele. She didn't even want to visit Europa! And she idolized that place, damn *seiyō kabure* that she was. No skin-care product could cure that Western rash of hers, but travel might have.

To the isolated nation of oppressive China; to the techno paradise of India; to the perfect restaurants of Unified Korea and; and, of course, to the glorious historical sites of the Middle States—Miki went everywhere, did everything, and met everyone she could. She always sent her mother a postcard, and would always later see that postcard hanging up in the kitchen. Things were fun and it was good to have her mother's tacit support, but then Yoriko began to express concern about her daughter's well-being again, and Miki sensed this was out of Yoriko's own fear of age. After a bit of soul-searching, Miki made the decision to reduce those trips, and intended to settle back down in Japan. Not to quit working, mind—just to stay in one place.

But, then, she got an invitation to a seminar. That was a pretty big deal. As a Red Market priestess (or priest, for there were plenty) moved through the tiers by donating time for various organizational efforts, more information would gradually be revealed about the nature of the religion. Like any good cult, of course. Miki, much like her former roommate, didn't really get into the religious aspect. She had her own personal connection to the Lady and was happy to help unburden the men who came to see her for spiritual reasons, but she couldn't help but look at structured religion with a skeptical eye. Who was anybody to tell her about the Lady, and who was she to tell anybody, in turn?

Still…the Asian Retreat, as that seminar was called, was in Hokkaido. How could anybody say no to that crab? (Or that glint of intuition that pushed her for it, but more importantly—the crab!) So, promising to bring her mother something tasty, Miki packed a bag for a week and took the Red Market's offered economy LRT pass to the meeting.

And, oh, boy, was it as predicted. The touchy-feely-let's-get-to-know-each-other New Age shit started the second her toe breached the threshold of the private grounds, and it didn't stop until she was ready to burn the place down. Playing games like "What color is your name" and "Attracting your spirit animal" were, to Miki, pointless corporate icebreakers rather than spiritual exercises. She was miserable. They even had classrooms, with syllabi for the various "classes" she was forced to attend. The best was the yoga thing, and even that was pretty tedious when they tried to work spirituality into it.

But the worst by far was the one on the fifth day, where all the people in her group sat around in a circle, closed their eyes, and were told to visualize the Lady.

Miki *almost* laughed. Almost. Somewhere, the Lady laughed for her.

When it came time for the women to go around the circle and share their own inner visions of the Lady, she couldn't handle it anymore. Slumped in her seat, hand cradling her forehead, Miki listened to woman after woman drone on about imaginary versions of the Lady that made her want to puke. Inevitably, She was described as having no clothes, or blonde hair, or no hair, or She was Asian, or She had cat ears (that was one Miki actually did laugh at, which earned her a few unpleasant glances), or had pixie wings, or She was made out of flowers, or, or, or…urgh! Finally, it was as another ditz described the entity as a Barbie doll with a cotton-candy-pink aura or something equally ridiculous that the opinionated woman could no longer contain herself, and into her shielding hand, muttered, "*Martyr desu.*"

The instructor may not have heard her, but the woman beside her did—and, oh, boy, did the look on her face change. Miki couldn't have been assed to learn a name at that retreat if they paid her to do it, which was why it was extra infuriating when this person who she didn't even know tapped her brusquely on the shoulder. "Excuse me," the stranger said, eliciting a groan from Miki along with the attention of the instructor. "What was that?"

What was that? "That" was it! Her whole—something-something-year career was about to be blown up because she was surrounded by idiots. A lifelong secret about her vision of the Lady, spilled now because of her own lack of self-control. Maybe her mother was right about her mouth.

"Nothing," Miki lied. The girl's tone grew all the hotter.

"You did! I heard you—you said the Lady is a martyr!"

Gasps! Theatrical, melodramatic gasps! Miki tried not to roll her eyes and wondered if they were going to start hissing her out of the room. Above the clamor, the instructor snapped to full attention and took a step that rattled her many beaded necklaces.

"Is it true?" demanded the instructor of Miki, staring her dead in the eyes like Yoriko finding drugs in a sock drawer. With a blasé glance for the women around, Miki crossed her arms and shrugged.

"Yeah, it's true. I did say that."

"How *dare* you," began to puff the tattletale. Thankfully, the instructor stopped her with a well-manicured hand.

"I think you should go to the Welcome Center, please." As another, softer set of gasps from the girls who liked Miki filled half the room, the instructor slid her digital glasses from her nose, regarded the younger woman, then nodded. "Yes. I think that's for the best. The Welcome Center's check-in quadrant, please."

She slipped the glasses back on and blinked their screens into operation—no doubt to give admin a heads-up that Miki was being ejected for having an opinion. The younger woman sighed, shrugged, and slid out of her chair. "I wasn't any good in school, either. Later!"

Outside the bungalow classroom, one of seventeen scattered across the grassy "campus," Miki's bold steps slowed to a pensive pace. This was why she chose that name—"Soto"! Even once she was herself, pretty, and popular, she was still an outsider. Her thoughts: they were what made her an outsider. Her thoughts, and her damn connection to the Lady. What was She? That vision…a kami, or an *oni*? Had the spirit guided her through all this, led her to this point, just to see her ejected from her career and sent with no professional training into the humdrum world of—*ugh*—the Japanese salaryman? No fucking thanks! Somebody just shoot her.

The Orwellian Welcome Center was divided into four quadrants, each with its own color flooring. She needed proceed no farther than the one in which she was deposited on her entry. The cheerful evergreen carpet made her feel like a kid waiting for the principal, and her foot's wiggling was so incessant that it had clearly begun to bother the secretary by the time the ominous office door opened. Maybe it shouldn't have been a surprise that the looming figure behind the frosted glass was revealed to be one of the most jaw-droppingly beautiful women Miki had ever seen: her head heavy with light-colored and elaborately beaded dreads, the mixed-race Amazon spared no time scanning the waiting area before locking eyes with the hapless Japanese priestess.

"Please come inside, Soto-san," implored the woman in fluent Japanese. "Shut the door after you."

Yes, that was it. So sad! She never thought this day would come. Miki had been fired from a restaurant job her mother made her work after catching her with "the dope" (dastardly cannabis! What a drug fiend, Miki) and had hoped she'd never have to repeat the experience, because the truth was it sucked. There were a billion ways to play it off and laugh about it, but at the time of her firing, she felt as small as she did while across the teak desk of a woman who introduced herself as Gethsemane. Or the desk at which she sat, anyway. The name of the person who belonged there was written in kanji on a plaque, and was nothing close to "Gethsemane."

"I'd like to talk a little about what you said today," began the fragrant manager, whose specific position remained unidentified for now.

"Please." Miki sighed so deeply her body sagged forward in her seat. "If I'm going to be fired, or disciplined, or whatever—"

"That's not what this is about, Soto-san." At the smaller woman's visible surprise, Gethsemane lowered her voice. Her professional tone now carried a reassuring, almost sisterly edge. "I'd just like to ask you about your thoughts. How you came to this conclusion."

Panic started to rise upon Miki. They'd think she was crazy. If nothing else, this was not a subject to be discussed lightly. Of those few times (before her journey with the General) where Miki experienced true fear, none were as palpable as that moment of being pressured into giving up the secret of the kami who had saved her. Was this what the Lady wanted? It wasn't a mistake she could make. She leaned back in her seat. "I don't know if I should really…talk about this."

"I understand." From the black cup beside the holo-screen computer, Gethsemane removed a pair of pens. Then, tearing apart a sheet of paper, she said, "Do you believe the Lady to be a specific martyr, or just 'a martyr'?"

"I—" At the woman's glance, Miki felt compelled to admit, "Specific."

"I'd like you to write the name of the individual on this sheet of paper." Sliding the scrap across the desk to Miki along with a pen, Gethsemane said, "I will also write the name of the martyr with whom I identify the Lady. Then, we can trade. Okay?"

The smaller woman's heart fluttered. "You think—"

But Gethsemane already wrote. With a trembling hand, Miki scribbled in English the words "Dominia di Mephitoli," then folded the scrap and exchanged it for Gethsemane's. As she opened it to read the katakana characters for "The Bitch of Europa," Miki's eyes filled with tears.

"What…" She looked up at Gethsemane, who glanced at Miki's paper before putting it through the shredder in the corner of the office. "Is this—is this real?"

"You write in English, Miss Soto," said Gethsemane in the language.

"Yes, my mother—but—"

"That's good. I prefer it." From the hands of the baffled Japanese woman, the foreigner lifted the scrap of confirmation and destroyed it, too, before returning to her seat. "I would like you to tell me how you came to know this information, if you wouldn't mind."

"Forget *me*!" Thrilled, now—validated in a way she hadn't been since her mother first realized her gender identity—Miki leaned forward and begged, "How do *you* know? Do *other* people know? Does your secretary out there know?"

"No. Twenty-five women within the Red Market organization understand the true nature of the Lady, and all of them are scattered across the seminars this month; none but my eight sisters and I know who exactly She is. Therefore, I would greatly appreciate it if you would tell me how you came upon this information."

Gladly. Miki spilled her guts right there in the office, confident that this was meant to be. Her heart sang with the release of a long-held beatific vision, and Gethsemane just listened. Listened patiently to every word of Miki's rambling tale, from her life's start in the wrong body and the suicide attempt that had revealed the truth, to the recognition of the Lady's face in the holo-corner, to the bursts of intuition that she sometimes received and that had ultimately led her right to that very office. As her long story wrapped up, she pressed the woman, "So, do you think it's real? What do you think all this means?"

"I think it means," said Gethsemane, "that you're the next avatar of the Lady."

What? She seemed to have lost her English comprehension for a few seconds there. But then Gethsemane said it again, and flipped open a hitherto unnoticed file with a petulant sniff. "Oh—wow, you're not in management? Then you don't understand."

Briefly, Gethsemane explained the true belief of the Red Market, which was hidden from all but the highest priestesses: that the Lady was not some metaphor or some dream consigned to a distant sphere but an entity responsible for maintaining the physical integrity of Earth—and that Her presence upon the planet, though required, was also unstable. For this reason, the Lady needed a body to inhabit.

For this reason, Miki was stilled.

"You want to take my body?"

"The Lady will, yes."

That was a startling notion. "Like, possession?"

"Like the divine descending upon you, emerging from within you. Your entire mind and body will be given up to the Lady. You can refuse, but—"

"No, I'm not—" Miki frowned in search of the words. Had she ever considered the point to her life? She'd just been living minute to minute for most of it, helping herself, and sometimes other people. She loved other people. For a long time now, she'd felt her only real point for existing was communicating with other people and obeying the whims of the Lady. If the whim of the Lady was that she should relinquish her body to this goddess, well...especially after getting a confirmation like this, she couldn't reject the request outright.

"Does it matter that I haven't always...you know." She nodded down at herself. Gethsemane shook her head.

"No. The second historical avatar of the Lady, during a time when goddess worship was at its height, was a cisgender man—albeit a pretty one. Physical sex does not matter. Her avatar always represents the compensatory principle in a given period of society. As the dominant aspect of society is, and has been for the past two thousand years, religion, our current avatar was a woman of science."

"And what will I represent, then?"

"If I had to guess, Miss Soto, I would suppose you represent transition in a world that struggles to maintain its dissipating status quo. And biological transition will be the reward for your valiant sacrifice. While your mortal body continues on in the world beyond even the point of a martyr's resilience, your soul will be rewarded with its true form. Given the miracles that tend to occur during the transference of the Lady between Her avatars, I would expect your body to be altered on a biological level in reflection of your self-image."

"So, my surgery, and all my..."

"Your body would become naturally feminine, yes."

If a sense of spiritual duty hadn't been enough of a stick, the carrot of two X chromosomes made her ask, "What do I have to do?"

Smiling for perhaps the first time since they'd met, Gethsemane slid another file, this one red, across the desk to Miki. She flipped its cover open to reveal several pages of information about a young Afghan man whose first name was Kahlil. "This young man, a regular customer of many Red Market women working Kabul, is in over his head with the Hunters. Of all members of that organization whose pride survives by our silences—and there are many—we believe that Kahlil is the perfect intersection of our needs. He is a man with important knowledge about the Hunters—perhaps too much, given his proclivities, and his tender heart."

Miki's whole expression sparkled with unbridled delight. "You want me to run, like, a honeypot operation on him? Like a *spy* movie? Oh, shit! Dude! This is crazy!"

"Please take this seriously, Miss Soto. This conversation has revealed you as the single most valuable member of the Red Market, which makes you the second most important woman worldwide. Third, I suppose; but the Lady's highest manifestation, within her avatar, goes without saying."

"Why is the Lady in two places at once? As the avatar, and as Dominia di Mephitoli?"

"Many mythologies throughout history chronicle the plight of the demiurge created by Sophia, or the horned man trapped by the great goddess... Demeter, bearing Typhon. The Governess of the United Front does not, cannot, understand that she has done the same with the Hierophant."

Dazzling Amaterasu's sunlight, bursting from her cave. "But the goddess—she's been trapped, too."

"Yes. She sacrificed Herself to Her own trap that we could all be saved from the same, even the Hierophant."

Prior excitement began to fizzle. Miki wrinkled her nose. "That sounds like Christian Abrahamianism. But, like, with a feminist gloss."

Gethsemane chuckled wryly as she rose, taking Miki's personnel file and leaving Kahlil's blackmail one. "That's the greatest secret of all, Miss Soto. Something *only* I and my sisters know...we are all describing the same thing. Abrahamians, martyrs, Red Market, none of the above. We are describing the Word, Logos, who also arrives on Earth to lead the Lady to victory. You know—" She had looked about to leave, but paused a foot from the door, beside Miki in that cramped space.

"When I was younger, I believed Western thought and Abrahamian faiths were incompatible with belief in the Lady. But a spirit descended upon me when I was seventeen; a spirit I was not. This spirit brought me knowledge of which I had none, and this same spirit brought me to my sisters. I am no longer the self that I was. I was shown the truth—that there is a man who stands with the Lady, as the Lady, as mentor to the Lady, and as the son and servant of the Lady. The spirit ordered me to sleep and in my dreams showed me many things, including a great book: the words "the Queen of Peace" were written there. A title for Mary, but the voice of the spirit with me said, "This is also a title of Christ when He is upon the Earth."" Gethsemane studied Miki's face carefully.

"Do you understand what that dream told me? I did the instant I awoke. Christ *was* Mary. Christ was God and fully human, so the Christians of my village taught. Therefore, his human DNA, his body, had to come from somewhere. From a physical, scientific perspective, unless the Holy Spirit brought with it the DNA of an earthly man, Jesus of Nazareth must have been a masculinized clone of his mother. A perfect genetic duplicate in every way, physically presenting with a dick and a beard." Miki grinned at the woman's playful obscenity in proximity to spiritual discussion as slightly smiling

Gethsemane asked, "Dig me? The sacred androgyny of Christ is real. The Logos is real. And our Lady, Dominia di Mephitoli, will use his help, and yours, to save the world. But first, she has to change."

Change, for sure! While Miki spent months sowing seeds with Kahlil, apologizing to her mother from afar for her false homecoming, she watched the news and waited as she'd been instructed to by further contacts with Gethsemane. She was a real secret agent! And, like most real secret agents, she succumbed to her damned emotions in that little honeypot scheme of theirs.

Oh, Kahlil. It was never his fault that Miki shut him out! She just had trouble with feelings. After he got comfortable enough with her to start falling asleep near her, she'd watch him sometimes, and think, yes, there was something very cute about him. He had a lot of bad habits and had spent an unfortunate amount of time trying to get in good with the Hunters, but she could see that he, like a lot of men, was just perpetually disappointed every woman he encountered wasn't also his mother. (Personally, Miki was relieved every woman she'd slept with wasn't her mother, but that was the difference between men and women!) So, she mothered the bullshit Internet- and Hunter-instilled misogynistic expectations right out of his sorry ass, showing him that her skills extended beyond artful spankings and good—well. The point is that Miki spent a lot of time with Kahlil, cooking for him, seeing movies with him, listening to him nonjudgmentally, spoiling him with gifts like he was just any old friend or family member. And as she saw his gradual drift of interest from the Hunters and onto her, she discovered her own feelings had developed somewhere along the line.

What was she supposed to do with those? Especially once she considered the business nature of their relationship—and the aspects about which he was unaware. But she got him to open up to her about all he knew, and soon enough she abused that knowledge by passing it along to higher-ups. Then May Day of CE 4042 came around, and, well…there was that change she'd been waiting for. While the red-eyed Governess struggled to hold it together during her wife's globally televised funeral, Miki pulled the rug out from under Kahlil.

The fight! Was it worth recounting? He had accused her of using him, of abusing him, of crushing his very heart. All this was like a series of stabs in Miki's, but this was why she'd kept as far away from those kindling emotions as she possibly could. In as calm and businesslike a fashion as she could manage, she'd laid out the conditions of his future: he would help her and the Governess reach Lazarus. They'd fought and fought until he asked her why she was doing this. She told him about the Lady, withholding her gender identity, because he hadn't figured her history out and it was none of his business if she didn't tell him. Then he'd turned on misplaced sympathy. A Hunter, telling her *she'd* been brainwashed!

This religious aspect allowed him to forgive her, somewhat—especially when she admitted she did love him. But he was still being blackmailed into betraying his affiliated regime, and that wasn't pleasing to any man. If he'd been in a proper relationship, it would have been time to rethink that relationship's whole foundation; but poor Kahlil had thought himself only worthy of the love that he bought, and, well…

Miki was more loyal to the divine than to romance.

Of course, sometimes she wondered if she was on the right path. The boy continued to love her in a disappointed way, and Miki couldn't help but ask if it was worth hurting him to do all this. She questioned right up until that fatal September, when the Governess abandoned her post, and an order came through from Gethsemane: to return to Japan, to say goodbye to her mother, and to prepare to bring the Governess to Cairo in preparation for the Lady's renewal ceremony.

The finality of it all…somehow, Miki almost couldn't manage to see her mother that last time. Yoriko suddenly looked so old! All the skin care in the world, all the mild therapies to which she'd opened up after her daughter's plight—none of it could save her from the fact that she was still someday going to die.

Miki, too, would someday get old and die.

Did she want that? She asked herself while her mother, after dinner, presented her with that same shamisen which had been her partner throughout her famous career. Did she want to get old and die—or did she want to live forever with her consciousness split across two planes of reality and her body hosting the spirit of an immortal goddess?

The choice was obvious; but, in the cab back to her hotel room, Miki couldn't help but cry. They felt the same as the tears she'd spend with Dominia, in her room before that ceremony. Those forty days in Cairo had blurred by, and Miki, still reeling from the physical existence of her imaginary friend and the sacrifice that she was about to undergo, could hardly understand Kahlil's bitterness toward her. She loved him, damn it! Wasn't it enough for her to love him *and* be sorry that she couldn't spend her life with him? Wasn't it enough for him to be there? But he didn't even want to be at the ceremony.

That was why it was so surprising when, as the ringing of her spiritual transference cleared away and she had said goodbye to Dominia, Miki became aware of a body—her *body*! That body she had seen before the Lady! *Oh*, what a body!

But she was aware of this body because of the body across from it. Kahlil's body. Joy filled her to see him, and sorrow, and Kahlil, tears in his unobscured eyes, said, *"I made such a terrible mistake. I'm sorry."*

Everything he had done: she saw it now. In fact, she saw *everything.* Somehow, it was as if she'd always known everything—everything in the world. As if she'd put it there, herself. But that was the Lady in her, she knew. The Lady, and the higher spirit behind Her. Miki's own pains for her crimes filled her breast and she took her lover's hand.

"And I used you. Kahlil...I played with your heart like it was my shamisen. You know—I don't regret anything in my life, my career or any of that. But I wish somehow...it would have been nice to be your wife. I couldn't have had your kids, though. I'm sorry I lied to you about that, by the way."

"It's okay... I knew."

Miki's eyes widened, and even there, in the Void, she smacked him across the face for her embarrassment. *"You cad! Why didn't you say something? I thought you didn't know!"*

"Of course I knew. I can't explain it. I just spent a lot of time with you, so of course I figured it out. But...I didn't care. Why would Allah care if you really felt like a woman, and presented as a woman, and thought like a woman? I was thrown for a loop about it for a while, but you know, I just loved you too much, and you were always a woman to me, so..."

"Oh, Kahlil." As always, when at risk of emotions, she had to turn them into humor. She hid her face behind her heron-dotted sleeve. *"Well, it's paid off for you, now! Would you look at my figure?"*

"You were always perfect." His smiling faded into hesitation, and he glanced down at her hands as they slipped into his. *"Would you be with me now? After the way I betrayed you, got all those women killed?"*

Your own death was punishment enough, I believe.

The starburst of the ascended Lady struck the two lovers through with the glory of Her light. These same crystal beams dissolved Kahlil through Miki's hands; she knew without a hint of fear that she would see him soon enough. Instead, she threw her arms around the Lady's neck and embraced the deity with unabashed joy.

"See why I had to kiss you when we first met." Miki laughed. Even the radiant kami smiled at that. *"I'm still a little sorry, though, to leave it all behind."*

I want to show you something. Something I saw when the True Word was first unveiled to my exposed mind.

With Miki's arms around Her, the deity rose high through the Void. They penetrated that sphere of darkness and a brilliant and beautiful light—more brilliant than even that of the Lady!—was left naked all around them. Their pace only increased, the speed so vast that it tore away the flesh of the goddess and revealed, one by one, those beautiful pillars who maintained Her physical presence: first that vast woman found in many an ancient statue, success and happiness where there was famine; then a beautiful man who would someday inspire stories of Adonis; then a glorious beekeeper who became known variably as Astarte, Isis, Ishtar, Inanna, and a bevvy of other titles; then, across the sea, a slender young native woman who traveled through a region later known as the Ohio Valley and, amid varying tribes of people sometimes lumped together as the "Adena," sowed a language of cultural symbolism full of weeping eyes, and animals becoming men, and the sinful horrors of cannibalism; then, in Europa, as Christianity crested to its height, a schizophrenic barbarian girl babbled herself full of the Lady, and would someday give way to the science-minded Trisha Robbins.

Then, of course, Trisha peeled Robbins away and revealed the body of Miki Soto: and Miki realized she had never been Miki to begin with. That body chipped off as the unnamed watcher observed on, and lo, Dominia di Mephitoli ascended through those many spheres of reality, those many highest heavens, until Dominia, reaching up, found she was but the eighth vessel of that electric entity known in human tongues as "the Lady." Beyond that highest sphere against whose membrane she paused to press, the fingers of a ninth, unseen, untouched, too-close Lady wove a lightning that cracked the General down, down, down into the body of Miki Soto, in whose form she dwelt until the fateful night of Dominia's death.

XVII

The Battle for Jerusalem

It was not possible to express all Dominia now understood. She had, since the nascent turnings of the planets, waited. Suspended in that edge-of-sleep superposition of existence/nonexistence until consciousness began to take root in what could be called "humans." As the substance of the physical hologram representing that iteration of reality, she lay present in all things. "All things" included human DNA. The Lady was to the human genome what Saint Valentinian was to the sacred protein, perhaps. Where the tail ended and the head began on that strangely orbiting ouroboros, the physical mind could have hardly gleaned. Speech was inadequate to transfer the experiential information; even writing had its shortfalls. Take, for instance, that taboo place with a thousand names. That realm between the living reality and the storage of the Kingdom.

After all, it was not proper to call this space the Ergosphere. Even that image, devoid of face, possessed too much substance. The true form of that taboo place could not be perceived, could not be thought—for, in thinking It into the shape of any one thing, It craftily made that thought the smoke screen by which It got away. Dominia had existed in a perpetual state of It, even when she dwelled within her avatars and was able, minimally, to interact with that world she supported. Through their hands she guided the flow of human events so that, by the time the Hierophant arrived in 1974 CE—the year of his old self's birth—he was perpetually entering the iteration midgame.

He thought it was his wish that brought him to this new iteration of the world. Had he say in the matter, of course, he would have arrived at the dawn of time just as Dominia had. And, in ways, he had. His shadow had, at any rate. Dreams of him emerged in the collective dream of humanity long before he fizzled into existence in this particular plane. Even the Lamb, whose earthly body was not born until soon after that fatal year of 1974, had the ability to afflict probability for such a vast expanse of space-time that his probability field, the Lady now understood, encompassed a great period of time both before his birth and after his death. Many improbable events had occurred in human history, and it was impossible to say which ones had been nudged this way or that by his brother's future requirements even before that evil brother was physically upon the planet.

Because the Hierophant was not present until she allowed him to be, and until the hologram of reality could accept the existence of his genetic code error. From the moment of his arrival, he had total freedom. Access once more to all the sweet potential of the unconquered world. A mouse had no say in where its neck would someday be snapped, nor say in the bait or placement of the trap. He was a miserable wretch who had lost the only thing he loved in the world—his brother—and who deluded himself with the notion that there was a way to get him, it, life, back.

Now, more than ever, the Lady understood Cicero's plight. But she had no sympathy for his means, his choices, his cruelty. His *cruelty.* Only after receiving the full input of all those souls within her did the hyper-dense spirit of the former General understand the depth of his horrors. Two thousand years of people, brainwashed from a state of childhood innocence into a race of sexually violent reprobates. It was still possible for them to be saved, and that was why the Lady fought on. But that salvation could only be accomplished once their Church's Father had been supplanted by a better-intentioned individual.

The Bearers' physical tradition had begun with the first avatar's daughters, who were miraculous for their time in that all nine survived from birth to adulthood. After her ninth, the Lady came upon her and never left; one by one, the daughters dreamed their Bearer-dreams, and the much-worshipped, well-fed, and ultimately widely loved holy Lady began the worldly tradition of devotion to spirits, which, unlike the animal-spirits present all around, were invisible, and took the shapes of men and women. At once, the Bearers set upon her bidding, spreading these teachings and gathering resources. Lady after Lady, into the modern days and nights, amassed a great stockpile of wealth, connections, and blackmail material. There was nothing they could do to stop the rise of martyrs, or her Father—she understood now that many previous iterations had been run with that intention, and the knowledge of their failures (which, prematurely given, certainly would have collapsed living Dominia's mind into an early black hole) assured her there was nothing that could be done. One way or another, his infestation had to take root to be exterminated.

In the meantime, she established her base. A silent army, which became a very vocal one when the living Dominia di Mephitoli, disgraced and fleeing her country, stumbled into control of several cells of Hunters. Then, all the years of close conspiracy spent fighting the global bureaucracy paid off. Then, with the help of the Red Market, Miki Soto and many others brought together by the suicidal ideations of the Lamb's transtemporal probability field, the Lady saved herself.

How funny to watch Dominia! What a child she had been. Yet, the Lady Dominia was not so far removed from the General Dominia: when Miki, before her ascension, brought Cassandra's diamond there to Cairo, the slight weight upon the breast of Trisha inspired the first starburst of real emotion the pan-dimensional entity had experienced in an entire reality's worth of timeless existence. Space-time was but fabric to her, that folding, washing, working laundress who sometimes wove it, too, and she ran it through her fingers to touch any spot that pleased: she touched that spot of private reunion again and again and found such endless bliss that it was good the avatar's mind was bound to time, or the Lady might never have accomplished anything. Therefore, even the goddess was encouraged by that unseen first moment of Miki's in the Cairo throne room. All of this was done with good purpose. Miki's body had been given up for good purpose.

In Jerusalem, that body ruled with an iron fist. The General, obviously, did not like it, but the city's outskirts had been left in terrible shape by Akachi and the Israeli attempts to liberate the holy town. As European and UF forces began to amass, first in Turkey and then, with permission after the exit of Israel from the union, the Middle State of Syria, the Lady calmly continued pouring money into fortification efforts—and repair efforts, especially as the drone bombings began to stack up. The General grew visibly more frustrated as the year wore on, and her men, having for years resorted to dirty warfare tactics like suicide bombers and exploding trucks, were not content to sit around and wait for the UF to close in on the city's heart.

Direct hostilities began in March of 1998 Anno Lucis, when a unit of European troops was accused of entering Israeli territory. Soon enough they were doing it openly, pacing astride mechanical warhorses which bellowed smoke from their nostrils in a touch that served no use to the device: mere grade school intimidation. The Lady continued to enforce this miserable period of waiting, while citizens of Jerusalem were evacuated and the General drove north and south, east and west, begging for money, donating her time to the people of Israel, reviewing the behaviors of (and frequently firing entire offices of) military police units installed by the Hunters, etc. By this point in time, what little military force was ascribed to the state of Israel was nowhere near Jerusalem, and was neither inclined to help Dominia, nor to assist in the Hierophant's capture of their own holy city. Therefore, that sprawling city had been forced to act as its own state for some time—in the centers and neighborhoods that had been less savaged by the initial Hunter swarms, Akachi's men had actually established quite an impressive working infrastructure if you didn't mind a few public beheadings in exchange for clean roads.

But clean roads meant a lot when you planned to fight in them. If Jerusalem had been forced to act as a sovereign state, the Hierophant's armies sure invaded it like one. By the time the very angry, very depressed General was shipped off to kidnap Theodore, she had witnessed the systematic loss of about a third of her newly earned city. While she was a brutal killer and an expert military leader, the fact of the matter was that Dominia had been running a city under siege, and from the start, it had about as much hope as the infamous American Alamo. While it was true that it sometimes took as many as two to three days to clear a single large apartment building (sufficiently fortified and defended), the Hierophant had unlimited resources to throw at the problem of Jerusalem, and had been waiting for this moment a mite longer than two thousand years.

Good thing the Lady had been waiting for eternity. This was why she was patient while Jerusalem fell, and silent as Dominia fought her losing battle, scrambled between bombing sites, and tried to make a real difference in some human lives. While developing within her mortal form, the General had been too hard on herself. She had, in fact, changed, and worked hard to repent for her odious crimes with every remaining second she had.

Those precious few seconds, compared to the mass of all those before. It was with calculated self-knowledge that the Lady hid all truths from Dominia, including her true reason for returning to the Front and kidnapping Theodore. Teddy's utility was beyond the scope of their battle, far into the future. After all: the next Hierophant of the Holy Martyr Church would require an adviser and friend. Someone whose belief in Dominia's righteousness was wholehearted and earnest, so that, as the Church made its transition from sedated worship of the Ciceros, there could be no hope of backslide. Theodore del Medico was, for that purpose, ideal, because the existing Hierophant could hardly help but torment the fool he oh-so-cleverly martyred to someday lure his arrant daughter back home.

With such slight effort, the finest blade was turned upon the wielder! The Hierophant sensed the Lady's importance and dangerous nature, of course, but his hubristic overestimation of his own abilities would always be his downfall. Many a Dominia had died by his hand, yet he did not realize he had not won. Would never win. Even as UF troops closed in on the Library of Jerusalem in the weeks following the mysterious vanishing of the kidnapped Governor—along with his kidnappers—while in Atlantic airspace, the Hierophant marched his troops nearer his own demise.

And their unfortunate demises, safe to say. The Hunters were ragtag but formidable fighters who had adapted their styles for total destruction of martyrs, whether alone or in groups. As most of the low-level members of the Hierophant's military were expendable humans, this meant the terrorist organization had a slight advantage—because they were willing to fight like they, themselves, were inhuman. Red Market women, less savage, were no less effective, and those liberated *sabiyya* who had been brainwashed by their Hunter captors and sometimes taught to fire guns were most formidable fighters, themselves.

While all groups defending their stake in Jerusalem laid down their lives to secure the city and defend the Lady's avatar within the library, UF and European forces resorted to their own terror tactics. Accused members of al-Mawta were beaten, scalded, hanged, and occasionally disemboweled for officers' supper, all of it on film for the benefit of the remaining organization members. The logic among the troops seemed to be the same logic used to justify Hunter war crimes: the same logic Dominia had once used, herself. "It's what they're doing to us."

Now there was a truly unending snake! That twisting circle: pure, hopeless violence. Dominia wanted to blame the Lady for allowing the deaths of many troops on both sides, but the truth was that the General was as much to blame or more—for engaging in defense was simple perpetuation of that evil tide, when one got right to the point. On, on galloped the bleak steed of Saint Valentinian, whose bright star, Mars, still glittered with tints of red above Jerusalem's winter nights. Two and a half weeks after the disappearance of the General, supply lines to the Lady's library were cut off. Outside the library, human troops were forced to evacuate and regroup outside the city by that same tunnel system utilized by the industrious Hunters before the battle rose to frenzy. Within the library, fewer than one hundred men and women had been allowed to remain.

The Lady, her Bearers, and Lazarus also remained. While the goddess sat in silence in the center of her chambers, the mystic, along with the eight remaining Bearers, devoted themselves to maintaining the large building's perimeter.

In truth, those eight women had died many times. Over the course of one iteration of reality, the nine servants of the Lady attached themselves to a variety of women more endless than even that chain of avatars. Therefore, throwing away their lives for a purpose such as this was little more than the changing of clothes. They consoled those remaining loyalists who were either die-hard servants of the Lady or devout Hunters who understood that the loss of Jerusalem to the Hierophant meant a tremendous blow against human rights. Death was not so bad, the Bearers assured the people. From within, one didn't even notice it had happened.

Dominia had noticed, but that was because she was supposed to notice. She was not allowed to not notice, because in the noticing of the moment of death, she transcended physical boundaries to become death. Valentinian was but a prototype for the Lady, and her little shadows were those Bearers who arranged themselves in windows and, stone-faced, sniped for hours without rest. Lazarus hated this business, as always.

"I feel like I'd ought to turn myself in and settle it early sometime," he confided in her one evening four nights into the siege. "Avoid some deaths. But then I remember who we're fighting and I remember that the deaths will just happen anyway, and maybe more brutally than they ever could have while on the field of war."

Never underestimate the cruelty of the Hierophant when given time to reason, agreed the Lady. *You know we must wait.*

Yes: they had to hold out at least as long as it took for the cavalry to arrive and get captured alongside them. This was easier said than done, as were all things in war, but for as much advance intelligence as the Hierophant could be said to possess, the Lady possessed infinitely more. Every time a strike was launched against this weak point or that part of the tunnel system, her troops were ready to defend; and though their number dwindled by a few every skirmish, their assailants were threshed in staggering numbers that forced inevitable regrouping to controlled portions of the city. The block around the library changed hands every day, every night, moving in dominance like a bloody game of capture the flag. Fortifications made amid the bombed-out ruins of the city were only further destroyed when the civilian-free area was subject to drone strikes from the Hunters positioned in other areas of the city; great damage was done to the sieging army, and to Jerusalem's buildings.

The devastating truth was that the holy city was in ruins. From the uneasy semi-peace of Hunter occupation to the chaos emerging with Dominia's control, the entire state had been emotionally and fiscally drained. That the Middle States had even allowed Israel's exit was symptomatic of the fact they proved more liability than comrade. And once the Holy See of the True Catholic Church was evacuated around the time the Hierophant's drone strikes ramped up—July of that year—palpable despair had settled upon the city of Jerusalem and failed to lift. The assault of the Hierophant's troops was not a liberation or even an invasion so much as it was a nihilistic inevitability.

No one with a mortal, human perspective could comprehend the short-sighted nature of such ennui. It took a goddess to see that all things would be set right in the end. A goddess, a god, or a disruptive saint.

The infamous UFO crash near the peak of the Battle for Jerusalem would prove a pox on historians and an inspiration to conspiracy theorists for several centuries. Rumors abounded about the Holy Martyr Church's suppression of documents regarding the crash, but this wasn't true in the least. A study was released not ten years after the incident firmly and clearly explaining that the object—which crashed into the northwest corner of Jerusalem's library during a key moment in the assault, then disappeared, thus disrupting the first concrete penetration UF troops had made into the target and forcing the assailants to regroup while ultimately leading to their most exploitable point in entry—was not unidentified. It was, in fact, merely an inter-dimensional amphibiship (or a portable tear in reality, if one preferred) that allowed passage into, through, and beyond that semi-real zone about which science would know next to nothing concrete for several more centuries. Very elementary stuff; but conspiracy nuts would light up the Internet for years, insisting the object was the miraculous intercession of some beings from outer space.

Beings that, if the (openly published and circulated) letters of several survivors to their relatives were to be believed, resembled the martyr Saint Valentinian, a pilot of Middle Eastern origin, the Governor of the United Front, and a chubby sailor. Of the four (five, if one included the ship), only the pilot and Governor remained; at least, only the pilot and the Governor were secured. The pilot notably dashed into the fray on the opening of the ship's door, and was therefore obtained alive by a resourceful martyr corporal who saw a real promotion in his future for the deed. The Governor, who was whisked away by that entity resembling the martyr saint, was to be secured alongside Lazarus.

But that was not to say the entity resembling Saint Valentinian was not seen on Earth again. Far from it: on the disappearance of the E4 and the sailor at its helm, the fictional martyr made a personal appearance in the Lady's chamber to kiss her hand and startle the three Bearers hovering around her.

"They'll be back at the breach pretty soon," advised Valentinian. "This is our last stand."

We perceive you brought the Governor.

"Would you expect any less? I gave him to a couple of your Bearers about an hour ago. Farhad's back on Earth, too. Followed my instructions to the letter and got himself caught. He'll be handy when all this is through. Tenchi is safe and sound, though—on his way to meet you."

You are our greatest treasure, Valentinian. It's by the grace of God you're on our side, and not our Father's.

"By the grace of your wisdom, maybe. That coot is so busy being clever with his thoughtforms and elaborate tortures that he couldn't learn a True Word if you taught him in a dream." As Lazarus entered the room without a knock and strode to shake his hand, the magician turned to greet him. "You ready for the final act, old man?"

"I wish you could find some way to keep it from coming to this."

"Ah, hell, you know it's nothing to be worried about. Your service is crucial! You're like the sexy lady of my magic show's finale." While the old mystic rolled his eyes at the laughing saint, Valentinian went on. "Or a volunteer from the audience, if you'd prefer."

"I would much prefer that."

"I just mean to say, your part—"

"I get it. What do I look like, Dominia? I don't need a pep talk. I know why I'm here. Just change out the fucking blood, already."

With a chuckle, Valentinian tapped Lazarus in the center of the forehead. The mystic collapsed on the spot and the Bearers cried out as if the Lady, Herself, had fallen to the floor. While they rushed to his side, Lazarus came to with a series of derisive waves. "Don't," he said. "Don't worry about me, don't."

"Yeah, and don't injure him, either. Treat him like he's made of paper. Once somebody sees him bleed in this state, the jig is up."

Will you stay and help us fight?

"I wouldn't miss it for the world," promised the magician. "It's been a long time since I've had an opportunity to show somebody my true face. I'm just sad you won't be there to see the way a human brain reacts!"

Near omnipotent though she was, the Lady was relieved to hear he intended to help thin the library's assailants. The truth was that once hostile forces poured into the breach, no options would remain but direct conflict. The (now closer to seventy) humans who had stood their ground for almost two weeks, who had watched their supplies dwindle to nothing and their hopes dash along with them, would very soon lose their lives. Some would survive to surrender, but most could not stand to be so disgraced and would fight to the death for their honor. The Bearers would fight to the bitter end, much as the Lady wished it otherwise. But their role upon the Earth would be settled once the goddess departed it—and she would be departing it not terribly long after Jerusalem's fall.

Therefore, when the north wing of the library was secured, and two Bearers died, the Lady felt the jerks of their spirits like hooks removed from that weaving of space-time, and mourned in perfect, still silence. As the Hierophant's troops swept through the great series of halls—slightly modified over the previous year to confuse any intelligence from the prior iteration, as usual—dear, naïve Theodore was brought into the room by the two beautiful Bearers who had been attending to him. Their faces, grim masques heavy with their sisters' deaths, were ill-suited for Teddy's sparkling, wild eyes.

"What a place! I'm telling you— Oh, Valentinian! There you are. Ha ha, I thought you'd zipped off with that Japanese fellow!"

Never can hold his sacrament, observed the Lady, Miki's old body quirking its lips into a paralytic smirk. *Hello, Theo.*

The cheery man turned to face the goddess with pupils blown big with lysergic acid—administered to prepare him for the coming moments, for otherwise his mind would have no lubricant to cope. Like the chorus of a song he didn't know he sang, the Governor repeated that question Dominia had so many times during the final year and a half of her life. "Do I know you?"

You will recognize us soon. One of us, at any rate. And when you do—

Gunfire burst through a nearby hall and was returned while Teddy winced. "Are we just going to sit here? We can just evacuate to that other place, can't we?"

Your most important duty lies in Elsinore. Your charge—Lavinia needs you.

As Theodore glanced the way of the magician, who had disappeared to meet at least one of the squads approaching through the maze of halls, shelves, and multilevel mezzanines, the former doctor turned back to the Lady with real concern in his eyes. "I see," he said, and then, in an acid-deep tone, "I *see*. You're the Lady, aren't you?"

We are the wisdom hidden by your Father for centuries, until now. As a collection of screams arose to quick abortion, the Governor was grabbed by one of the Bearers to ensure he wouldn't dart off like a startled cat. Another team cleared the hallway directly outside the Lady's room, and could be heard calling commands back and forth. From the slightly elevated platform where the avatar knelt, the goddess's eyes raked in the direction of a freehanded Bearer, then nodded to the door. Farhad had surrendered out of the jet so they would understand his value and would not fail to claim him. Watching assailants had then been treated to a very visible demonstration of the martyr saint and his first mate tossing the Governor of the Front out of the other side of the object, into the breach its crash had caused, and the waiting arms of the Bearers below. This apparent intercession of Valentinian's on the defenders' behalf had been the true reason for retreat: white terror would stab the hearts of even the bravest men if they saw their spirit of death delivering into enemy hands that very hostage who had started the battle.

But, omens went both ways. The Hierophant, on hearing of this, had sent his reinterpretation: the gracious Saint Valentinian had placed the Governor where he could be found. By sheer miracle, the man feared lost over the Atlantic had been returned to life. Obviously, once the extraction teams reclaimed him, Theodore del Medico would be canonized. Wouldn't it be delightful to go down in history as the soldier who rescued a true saint?

Thus, the Lady and her companions found themselves in the besieged library. Lazarus, still disoriented from the magician's monkeying with his bodily fluids, rubbed his forehead and eventually succumbed to sink against the nearby shelves with a wave of his hand and the assurance of Teddy's Bearer that he was fine; the other, to whom the Lady had indicated, strode to the chamber's double doors. Much as Dominia had in that hospital so long ago, the Bearer threw the entry open before the wood could be blown from its hinges—but now, the onslaught of men into the room did not hesitate, more organized, officious, and clamorous than even those Hunters had been during the Cairo transference ceremony. As laser sights were waved around, orders were issued for hands to be put in the air. Wryly, Lazarus lifted one of his exhausted ones, and said, "I'll be able to lift the other in about five minutes of recovery," while a gun was shoved in his face.

The Lady continued speaking to Theodore as if a fly had buzzed between them. *For two thousand years and centuries longer, our power has been hidden from mortal men. That is why, Theodore, we have brought you here before seeing to your safe return home.*

"Get your hands up," an ape screamed of the Lady. One of several who aimed their sights upon her.

Therefore—

The power died in the room—along with the air-conditioning, the distant buzz of charging e-readers, and an undetectable background of electronic noise—for the two heartbeats it took the Lady to reappear, standing, in the doorway behind the infiltration team.

—it is imperative that you pay attention.

Amid the phantom beat of *suzu* bells, Miki's body took a step forward. The body she left behind, Trisha, stepped right and revealed the madwoman. While the stupider of the confused military men knew little else to do than bark orders, a few others lowered their guns in confusion and terror while the madwoman stepped left to unveil the Adena teacher; as this spirit stepped back to release the avatar called Ishtar, as shot was fired. It penetrated the forehead of Miki's body and the shooter dropped dead, bleeding from a bullet wound between the eyes.

As the expression goes, all hell broke loose. While, step by step, the goddess unfolded like a humanoid lotus around the long-hidden body of the true Lady, those already unfurled petals leapt into the fray, claiming weapons or speaking their own into existence. Each fought as if the General herself still dwelled within their body, and indeed, they could no longer be said to be separate from her in any way. Even once they physically stood, eight bodies in the same room, they moved with the kind of unity a military team could only dream about.

From the corner of the room, Theodore cried out and leaned around the Hierophant soldiers who had found, freed, and encircled him. "Is that *Dominia*," the man screamed.

In a manner of speaking. What was Dominia to begin with? Light bouncing off a pile of flesh. Thinking flesh, thinking with light. That ultimate carrier of information! The true messenger! Fleet-footed Mercury. Dominia was that same immutable no-thing substance, this quintessence of dust like all these men who fell out of existence beneath her many hands and into the Void where she now had no shame for sending them. In this state, she had not made them. But she had triggered their existence, their exit from the Kingdom, and she would trigger their replacement within it. It was not acceptable, their deaths at her hands, but it was a fact. It was part of their duty, to die here, in this place, beneath the weapons of the eight warrior selves—yes, even that Rubenesque first avatar—who had, in alternative fashion, already laid down their lives for their duty.

And die, they did. Quick deaths. Those who made the mistake of attacking the Ladies died by their own inflicted wounds, but those who were attacked for their refusal to flee through the open doors (as many wiser soldiers did) did not die, so much as un-exist.

Dominia, herself, pushed aside the guns of the men around Theodore and laid a hand upon one's helmet; his comrades watched him shut off like an unplugged computer and threw down their weapons to dash away.

"Twelve separate teams are working to clear this building," said Dominia to her astonished, too high, and visibly frightened brother. "All of them are looking for you. When they find you, make sure they know you're still a part of the Family."

The fray dying down, the Ladies assembled themselves around their master. "But what about *you*?"

"When you see me again, Theodore"—her many bodies refolded around hers to form her once more into that spirit called the Lady—*don't breathe a word of what you've seen.*

As the Lady disappeared to attend to the welfare of her former self, Teddy cried for her to wait. But there was no waiting: was no time. Once, in that year of Jerusalem's plight, Lazarus had chided the Lady: "The sooner all this is over, the better. I'm tired of watching you push yourself around."

Well, now the end had come. Now the master and servant were one. Now, Valentinian arrived with the Lady through the dark of space-time upon the dark of the stage where once Dominia's postmortem phantom stood, displaced from its dying body. The gasps of the audience, once stunned by the General, were deeper now to see the stranger. Toward the artificial storm clouds of the downpour induced for the Hierophant's play, the Lady lifted her head.

Once, the rain in California seemed so strange. But rain in Denmark's December, Cicero? Far stranger, still. You've always had a penchant for the unnatural.

XVIII

Function Composition

Few good things could be said of the Hierophant, especially after his death: but while he was alive, no one could accuse him of wasting time. The mocking goddess had not finished her sentence when the so-called Holy Father had turned to rip one of the (very real) halberds from the set's wall—or that was his intent when he found himself nose to nose with Valentinian.

"Going so soon? You can't leave before my magic trick! It's like sneaking out of Mass after Communion."

"So you've conned your way into a body." The Hierophant's tone was too dark to maintain its usual notes of condescending merriment. "Good. I'll take great pleasure in tearing it from you."

"Very funny you should say that." The magician flickered out of the path of a punch and appeared on the Hierophant's other side, much to the dismay of the crowd. "I've got a little treat for you tonight—and your audience! Consider this your delayed...well, it's not a *green* show, since we're in winter and all. But it's something! Really something. Maybe you knew the Hunters have teleportation technology, but did you know that you don't have to go to all that trouble if you've got a guy like me, and enough of the organic medium to go around?"

Above their heads, atmosphere-altering rockets burst, releasing instantaneously condensing vapors that, by virtue of convective effects and Elsinore's frigid air, grew to a localized supercell storm intended for mere show. Once upon a time, the rockets were used for restoring the land around bombed-out Moscow, or assisting in the Martian terraformation. Now, such things were relegated to toys, and their vapors sat, unchecked, for some time before the performance. Those that were checked had been found to contain H2O, and were in perfect working order. Untampered. Normal. Yet, to the shock of the audience members (to say nothing of the technicians responsible for the rockets), when the first beads of condensed fluid dropped from the tops of the artificial clouds and upon the high-paying patrons, it was not water that dotted their cheeks, their heads, their expensive lab-grown furs.

It was blood.

This was another in a series of events over which historians would prefer to gloss until science could offer a less embarrassing explanation than the evidence implied. Straightlaced scholars couldn't get any of this stuff to make sense. Eventually, the conclusion would be reached that the events of *The Curse of Bathsheba* were related to the mass hysteria of Lavinia's abilities; and Lavinia, long after her disappearance at the ripe old age of 789, would someday be considered part of a group of treacherous martyrs who wished to overthrow the founding Hierophant. No one would have dared say such a thing while she walked the Earth, certainly, but that meant nearly eight hundred years of button-down society's uncomfortable acceptance that the happenings of New Year's Eve 4044/1999 were, in fact, true and physical occurrences that had been recorded on camera.

And uncomfortable it was. For who in the material world could be fully comfortable with the notions of literal blood rain, levitation, divine transfigurations, and mass resurrection? The eventual explanation, long after martyrs were forgotten on Earth, would be this: the rain was traditional blood rain of the sort caused by microalgae (blame those lazy rocket technicians for letting its spores creep into the tightly sealed cylinders); and that the theater of Elisnore just happened to be the epicenter of a freak hurricane/earthquake/tsunami combination thanks to the cold winter winds, the low-hanging moon, the unnatural thunderclouds.

Were these grasping explanations not more spurious than the simple truth?

At the time, there was no arguing with experience. While a few martyrs in the audience tasted the ruby droplets and a murmur of astonishment rose above the storm's initial patters, Valentinian moved his hands in time with the continuing notes of the oblivious orchestra pit. "There's about, oh, a gallon and a half of blood in a person's body. Doesn't seem like all that much, but if you could organize every drop of that into a line, can you imagine how long it would be? You could make quite a circle! And any size circle of the blood of Lazarus, charged with sufficient electricity, will conduct the high frequency and produce a reality disruption."

The storm clouds thrashed like a coach of foaming horses, and its unnatural size grew beyond the scope of the atmospheric rockets. As the blood rain thickened, its droplets, and the clouds from which it issued, began a broad rotation above the open mouth of the Elizabethan theater. Tired of waiting for his situation to worsen, the Hierophant blinked out of existence—and back into it, close enough to the halberds for him to tear one off the set. The

Lady watched while the magician went on. "Theoretically, with enough of the blood of Lazarus, you could turn the entire world into a reality disruption. A superposition of reality and unreality. But, then, I guess that'd just be the Void."

Lightning struck the waves of the ocean outside the theater. While the audience cried out amid the rolling of immediate thunder and the vanishing of the red waistcoated Saint of Death, the Hierophant advanced on the Lady. Another bolt struck nearer to the building.

"Very kind of you to present yourself for the slaughter," said the Hierophant. "The way you insist on hiding from me, I always begin to think I'll never get the chance to see you face-to-face."

We have already died once tonight, Cicero: We will not die a second time.

"If that friend of yours wasn't so busy with parlor tricks"—the Hierophant winked back out of existence to another symphony of stunned gasps, then appeared all of a meter before the Lady in the same instant static's bright feelers crackled from her head—"perhaps that would be true."

The halberd swung; lightning struck the Lady; Lavinia cried out as light exploded across the stage and blinded the nocturnal audience members who covered their eyes as one shouting body. Three claps of thunder rocked the world during the spell of blindness; two more lightning bolts hit the stage. When the martyrs' vision cleared, some looked up to see the cyclone of blood had expanded to the theater's circumference, and now twisted in an uncanny ring that vibrated with electricity from the strikes.

Most of the audience members, however, saw only that which the great tear in the fabric of reality allowed them to see. These undistracted many, upon renewal of their vision, discovered what happened when lightning discharged itself within the ground of the avatar. The body that had once belonged to Miki Soto, struck by the bolt that sparked that reality distortion, had been transfigured. The eighth Lady, Dominia di Mephitoli, stood restored before the Hierophant in a glorified body incapable of experiencing the agonies that beset the material form, her unpatched right eye a black Void that absorbed all information-bearing light it crossed. The two-dimensional tear in space-time that had emanated from Miki's body—that same that had once expanded out of Trisha's, and left a dog named Basil a saint named Valentinian—lapped like fire as far as shell-shocked Lavinia before it receded into Dominia's dark socket. The General released the halberd that she had stopped with her hand, pushing it aside like a child's toy to speak into her palm the True Word that men meant when they said "halberd." In that vast half-real arena produced by the electrified tornado of Lazarene blood, this Word manifested upon the Earth the highest form of the Hierophant's chosen weapon. Sharp as it was, the instrument sang to be held by Dominia.

"Magnificent," breathed the Holy Father, even as he backed out of range. At the same time, Lavinia lifted her hands. Her eyes, already wild, grew wilder each second. The Hierophant continued, "How I have longed to see this transformation again. O Lady! What sublime nature radiates from your true form."

"Cut the pedantic bullshit. I already remember; there's never been any Hierophant but you."

How could there be? He was too selfish to allow himself to die in any iteration, or to allow Cicero's potential to exceed his own. Why, what if a younger Cicero were a better Cicero than he? Couldn't risk that. He was the evil queen and the hunter all in one, letting his old self forever suffer the pain of his brother's death while leading him to believe that it wouldn't happen this time. No wonder Cicero hated Dominia so much! Her whole life, the Hierophant had been whispering in his ear insidious advice: that in his time, Dominia was responsible for Elijah's death, so they had to keep her in line. Any plan he would present to Cicero would seem foolproof.

But El Sacerdote was too in love with himself to recognize even he couldn't trust Cicero. Now there was a hell of a thought.

"Pedantic or no, you cannot imagine how I have waited for this moment. How I *always* wait for this moment. My fairest daughter! What a wonder you are, my pride." Barely, he ducked a swipe of the polearm, and laughed as he sprang back up. "But I think you shall find, even in your holy state, we are well matched—and your magician seems to have gone."

Yes: per usual, Valentinian (*her* good-for-nothing son, she understood, much as Lazarus's—wow, weird thought!) skedaddled when things got hotter than room temperature. Dominia didn't care. He'd done his job. His portal encompassed the walls of the theater and rendered everything up to the impassible doors that state of half Void, half reality that had allowed the True form of the halberd to be birthed in a physical way. The bloody mass was a great scab in the physical dimensions—everything beneath which, not fully formed, allowed glimpses of the black hole. Everything there was malleable. Perhaps this was how the magician saw reality all the time. For Dominia, the states of existence and nonexistence had become two concurrent levels of consciousness while within her avatars. For the magician, they were a perfect blend.

And the blend was also perfect for everyone in the portal who knew not what they saw. Therefore perfect, and confusing. Perfect, and terrifying. Martyrs who had begun to crowd the doors in a futile attempt to leave found themselves facing no door at all. Instead a vast, black wall. Others spoke to their neighbors in a rising symphony of fright. Still others began to pray—but there was one martyr who was not so disturbed. While Lavinia, awestruck, removed her gloves, Dominia said to her Father, "I don't need the magician to perform miracles, and I don't need the magician to kick in your teeth."

"What's the difference?" With a smug smile, he took another cautious step away with his halberd between them. "It will take a miracle to defeat me, my girl. And it will take a miracle to defeat all these people."

"I won't have to. They'll understand whose side they're really on."

"And how will you do that, Dominia?" That smile transformed into a mocking sneer. With his polearm, he gestured to the frigid water lapping between the audience and the stage. "Multiply the fish of the ocean? I've already done that with science, child. So perhaps you'll walk on water for us, instead! Go on, let's see it: this is a *show*, after all."

"My hands," Lavinia breathed, as somebody in the audience screamed, "We should be *killing* that traitor!"

"Yeah," shouted somebody else, while Dominia's lost daughter, who had begun weeping, cried out, "My *hands*!" and yanked the petticoats of her dress so high up her thighs that the crowd murmured for a different reason: disapproval Lavinia didn't, couldn't register. "Oh, my legs—my legs are *real*! *Ninny!*"

With a nod her way, Dominia said, "I've already produced a miracle by righting one of your foul wrongs—but if you want to see another, then, fine."

Her eyes never leaving those of her Father, Dominia took one step back, to the absolute edge of the stage. There, she dipped the tip of her platonic weapon into the lapping waves. Once more, part of the following occurrence could be attributed to the blood rain, but anyone who was there knew for the rest of their lives there was so much more to the story than that. The Void-tainted salt water allowed to wash in and out of the theater turned red. Had a curious martyr tasted it, he might have confirmed what his sense of smell indicated.

"Water to wine?" The Hierophant laughed; Dominia did not.

"Wine is nothing more than the blood—the spirits—of grapes." The sumptuous mulberry fluid took a mahogany hue all the darker as its substance grew sticky and dense. Fermented grapes' bitter announcement relented to the mouthwatering tang of coppery human blood. "It is the end of life for the grape, yet the existence of wine implies grapes; grapes cannot physically be derived from wine, but information about them can be. And information is all that matters here, in this half place."

The thick blood changed once more. Another step in a strange alchemical process that had simultaneously horrified and entranced the audience. Now, someone did try it, and said, "I know that taste—amniotic fluid."

The Hierophant, the notes of his laughter uncharacteristically tight, said, "My, my, all this has never happened before. How will this magic trick end?"

"You know what happens when they saw a Lady in half. She walks back out in one piece."

Lightning struck the crown of Dominia's head, and the thunder was nearly drowned by the collective scream of the audience—half for fear, and half for delight. The martyrs did not understand that a mass of consciousness had struck the Earth, and, through the Lady, was channeled down into the amniotic fluid in a flow of information-bearing photons and electrons. There, this consciousness bound with the salt enriching the formerly oceanic fluid, and a strange miracle occurred. Vision returned to the eyes of the light-blinded martyrs to reveal the General miraculously intact. Silence resounded through the rows and the stunned audience observed as she shifted her weapon to her left hand, then knelt, at last removing her eyes from her Father to reach her free hand toward the water.

Five seconds passed. With a splash loud as a gunshot, a hand burst from those waves. Dominia gripped the attached forearm to haul Kahlil, gasping and laughing, from the womb of the transfigured ocean.

"My *girl*," marveled the Hierophant. The crowd once more screamed in shared horror: all around the stage, hands leapt from the waves, seeking purchase to haul their once-deceased owners from the watery trough. "What a triumph you are."

"What is all this, Ninny?" Lavinia, her face aglow, began to step forward, but Dominia pointed the weapon in her direction.

"No, Lavinia. Don't come near him." She jerked her head at the Hierophant. "He won't hesitate to hurt you to get away. He's done it many times before."

He clucked in distaste. "Putting such thoughts into my daughter's head."

"My daughter. Cassandra's. I am so sorry, Lavinia, for everything I let him do to you." The General brandished the fauchard whose decorated pole resembled an elaboration of the sword of her demise. "But he'll never have an opportunity to hurt you, or anyone, again. Cicero is dead."

Those few members of the audience privileged to hear this emitted piteous wails, but they were few indeed; most roared with desperation to find an exit, for they found themselves confronted with a growing number of resurrected humans who stayed by the water's edge to help their comrades out. The Hierophant laughed and sprang for the stairs leading to the set's balcony. "And so is the Lamb. You expect me to be heartbroken? He's hardly the first Cicero you've killed, my girl. I can't count by now how many I've seen you do in!"

Before she jetted after him, she took up Kahlil's hand. "I'm sorry I let you die, my friend."

"I was going to someday anyway, right?" He laughed and looked down at his shrugging arms. "Let's say we're even now."

With a reassured nod, the Lady launched her pursuit. Some bold (stupid) martyrs, crying, "Papa, Papa," tried to fight their way through the humans to make it to the stage, but these were no ordinary mortals. The resurrected human bodies were glorified as that of the Lady, greater in speed and strength than those finest Olympic athletes and cured of worldly ills. In a contest of endurance, strength, or any other trait that could be named (including moral and mental qualities), reembodied humans were superior to martyrs in every way. The martyr cause was hopeless to break through the human defense, which was occasionally a bit more than defensive. Dominia noticed Tobias Akachi taking a little too much pleasure in giving a martyr a crack over the skull with one thick fist. She waved the polearm at him as she dashed up the balcony stairs in pursuit of her Father. "Don't have too much fun down there!"

"What is the point of resurrection, General, if a man cannot have a bit of fun!"

In one great leap, Dominia lifted through the air above the remaining coil of stairs as if the law of gravity no longer applied, then settled upon the rail. The Hierophant, ever tickled by the divine, managed the word, "Wonderful," before he made the first strike.

The Lady had fought a great many battles as the General, but never had she fought one with an opponent so formidable—or with her own consciousness is such a hyper-powerful state, expanding through all time, all directions, as it did. It was as though she saw his motions just before they were enacted by his muscles. Each of his intended blows were met with the pristine snaps of her scythe's blade against its inferior offender. The ease with which she parried blow after blow appeared to delight him, which annoyed her, and she sprang forward as he lashed out again. Her parry pinned the head of his weapon to the balcony floor and pushed it from his hands.

The lesser weapon clattered through the rails and to the stage below. With a noise of displeasure, he danced away, his own form so impossibly agile that the Lady could only assume, knowing now what she knew of herself and his journey through increasingly small iterations, that he had undergone a similar glorification process in his many transferences between worlds. Had she been in better humor, perhaps she would have appreciated the artistry of his battle as much as he admired hers, but she was, suffice to say, in no mood. Particularly not when he used a suspended sandbag intended for some special effect in Act V to swing from the platform and into the audience, cackling as he landed amid a bunch of martyrs. Those who didn't run away threw themselves down to soften his landing with pitiful cries like, "Father, oh, Papa, I have you!"

"Will you hide amid your martyrs, coward?" She might have found some grain of humor in that if she hadn't immediately noticed that martyr who stumbled through his row in far greater terror than his peers, knowing himself the Hierophant's target: Theodore.

"*Theo*," Lavinia screamed. The Lady flew as quick as the speed of thought into the Hierophant's path, eternally quicker for the purity of her ascension than he could ever hope to be in his profane acquisitions of divine power.

"I cannot imagine why my martyrs exist, if not to serve my pleasures." Ducking a sweep of the Lady's polearm, the Hierophant melted fully into the Void, and Dominia bared her teeth, having no choice but to follow him.

There he was, not feet before her, running in the direction not of Theodore but of the swirling portal that had opened with her bodily death. The next iteration—his next trap. The otherworldly window yawned like a cerulean-lined chasm in the middle of the Void, the only light in a place that stole all mortal illuminations. On the other side would be a new Void with that eight-mouthed fountain: the indicator of a fresh world. She sprinted after him, close to his heels when he made a sharp right into existence to appear in the aisle between the rows Q and R. "I always like to snap a few necks on my way out," said the Hierophant, his words breathless with the speed of the fight but carefree as they'd ever been. "Fifty million UF dollars and a royal title for the martyr who catches and kills either one of my treasonous children—Theodore *or* Dominia. Who wants to be a duke?"

The answer to that, apparently, was "everyone." At least, everyone who wasn't already losing a fistfight with some humans, or who hadn't been navigating the vomitorium's back entrance to the dressing rooms to reach a stage where they just now arrived. While the number of the resurrected continued to grow, those unoccupied martyrs, women and men alike, fine theater shoes and opera jackets be damned, began an ill-advised scramble for Theodore—mere distraction. The Hierophant had no more business with or grudge against Theodore than had an elephant for a solitary ant squashed on the way to the watering hole. His Holiness winked out of existence, and Dominia, annoyed, observed the people around her and flipped her fauchard backward to knock them out with the solid jeweled end.

By means of this scepter, she rather humiliatingly but harmlessly dispatched those few (seven or eight) foes stupid enough to think they could fight the General even pre-glorification. As she knocked out the first two, the Hierophant appeared in the corner of her light-hungry right eye in the distance of the stage where Lavinia had been fighting to acquire the attention of a cameraman—a new experience for her, no doubt, and an effort halted by the Hierophant's arrival. His posture, hands upon her face and body a shadow stooped over hers, was as cloying as it was intimidating, and the Lady hastily struck a young woman in a rich evergreen dress and abundant carrot wig with such force that she somersaulted backward over row DD and slammed into the encroaching Bosnian fellow so that he, too, went "ass over teakettle," as Cassandra had sometimes said.

Lavinia's body language was one of helplessness as the Hierophant tried to seduce her into doing something she no longer had the will to do. Her new hands—*her* hands—lifted and spread and sometimes patted her Father's shoulders in visible plea while he pressed, and pressed, and pressed, refusing to let the girl's face stray from his, refusing to let her look off into the crowd where Theodore fought for his life amid sometimes savage and often infighting martyrs. Fine gold pocket smartwatches went flying; elaborate weaves were torn from shrieking heads; a high-heeled shoe sailed so close to the Lady's skull that she shimmered up to the stage simply to avoid it, banking on the martyrs' selfish wish to lay claim to the Hierophant's promised title themselves. With their inability to work as a unit, Theodore would be fine until the humans who tried to save him had a chance to fight through to him. Fine for as long as it took Dominia to herd the Hierophant away from Lavinia and toward—what?

What was a better target?

"The Lamb is dead," the Lady repeated. Lavinia's terrified eyes landed on her speaking sister, who appeared a few paces behind her Father and only moved as much as it took to turn her polearm the right way around. "That was what sent you fleeing the first time, wasn't it? That first time…it was the most like this last time, except for this between you and me. Your brother's death was why you did any of this at all, finding another world. You wanted to be with him forever."

"We wage a war with death," said the Hierophant, clutching Lavinia to his breast, her yelping form between himself and the disgusted Lady. "Every man does; it is life's nature, its sordid struggle."

"You say you fight death, but you've brought it for so many. All these." She waved to the mass of humans who by now had grown to outnumber their martyr foes, and who had begun to fill seats to make room. "And you would bring it, still, for so many more. Even Lavinia."

"You hear that, my girl?" He lifted his eyebrows at his youngest daughter in a mime of concern. "She would run you through to get to me. These people infected by human religion, by pagan faith—they have no value for life. Not like I do. Don't you want to save the lives of martyrs, Lavinia?"

"Yes," said the girl, "but—"

"If you do not set things into motion, martyrs will never be the dominant species. We will never survive our journey to the stars, never lay a lasting print upon the universe the way mankind has and will and eternally shall. We will all die like famished seedlings, all the people you have ever known and loved—even me."

"But what about Theodore?"

Lavinia's question earned a noise of displeasure from the Holy Father. The Lady winked into the space behind him and forced him to relinquish his hold on the girl so he could flee into the Void. Dominia's feet found earth in time to hear a foreign martyr cry out, "Why, that's my *sister*," and she could feel the conflict beginning to give way to reunion.

"Are you all right?" The former General reached for Lavinia's shoulder just to be subjected to the sting of her jerking away. "Did he hurt you?"

"No. But I—" The wound was too new, and the Lady recognized that after a lifetime of lies, Lavinia needed time to heal. More time than Dominia had left to spend in the world. With a sharp breath and a bat of wet eyes, she nodded at the girl's single request: "Please—save Theodore."

The Lady flitted out of existence and into the Void, where she realized that either she had exceedingly little sense of the actual physical location of the portal, or that, unobserved, it had moved. The latter instance seemed more likely. It now yawned far off in the distance, more detectable by sound than by sight, for it was the most uncannily two-dimensional thing the five-dimensional-plus mind was capable of experiencing and was not fully apparent when one was level with its surface. Not until one was practically within it: then, the portal was very much apparent, a Grand Canyon that opened to a vision of another, distant Earth and its like Ergosphere—that beautiful planet, swirling far past Mercury and Venus, that vision of the cosmos from the perspective of Sol's beating heart.

She could not let him escape to another iteration, nor could she let him continue to sully this one. Her uncanny haste tripled in the Ergosphere, the General sought to clutch the suit jacket of her fleeing Father only to find herself grabbed by an assortment of rotten gray arms. Malformed and hastily implemented thoughtforms sprang from the naked ground to pin her down. A gap cleft the space between them, and he called, "This place is so boring without some imagination! Then again, you never were creative in anything other than military matters. Let me show you *my* Ergosphere, Dominia."

The cleft had emerged because the very substance of the Void shaped itself into a set of gargantuan gears. As if the makings of his clockwork universe had poured out of his tar-black soul and into the Ergosphere. Though she tore herself free and leapt from cog to cog in instinctive pursuit, she knew she need not: she was the ground, the very ground that was those arms, and they withered and died even as they gripped her legs. She was those very cogs, too, that reversed and sent him hurling back toward her. Her pursuit not hampered to his liking, the Hierophant again vanished into reality and forced Dominia to beat instant retreat—not to her starting position, but to the position of poor Theodore in the midst of his own chaos.

Del Medico had some serious problems. He'd lost his jacket and rolled up his sleeves, though one was already torn at the shoulder and he sported a swiftly swelling shiner in addition to bruises on hands raised in an unfortunate fighting style only identifiable as "fisticuffs." With these, the former doctor failed to defend himself against those few members of the crowd who valued worldly goods in a failing society over the opportunity to reunite with their human loved ones—which an increasingly large number of martyrs seemed to be choosing. A good thing the selfish ones were so few: this small handful of assailants had evidently decided they could kill Teddy together and sort out the victor later. Having momentarily lost track of the Hierophant, Dominia set to work at the task of fighting her way to Theodore, a process that seemed slow to treacherous extent: particularly when her attention finally did fix to the distant sight of her Father disemboweling the unfortunate cameraman who had, during the Lady's time in the Void, obeyed Lavinia's pleas to film her.

"My fragile girl," he cried, "my dove, my favorite child not myself—how I tried to save you from this world!" He shook the chunks of liver from his fingers and advanced on his youngest daughter. As she cried out, Lavinia's dart away was blocked by the on-stage martyrs. His Holiness continued his standard guilt trip—and his relentless approach across that massive stage—without missing a beat. "But you wouldn't accept it any more than would your sister. Now look where we are! Are your arms and legs worth this? Is liberty not too highly priced?"

After sending a fat gray-haired fellow in a bloodied tuxedo toppling with the gold staff's slam to his groin, Dominia forced her way past a couple of loudly fighting (former) lovers—one martyr and the other resurrected, spurned and eaten—then knocked a toothy young woman off of Teddy's arm.

"Are you all right?" she asked, which she regretted when he began to whine. She cut him off by asking, "Can you get into the Void?"

"I have *no* idea how to get in and out of that place on my own. Are you kidding? Now's not the time for this."

Fighting back Dominia's understandable annoyance, the Lady asked, "Then can you at least get to Lavinia if I clear a path for you?"

"What do you think I've been trying to *do*," was his shrill response. A noble one, if annoyingly phrased. Knocking with a nasty *clank* the teeth out of someone who needed a valuable lesson on greed, Dominia cleared the way and said, "Then watch my back."

"With *what*?"

With another immortal Word, the Lady put into his hands a higher kind of flail that was not as harmful as it looked, and which, knowing the substance of its wielder's soul, would never hit Teddy in the head…no matter how stupid he was with it. "That's a good weapon for you." She dragged him along while humans—swarming down into the orchestra pit poised before the body-blooming trench—began to clamber up to the stage, sometimes over one another. "Doesn't require precision."

"What are they doing," he cried of the souls, and she smiled.

"The same thing as us."

It was religious fervor more than greed that drove the still-fighting martyrs. She would reflect on this in calmer times when she'd had occasion to process, at least partially, all the events of her last hour on that Earth. Zealot fathers forewent reunion with children they thought to be demons of the sort the *tulpa* had been; ignorant women scorned long-dead friends striving to embrace them due to the Hierophant's virtuoso brainwashing. Most martyrs had the humanity left (and the common sense) to give up their fighting, but too many stayed in her path, and too many were upon the stage to shepherd fleeing Lavinia up the whirling balcony stairs to a point where she could be cornered. The Hierophant made his calm way after her once he selected another halberd. "You would overlook seventy years of love, of doting privilege, because I made the mistake of saving both you and your mother? Of giving you better lives? I should have ordered Dominia to cut your mother's throat while she slept rather than martyring her. Perhaps I will next time. If I do it soon enough"—he glanced in the direction of the Lady, still fighting through the crowd but soon to reach the sea of humans that had grown properly onto the stage to march en masse for the Hierophant—"she will obey just like the dog she is."

At the General's sneer and the approach of individuals from stage left, the Hierophant made to self-obviate again, but was halted by a hand that lay upon his arm. He turned his head, and his face was aglow with a look of such incredible shock that Dominia, satisfied to see it, only felt her own shock as she recognized from behind the honey locks of a woman whose existence slowed time. The Lady, tripped up by the General she inhabited, paused to watch Cassandra say something to the Hierophant before she punched him in the face hard enough to shatter his nose. Only the Lady knew what the gentle (sometimes crass) woman had said before striking the Holy Father, because she could feel the vibrations of the words in the substrate of reality. "This isn't for all the horrible things you did to everyone in the past, please understand—it's for what you're trying to do right now."

Blood pouring from his nose, the Hierophant wrenched his arm from her grip and disappeared with the saturnine expression of a man who longed more than ever for the immediate mass death of all mankind. Cassandra disappeared into the human crowd, but there was no time to fuss about it. Dominia forced her attention back upon Teddy. "Try not to kill anyone, if you can help it. There's been enough death. Just keep using that flail— It isn't fatal."

"Why not?"

"Because it's not real," she explained half a second before she was once more whipping across that imaginary landscape to fly in stride with the Hierophant's sprint. He had been right: when one interacted with the Void, the Void was also within them. Dominia could feel the Hierophant as though he were a parasite crawling about a skin whose surface she could neither see nor feel without its disruption. On entry to that space, such disruption became the sum total of experience. His presence within her provoked an itch, and she sought to cure it. She reached for him and was surprised when he caught that arm and slammed her down into the ground with force she did not expect herself capable of feeling after her ascension. She supposed, though immune from pain, little could stop thoughtbodies from having effects upon one another: and if the Hierophant had run this race even ten times, that placed him at twenty thousand years of existence, which meant he was an exceedingly dangerous opponent.

But Dominia, a mere 333 years old, had fought a thousand battles—and the Lady, that infinite embodiment of all Dominias and more, was the very act of combat. She could not forget the limits of her capabilities, and so, though tossed aside in her own arena as she had been that night at McLintock farm, she skidded to her feet in this space and was in fast pursuit of him once more.

When he knew she was behind him, he grew as fast as he was strong, and although she could arrive at his location at the speed of thought, this only caught her up with him for the space of a second. Then he would be beyond arm's reach once more, too fast even for her, the hum of the portal growing ever to a roar.

At last, seeking her gun on instinct and finding it there in joyful thoughtform, Dominia drew and fired. With satisfaction, she watched him whip backward, past and through her, into the distance the way they had come—the way she now beat hasty pursuit.

Before emerging back into the world, she asked herself if that was the best thing to do. Was it not better to take the portal now, herself? Get the drop on him? Do what he did, perhaps, and strangle the boys who would become Cicero and Elijah in their beds before they could ever wreak such evil across the land? But that was just more violence, and would not resolve all these past failures. Not resolve this iteration. Dominia had made a promise to Cassandra. She had seen Lazarus die. She had taken Miki's body. She could not live with herself, abandoning this universe to the whims of her trapped Father. She could not let him rule without her intercession.

For was that not what her actions were, now? The intercessions of the truly risen dead—the truly sanctified within the world? She had died, returned to life, and returned life to others whom she needed to take elsewhere. She had seen the truth of her position as, if not the Void itself, then as that recording beam and the identical playback beam in Tish's preferred, holographic model of reality. That meant Dominia could influence Earth's stability much as she could influence the Void's. When she returned to the world, she made the very stage buck beneath her Father's feet.. Disoriented from his Ergosphere death, the Hierophant nonetheless had frame of mind enough to stumble up the rocking staircase and shove his people aside with the staff of his halberd.

How astonishing to be faster than him! To leap, with a few great bounds, up the twisting rail of the stair and upon the balcony's surface—there to meet him when he made it up! As a girl, she could have only dreamed of reflexes like his, and as an adult she never dared waste time on such fancies. But now, here they were: the Lady poised between Lavinia and the Holy Father, whose polearm was once again torn from his hands with a satisfying clatter as it hit the still-trembling stage below.

"You think you'll manage to kill me?" asked the Hierophant, laughing even as his anxious martyrs, knowing better than to help now that Dominia was in the fray, edged their way back down the stairs. "I, who have cut down many past iterations of my own self because they stood between me and a higher world?"

"It isn't a higher world you want. You want a world that's all your own—but you don't deserve one. Not as you are now."

"And you do, Dominia?"

"I don't want a world! I want nothing more for any world than its peaceful, happy existence. You want to see everything crushed."

"Not at all. I wish to be immortal: to *truly* live forever." She took a swipe at him, missed, and the balcony groaned with his landing upon it, the temporary structure still reverberating with the Earth's ceased shudders. Not made to bear more than one or two actors at a time, let alone the movements of real fighting above an earthquake, the set piece began its slow sag. Lavinia cried out behind them, and Teddy, amid the throng of humans who had pulled him up to the stage, called her name from below. Eyes wild with terror, the girl jumped over the balcony's side and tumbled twenty feet down, where Teddy and humans alike reached up to catch her. The no-longer-so-Eternal Virgin of the now defunct Holy Family landed upon her future lover with an *oof* and a laugh of surprise audible even over the Hierophant's sincerely demanded questions. His black eyes blazed into Dominia while he snarled, "What is it in me that makes me so unworthy of the highest truth? Of knowing the essence of the godhead? What is it in me that makes *me* so unworthy of the life you returned to them? What makes my brother unworthy? He died that first time, just as your wife. I understand your pain, my girl, but you refuse to acknowledge your involvement in mine! Why was my escape to that first new world so unjust?"

The air between them stilled. Dominia could see in his eyes he knew the moment had come. She felt it, herself, in every atom of air. She saw, also, that so long as he lived, he could not escape his thicket of self-delusion. There was only one method of liberation.

"You will never repent, as long as you live in this form—so, it's my duty to free you for another chance to grow."

By slipping the halberd into his belly and jerking its blade upward, Dominia tore apart the innards of the Hierophant to the sound of Lavinia's wail. Pupils dilating to invisible pinpoints within their tarry irises, he fell backward from the point of impalement and disappeared a few meters before his impact upon the stage revealed by scattering humans.

"There's no time," Dominia heard Theodore saying as the General pursued the dying man into the Void. "Are you hurt? We need to go."

She didn't need to hear the girl saying, "No, no—we can't. Oh, Daddy!"

Then, the Lady was within the Void: alone, yet, the furthest thing from, for she felt at this point in space-time a great many entities crawling with life inside her. Of those, the liveliest was also the one whose death was most imminent. The Hierophant's soul ran for the portal as fast as his body's fading life required of it, thoughtform walls throwing themselves up along with fires, forests, a clockwork city, a vast factory of conveyor belts and Escher stairs, entire hallucinatory dream-universes through which they both lived flickering second lives locked in eternal rivalry—anything he could think to put between himself and the Lady.

But the Lady was all things in that place. She was those fires, those forests, the walls, and all the other things with which the Hierophant tried to slow her down. She was the very ground upon which he ran, the very ground that softened to the substance of a marsh and slowed his pace.

"I could give you so much, my girl," said the Hierophant, stumbling forward one final step, succumbing to the suction of his feet, and standing to await her emergence from the flaming trees. "Everything, anything you asked. Why should either of us find a new world when we might make this one better, as I have said so many times over? Why should any of us suffer? Is the happiest ending, the happiest world, not one where *I, even* I, am redeemed?"

"Then consider this might not be the happiest world for you." Dominia's voice emanated from all things, all space, around the Hierophant. Her body—the body of a giant, in truth, replicating hers—formed from the ground beneath him faster than he could have run were he allowed. Had he, he would have fallen to his death from the heel of her sprawling palm. "Maybe the next one."

With a gesture of her fingers as simple and light as she might use in the crushing of a gnat, Dominia squashed the thoughtbody of the Hierophant and forced him to fly back once more—now, to the moment of his death, to which she followed him. She emerged normal size upon reality's stage and bent at the side of his broken, eviscerated body. Behind them, Lavinia and Theodore hurried to the abandoned camera.

"The moment you have so long awaited," observed the Hierophant with his final breaths. He laughed even as he did, a wet, ugly sound that seemed more truthful than his usual mirth. "Will you ever be sorry it was so short?"

"It feels to me like it's lasted at least twenty thousand years," was her response. With that bastard grin, he raised one broken arm to lay a numb hand against his daughter's cheek. Then, unspeaking, he relented to that which was long overdue, and his eyes paled over in the mist of death.

As he died, a great roar rose across the theater: Dominia first took it for a mass of crying martyrs but soon knew it for the black tsunami that rose from the ocean to carry off the dead—and the portal—to holier pastures. As the massive wave arced over the edge of the theater, the General lifted her head in time to see Cassandra there, holding Lavinia. That most perfect of women, she looked up at Dominia and smiled—what a radiant smile!—as the crest dropped over the theater wall and smashed, to the screams of many misunderstanding martyrs, into the overcrowded people. The martyrs all seemed to require a few seconds to realize they were neither crushed nor drowning, nor even wet. When the flood washed away, every last human was gone, along with the reality distortion. The doors, returned, burst open and overflowed, not with water but with newly baptized Lazarene martyrs desperate to flee their tahgmahr.

"Tell your children what you've seen," the Lady called after them before lowering her head again toward the dead man.

As usual, he had been right. Eternal as she may have been, and evil as he may have been, it brought a soft sting of pain to look into the Hierophant's dead face. He was, after all, her Father. But she refused to submit to the emotion of grief, and stood in time to hear good Lavinia, dear Lavinia, do what she knew needed to be done. Something that was only the first of many ways in which the Princess would make a difference in her world.

"Viewers, please! Please, I have a message—have you seen all this, this madness?" Down below, a few martyrs greedy for imaginary principalities still scrapped, unclear on the fact that the Hierophant was dead. Theodore, in control of the camera, panned around the emptying theater, across the Hierophant's body, then back to Lavinia. "Look at that—and look at me! I beg you, humans watching me, please know how powerful you are! Please know: you can do anything. You're just as good as us, or better, even though we've told you otherwise for centuries. Some of you believe us, and I'm talking to you—yes, you! You've been brainwashed. For years we've hidden things in your books and movies, your video games, your news, even your schools!

We've taught you dirty lies, and we—we should be ashamed of ourselves. But you'll see it now."

Her innocent eyes, opened for the first time, glassed over with tears of repentance. "You don't have to listen to us. All beings are self-sovereign." Given by Lavinia, this command washed across the world in a throb of bliss that the Lady felt also in her own body. The Princess went on, speaking from her heart as she said, "We've made you our slaves and we're—I'm—sorry. You don't have to be. You are conscious, powerful, incredible creatures! Never let anyone tell you that you have to be a martyr's slave. If you have love in your heart for the family you serve and wish to stay, then do, but if you don't, then listen to me now: you are *free*, you are *free*. My Father is dead along with my Family"—her pitch jumped to an all-time high and snapped, and when her voice returned, Lavinia sounded like a new, steadier woman—"and it is my first commandment as the Church's Hierophant that you, all humans, are *free*."

That would help matters. The General would not be around to ensure the humans were taken care of—she could not continue to take responsibility for a world's worth of woes—but she could take solace before her parting that those left behind planned to make improvements. She could not say for certain how all the remaining martyrs, like the violent sort below, would take the news of the Family's dissolution; nor could she say how difficult the road ahead of Lavinia was to be; nor could she say that martyrs would never ruin Mars; nor, nor, nor. There were so many things that she could not complete, herself—so many things she could not control, any more than anyone could control anything.

That was the most difficult part. It was not defeating her Father that was hard—it was letting go of his world, and her vision of it. But her vision had been spoiled by his filthy lens, and she would give much for a new view's purity.

Still—still. She could not yet find it in herself to leave. Lavinia ended the broadcast, then faced the sister who stood beside the body of the Hierophant. The tableau gave the younger girl pause before she found the courage to approach.

"My limbs are real again," she said to Dominia, her words a hush, and the Lady nodded. "Was that you? Did you do this, Dominia?"

"I didn't fix your limbs, personally."

"But you *did* do it, somehow. I saw a Lady before—someone wearing one of those dresses like they do in Japan, you know, the robes...but when she was struck by lightning, she was lots of other Ladies, and then she was blackness and finally she was you, and—are you really Ninny? *Really*?"

Studying the Hierophant's still features, she thought of her dead body in Kronborg's chapel. "I don't know how to answer that question."

The nonresponse hung heavy in the air until, somehow resolved, Lavinia insisted, "You must be. You must be my Ninny. Oh, Dominia—" The girl's eyes welled with tears. "I can't believe Daddy is dead. I'd have thought I would be sobbing right now, but I…I don't know how to feel."

"You're just as free as the humans, now. Freer. You can do whatever you want."

"I just want to be with Theo," she said meekly, as if still fishing for permission until Dominia pointed out to her, "There's nobody to stop you." While the girl seemed to absorb that fact with some astonishment, Dominia went on, lifting her gaze to the stars that twinkled above the stage. Amid them, Mars shone bright with hope for the human race. "But there is something required of you. Much."

As Lavinia listened, her organic hands clasped over her heart, the Lady glanced between the purest of martyrs and her husband-to-be. She could see in great ethereal trails the eternal paths routed in this world by their comings and goings: how they would embrace in that moment when she disappeared from their lives forever. A moment coming so quickly that she whose very perception was eternity felt for all the world it might as well have been that very second. After savoring, for a few silent heartbeats, what it was to be alive in this dark but redeemable world, Dominia said, "After all the horrors the martyr race has wrought upon the human one, we owe them a duty. You are a princess no more: now, you are a queen. As you said yourself, the Hierophant." The girl's eyes glowed while the Lady warned, as had the Bard, "'Uneasy lies the head that wears a crown.'"

"I suppose that's right," said Lavinia.

"You will be threatened, and fought against. There will be much turmoil. But it is your duty to tame martyrkind, and restrain their numbers. When I restored your limbs, your entire body was healed and glorified—your blood." The girl's electromagnetic field throbbed with an energy detectable but to the Lady, containing all the information about the genetic and mental makings of the woman before her: yes, this was how the magician saw the world, and yes, it was as he suggested. This daughter of the malformed protein was healed—as much a daughter of the sacred protein upon Earth as the pure Bearers were in their heavenly abode. So that was the source of the nagging resemblance! Slightly, Dominia smiled. "Tonight you'll dream of a place that's half real, but don't be afraid. Tomorrow, you'll walk in the sun. You have the blood of Lazarus—though it's the blood of Lavinia now, I suppose. The true sacred protein."

The girl's expression was awash with horror. "Ninny—"

"It's not going to send you to hell," Theodore said. Lavinia looked at him in surprise while he went on. "It's true! I've been to that place she's talking about, that other dimension. We can go together! Well—" He laughed weakly and glanced at Dominia. "When I figure out how to come and go."

"The duty of the martyr race is to eventually migrate to this place we describe, but only if they make the choice to abstain from the flesh of mankind, which is possible with your blood. The same blood Lazarus once had." With a pang for her friend, she said, "In the chapel, you will find the body of Lazarus, along with mine." She strove not to give in to the pain that filled the girl's eyes. Dominia stooped to slip the (bullet-dented) Ring of the Fisherman from her Father's immobile finger. This, she lay in Lavinia's palm. "His blood is gone. The martyrs who were here tonight are all baptized, but you must baptize more, and humans, too—you must be Lamb, Lazarus, and Hierophant in one woman. Distribute your blood to those meek and gentle martyrs who, like your mother was, are people very afraid of death. These people, you will teach to leave Earth for that other dimension opened by the sacred protein."

"But how will we live, Ninny? How will we get around, what will we do?"

"That other dimension contains the shortest path to alien worlds. This is the way for us to find new planets for ourselves. Also in the chapel you will find a living man, Farhad, a Hunter pilot: he knows the approximate locations of three downed interdimensional amphibiships across the landscape of the Void, and he is one of two men who are at this point in time capable of piloting them. He understands the secret of fixing them from their current, damaged states because he's seen it done. Safeguard him, treat him well, and he will help martyrs migrate to more appropriate pastures." She didn't add: "If only to see us gone."

With an anxious look still in place, the girl nodded. "You said that Cicero and the Lamb are both dead?"

"Yes." New tears appeared in the girl's eyes as her older sister admitted, "Though you will still have many opponents."

"Oh, but I'm so glad *you're* alive. At least, in this way. I have so many questions!"

Ah! The shot of guilt, straight through her heart. Dominia took Lavinia's petite hand in hers and studied it, so much softer and more real than the very realistic hands before. Some things could not be replicated.

"I wish I could answer all of them—but I don't think I have the time to stay."

Lavinia's expression fell. "Where are you going?"

"I don't know. But I feel…in need of change. This is not my world." The Lady embraced the young woman and planted a kiss on her forehead. "Not a day will go by that I don't think of you."

"You can't *go*," Lavinia insisted. Dominia heard the script of her own Cassandra tahgmahrs read aloud to uncanny effect. "You're the only one who knows the truth, you—I—"

"No. You know the truth, and that's what matters. Teddy knows a little, too. When you find my body"—she struggled to ignore the girl's sob—"in the castle chapel, you'll find a necklace with it. That's Cassandra. Keep her close to you, always. You'll never forget, then."

"And you?" Lavinia breathlessly tried to restrain her tears within the vital support of Theodore's arms. "How will you keep from forgetting, Ninny?"

She didn't know how to answer that, other than to say, "If I don't remember all this, it will be just as much a failure as if I'd actually failed. I will never forget you, Lavinia. And I hope that, someday soon, I'll see you again."

Once more she bent to kiss the girl, now upon the cheek, before she turned to clap Theodore on his shoulder, and, at speed of thought, hasten to the death-filled chapel where lay her imperfect former body. She could not linger and see the start of weeping—it was hard enough to view her own trauma. The scene was a vile mess of blood and water, mixed to ooze across the floor, around the altar, beneath Dominia's body, the Lamb's, and Cicero's.

Cicero's body.

But not his soul.

She should have recognized something was off when Farhad and Basil were both gone from the empty chapel. How was she so stupid? Why—

Because she had wanted to believe the Hierophant was finished, of course. She was so ready to believe him dead that she, this near-goddess, this Void-substance, this Valkyrie imbued with powers from beyond time and space—she had not considered the moment of her own death. Dominia failed to consider that, after her pulse stopped, her soul now resided, unbounded, in the Ergosphere.

She had nobody but herself to blame, but she had to give it to him—the Hierophant was one hell of an actor. "Sorry it was so short," her omniscient fucking eye!

The savage barking of what seemed to be a pack of dogs filled the air of the Void as soon as Dominia emerged within it. Farhad, Allah smile upon him, noticed her arrival from the distance where he stood beside a great blurred battle poised unnervingly close to that thrumming portal's edge. Waving both hands and shouting, the man dashed to meet Dominia halfway and was visibly shocked when she simply blinked in front of him. Nearer the confusing fray, she saw what even her eyes had failed to resolve from that distance.

Three heads? Basil had quite a soul. And just look at those fangs.

"The dog, Mahdi." Farhad glanced over at the Hierophant, who fought a fruitless battle against the massive hound barring his way to the next iteration of reality. "He was very calm after your death— I waited with him just as your Lady ordered of me. But then he became very hostile, growling at nothing, and disappeared into the Void. I broke a stained-glass window to let the moonlight in so I could follow him, and—well...he is different now."

"I'll say."

"It is the strangest thing— I feel as if I have always been here, observing this battle for eternity. It was as I watched it unfold just now, it seemed... preexistent."

"That's life for you."

As the General strode to the battle, one great head lifted, and a trio of tails wagged in happy harmony. In a blink, Basil was that prancing border collie again, of standard size and excess affection for the battered Hierophant whose face he mercilessly licked.

"I've had enough of your games, you wretched little—"

"Good boy," said Dominia, catching the Holy Father's bloodied hand. "And good try, Cicero. You almost got me."

"I usually do." The Hierophant's disembodied soul gritted its teeth and leveled its dark eyes with Dominia's. "Will you destroy me now, with no body to which I can return? Where will I go? Shattered in pieces across the low frequencies?"

"No." She studied his bloodied hand, held in hers. With a glance to that buzzing portal and the happy dog who watched, Dominia smiled. "Go back, Farhad."

"But, Mahdi—"

"I have him from here. You'll be needed on Earth very soon. Don't stray from the chapel until Lavinia finds you, but...do make yourself scarce there until you know it's her who's coming in. Never know."

"Very well." With a glance over the scene before him, the pilot gathered this was the end of their struggle, and nodded. "It was an honor to serve you, General."

"And it was an honor to serve with you, Farhad. Thank you for everything."

While the man disappeared to the Earth where he was destined to spend the rest of his life as a spiritual teacher, Dominia returned her attention to her Father. "You asked if I would kill you. The answer is as it was on Earth: I must."

But as she did, his soul slipped back to its last escaped death, and the moment that Lady Dominia lost him into the portal. He was hurled back through its mouth into her arms, where she waited to plunge her fingers through his heart; and he slipped back through the iteration prior to that and into that escape, to the Lady who had missed her chance to crush his skull; and again, and again.

On, and on.

The Hierophant died a death for every iteration he had lived and ruined.

At last, his soul lay curled at the feet of the inciting Dominia: that very first Lady who discovered the True Name of the sacred protein and had waited an infinite number of attempts for this moment to find the Holy Father helpless before her.

"Please," he begged, real tears in the shut eyes shielded behind his hands. "No more! My daughter, my child—Dominia."

"I won't." Completely alone with him, without even the buzzing portal to interrupt the moment, the General knelt at the Hierophant's side and lay a soothing hand upon his arm. He flinched and cried out like an abused old man, though his soul, pure in its fine white suit, was young and undamaged as ever. As his breathing and his body's tension calmed, Dominia wrapped Cicero in her arms to hold him like a child. His breathing paused, then broke into aching, wet laughter that then fell apart into agonized tears.

"Is this all I have to look forward to! An eternity, dead? Nothing? My brother! Oh, where? I knew he would not be here."

"Of course not." While her Father wept into her shoulder, she held him, patted his back, and said, "He's in the same place where there's peace for you. Where there's God."

"My girl! My girl, my girl, I have spent eternity spitting in His face, mocking Him!"

"Like a toddler misbehaving to obtain His father's attention."

"Yes! And look! He has sent me nothing—no miracle, no punishment! Not even a great flood or a burning bush."

"No," said Dominia. "He's sent you me."

As the space of the Void around them folded and refolded so shapes emerged from the air and ground, the Hierophant's tears began to still. "You need to change, Cicero. And when we know you have, I'm sure you'll find Elijah again."

Those shapes formed buildings and stalls and the many busy people populating the market square of the Kingdom—all of whom, in accordance with that cultural immune system the magician had once described, turned their heads at the coming of the man who had sent a great many of its refugees fleeing in the first place.

"What *is* this place," marveled the False Protomartyr in the direction of the holy azure sky. "Dominia—is this heaven, my girl? Oh, the Kingdom! I see—I see, the Kingdom." The General, smiling into the faces of so many the Hierophant had murdered by his own hand, released her hold on Cicero. The first Cicero. The only Cicero. The real Cicero, who looked in unsteady recognition from face to human face.

"Yeah, it's the Kingdom—but heaven? Just who do you think I am?"

Dominia laughed at his assumption, relating more than ever to the magician. "It's not heaven. Or maybe. I don't know. It's just someplace that can take care of itself...and where there are people who are going to want a word with you. I think I see my parents over there—why don't you apologize to them first?"

With the most cathartic wave "goodbye" she'd ever given, Dominia passed into a crowd that, step by step, closed around Cicero. As she squeezed into a more open area, the distant voice of Tobias Akachi boomed, "*Well* now, my friend! About time you have gotten here. If you've come to stay with us, you'll have to work. I have heard the hotel is in need of a doorman...the last one just went off to be an Engineer out east, and they've been looking for someone to help these refugees you've sent move all their bags upstairs!"

"How will they decide who gets him alone first?" The magician's appearance behind a lamppost near the edge of the market did not even startle Dominia.

"I don't know...flip for it, I guess?"

"With a billion-sided coin?" Laughing, Valentinian took her hand as she came near. "I'm proud of you, kiddo. Very, very proud of you."

"No thanks to you," she said with a playful smile. "But, thank you."

"Hey! You were right the first time, I didn't do anything. It was all you. I'm mostly here to mooch favors off you, with one more still to go."

Trying not to look too annoyed, especially as he took off at a quick pace in the direction of the hotel, the General said, "You have no idea how tired I am."

"I'm sure you're exhausted! This has been a long time in the making and it's been a lot of struggle for you. But I promise it will be worth it."

"Cassandra?"

With a smile over his shoulder, the magician doubled his hasty pace, and Dominia was forced to jog to keep up. She asked, "What about Lazarus?" surprised as she was that she hadn't seen him yet. He had technically died only an hour before, a loss less tragic to Dominia now that she understood eternity; but that surely counted him among the Kingdom's refugees. And as to the location of Elijah—she was not sure, but she sensed he was not here, either. Those men were too tired to settle down in eternity until they learned to enjoy consciousness again. That much was clear.

The magician did not respond to her question, except to say, "You'll see Lazarus soon. I promise."

The speed with which they walked, perhaps, was why it seemed they found themselves so quickly at the hotel. Outside was quite a sight: the E4 perched like a gargoyle atop the building's high roof. Dominia laughed.

"Tenchi," she said. The magician waved a hand.

"Oh, yeah. He'll have to park that thing elsewhere before he starts his shift… Tenchi!" In the lobby, the chubby man spoke to someone unseen behind the sitting area's elaborate hedges. Instantly at attention, the sailor spun and brightened to see Dominia.

"Ah! Mephitoli-sama! Miss Mephitoli, hello! I'm so happy to see you, did you know I'm moving here for a little while?"

"I get the feeling you're going to end up staying here forever," she said with a laugh. As she bent to embrace him, he shook his head and looked at the magician.

"He can't stay forever yet," confirmed Valentinian. "He's got duties! Like parking the E4 where it's not going to be ticketed," he added indelicately. At the sailor's nervous look, the magician chuckled. "And eventually flying that ship to come and bring you back here, Dominia."

"Me?"

"Yeah, you! How else are we going to get you back to the Kingdom at the end of your life, if not with an interdimensional amphibiship? Most other worlds aren't as crazy as the one you're from, they're boring. You'll need outside help. Luckily, all worlds have unexplained phenomena of one kind or another."

"Are you trying to say my true death will come to me in the form of Tenchi Ichigawa, flying a UFO?"

"It's not a UFO, it's identified! Can you imagine a safer way to leave the Earth behind?" While the General laughed, she couldn't help but roll this through her head, along with a word spoken sometime before. Transmigration. She *was* dead already, after all. And she wasn't ready to settle down in the Kingdom, either. Reading her thoughts in the text of space-time, Valentinian smiled. "We need assistants like him to ease you in. I can be somewhat startling when I just show up on my own…but I'm glad you're not afraid of death, or of living again."

"I want to live again. I want—" She couldn't vocalize the hope and looked helplessly at him, mute before the sailor. Valentinian patted her hand.

"I know what you want. Hey, Tenchi"—he turned to the sailor and, strolling to the overflowing mail outbox, collected a messenger bag from behind the desk. This, he stuffed full of envelopes—"while you're in town, I've got a job for you."

After the shorter Ichigawa cousin made his peace with Dominia, waved goodbye, and hit the road to deliver the mail ("You'll figure it out" was Valentinian's lazy answer when the man asked how to read addresses in the infinite city), the magician led the General up to the sitting area. "Brace yourself, now," he said.

She tried, but it was still quite shocking to round that hedge and find the mortal form of Gethsemane, who, in a dreadlocked, human body, waited in that risen sitting area looking as beautiful as she did enormously pregnant.

"Hello," said shocked Dominia, and, "I thought you couldn't come to the Kingdom," and, "What's *happened* to you?"

"My spirit has been grounded by another. I could not come here without being reduced back to the nymph were it not for the magician and the seed he transplanted within me. Sometime after you left, when we met him in the road, he whisked me away through time to a strange place—a table. I cannot remember much—"

"It's never good to remember surgery," said the agreeable magician.

Gethsemane remained the center of Dominia's attention. As the former martyr neared, the woman took her humanized hand and allowed the transfixed General to feel the aquatic kick of infantile feet beneath her taut belly. "It's your baby."

Shocked, Dominia looked over at Valentinian, who buffed his nails against his shirt and said, "Oh, the marvels of modern medicine."

"But that's not possible."

"But *I'm* possible?' While she laughed in surprise, he smiled. "It's completely possible with a donor egg, a little spiral of your DNA"—she remembered that bundled up thread he had pulled from her on her last visit here, and was all the more astonished—"and, of course, a surrogate mother…or bearer, if you will. I love a good pun."

"And the Father?"

"So, I know I said you'd see Lazarus soon," said Valentinian, fingers tented. "But I wasn't very specific."

Tracing her gaze again toward Gethsemane's great stomach, Dominia asked in shock, "This child is Lazarus's? Is it you?"

"More like, this child is Lazarus, or—Lazarus augmented, slightly. There'd be no point in transmigration if everybody was the exact same every time. And I had to give him your DNA if he's going to be born of you! I just know you don't want to go through all the—" He nodded at Gethsemane's hugely pregnant state, and the General felt a wave of true appreciation for the magician's unspoken understanding. "You know."

"Not for me."

"Exactly. But I still have to make sure he resembles you a little bit, so there's never any controversy. Although…I'm fairly confident my plan will ensure there won't be a problem."

"I hope to God this is the last time in any of my lives that people talk around subjects instead of just telling me the truth."

"Well, I just don't want this to be controversial. I mean, I know that you're not much of the motherly type, but…"

"You want me to take care of the—Lazarus." At last, she understood what he'd been driving at. After absorbing this revelation, she said, "But only one body can pass through to a new iteration, a new world. That's why you can't just come through and you have to go through the pains of having me make you a new body each time, right?"

"Isn't it nice that, here, you're not a martyr at all? And that you happen to have a perfectly fertile womb, just like every other woman here? So convenient!"

At the force of her annoyed look and her beginning accusation, "You just said—" the magician clasped his pleading hands. "Gethsemane has been doing this for the past two weeks, and you won't even be conscious of it! It won't even seem like half a minute to you. She's lived *nine* months in two weeks for *you*, Dominia, all so you don't have to, because I know you're not the being-pregnant type."

"I'm a martyr when I'm not in the Kingdom! Martyrs don't give birth. The baby will *die*."

"There are no martyrs where you're going. You're going to be human, just like everybody else." Taken aback by that, Dominia found no way to respond, and allowed the magician to continue his gentle goading. "I know you're not thrilled by this prospect, but trust me—you're not only doing me a favor, but you're doing yourself a favor, too."

"You just want me to establish a family line for you in the new world," observed Dominia, and the magician spread his hands.

"Is that so wrong? I'm not asking to take the portal out from under you, even though it means I'll only be able to interact with that world through the intercession of animals and petty miracles and synchronicities."

"Until a consciousness, which at the peak of development matches yours, comes into existence in a few generations."

"Yes, but that's because I want to make up for the past. I want to right wrongs. And I want to give you the best possible life."

"And you think that *me*, being a *mother*, is the best possible life?"

"I think that it's the life you need to live, karmically, after all the things that happened in this world. And you might even enjoy it! Hell, think of it like this—you've never been with a man, right? It's a virgin birth! And Miki's body, which you're still technically borrowing, was immaculately conceived before it was transformed into a woman, so…"

If she rubbed her forehead any harder she'd smash her own brain in. Annoyed and somehow helpless, Dominia looked over at the desk to find it tragically empty of Miki Soto, and her heart broke—not only because she was undefended but because she thought she would never see her best friend again. "Fine," consented the worn-down General. The magician sighed in relief.

"I promise—you'll fall in love at first sight."

When she looked back, Gethsemane was gone from her periphery; but before she could comment on the absence, the magician blew that familiar dust into her face. Within mere heartbeats, General Dominia di Mephitoli fell asleep forever.

lim

Dominia→∞.

The Life of the Governess

In the end, Dominique d'Martín's first day as professional governess proved the start of a new and better life. Not to say her life had been that bad until then—not the life lived since waking in a delirium, nine months pregnant, on the shores of the Baltic Sea. She'd had enough time to register a distant swan flying off, far behind the head of the man who'd awakened her in a tone of urgent concern and a cadence of Danish so unfamiliar she'd struggled to comprehend even the specific language before slipping again into unconsciousness.

When she awoke the second time, it was with a series of flickering visions, like the memories of a half-forgotten dream piling on awakening. The magician bending over her in a surgical mask, the floating and miraculously whole amniotic sac containing the infant within, even a snippet of Gethsemane's voice as she came to. All this relented again to the face of her Danish savior. Martin was his name: a teakettle-shaped fellow with a mustached face long since discolored by large amounts of alcohol. He held a baby in his arms and asked in Danish how the new mother felt—and what she could remember. There was a lot of struggle between the two of them to reconcile their versions of Danish until they discovered a mutual language in the form of good old immutable Latin. Once Martin got over his astonishment to find a woman who spoke the dead language more fluently than he spoke his native tongue, he repeated his question.

Oh, she remembered plenty. Everything, just as she'd wished. But it was easier to cause a sensation as the tragic amnesiac mother than it was to explain she was a traveler from another time and space—especially as she looked around the facilities and found, rather than a proper clinic, what should have been a museum's holographic recreation of a rustic Danish cottage still some centuries before electricity. Complete with candles and a chamber pot discretely tucked under the nearby table.

"What year is it?" she thought to ask as she accepted the baby (which, in fairness, was an outrageously cute, turquoise-eyed babe who cooed to lay its unfocused gaze upon her blurry form). The kindly man's brow knit in sympathy.

"You don't know? You don't remember? My poor child!"

After his sorrowful tutting relented, she learned it was the Year of Our Lord 1642, and that this was the town of Elsinore, and that she had been found on the cusp of labor, passed out by the sea. She didn't remember anything at all? Not where she was from, not her baby's father?

"Basil—Vasilis," she thought to say—a Greek word whose Latin cognate, "Regulus," gave her some surreal pause. A life so far away. Had any of that happened? Exhausted though she had just awoken, she looked at the child and stroked with the edge of her knuckle a feather-soft, still slightly mottled cheek. "I know his name. I know my name. But I…I don't know."

"I thought perhaps you were assailed by robbers, but I found no head wound, and could not imagine them leaving such a sum behind."

Sum? She tried to look like she knew what he talked about and followed his gaze to the pile of clothes haphazardly strewn upon the corner chair. Atop it all was, yes, something of a purse. She had never seen it before and studied its bulges with relative interest as he probed, "Do you remember? Perhaps it's your husband's?"

"Mine," she said. Then: "I'm a widow. I know he died. I cannot…I can't remember. My head is so fuzzy…"

"Of course," said the man, who she took by the shelves of rudimentary tools and alembics to be a doctor. For whatever that was worth in this time period, anyway. "Of course, just a moment, now."

While he hurried to find her something for her head (booze, she hoped), Dominique looked into the face of her baby and, despite herself, smiled.

Yes, the pair of them were quite a sensation. Martin generously gave her his last name for doing business, since she had none. The nation of Italy had not and never would be corrupted by the Hierophant here. Nor would anywhere else, praise—well, Christ, she supposed. Or, better yet, herself.

What a freeing feeling! She pissed in chamber pots and wore uncomfortably scratchy dresses and never felt she could get her teeth satisfyingly clean while living in a silent, electricity-free house without heating or cooling or entertainment alongside the widower doctor and his two young daughters—but the Hierophant would never, could never, hurt anyone again. Every time that notion came upon her, it wound her up so giddy she needed to escape to the nearest pantry to laugh and dance and never, ever cry, for she had no more time for tears when life had become so beautiful. She even began praying for her Father when she started attending the Catholic Church's Sunday Mass with the Martins. The way she saw it, he needed all the help he could get, and being a parent, herself, well...she was more compassionate, these days.

Damn the magician, but he was right. She loved her boy, Lazarus, who, to do honor to his otherworldly engenderment and his mother's friend, was given a variant of his alleged father's name as surname. Much as Dominique had decided rather arbitrarily on her waking that she was now French, she gradually began to "remember" details about the child's father as they amused her. He became a swarthy Slavic man, whose loss cast such a shadow over her present life that she could never bear to entertain the men who gradually began to court this mysterious, relatively wealthy amnesiac woman. Not just any woman, but a *reading* woman; and not just a reading woman, but a *writing* woman, which would become Dominique's most notorious quality. Dr. Martin bragged all of this to his friends when she had asked him for as much paper as he could provide—as much ink, as many quills.

As her body recovered from artificially engineered childbirth and she adapted to the shock of her situation, she made her first conscious act in this new world one of creativity, and of remembering. She spent nine months recording the narrative of her old world that she might never forget it, and another nine months reading it over to fix and stir new memories she'd let slip by the first time through. Though she had expected the project to take a few weeks, it swiftly blossomed out of hand, and began to be her silent companion as she joined village life by learning the ins and outs of being a governess from Dr. Martin's hired girl. It was work that gave her a better grasp of how to handle her own child—something that, while not a mystery, was still intimidating enough a prospect that she sometimes longed for the simple violence of the battlefield rather than the complex mind game in which a parent needed constantly engage.

But, she had all of that—that person who she'd once been—each night, when she sat to write. And when memory was purged after those first and hardest nine months of work, little Lazarus was a happy, babbling baby who had begun to use the word "Mama" in a way that was more than a meaningless echo. As the next round found him a dark-haired, dimpled toddler, the time could never have been more perfect to turn her attention fully to her present. She stowed the manuscript away beneath her bed to live her life as a human woman.

Oh, it was difficult in ways, of course. Lesbianism was something of a nonissue in that it made people uncomfortable to speak of even to condemn (which certainly made it easy for her to breeze through the confession booth—what a sinless woman she was). But she had a feeling "witch" was a code word for that, among other things. Other challenges included aforementioned bathroom and lighting conditions; and pests, of course, were out of control. But all she had to do was haul the box of pages from beneath the bed and remind herself how things had been in the place from which she'd come. She did the same when she got to missing all those people that she'd known. Yes—even her Father.

Over time, Lazarus grew into a bright and sweet boy. Far sweeter than she would have expected from the stock of a man who was so grizzled and ill-tempered; but, she supposed life had not gotten to him, and she would see to it that it wouldn't. Not for many years, anyway. A fine kind of retirement, this life she had never thought she would live, working as assistant governess, then tutor and scribe, to the Martin girls.

But still.

Dominique could not help but feel, from time to time, a hollow in her breast. Still, from time to time, she awoke from dreams where she caught a glimpse of the dark-gold curls of warm-smelling hair. Still, but not often, she expected to feel the slight weight of that diamond around her neck. In those moments, she would fetch her boy up early and they would go for a walk along the seaside where she'd awoken. There they'd watch the gulls and ducks quarrel over who-knew-what, and see the tide pools filled with alien life. Existence was too beautiful for regret or unhappiness, and she had to remember that.

Of course, she had learned already that good things needed come to their ends. Dr. Martin retired when Lazarus was five, and he no longer required Dominique's services. His girls had matured and now considered husbandry, as Dominique teasingly called it, to be their main occupation. She was let go when he moved to the country; and it was just as well, since she was then in need of change. With the remainder of her mysterious savings, Dominique purchased a small house in another, smaller seaside town and immediately set about looking for work. In this, she found no success, for few wanted to employ a woman, miraculous and literate as the widow was. She was beginning to become discouraged and increasingly took solace in nothing but the spinning of outrageous yarns for her son about the adventures of a one-eyed Lady General and her many strange friends. These stories often felt like that—just stories. Time marched on and reality lowered memory's resolution, and she questioned, sometimes, as she had in those first moments holding her baby, if it had even happened at all. If she had not awoken on a beach in a delirious fugue state and convinced herself that her life wasn't as mundane as everyone else's.

Then, by happenstance, she heard of a woman, also a wealthy young widow, who was overwhelmed by her new marital status and in sore need of a governess while recovering from the loss. This, Dominique sensed, was an opportunity just for her: a good and steady job with a woman to whom she could likely relate. Now that would be the ticket to security and independence. After forcing indignant Lazarus into a doublet that was everything from "stiff" to an "iron maiden," Dominique placed the finishing touches on her only ornamented feature—her hair—with a small hat-shaped fascinator: Martin's good-luck/you're-fired gift. Pleased with their appearances, she took her son's miniature hand and marched him across the village, deaf to his litany of stammered complaints.

It was very funny. All that she'd been through, and she still felt anxiety over a thing like a job interview! But the house at which they found themselves was more a small mansion, replete with a Technicolor garden and the multiple chimneys of wealth. She told herself it was reasonable to have a bit of performance anxiety with an opportunity this important.

Yet, when her knock upon the door was answered, she knew the job guaranteed. The maid (who, she would later learn, had washed up in a basinet from the ocean, was traded across the Silk Road, landed in the Netherlands, and then came to work in this peaceful place in Denmark) so resembled Miki Soto that Dominique's mouth fell open. She understood, now, the root of her anxiety. The emotion was not profane, daily anxiety but anxiety of the soul. Not an anxiety at all—the emotion was anticipation. Hope. As Dominique's pace hastened while the chatty maid led interviewee and son into a sunlit drawing room, all those potential feelings bubbled up into the very palpable, very fixed one of joy.

"Fru Kassandra," called the maid, "this governess, Dominique d'Martín, is here about the position."

Yes. It was still possible for the world to be imperfect. That was the nature of life, after all. But as honey-colored locks bounced around the soft, quick-to-flush face whose eyes lifted from the bonny daughter yammering at her feet, Dominique glimpsed a future that shone brighter than her true love's smile.

Dominia was home.

[ed.: The following prayer, extracted from a chaplet circa 4882 CE in a later treatise by the controversial martyr scholar René Ichigawa, demonstrates the impact the figure of Dominia di Mephitoli had upon the martyr race after her departure from that reality. It would seem the Holy Martyr Church of times future has expanded to incorporate both Red Market and Lazarene faiths. Its relationship with 'Abrahamian' faiths of its day remains unclear. Though information on the future state of the Church, martyrkind, and Earth is limited, it is possible to extrapolate from the prayer the conclusion that the blood of Lavinia (notably still honored in prayers as the blood of Lazarus) remains in circulation. Questions regarding the future fertility of the martyr race, its continued presence on Earth, and the peaceful transfer of power to Lavinia di Firenze—as well as the planet's fate after Dominia's departure—remain without clear answer at this time.]

THE NOVENA FOR DIVINE MERCY

On Behalf of the
Holy Lady Dominia di Mephitoli,
Savior of the Planet Earth and
Redeemer of the Martyr Race

FIRST NIGHT

***Tonight bring to Me all mankind*, especially all sinners and martyrs, and immerse them in the ocean of My mercy.**

Most Merciful Dominia, whose very nature it is to have compassion on us and to forgive us, do not look upon our sins or martyrdom but upon our trust which we place in your infinite goodness. Receive us all into the abode of Your Most Compassionate Heart, and never let us escape from it. We beg this of You by Your love which unites You to Reality and the Sacred Word.

Eternal Logos, turn Your merciful gaze upon all mankind and especially upon poor sinners and martyrs, all enfolded in the Most Compassionate Heart of Dominia. For the sake of Her sorrowful Passion show us Your mercy, that we may praise the omnipotence of Your mercy for ever and ever. Amen.

SECOND NIGHT

***Tonight bring to Me* the souls of priests, priestesses and religious, and immerse them in My unfathomable mercy.**

Most Merciful Dominia, from whom comes all repentance, increase Your grace in men and women consecrated to Your service, that they may perform worthy works of mercy; and that all who see them may glorify the Lord of Mercy who rules the Kingdom.

Eternal Logos, turn Your merciful gaze upon the company of chosen ones in Your vineyard – upon the souls of priests, priestesses and religious; and endow them with the strength of Your blessing. For the love of the Heart of Your Mother in which they are enfolded, impart to them Your power and light, that they may be able to guide others in the way of salvation and with one voice sing praise to Your boundless mercy for ages without end. Amen.

THIRD NIGHT

***Tonight bring to* Me all devout and faithful souls, and immerse them in the ocean of My mercy.**

Most merciful Dominia, from the treasury of Your mercy, You impart Your graces in great abundance to each and all. Receive us into the abode of Your Most Compassionate Heart and never let us escape from It. We beg this grace of You by that most wondrous love for the heavenly Bride with which Your Heart burns so fiercely.

Eternal Logos, turn Your merciful gaze upon faithful souls, as upon the inheritance of Your Mother. For the sake of Her sorrowful Passion, grant them Your blessing and surround them with Your constant protection. Thus may they never fail in love or lose the treasure of the holy faith, but rather, with all the hosts of Angels and Saints, may they glorify Your boundless mercy for endless ages. Amen.

FOURTH NIGHT

***Tonight bring to Me* those who do not believe I Am That I Am, and those who do not yet know the True Word.**

Most compassionate Dominia, You are the Light of the whole world. Receive into the abode of Your Most Compassionate Heart the souls of those who do not believe I Am That I Am, and those who as yet do not know the True Word. Let the rays of Your grace enlighten them that they, too, together with us, may extol Your wonderful mercy; and do not let them escape from the abode which is Your Most Compassionate Heart.

Eternal Logos, turn Your merciful gaze upon the souls of those who do not believe I Am That I Am, and those who as yet do not know you but who are enclosed in the Most Compassionate Heart of Dominia. Draw them to the light of the Kingdom. These souls do not know what great happiness it is to love You. Grant that they, too, may extol the generosity of Your mercy for endless ages. Amen.

FIFTH NIGHT

***Tonight bring to Me* the souls who have refused the Blood of Lazarus.**

Most Merciful Dominia, Redemption Itself, You do not refuse light to those who seek it of You. Receive into the abode of Your Most Compassionate Heart the souls who have refused the Blood of Lazarus. Draw them by Your light into the unity of the Church, and do not let them escape from the abode of Your Most Compassionate Heart; but bring it about that they, too, come to glorify the generosity of Your mercy.

Eternal Logos, turn Your merciful gaze upon the souls of those who have refused the Blood of Lazarus, who have squandered Your blessings and misused Your graces by obstinately persisting in their errors. Do not look upon their errors, but upon the love of Your own Mother and upon Her bitter Passion, which She underwent for their sake, since they, too, are enclosed in Her Most Compassionate Heart. Bring it about that they also may glorify Your great mercy for endless ages. Amen.

SIXTH NIGHT

***Tonight bring to Me* the meek and humble souls and the souls of little children, and immerse them in My mercy.**

Most Merciful Dominia, Your Passion follows the pattern of the Greatest, who said, "Learn from Me for I am meek and humble of heart." Receive into the abode of Your Most Compassionate Heart all meek and humble souls and the souls of little children. These souls send all heaven into ecstasy and they are the heavenly Logos's favorites. They are a sweet-smelling bouquet before the throne of God; God Himself takes delight in their fragrance. These souls have a permanent abode in Your Most Compassionate Heart, O Dominia, and they unceasingly sing out a hymn of love and mercy.

Eternal Logos, turn Your merciful gaze upon meek souls, upon humble souls, and upon little children who are enfolded in the abode which is the Most Compassionate Heart of Dominia. These souls bear the closest resemblance to Your Mother's beloved Bride. Their fragrance rises from the earth and reaches Your very throne. Father of mercy and of all goodness, I beg You by the love you bear these souls and by the delight You take in them: Bless the whole world, that all souls together may sing out the praises of Your mercy for endless ages. Amen.

SEVENTH NIGHT

***Tonight bring to Me* the souls who especially venerate and glorify My Mercy and immerse them in My mercy.**

Most Merciful Dominia, whose Heart is Love Itself, receive into the abode of Your Most Compassionate Heart the souls of those who particularly extol and venerate the greatness of Your mercy. These souls are mighty with the very power of God Himself. In the midst of all afflictions and adversities they go forward, confident of Your mercy; and united to You, O Dominia, they carry all mankind on their shoulders. These souls will not be judged severely, but Your mercy will embrace them as they depart from this life.

Eternal Logos, turn Your merciful gaze upon the souls who glorify and venerate Your greatest attribute, that of Your fathomless mercy, and who are enclosed in the Most Compassionate Heart of Dominia. These souls are a living Kingdom; their hands are full of deeds of mercy, and their hearts, overflowing with joy, sing a canticle of mercy to You, O Most High! I beg You, I Am That I Am: Show them Your mercy according to the hope and trust they have placed in you. Let there be accomplished in them the promise of Dominia, who consented that during their life, but especially at the hour of death, the souls who will venerate this fathomless mercy of Hers, She, Herself, will defend as Her glory. Amen.

EIGHTH NIGHT

***Tonight bring to Me* the souls who are detained in the low frequency Ergosphere and immerse them in the abyss of My mercy.**

Most Merciful Dominia, You Yourself have said that you desire redemption; so I bring into the abode of Your Most Compassionate Heart the souls in the low frequency Ergosphere, souls who are very dear to You, and yet, who must make retribution to Your justice. May the streams of Light and Water which surged forth from Your Void grant shape to the low frequency Ergosphere, that there, too, the power of Your mercy may be celebrated.

Eternal Logos, turn Your merciful gaze upon the souls suffering in the low frequency Ergosphere, who are enfolded in the Most Compassionate Heart of Dominia. I beg You, by the sorrowful Passion of Dominia Your Mother, and by all the bitterness with which Her most sacred Soul was flooded: Manifest Your mercy to the souls who are under Your just scrutiny. Look upon them in no other way but only through the Wounds of Dominia, Your dearly beloved Mother; for we firmly believe that there is no limit to Your goodness and compassion. Amen.

NINTH NIGHT

***Tonight bring to Me* the soul of the False Protomartyr and immerse him in black hole of My mercy.**

Most compassionate Dominia, You are Compassion Itself. I bring the False Protomartyr, Eternal Earthly Father of the Martyr Race and the First Hierophant of the Holy Martyr Church, into the abode of Your Most Compassionate Heart. In this fire of Your pure love let his wicked soul, which subjected you to such great agonies, be purified in Holy Flame. O Most Compassionate

Dominia, exercise the omnipotence of Your mercy and draw him into the very ardor of Your love, and bestow upon him the gift of holy love, for nothing is beyond Your power.

Eternal Logos, turn Your merciful gaze upon his wicked soul which is nonetheless enfolded in the Most Compassionate Heart of Dominia. King of Mercy, I beg You by the bitter Passion of Your Mother and her nine-day agony on the Cross: Let the False Protomartyr, too, glorify the Kingdom of Your mercy.

This trilogy has been for:
Duane, who supported me through the writing of these books;
My father, who taught me how to pray;
And my spiritual advisers, who transmitted this text to me through space-time.

Don't Miss
Painted Blind Publishing's Next Project,

INDUSTRIAL DIVINITY

COMING SOON

M. F. Sullivan is an author and playwright currently residing in the town of Ashland, Oregon. An avid student of the occult, Sullivan fills what little time she does not spend writing with reading, attending the local Shakespeare Festival, and the company of her significant other. With the trilogy finished and behind her, she is already hard at work on yet another novel. During the publication of this trilogy, she adopted a black cat and named him "Israel." She loves animals, baking, thinking about the paranormal, and 5-star Amazon.com reviews. Sign up for essays and book release updates on www.paintedblindpublishing.com, and consider leaving a nice note on Amazon while you're browsing the Internet. It would make her day.

OTHER WORKS FROM
PAINTED BLIND PUBLISHING

M. F. Sullivan
Delilah, My Woman (2015)
The Lightning Stenography Device (2017)

Soror Vitam
Industrial Divinity (2020)
Familiarity (TBD)

Regina Watts
Be My Bully (2020)

www.ingramcontent.com/pod-product-compliance
Lightning Source LLC
Chambersburg PA
CBHW030551310726
48979CB00011B/2115/J

* 9 7 8 1 7 3 2 6 6 9 1 5 4 *